JAY FOSGITT

BODIE TROLL ™

kaboom! ™

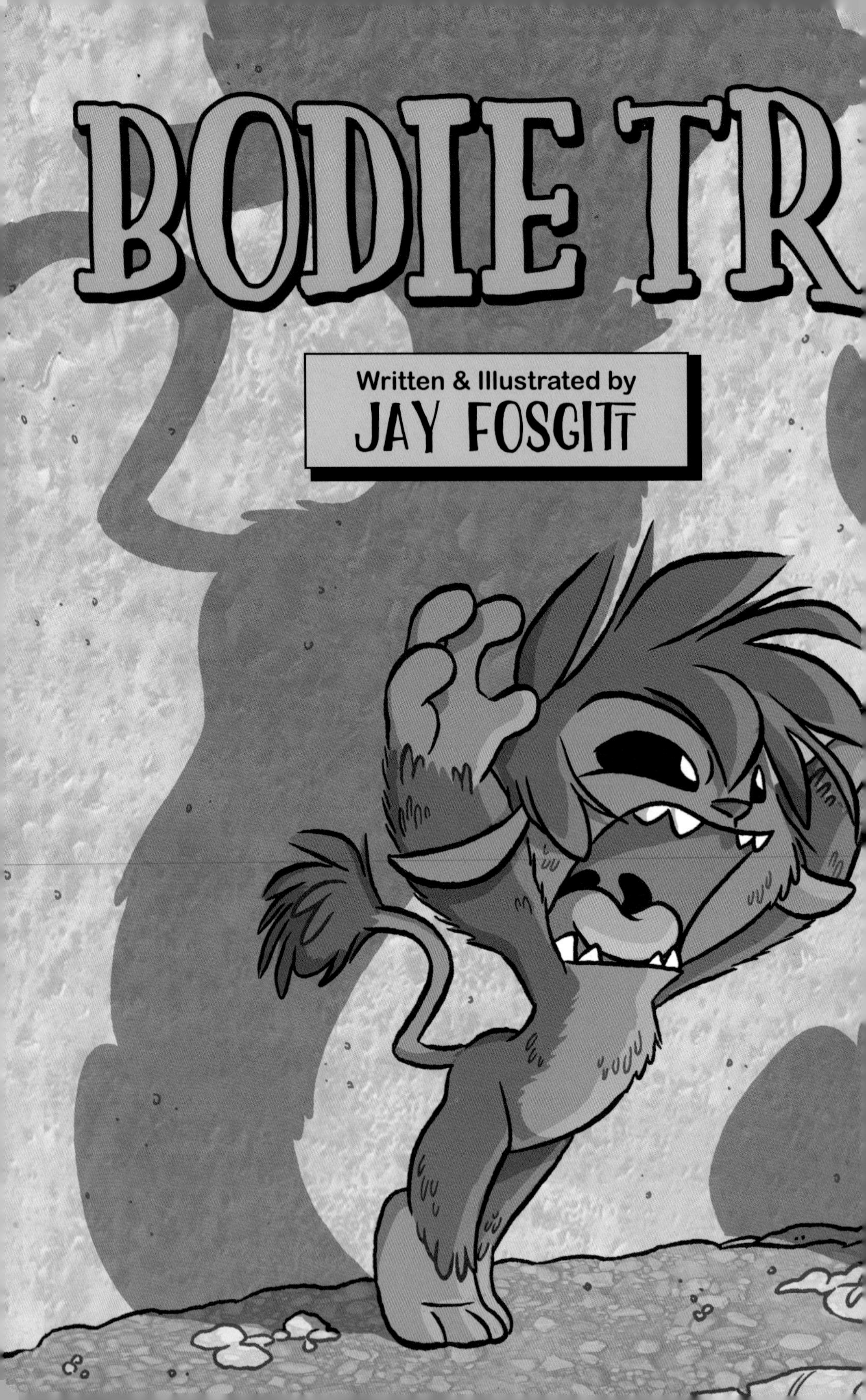
BODIE TR
Written & Illustrated by
JAY FOSGITT

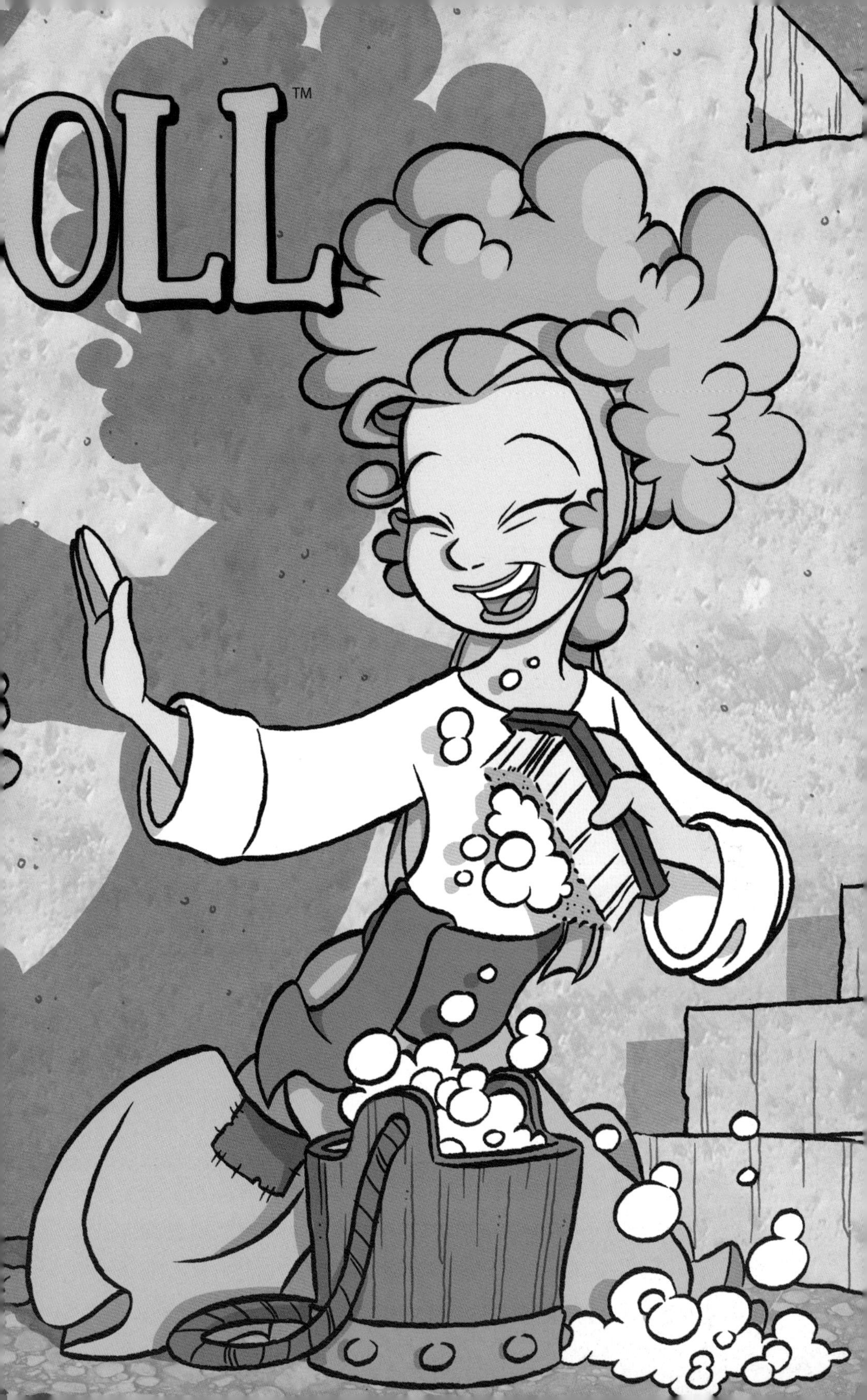
OLL™

Designer
Michelle Ankley

Associate Editor
Chris Rosa

Editor
Whitney Leopard

Special Thanks to Jay Jacot

Ross Richie CEO & Founder
Matt Gagnon Editor-in-Chief
Filip Sablik President of Publishing & Marketing
Stephen Christy President of Development
Lance Kreiter VP of Licensing & Merchandising
Phil Barbaro VP of Finance
Arune Singh VP of Marketing
Bryce Carlson Managing Editor
Mel Caylo Marketing Manager
Scott Newman Production Design Manager
Kate Henning Operations Manager
Sierra Hahn Senior Editor
Dafna Pleban Editor, Talent Development
Shannon Watters Editor
Eric Harburn Editor
Whitney Leopard Editor
Cameron Chittock Editor
Chris Rosa Associate Editor
Matthew Levine Associate Editor

Sophie Philips-Roberts Assistant Editor
Amanda LaFranco Executive Assistant
Katalina Holland Editorial Administrative Assistant
Jillian Crab Production Designer
Michelle Ankley Production Designer
Kara Leopard Production Designer
Marie Krupina Production Designer
Grace Park Production Design Assistant
Chelsea Roberts Production Design Assistant
Elizabeth Loughridge Accounting Coordinator
Stephanie Hocutt Social Media Coordinator
José Meza Event Coordinator
Holly Aitchison Operations Coordinator
Megan Christopher Operations Assistant
Rodrigo Hernandez Mailroom Assistant
Morgan Perry Direct Market Representative
Cat O'Grady Marketing Assistant
Liz Almendarez Accounting Administrative Assistant
Cornelia Tzana Administrative Assistant

kaboom!™ **BODIE TROLL, February 2018.** Published by KaBOOM!, a division of Boom Entertainment, Inc. Bodie Troll is ™ & © 2018 Jay Fosgitt. Originally published in single magazine form as BODIE TROLL No. 1-4, ATOMIC ROBO/BODIE TROLL FREE COMIC BOOK DAY 2013, ATOMIC ROBO/BODIE TROLL/HAUNTED FREE COMIC BOOK DAY 2014, BODIE TROLL: FUZZY MEMORIES, BODIE TROLL/DRONE/AGENT 42 FREE COMIC BOOK DAY 2015. ™ & © 2012-2015 Jay Fosgitt. All rights reserved. KaBOOM!™ and the KaBOOM! logo are trademarks of Boom Entertainment, Inc., registered in various countries and categories. All characters, events, and institutions depicted herein are fictional. Any similarity between any of the names, characters, persons, events, and/or institutions in this publication to actual names, characters, and persons, whether living or dead, events, and/or institutions is unintended and purely coincidental. KaBOOM! does not read or accept unsolicited submissions of ideas, stories, or artwork.

BOOM! Studios, 5670 Wilshire Boulevard, Suite 450, Los Angeles, CA 90036-5679. Printed in China. First Printing.

ISBN: 978-1-68415-124-0, eISBN: 978-1-61398-863-3

Contents

Bodie's Bargain 6
with pages 1-4 colored by Evan "Doc" Shaner

Make Up Mix Up 30

Bouncing Baby Bodie 54

The Sky's the Limit 80

Haunted Harvest 104

Playing for Keeps 118

Bagging A Bodie 136

Bittersweet 162

Prose and Cons 188
with colors by Nathan Pride

Bodie Grows Two Feet 208

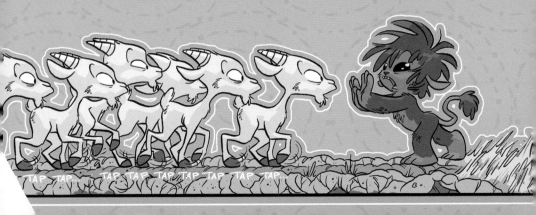

CHAPTER 1
BODIE'S BARGAIN

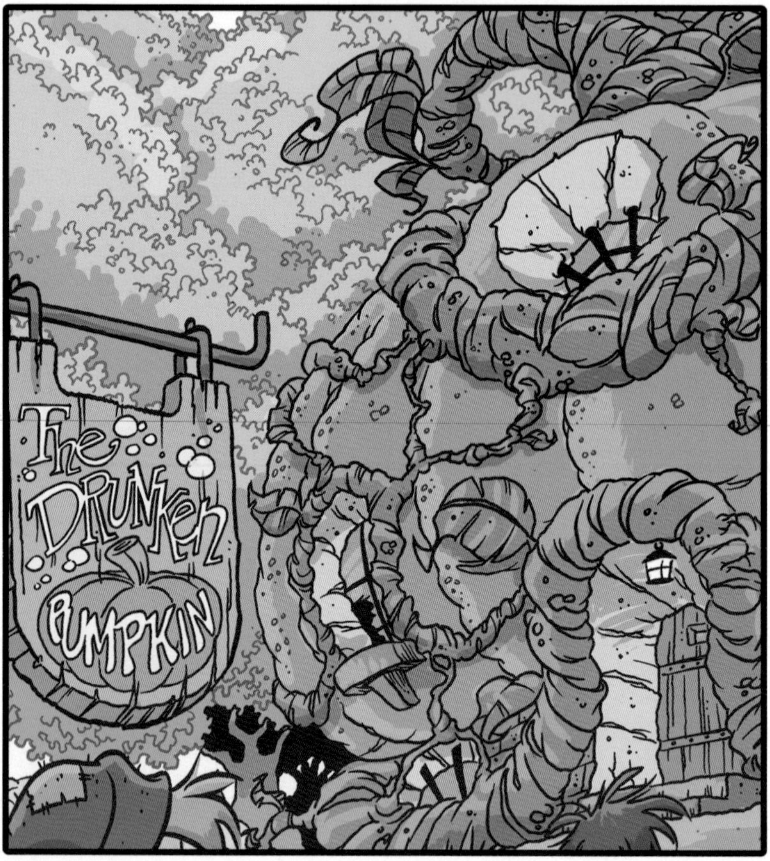
The Drunken Pumpkin

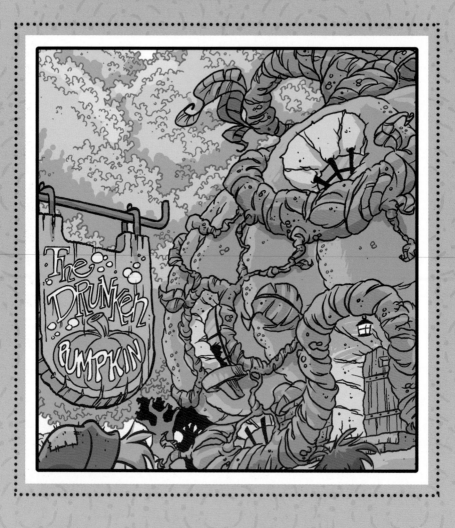

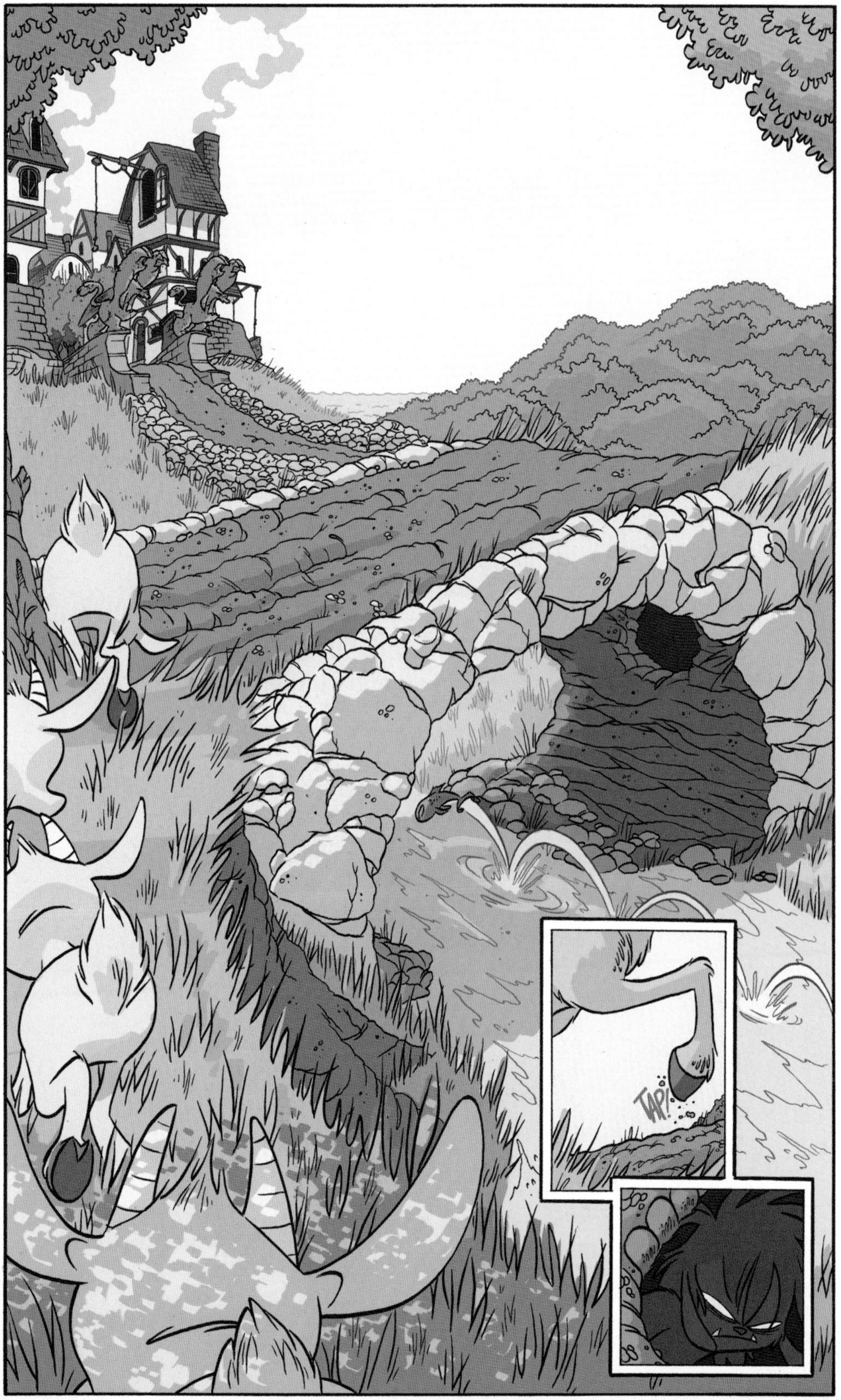
TAP!

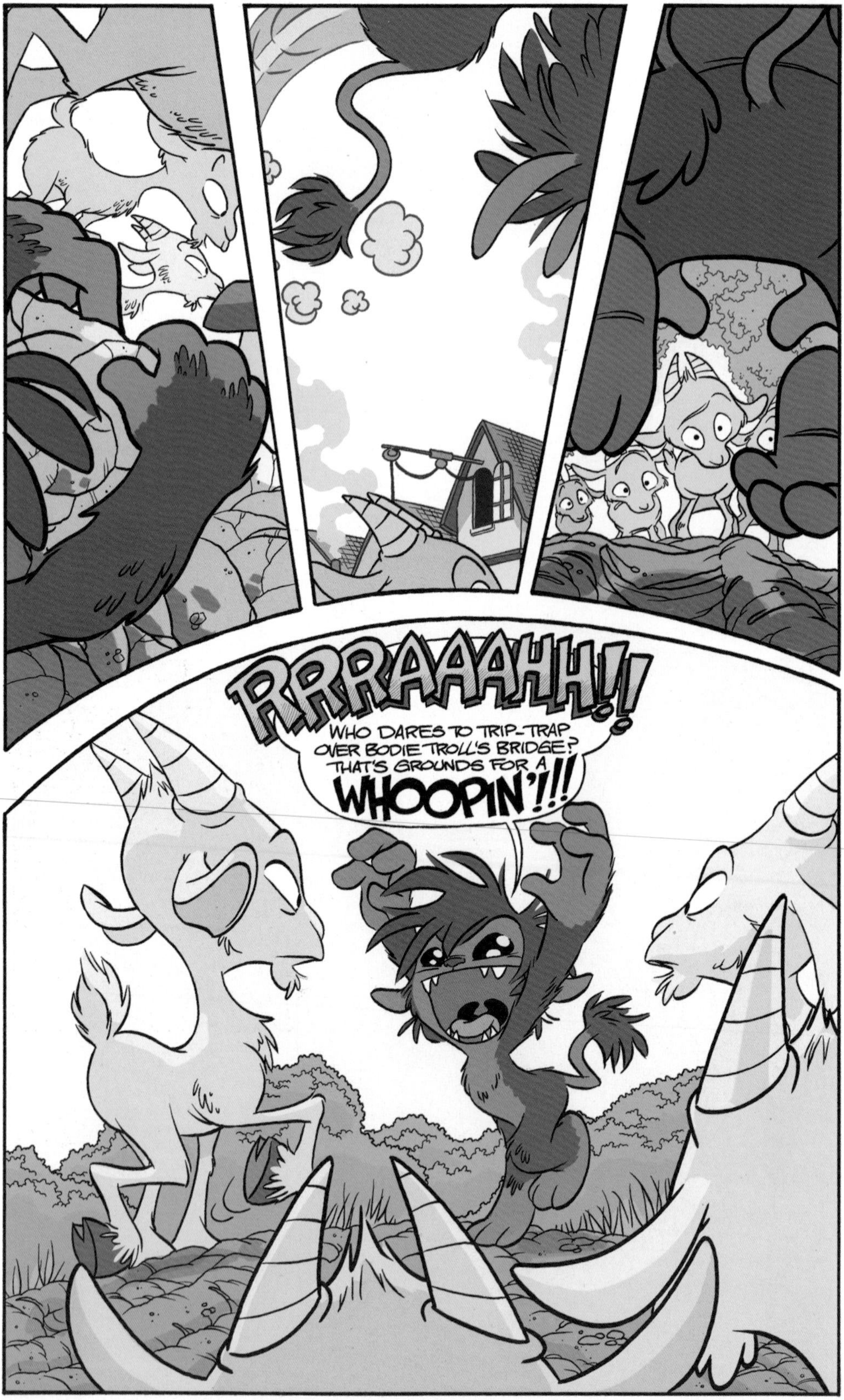
RRRAAAHH!!
WHO DARES TO TRIP-TRAP OVER BODIE TROLL'S BRIDGE? THAT'S GROUNDS FOR A WHOOPIN'!!!

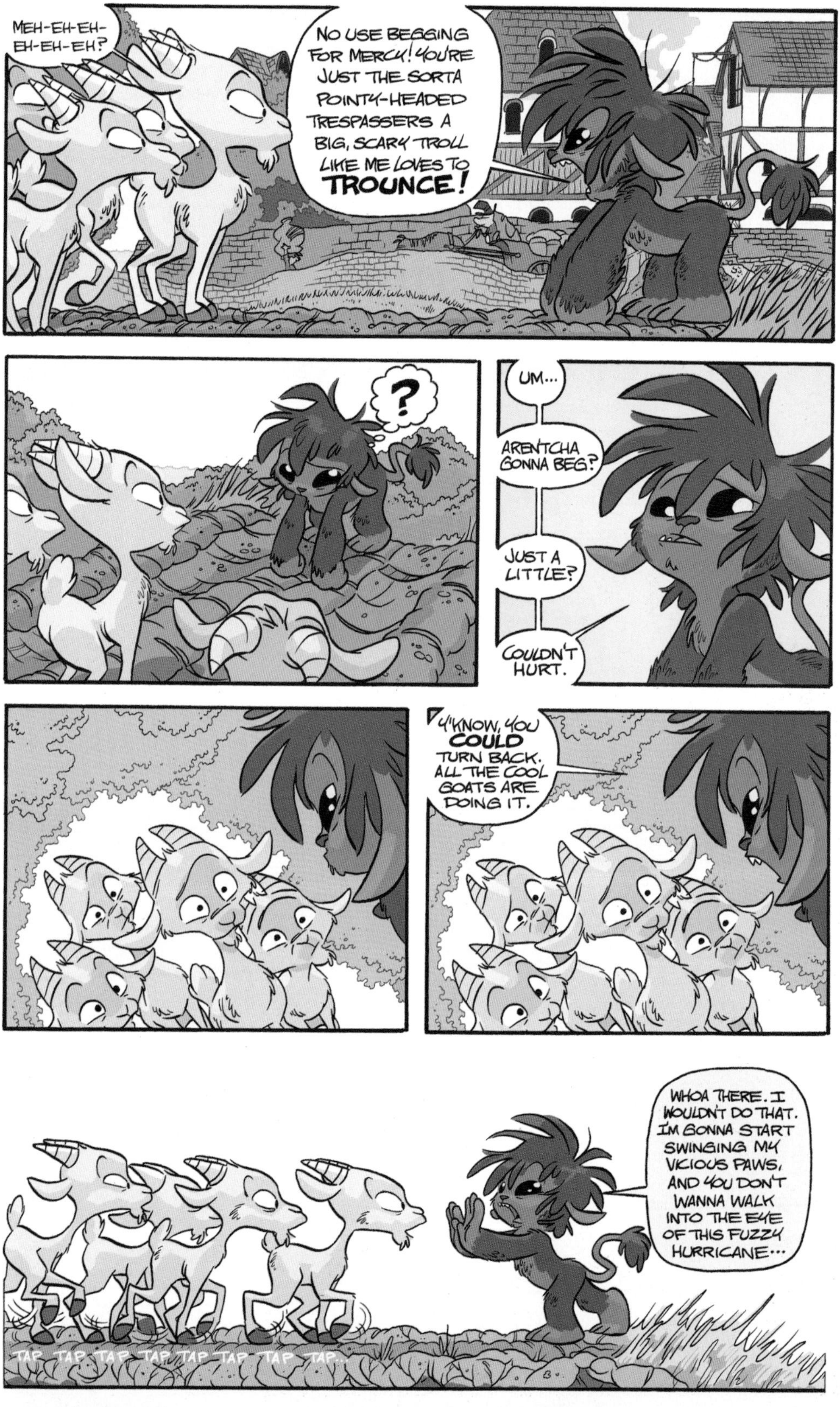
MEH-EH-EH-EH-EH-EH?
NO USE BEGGING FOR MERCY! YOU'RE JUST THE SORTA POINTY-HEADED TRESPASSERS A BIG, SCARY TROLL LIKE ME LOVES TO TROUNCE!
?
UM...
ARENT'CHA GONNA BEG?
JUST A LITTLE?
COULDN'T HURT.
Y'KNOW, YOU COULD TURN BACK. ALL THE COOL GOATS ARE DOING IT.
WHOA THERE. I WOULDN'T DO THAT. I'M GONNA START SWINGING MY VICIOUS PAWS, AND YOU DON'T WANNA WALK INTO THE EYE OF THIS FUZZY HURRICANE...
TAP TAP TAP TAP TAP TAP TAP TAP...

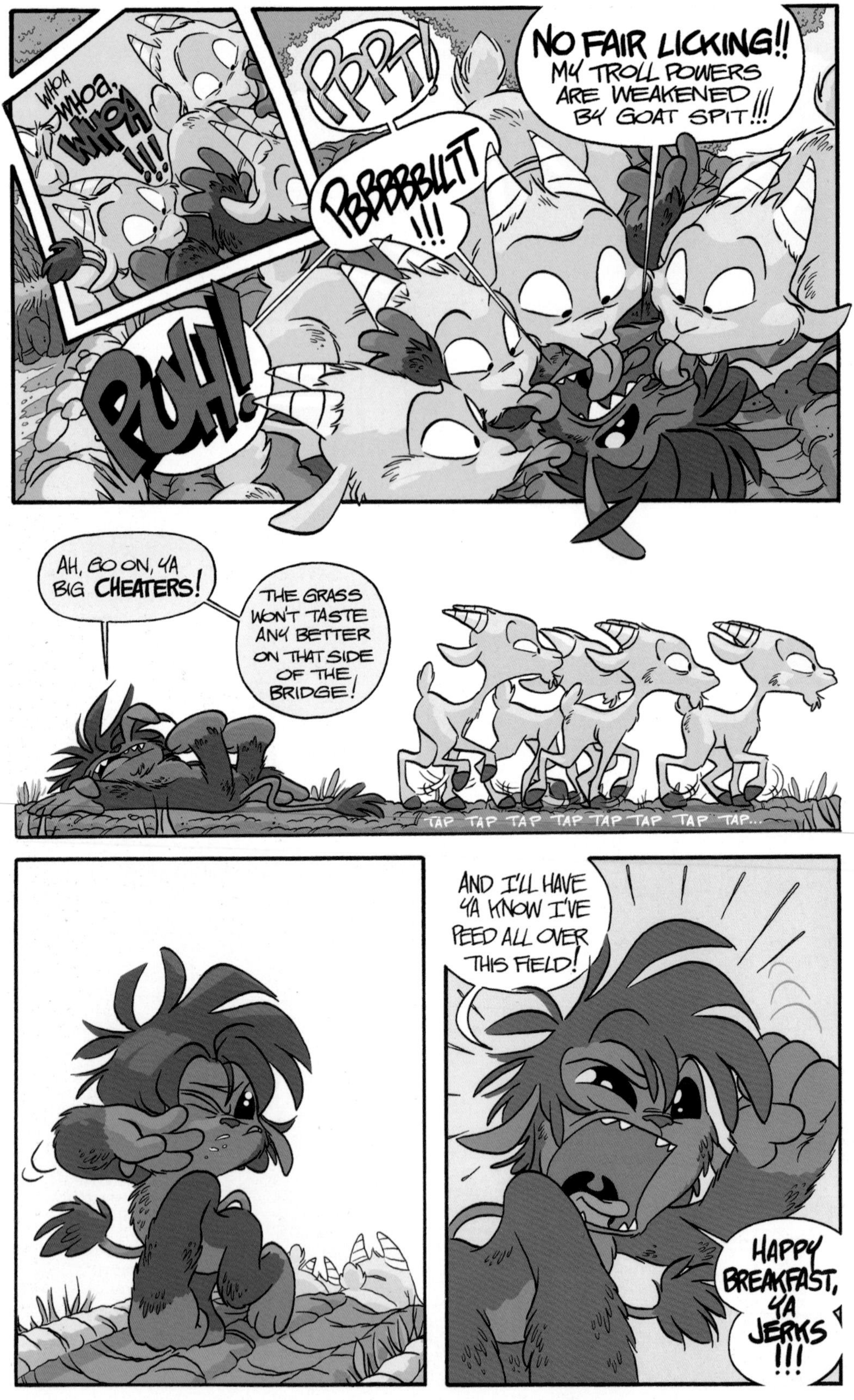
WHOA WHOA, WHOA!!!
PPPT!
PBBBBBLLTT!!!
PUH!
NO FAIR LICKING!! MY TROLL POWERS ARE WEAKENED BY GOAT SPIT!!!
AH, GO ON, YA BIG CHEATERS!
THE GRASS WON'T TASTE ANY BETTER ON THAT SIDE OF THE BRIDGE!
TAP TAP TAP TAP TAP TAP TAP TAP...
AND I'LL HAVE YA KNOW I'VE PEED ALL OVER THIS FIELD!
HAPPY BREAKFAST, YA JERKS!!!

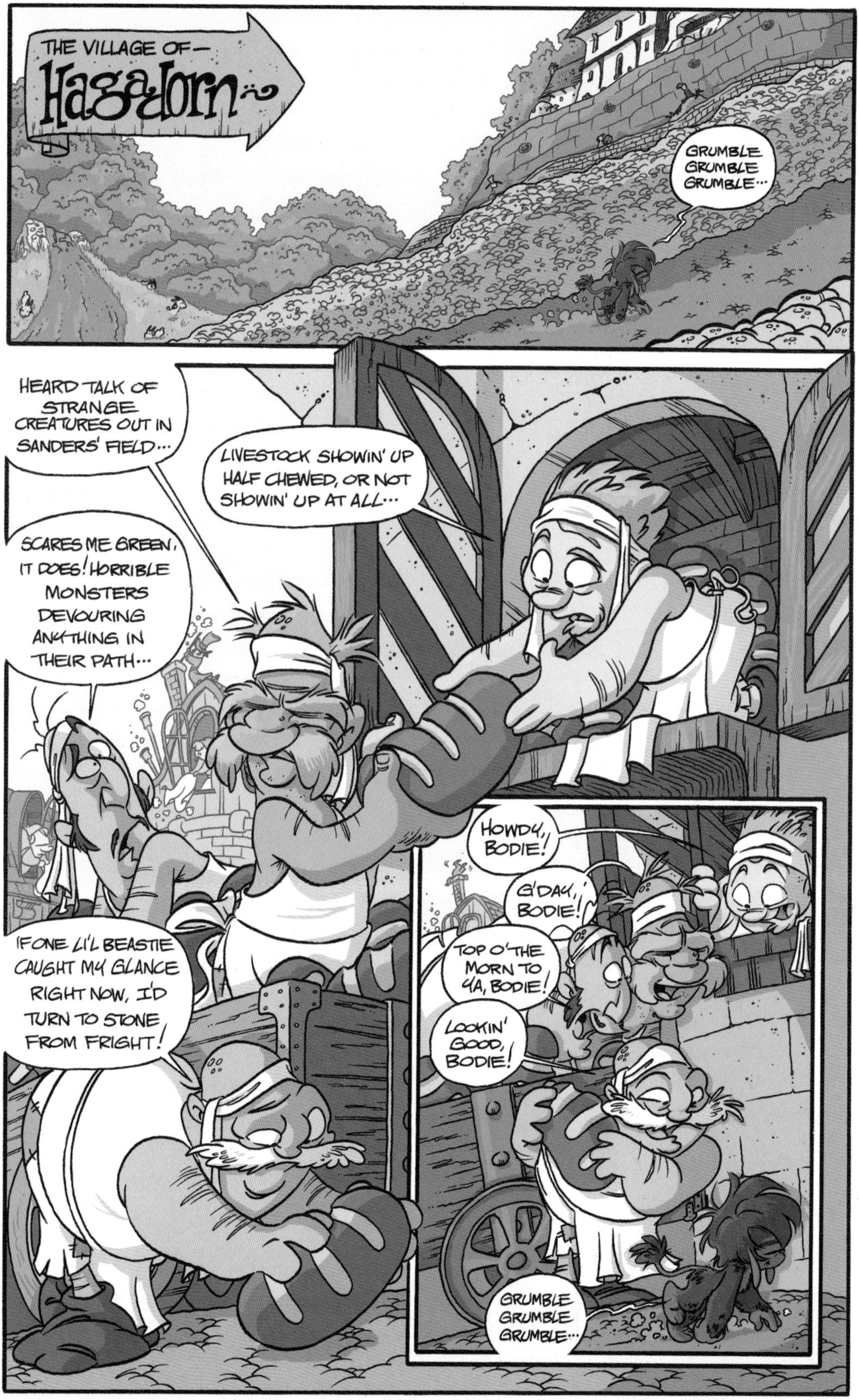
THE VILLAGE OF—
Hagadorn
GRUMBLE GRUMBLE GRUMBLE...
HEARD TALK OF STRANGE CREATURES OUT IN SANDERS' FIELD...
LIVESTOCK SHOWIN' UP HALF CHEWED, OR NOT SHOWIN' UP AT ALL...
SCARES ME GREEN, IT DOES! HORRIBLE MONSTERS DEVOURING ANYTHING IN THEIR PATH...
IF ONE LI'L BEASTIE CAUGHT MY GLANCE RIGHT NOW, I'D TURN TO STONE FROM FRIGHT!
HOWDY, BODIE!
G'DAY, BODIE!
TOP O' THE MORN TO YA, BODIE!
LOOKIN' GOOD, BODIE!
GRUMBLE GRUMBLE GRUMBLE...

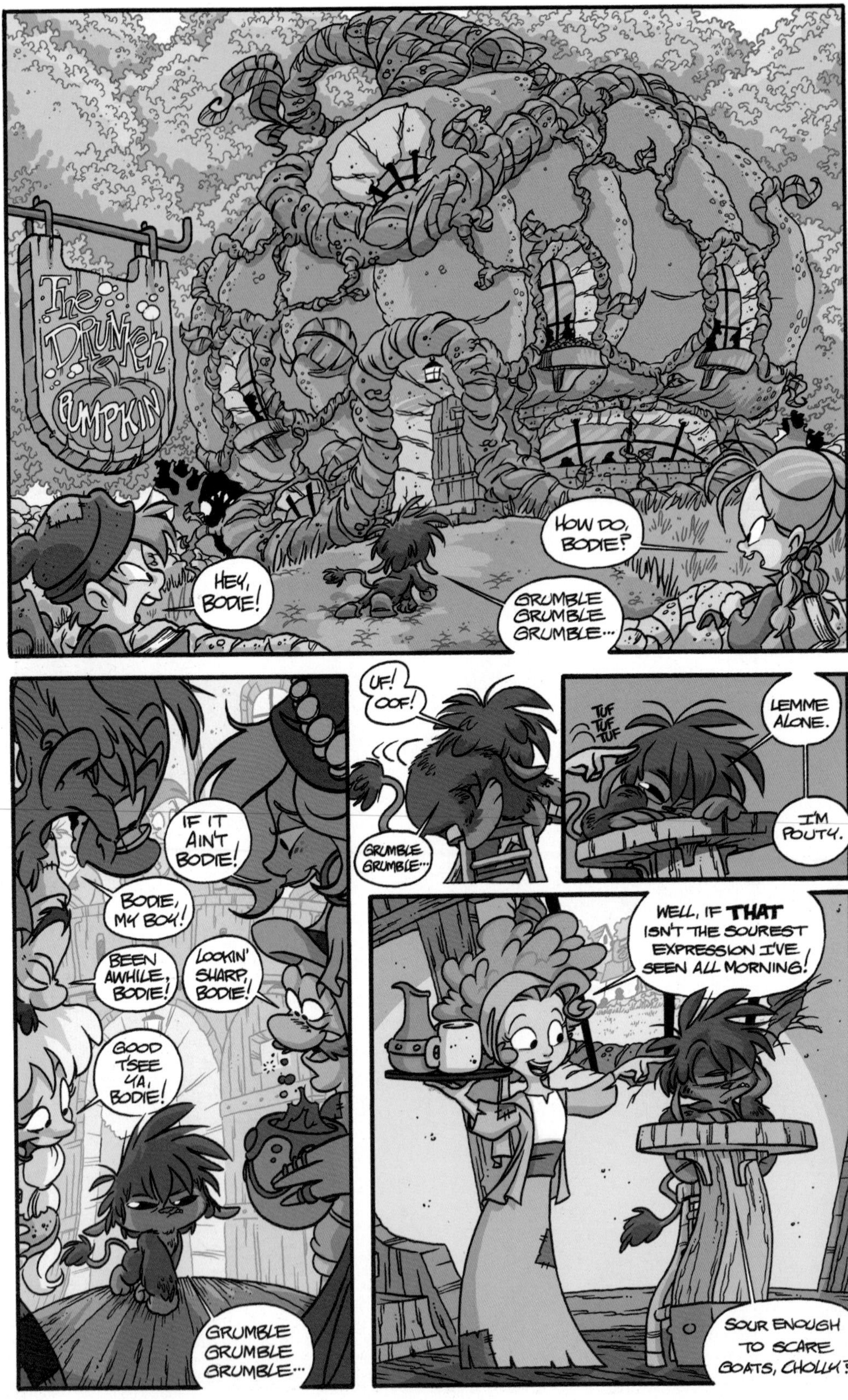
The Drunken Pumpkin
HEY, BODIE!
HOW DO, BODIE?
GRUMBLE GRUMBLE GRUMBLE...
IF IT AIN'T BODIE!
BODIE, MY BOY!
BEEN AWHILE, BODIE!
LOOKIN' SHARP, BODIE!
GOOD T'SEE YA, BODIE!
GRUMBLE GRUMBLE GRUMBLE...
UF! OOF!
GRUMBLE GRUMBLE...
TUF TUF TUF
LEMME ALONE.
I'M POUTY.
WELL, IF THAT ISN'T THE SOUREST EXPRESSION I'VE SEEN ALL MORNING!
SOUR ENOUGH TO SCARE GOATS, CHOLLY?

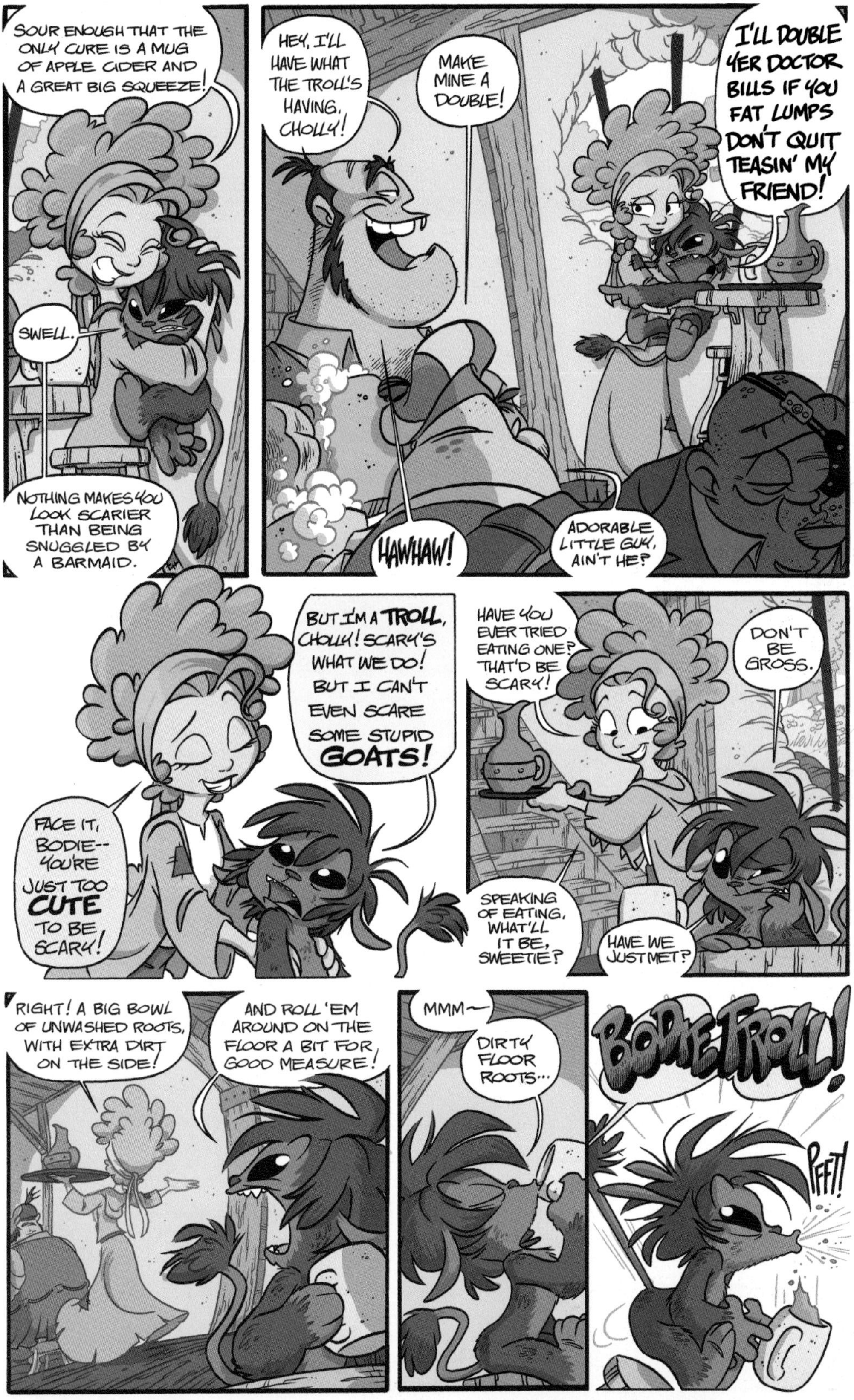
SOUR ENOUGH THAT THE ONLY CURE IS A MUG OF APPLE CIDER AND A GREAT BIG SQUEEZE!
SWELL.
NOTHING MAKES YOU LOOK SCARIER THAN BEING SNUGGLED BY A BARMAID.
HEY, I'LL HAVE WHAT THE TROLL'S HAVING, CHOLLY!
MAKE MINE A DOUBLE!
HAWHAW!
I'LL DOUBLE YER DOCTOR BILLS IF YOU FAT LUMPS DON'T QUIT TEASIN' MY FRIEND!
ADORABLE LITTLE GUY, AIN'T HE?
BUT I'M A TROLL, CHOLLY! SCARY'S WHAT WE DO! BUT I CAN'T EVEN SCARE SOME STUPID GOATS!
FACE IT, BODIE--YOU'RE JUST TOO CUTE TO BE SCARY!
HAVE YOU EVER TRIED EATING ONE? THAT'D BE SCARY!
DON'T BE GROSS.
SPEAKING OF EATING, WHAT'LL IT BE, SWEETIE?
HAVE WE JUST MET?
RIGHT! A BIG BOWL OF UNWASHED ROOTS, WITH EXTRA DIRT ON THE SIDE!
AND ROLL 'EM AROUND ON THE FLOOR A BIT FOR GOOD MEASURE!
MMM~
DIRTY FLOOR ROOTS...
BODIE TROLL!
PFFT!

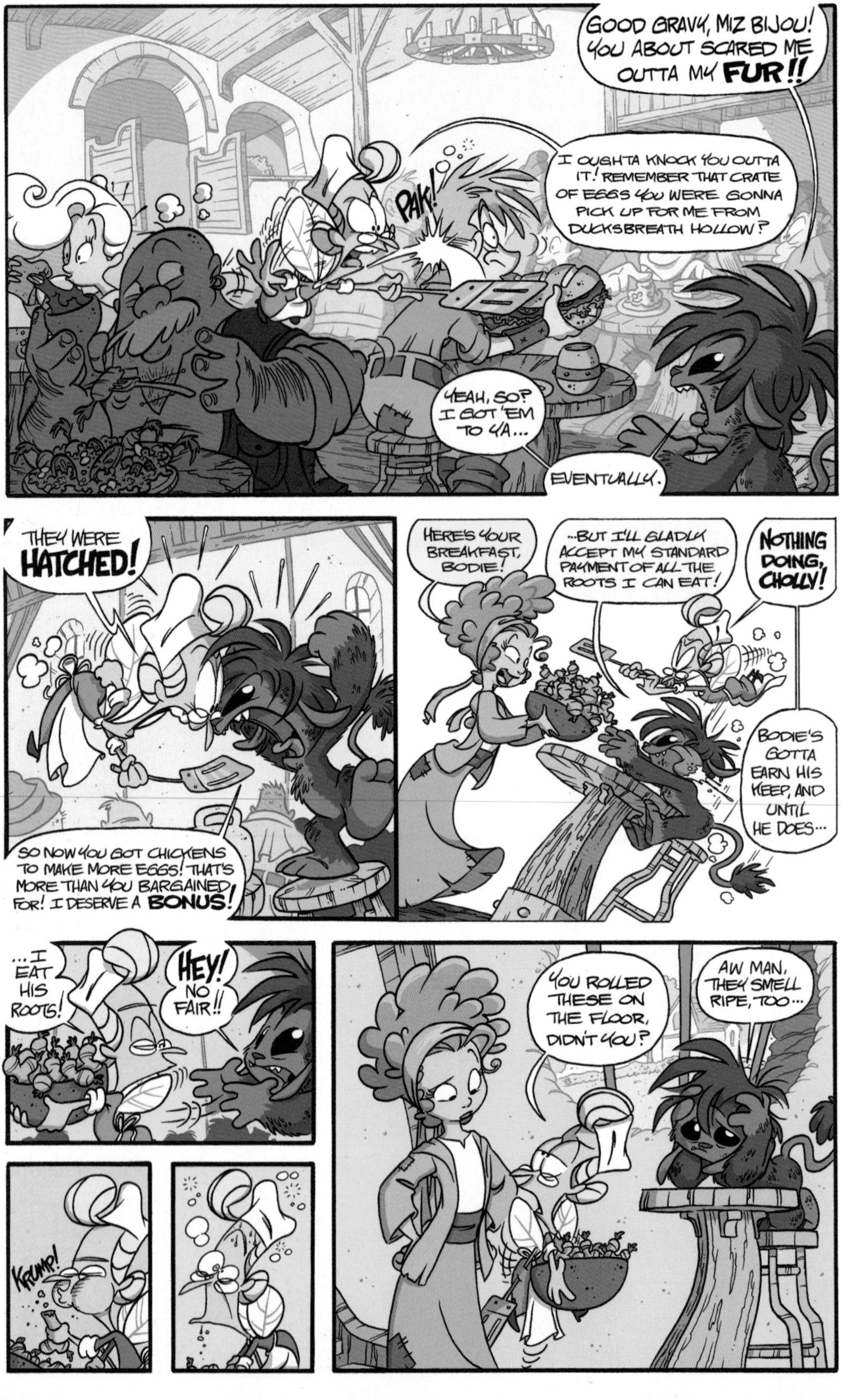
GOOD GRAVY, MIZ BIJOU! YOU ABOUT SCARED ME OUTTA MY FUR!!
I OUGHTA KNOCK YOU OUTTA IT! REMEMBER THAT CRATE OF EGGS YOU WERE GONNA PICK UP FOR ME FROM DUCKSBREATH HOLLOW?
PAK!
YEAH, SO? I GOT 'EM TO YA...
EVENTUALLY.
THEY WERE HATCHED!
SO NOW YOU GOT CHICKENS TO MAKE MORE EGGS! THAT'S MORE THAN YOU BARGAINED FOR! I DESERVE A BONUS!
HERE'S YOUR BREAKFAST, BODIE!
...BUT I'LL GLADLY ACCEPT MY STANDARD PAYMENT OF ALL THE ROOTS I CAN EAT!
NOTHING DOING, CHOLLY!
BODIE'S GOTTA EARN HIS KEEP, AND UNTIL HE DOES...
... I EAT HIS ROOTS!
HEY! NO FAIR!!
KRUMP!
YOU ROLLED THESE ON THE FLOOR, DIDN'T YOU?
AW MAN, THEY SMELL RIPE, TOO...

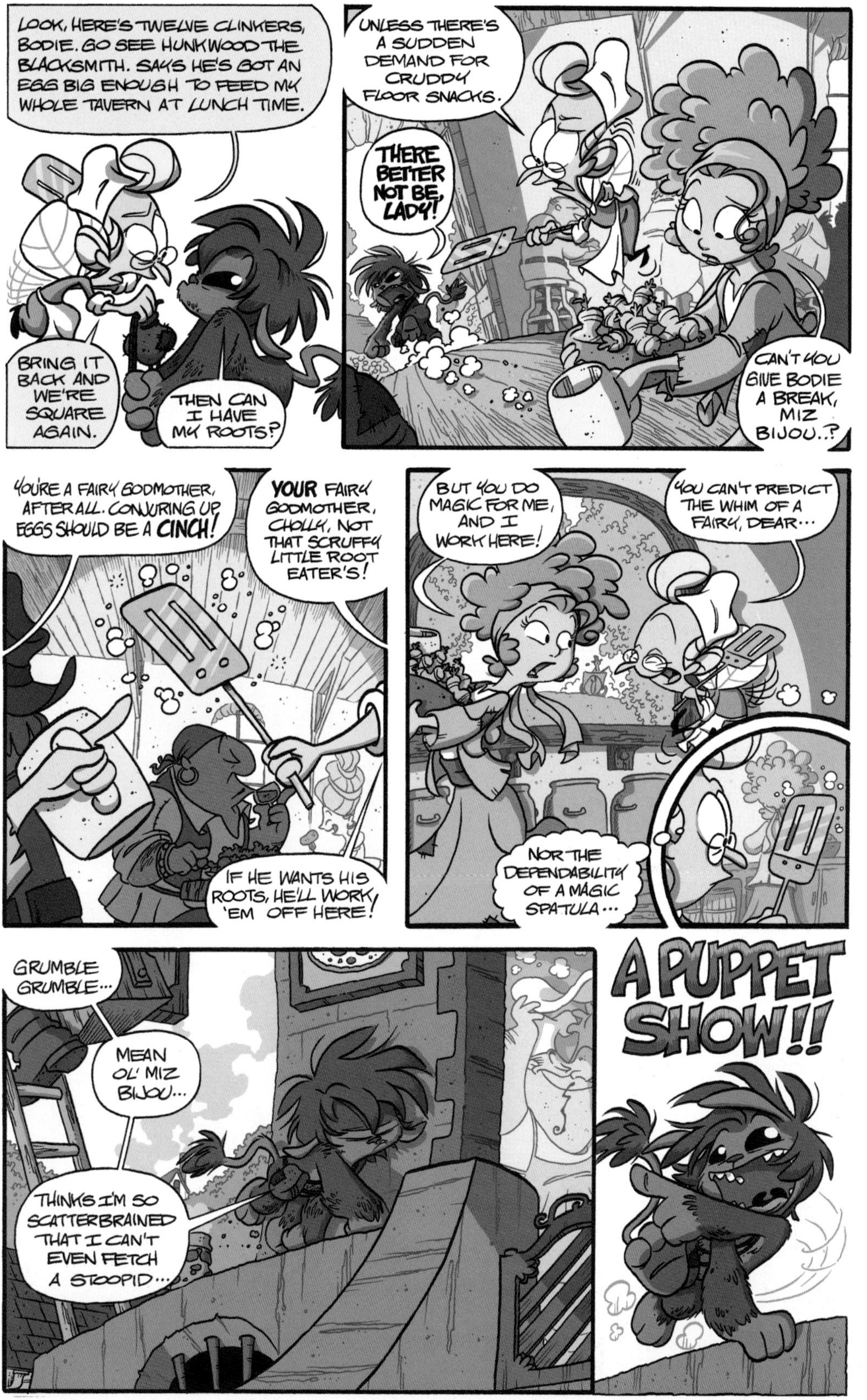
LOOK, HERE'S TWELVE CLINKERS, BODIE. GO SEE HUNKWOOD THE BLACKSMITH. SAYS HE'S GOT AN EGG BIG ENOUGH TO FEED MY WHOLE TAVERN AT LUNCH TIME.
BRING IT BACK AND WE'RE SQUARE AGAIN.
THEN CAN I HAVE MY ROOTS?
UNLESS THERE'S A SUDDEN DEMAND FOR CRUDDY FLOOR SNACKS.
THERE BETTER NOT BE, LADY!
CAN'T YOU GIVE BODIE A BREAK, MIZ BIJOU..?
YOU'RE A FAIRY GODMOTHER, AFTER ALL. CONJURING UP EGGS SHOULD BE A CINCH!
YOUR FAIRY GODMOTHER, CHOLLY, NOT THAT SCRUFFY LITTLE ROOT EATER'S!
IF HE WANTS HIS ROOTS, HE'LL WORK 'EM OFF HERE!
BUT YOU DO MAGIC FOR ME, AND I WORK HERE!
YOU CAN'T PREDICT THE WHIM OF A FAIRY, DEAR...
NOR THE DEPENDABILITY OF A MAGIC SPATULA...
GRUMBLE GRUMBLE...
MEAN OL' MIZ BIJOU...
THINKS I'M SO SCATTERBRAINED THAT I CAN'T EVEN FETCH A STOOPID...
A PUPPET SHOW!!

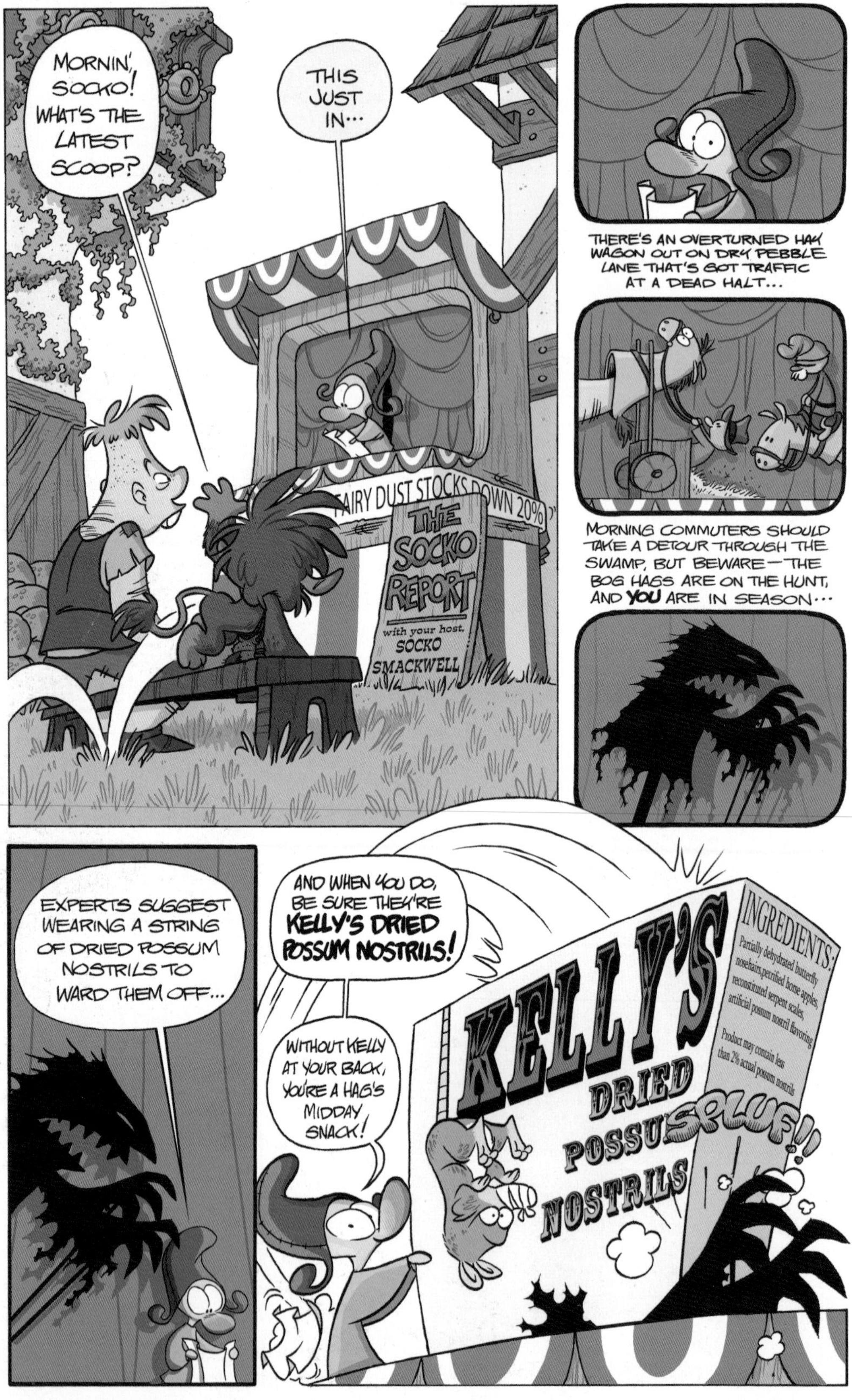
MORNIN', SOCKO! WHAT'S THE LATEST SCOOP?
THIS JUST IN...
FAIRY DUST STOCKS DOWN 20%
THE SOCKO REPORT
with your host. SOCKO SMACKWELL
THERE'S AN OVERTURNED HAY WAGON OUT ON DRY PEBBLE LANE THAT'S GOT TRAFFIC AT A DEAD HALT...
MORNING COMMUTERS SHOULD TAKE A DETOUR THROUGH THE SWAMP, BUT BEWARE—THE BOG HAGS ARE ON THE HUNT, AND YOU ARE IN SEASON...
EXPERTS SUGGEST WEARING A STRING OF DRIED POSSUM NOSTRILS TO WARD THEM OFF...
AND WHEN YOU DO, BE SURE THEY'RE KELLY'S DRIED POSSUM NOSTRILS!
WITHOUT KELLY AT YOUR BACK, YOU'RE A HAG'S MIDDAY SNACK!
KELLY'S
DRIED
POSSU
NOSTRILS
INGREDIENTS:
Partially dehydrated butterfly nosehairs,petrified horse apples, reconstituted serpent scales, artificial possum nostril flavoring
Product may contain less than 2% actual possum nostrils
SPLUF!!

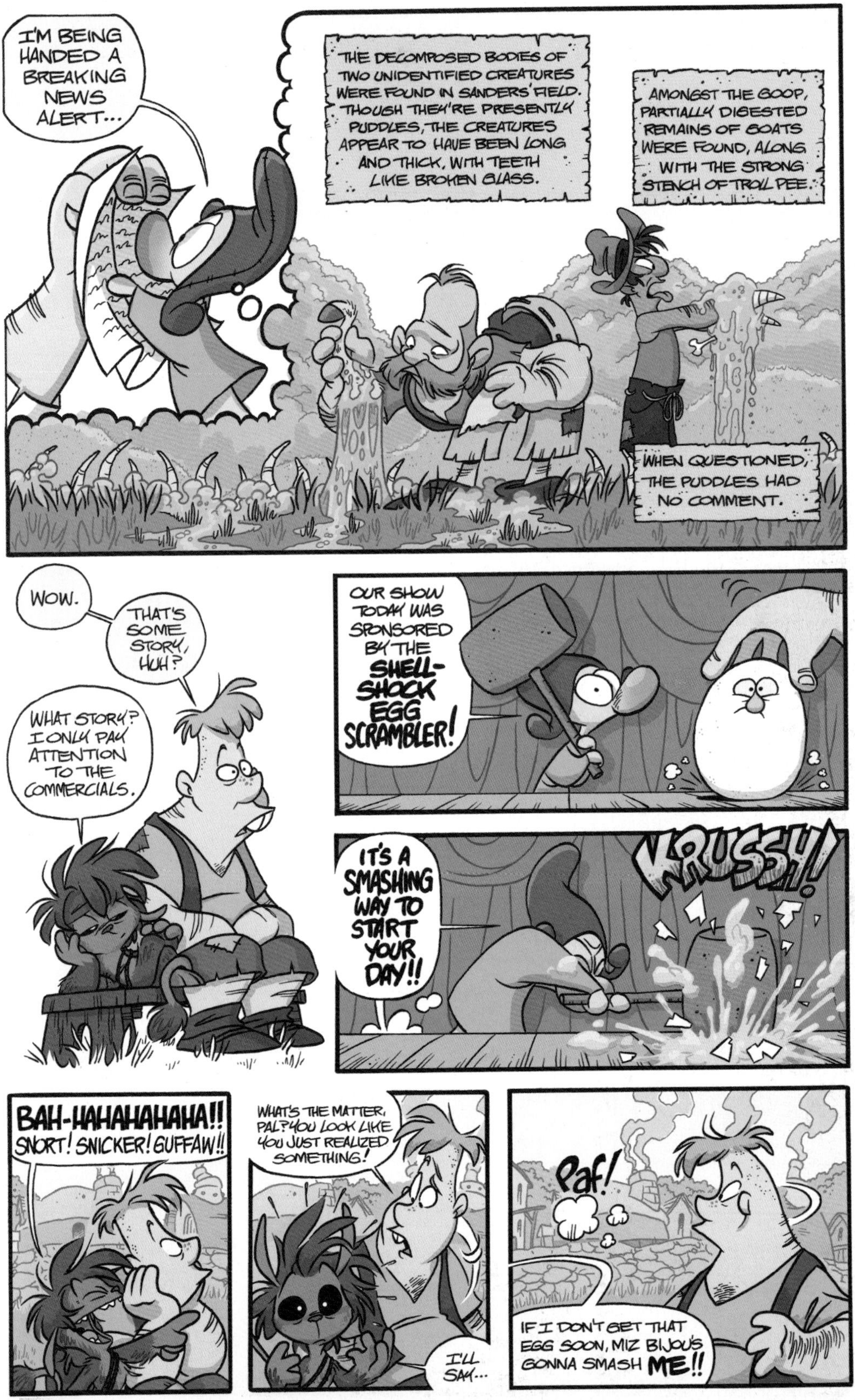
I'M BEING HANDED A BREAKING NEWS ALERT...
THE DECOMPOSED BODIES OF TWO UNIDENTIFIED CREATURES WERE FOUND IN SANDERS' FIELD. THOUGH THEY'RE PRESENTLY PUDDLES, THE CREATURES APPEAR TO HAVE BEEN LONG AND THICK, WITH TEETH LIKE BROKEN GLASS.
AMONGST THE GOOP, PARTIALLY DIGESTED REMAINS OF GOATS WERE FOUND, ALONG WITH THE STRONG STENCH OF TROLL PEE.
WHEN QUESTIONED, THE PUDDLES HAD NO COMMENT.
WOW.
THAT'S SOME STORY, HUH?
WHAT STORY? I ONLY PAY ATTENTION TO THE COMMERCIALS.
OUR SHOW TODAY WAS SPONSORED BY THE SHELL-SHOCK EGG SCRAMBLER!
IT'S A SMASHING WAY TO START YOUR DAY!!
KRUSSH!
BAH-HAHAHAHAHA!! SNORT! SNICKER! GUFFAW!!
WHAT'S THE MATTER, PAL? YOU LOOK LIKE YOU JUST REALIZED SOMETHING!
I'LL SAY...
PAF!
IF I DON'T GET THAT EGG SOON, MIZ BIJOU'S GONNA SMASH ME!!

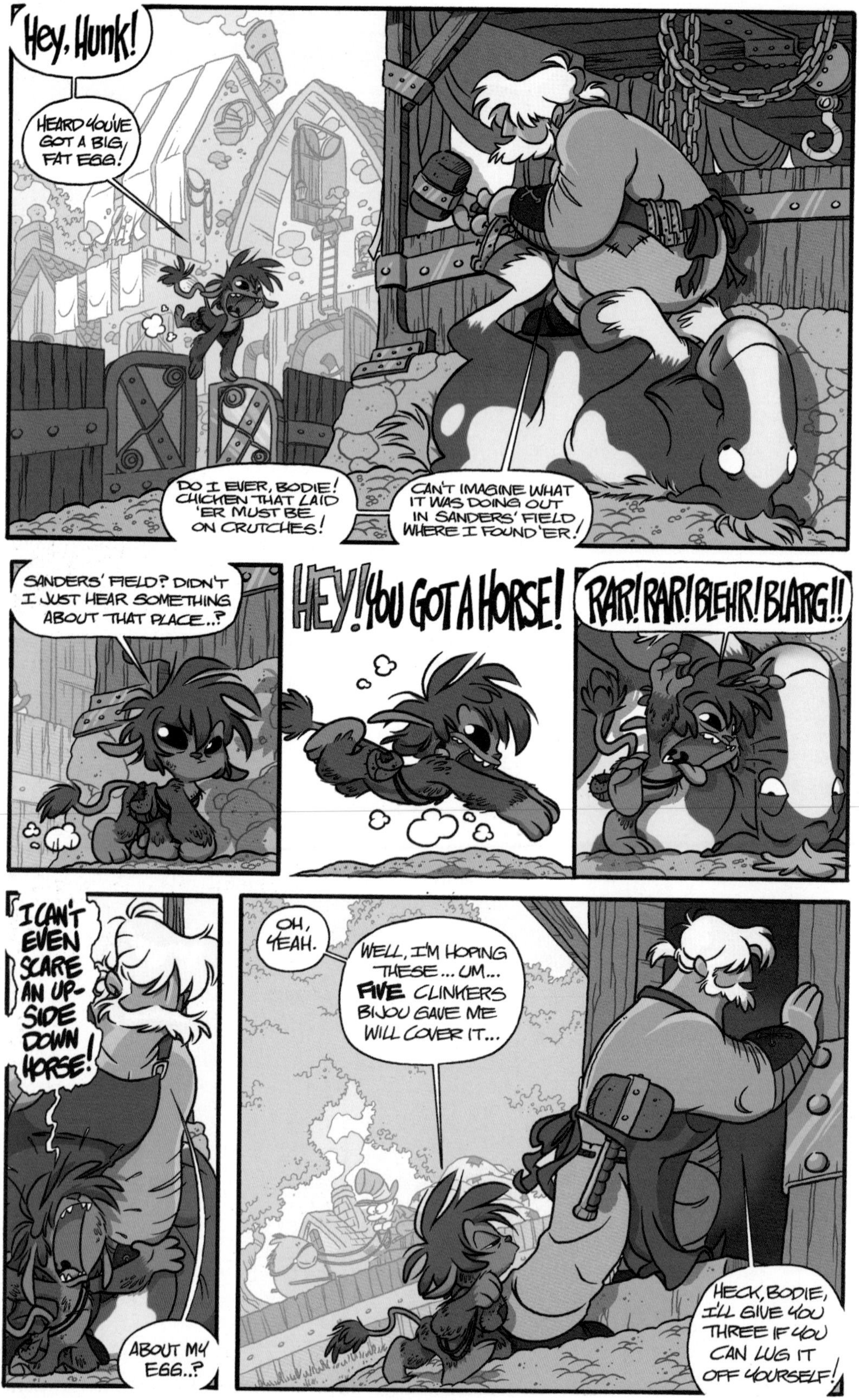
Hey, Hunk!
HEARD YOU'VE GOT A BIG, FAT EGG!
DO I EVER, BODIE! CHICKEN THAT LAID 'ER MUST BE ON CRUTCHES!
CAN'T IMAGINE WHAT IT WAS DOING OUT IN SANDERS' FIELD WHERE I FOUND 'ER!
SANDERS' FIELD? DIDN'T I JUST HEAR SOMETHING ABOUT THAT PLACE..?
HEY! YOU GOT A HORSE!
RAR! RAR! BLEHR! BLARG!!
I CAN'T EVEN SCARE AN UP-SIDE DOWN HORSE!
ABOUT MY EGG..?
OH, YEAH.
WELL, I'M HOPING THESE... UM... FIVE CLINKERS BIJOU GAVE ME WILL COVER IT...
HECK, BODIE, I'LL GIVE YOU THREE IF YOU CAN LUG IT OFF YOURSELF!

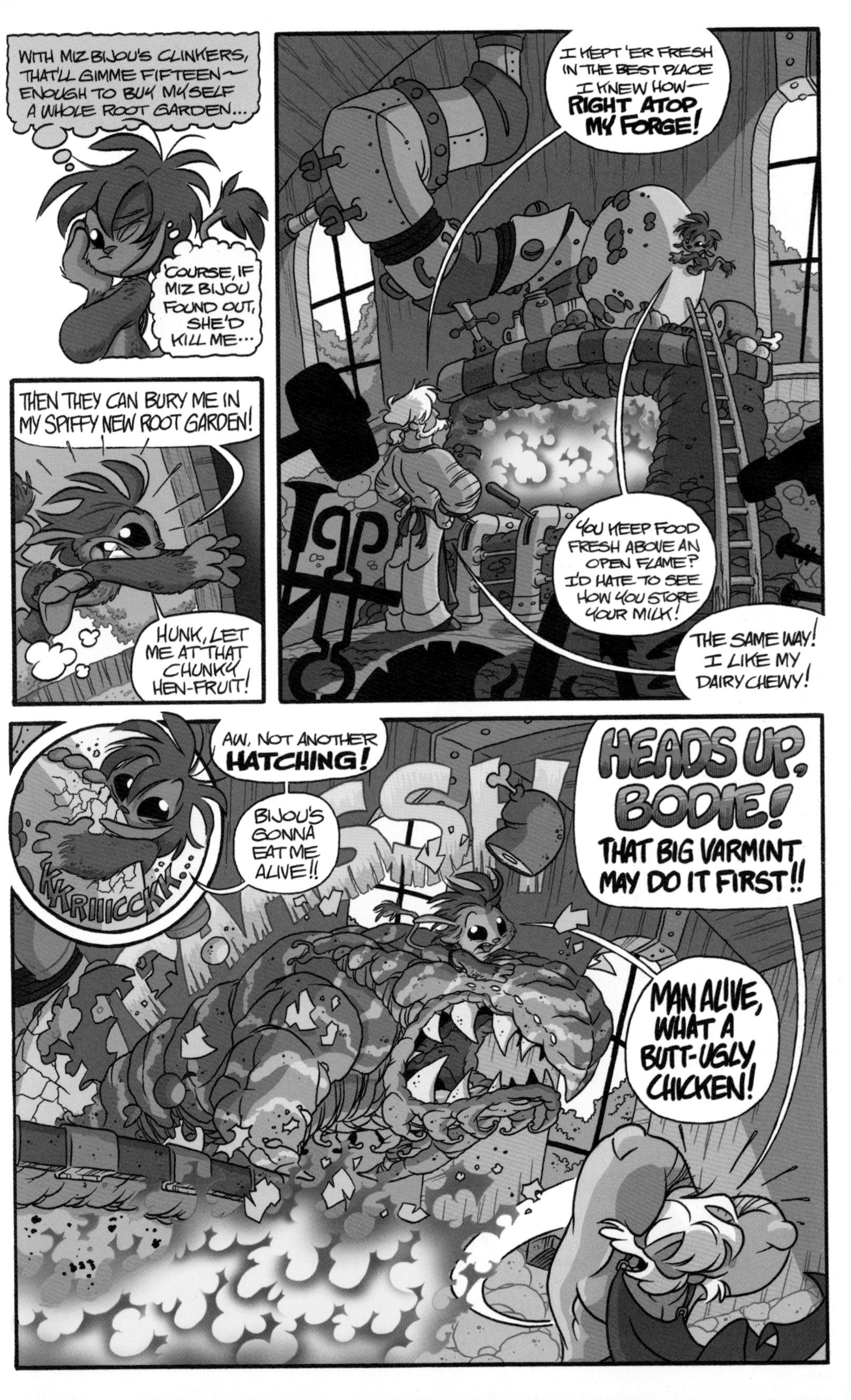
WITH MIZ BIJOU'S CLINKERS, THAT'LL GIMME FIFTEEN— ENOUGH TO BUY MYSELF A WHOLE ROOT GARDEN...
'COURSE, IF MIZ BIJOU FOUND OUT, SHE'D KILL ME...
THEN THEY CAN BURY ME IN MY SPIFFY NEW ROOT GARDEN!
HUNK, LET ME AT THAT CHUNKY HEN-FRUIT!
I KEPT 'ER FRESH IN THE BEST PLACE I KNEW HOW— RIGHT ATOP MY FORGE!
YOU KEEP FOOD FRESH ABOVE AN OPEN FLAME? I'D HATE TO SEE HOW YOU STORE YOUR MILK!
THE SAME WAY! I LIKE MY DAIRY CHEWY!
AW, NOT ANOTHER HATCHING!
BIJOU'S GONNA EAT ME ALIVE!!
KKRIIICCKK
HEADS UP, BODIE! THAT BIG VARMINT MAY DO IT FIRST!!
MAN ALIVE, WHAT A BUTT-UGLY CHICKEN!

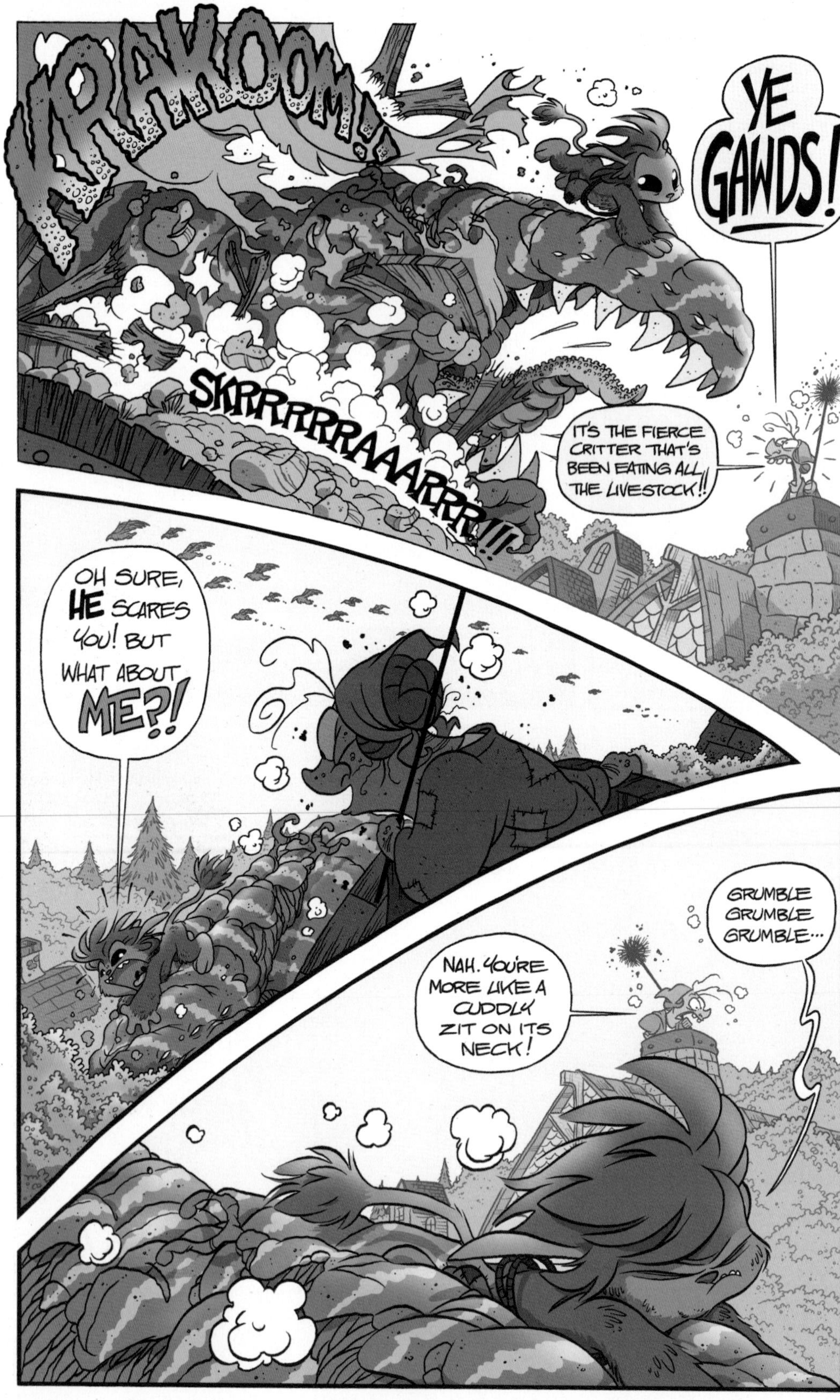
KRAKOOM!!
YE GAWDS!
SKRRRRRRRAAARRRR!!!
IT'S THE FIERCE CRITTER THAT'S BEEN EATING ALL THE LIVESTOCK!!
OH SURE, HE SCARES YOU! BUT WHAT ABOUT ME?!
GRUMBLE GRUMBLE GRUMBLE...
NAH. YOU'RE MORE LIKE A CUDDLY ZIT ON ITS NECK!

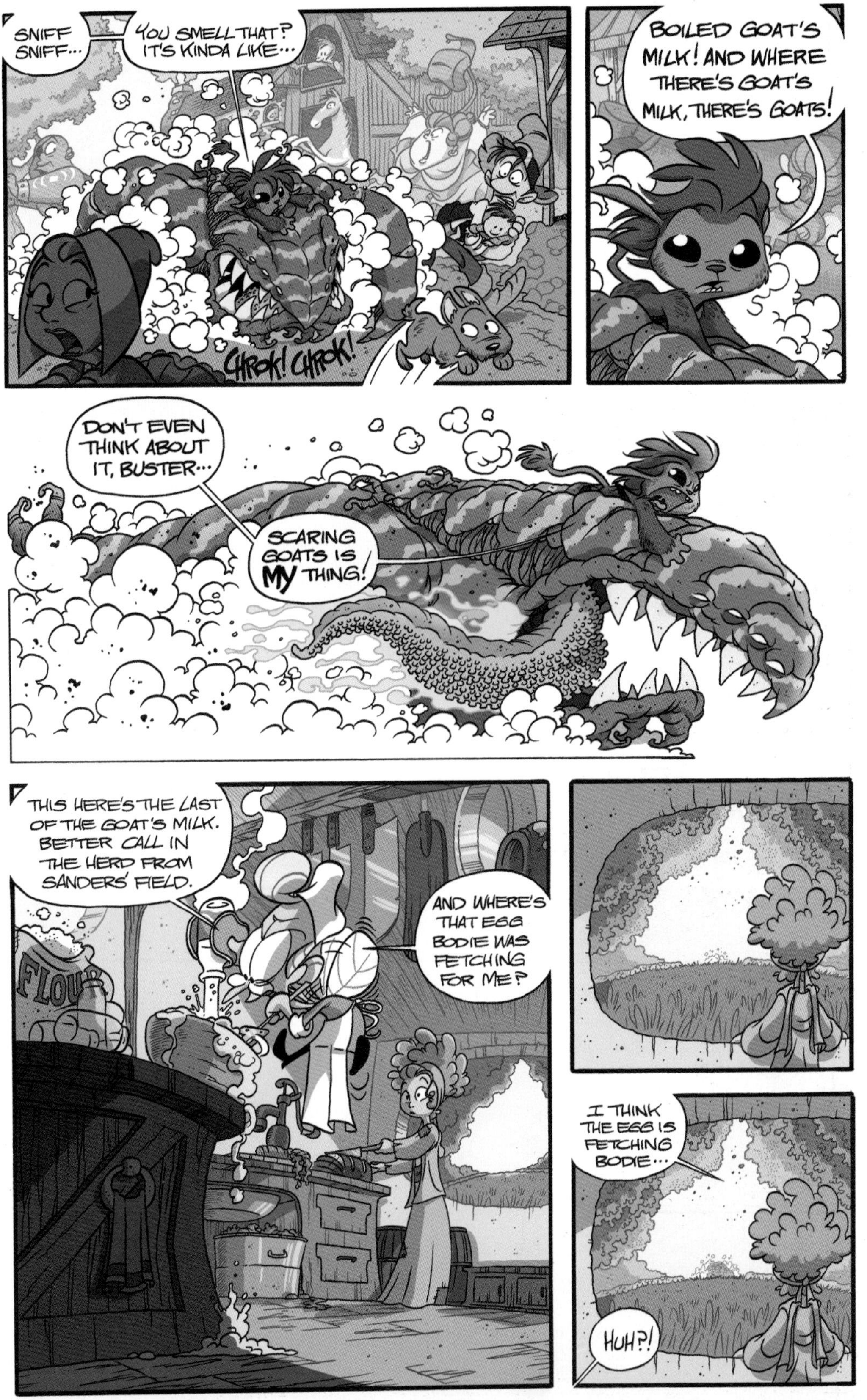
SNIFF SNIFF...
YOU SMELL THAT? IT'S KINDA LIKE...
CHROK! CHROK!
BOILED GOAT'S MILK! AND WHERE THERE'S GOAT'S MILK, THERE'S GOATS!
DON'T EVEN THINK ABOUT IT, BUSTER...
SCARING GOATS IS MY THING!
THIS HERE'S THE LAST OF THE GOAT'S MILK. BETTER CALL IN THE HERD FROM SANDERS' FIELD.
FLOUR
AND WHERE'S THAT EGG BODIE WAS FETCHING FOR ME?
I THINK THE EGG IS FETCHING BODIE...
HUH?!

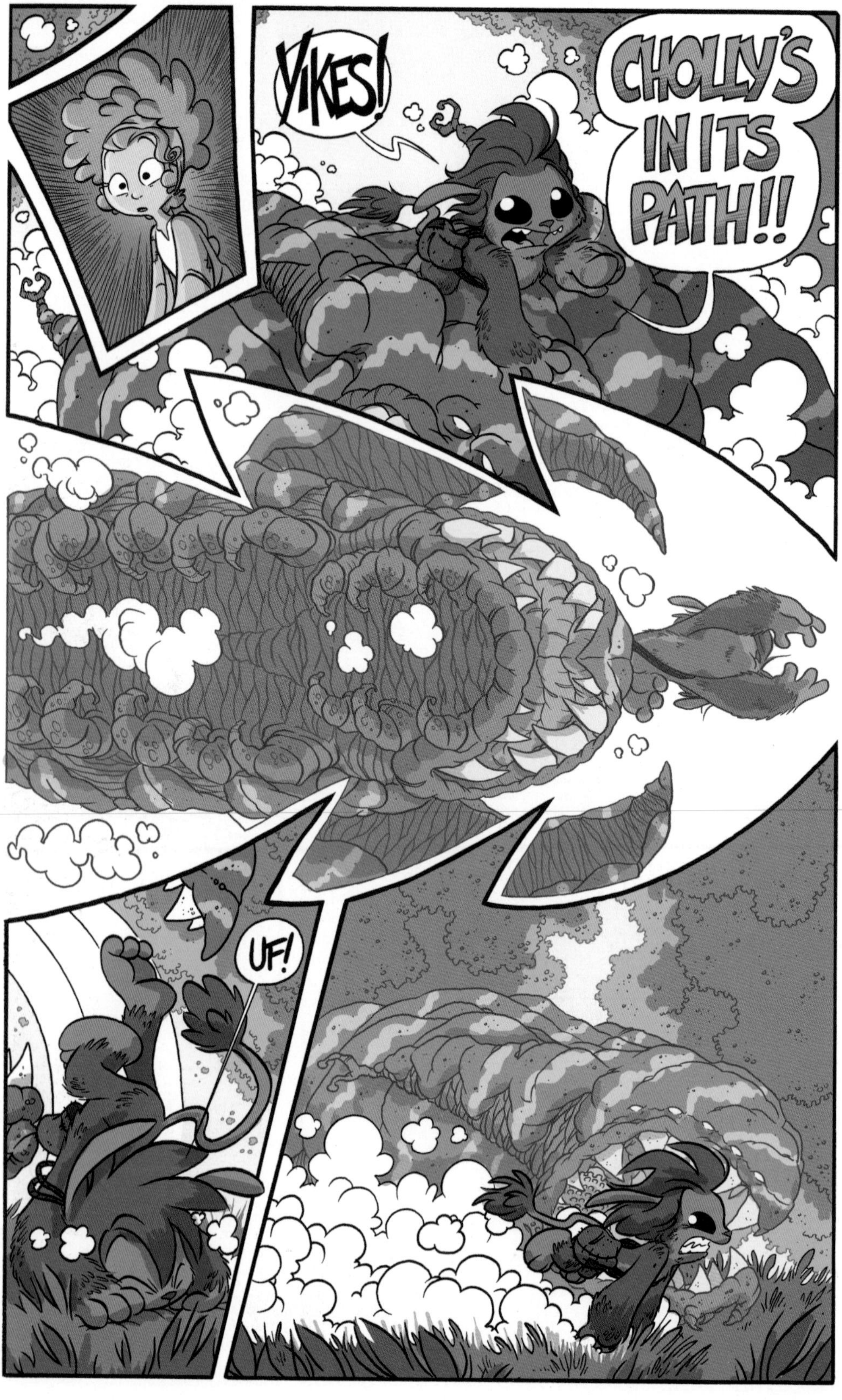
YIKES!
CHOLLY'S IN ITS PATH!!
UF!

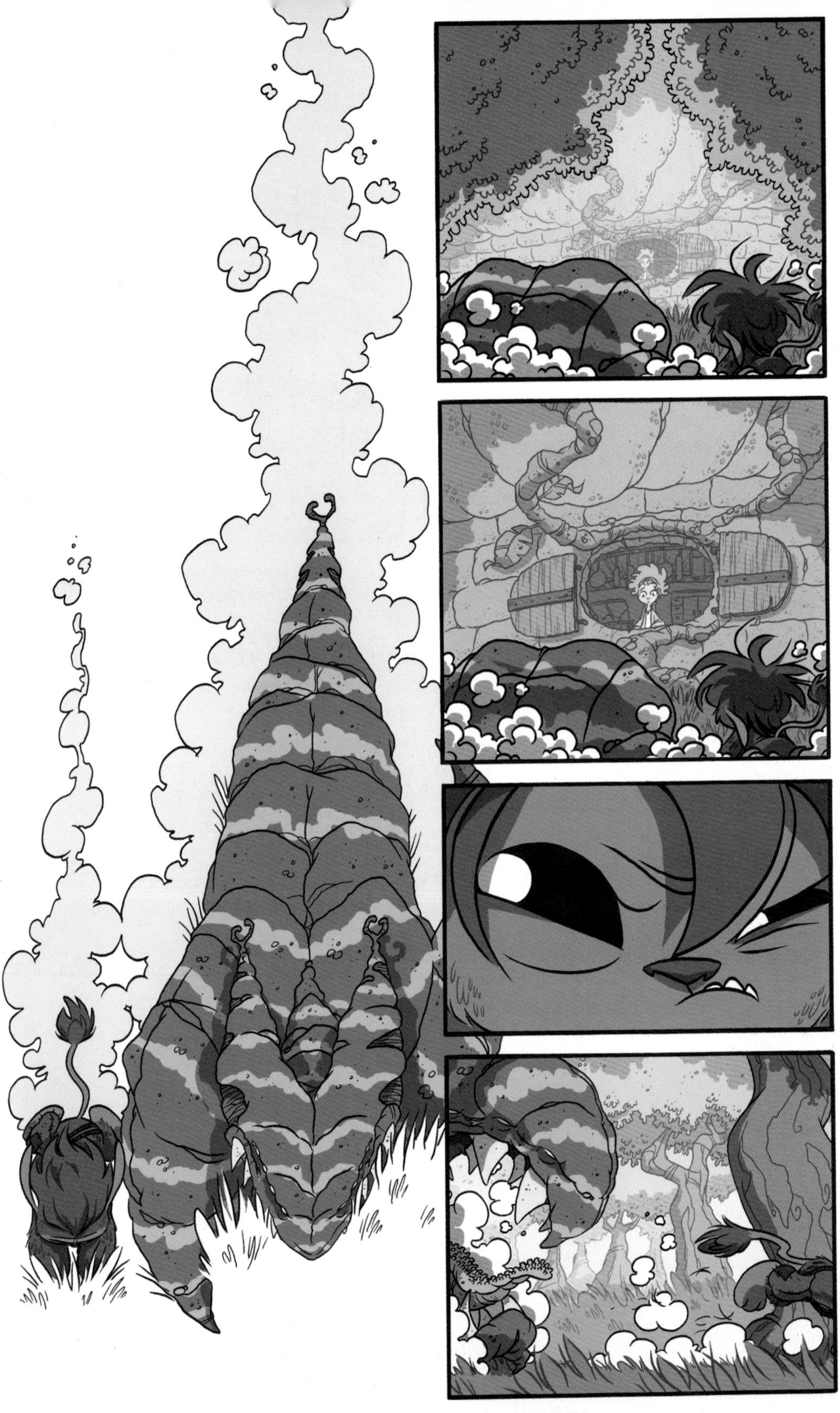

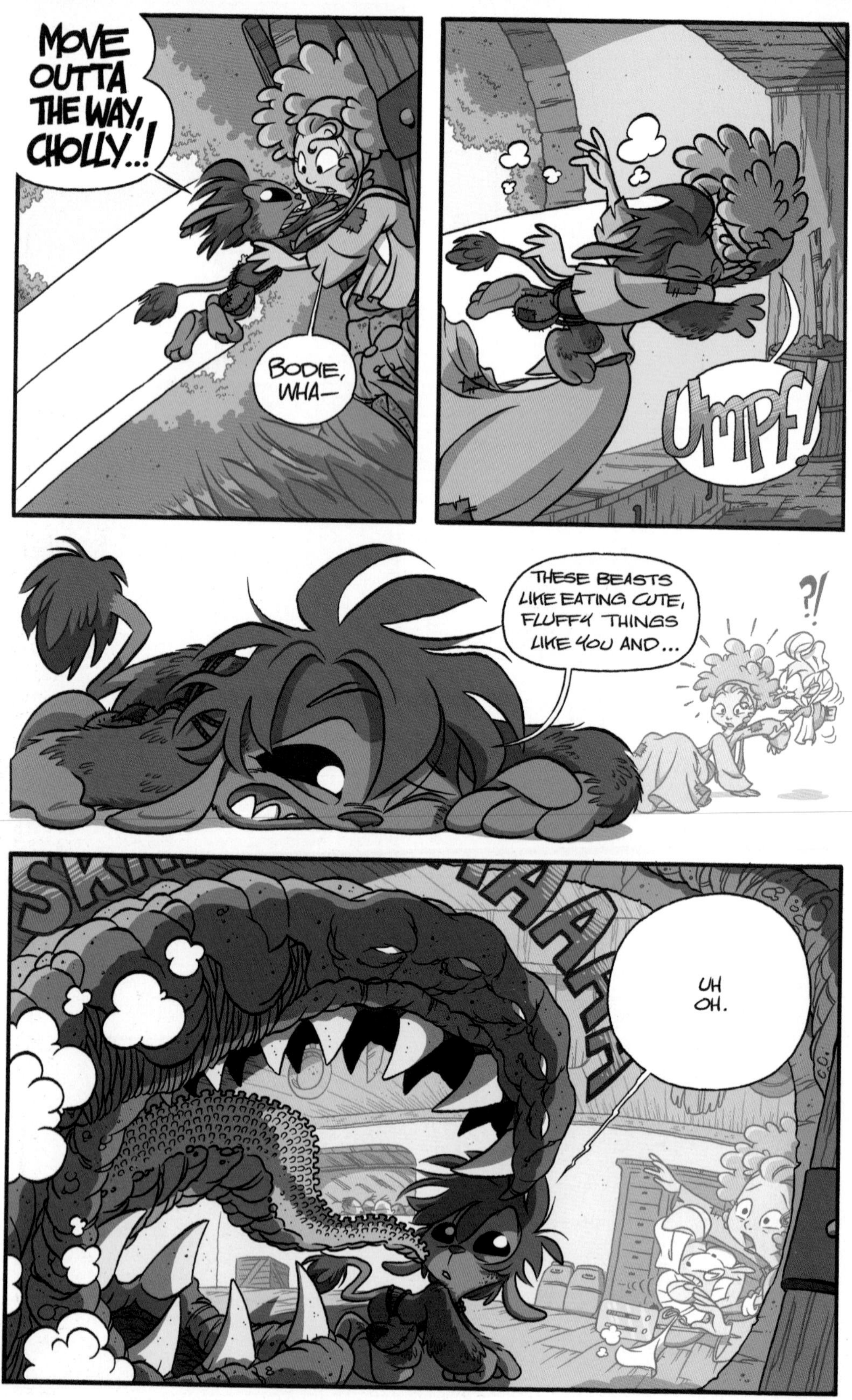
MOVE OUTTA THE WAY, CHOLLY..!
BODIE, WHA—
UMPF!
THESE BEASTS LIKE EATING CUTE, FLUFFY THINGS LIKE YOU AND...
?!
UH OH.

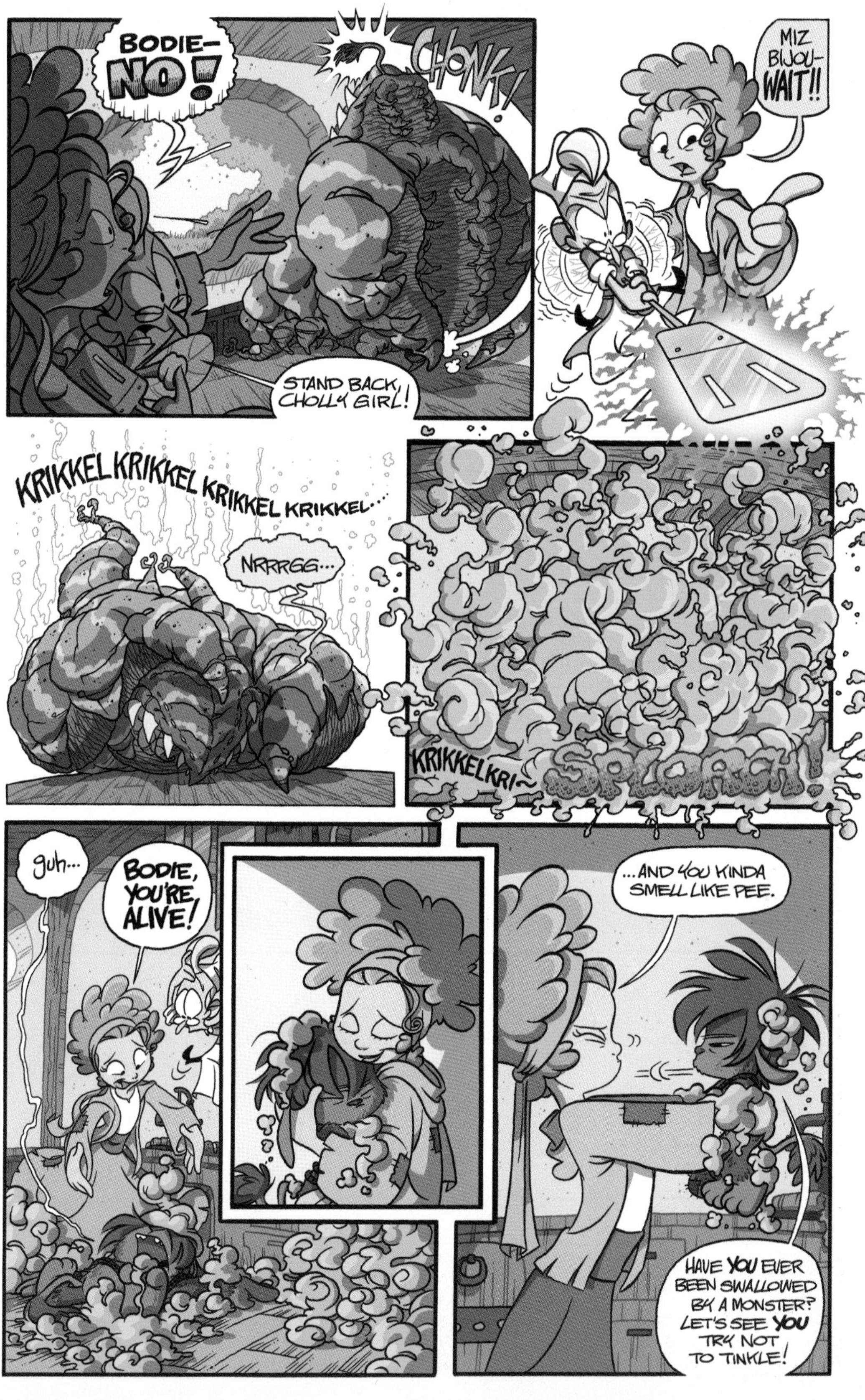

BODIE–NO!
CHONK!
MIZ BIJOU–WAIT!!
STAND BACK, CHOLLY GIRL!
KRIKKEL KRIKKEL KRIKKEL KRIKKEL...
NRRRGG...
KRIKKELKRI~ SPLOOSH!
guh...
BODIE, YOU'RE ALIVE!
...AND YOU KINDA SMELL LIKE PEE.
HAVE YOU EVER BEEN SWALLOWED BY A MONSTER? LET'S SEE YOU TRY NOT TO TINKLE!

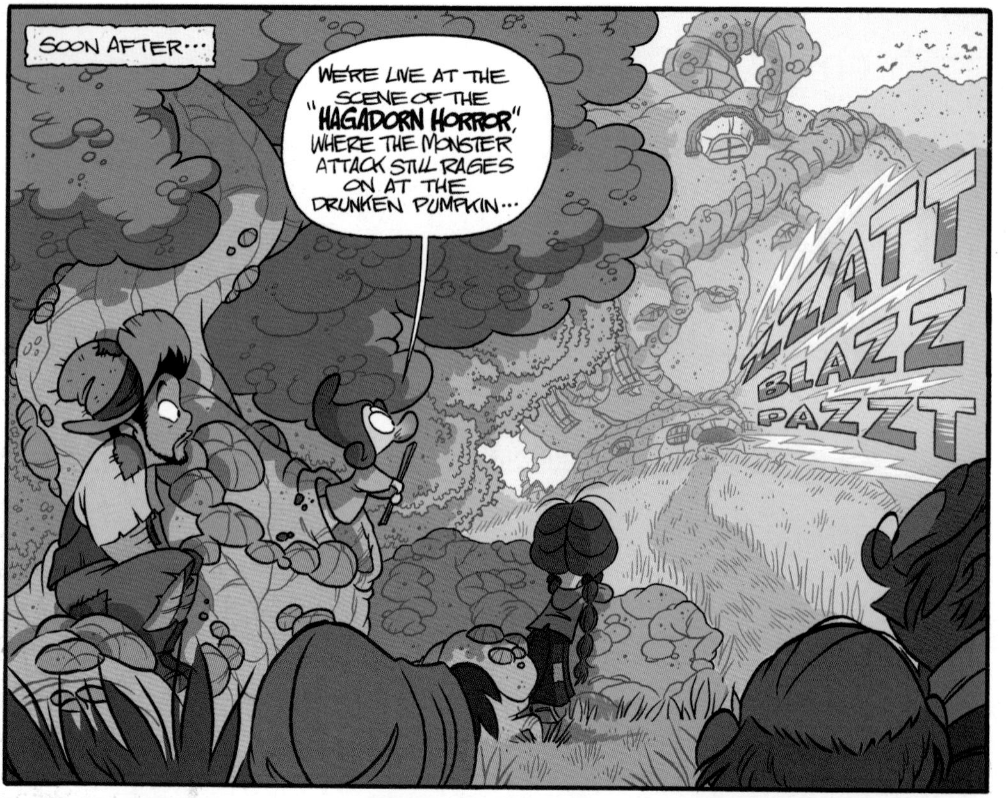
SOON AFTER…
WE'RE LIVE AT THE SCENE OF THE "HAGADORN HORROR," WHERE THE MONSTER ATTACK STILL RAGES ON AT THE DRUNKEN PUMPKIN…
ZZZATT
BLAZZ
PAZZZT

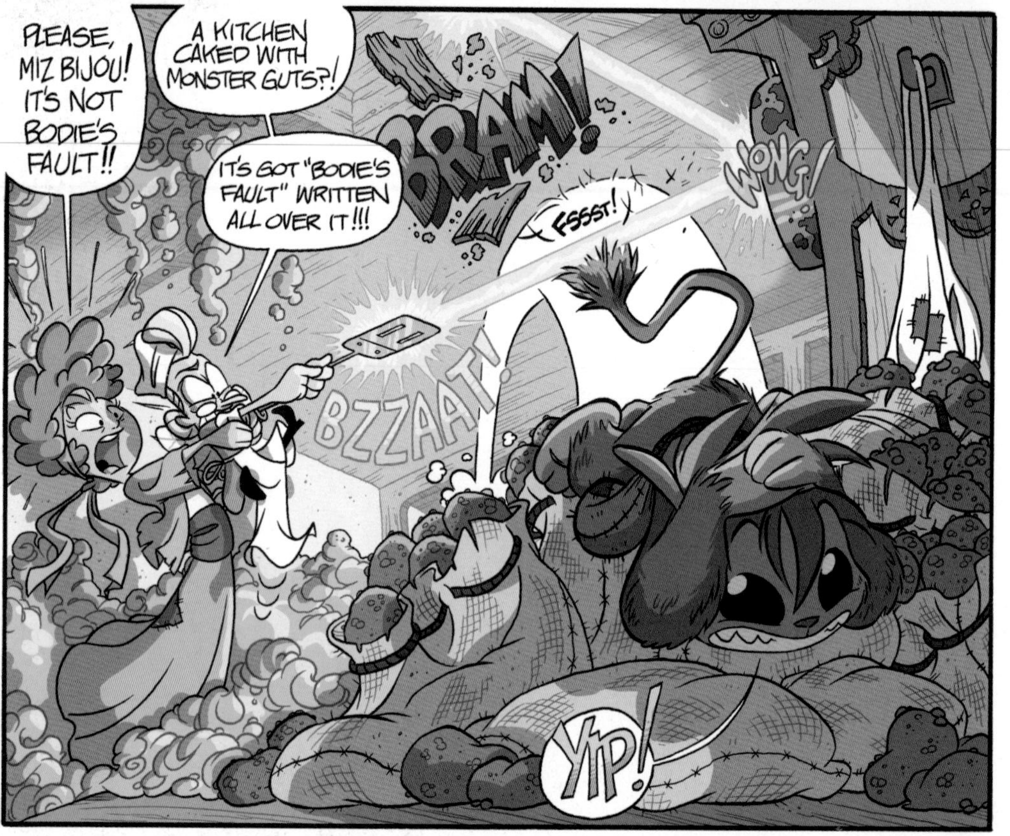
PLEASE, MIZ BIJOU! IT'S NOT BODIE'S FAULT!!
A KITCHEN CAKED WITH MONSTER GUTS?!
IT'S GOT "BODIE'S FAULT" WRITTEN ALL OVER IT!!!
BRAM!
WONG!
FSSST!
BZZAAT!
YIP!

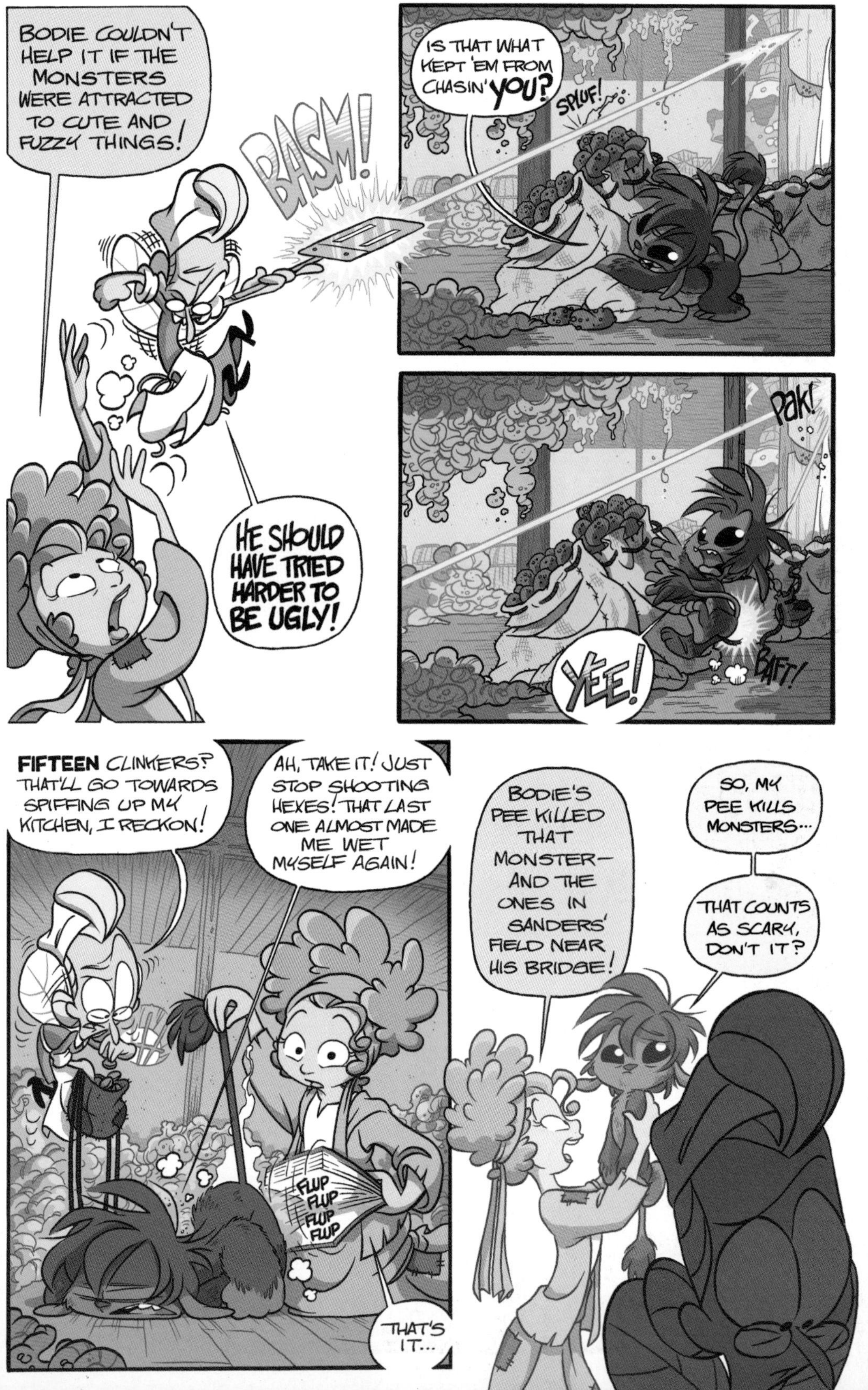
BODIE COULDN'T HELP IT IF THE MONSTERS WERE ATTRACTED TO CUTE AND FUZZY THINGS!
BASM!
HE SHOULD HAVE TRIED HARDER TO BE UGLY!
IS THAT WHAT KEPT 'EM FROM CHASIN' YOU?
SPLUF!
PAK!
YEE!
BAFT!
FIFTEEN CLINKERS? THAT'LL GO TOWARDS SPIFFING UP MY KITCHEN, I RECKON!
AH, TAKE IT! JUST STOP SHOOTING HEXES! THAT LAST ONE ALMOST MADE ME WET MYSELF AGAIN!
FLUP FLUP FLUP FLUP
THAT'S IT...
BODIE'S PEE KILLED THAT MONSTER— AND THE ONES IN SANDERS' FIELD NEAR HIS BRIDGE!
SO, MY PEE KILLS MONSTERS...
THAT COUNTS AS SCARY, DON'T IT?

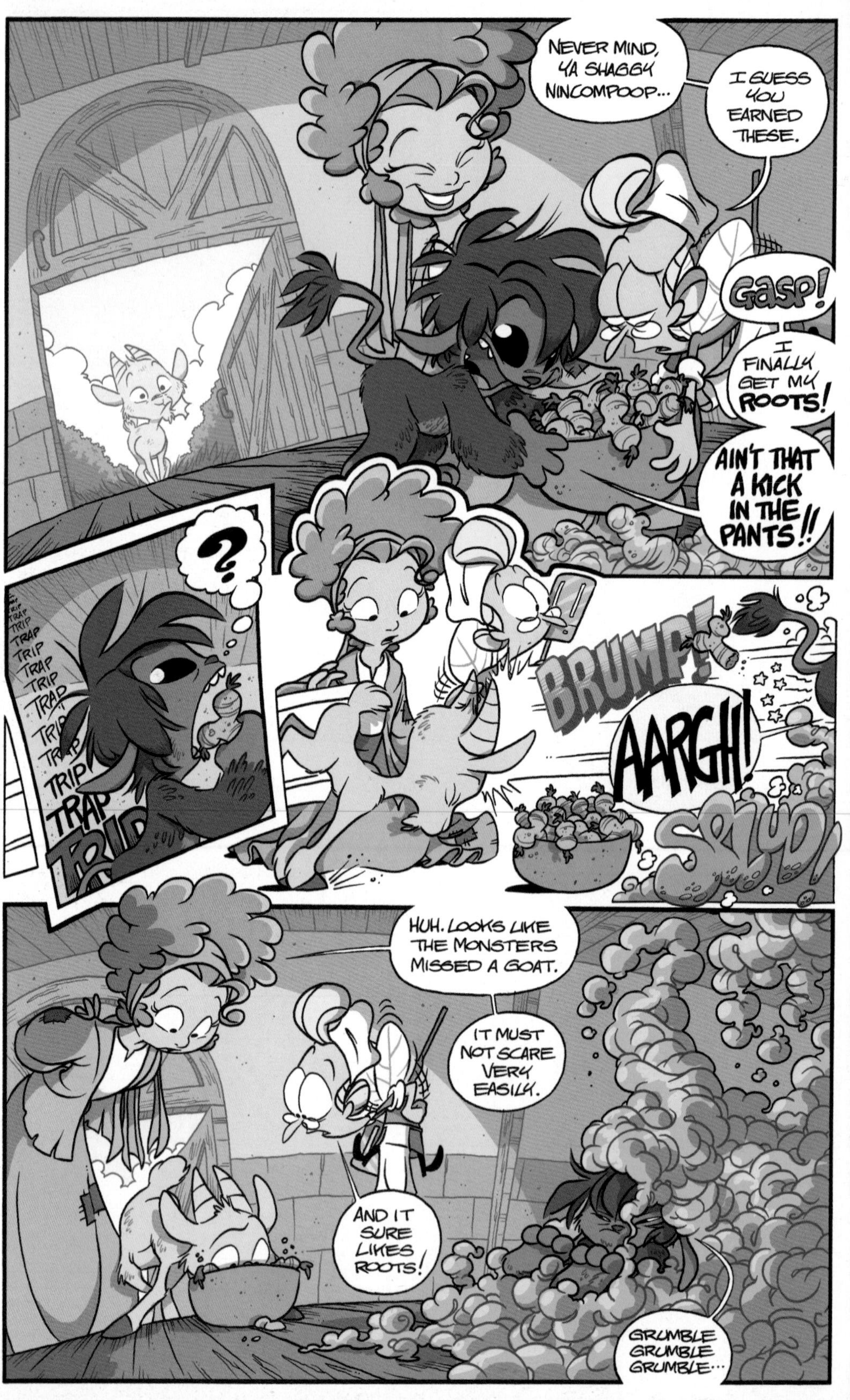

NEVER MIND, YA SHAGGY NINCOMPOOP...
I GUESS YOU EARNED THESE.
GASP!
I FINALLY GET MY ROOTS!
AIN'T THAT A KICK IN THE PANTS!!
?
TRIP TRAP TRIP TRAP TRIP TRAP TRIP TRAP TRIP TRAP TRIP
BRUMP!
AARGH!
SPLUD!
HUH. LOOKS LIKE THE MONSTERS MISSED A GOAT.
IT MUST NOT SCARE VERY EASILY.
AND IT SURE LIKES ROOTS!
GRUMBLE GRUMBLE GRUMBLE...

CHAPTER 2

MAKE UP MIX UP

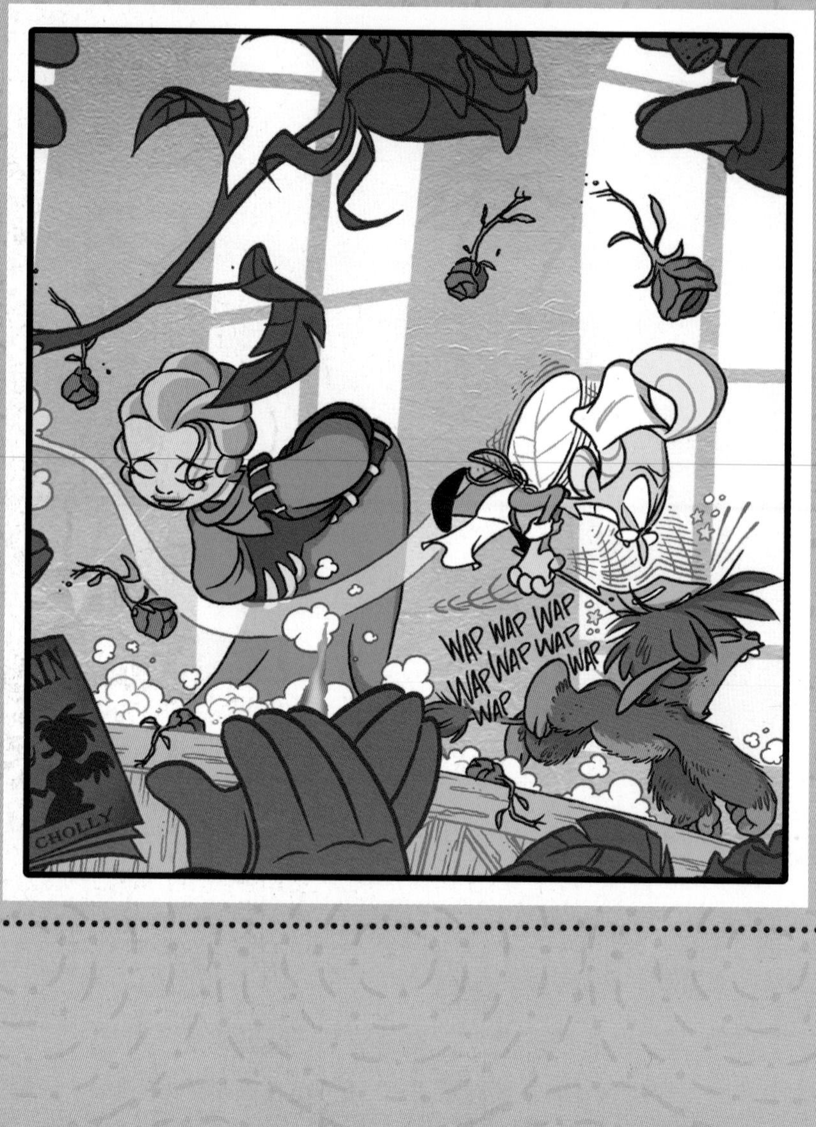
WAP WAP WAP
WAP WAP WAP
WAP
WAP
WAP
CHOLLY

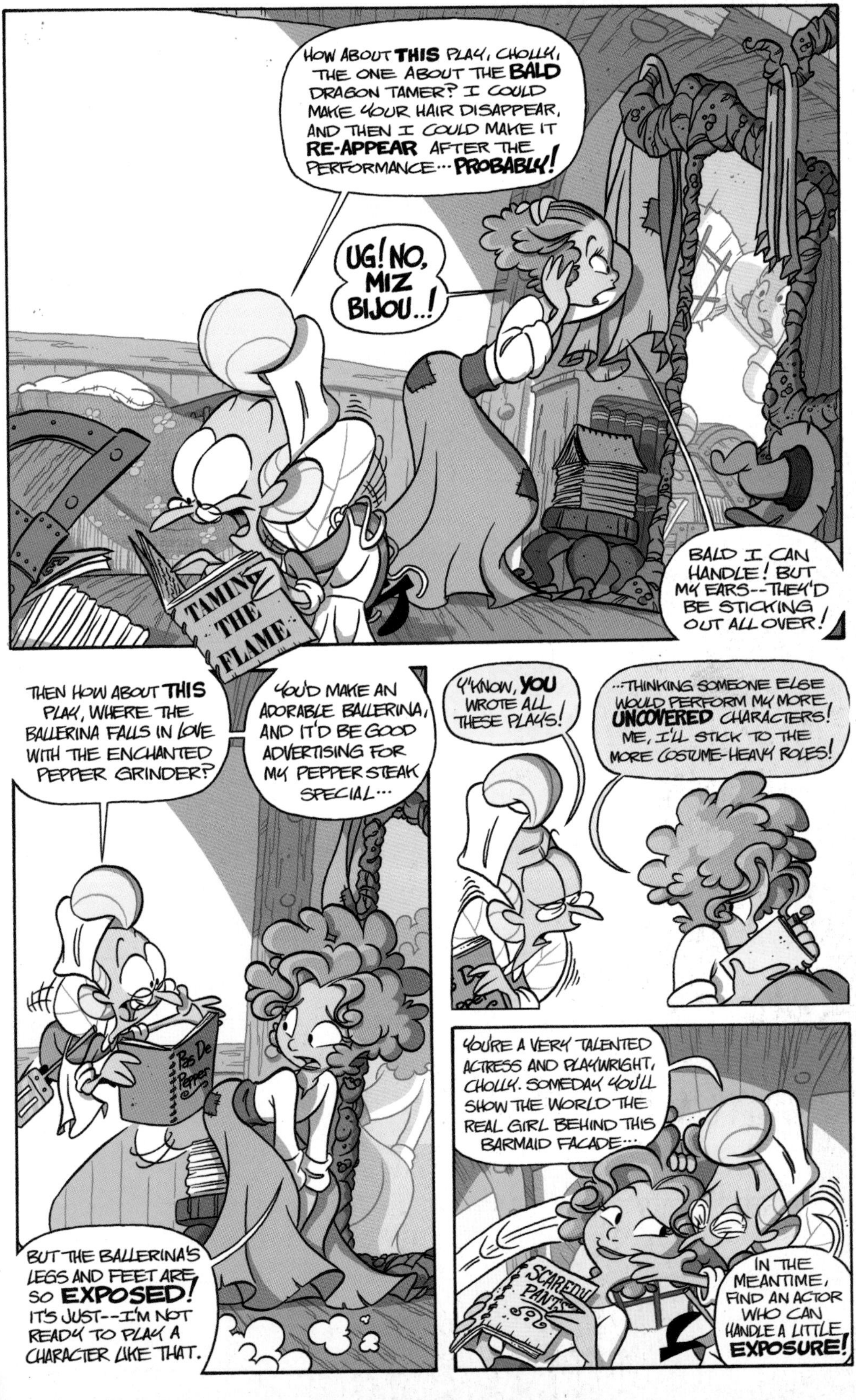
HOW ABOUT THIS PLAY, CHOLLY, THE ONE ABOUT THE BALD DRAGON TAMER? I COULD MAKE YOUR HAIR DISAPPEAR, AND THEN I COULD MAKE IT RE-APPEAR AFTER THE PERFORMANCE... PROBABLY!
UG! NO, MIZ BIJOU..!
BALD I CAN HANDLE! BUT MY EARS--THEY'D BE STICKING OUT ALL OVER!
TAMING THE FLAME
THEN HOW ABOUT THIS PLAY, WHERE THE BALLERINA FALLS IN LOVE WITH THE ENCHANTED PEPPER GRINDER?
YOU'D MAKE AN ADORABLE BALLERINA, AND IT'D BE GOOD ADVERTISING FOR MY PEPPER STEAK SPECIAL...
Pas De Pepper
BUT THE BALLERINA'S LEGS AND FEET ARE SO EXPOSED! IT'S JUST--I'M NOT READY TO PLAY A CHARACTER LIKE THAT.
Y'KNOW, YOU WROTE ALL THESE PLAYS!
...THINKING SOMEONE ELSE WOULD PERFORM MY MORE UNCOVERED CHARACTERS! ME, I'LL STICK TO THE MORE COSTUME-HEAVY ROLES!
YOU'RE A VERY TALENTED ACTRESS AND PLAYWRIGHT, CHOLLY. SOMEDAY YOU'LL SHOW THE WORLD THE REAL GIRL BEHIND THIS BARMAID FACADE...
SCAREDY PANTS
IN THE MEANTIME, FIND AN ACTOR WHO CAN HANDLE A LITTLE EXPOSURE!

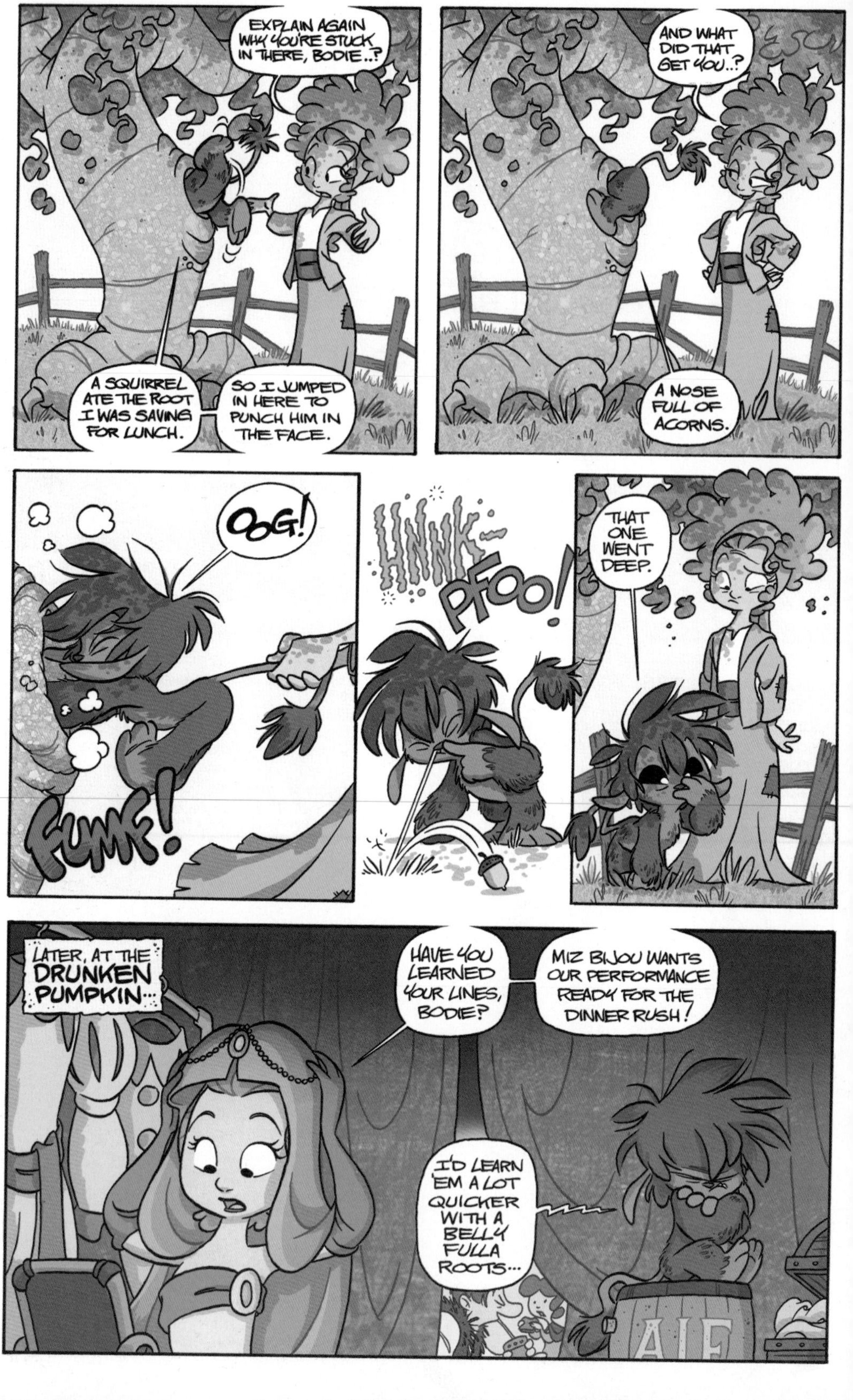
EXPLAIN AGAIN WHY YOU'RE STUCK IN THERE, BODIE..?
A SQUIRREL ATE THE ROOT I WAS SAVING FOR LUNCH.
SO I JUMPED IN HERE TO PUNCH HIM IN THE FACE.
AND WHAT DID THAT GET YOU..?
A NOSE FULL OF ACORNS.
OOG!
FUMF!
HNNK--
PFOO!
THAT ONE WENT DEEP.
LATER, AT THE DRUNKEN PUMPKIN...
HAVE YOU LEARNED YOUR LINES, BODIE?
MIZ BIJOU WANTS OUR PERFORMANCE READY FOR THE DINNER RUSH!
I'D LEARN 'EM A LOT QUICKER WITH A BELLY FULLA ROOTS...
ALE

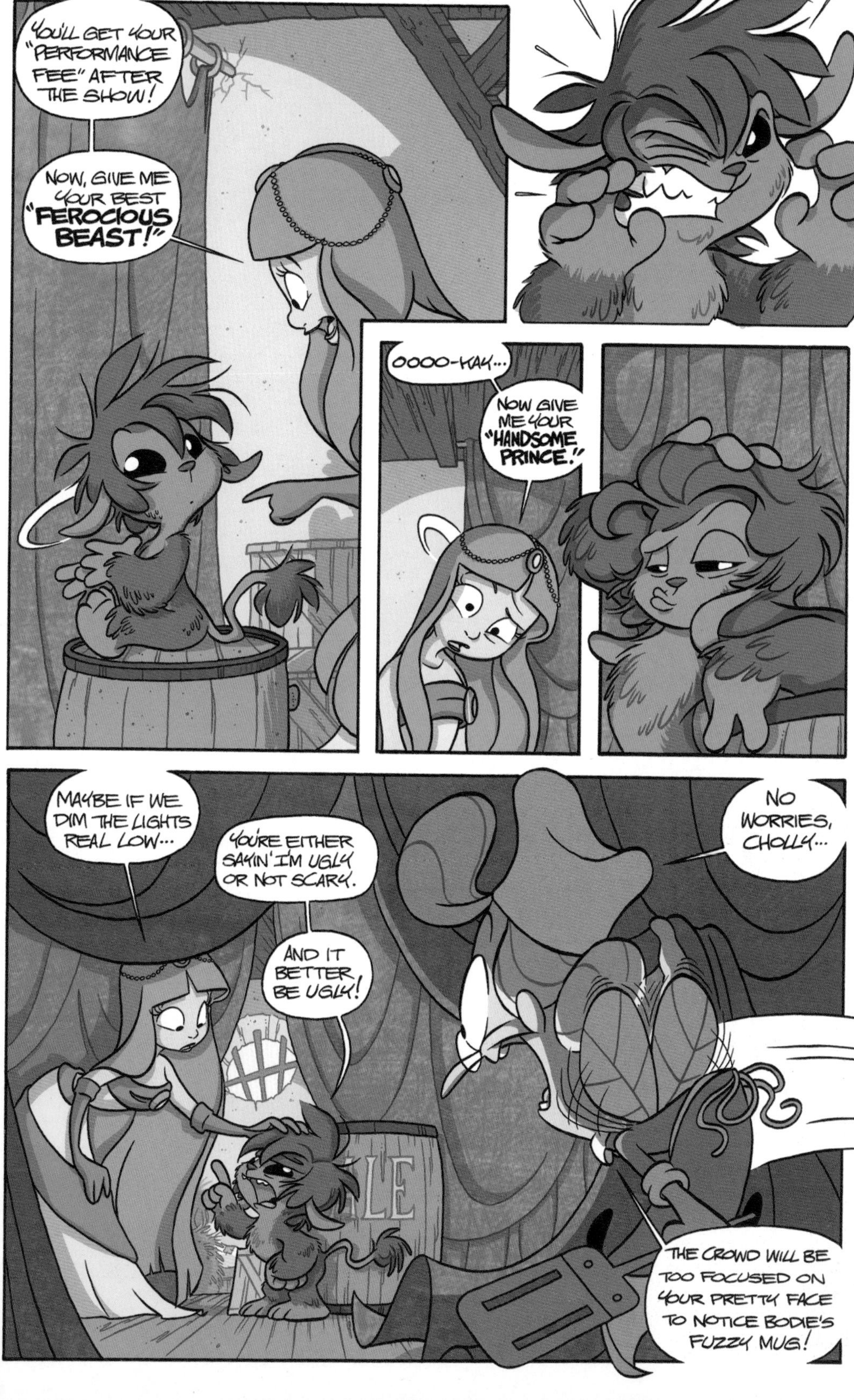
YOU'LL GET YOUR "PERFORMANCE FEE" AFTER THE SHOW!
NOW, GIVE ME YOUR BEST "FEROCIOUS BEAST!"
OOOO-KAY...
NOW GIVE ME YOUR "HANDSOME PRINCE."
MAYBE IF WE DIM THE LIGHTS REAL LOW...
YOU'RE EITHER SAYIN' I'M UGLY OR NOT SCARY.
AND IT BETTER BE UGLY!
NO WORRIES, CHOLLY...
THE CROWD WILL BE TOO FOCUSED ON YOUR PRETTY FACE TO NOTICE BODIE'S FUZZY MUG!

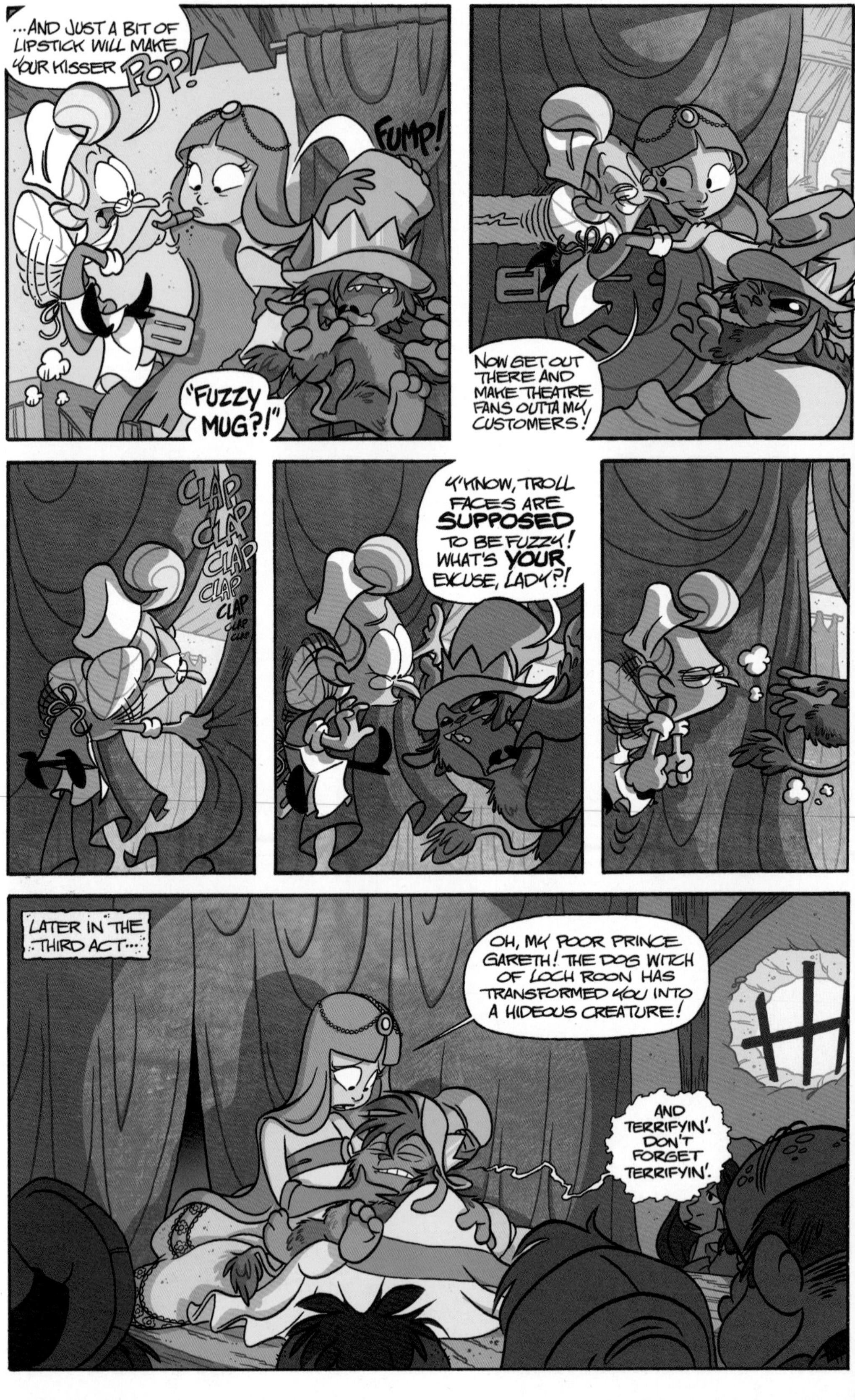
...AND JUST A BIT OF LIPSTICK WILL MAKE YOUR KISSER POP!
FUMP!
"FUZZY MUG?!"
NOW GET OUT THERE AND MAKE THEATRE FANS OUTTA MY CUSTOMERS!
CLAP CLAP CLAP CLAP CLAP CLAP CLAP
Y'KNOW, TROLL FACES ARE SUPPOSED TO BE FUZZY! WHAT'S YOUR EXCUSE, LADY?!
LATER IN THE THIRD ACT...
OH, MY POOR PRINCE GARETH! THE DOG WITCH OF LOCH ROON HAS TRANSFORMED YOU INTO A HIDEOUS CREATURE!
AND TERRIFYIN'. DON'T FORGET TERRIFYIN'.

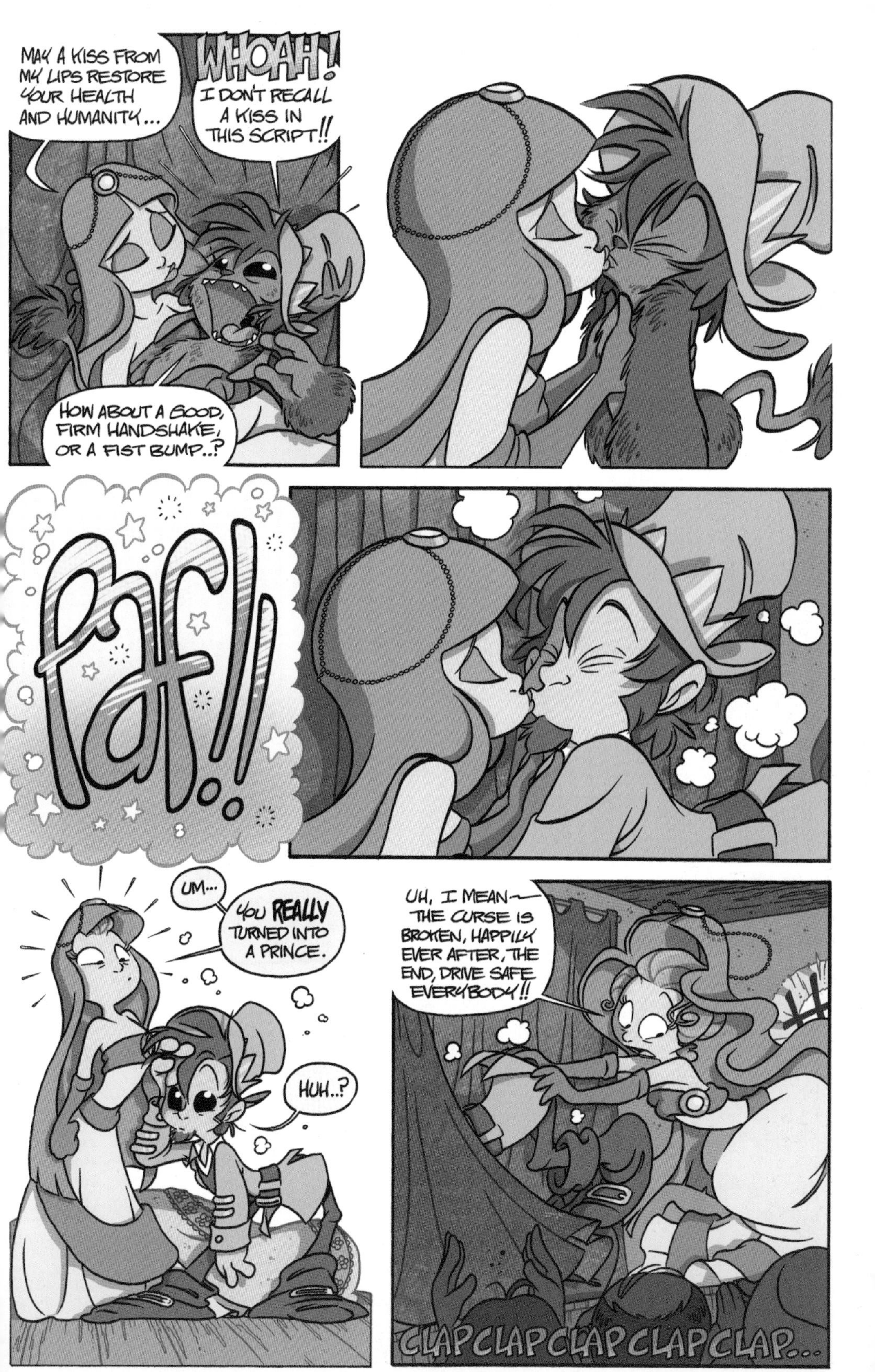
MAY A KISS FROM MY LIPS RESTORE YOUR HEALTH AND HUMANITY...
WHOAH!
I DON'T RECALL A KISS IN THIS SCRIPT!!
HOW ABOUT A GOOD, FIRM HANDSHAKE, OR A FIST BUMP..?
PAF!!
UM...
YOU REALLY TURNED INTO A PRINCE.
HUH..?
UH, I MEAN— THE CURSE IS BROKEN, HAPPILY EVER AFTER, THE END, DRIVE SAFE EVERYBODY!!
CLAP CLAP CLAP CLAP CLAP...

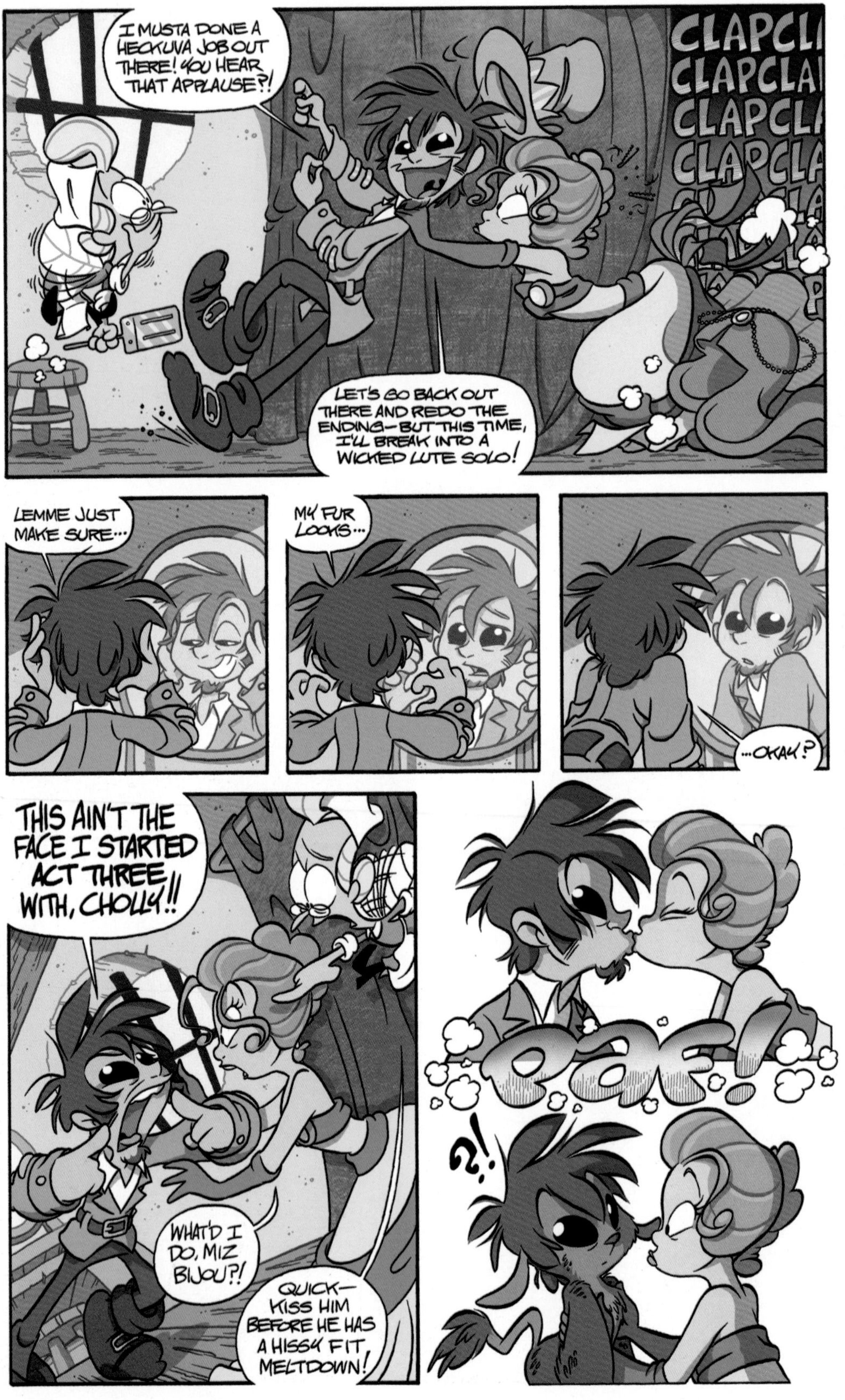
CLAPCLA
I MUSTA DONE A HECKUVA JOB OUT THERE! YOU HEAR THAT APPLAUSE?!
LET'S GO BACK OUT THERE AND REDO THE ENDING—BUT THIS TIME, I'LL BREAK INTO A WICKED LUTE SOLO!
LEMME JUST MAKE SURE...
MY FUR LOOKS...
...OKAY?
THIS AIN'T THE FACE I STARTED ACT THREE WITH, CHOLLY!!
WHAT'D I DO, MIZ BIJOU?!
QUICK— KISS HIM BEFORE HE HAS A HISSY FIT MELTDOWN!
PAF!
?!

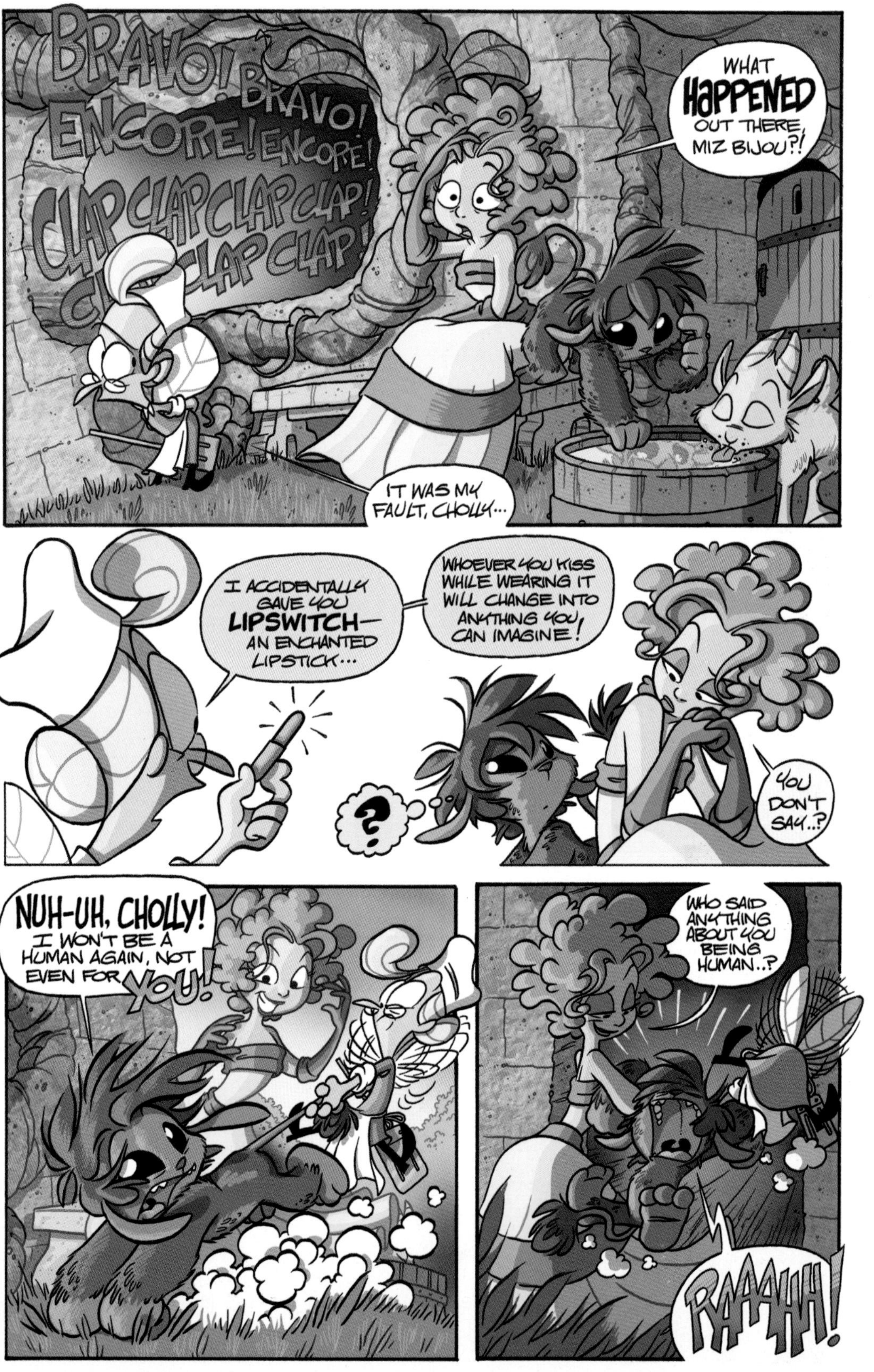

BRAVO! BRAVO!
ENCORE! ENCORE!
CLAP CLAP CLAP CLAP! CLAP CLAP CLAP!
WHAT HAPPENED OUT THERE, MIZ BIJOU?!
IT WAS MY FAULT, CHOLLY...
I ACCIDENTALLY GAVE YOU LIPSWITCH— AN ENCHANTED LIPSTICK...
WHOEVER YOU KISS WHILE WEARING IT WILL CHANGE INTO ANYTHING YOU CAN IMAGINE!
?
YOU DON'T SAY..?
NUH-UH, CHOLLY! I WON'T BE A HUMAN AGAIN, NOT EVEN FOR YOU!
WHO SAID ANYTHING ABOUT YOU BEING HUMAN..?
RAAAHH!

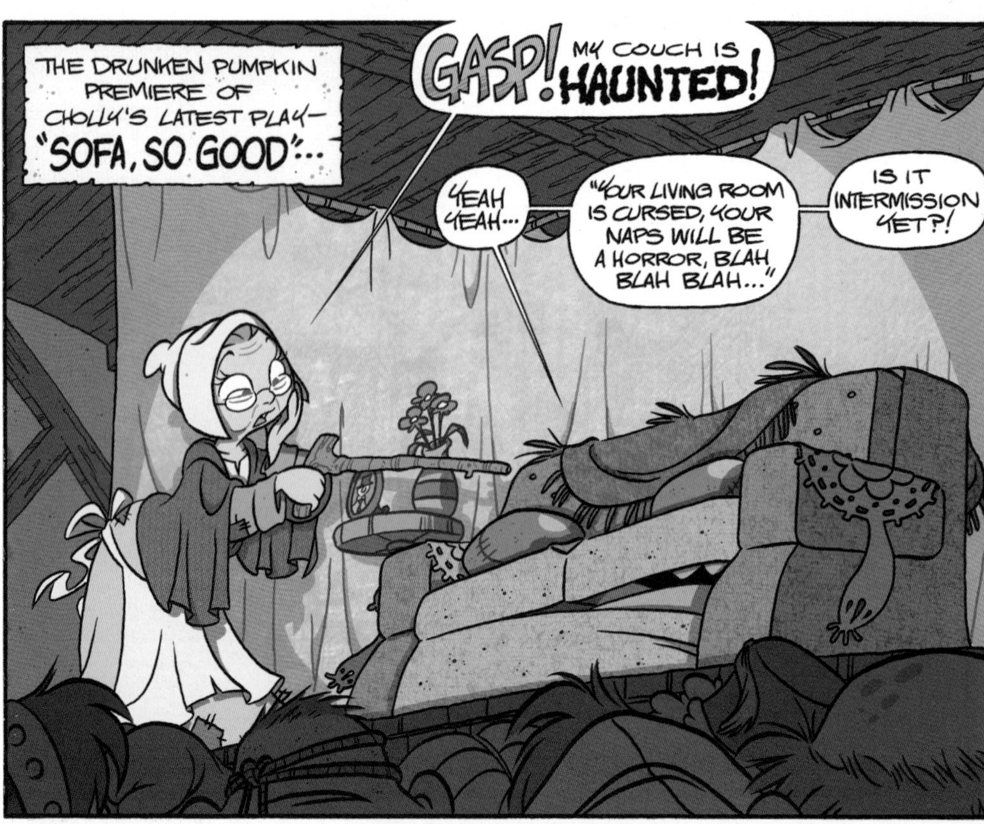
THE DRUNKEN PUMPKIN PREMIERE OF CHOLLY'S LATEST PLAY— "SOFA, SO GOOD"...
GASP! MY COUCH IS HAUNTED!
YEAH YEAH...
"YOUR LIVING ROOM IS CURSED, YOUR NAPS WILL BE A HORROR, BLAH BLAH BLAH..."
IS IT INTERMISSION YET?!

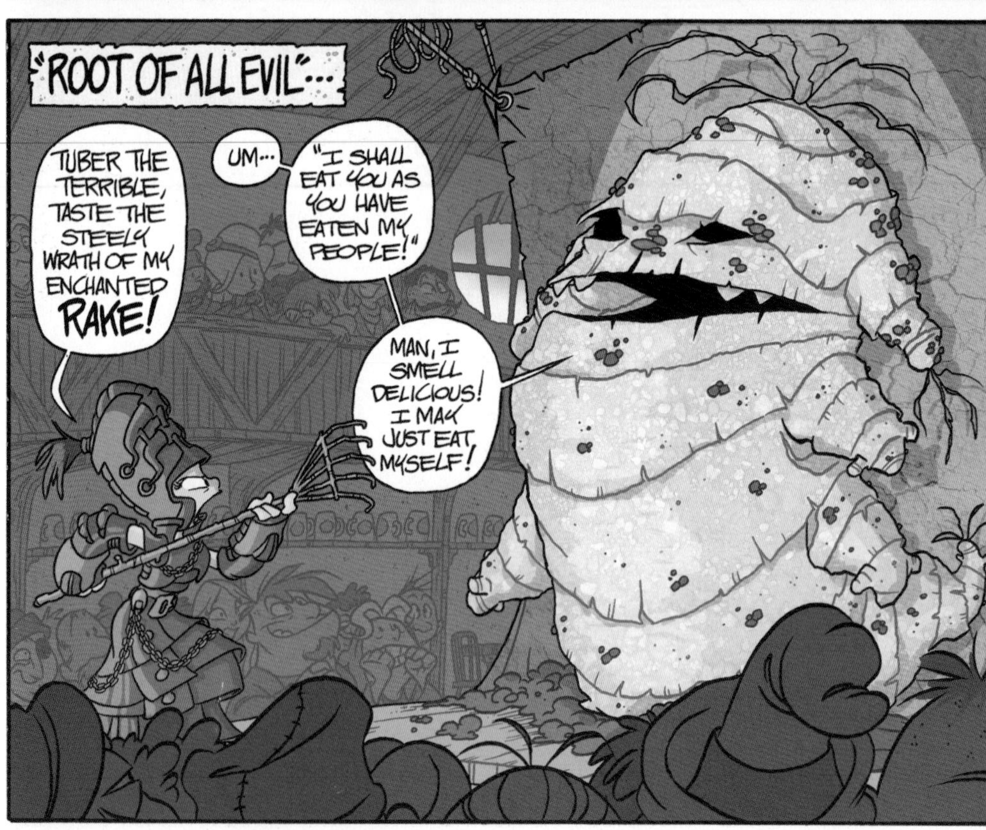
"ROOT OF ALL EVIL"...
TUBER THE TERRIBLE, TASTE THE STEELY WRATH OF MY ENCHANTED RAKE!
UM...
"I SHALL EAT YOU AS YOU HAVE EATEN MY PEOPLE!"
MAN, I SMELL DELICIOUS! I MAY JUST EAT MYSELF!

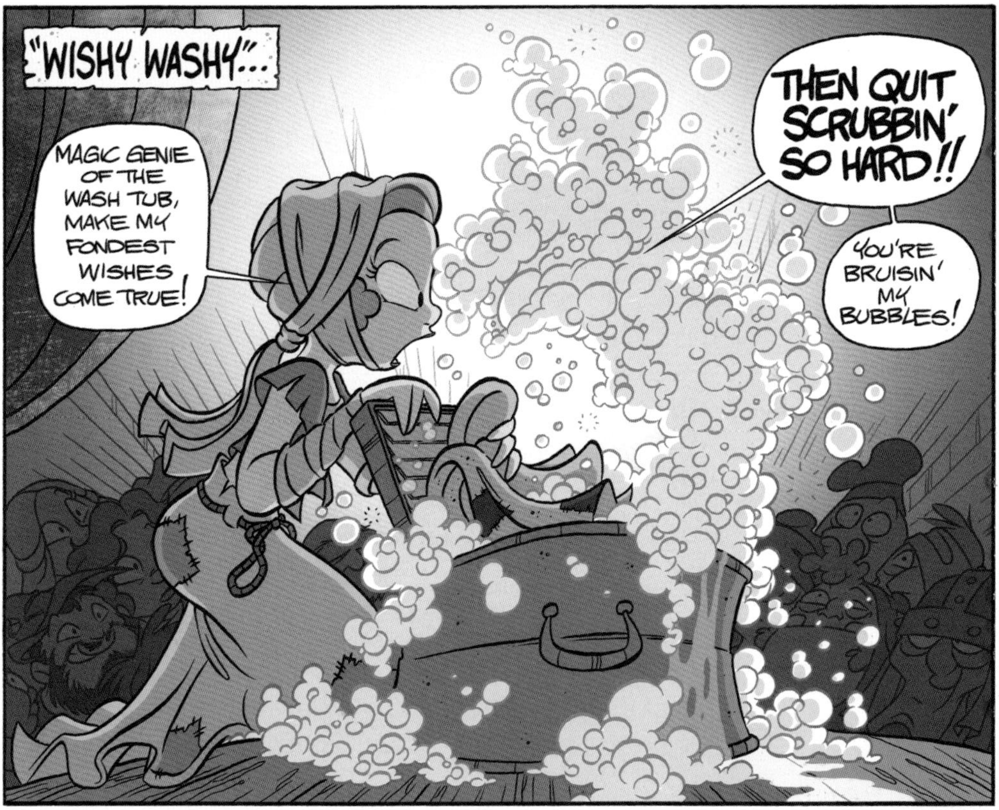
"WISHY WASHY"...
MAGIC GENIE OF THE WASH TUB, MAKE MY FONDEST WISHES COME TRUE!
THEN QUIT SCRUBBIN' SO HARD!!
YOU'RE BRUISIN' MY BUBBLES!

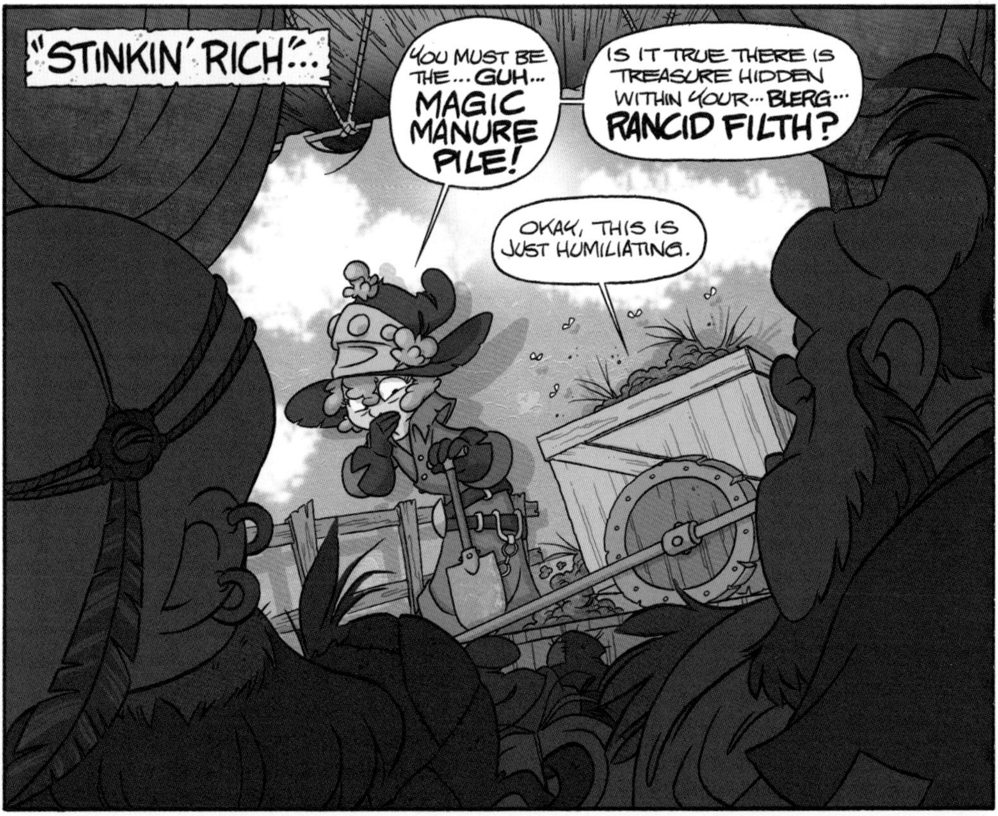
"STINKIN' RICH"...
YOU MUST BE THE... GUH... MAGIC MANURE PILE!
IS IT TRUE THERE IS TREASURE HIDDEN WITHIN YOUR... BLERG... RANCID FILTH?
OKAY, THIS IS JUST HUMILIATING.

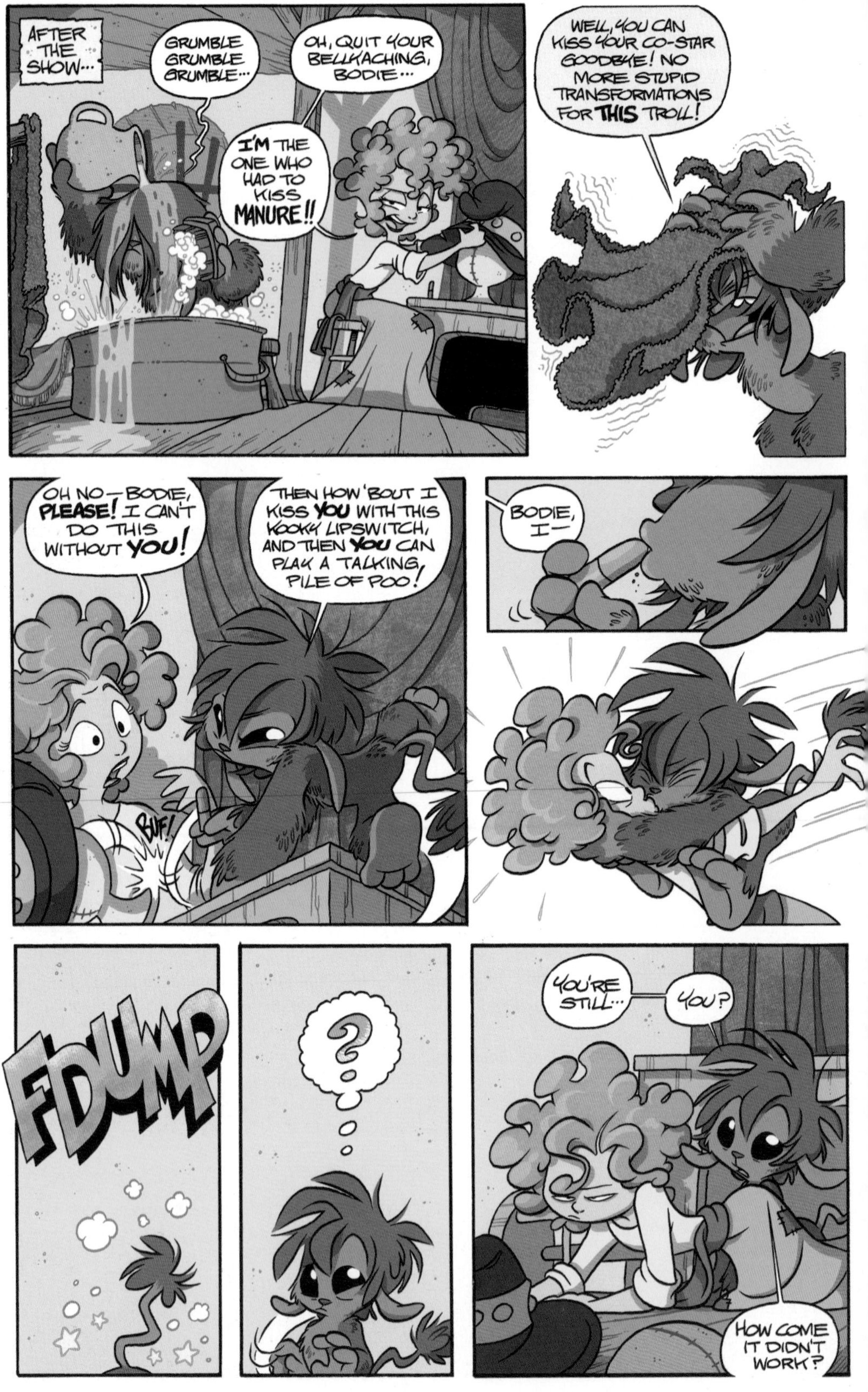
AFTER THE SHOW...
GRUMBLE GRUMBLE GRUMBLE...
OH, QUIT YOUR BELLYACHING, BODIE...
I'M THE ONE WHO HAD TO KISS MANURE!!
WELL, YOU CAN KISS YOUR CO-STAR GOODBYE! NO MORE STUPID TRANSFORMATIONS FOR THIS TROLL!
OH NO—BODIE, PLEASE! I CAN'T DO THIS WITHOUT YOU!
THEN HOW 'BOUT I KISS YOU WITH THIS KOOKY LIPSWITCH, AND THEN YOU CAN PLAY A TALKING PILE OF POO!
BUF!
BODIE, I—
FDUMP
?
YOU'RE STILL...
YOU?
HOW COME IT DIDN'T WORK?

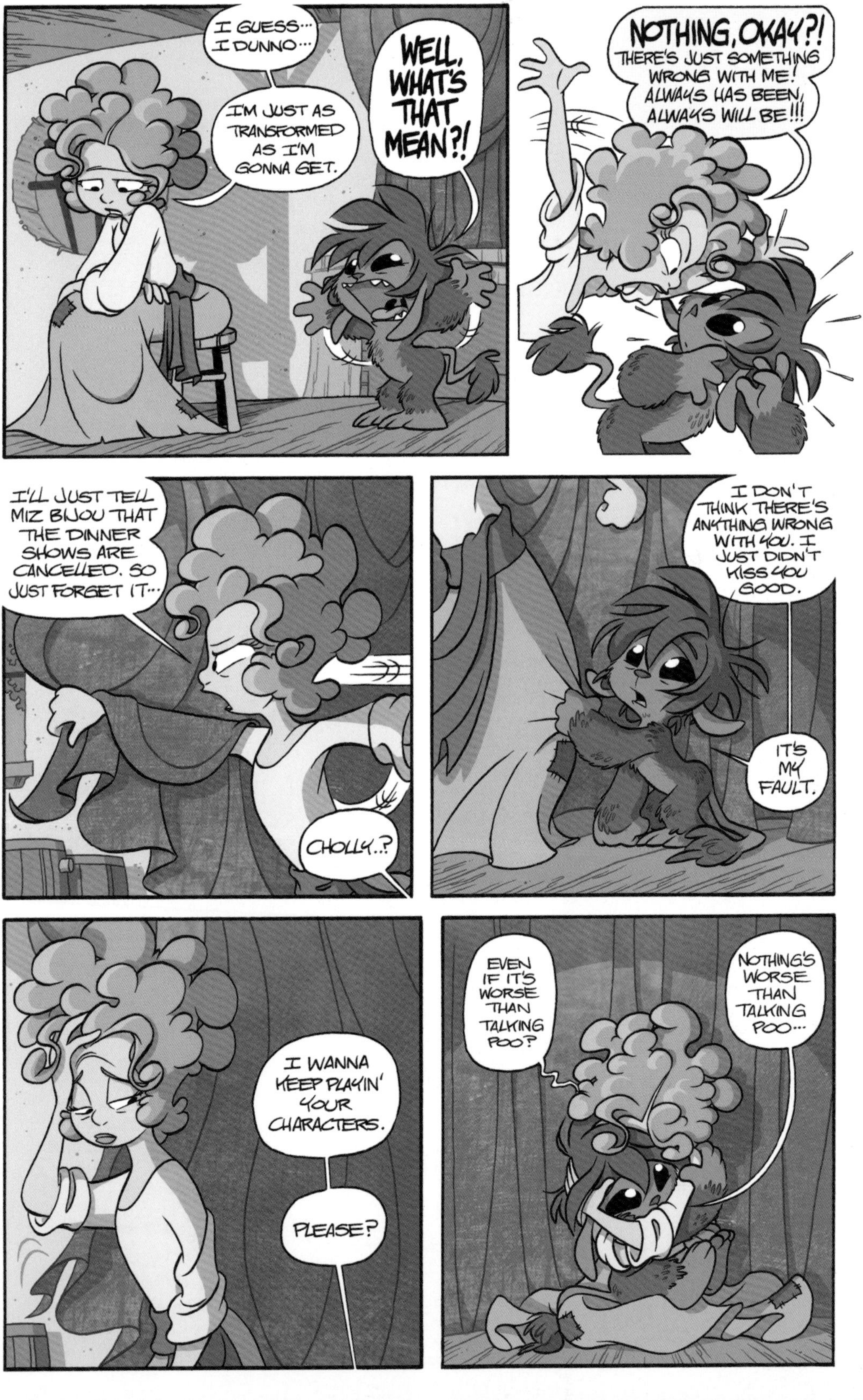
I GUESS...
I DUNNO...
I'M JUST AS TRANSFORMED AS I'M GONNA GET.
WELL, WHAT'S THAT MEAN?!
NOTHING, OKAY?! THERE'S JUST SOMETHING WRONG WITH ME! ALWAYS HAS BEEN, ALWAYS WILL BE!!!
I'LL JUST TELL MIZ BIJOU THAT THE DINNER SHOWS ARE CANCELLED. SO JUST FORGET IT...
CHOLLY..?
I DON'T THINK THERE'S ANYTHING WRONG WITH YOU. I JUST DIDN'T KISS YOU GOOD.
IT'S MY FAULT.
I WANNA KEEP PLAYIN' YOUR CHARACTERS.
PLEASE?
EVEN IF IT'S WORSE THAN TALKING POO?
NOTHING'S WORSE THAN TALKING POO...

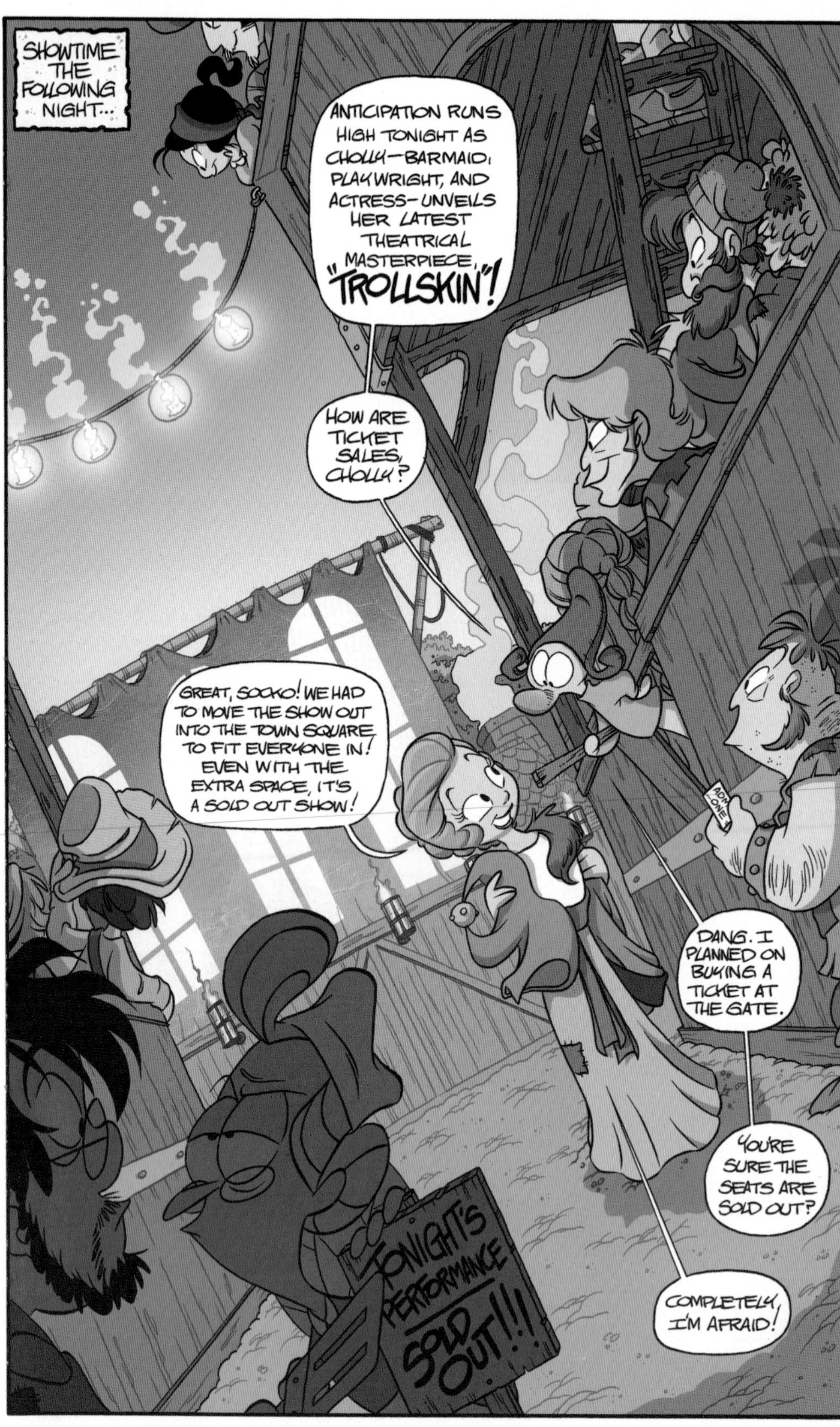
SHOWTIME THE FOLLOWING NIGHT...
ANTICIPATION RUNS HIGH TONIGHT AS CHOLLY—BARMAID, PLAYWRIGHT, AND ACTRESS—UNVEILS HER LATEST THEATRICAL MASTERPIECE, "TROLLSKIN"!
HOW ARE TICKET SALES, CHOLLY?
GREAT, SOCKO! WE HAD TO MOVE THE SHOW OUT INTO THE TOWN SQUARE TO FIT EVERYONE IN! EVEN WITH THE EXTRA SPACE, IT'S A SOLD OUT SHOW!
DANG. I PLANNED ON BUYING A TICKET AT THE GATE.
YOU'RE SURE THE SEATS ARE SOLD OUT?
COMPLETELY, I'M AFRAID!
TONIGHT'S PERFORMANCE SOLD OUT!!!

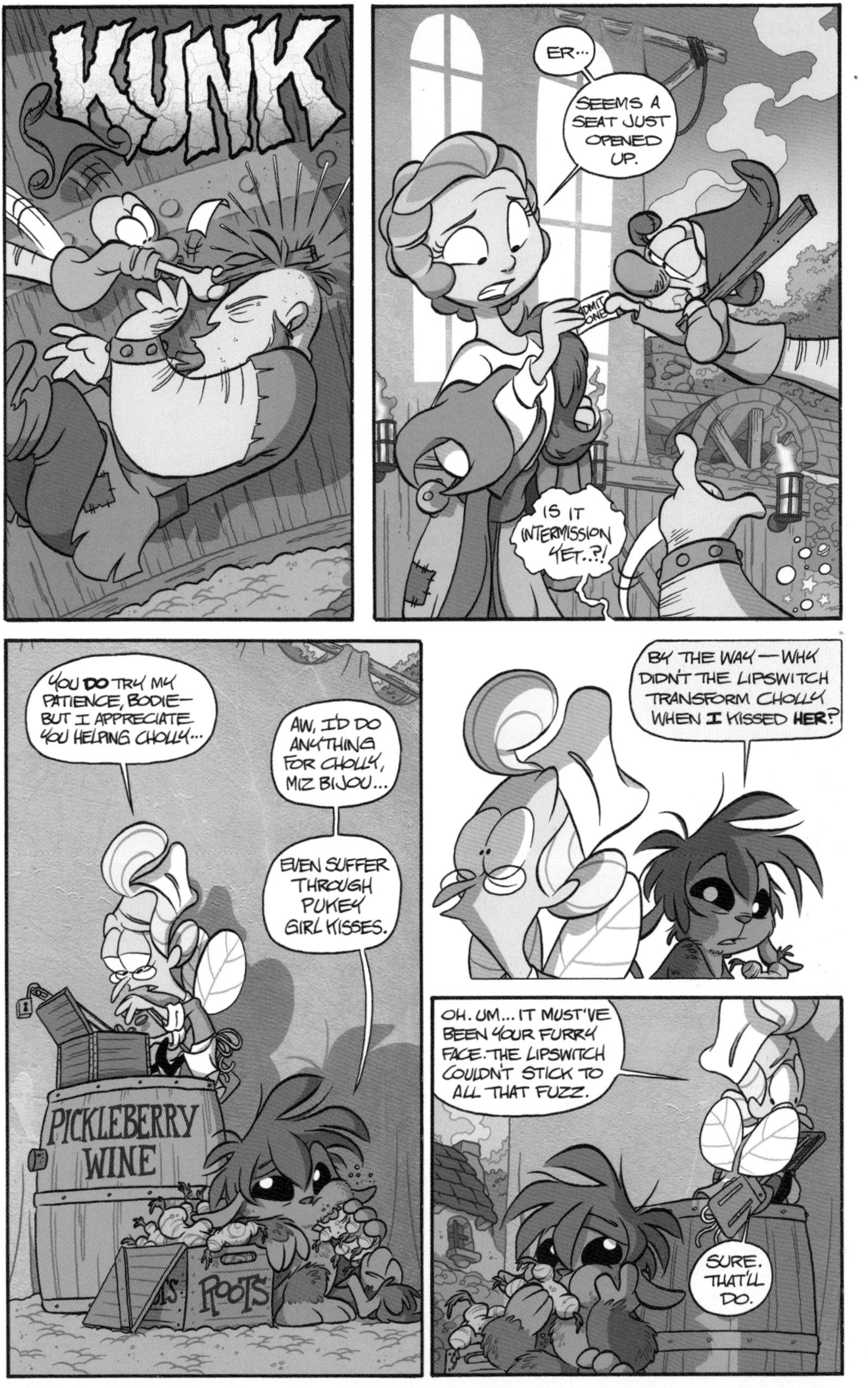
KUNK
ER...
SEEMS A SEAT JUST OPENED UP.
ADMIT ONE
IS IT INTERMISSION YET..?!
YOU DO TRY MY PATIENCE, BODIE— BUT I APPRECIATE YOU HELPING CHOLLY...
AW, I'D DO ANYTHING FOR CHOLLY, MIZ BIJOU...
EVEN SUFFER THROUGH PUKEY GIRL KISSES.
PICKLEBERRY WINE
ROOTS
BY THE WAY— WHY DIDN'T THE LIPSWITCH TRANSFORM CHOLLY WHEN I KISSED HER?
OH. UM... IT MUST'VE BEEN YOUR FURRY FACE. THE LIPSWITCH COULDN'T STICK TO ALL THAT FUZZ.
SURE. THAT'LL DO.

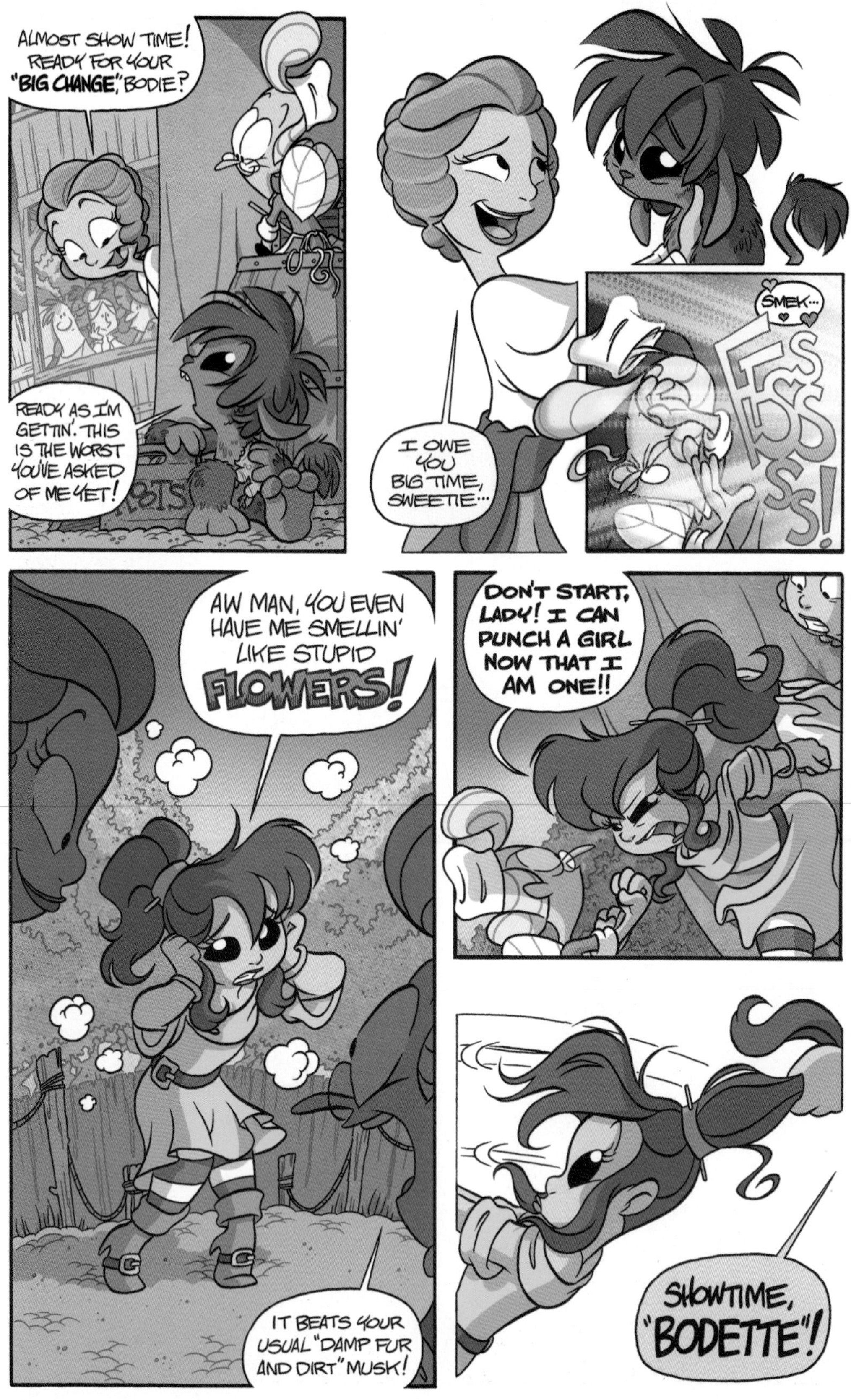
ALMOST SHOW TIME! READY FOR YOUR "BIG CHANGE," BODIE?
READY AS I'M GETTIN'. THIS IS THE WORST YOU'VE ASKED OF ME YET!
I OWE YOU BIG TIME, SWEETIE...
SMEK...
FSSSSSS!
AW MAN, YOU EVEN HAVE ME SMELLIN' LIKE STUPID FLOWERS!
IT BEATS YOUR USUAL "DAMP FUR AND DIRT" MUSK!
DON'T START, LADY! I CAN PUNCH A GIRL NOW THAT I AM ONE!!
SHOWTIME, "BODETTE"!

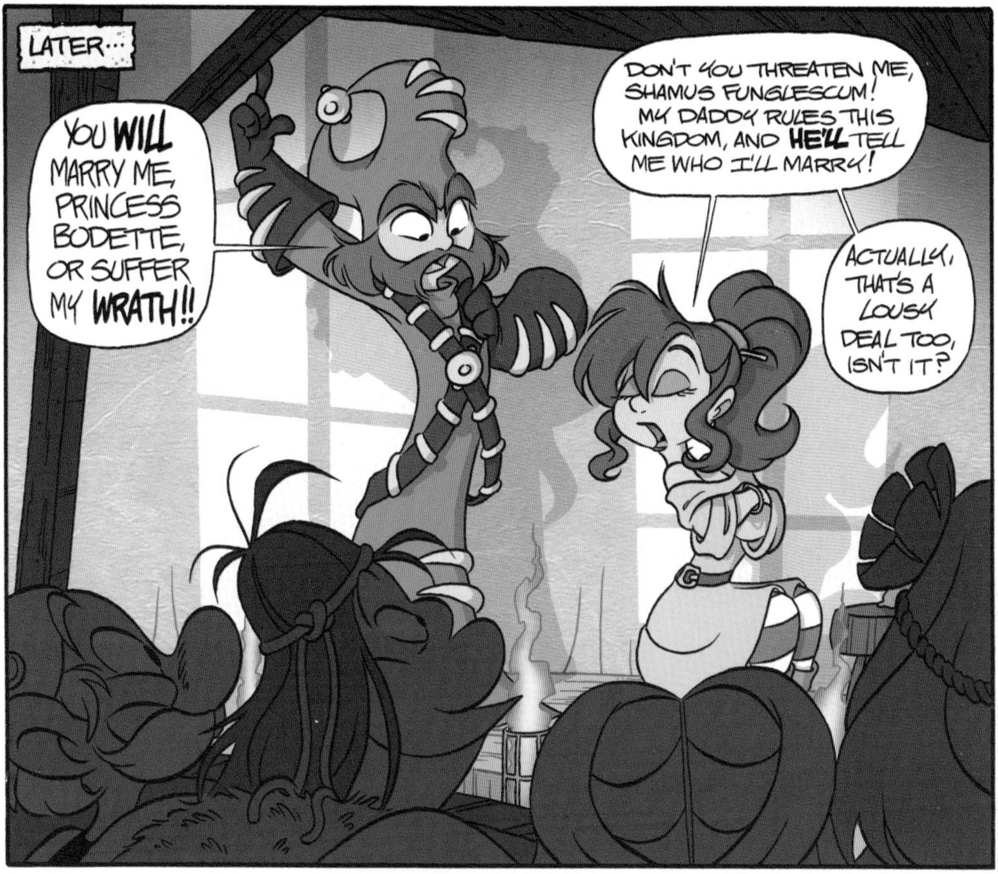
LATER...
YOU WILL MARRY ME, PRINCESS BODETTE, OR SUFFER MY WRATH!!
DON'T YOU THREATEN ME, SHAMUS FUNGLESCUM! MY DADDY RULES THIS KINGDOM, AND HE'LL TELL ME WHO I'LL MARRY!
ACTUALLY, THAT'S A LOUSY DEAL TOO, ISN'T IT?

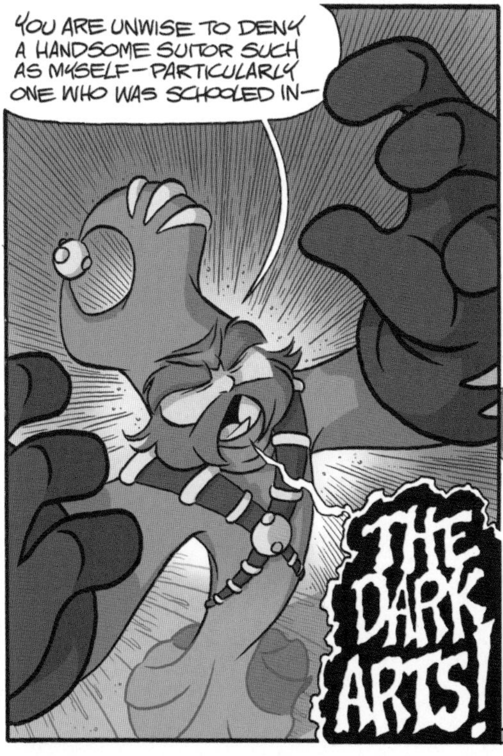
YOU ARE UNWISE TO DENY A HANDSOME SUITOR SUCH AS MYSELF—PARTICULARLY ONE WHO WAS SCHOOLED IN—
THE DARK ARTS!

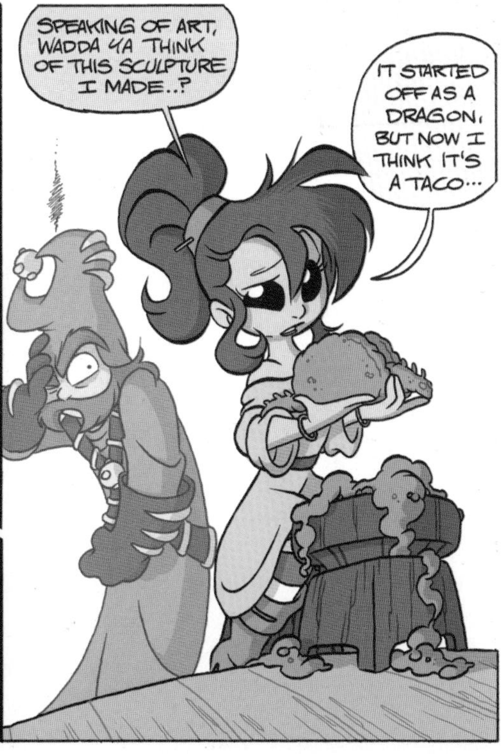
SPEAKING OF ART, WADDA YA THINK OF THIS SCULPTURE I MADE..?
IT STARTED OFF AS A DRAGON, BUT NOW I THINK IT'S A TACO...

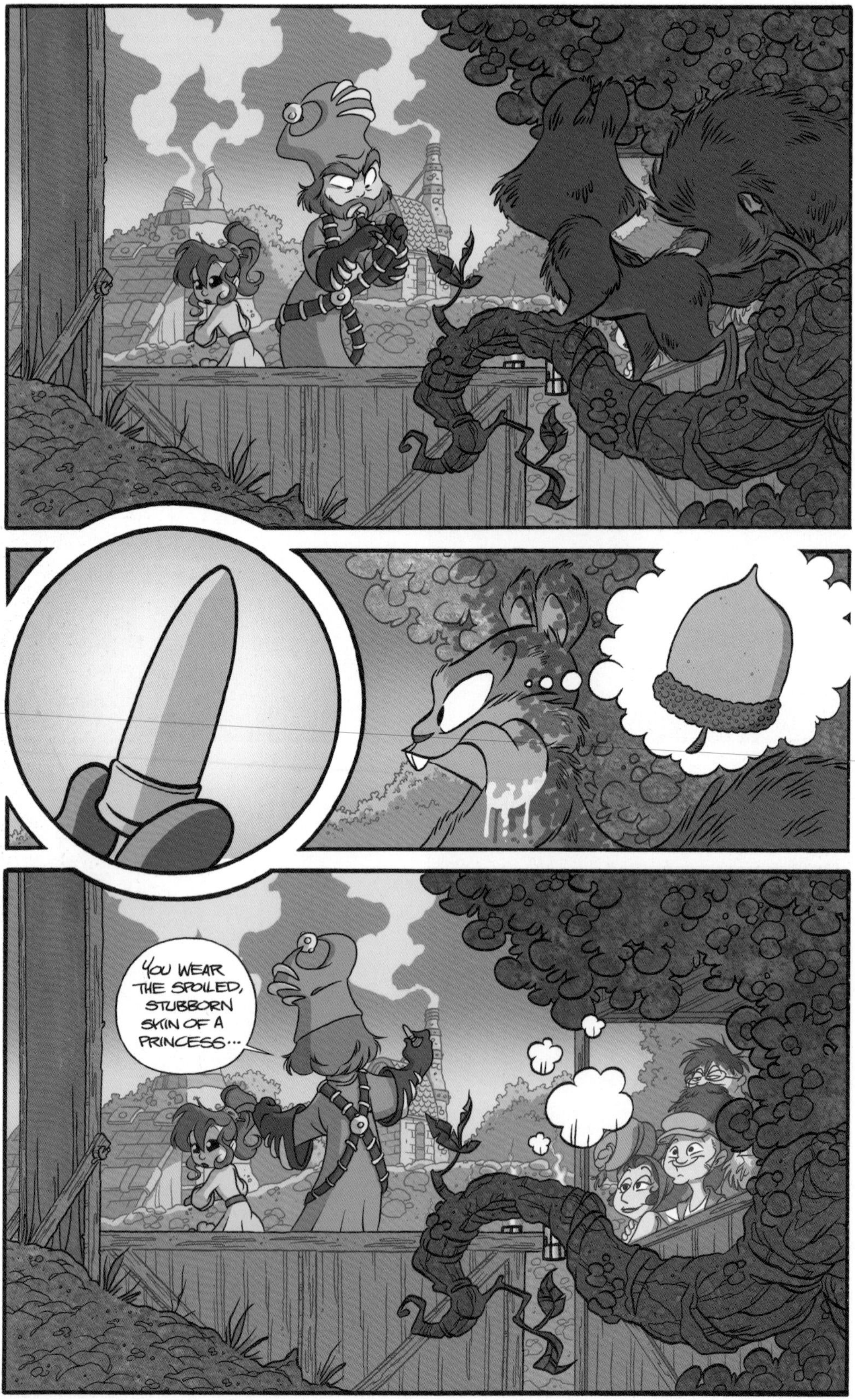
YOU WEAR THE SPOILED, STUBBORN SKIN OF A PRINCESS...

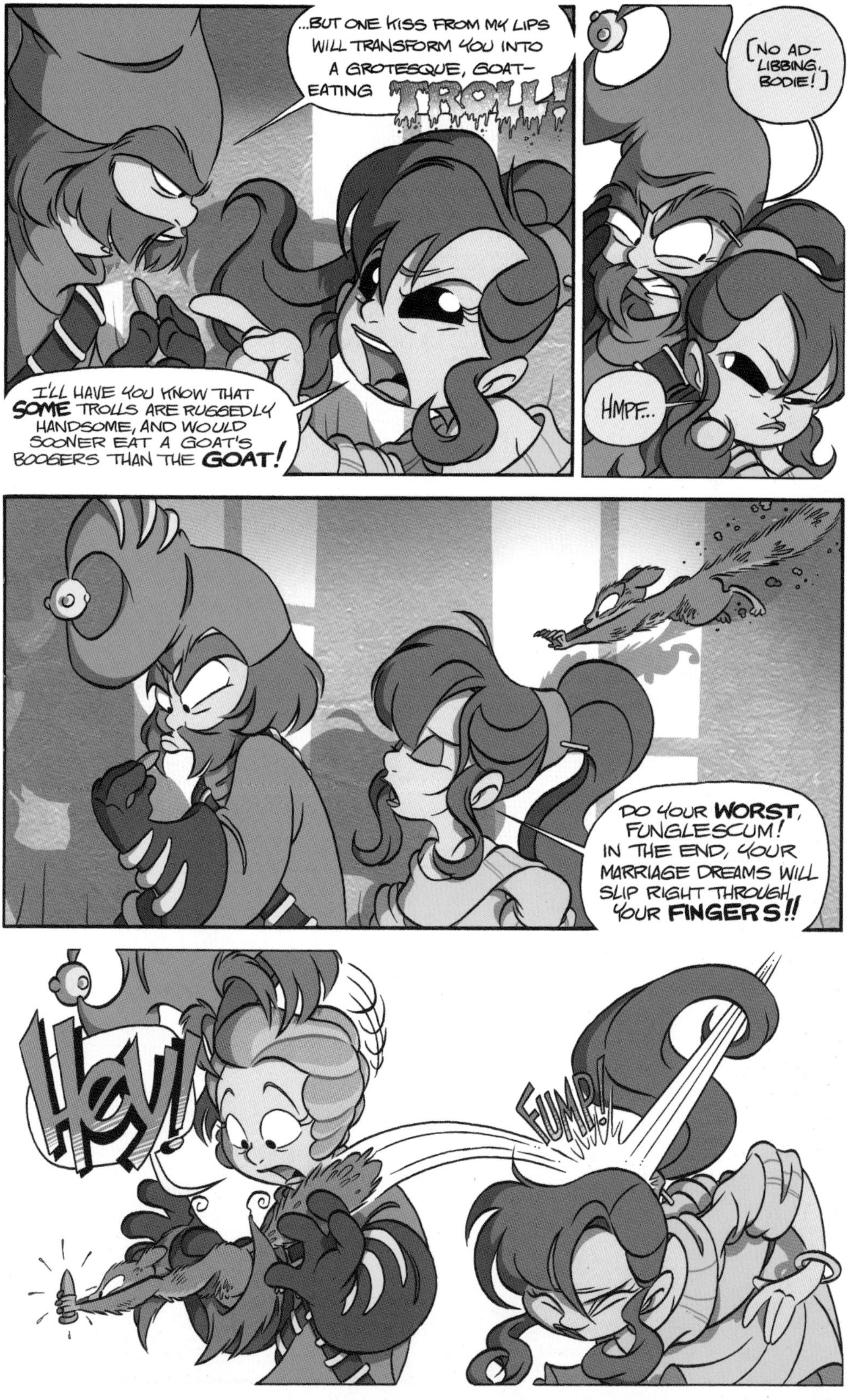
...BUT ONE KISS FROM MY LIPS WILL TRANSFORM YOU INTO A GROTESQUE, GOAT-EATING TROLL!
I'LL HAVE YOU KNOW THAT SOME TROLLS ARE RUGGEDLY HANDSOME, AND WOULD SOONER EAT A GOAT'S BOOGERS THAN THE GOAT!
[NO AD-LIBBING, BODIE!]
HMPF...
DO YOUR WORST, FUNGLESCUM! IN THE END, YOUR MARRIAGE DREAMS WILL SLIP RIGHT THROUGH YOUR FINGERS!!
HEY!
FUMP!

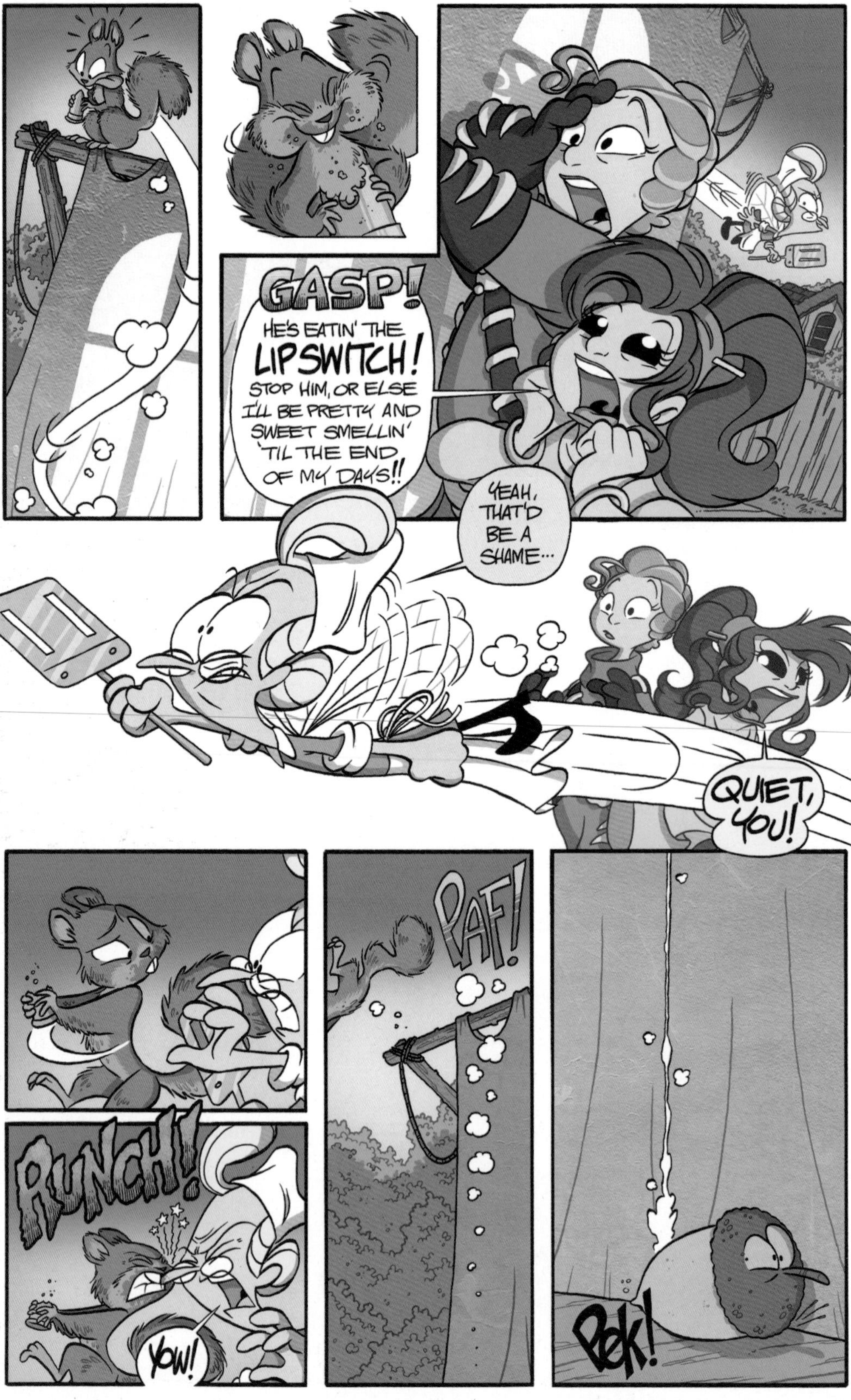
GASP!
HE'S EATIN' THE LIPSWITCH! STOP HIM, OR ELSE I'LL BE PRETTY AND SWEET SMELLIN' 'TIL THE END OF MY DAYS!!
YEAH, THAT'D BE A SHAME...
QUIET, YOU!
RUNCH!
YOW!
PAF!
BEK!

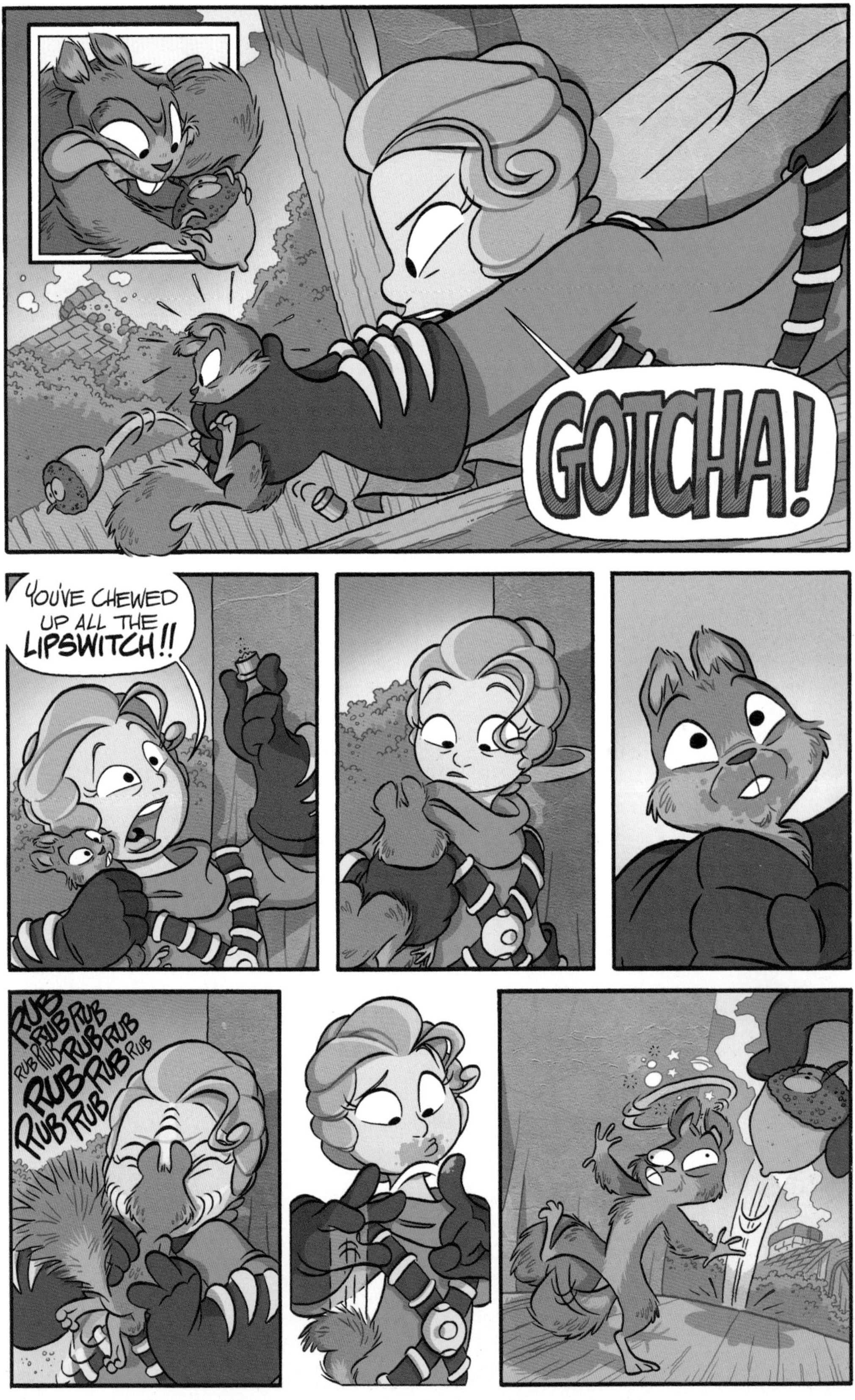
GOTCHA!
YOU'VE CHEWED UP ALL THE LIPSWITCH!!
RUB RUB RUB RUB RUB RUB RUB RUB RUB RUB RUB RUB RUB RUB

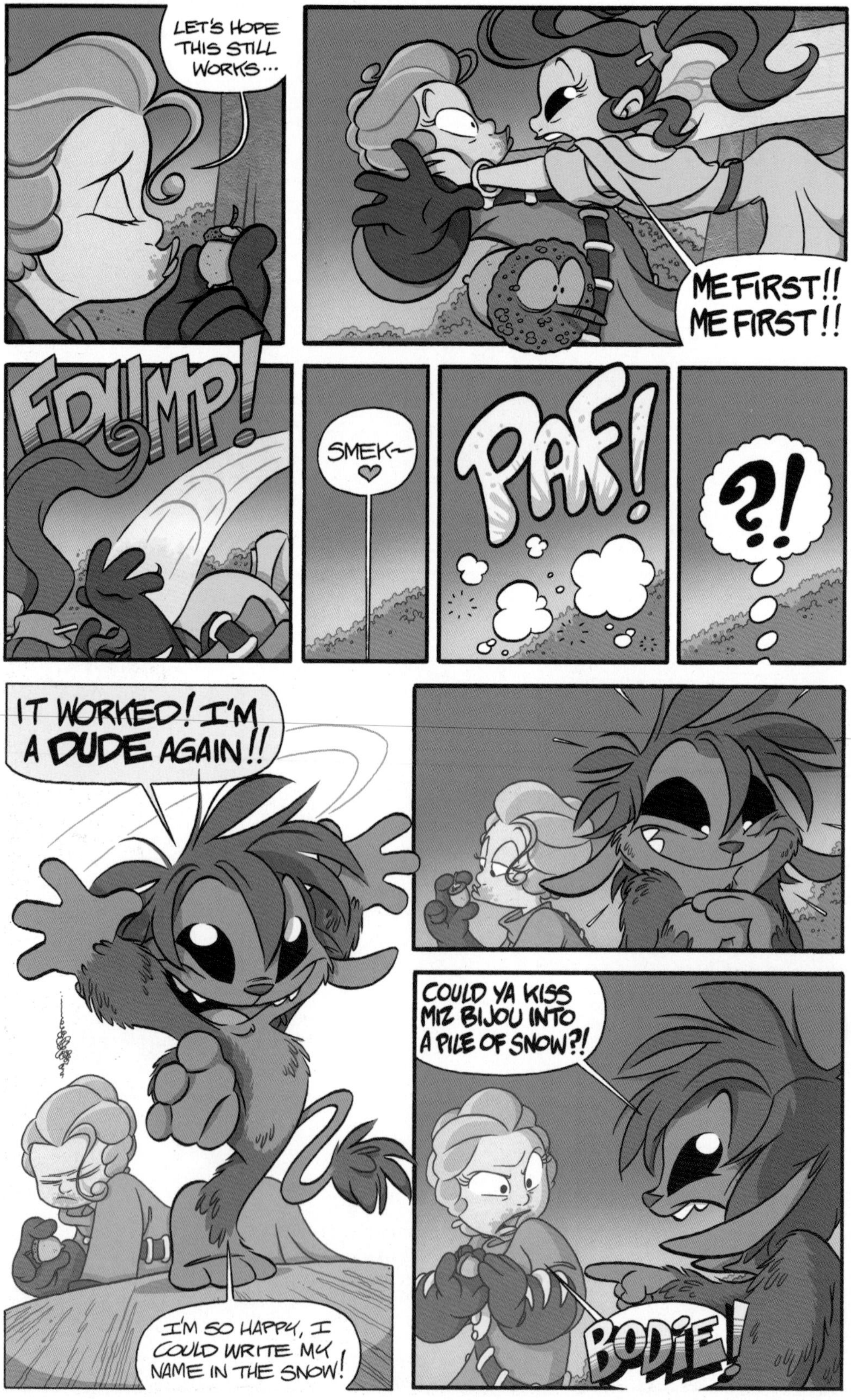
LET'S HOPE THIS STILL WORKS...
ME FIRST!! ME FIRST!!
FDUMP!
SMEK~ ♥
PAF!
?!
IT WORKED! I'M A DUDE AGAIN!!
I'M SO HAPPY, I COULD WRITE MY NAME IN THE SNOW!
COULD YA KISS MIZ BIJOU INTO A PILE OF SNOW?!
BODIE!

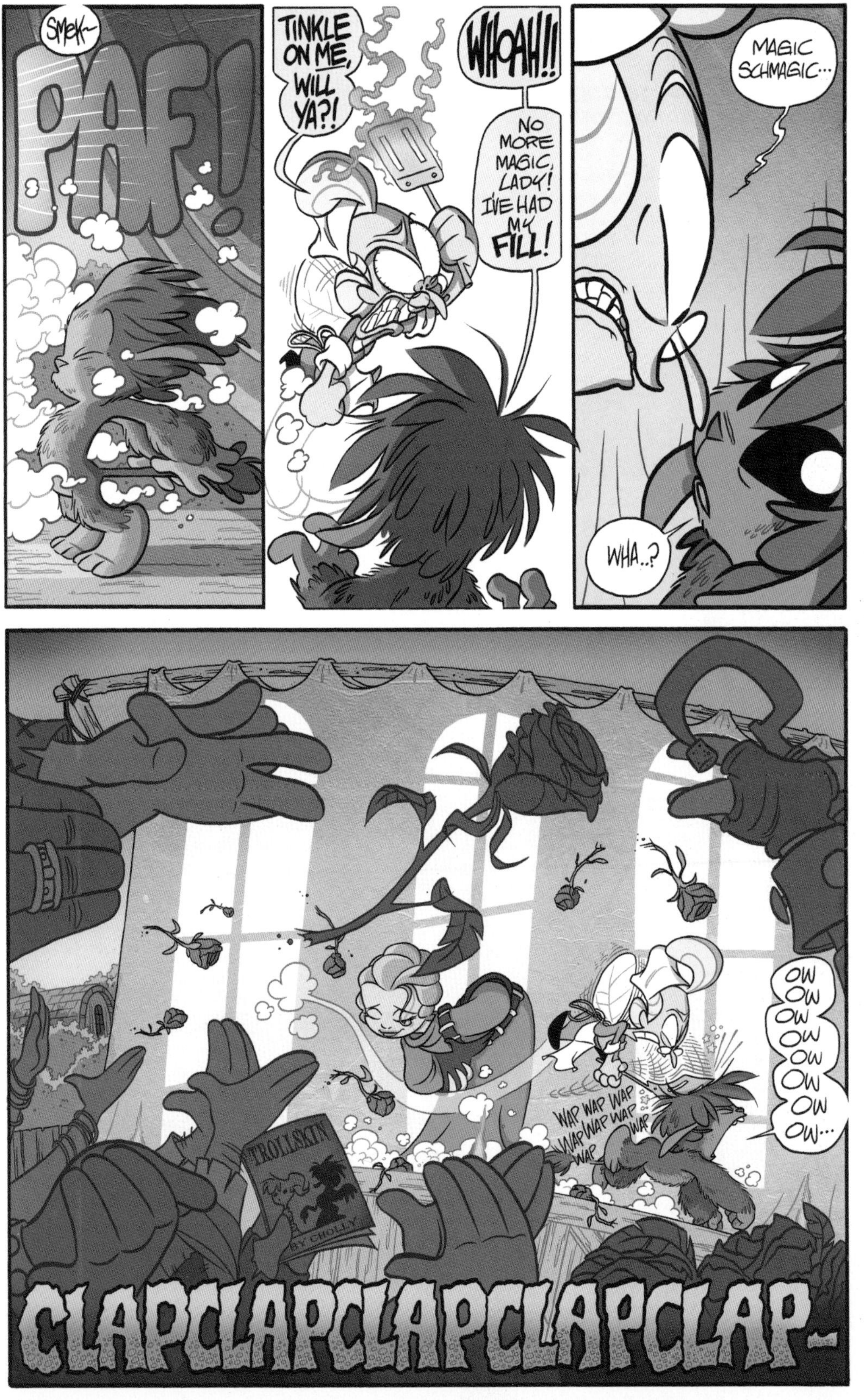
SMEK~
PAF!
TINKLE ON ME, WILL YA?!
WHOAH!!
NO MORE MAGIC, LADY! I'VE HAD MY FILL!
MAGIC SCHMAGIC...
WHA..?
TROLLSKIN
BY CHOLLY
WAP WAP WAP WAP WAP WAP WAP WAP
OW OW OW OW OW OW OW OW...
CLAPCLAPCLAPCLAPCLAP~

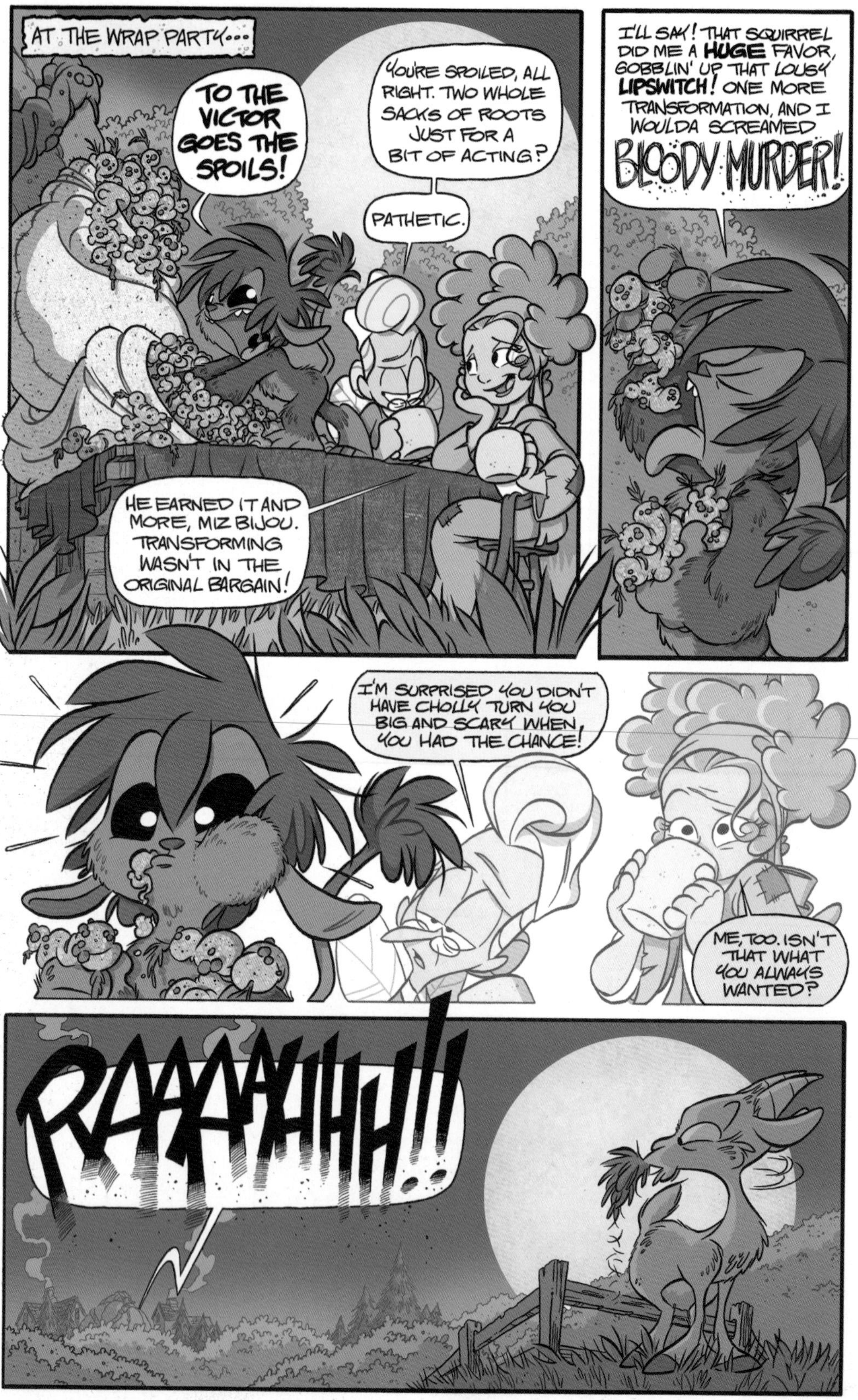
AT THE WRAP PARTY...
TO THE VICTOR GOES THE SPOILS!
YOU'RE SPOILED, ALL RIGHT. TWO WHOLE SACKS OF ROOTS JUST FOR A BIT OF ACTING?
PATHETIC.
HE EARNED IT AND MORE, MIZ BIJOU. TRANSFORMING WASN'T IN THE ORIGINAL BARGAIN!
I'LL SAY! THAT SQUIRREL DID ME A HUGE FAVOR, GOBBLIN' UP THAT LOUSY LIPSWITCH! ONE MORE TRANSFORMATION, AND I WOULDA SCREAMED BLOODY MURDER!
I'M SURPRISED YOU DIDN'T HAVE CHOLLY TURN YOU BIG AND SCARY WHEN YOU HAD THE CHANCE!
ME, TOO. ISN'T THAT WHAT YOU ALWAYS WANTED?
RAAAAHHHH!!!

CHAPTER 3
BOUNCING BABY BODIE

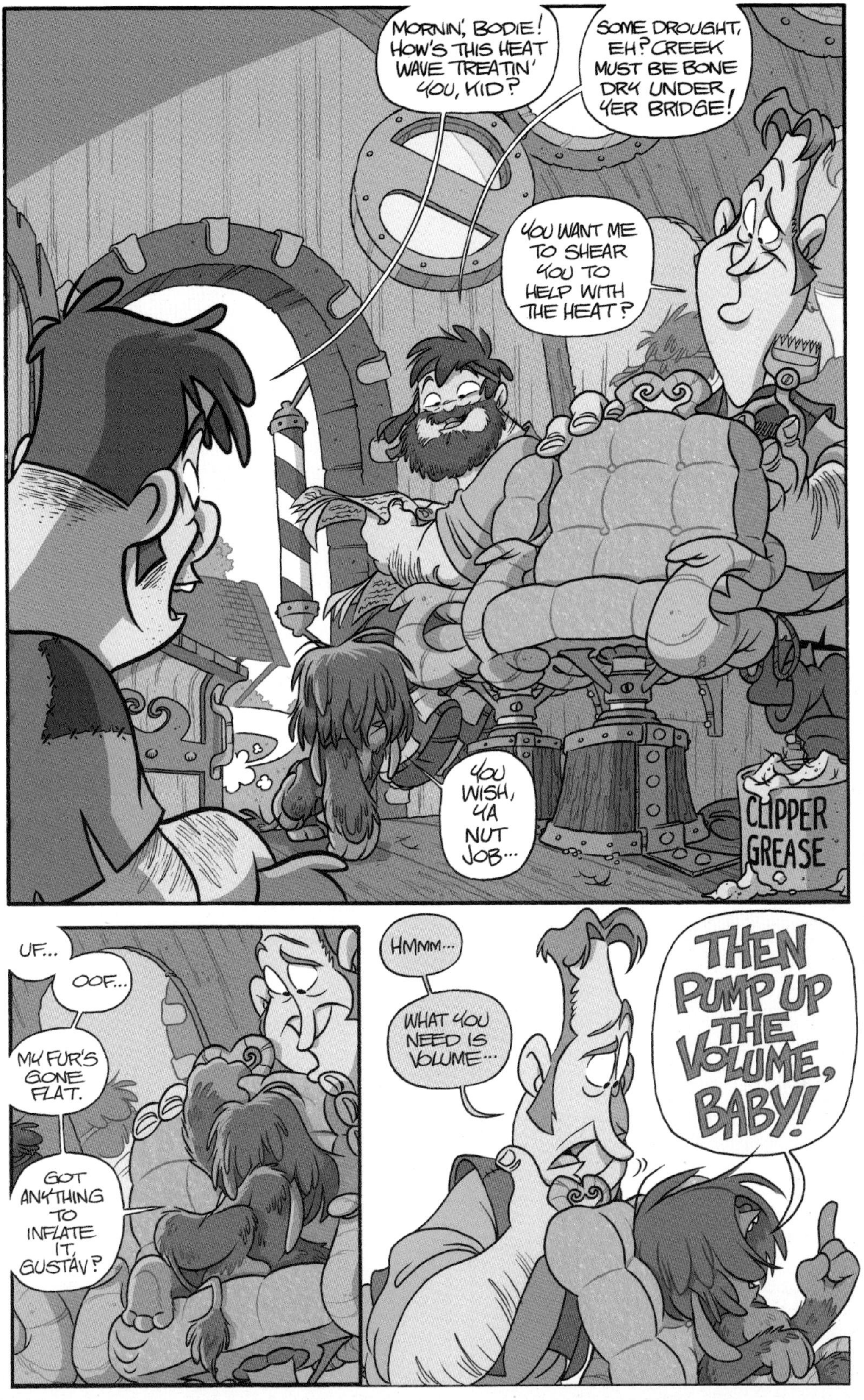
MORNIN', BODIE! HOW'S THIS HEAT WAVE TREATIN' YOU, KID?
SOME DROUGHT, EH? CREEK MUST BE BONE DRY UNDER YER BRIDGE!
YOU WANT ME TO SHEAR YOU TO HELP WITH THE HEAT?
YOU WISH, YA NUT JOB...
CLIPPER GREASE
UF...
OOF...
MY FUR'S GONE FLAT.
GOT ANYTHING TO INFLATE IT, GUSTAV?
HMMM...
WHAT YOU NEED IS VOLUME...
THEN PUMP UP THE VOLUME, BABY!

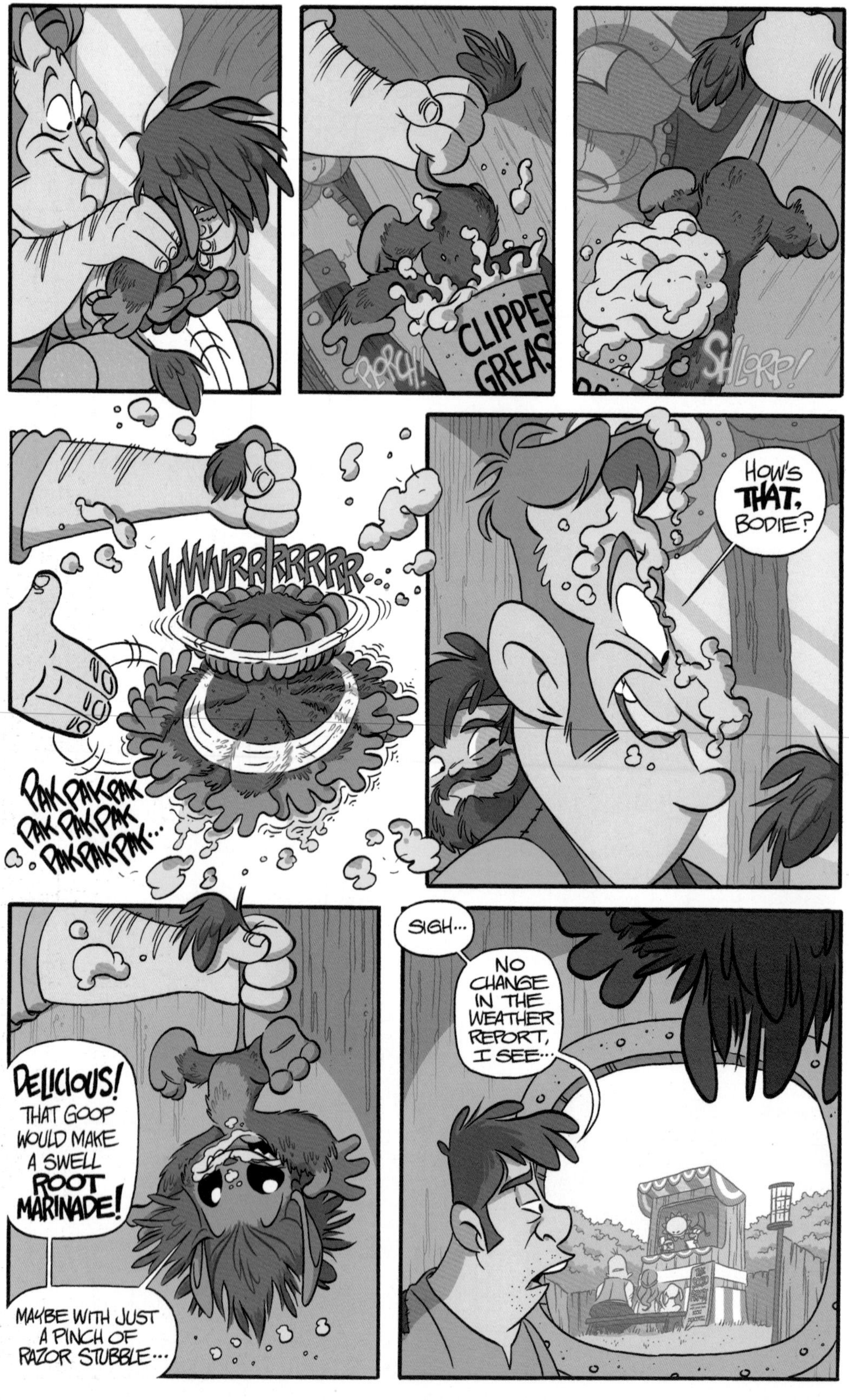
CLIPPER GREAS
PLORCH!
SHLORP!
WWWRRRRRRRR
PAK PAK PAK
PAK PAK PAK
PAK PAK PAK...
HOW'S THAT, BODIE?
DELICIOUS! THAT GOOP WOULD MAKE A SWELL ROOT MARINADE!
MAYBE WITH JUST A PINCH OF RAZOR STUBBLE...
SIGH...
NO CHANGE IN THE WEATHER REPORT, I SEE...

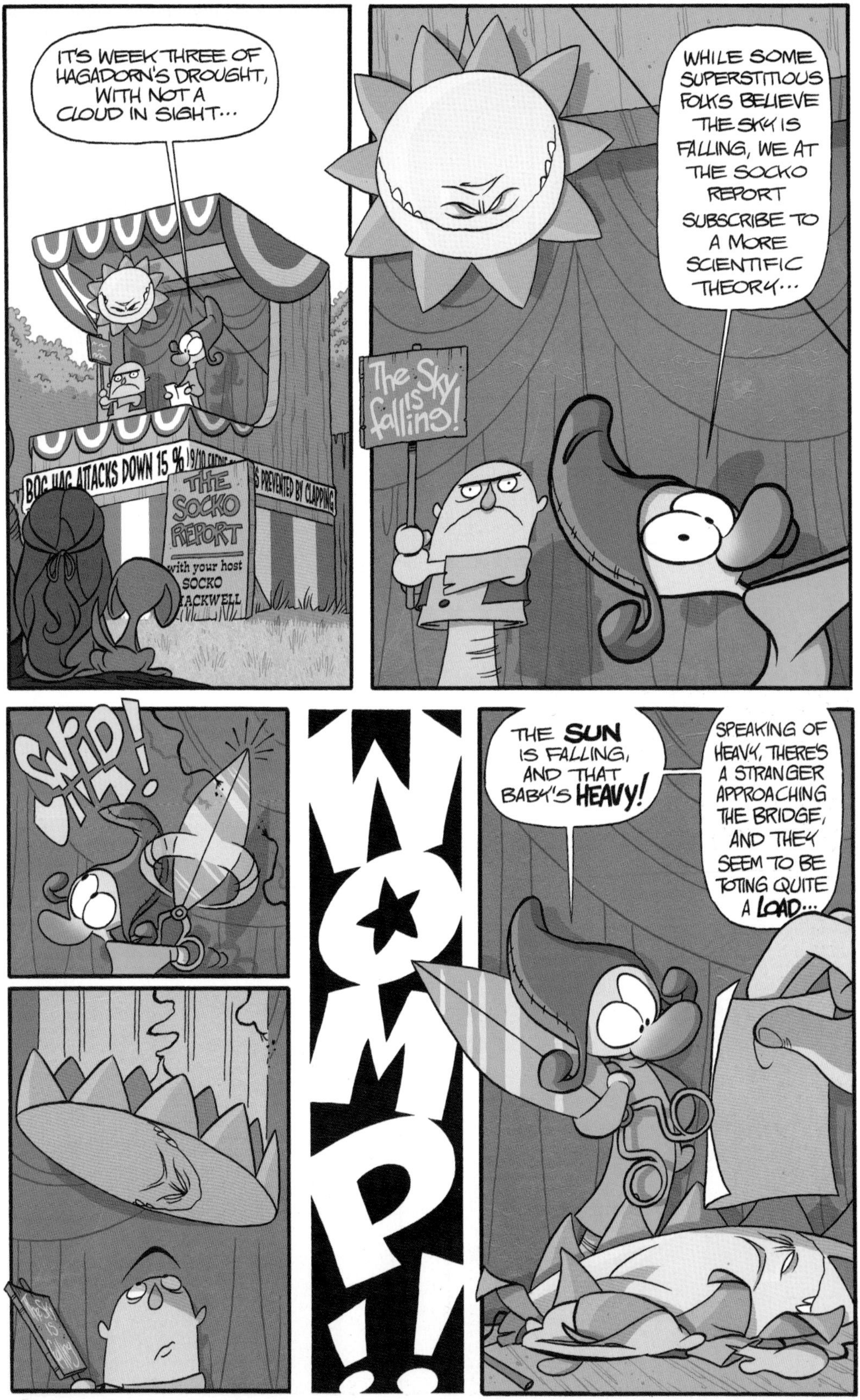

IT'S WEEK THREE OF HAGADORN'S DROUGHT, WITH NOT A CLOUD IN SIGHT...
BOG HAG ATTACKS DOWN 15 %
PREVENTED BY CLAPPING
THE SOCKO REPORT
with your host
SOCKO
WHILE SOME SUPERSTITIOUS FOLKS BELIEVE THE SKY IS FALLING, WE AT THE SOCKO REPORT SUBSCRIBE TO A MORE SCIENTIFIC THEORY...
The Sky is falling!
WOMP!!
THE SUN IS FALLING, AND THAT BABY'S HEAVY!
SPEAKING OF HEAVY, THERE'S A STRANGER APPROACHING THE BRIDGE, AND THEY SEEM TO BE TOTING QUITE A LOAD...

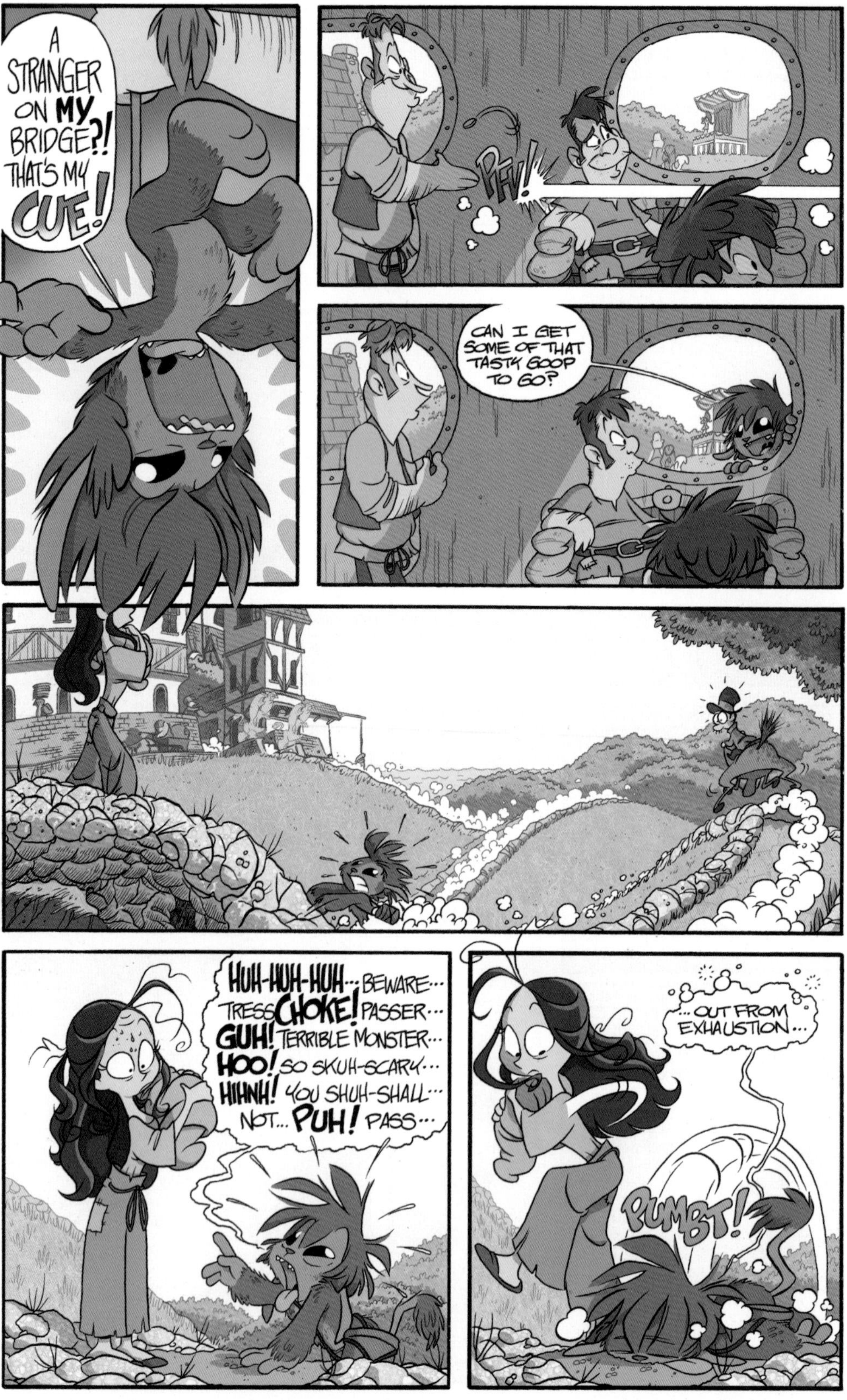
A STRANGER ON MY BRIDGE?! THAT'S MY CUE!
PFFT!
CAN I GET SOME OF THAT TASTY GOOP TO GO?
HUH-HUH-HUH... BEWARE... TRESS CHOKE! PASSER... GUH! TERRIBLE MONSTER... HOO! SO SKUH-SCARY... HIHNH! YOU SHUH-SHALL... NOT... PUH! PASS...
...OUT FROM EXHAUSTION...
PUMBT!

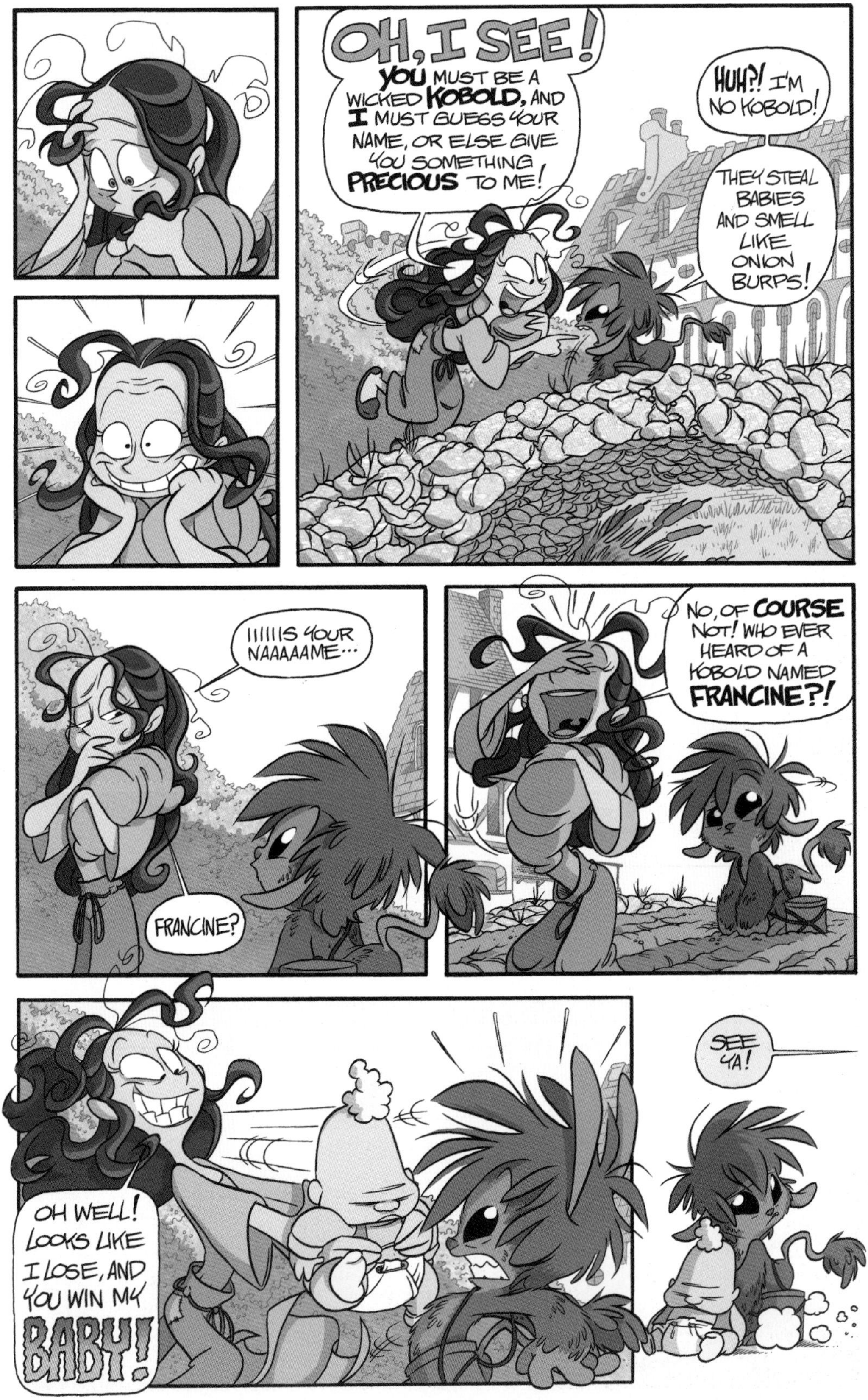
OH, I SEE! YOU MUST BE A WICKED KOBOLD, AND I MUST GUESS YOUR NAME, OR ELSE GIVE YOU SOMETHING PRECIOUS TO ME!
HUH?! I'M NO KOBOLD!
THEY STEAL BABIES AND SMELL LIKE ONION BURPS!
IIIIIIS YOUR NAAAAAME...
FRANCINE?
NO, OF COURSE NOT! WHO EVER HEARD OF A KOBOLD NAMED FRANCINE?!
OH WELL! LOOKS LIKE I LOSE, AND YOU WIN MY BABY!
SEE YA!

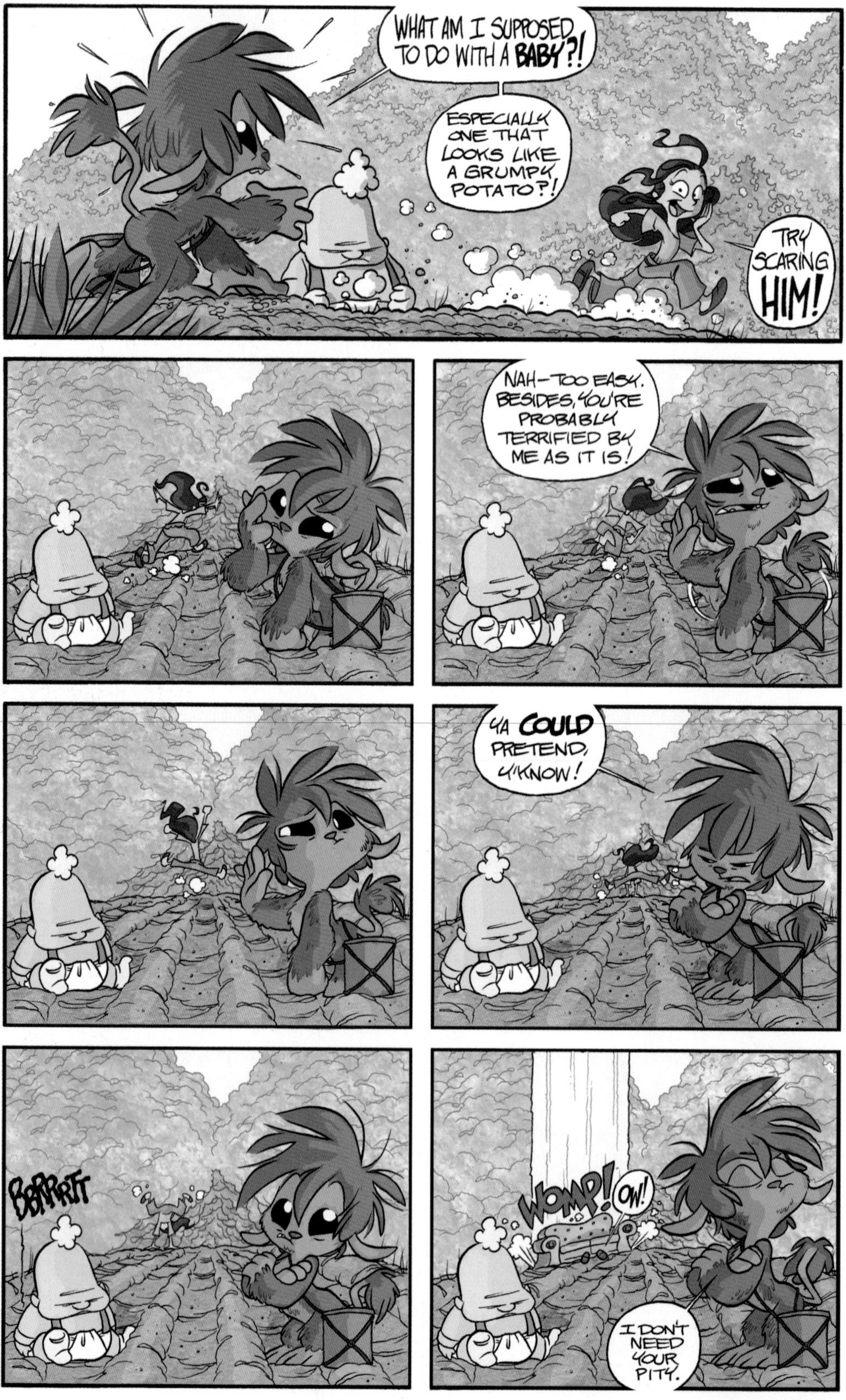
WHAT AM I SUPPOSED TO DO WITH A BABY?!
ESPECIALLY ONE THAT LOOKS LIKE A GRUMPY POTATO?!
TRY SCARING HIM!
NAH—TOO EASY. BESIDES, YOU'RE PROBABLY TERRIFIED BY ME AS IT IS!
YA COULD PRETEND, Y'KNOW!
BBRRRRTT
WOMP!
OW!
I DON'T NEED YOUR PITY.

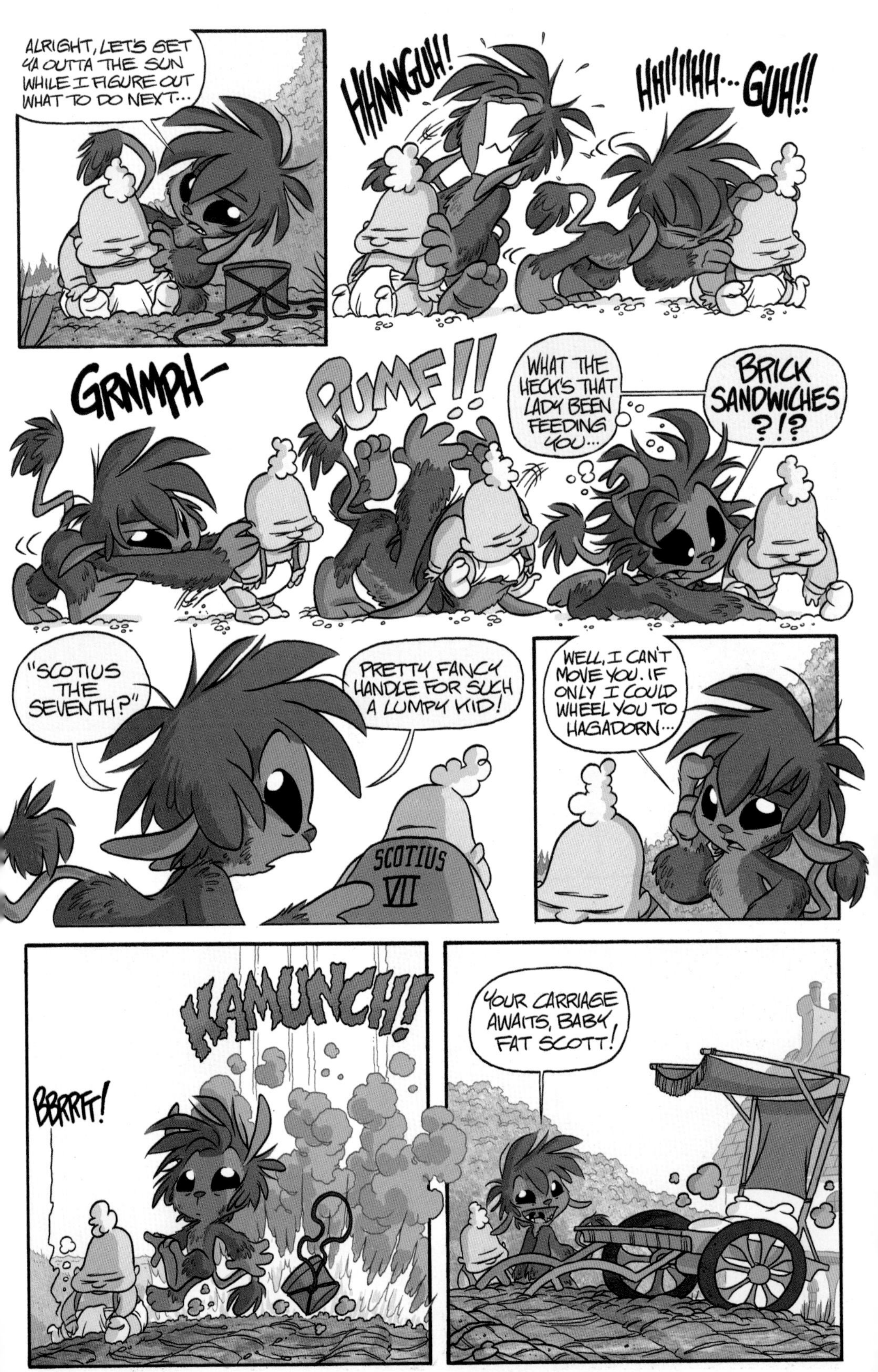

ALRIGHT, LET'S GET YA OUTTA THE SUN WHILE I FIGURE OUT WHAT TO DO NEXT...
HHNNGUH!
HHIIIHH...GUH!!
GRNMPH-
PUMF!!
WHAT THE HECK'S THAT LADY BEEN FEEDING YOU...
BRICK SANDWICHES ?!?
"SCOTIUS THE SEVENTH?"
PRETTY FANCY HANDLE FOR SUCH A LUMPY KID!
SCOTIUS VII
WELL, I CAN'T MOVE YOU. IF ONLY I COULD WHEEL YOU TO HAGADORN...
KAMUNCH!
BBRRFT!
YOUR CARRIAGE AWAITS, BABY FAT SCOTT!

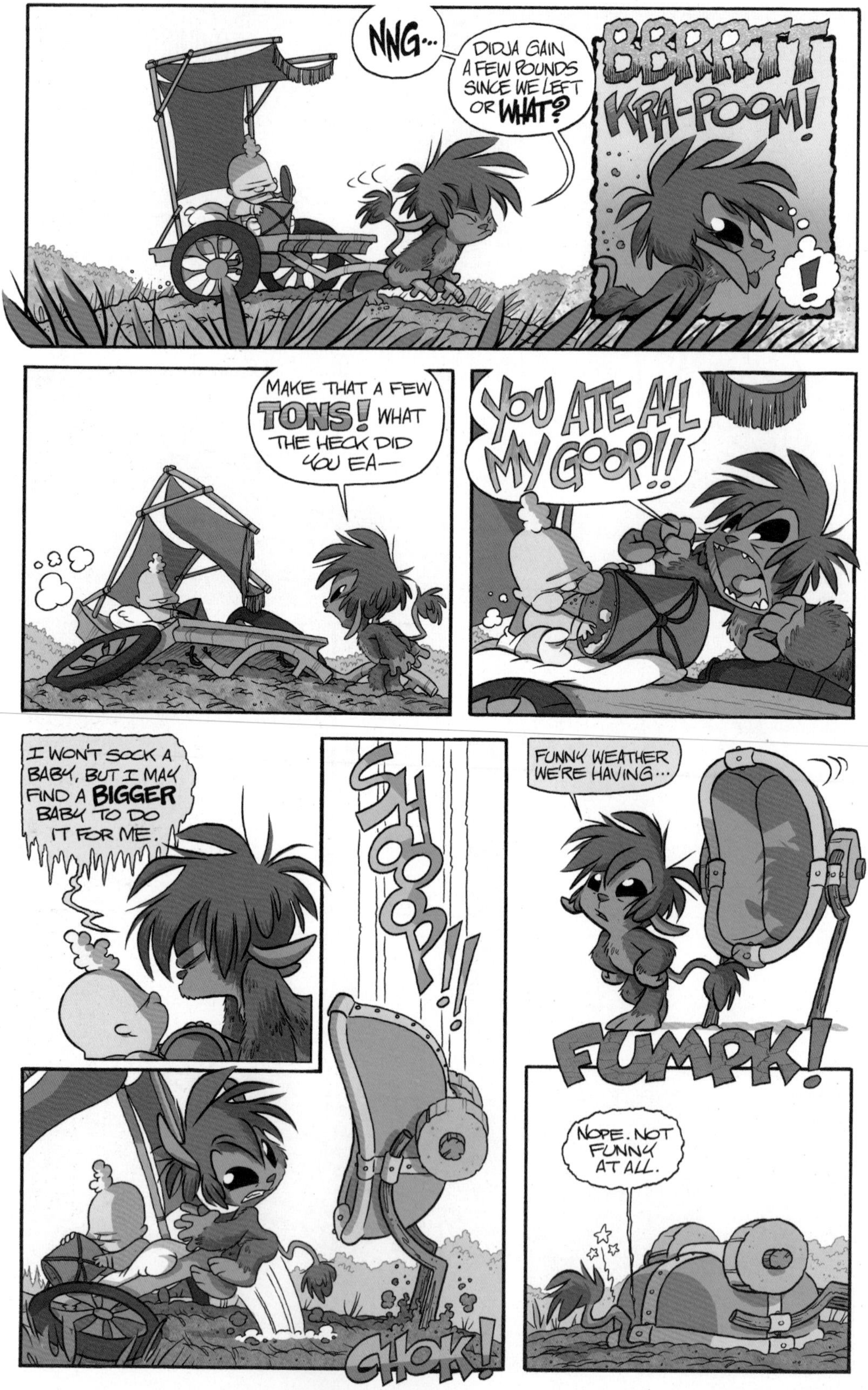
NNG...
DIDJA GAIN A FEW POUNDS SINCE WE LEFT OR WHAT?
BBRRRTT
KRA-POOM!
!
MAKE THAT A FEW TONS! WHAT THE HECK DID YOU EA—
YOU ATE ALL MY GOOP!!
I WON'T SOCK A BABY, BUT I MAY FIND A BIGGER BABY TO DO IT FOR ME.
SHOOOP!!
FUNNY WEATHER WE'RE HAVING...
FUMPK!
CHOK!
NOPE. NOT FUNNY AT ALL.

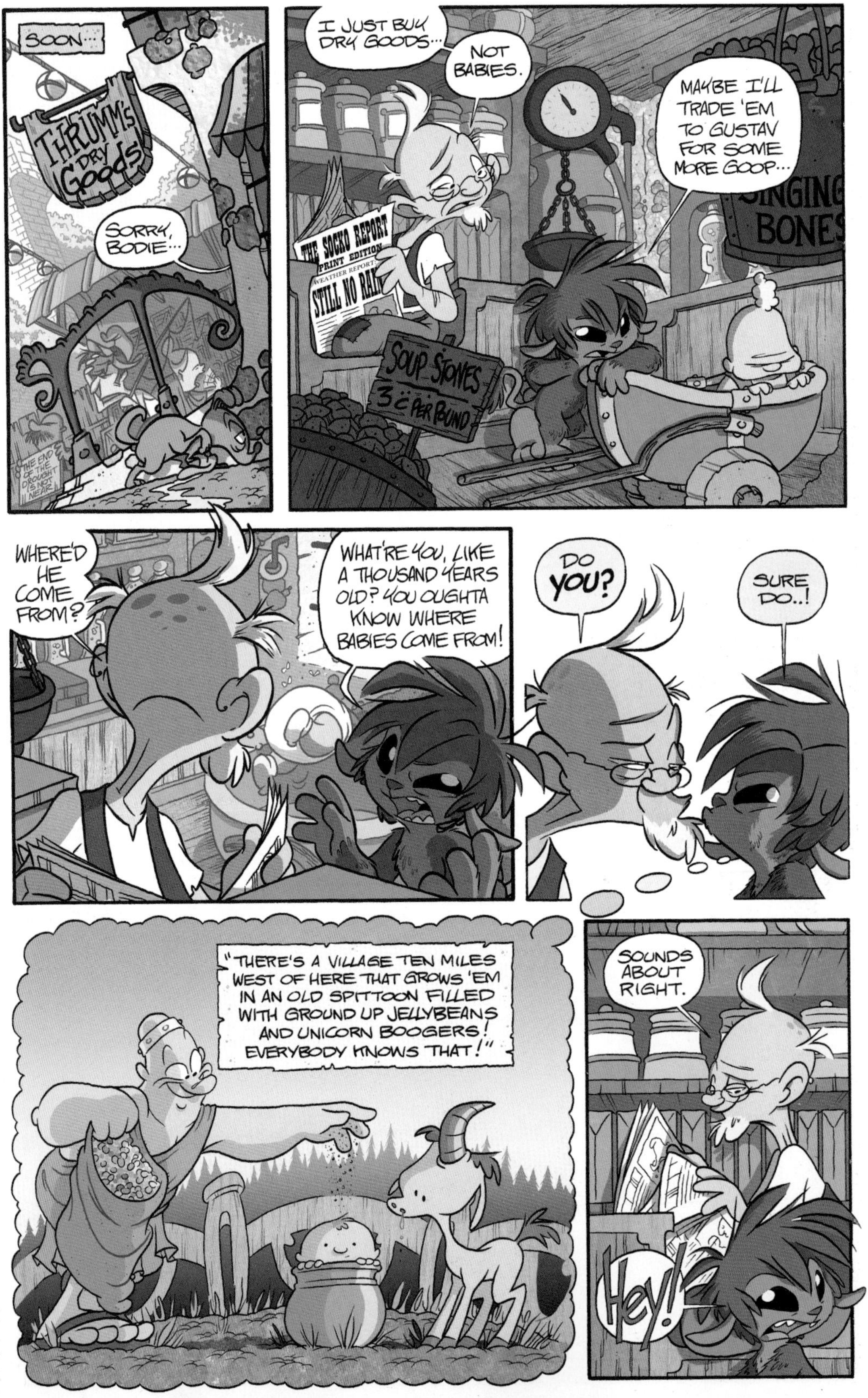
SOON...
THRUMM'S DRY GOODS
SORRY, BODIE...
THE END OF THE DROUGHT IS NOT NEAR
I JUST BUY DRY GOODS...
NOT BABIES.
THE SOCKO REPORT
PRINT EDITION
WEATHER REPORT:
STILL NO RAI
SOUP STONES
3¢ PER POUND
MAYBE I'LL TRADE 'EM TO GUSTAV FOR SOME MORE GOOP...
SINGING BONES
WHERE'D HE COME FROM?
WHAT'RE YOU, LIKE A THOUSAND YEARS OLD? YOU OUGHTA KNOW WHERE BABIES COME FROM!
DO YOU?
SURE DO..!
"THERE'S A VILLAGE TEN MILES WEST OF HERE THAT GROWS 'EM IN AN OLD SPITTOON FILLED WITH GROUND UP JELLYBEANS AND UNICORN BOOGERS! EVERYBODY KNOWS THAT!"
SOUNDS ABOUT RIGHT.
HEY!

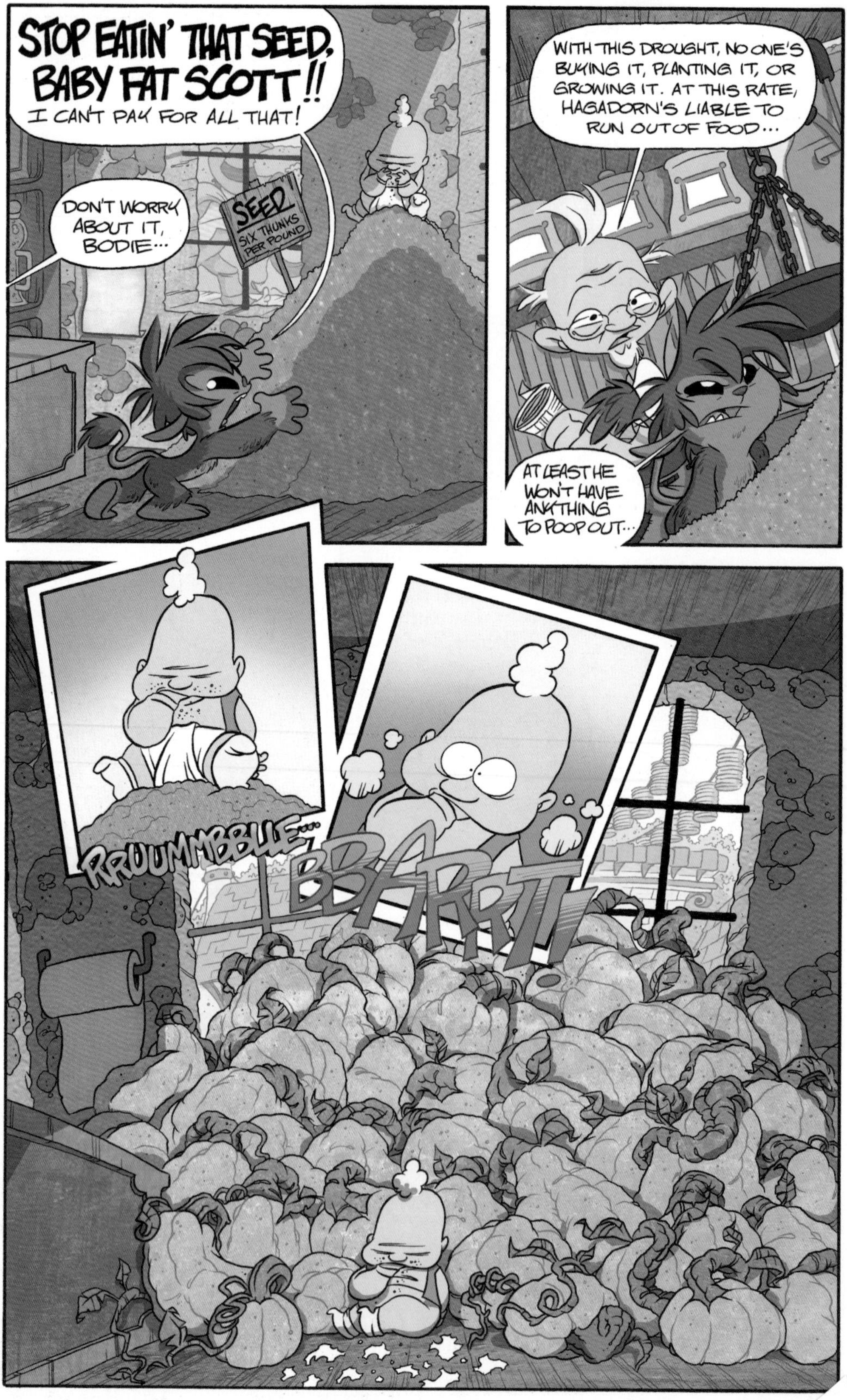
STOP EATIN' THAT SEED, BABY FAT SCOTT!! I CAN'T PAY FOR ALL THAT!
SEED SIX THUNKS PER POUND
DON'T WORRY ABOUT IT, BODIE...
WITH THIS DROUGHT, NO ONE'S BUYING IT, PLANTING IT, OR GROWING IT. AT THIS RATE, HAGADORN'S LIABLE TO RUN OUT OF FOOD...
AT LEAST HE WON'T HAVE ANYTHING TO POOP OUT...
RRUUMMBBLLE....
BBARRRT!!

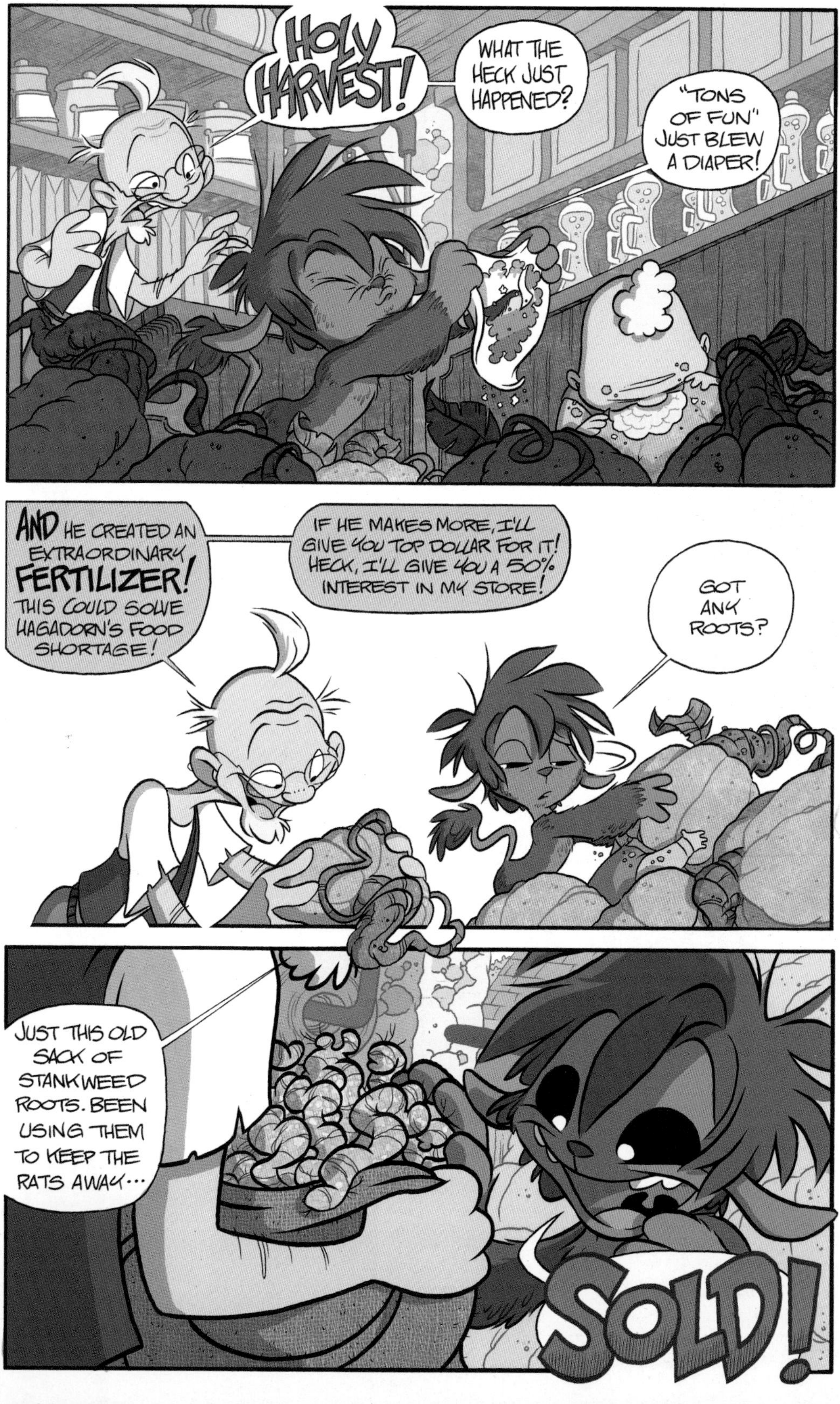
HOLY HARVEST!
WHAT THE HECK JUST HAPPENED?
"TONS OF FUN" JUST BLEW A DIAPER!
AND HE CREATED AN EXTRAORDINARY FERTILIZER! THIS COULD SOLVE HAGADORN'S FOOD SHORTAGE!
IF HE MAKES MORE, I'LL GIVE YOU TOP DOLLAR FOR IT! HECK, I'LL GIVE YOU A 50% INTEREST IN MY STORE!
GOT ANY ROOTS?
JUST THIS OLD SACK OF STANKWEED ROOTS. BEEN USING THEM TO KEEP THE RATS AWAY...
SOLD!

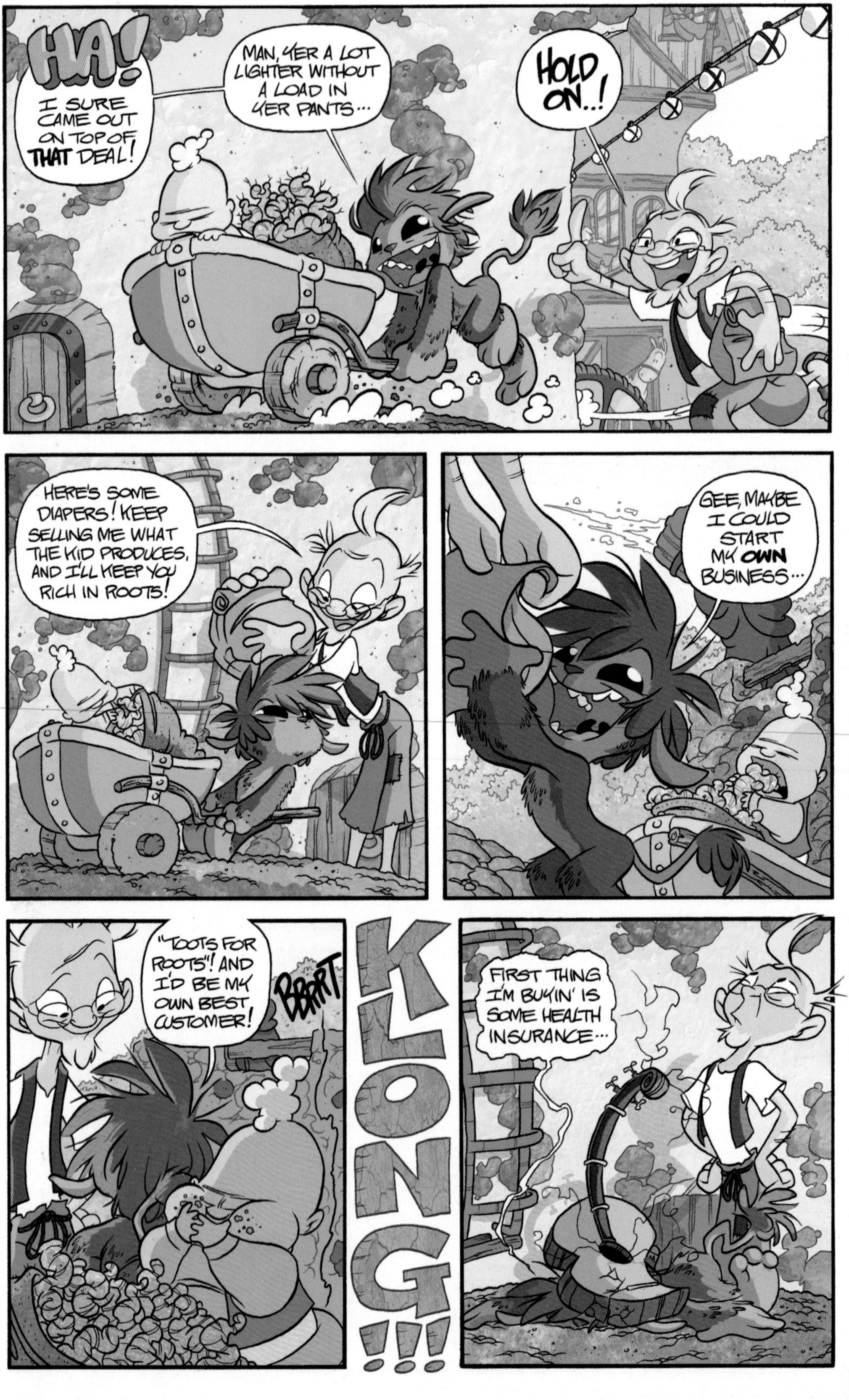
HA!
I SURE CAME OUT ON TOP OF THAT DEAL!
MAN, YER A LOT LIGHTER WITHOUT A LOAD IN YER PANTS...
HOLD ON..!
HERE'S SOME DIAPERS! KEEP SELLING ME WHAT THE KID PRODUCES, AND I'LL KEEP YOU RICH IN ROOTS!
GEE, MAYBE I COULD START MY OWN BUSINESS...
"TOOTS FOR ROOTS"! AND I'D BE MY OWN BEST CUSTOMER!
BBRRT
KLONG!!!
FIRST THING I'M BUYIN' IS SOME HEALTH INSURANCE...

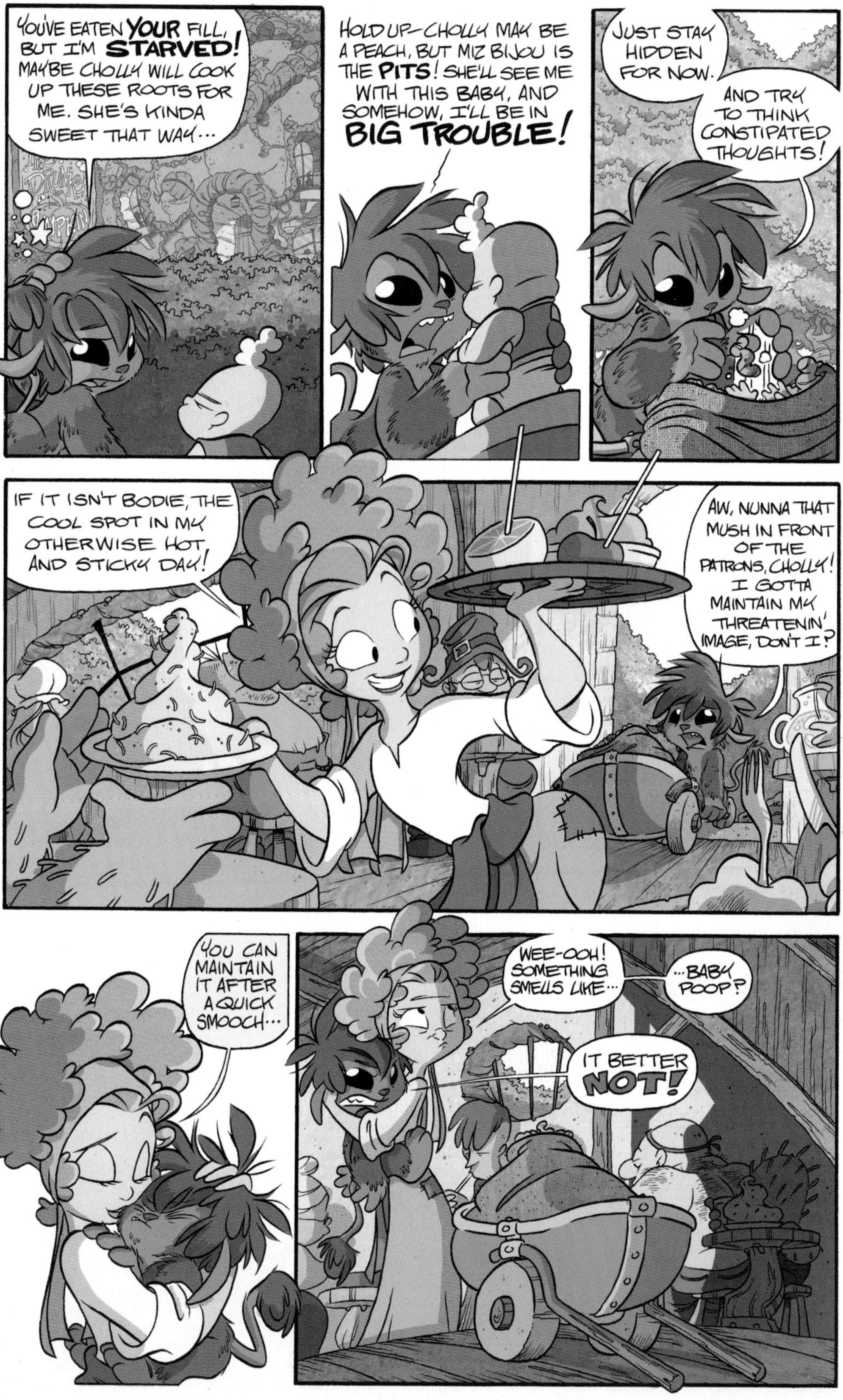
YOU'VE EATEN YOUR FILL, BUT I'M STARVED! MAYBE CHOLLY WILL COOK UP THESE ROOTS FOR ME. SHE'S KINDA SWEET THAT WAY...
HOLD UP--CHOLLY MAY BE A PEACH, BUT MIZ BIJOU IS THE PITS! SHE'LL SEE ME WITH THIS BABY, AND SOMEHOW, I'LL BE IN BIG TROUBLE!
JUST STAY HIDDEN FOR NOW.
AND TRY TO THINK CONSTIPATED THOUGHTS!
IF IT ISN'T BODIE, THE COOL SPOT IN MY OTHERWISE HOT AND STICKY DAY!
AW, NUNNA THAT MUSH IN FRONT OF THE PATRONS, CHOLLY! I GOTTA MAINTAIN MY THREATENIN' IMAGE, DON'T I?
YOU CAN MAINTAIN IT AFTER A QUICK SMOOCH...
WEE-OOH! SOMETHING SMELLS LIKE...
...BABY POOP?
IT BETTER NOT!

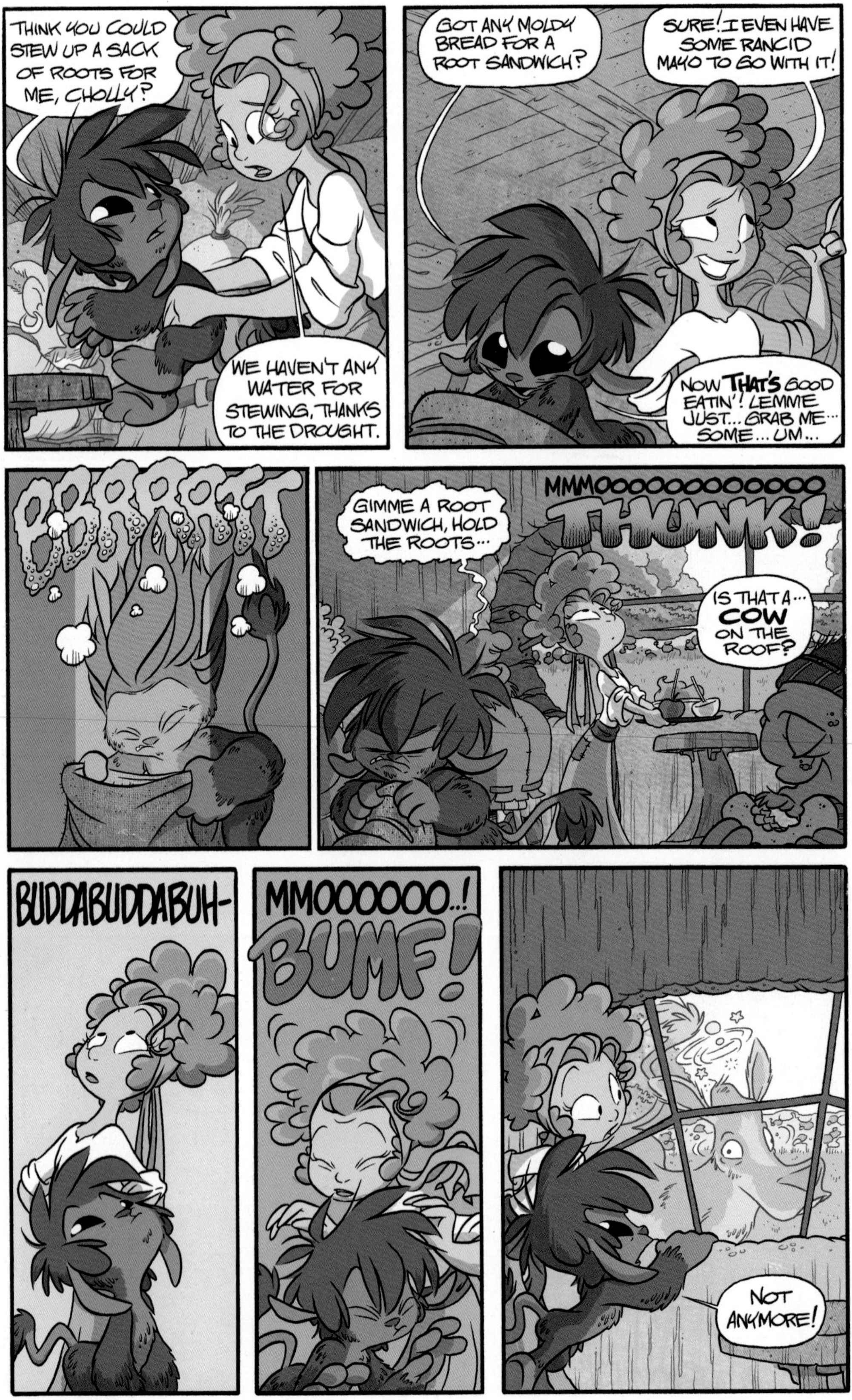
THINK YOU COULD STEW UP A SACK OF ROOTS FOR ME, CHOLLY?
WE HAVEN'T ANY WATER FOR STEWING, THANKS TO THE DROUGHT.
GOT ANY MOLDY BREAD FOR A ROOT SANDWICH?
SURE! I EVEN HAVE SOME RANCID MAYO TO GO WITH IT!
NOW THAT'S GOOD EATIN'! LEMME JUST... GRAB ME... SOME... UM...
BBRRRTT
GIMME A ROOT SANDWICH, HOLD THE ROOTS...
MMMOOOOOOOOOOOOO
THUNK!
IS THAT A... COW ON THE ROOF?
BUDDABUDDABUH-
MMOOOOOOO..!
BUMF!
NOT ANYMORE!

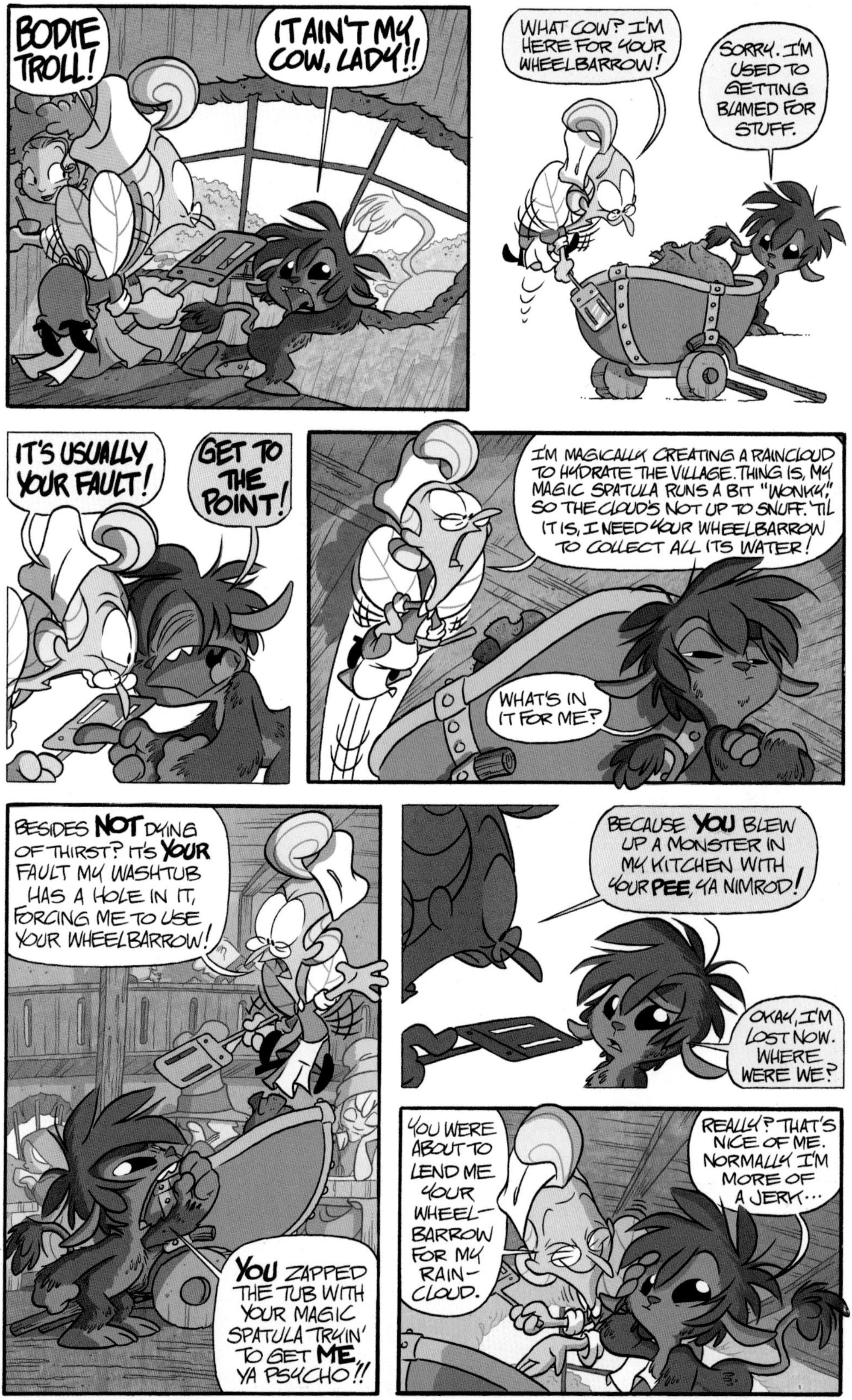
BODIE TROLL!
IT AIN'T MY COW, LADY!!
WHAT COW? I'M HERE FOR YOUR WHEELBARROW!
SORRY. I'M USED TO GETTING BLAMED FOR STUFF.
IT'S USUALLY YOUR FAULT!
GET TO THE POINT!
I'M MAGICALLY CREATING A RAINCLOUD TO HYDRATE THE VILLAGE. THING IS, MY MAGIC SPATULA RUNS A BIT "WONKY," SO THE CLOUD'S NOT UP TO SNUFF. 'TIL IT IS, I NEED YOUR WHEELBARROW TO COLLECT ALL ITS WATER!
WHAT'S IN IT FOR ME?
BESIDES NOT DYING OF THIRST? IT'S YOUR FAULT MY WASHTUB HAS A HOLE IN IT, FORCING ME TO USE YOUR WHEELBARROW!
YOU ZAPPED THE TUB WITH YOUR MAGIC SPATULA TRYIN' TO GET ME, YA PSYCHO!!
BECAUSE YOU BLEW UP A MONSTER IN MY KITCHEN WITH YOUR PEE, YA NIMROD!
OKAY, I'M LOST NOW. WHERE WERE WE?
YOU WERE ABOUT TO LEND ME YOUR WHEEL-BARROW FOR MY RAIN-CLOUD.
REALLY? THAT'S NICE OF ME. NORMALLY I'M MORE OF A JERK...

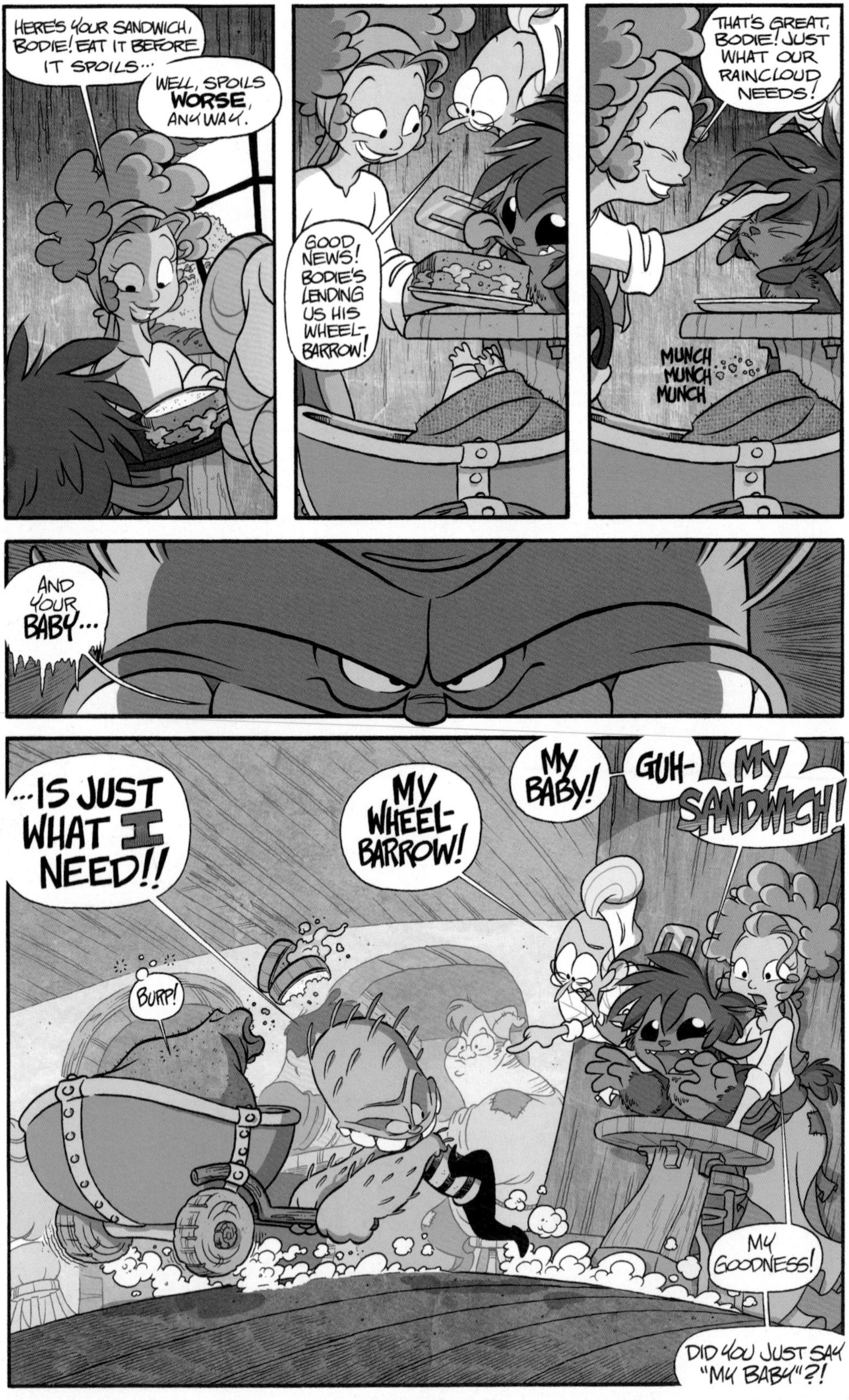
HERE'S YOUR SANDWICH, BODIE! EAT IT BEFORE IT SPOILS...
WELL, SPOILS WORSE, ANYWAY.
GOOD NEWS! BODIE'S LENDING US HIS WHEEL-BARROW!
THAT'S GREAT, BODIE! JUST WHAT OUR RAINCLOUD NEEDS!
MUNCH MUNCH MUNCH
AND YOUR BABY...
...IS JUST WHAT I NEED!!
MY WHEEL-BARROW!
MY BABY!
GUH-
MY SANDWICH!
BURP!
MY GOODNESS!
DID YOU JUST SAY "MY BABY"?!

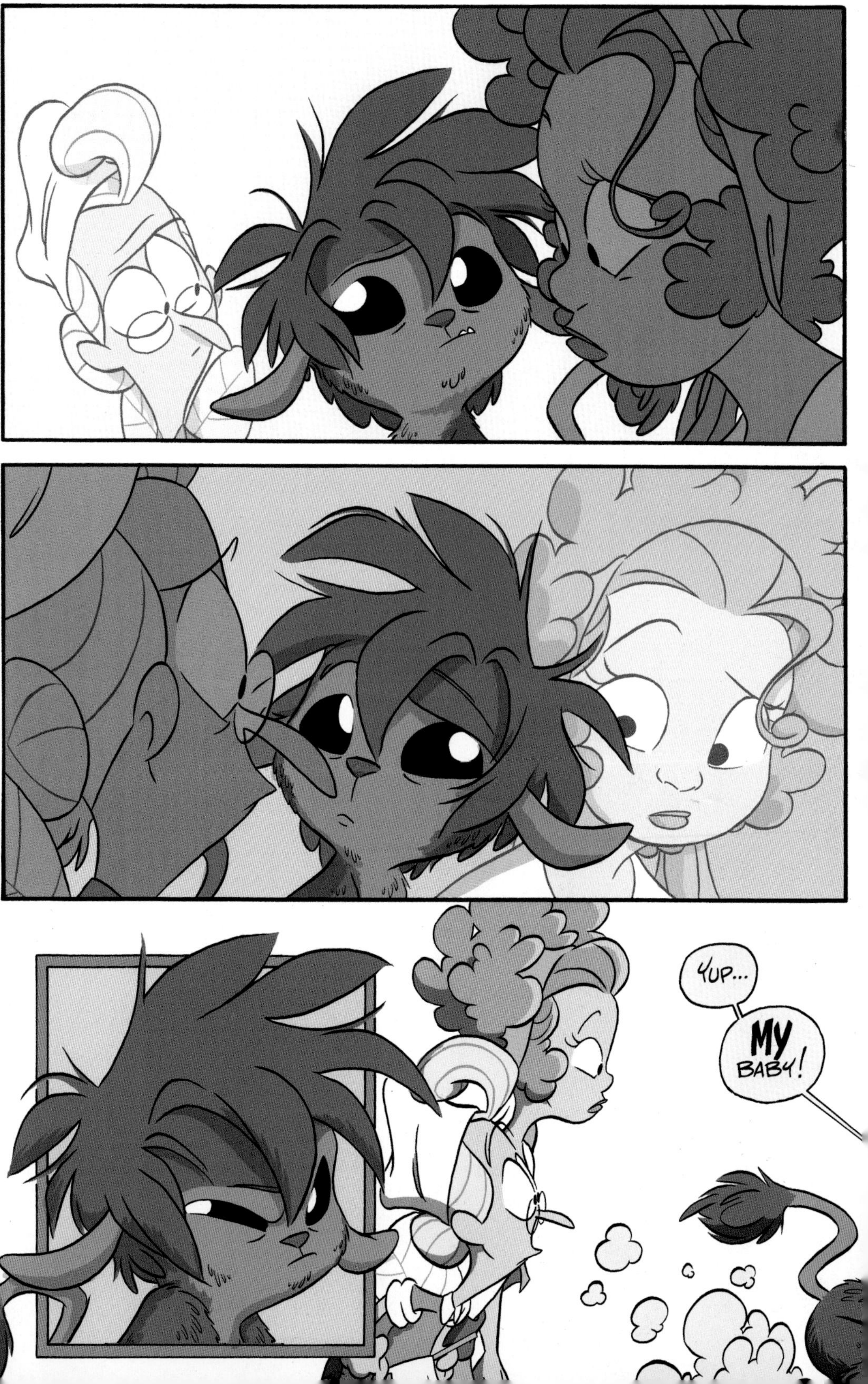
YUP...
MY BABY!

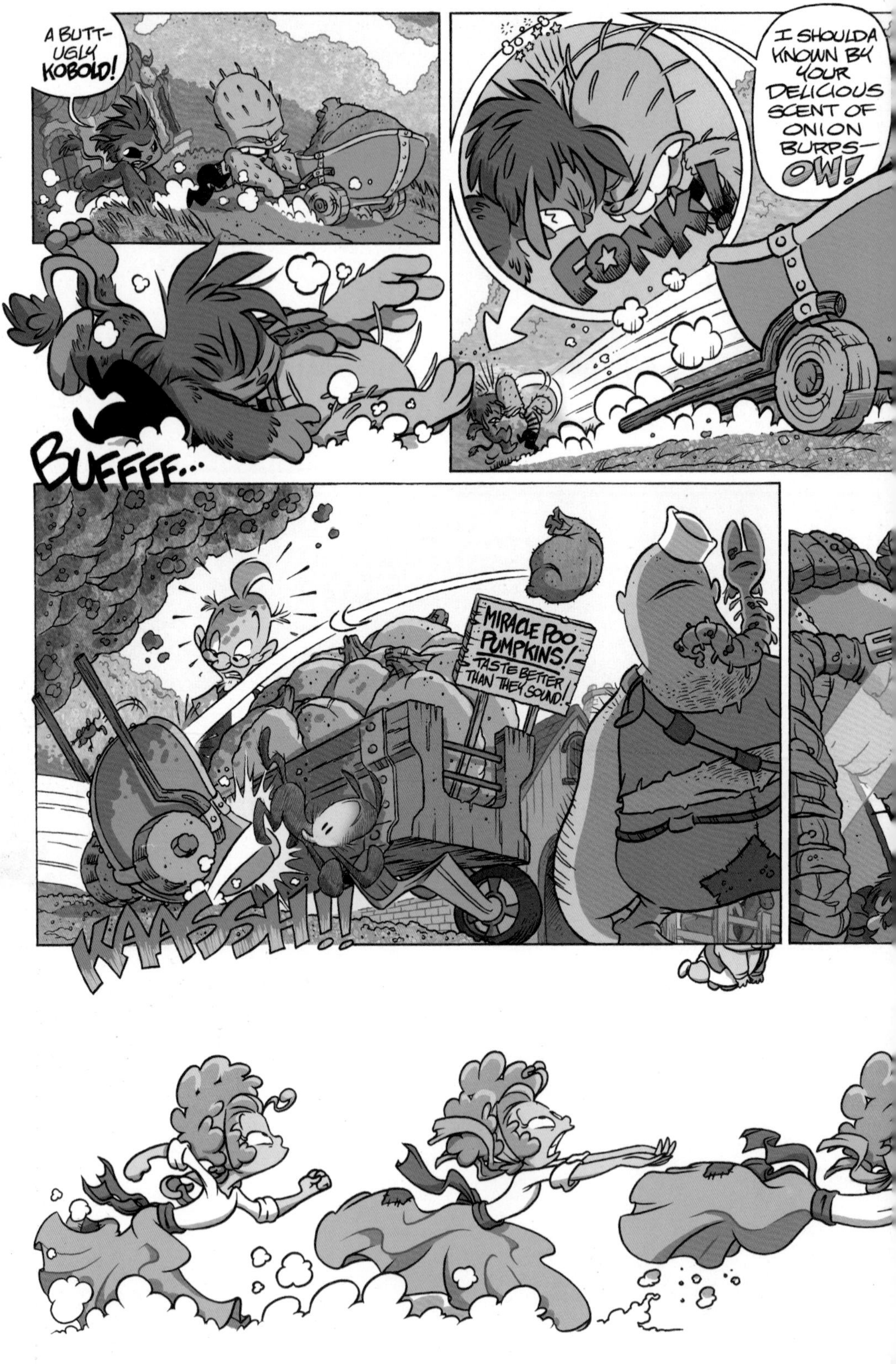
A BUTT-UGLY KOBOLD!
I SHOULDA KNOWN BY YOUR DELICIOUS SCENT OF ONION BURPS—OW!
CONK!
BUFFFF...
MIRACLE POO PUMPKINS! TASTE BETTER THAN THEY SOUND!
KAASSH!!

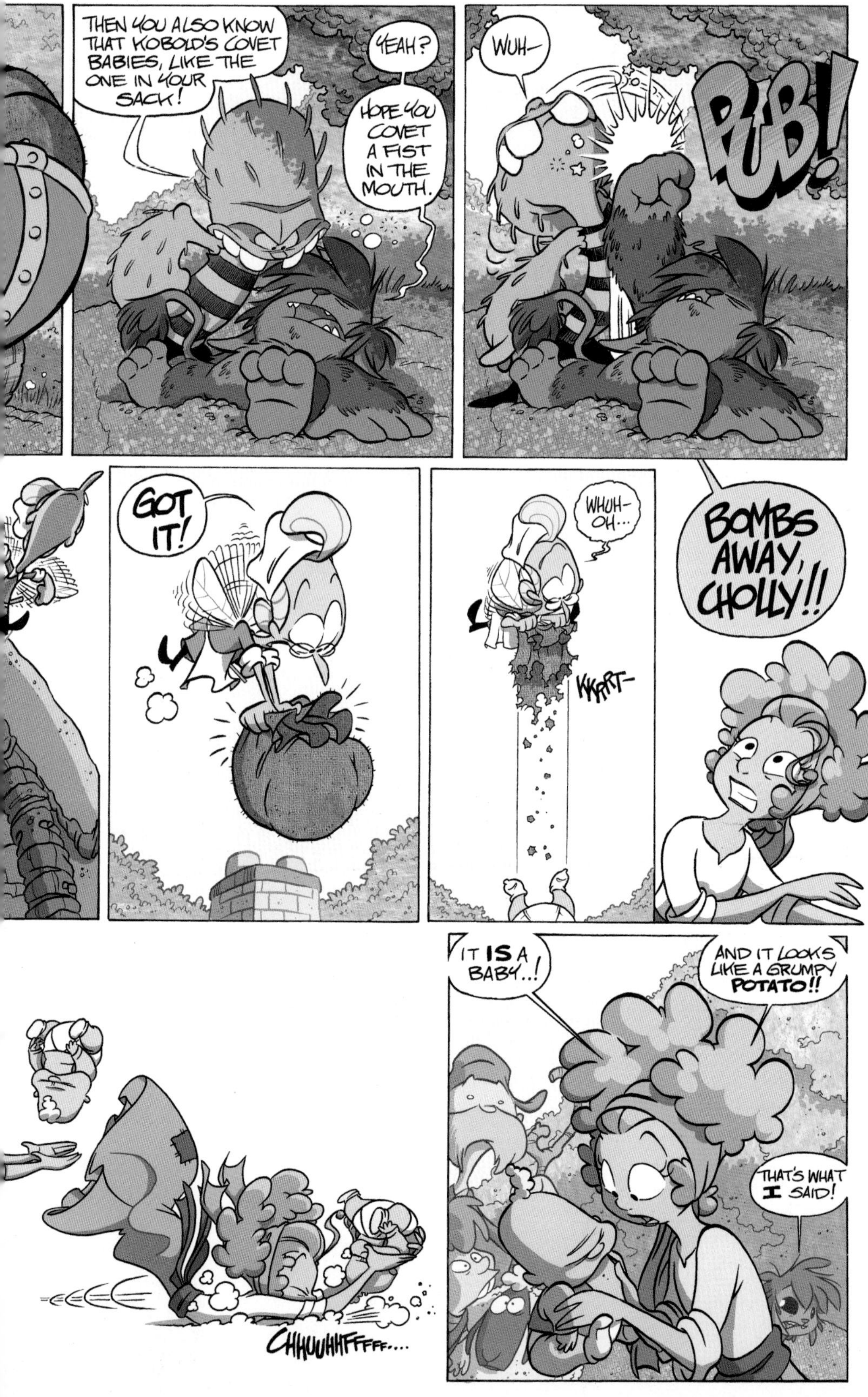
THEN YOU ALSO KNOW THAT KOBOLD'S COVET BABIES, LIKE THE ONE IN YOUR SACK!
YEAH?
HOPE YOU COVET A FIST IN THE MOUTH.
WUH-
BUB!
GOT IT!
WHUH-OH...
KKRRT-
BOMBS AWAY, CHOLLY!!
CHHUUHHFFFFF....
IT IS A BABY..!
AND IT LOOKS LIKE A GRUMPY POTATO!!
THAT'S WHAT I SAID!

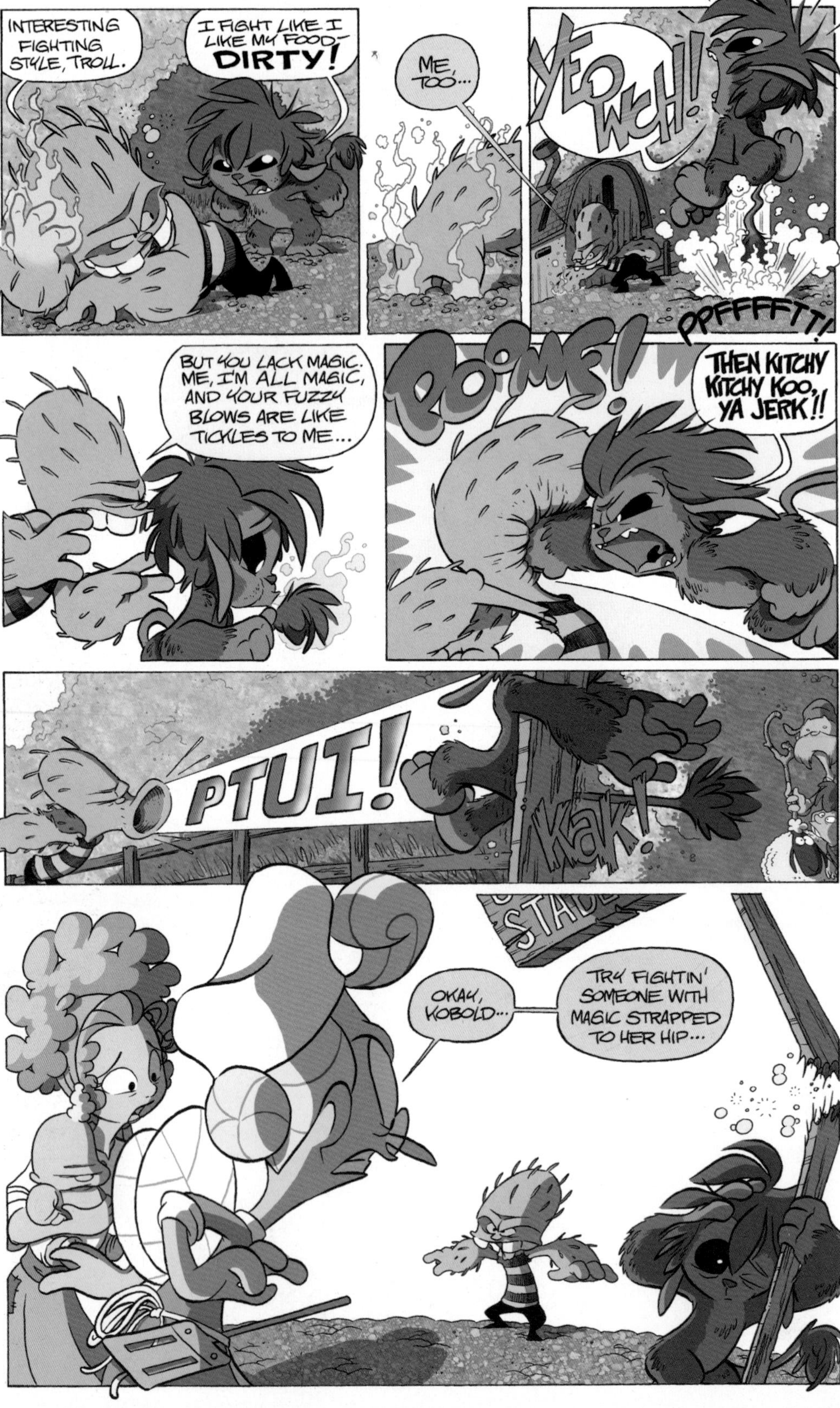
INTERESTING FIGHTING STYLE, TROLL.
I FIGHT LIKE I LIKE MY FOOD– DIRTY!
ME, TOO...
YEOWCH!!
PPFFFFTT!!
BUT YOU LACK MAGIC. ME, I'M ALL MAGIC, AND YOUR FUZZY BLOWS ARE LIKE TICKLES TO ME...
POOMF!
THEN KITCHY KITCHY KOO, YA JERK!!
PTUI!
KAK!
STABL
OKAY, KOBOLD...
TRY FIGHTIN' SOMEONE WITH MAGIC STRAPPED TO HER HIP...

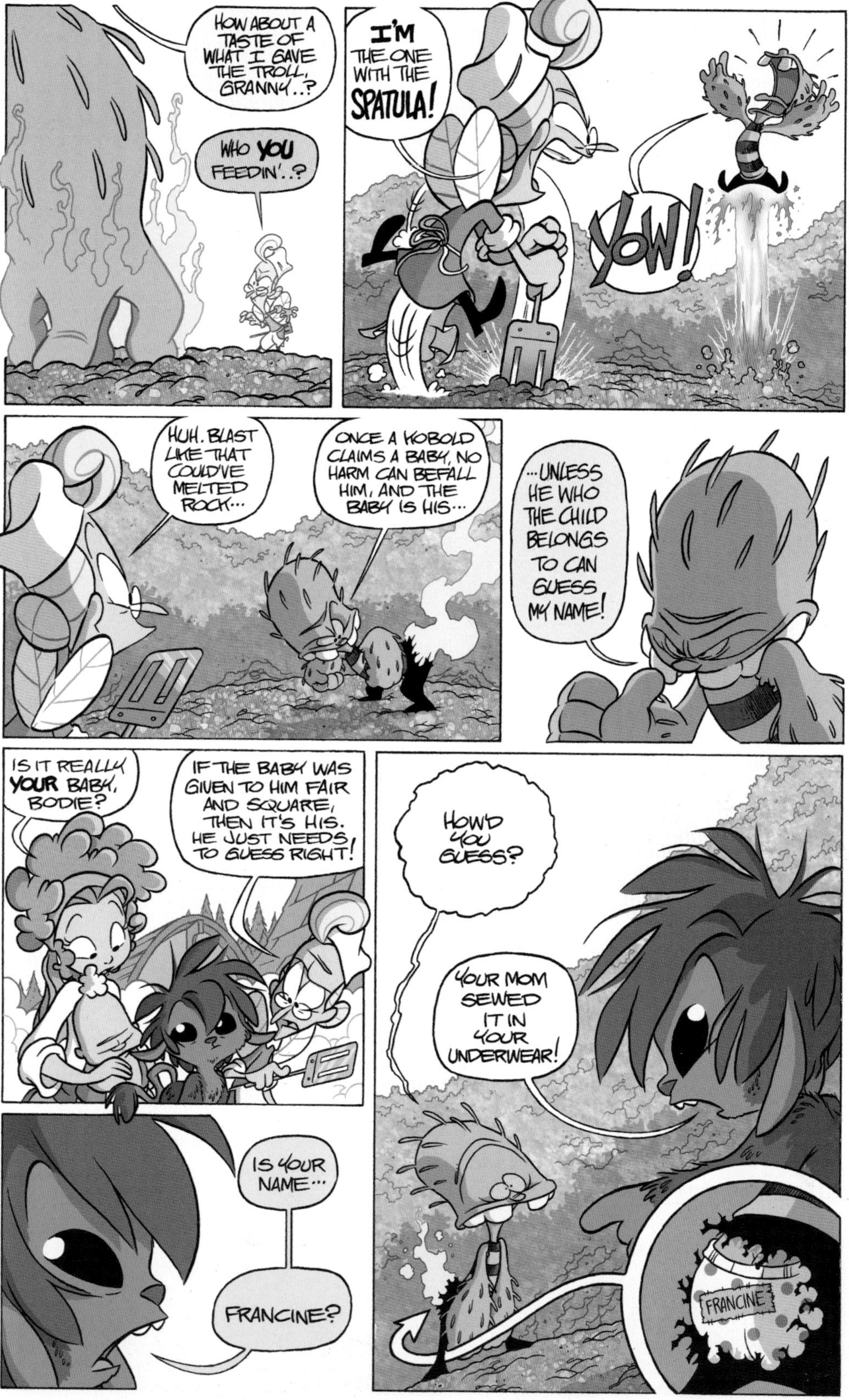

HOW ABOUT A TASTE OF WHAT I GAVE THE TROLL, GRANNY..?
WHO YOU FEEDIN'..?
I'M THE ONE WITH THE SPATULA!
YOW!
HUH. BLAST LIKE THAT COULD'VE MELTED ROCK...
ONCE A KOBOLD CLAIMS A BABY, NO HARM CAN BEFALL HIM, AND THE BABY IS HIS...
...UNLESS HE WHO THE CHILD BELONGS TO CAN GUESS MY NAME!
IS IT REALLY YOUR BABY, BODIE?
IF THE BABY WAS GIVEN TO HIM FAIR AND SQUARE, THEN IT'S HIS. HE JUST NEEDS TO GUESS RIGHT!
HOW'D YOU GUESS?
YOUR MOM SEWED IT IN YOUR UNDERWEAR!
FRANCINE
IS YOUR NAME...
FRANCINE?

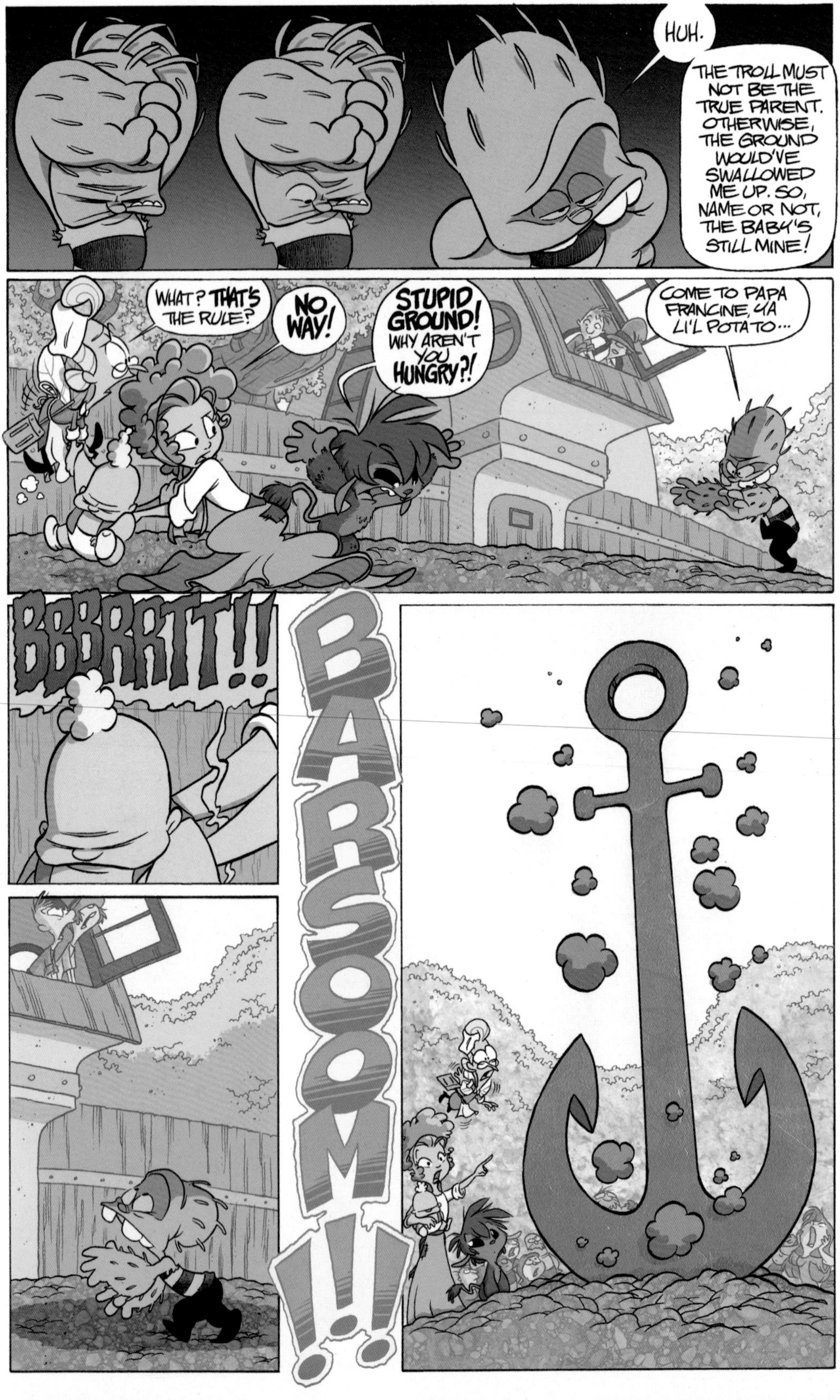
HUH.
THE TROLL MUST NOT BE THE TRUE PARENT. OTHERWISE, THE GROUND WOULD'VE SWALLOWED ME UP. SO, NAME OR NOT, THE BABY'S STILL MINE!
WHAT? THAT'S THE RULE?
NO WAY!
STUPID GROUND! WHY AREN'T YOU HUNGRY?!
COME TO PAPA FRANCINE, YA LI'L POTATO...
BBBRRRTT!!
BARSOOM!!

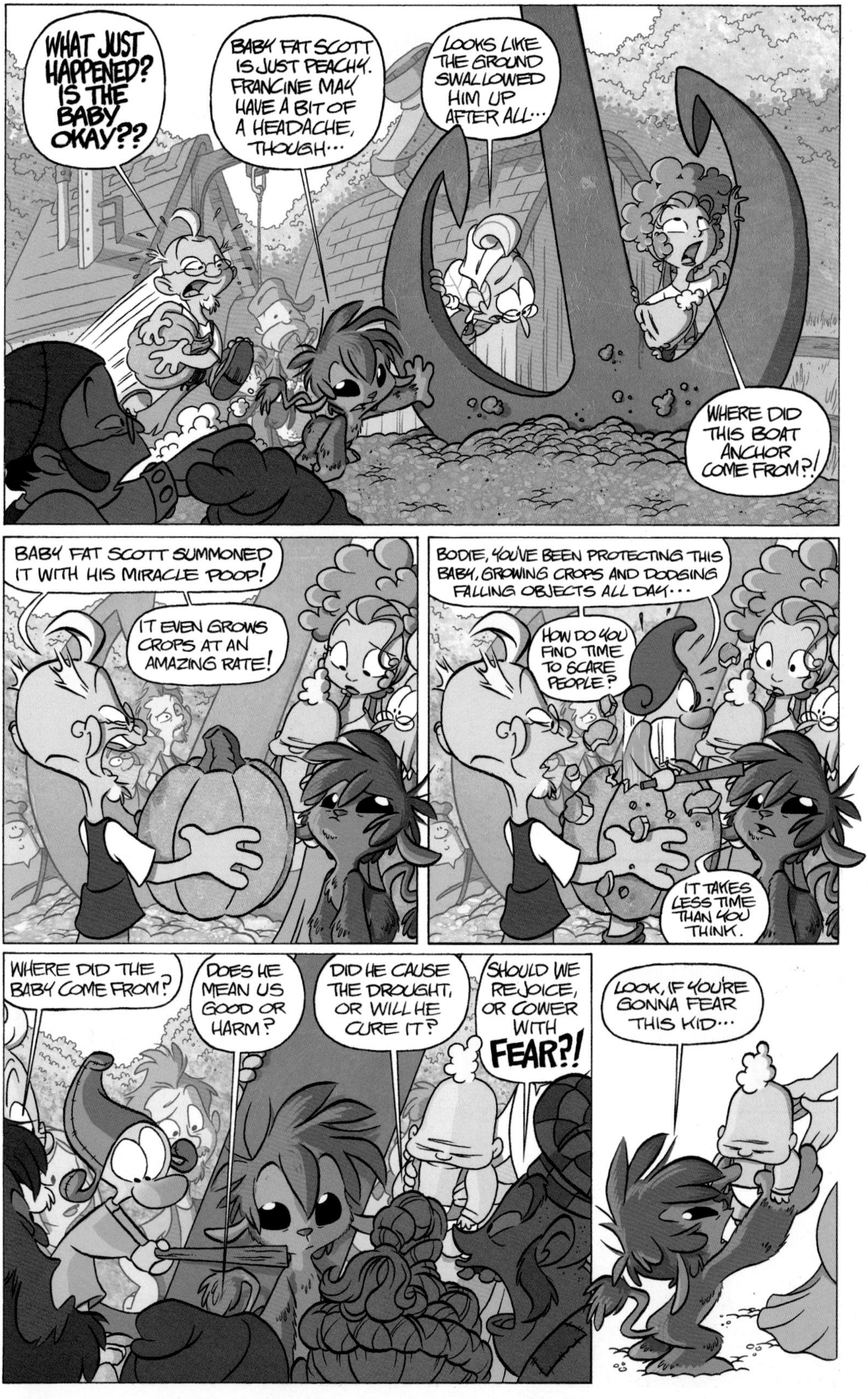
WHAT JUST HAPPENED? IS THE BABY OKAY??
BABY FAT SCOTT IS JUST PEACHY. FRANCINE MAY HAVE A BIT OF A HEADACHE, THOUGH...
LOOKS LIKE THE GROUND SWALLOWED HIM UP AFTER ALL...
WHERE DID THIS BOAT ANCHOR COME FROM?!
BABY FAT SCOTT SUMMONED IT WITH HIS MIRACLE POOP!
IT EVEN GROWS CROPS AT AN AMAZING RATE!
BODIE, YOU'VE BEEN PROTECTING THIS BABY, GROWING CROPS AND DODGING FALLING OBJECTS ALL DAY...
HOW DO YOU FIND TIME TO SCARE PEOPLE?
IT TAKES LESS TIME THAN YOU THINK.
WHERE DID THE BABY COME FROM?
DOES HE MEAN US GOOD OR HARM?
DID HE CAUSE THE DROUGHT, OR WILL HE CURE IT?
SHOULD WE REJOICE, OR COWER WITH FEAR?!
LOOK, IF YOU'RE GONNA FEAR THIS KID...

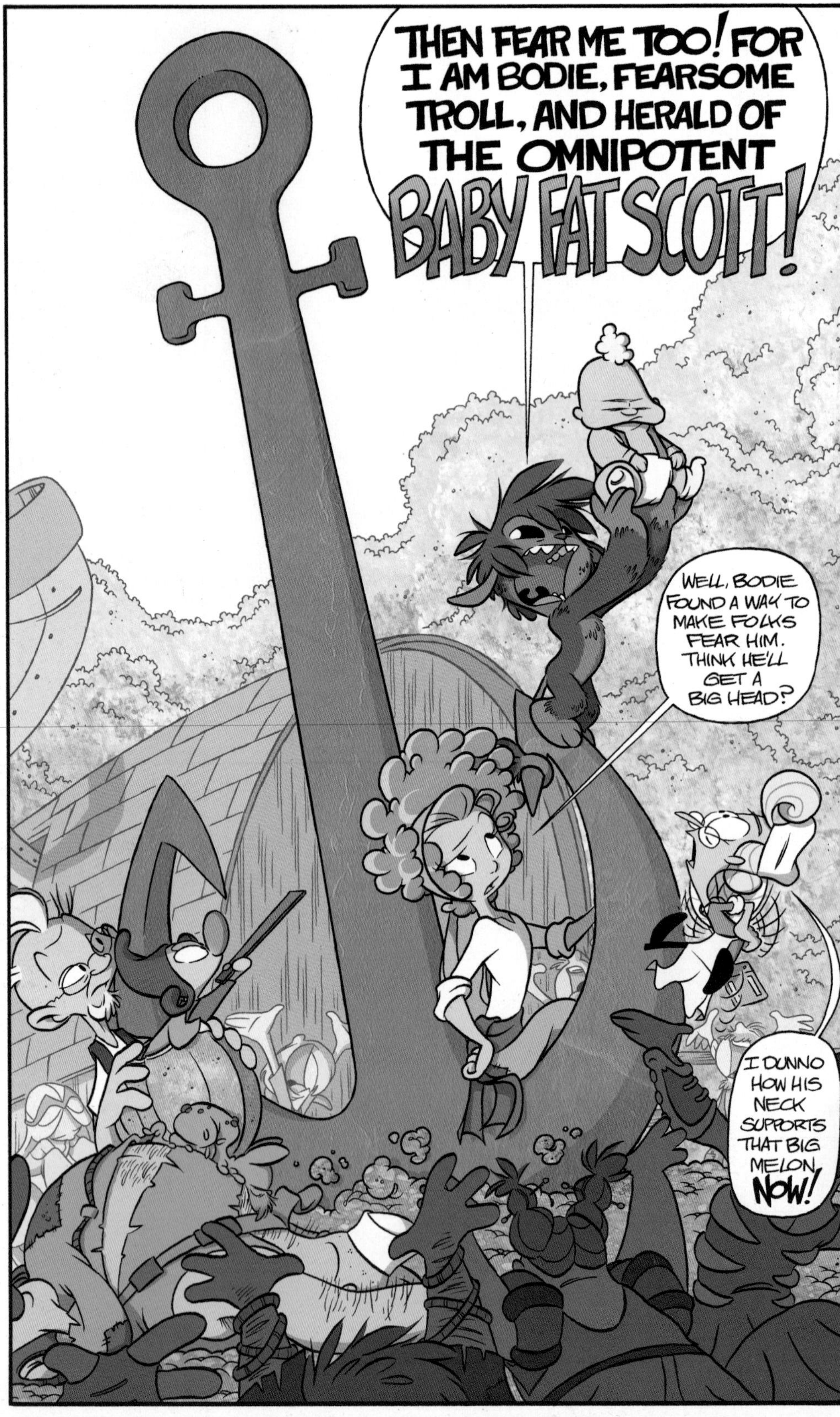
THEN FEAR ME TOO! FOR I AM BODIE, FEARSOME TROLL, AND HERALD OF THE OMNIPOTENT BABY FAT SCOTT!
WELL, BODIE FOUND A WAY TO MAKE FOLKS FEAR HIM. THINK HE'LL GET A BIG HEAD?
I DUNNO HOW HIS NECK SUPPORTS THAT BIG MELON, NOW!

CHAPTER 4
THE SKY'S THE LIMIT

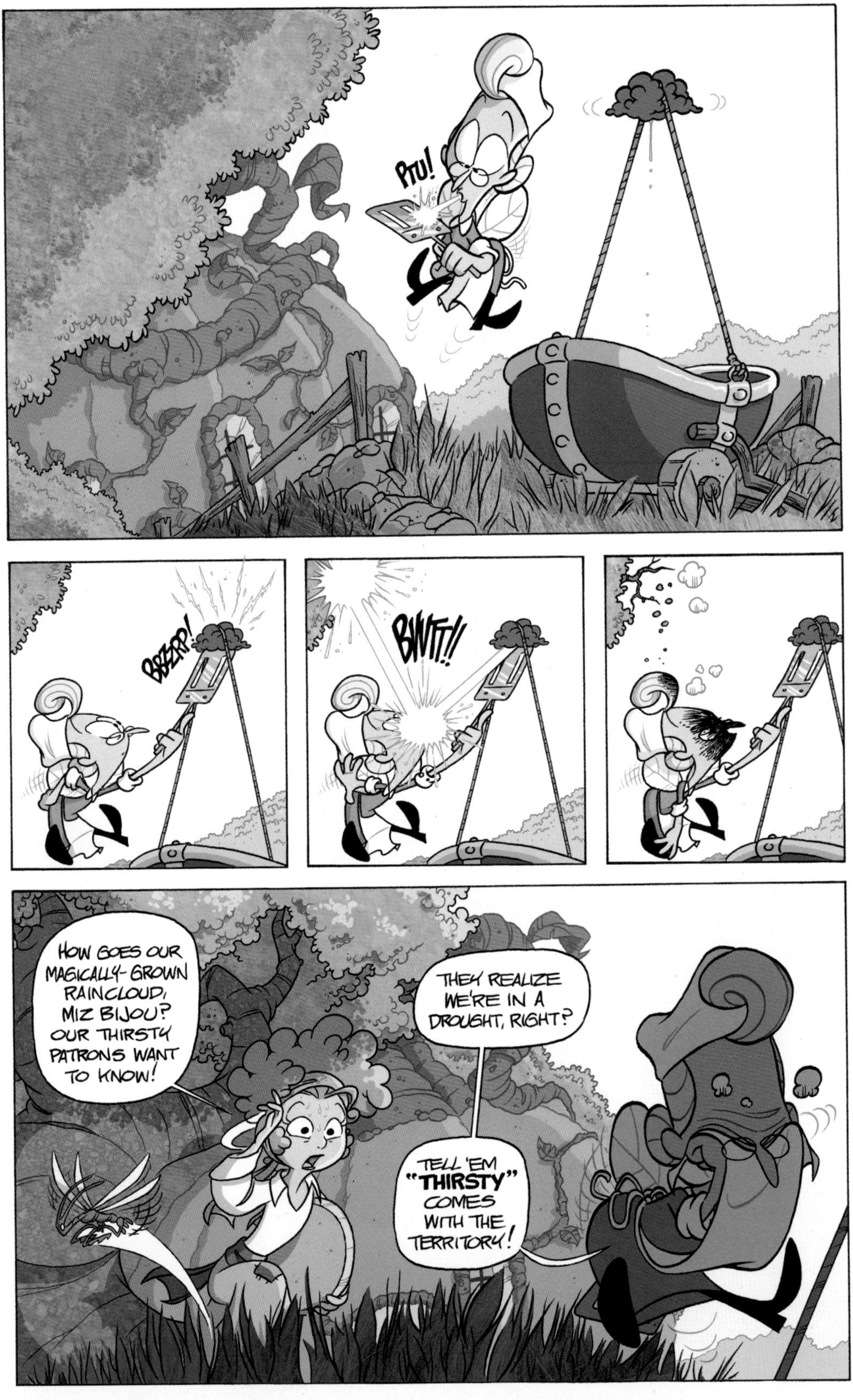
PTU!
BZZZRP!
BWTT!!
HOW GOES OUR MAGICALLY-GROWN RAINCLOUD, MIZ BIJOU? OUR THIRSTY PATRONS WANT TO KNOW!
THEY REALIZE WE'RE IN A DROUGHT, RIGHT?
TELL 'EM "THIRSTY" COMES WITH THE TERRITORY!

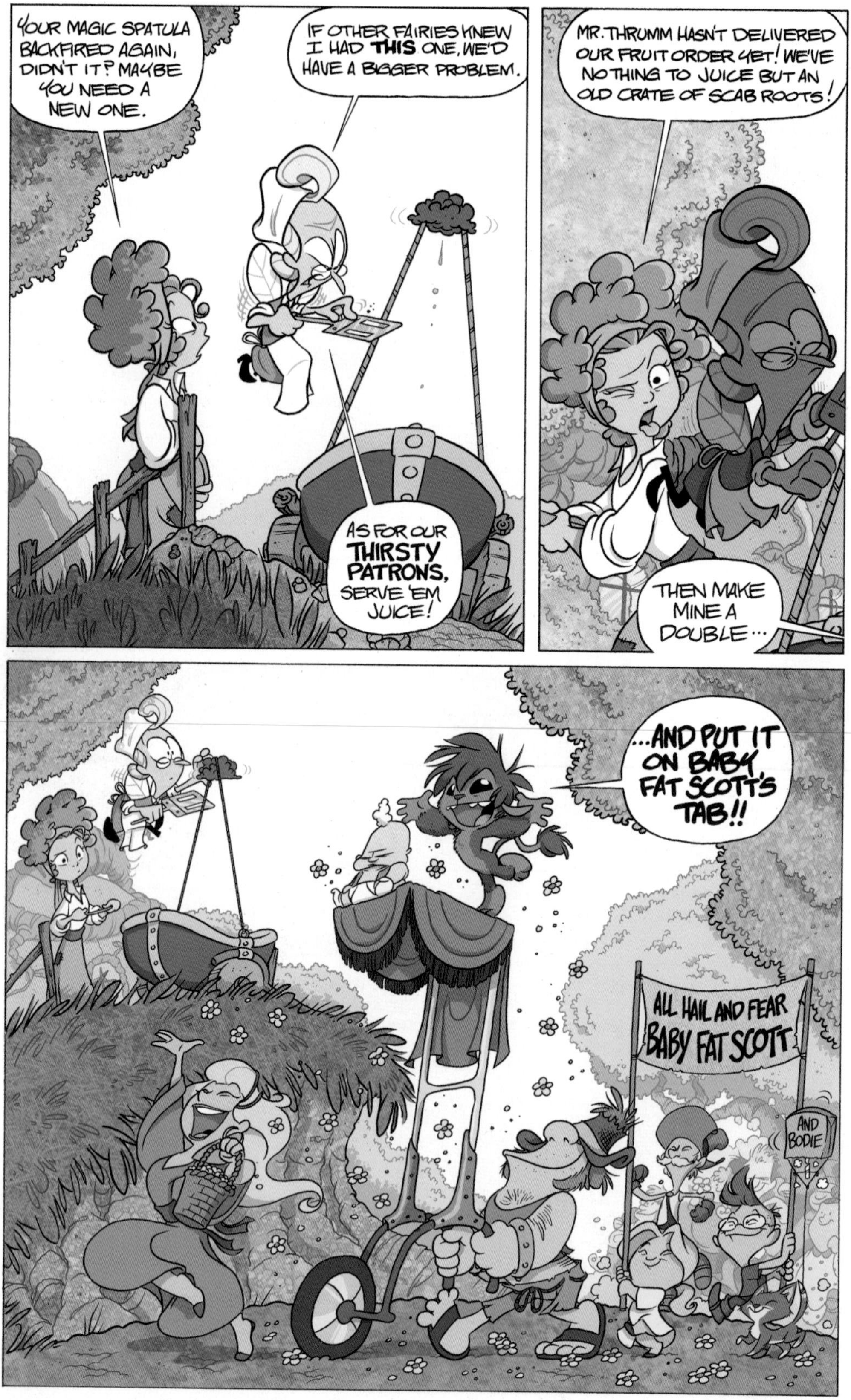
YOUR MAGIC SPATULA BACKFIRED AGAIN, DIDN'T IT? MAYBE YOU NEED A NEW ONE.
IF OTHER FAIRIES KNEW I HAD THIS ONE, WE'D HAVE A BIGGER PROBLEM.
AS FOR OUR THIRSTY PATRONS, SERVE 'EM JUICE!
MR. THRUMM HASN'T DELIVERED OUR FRUIT ORDER YET! WE'VE NOTHING TO JUICE BUT AN OLD CRATE OF SCAB ROOTS!
THEN MAKE MINE A DOUBLE...
...AND PUT IT ON BABY FAT SCOTT'S TAB!!
ALL HAIL AND FEAR BABY FAT SCOTT
AND BODIE

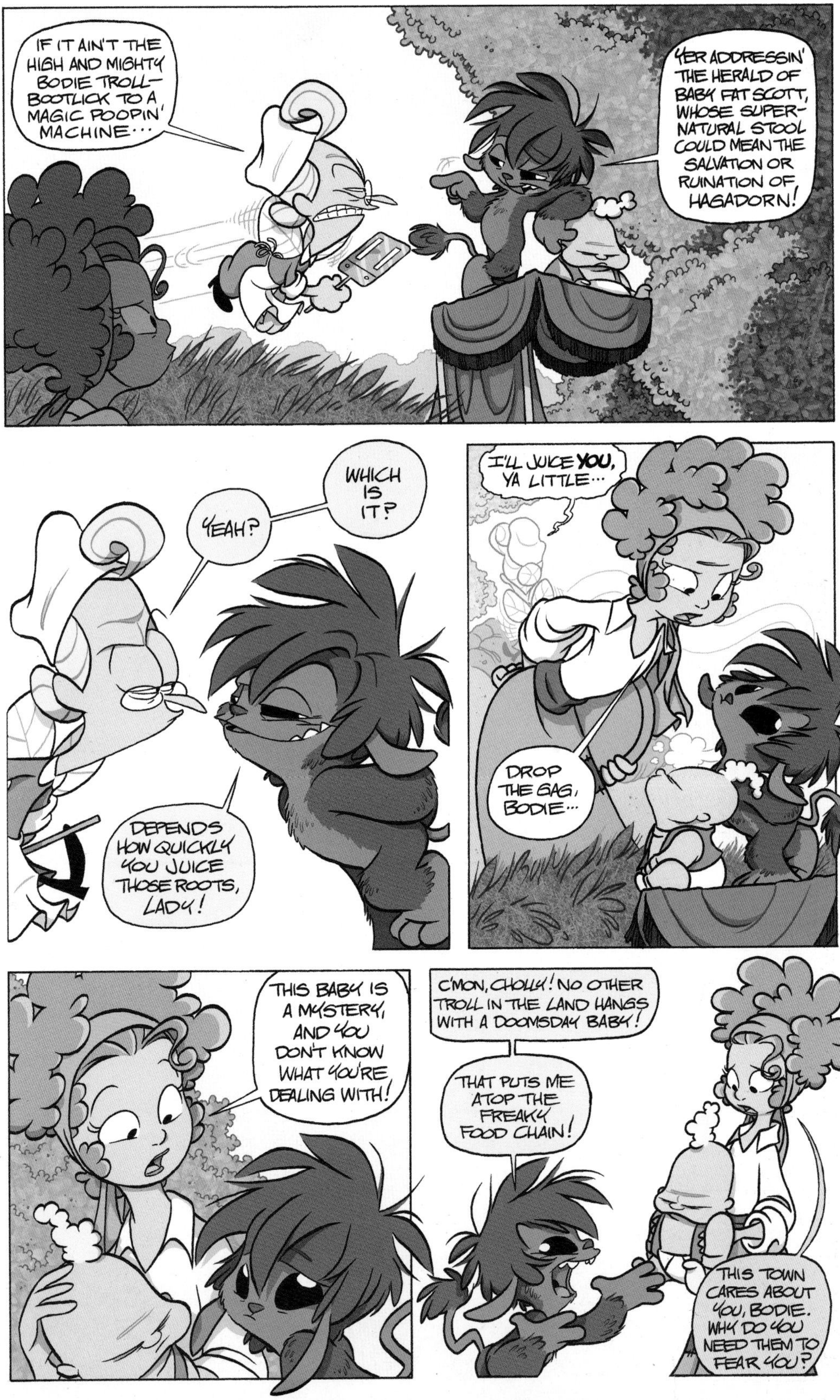
IF IT AIN'T THE HIGH AND MIGHTY BODIE TROLL— BOOTLICK TO A MAGIC POOPIN' MACHINE...
YER ADDRESSIN' THE HERALD OF BABY FAT SCOTT, WHOSE SUPER-NATURAL STOOL COULD MEAN THE SALVATION OR RUINATION OF HAGADORN!
YEAH?
WHICH IS IT?
DEPENDS HOW QUICKLY YOU JUICE THOSE ROOTS, LADY!
I'LL JUICE YOU, YA LITTLE...
DROP THE GAG, BODIE...
THIS BABY IS A MYSTERY, AND YOU DON'T KNOW WHAT YOU'RE DEALING WITH!
C'MON, CHOLLY! NO OTHER TROLL IN THE LAND HANGS WITH A DOOMSDAY BABY!
THAT PUTS ME ATOP THE FREAKY FOOD CHAIN!
THIS TOWN CARES ABOUT YOU, BODIE. WHY DO YOU NEED THEM TO FEAR YOU?

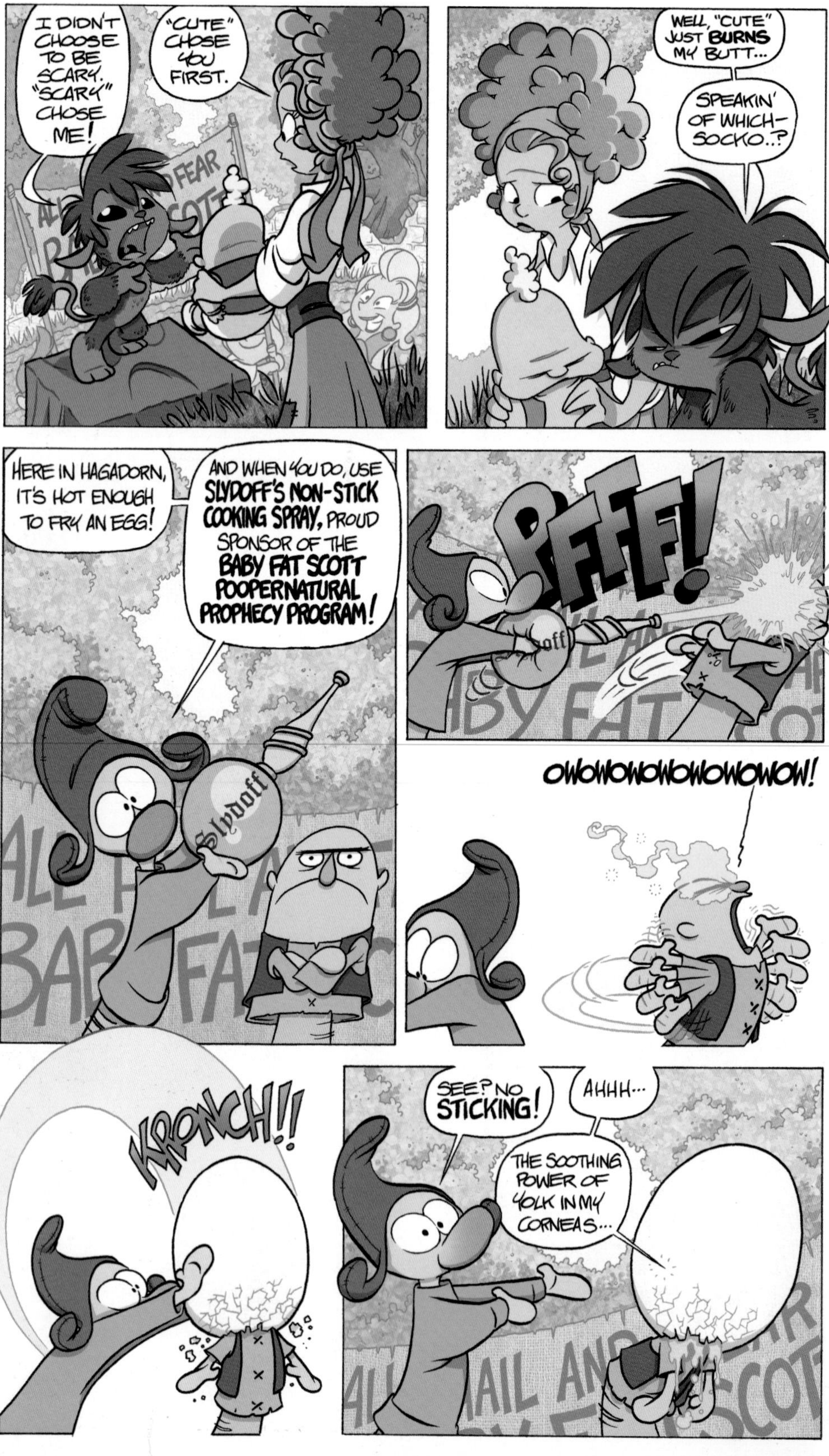
I DIDN'T CHOOSE TO BE SCARY. "SCARY" CHOSE ME!
"CUTE" CHOSE YOU FIRST.
WELL, "CUTE" JUST **BURNS** MY BUTT...
SPEAKIN' OF WHICH- SOCKO..?
HERE IN HAGADORN, IT'S HOT ENOUGH TO FRY AN EGG!
AND WHEN YOU DO, USE **SLYDOFF'S NON-STICK COOKING SPRAY,** PROUD SPONSOR OF THE **BABY FAT SCOTT POOPERNATURAL PROPHECY PROGRAM!**
Slydoff
OWOWOWOWOWOWOWOW!
KRONCH!!
SEE? NO **STICKING!**
AHHH...
THE SOOTHING POWER OF YOLK IN MY CORNEAS...

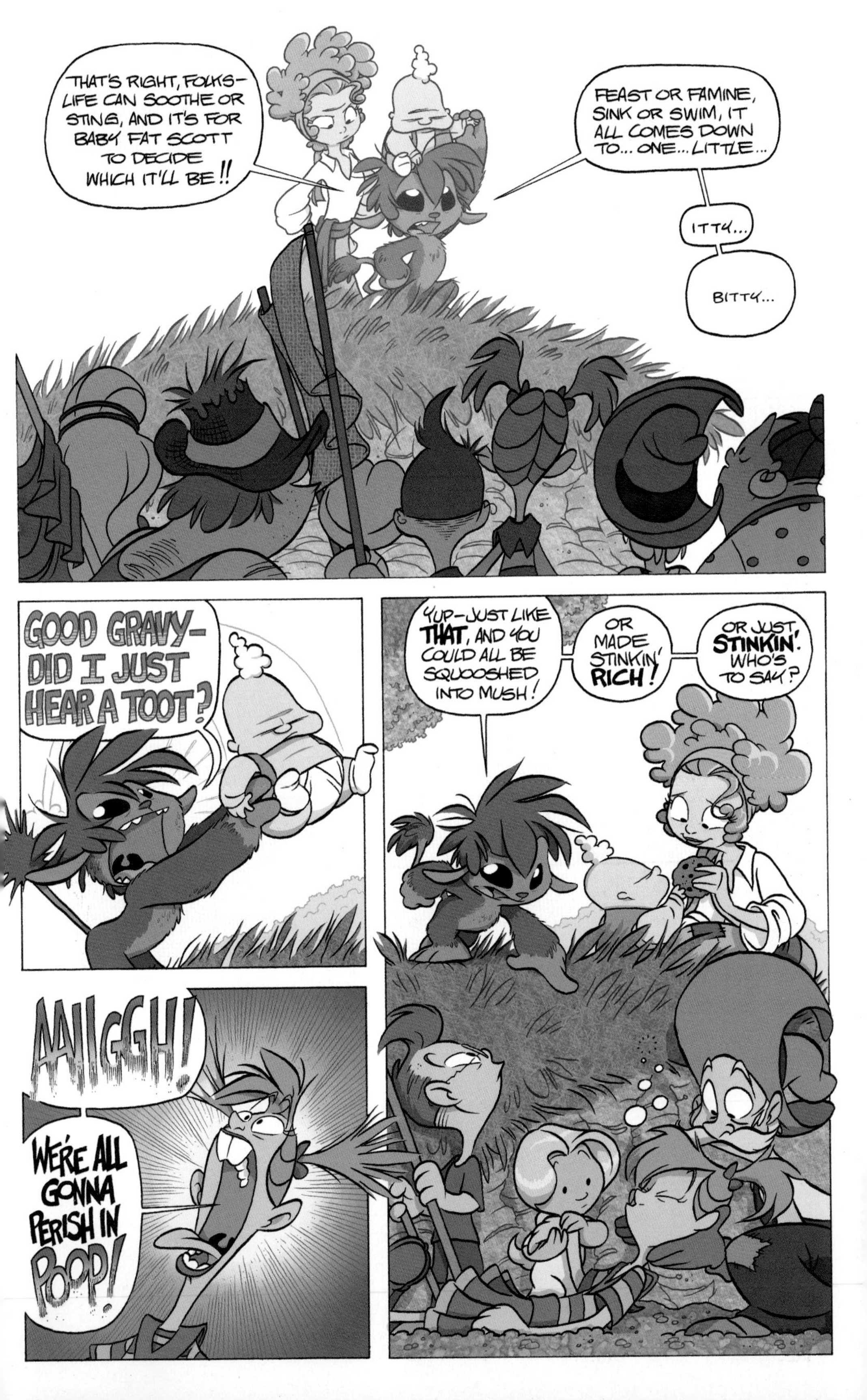
THAT'S RIGHT, FOLKS-LIFE CAN SOOTHE OR STING, AND IT'S FOR BABY FAT SCOTT TO DECIDE WHICH IT'LL BE!!
FEAST OR FAMINE, SINK OR SWIM, IT ALL COMES DOWN TO... ONE... LITTLE...
ITTY...
BITTY...
GOOD GRAVY-DID I JUST HEAR A TOOT?
YUP-JUST LIKE THAT, AND YOU COULD ALL BE SQUOOSHED INTO MUSH!
OR MADE STINKIN' RICH!
OR JUST STINKIN'. WHO'S TO SAY?
AAIIGGH!
WE'RE ALL GONNA PERISH IN POOP!

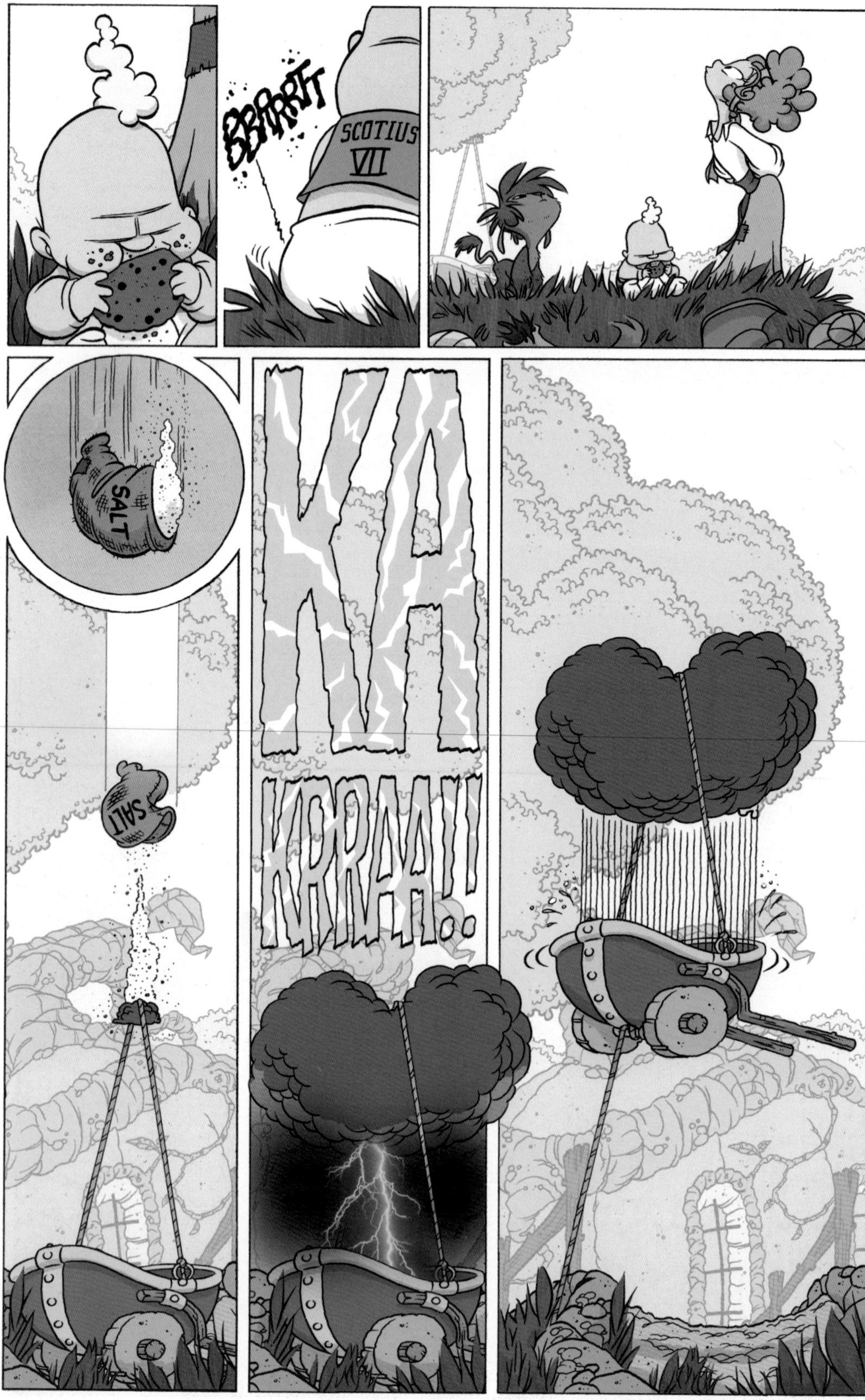
BBRRRFT
SCOTIUS VII
SALT
SALT
KA KRRAA!!..

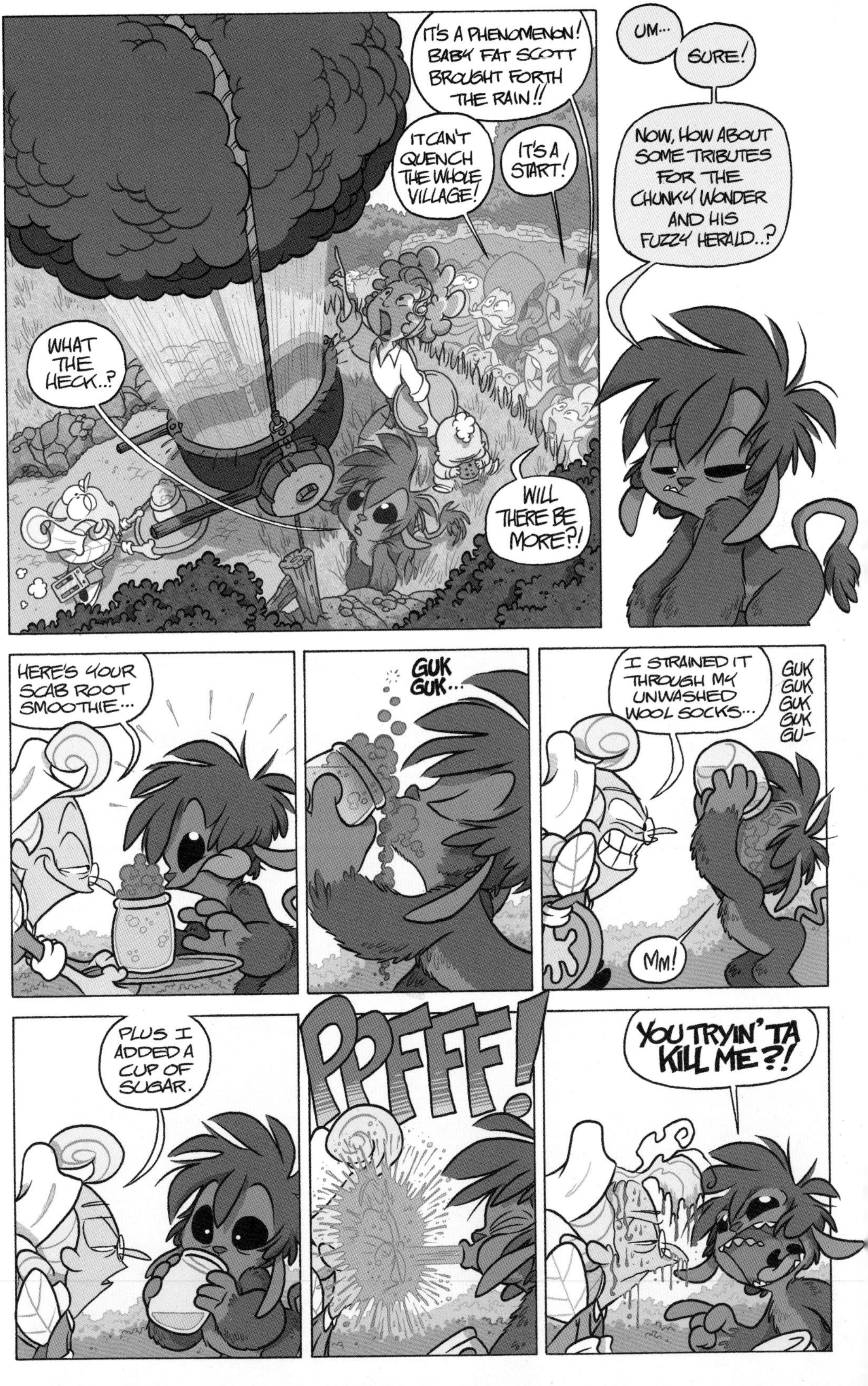
IT'S A PHENOMENON! BABY FAT SCOTT BROUGHT FORTH THE RAIN!!
IT CAN'T QUENCH THE WHOLE VILLAGE!
IT'S A START!
WHAT THE HECK..?
WILL THERE BE MORE?!
UM...
SURE!
NOW, HOW ABOUT SOME TRIBUTES FOR THE CHUNKY WONDER AND HIS FUZZY HERALD..?
HERE'S YOUR SCAB ROOT SMOOTHIE...
GUK GUK...
I STRAINED IT THROUGH MY UNWASHED WOOL SOCKS...
GUK GUK GUK GUK GU–
MM!
PLUS I ADDED A CUP OF SUGAR.
PPFFFF!
YOU TRYIN' TA KILL ME?!

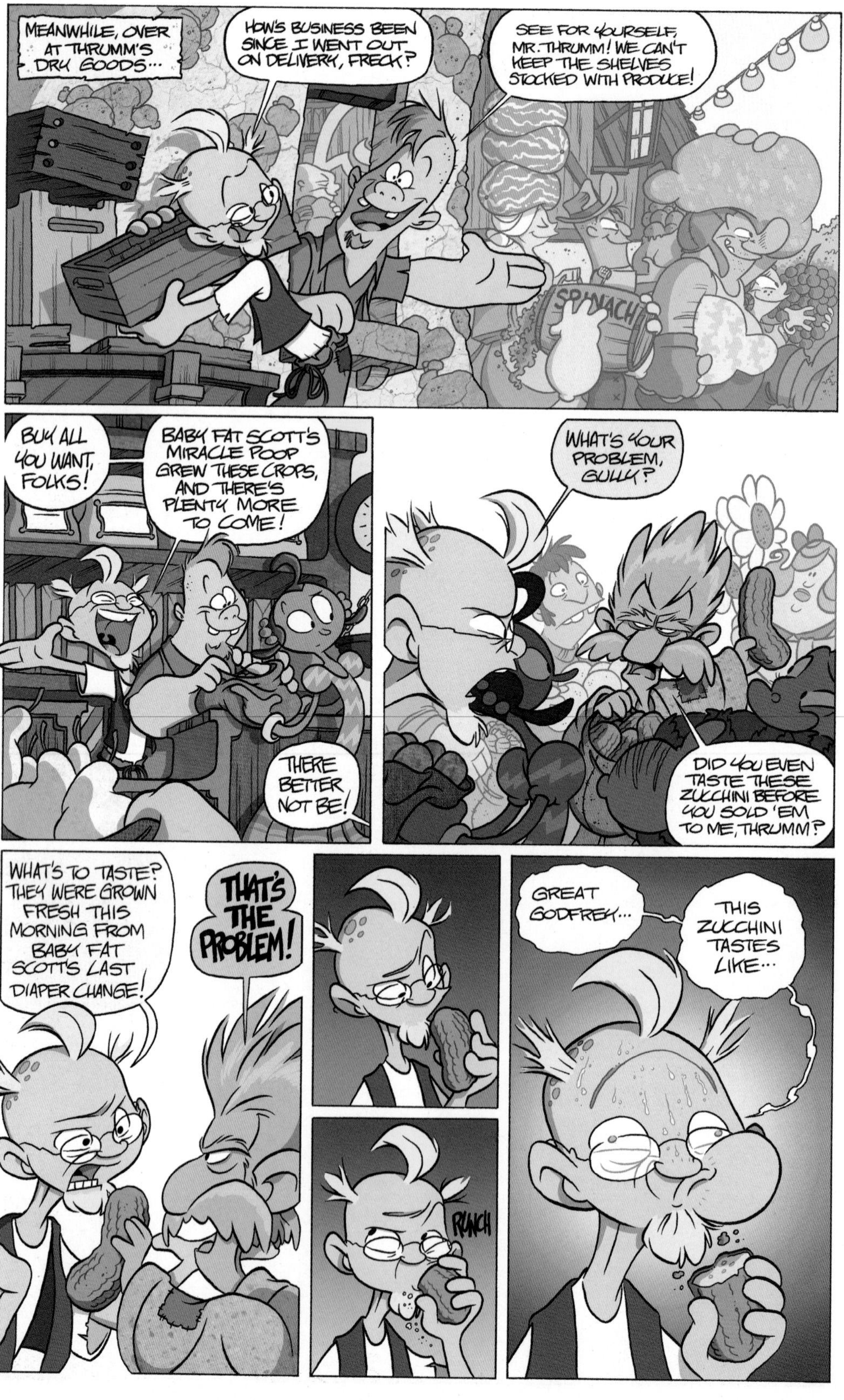

MEANWHILE, OVER AT THRUMM'S DRY GOODS...
HOW'S BUSINESS BEEN SINCE I WENT OUT ON DELIVERY, FRECK?
SEE FOR YOURSELF, MR. THRUMM! WE CAN'T KEEP THE SHELVES STOCKED WITH PRODUCE!
SPINACH
BUY ALL YOU WANT, FOLKS!
BABY FAT SCOTT'S MIRACLE POOP GREW THESE CROPS, AND THERE'S PLENTY MORE TO COME!
THERE BETTER NOT BE!
WHAT'S YOUR PROBLEM, GULLY?
DID YOU EVEN TASTE THESE ZUCCHINI BEFORE YOU SOLD 'EM TO ME, THRUMM?
WHAT'S TO TASTE? THEY WERE GROWN FRESH THIS MORNING FROM BABY FAT SCOTT'S LAST DIAPER CHANGE!
THAT'S THE PROBLEM!
RUNCH
GREAT GODFREY...
THIS ZUCCHINI TASTES LIKE...

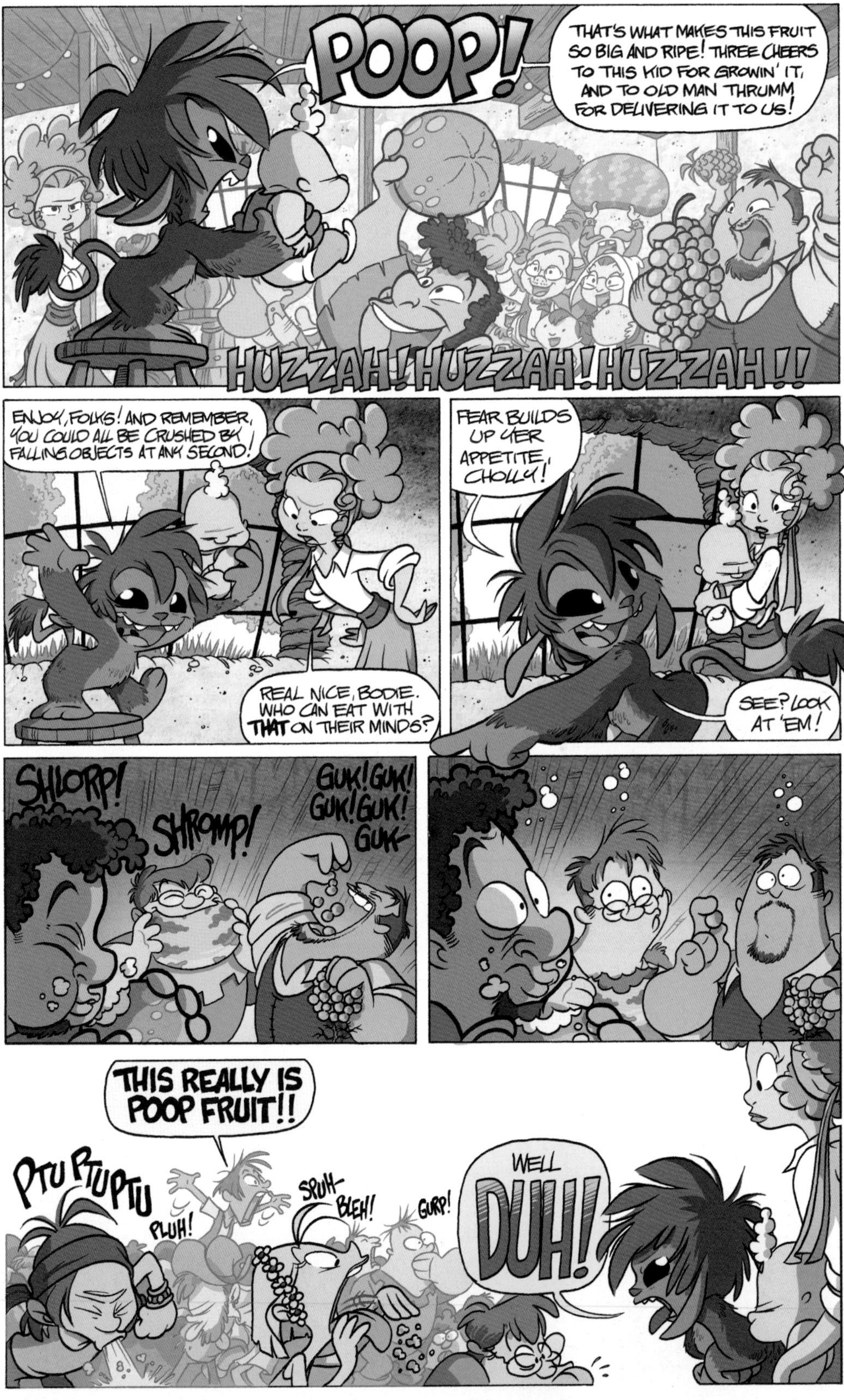
POOP!
THAT'S WHAT MAKES THIS FRUIT SO BIG AND RIPE! THREE CHEERS TO THIS KID FOR GROWIN' IT, AND TO OLD MAN THRUMM FOR DELIVERING IT TO US!
HUZZAH! HUZZAH! HUZZAH!!
ENJOY, FOLKS! AND REMEMBER, YOU COULD ALL BE CRUSHED BY FALLING OBJECTS AT ANY SECOND!
REAL NICE, BODIE. WHO CAN EAT WITH THAT ON THEIR MINDS?
FEAR BUILDS UP YER APPETITE, CHOLLY!
SEE? LOOK AT 'EM!
SHLORP!
SHROMP!
GUK! GUK! GUK! GUK! GUK
THIS REALLY IS POOP FRUIT!!
PTU PTU PTU
PLUH!
SPUH-BLEH!
GURP!
WELL DUH!

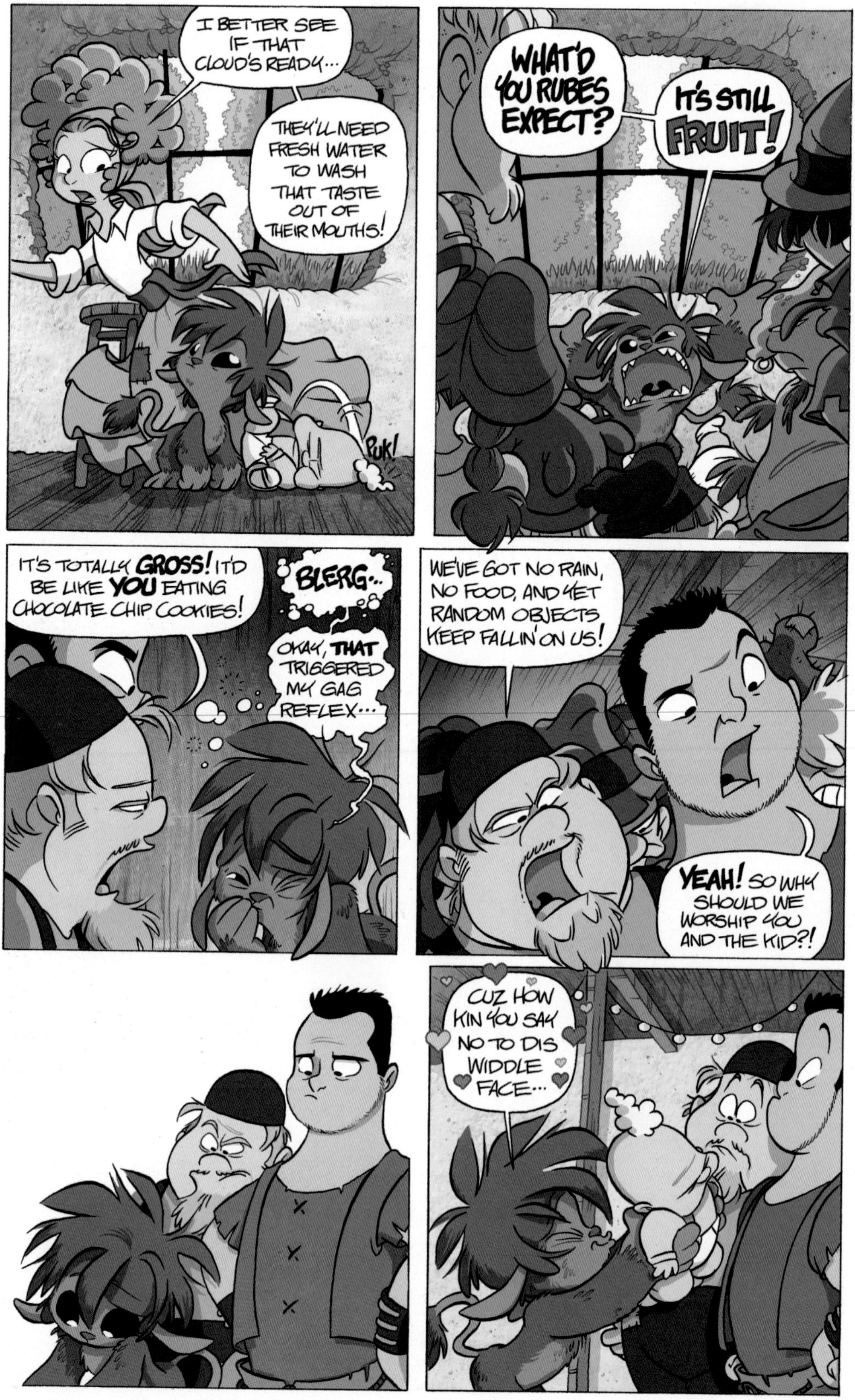
I BETTER SEE IF THAT CLOUD'S READY...
THEY'LL NEED FRESH WATER TO WASH THAT TASTE OUT OF THEIR MOUTHS!
PUK!
WHAT'D YOU RUBES EXPECT?
IT'S STILL FRUIT!
IT'S TOTALLY GROSS! IT'D BE LIKE YOU EATING CHOCOLATE CHIP COOKIES!
BLERG...
OKAY, THAT TRIGGERED MY GAG REFLEX...
WE'VE GOT NO RAIN, NO FOOD, AND YET RANDOM OBJECTS KEEP FALLIN' ON US!
YEAH! SO WHY SHOULD WE WORSHIP YOU AND THE KID?!
CUZ HOW KIN YOU SAY NO TO DIS WIDDLE FACE...

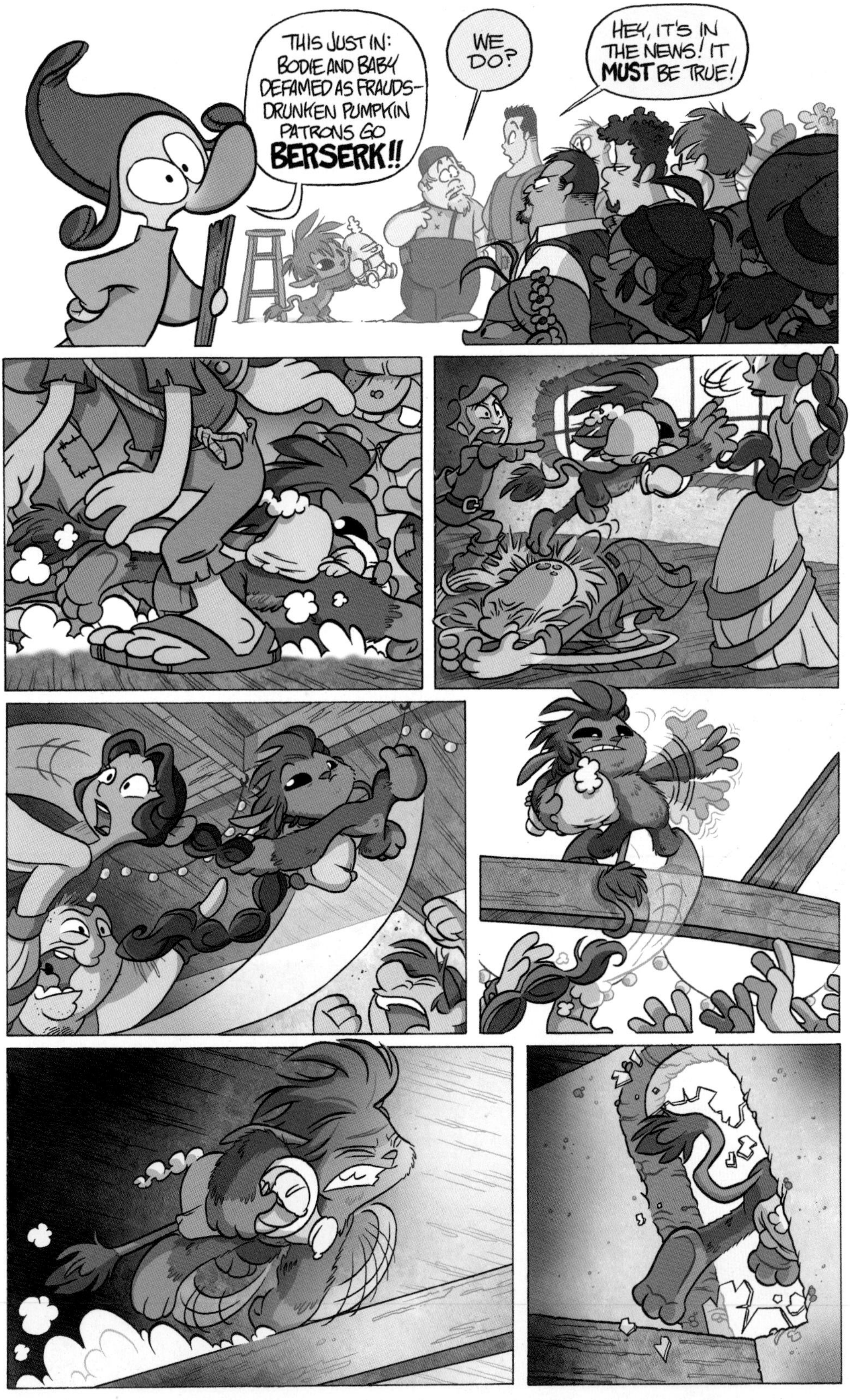

THIS JUST IN: BODIE AND BABY DEFAMED AS FRAUDS- DRUNKEN PUMPKIN PATRONS GO **BERSERK!!**
WE DO?
HEY, IT'S IN THE NEWS! IT **MUST** BE TRUE!

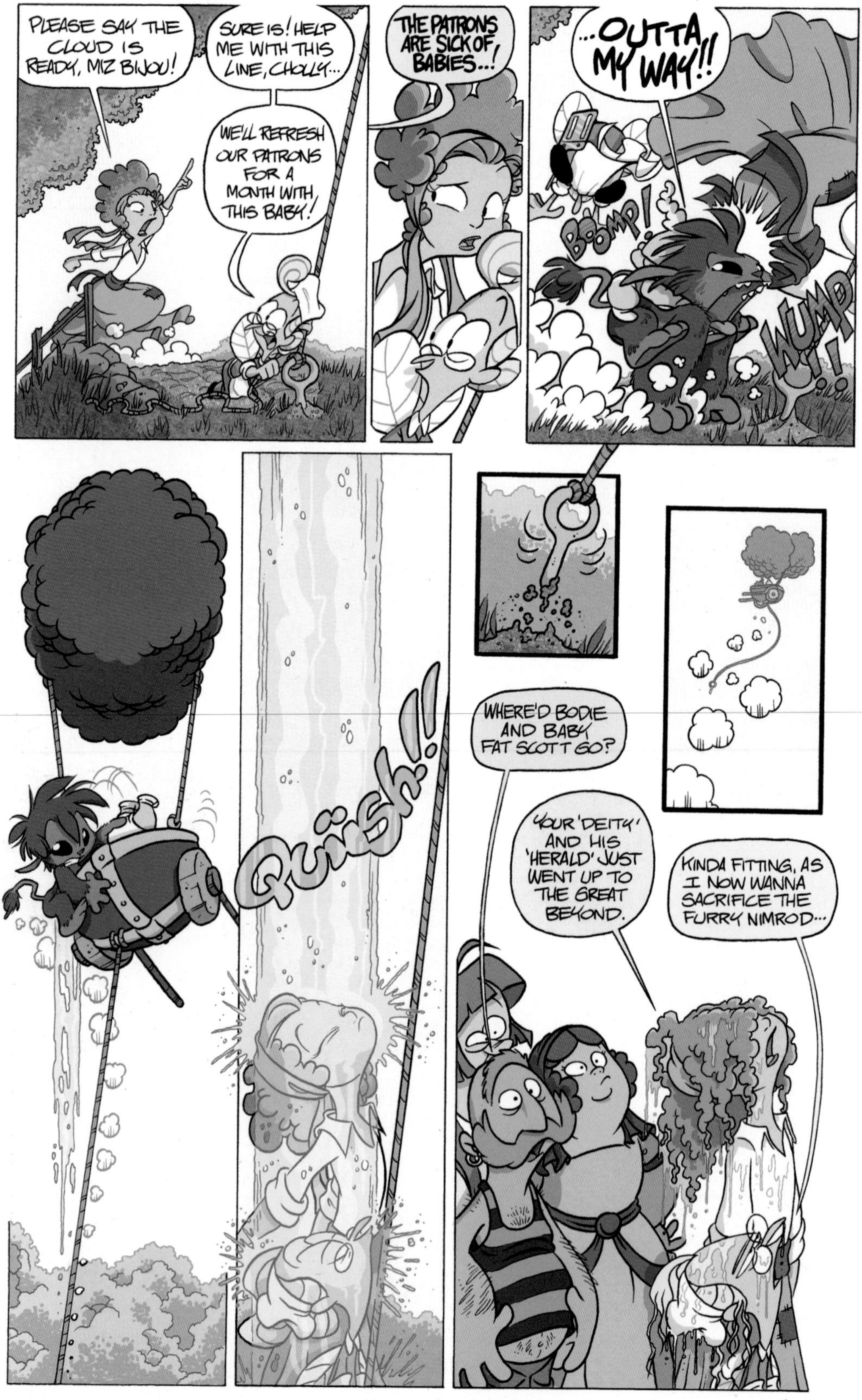
PLEASE SAY THE CLOUD IS READY, MIZ BIJOU!
SURE IS! HELP ME WITH THIS LINE, CHOLLY...
WE'LL REFRESH OUR PATRONS FOR A MONTH WITH THIS BABY!
THE PATRONS ARE SICK OF BABIES...!
...OUTTA MY WAY!!
BOOMP!
WUMP!!
QUISH!!
WHERE'D BODIE AND BABY FAT SCOTT GO?
YOUR 'DEITY' AND HIS 'HERALD' JUST WENT UP TO THE GREAT BEYOND.
KINDA FITTING, AS I NOW WANNA SACRIFICE THE FURRY NIMROD...

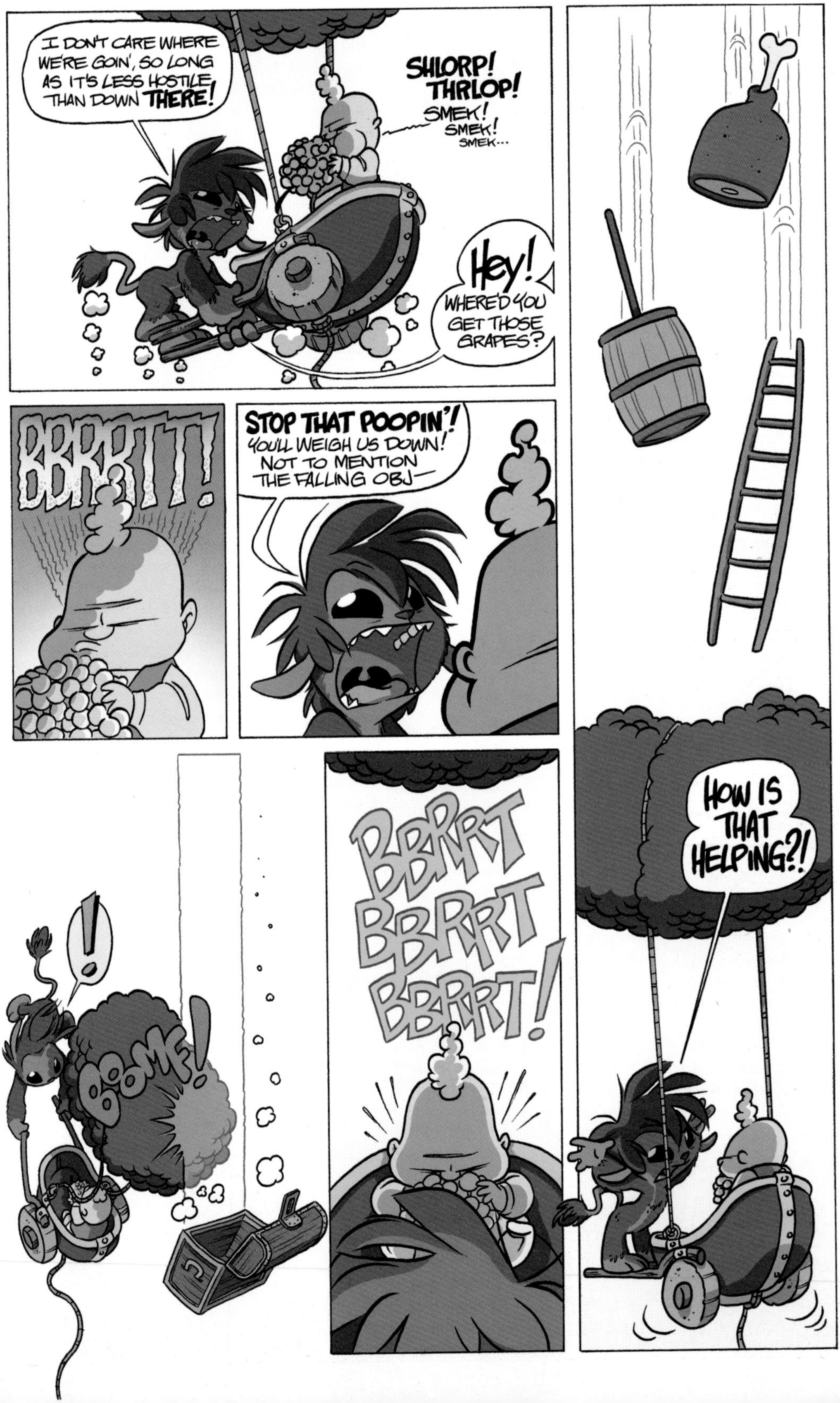
I DON'T CARE WHERE WE'RE GOIN', SO LONG AS IT'S LESS HOSTILE THAN DOWN THERE!
SHLORP! THRLOP!
SMEK! SMEK! SMEK...
Hey! WHERE'D YOU GET THOSE GRAPES?
BBRRTTT!
STOP THAT POOPIN'! YOU'LL WEIGH US DOWN! NOT TO MENTION THE FALLING OBJ—
!
BOOMF!
BBRRRT BBRRRT BBRRRT!
HOW IS THAT HELPING?!

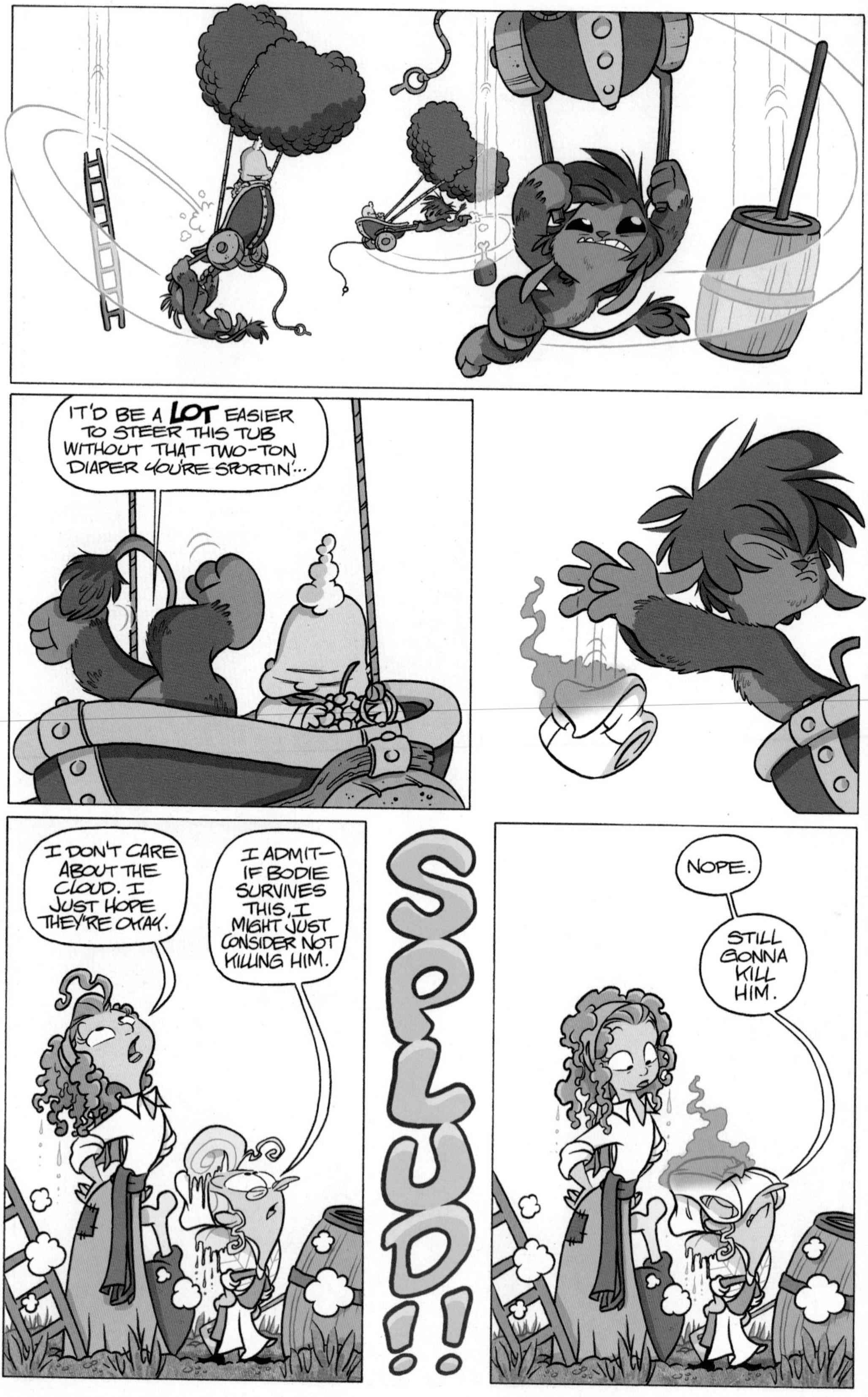
IT'D BE A LOT EASIER TO STEER THIS TUB WITHOUT THAT TWO-TON DIAPER YOU'RE SPORTIN'...
I DON'T CARE ABOUT THE CLOUD. I JUST HOPE THEY'RE OKAY.
I ADMIT— IF BODIE SURVIVES THIS, I MIGHT JUST CONSIDER NOT KILLING HIM.
SPLUD!!
NOPE.
STILL GONNA KILL HIM.

IT'S THE GRAPES! THEY'RE INFUSED WITH YOUR POOP, SO THEY'RE MAKING YOU GO RAPID-FIRE!!
BRRT! BBRRT! BRT!!
GAWP-
THAT MEANS STOP EATIN' 'EM, GENIUS!!
SPAK!
BBRRT BRRT BRRT BRRT BRRT BRRT

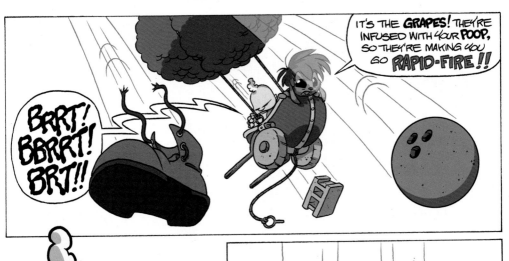

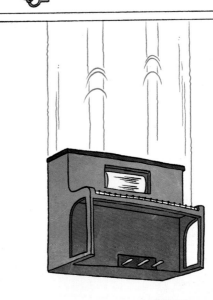

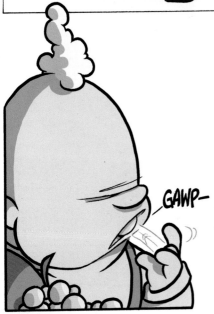

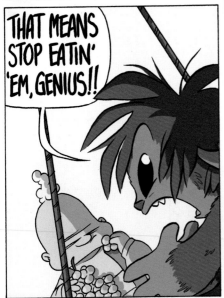

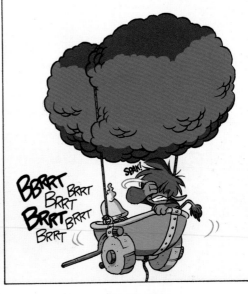

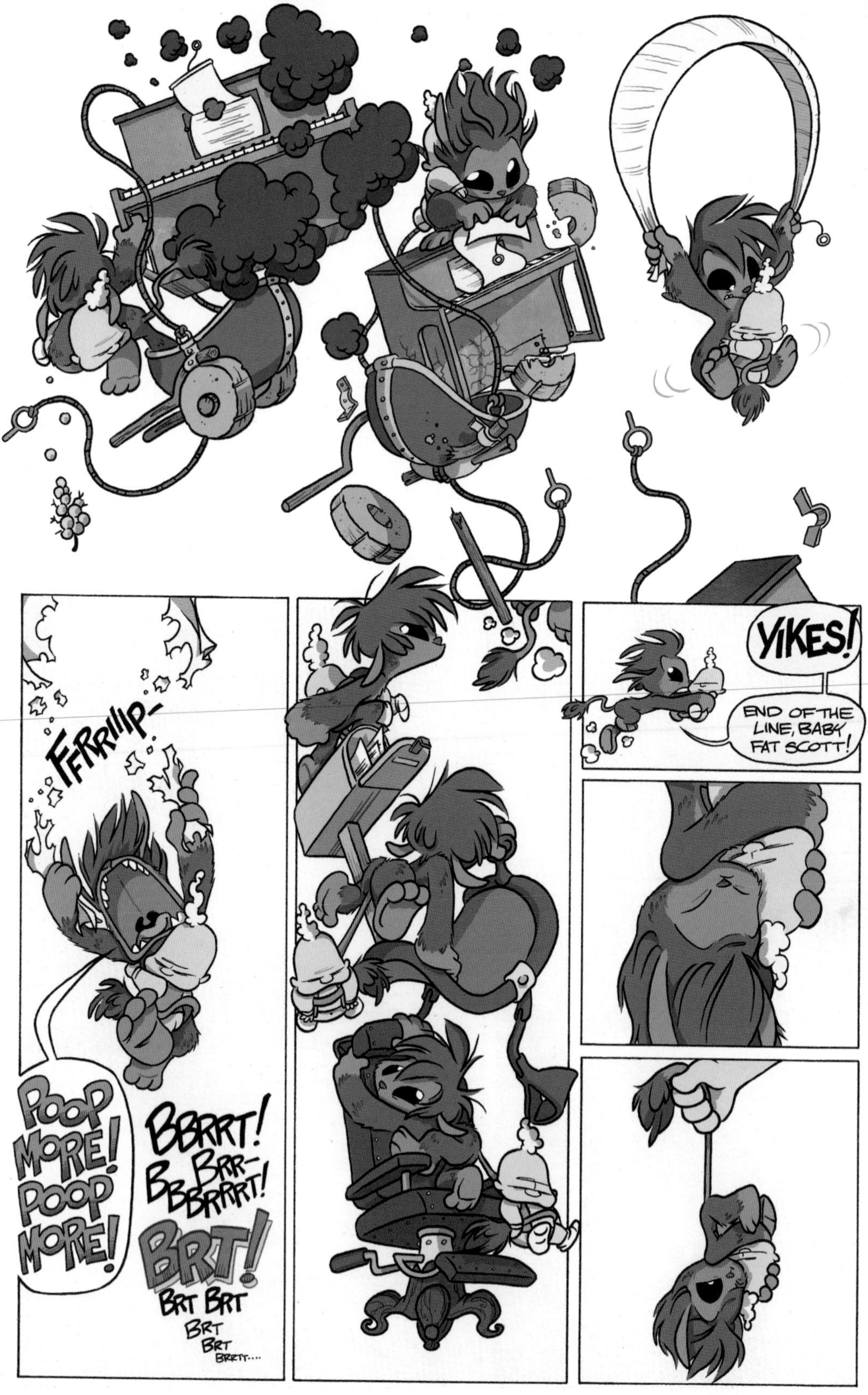
FFRRIIIP-
POOP MORE! POOP MORE!
BBRRT! BBBRRR-BRRRT!
BRT!
BRT BRT
BRT
BRT
BRRTT....
YIKES!
END OF THE LINE, BABY FAT SCOTT!

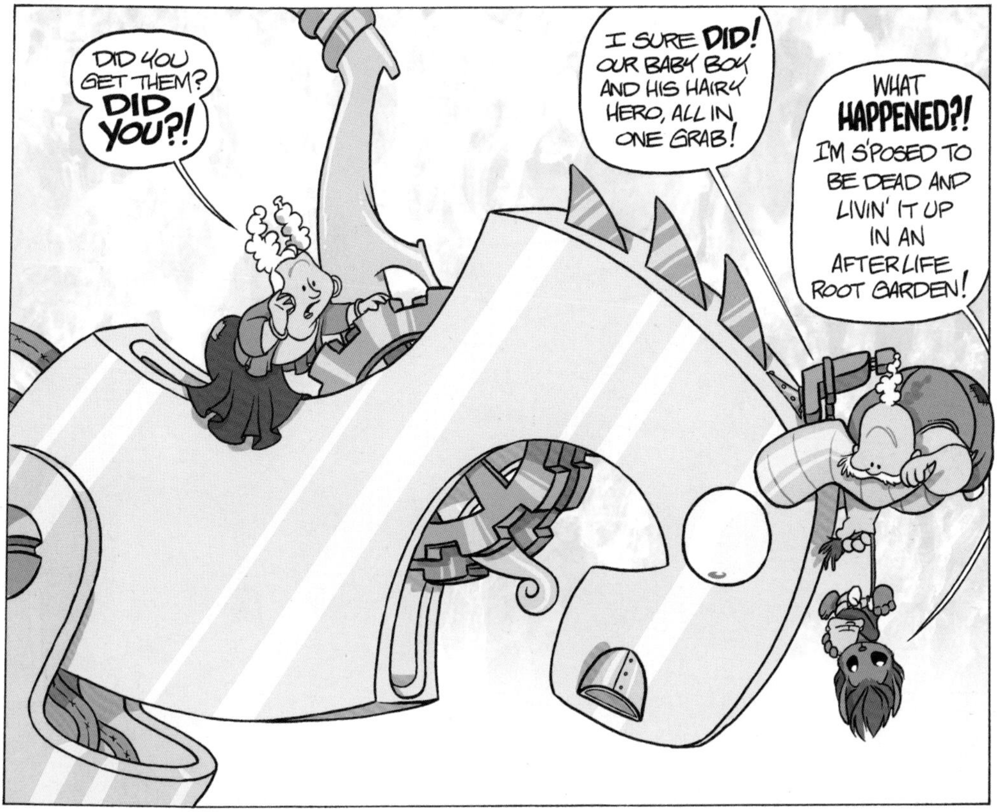

DID YOU GET THEM? DID YOU?!
I SURE DID! OUR BABY BOY AND HIS HAIRY HERO, ALL IN ONE GRAB!
WHAT HAPPENED?! I'M S'POSED TO BE DEAD AND LIVIN' IT UP IN AN AFTERLIFE ROOT GARDEN!

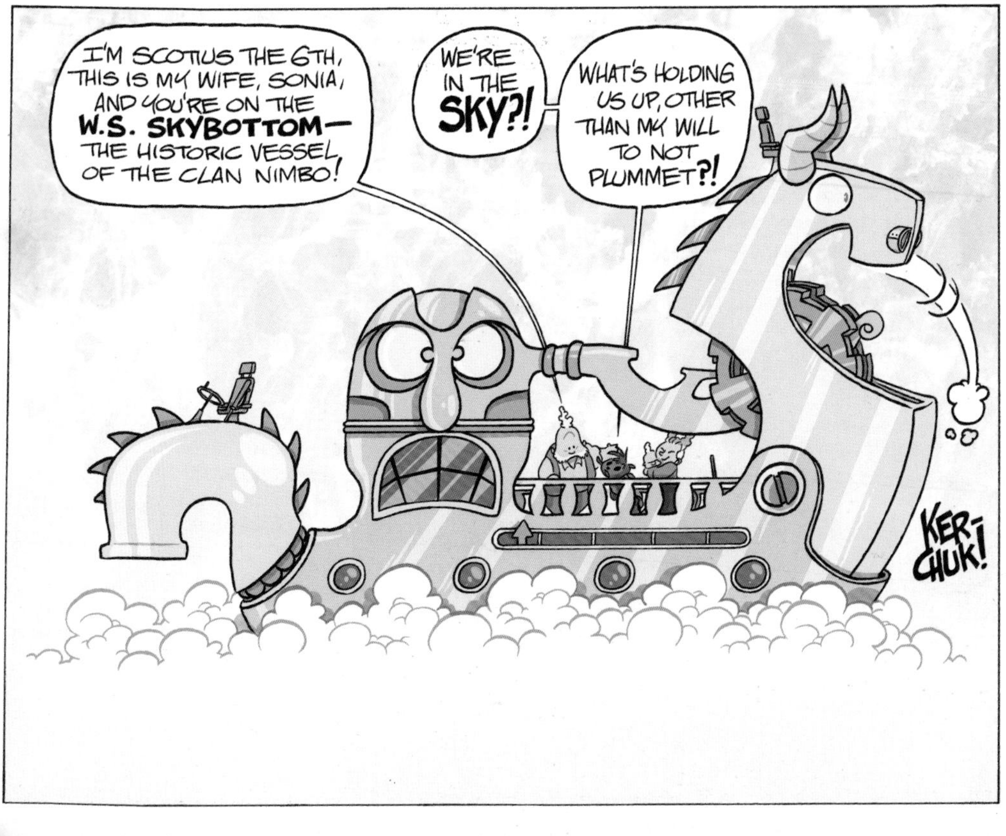

I'M SCOTIUS THE 6TH, THIS IS MY WIFE, SONIA, AND YOU'RE ON THE W.S. SKYBOTTOM— THE HISTORIC VESSEL OF THE CLAN NIMBO!
WE'RE IN THE SKY?!
WHAT'S HOLDING US UP, OTHER THAN MY WILL TO NOT PLUMMET?!
KER-CHUK!

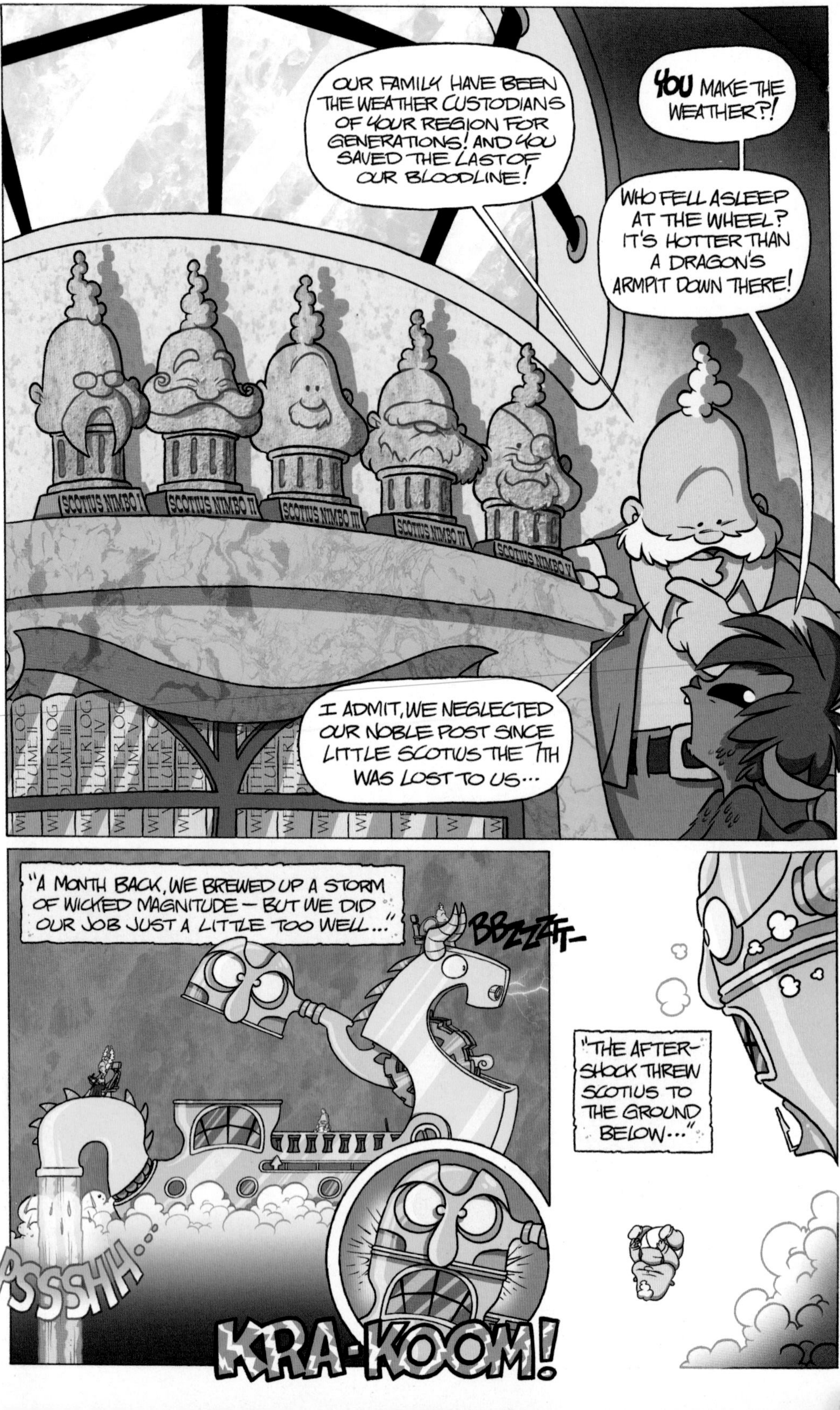
OUR FAMILY HAVE BEEN THE WEATHER CUSTODIANS OF YOUR REGION FOR GENERATIONS! AND YOU SAVED THE LAST OF OUR BLOODLINE!
YOU MAKE THE WEATHER?!
WHO FELL ASLEEP AT THE WHEEL? IT'S HOTTER THAN A DRAGON'S ARMPIT DOWN THERE!
SCOTIUS NIMBO I
SCOTIUS NIMBO II
SCOTIUS NIMBO III
SCOTIUS NIMBO IV
SCOTIUS NIMBO V
I ADMIT, WE NEGLECTED OUR NOBLE POST SINCE LITTLE SCOTIUS THE 7TH WAS LOST TO US...
"A MONTH BACK, WE BREWED UP A STORM OF WICKED MAGNITUDE — BUT WE DID OUR JOB JUST A LITTLE TOO WELL..."
BBZZZATT—
PSSSHH...
KRA-KOOM!
"THE AFTER-SHOCK THREW SCOTIUS TO THE GROUND BELOW..."

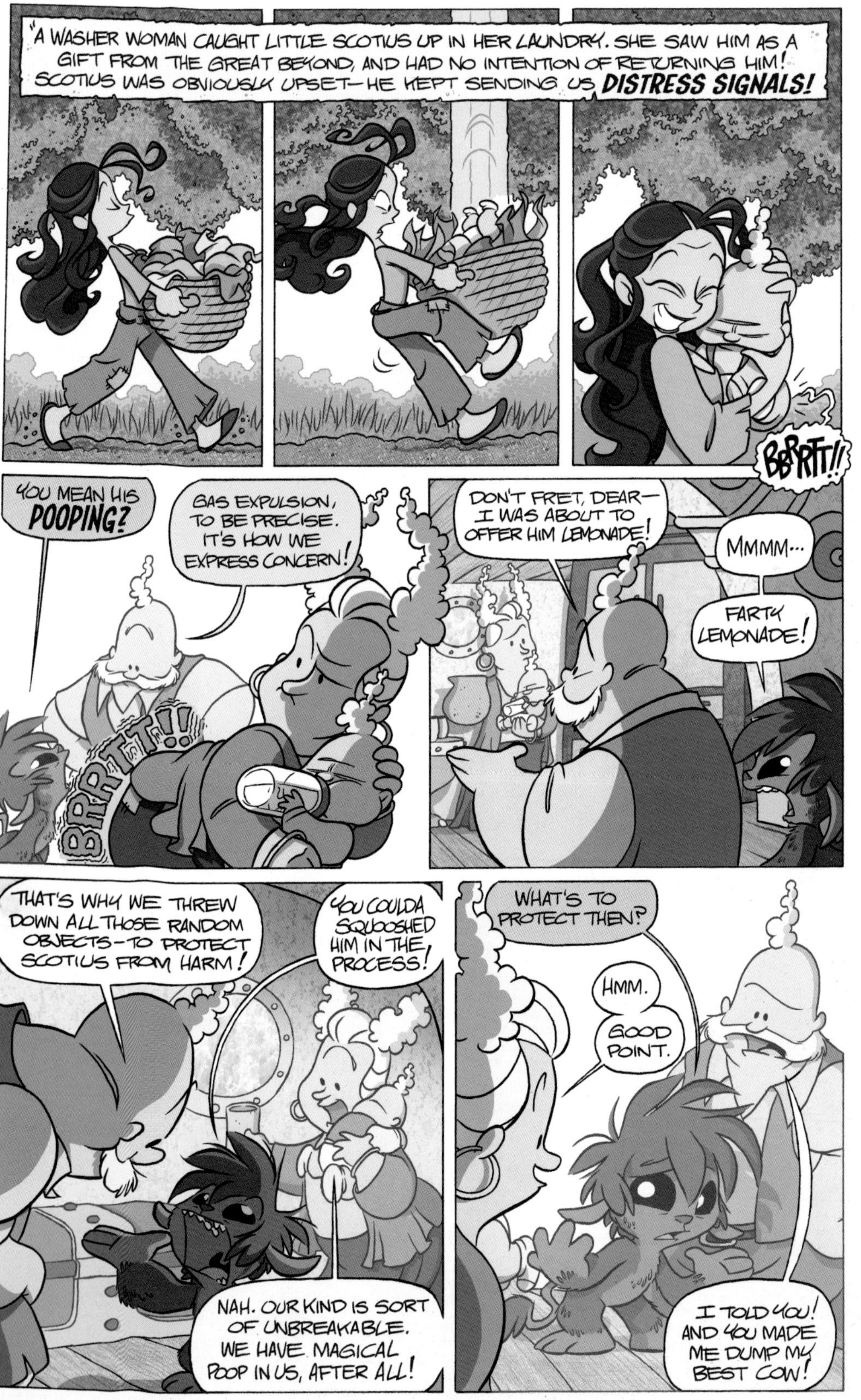
"A WASHER WOMAN CAUGHT LITTLE SCOTIUS UP IN HER LAUNDRY. SHE SAW HIM AS A GIFT FROM THE GREAT BEYOND, AND HAD NO INTENTION OF RETURNING HIM! SCOTIUS WAS OBVIOUSLY UPSET—HE KEPT SENDING US DISTRESS SIGNALS!
BBRRFT!!
YOU MEAN HIS POOPING?
GAS EXPULSION, TO BE PRECISE. IT'S HOW WE EXPRESS CONCERN!
BRRTTT!!
DON'T FRET, DEAR—I WAS ABOUT TO OFFER HIM LEMONADE!
MMMM...
FARTY LEMONADE!
THAT'S WHY WE THREW DOWN ALL THOSE RANDOM OBJECTS—TO PROTECT SCOTIUS FROM HARM!
YOU COULDA SQUOOSHED HIM IN THE PROCESS!
NAH. OUR KIND IS SORT OF UNBREAKABLE. WE HAVE MAGICAL POOP IN US, AFTER ALL!
WHAT'S TO PROTECT THEN?
HMM.
GOOD POINT.
I TOLD YOU! AND YOU MADE ME DUMP MY BEST COW!

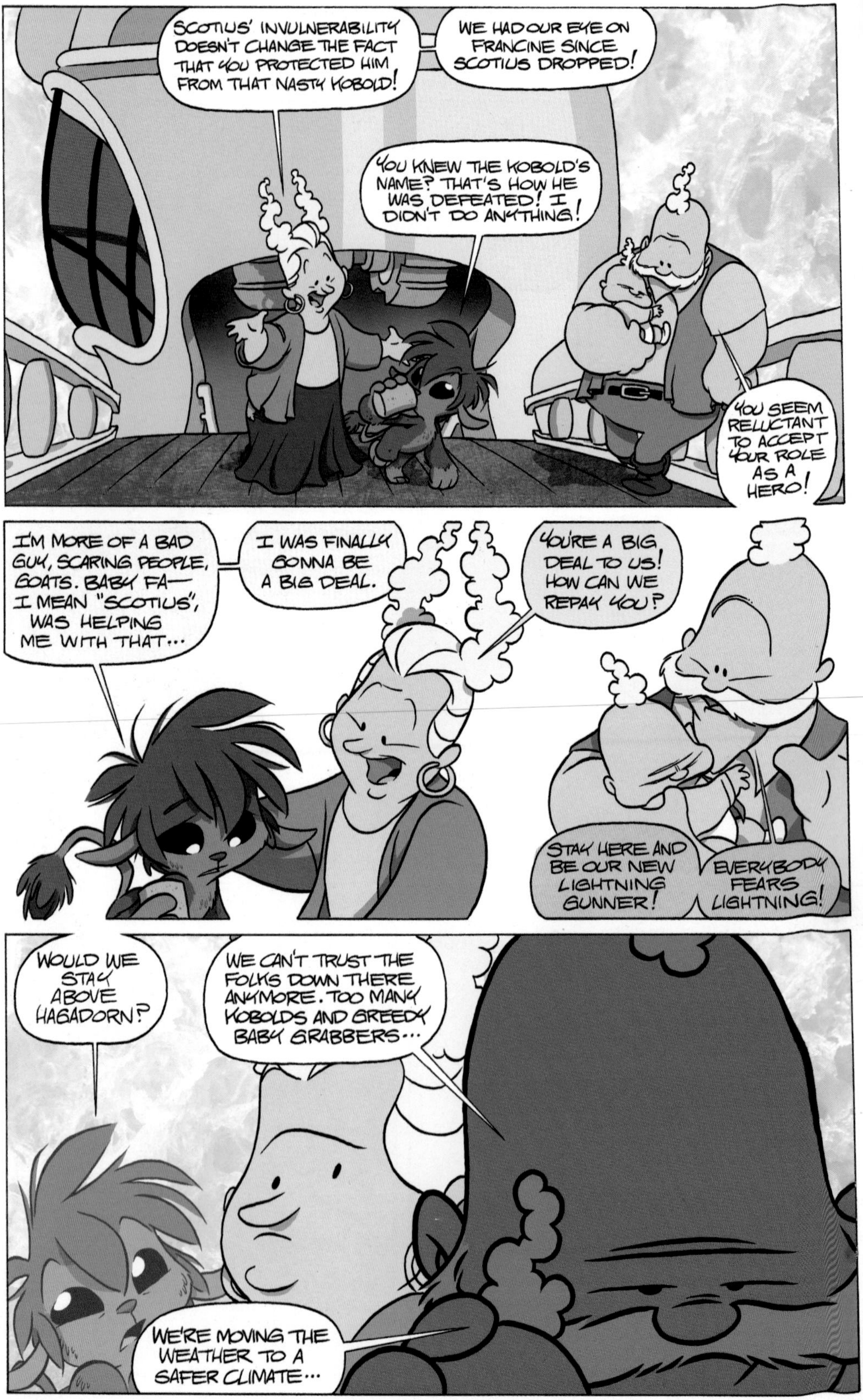
SCOTIUS' INVULNERABILITY DOESN'T CHANGE THE FACT THAT YOU PROTECTED HIM FROM THAT NASTY KOBOLD!
WE HAD OUR EYE ON FRANCINE SINCE SCOTIUS DROPPED!
YOU KNEW THE KOBOLD'S NAME? THAT'S HOW HE WAS DEFEATED! I DIDN'T DO ANYTHING!
YOU SEEM RELUCTANT TO ACCEPT YOUR ROLE AS A HERO!
I'M MORE OF A BAD GUY, SCARING PEOPLE, GOATS. BABY FA— I MEAN "SCOTIUS", WAS HELPING ME WITH THAT...
I WAS FINALLY GONNA BE A BIG DEAL.
YOU'RE A BIG DEAL TO US! HOW CAN WE REPAY YOU?
STAY HERE AND BE OUR NEW LIGHTNING GUNNER!
EVERYBODY FEARS LIGHTNING!
WOULD WE STAY ABOVE HAGADORN?
WE CAN'T TRUST THE FOLKS DOWN THERE ANYMORE. TOO MANY KOBOLDS AND GREEDY BABY GRABBERS...
WE'RE MOVING THE WEATHER TO A SAFER CLIMATE...

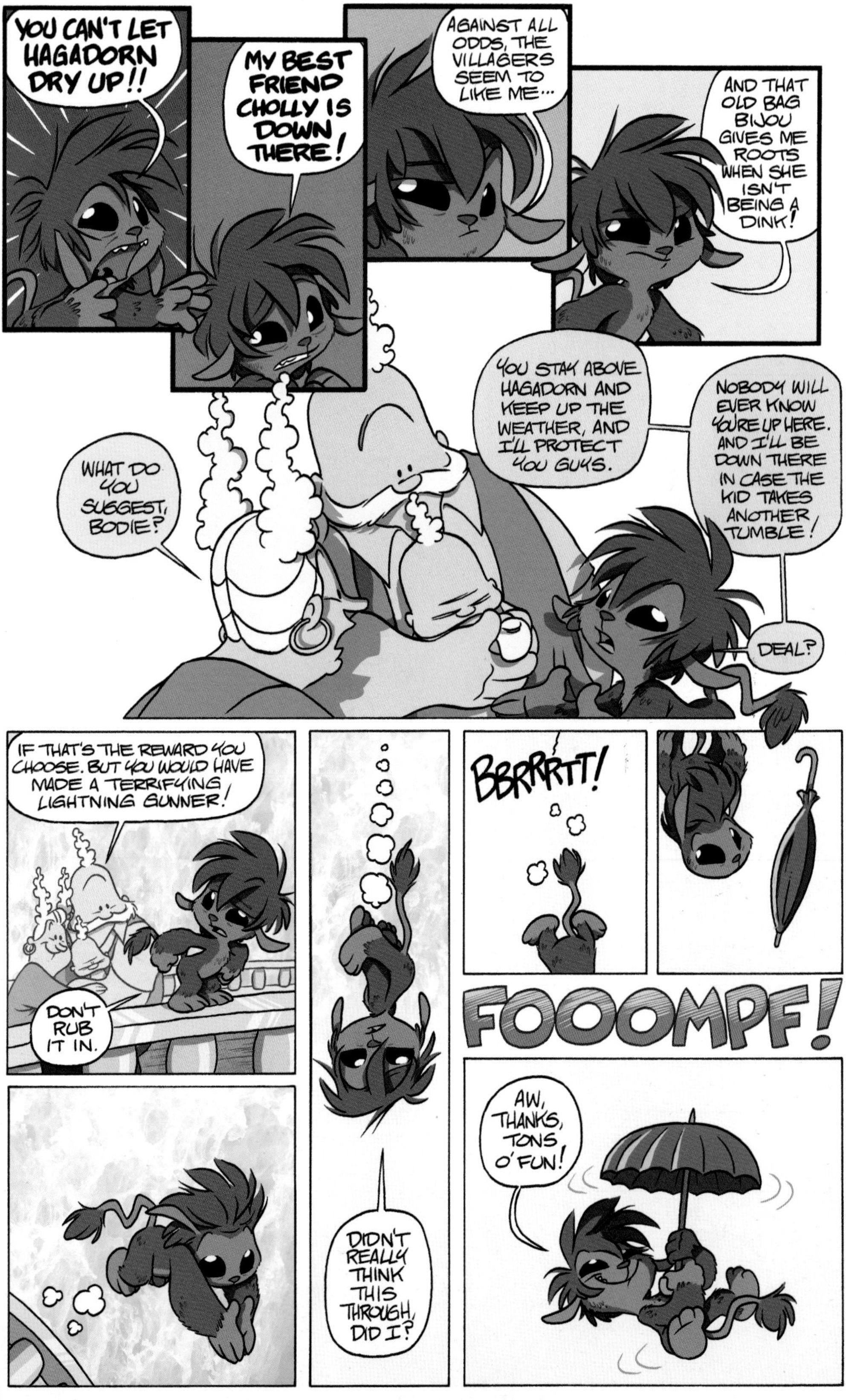
YOU CAN'T LET HAGADORN DRY UP!!
MY BEST FRIEND CHOLLY IS DOWN THERE!
AGAINST ALL ODDS, THE VILLAGERS SEEM TO LIKE ME...
AND THAT OLD BAG BIJOU GIVES ME ROOTS WHEN SHE ISN'T BEING A DINK!
WHAT DO YOU SUGGEST, BODIE?
YOU STAY ABOVE HAGADORN AND KEEP UP THE WEATHER, AND I'LL PROTECT YOU GUYS.
NOBODY WILL EVER KNOW YOU'RE UP HERE. AND I'LL BE DOWN THERE IN CASE THE KID TAKES ANOTHER TUMBLE!
DEAL?
IF THAT'S THE REWARD YOU CHOOSE. BUT YOU WOULD HAVE MADE A TERRIFYING LIGHTNING GUNNER!
DON'T RUB IT IN.
DIDN'T REALLY THINK THIS THROUGH, DID I?
BBRRRTTT!
FOOOMPF!
AW, THANKS, TONS O' FUN!

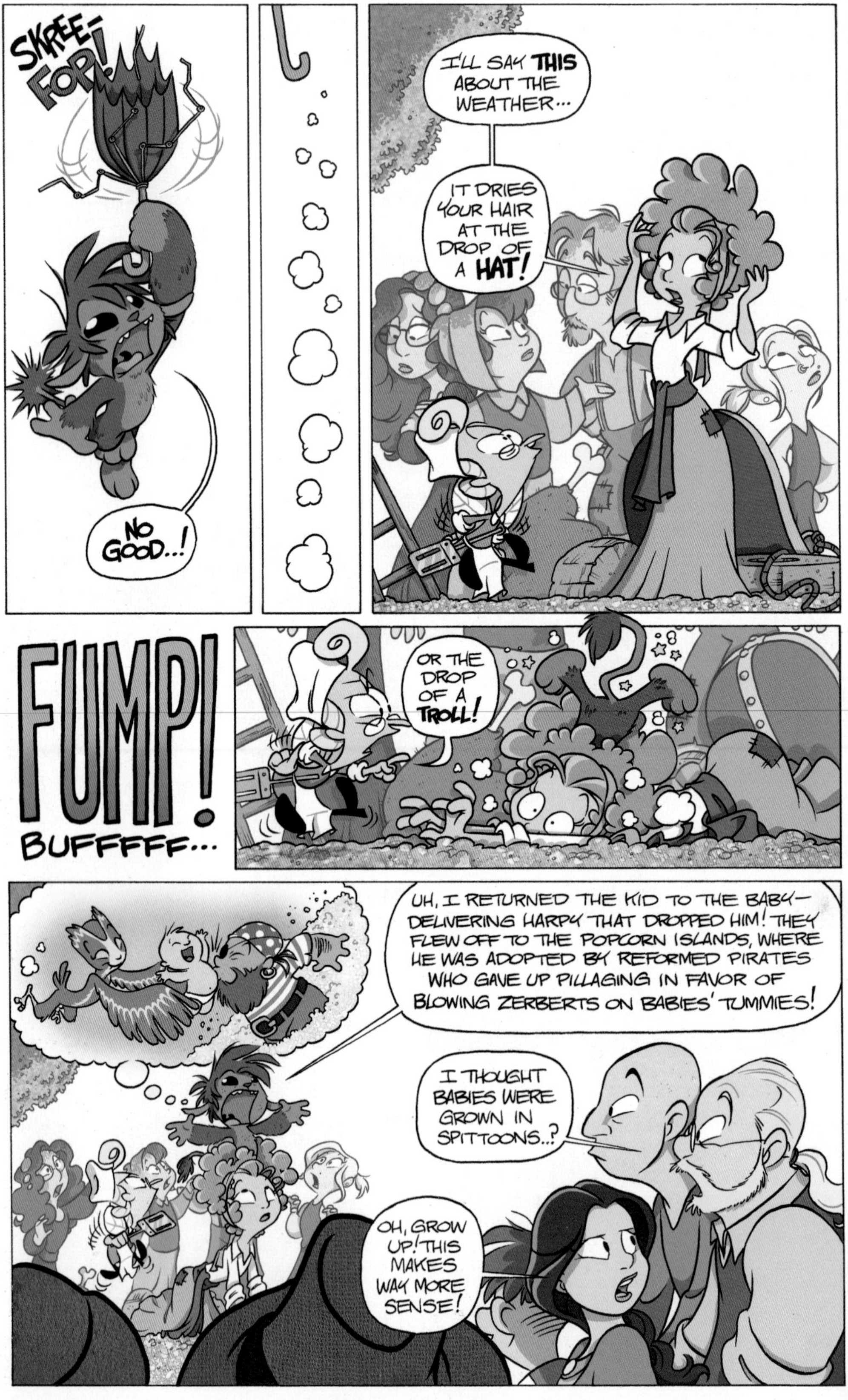
SKREE-FOP!
NO GOOD...!
I'LL SAY THIS ABOUT THE WEATHER...
IT DRIES YOUR HAIR AT THE DROP OF A HAT!
FUMP!
BUFFFFF...
OR THE DROP OF A TROLL!
UH, I RETURNED THE KID TO THE BABY-DELIVERING HARPY THAT DROPPED HIM! THEY FLEW OFF TO THE POPCORN ISLANDS, WHERE HE WAS ADOPTED BY REFORMED PIRATES WHO GAVE UP PILLAGING IN FAVOR OF BLOWING ZERBERTS ON BABIES' TUMMIES!
I THOUGHT BABIES WERE GROWN IN SPITTOONS..?
OH, GROW UP! THIS MAKES WAY MORE SENSE!

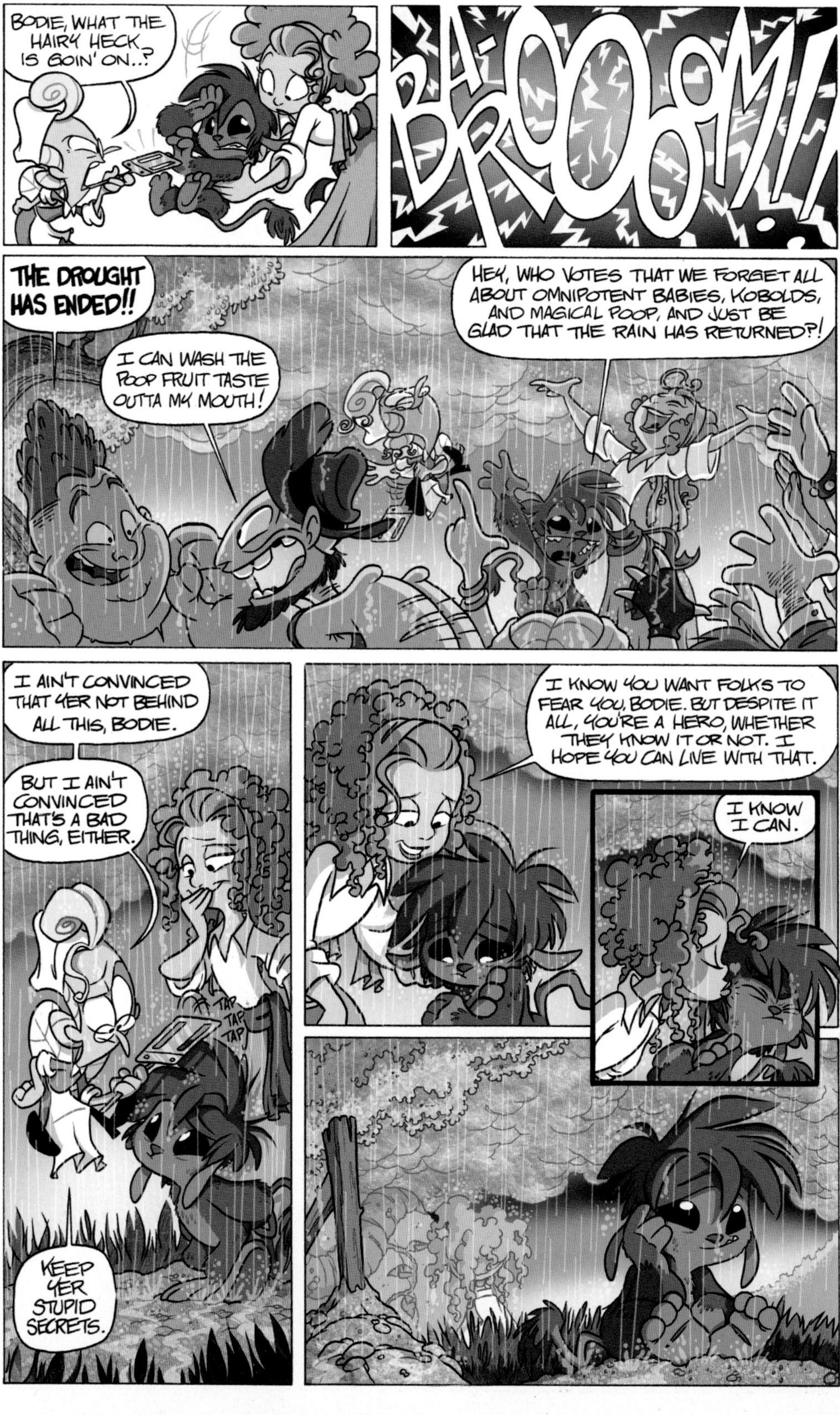
BODIE, WHAT THE HAIRY HECK IS GOIN' ON...?
BA-DROOOOOM!!
THE DROUGHT HAS ENDED!!
I CAN WASH THE POOP FRUIT TASTE OUTTA MY MOUTH!
HEY, WHO VOTES THAT WE FORGET ALL ABOUT OMNIPOTENT BABIES, KOBOLDS, AND MAGICAL POOP, AND JUST BE GLAD THAT THE RAIN HAS RETURNED?!
I AIN'T CONVINCED THAT YER NOT BEHIND ALL THIS, BODIE.
BUT I AIN'T CONVINCED THAT'S A BAD THING, EITHER.
TAP TAP TAP
KEEP YER STUPID SECRETS.
I KNOW YOU WANT FOLKS TO FEAR YOU, BODIE. BUT DESPITE IT ALL, YOU'RE A HERO, WHETHER THEY KNOW IT OR NOT. I HOPE YOU CAN LIVE WITH THAT.
I KNOW I CAN.

CHAPTER 5
HAUNTED HARVEST

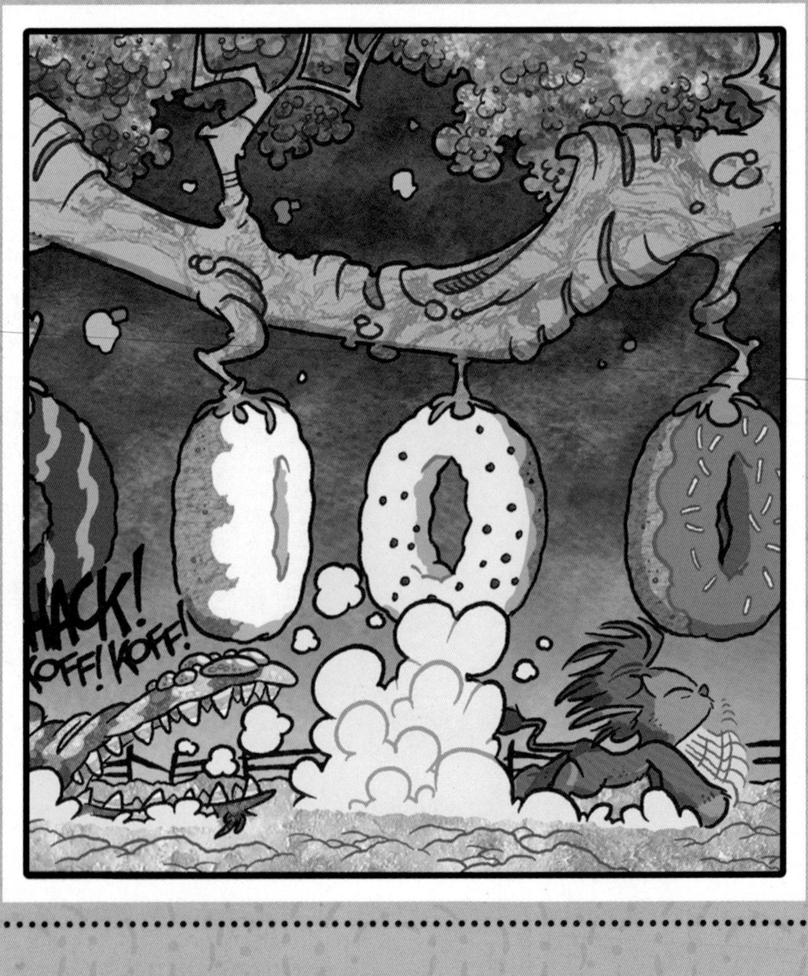
HACK!
KOFF! KOFF!

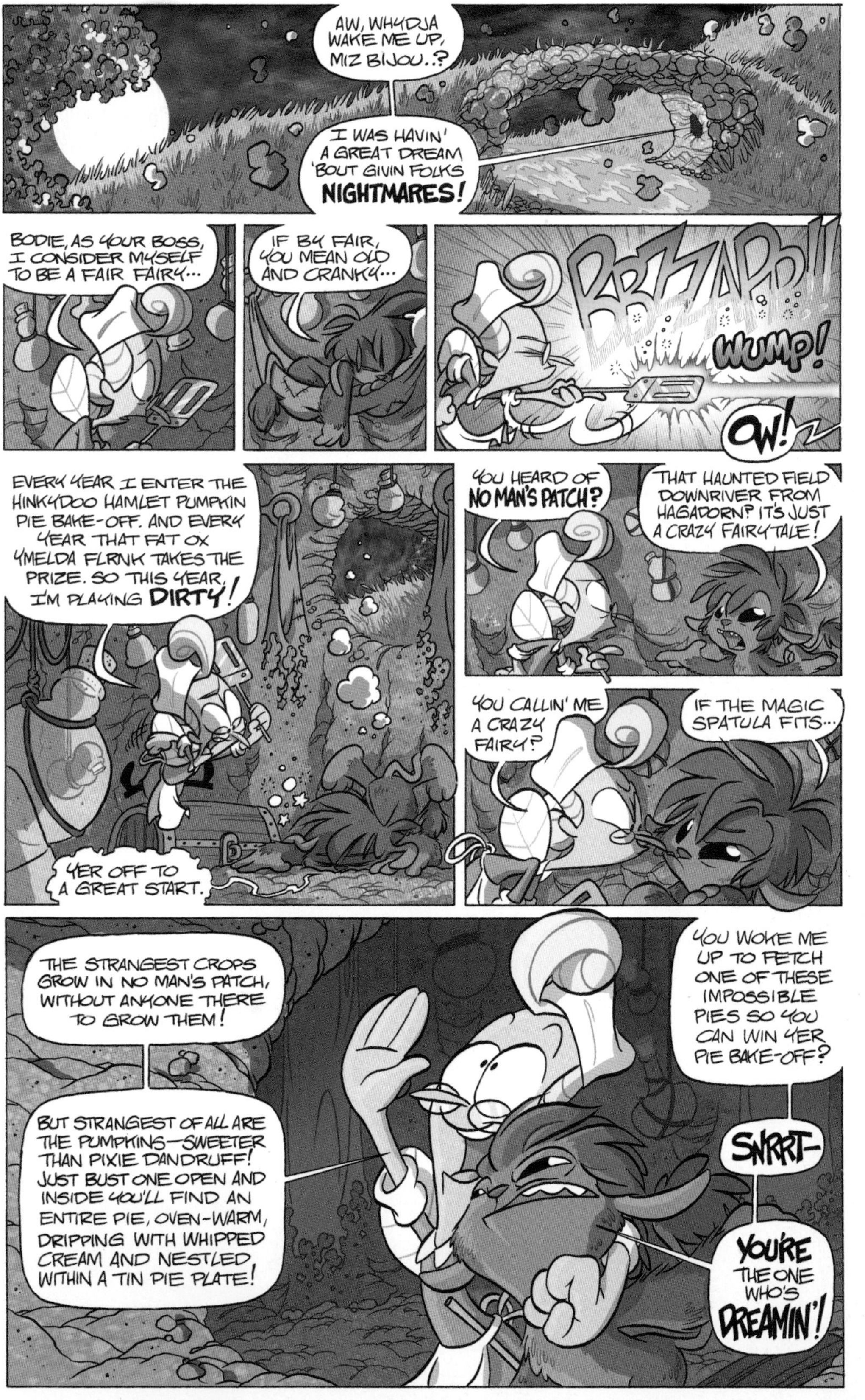
AW, WHYDJA WAKE ME UP, MIZ BIJOU..?
I WAS HAVIN' A GREAT DREAM 'BOUT GIVIN FOLKS NIGHTMARES!
BODIE, AS YOUR BOSS, I CONSIDER MYSELF TO BE A FAIR FAIRY...
IF BY FAIR, YOU MEAN OLD AND CRANKY...
BRZZAPP!!!
WUMP!
OW!
EVERY YEAR I ENTER THE HINKYDOO HAMLET PUMPKIN PIE BAKE-OFF. AND EVERY YEAR THAT FAT OX YMELDA FLRNK TAKES THE PRIZE. SO THIS YEAR, I'M PLAYING DIRTY!
YER OFF TO A GREAT START.
YOU HEARD OF NO MAN'S PATCH?
THAT HAUNTED FIELD DOWNRIVER FROM HAGADORN? IT'S JUST A CRAZY FAIRY TALE!
YOU CALLIN' ME A CRAZY FAIRY?
IF THE MAGIC SPATULA FITS...
THE STRANGEST CROPS GROW IN NO MAN'S PATCH, WITHOUT ANYONE THERE TO GROW THEM!
BUT STRANGEST OF ALL ARE THE PUMPKINS—SWEETER THAN PIXIE DANDRUFF! JUST BUST ONE OPEN AND INSIDE YOU'LL FIND AN ENTIRE PIE, OVEN-WARM, DRIPPING WITH WHIPPED CREAM AND NESTLED WITHIN A TIN PIE PLATE!
YOU WOKE ME UP TO FETCH ONE OF THESE IMPOSSIBLE PIES SO YOU CAN WIN YER PIE BAKE-OFF?
SNRRT-
YOU'RE THE ONE WHO'S DREAMIN'!

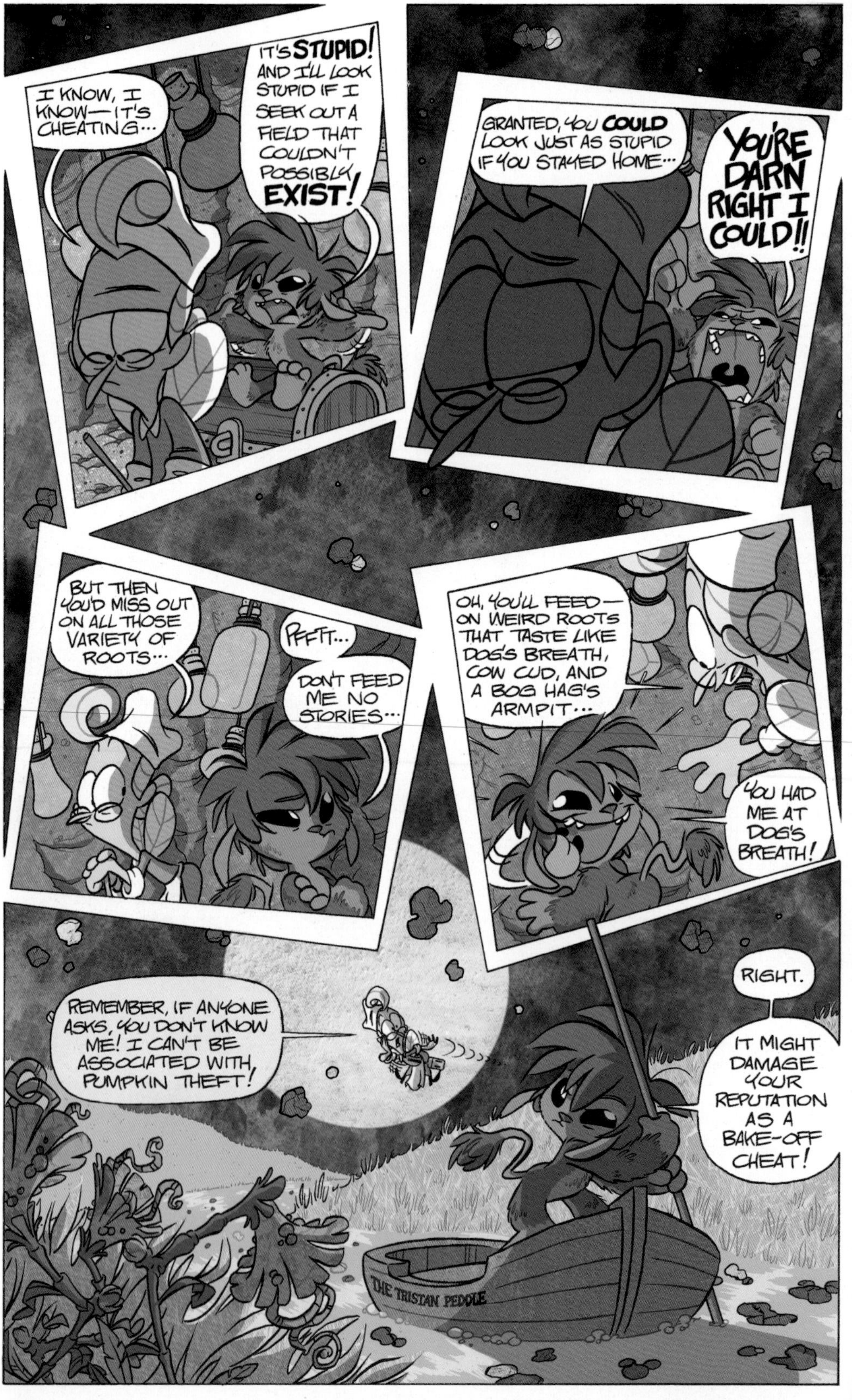
I KNOW, I KNOW—IT'S CHEATING...
IT'S STUPID! AND I'LL LOOK STUPID IF I SEEK OUT A FIELD THAT COULDN'T POSSIBLY EXIST!
GRANTED, YOU COULD LOOK JUST AS STUPID IF YOU STAYED HOME...
YOU'RE DARN RIGHT I COULD!!
BUT THEN YOU'D MISS OUT ON ALL THOSE VARIETY OF ROOTS...
PFFFT...
DON'T FEED ME NO STORIES...
OH, YOU'LL FEED—ON WEIRD ROOTS THAT TASTE LIKE DOG'S BREATH, COW CUD, AND A BOG HAG'S ARMPIT...
YOU HAD ME AT DOG'S BREATH!
REMEMBER, IF ANYONE ASKS, YOU DON'T KNOW ME! I CAN'T BE ASSOCIATED WITH PUMPKIN THEFT!
RIGHT.
IT MIGHT DAMAGE YOUR REPUTATION AS A BAKE-OFF CHEAT!
THE TRISTAN PEDDLE

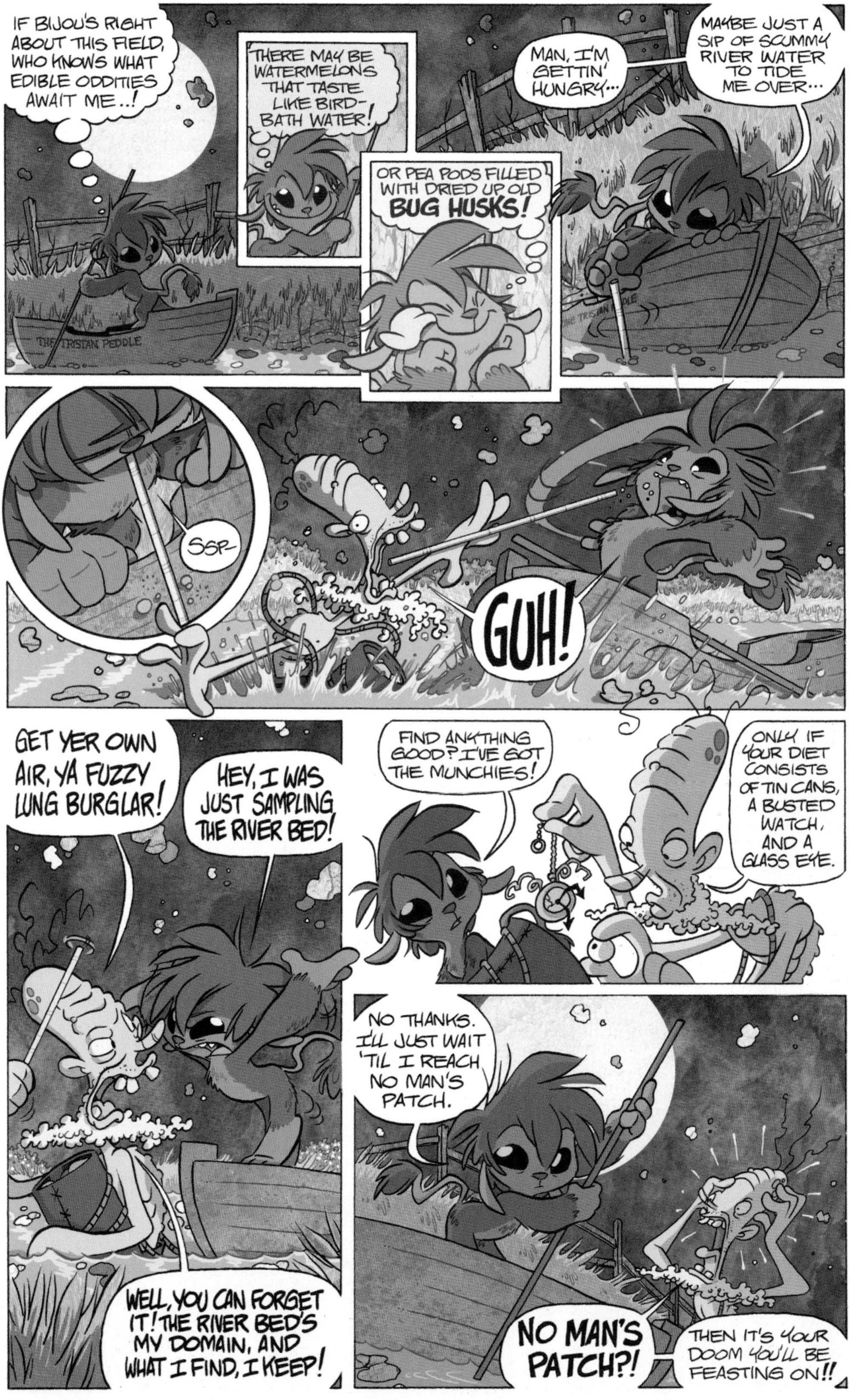
IF BIJOU'S RIGHT ABOUT THIS FIELD, WHO KNOWS WHAT EDIBLE ODDITIES AWAIT ME..!
THE TRISTAN PEDDLE
THERE MAY BE WATERMELONS THAT TASTE LIKE BIRD-BATH WATER!
OR PEA PODS FILLED WITH DRIED UP OLD BUG HUSKS!
MAN, I'M GETTIN' HUNGRY...
MAYBE JUST A SIP OF SCUMMY RIVER WATER TO TIDE ME OVER...
SSP-
GUH!
GET YER OWN AIR, YA FUZZY LUNG BURGLAR!
HEY, I WAS JUST SAMPLING THE RIVER BED!
WELL, YOU CAN FORGET IT! THE RIVER BED'S MY DOMAIN, AND WHAT I FIND, I KEEP!
FIND ANYTHING GOOD? I'VE GOT THE MUNCHIES!
ONLY IF YOUR DIET CONSISTS OF TIN CANS, A BUSTED WATCH, AND A GLASS EYE.
NO THANKS. I'LL JUST WAIT 'TIL I REACH NO MAN'S PATCH.
NO MAN'S PATCH?!
THEN IT'S YOUR DOOM YOU'LL BE FEASTING ON!!

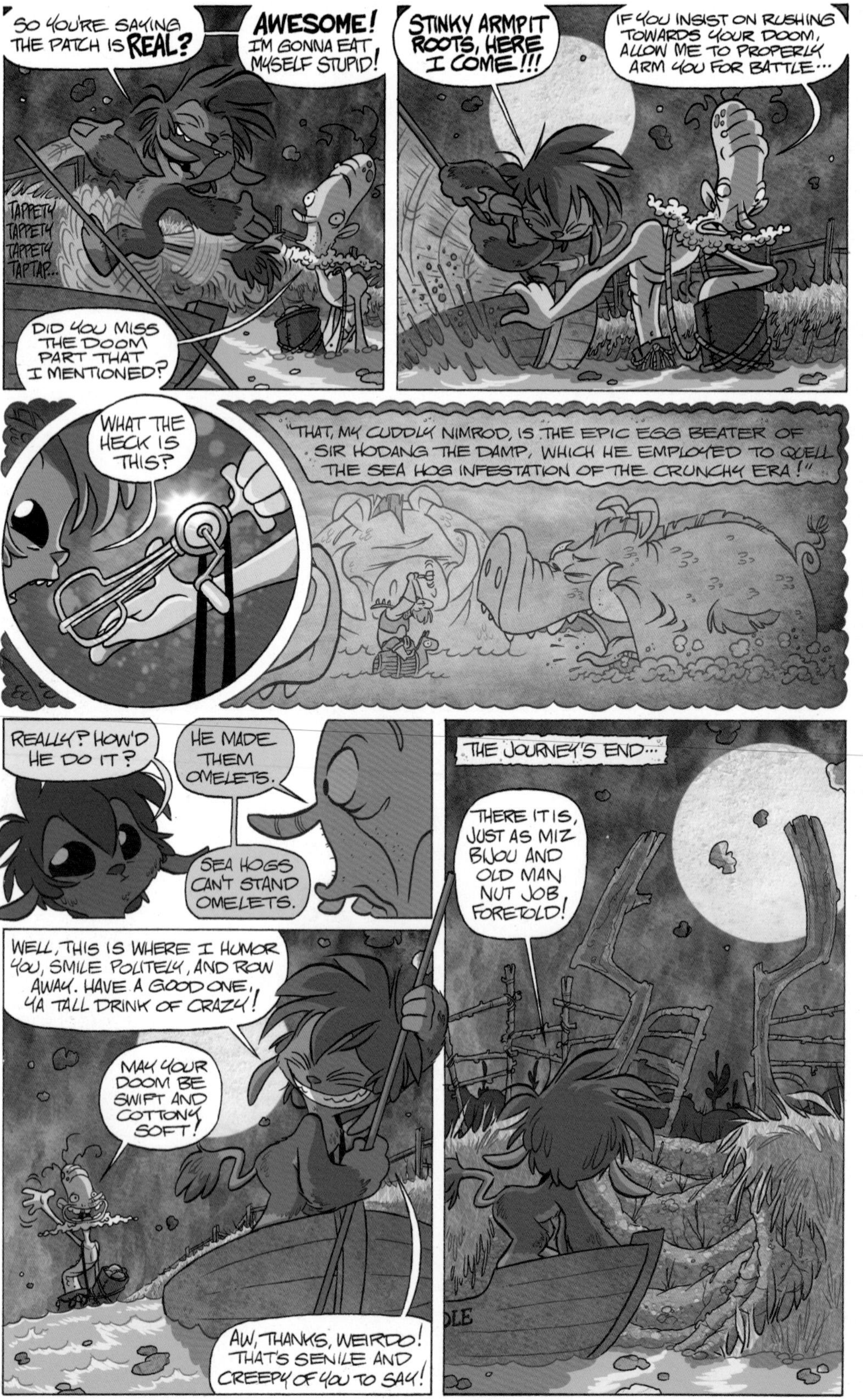
SO YOU'RE SAYING THE PATCH IS REAL?
AWESOME! I'M GONNA EAT MYSELF STUPID!
TAPPETY TAPPETY TAPPETY TAPTAP...
DID YOU MISS THE DOOM PART THAT I MENTIONED?
STINKY ARMPIT ROOTS, HERE I COME!!!
IF YOU INSIST ON RUSHING TOWARDS YOUR DOOM, ALLOW ME TO PROPERLY ARM YOU FOR BATTLE...
WHAT THE HECK IS THIS?
"THAT, MY CUDDLY NIMROD, IS THE EPIC EGG BEATER OF SIR HODANG THE DAMP, WHICH HE EMPLOYED TO QUELL THE SEA HOG INFESTATION OF THE CRUNCHY ERA!"
REALLY? HOW'D HE DO IT?
HE MADE THEM OMELETS.
SEA HOGS CAN'T STAND OMELETS.
WELL, THIS IS WHERE I HUMOR YOU, SMILE POLITELY, AND ROW AWAY. HAVE A GOOD ONE, YA TALL DRINK OF CRAZY!
MAY YOUR DOOM BE SWIFT AND COTTONY SOFT!
AW, THANKS, WEIRDO! THAT'S SENILE AND CREEPY OF YOU TO SAY!
THE JOURNEY'S END...
THERE IT IS, JUST AS MIZ BIJOU AND OLD MAN NUT JOB FORETOLD!

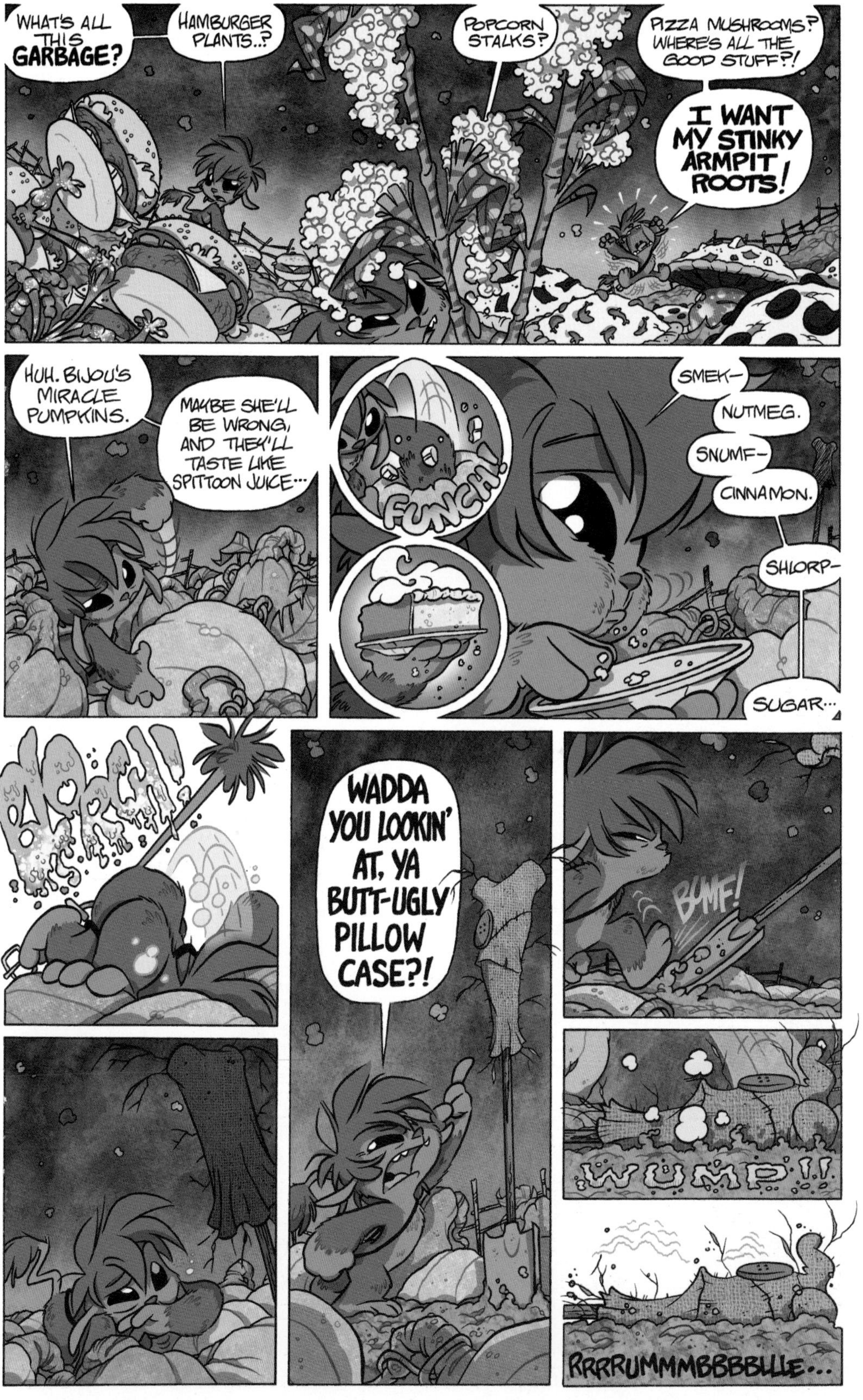
WHAT'S ALL THIS GARBAGE?
HAMBURGER PLANTS..?
POPCORN STALKS?
PIZZA MUSHROOMS? WHERE'S ALL THE GOOD STUFF?!
I WANT MY STINKY ARMPIT ROOTS!
HUH. BIJOU'S MIRACLE PUMPKINS.
MAYBE SHE'LL BE WRONG, AND THEY'LL TASTE LIKE SPITTOON JUICE...
FUNCH!
SMEK-
NUTMEG.
SNUMF-
CINNAMON.
SHLORP-
SUGAR...
WADDA YOU LOOKIN' AT, YA BUTT-UGLY PILLOW CASE?!
BUMF!
WUMP!!
RRRRUMMMBBBBLLLE...

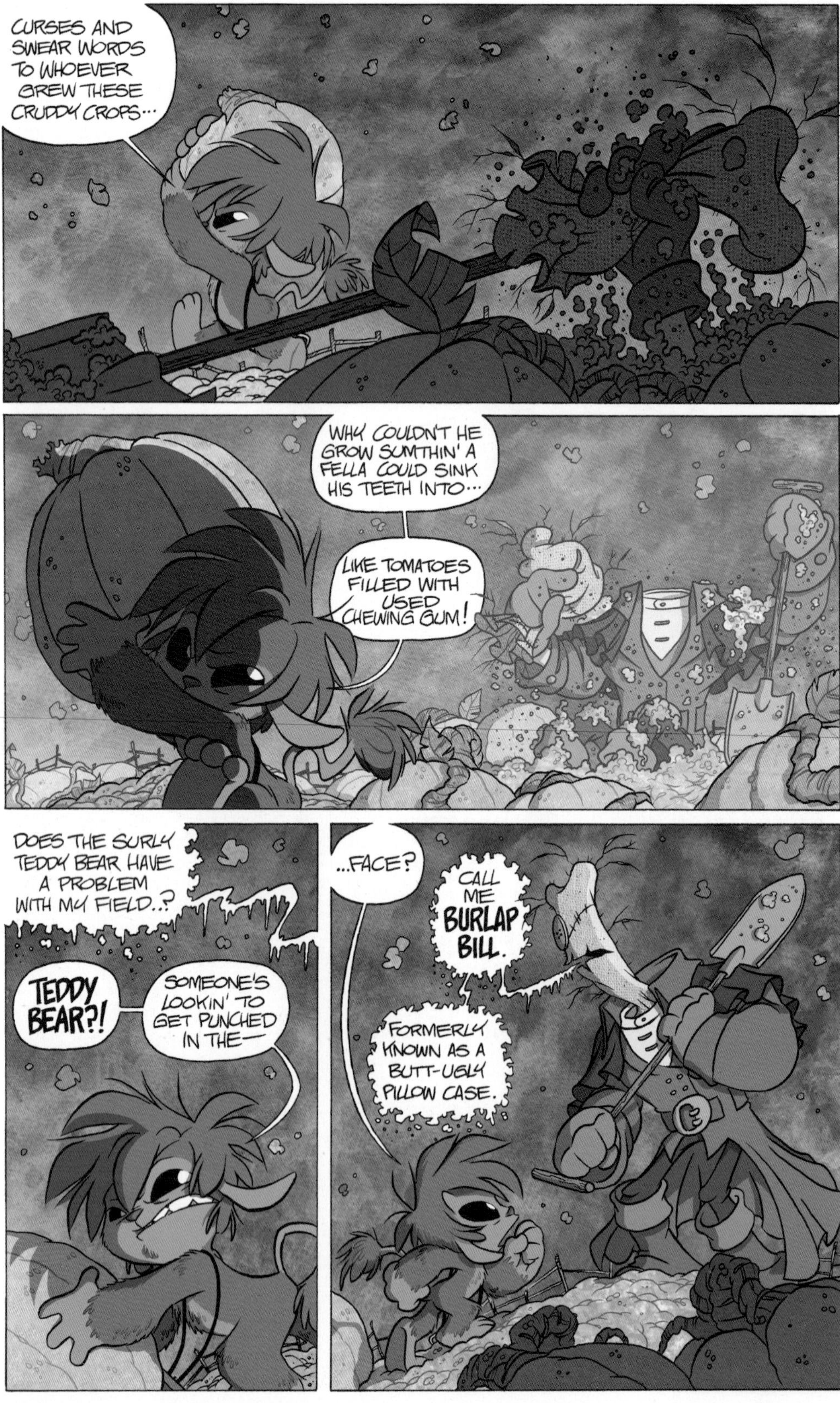
CURSES AND SWEAR WORDS TO WHOEVER GREW THESE CRUDDY CROPS...
WHY COULDN'T HE GROW SUMTHIN' A FELLA COULD SINK HIS TEETH INTO...
LIKE TOMATOES FILLED WITH USED CHEWING GUM!
DOES THE SURLY TEDDY BEAR HAVE A PROBLEM WITH MY FIELD..?
TEDDY BEAR?!
SOMEONE'S LOOKIN' TO GET PUNCHED IN THE—
...FACE?
CALL ME BURLAP BILL.
FORMERLY KNOWN AS A BUTT-UGLY PILLOW CASE.

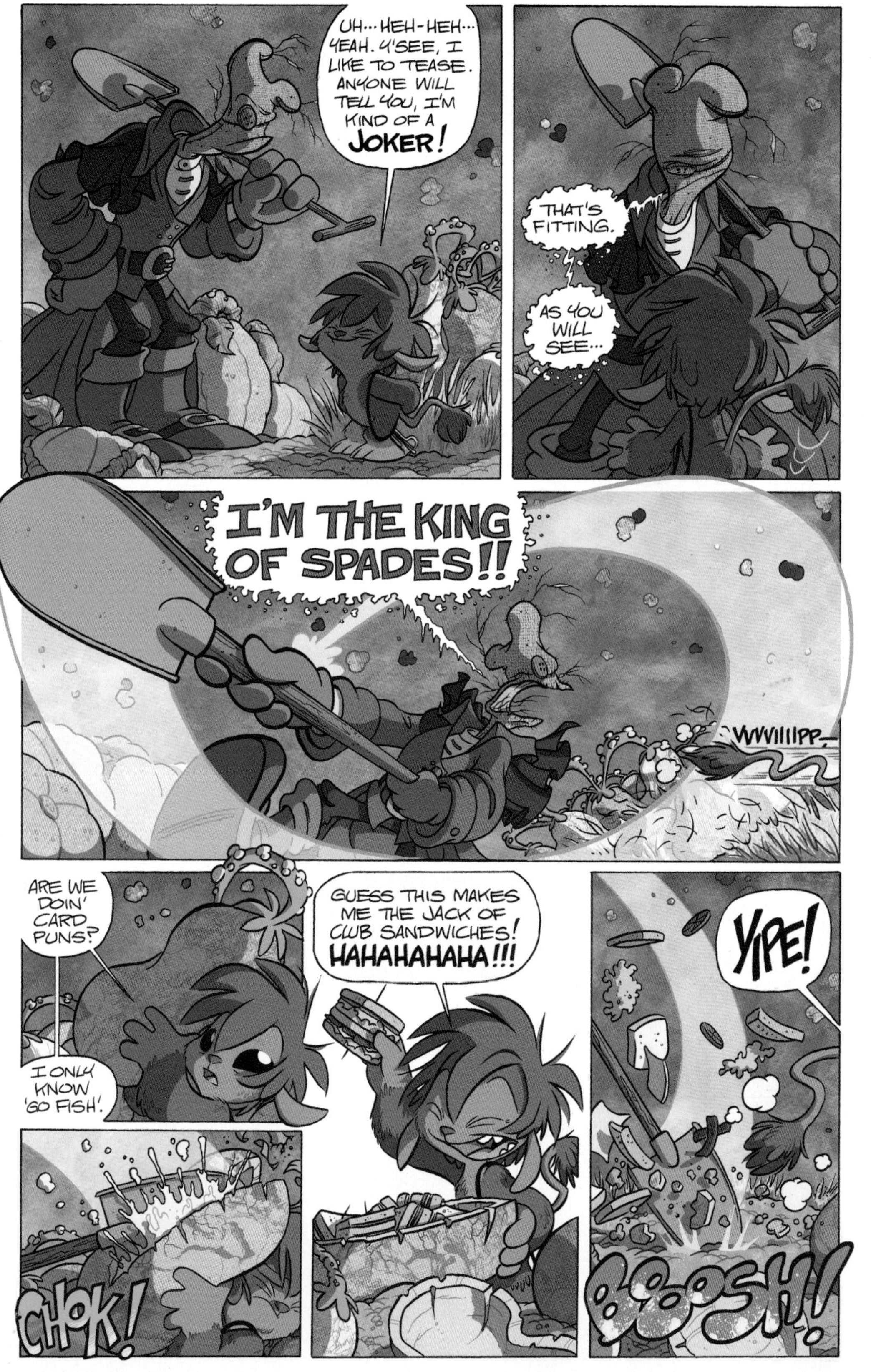
UH... HEH-HEH... YEAH. Y'SEE, I LIKE TO TEASE. ANYONE WILL TELL YOU, I'M KIND OF A JOKER!
THAT'S FITTING.
AS YOU WILL SEE...
I'M THE KING OF SPADES!!
VVVIIIIPP
ARE WE DOIN' CARD PUNS?
I ONLY KNOW 'GO FISH'.
GUESS THIS MAKES ME THE JACK OF CLUB SANDWICHES! HAHAHAHAHA!!!
YIPE!
CHOK!
BOOSH!

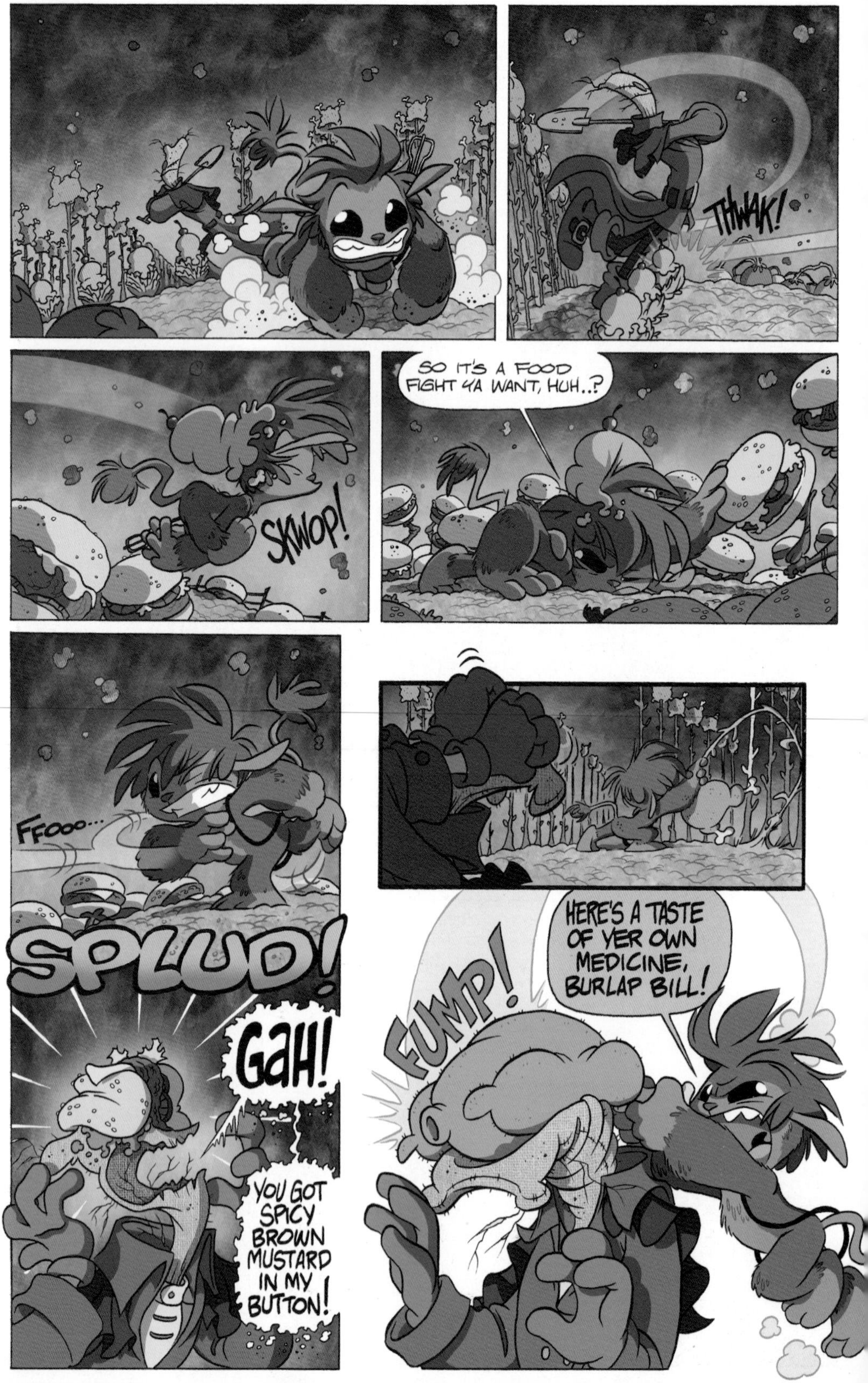
THWAK!
SKWOP!
SO IT'S A FOOD FIGHT YA WANT, HUH..?
FFOOO...
SPLUD!
GAH!
YOU GOT SPICY BROWN MUSTARD IN MY BUTTON!
HERE'S A TASTE OF YER OWN MEDICINE, BURLAP BILL!
FUMP!

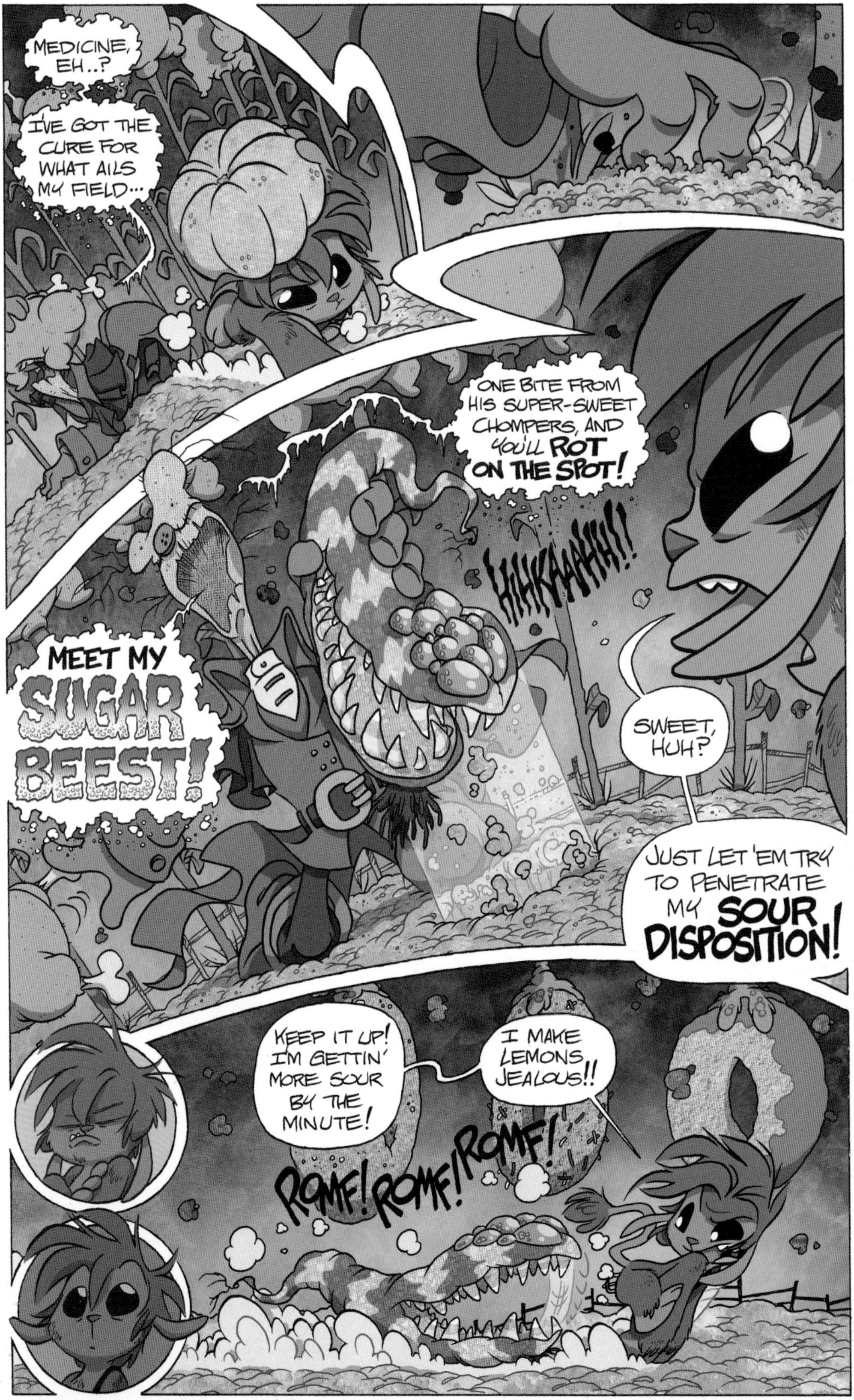
MEDICINE, EH...?
I'VE GOT THE CURE FOR WHAT AILS MY FIELD...
ONE BITE FROM HIS SUPER-SWEET CHOMPERS, AND YOU'LL ROT ON THE SPOT!
HHKAAHH!!
MEET MY SUGAR BEEST!
SWEET, HUH?
JUST LET 'EM TRY TO PENETRATE MY SOUR DISPOSITION!
KEEP IT UP! I'M GETTIN' MORE SOUR BY THE MINUTE!
I MAKE LEMONS JEALOUS!!
ROMF! ROMF! ROMF!

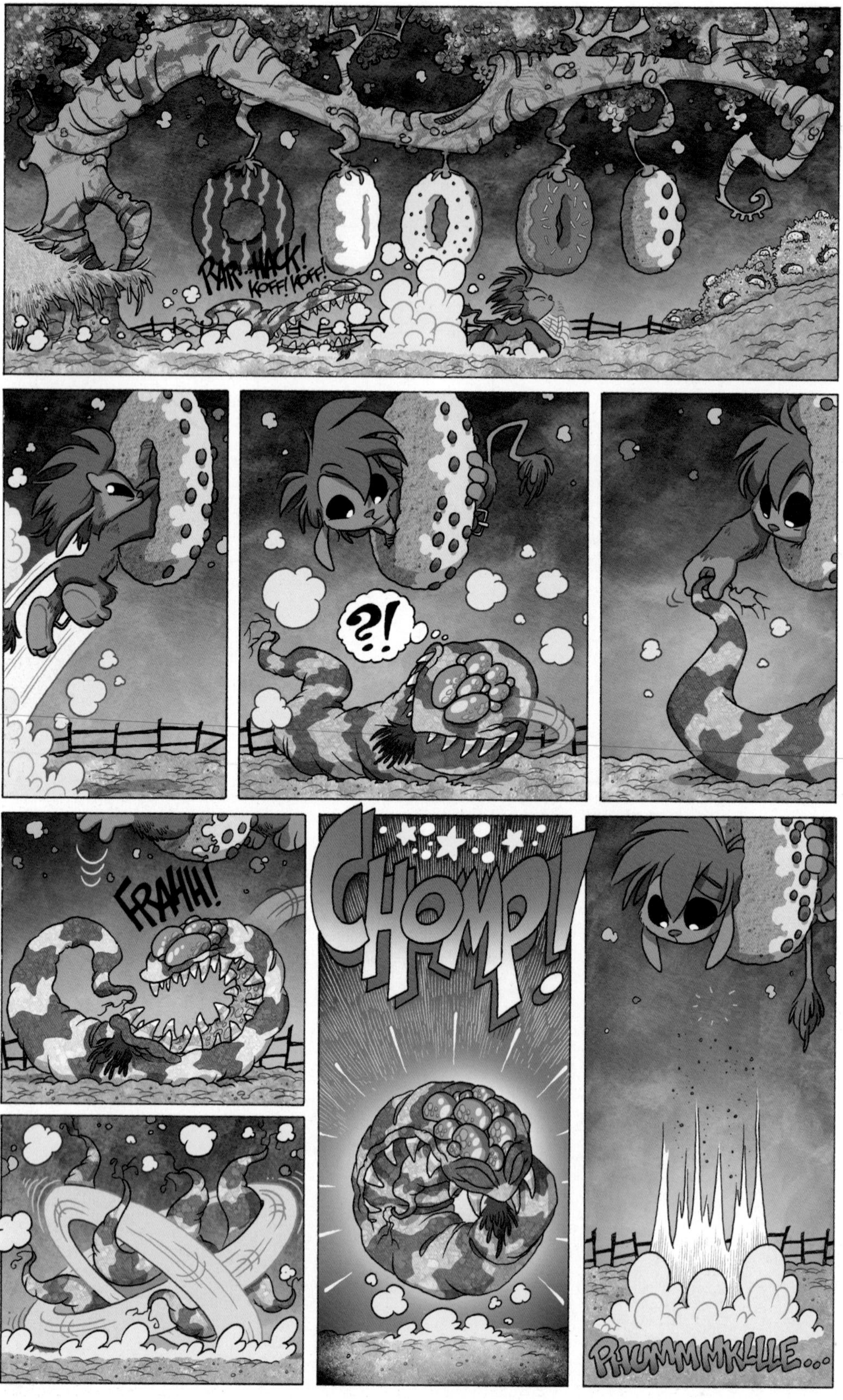
RAR..HACK!
KOFF! KOFF!
?!
FRAHH!
CHOMP!
PHUMMMKLLLE...

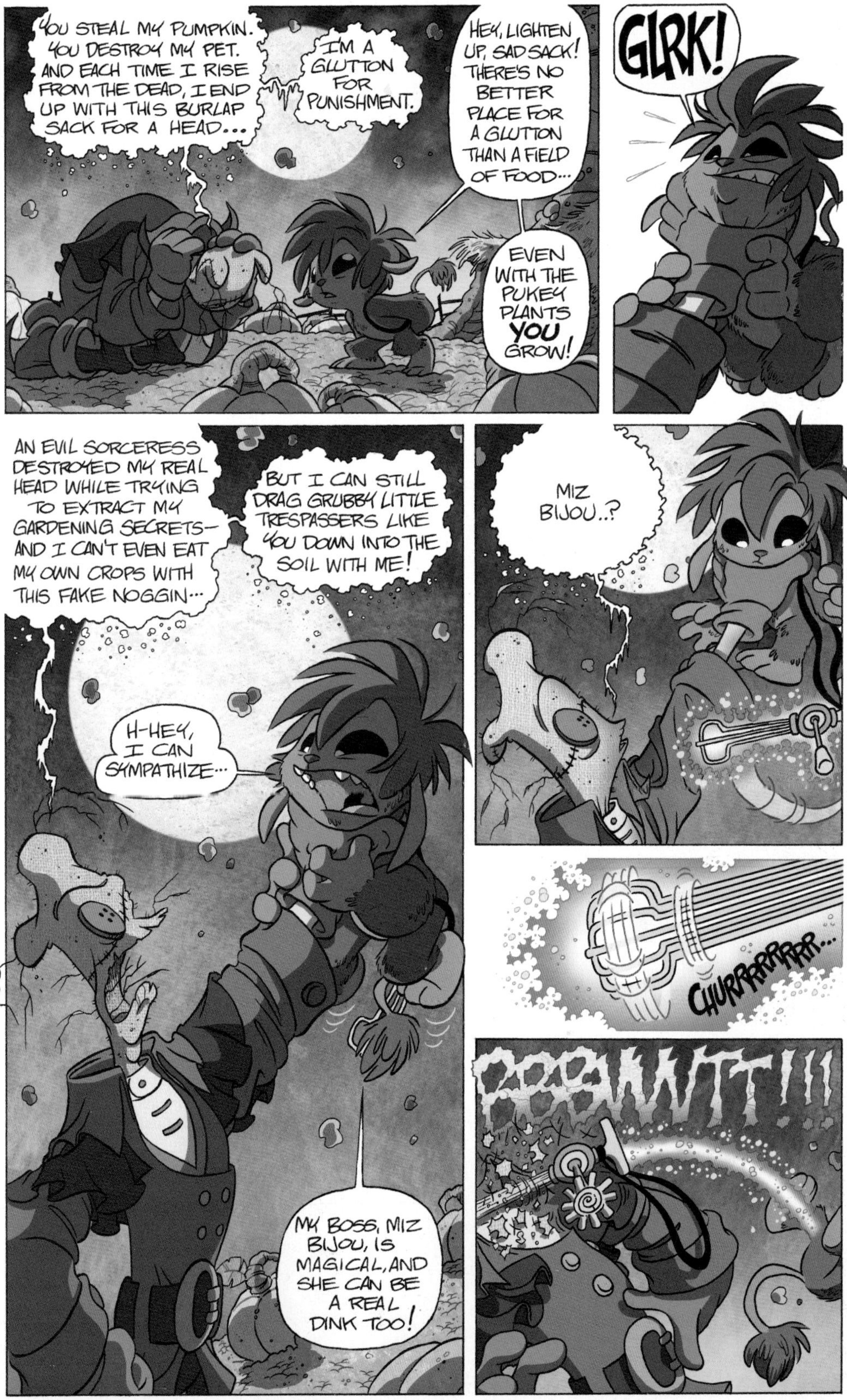

YOU STEAL MY PUMPKIN. YOU DESTROY MY PET. AND EACH TIME I RISE FROM THE DEAD, I END UP WITH THIS BURLAP SACK FOR A HEAD...
I'M A GLUTTON FOR PUNISHMENT.
HEY, LIGHTEN UP, SAD SACK! THERE'S NO BETTER PLACE FOR A GLUTTON THAN A FIELD OF FOOD...
EVEN WITH THE PUKEY PLANTS YOU GROW!
GLRK!
AN EVIL SORCERESS DESTROYED MY REAL HEAD WHILE TRYING TO EXTRACT MY GARDENING SECRETS-- AND I CAN'T EVEN EAT MY OWN CROPS WITH THIS FAKE NOGGIN...
BUT I CAN STILL DRAG GRUBBY LITTLE TRESPASSERS LIKE YOU DOWN INTO THE SOIL WITH ME!
H-HEY, I CAN SYMPATHIZE...
MY BOSS, MIZ BIJOU, IS MAGICAL, AND SHE CAN BE A REAL DINK TOO!
MIZ BIJOU..?
CHURRRRRRR...
PPPWTT!!!

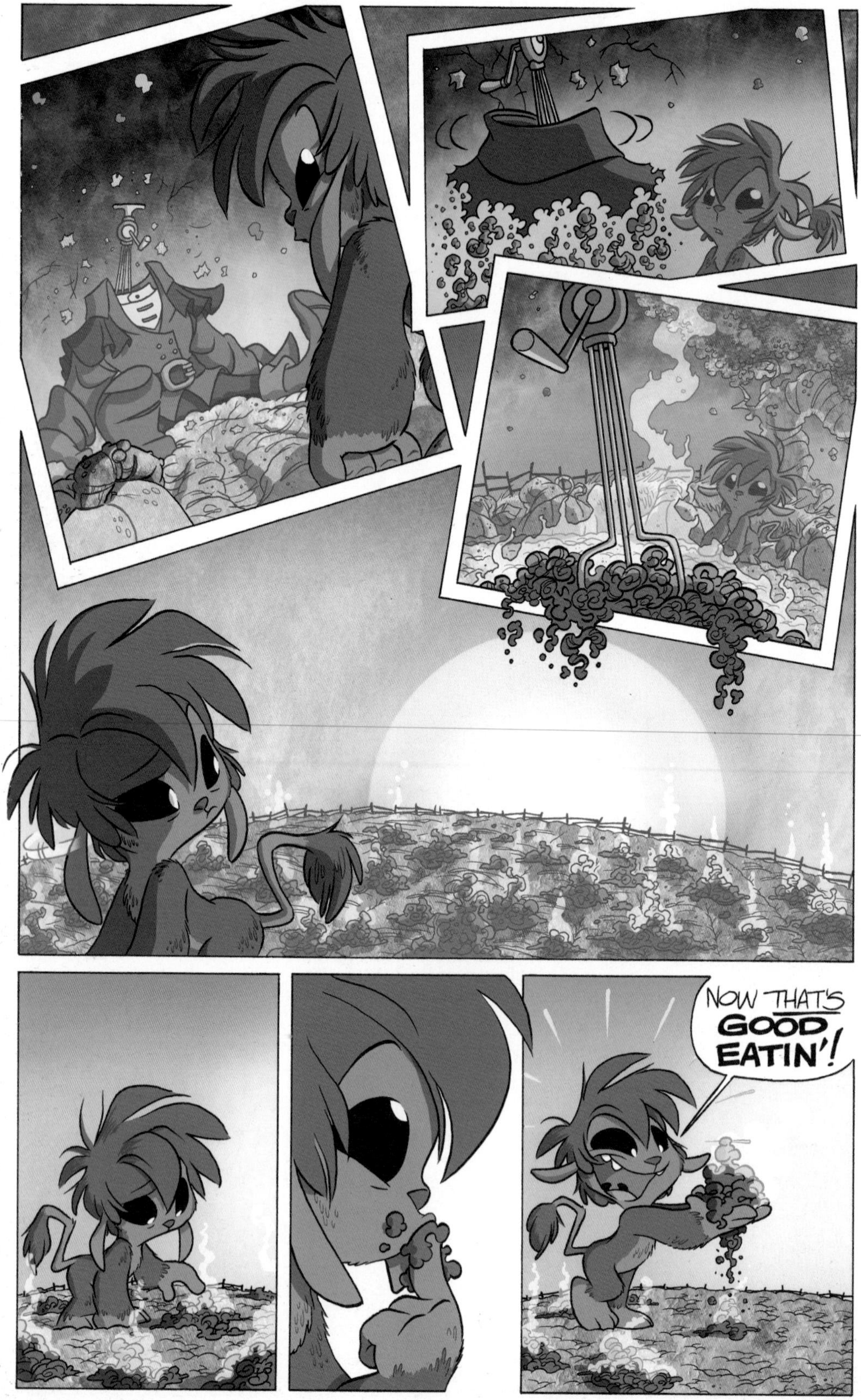
NOW THAT'S GOOD EATIN'!

CHAPTER 6
PLAYING FOR KEEPS

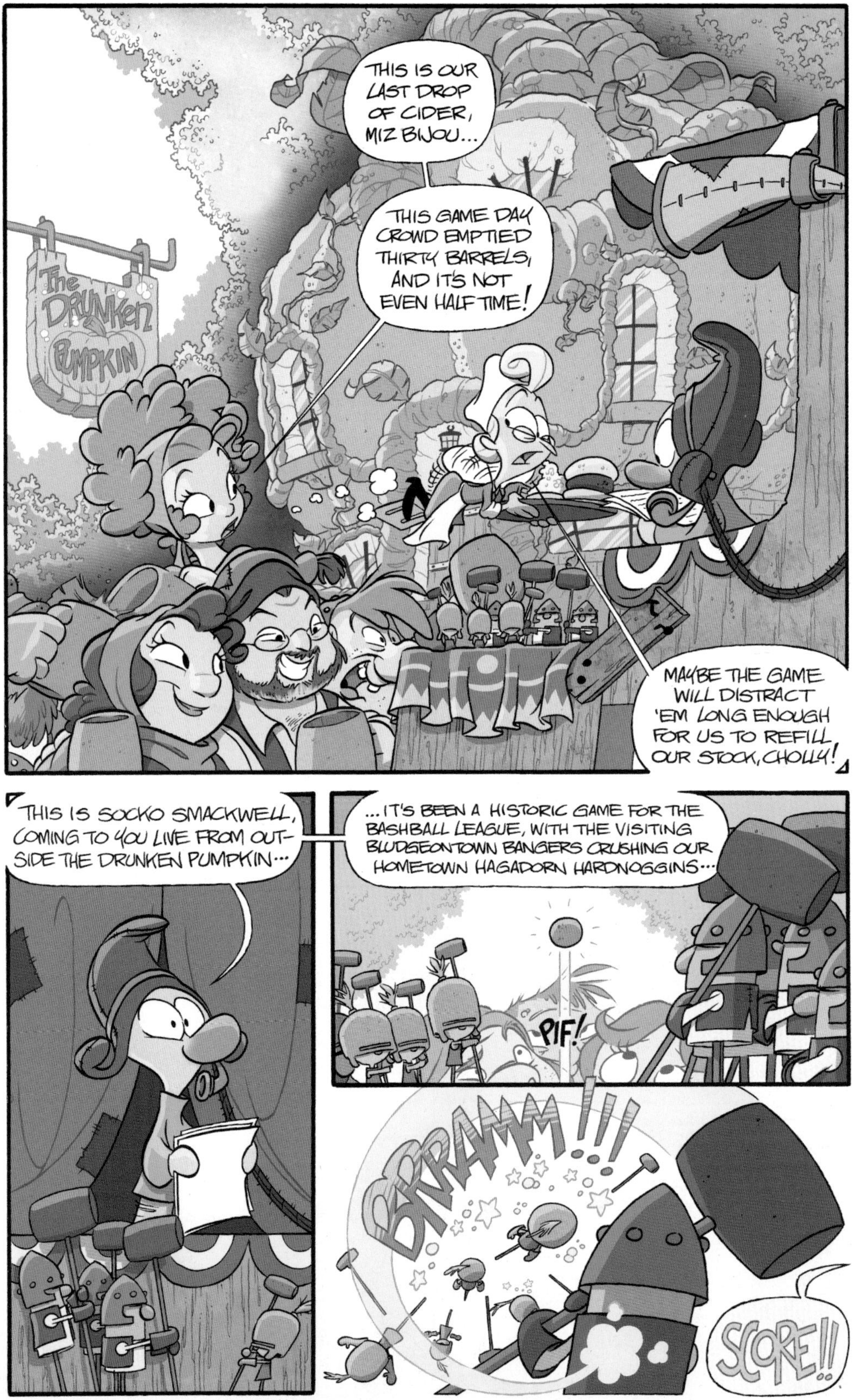

THIS IS OUR LAST DROP OF CIDER, MIZ BIJOU...
THIS GAME DAY CROWD EMPTIED THIRTY BARRELS, AND IT'S NOT EVEN HALF TIME!
The DRUNKEN PUMPKIN
MAYBE THE GAME WILL DISTRACT 'EM LONG ENOUGH FOR US TO REFILL OUR STOCK, CHOLLY!
THIS IS SOCKO SMACKWELL, COMING TO YOU LIVE FROM OUTSIDE THE DRUNKEN PUMPKIN...
...IT'S BEEN A HISTORIC GAME FOR THE BASHBALL LEAGUE, WITH THE VISITING BLUDGEONTOWN BANGERS CRUSHING OUR HOMETOWN HAGADORN HARDNOGGINS...
PIF!
BRRAMM!!!
SCORE!!

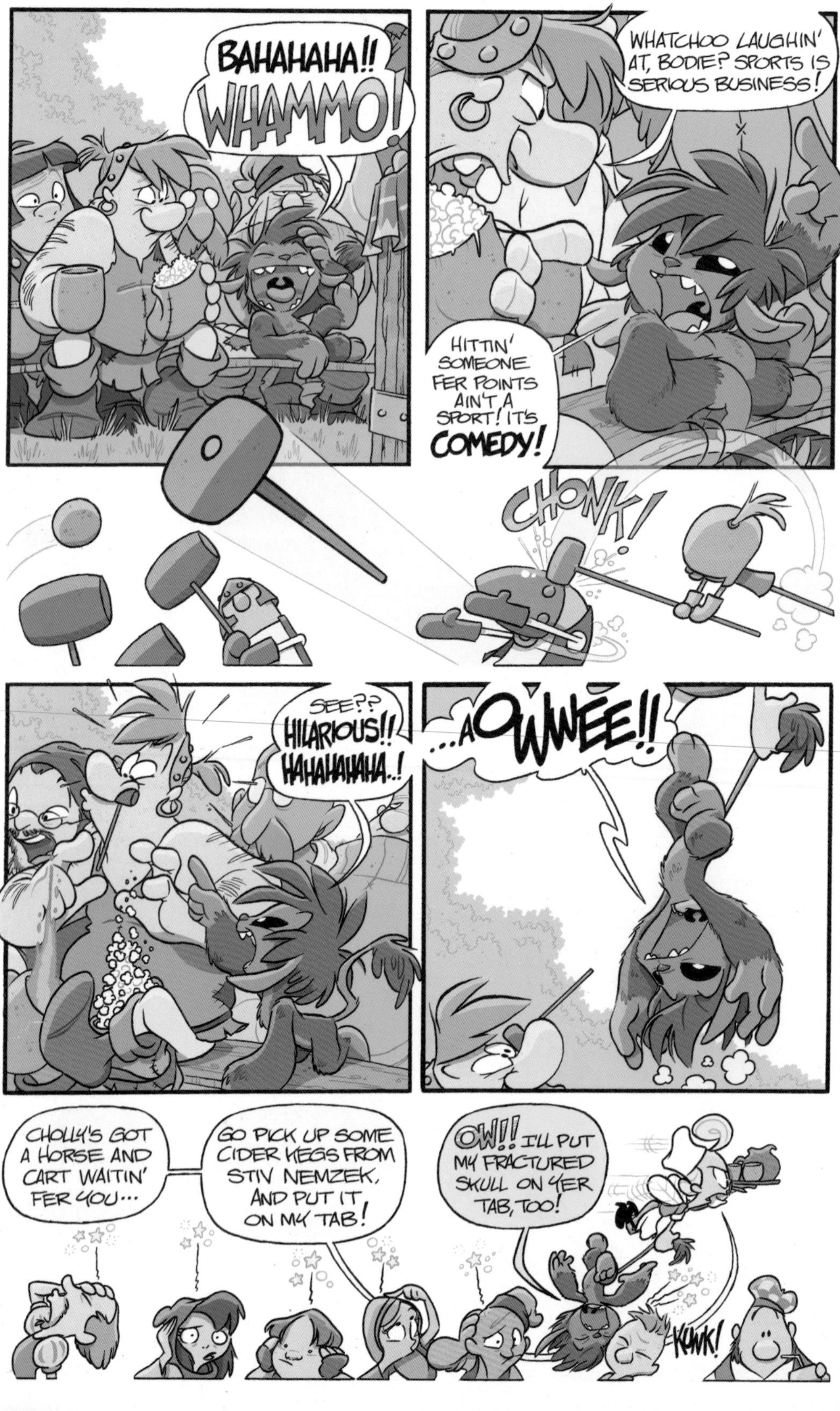
BAHAHAHA!!
WHAMMO!
WHATCHOO LAUGHIN' AT, BODIE? SPORTS IS SERIOUS BUSINESS!
HITTIN' SOMEONE FER POINTS AIN'T A SPORT! IT'S COMEDY!
CHONK!
SEE?? HILARIOUS!! HAHAHAHAHA..!
...AOWWEE!!
CHOLLY'S GOT A HORSE AND CART WAITIN' FER YOU...
GO PICK UP SOME CIDER KEGS FROM STIV NEMZEK, AND PUT IT ON MY TAB!
OW!! I'LL PUT MY FRACTURED SKULL ON YER TAB, TOO!
KUNK!

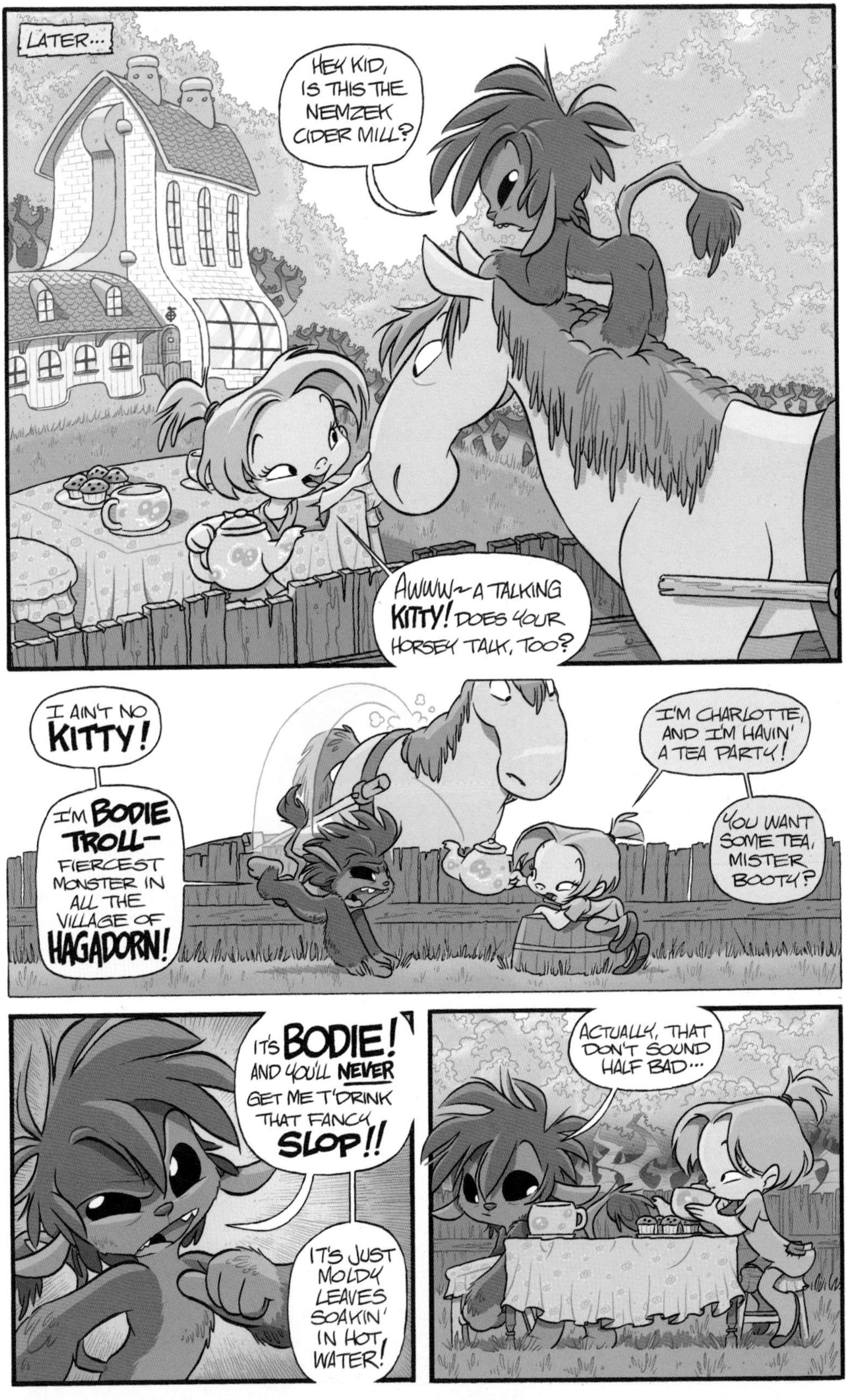
LATER...
HEY KID, IS THIS THE NEMZEK CIDER MILL?
AWWW~ A TALKING KITTY! DOES YOUR HORSEY TALK, TOO?
I AIN'T NO KITTY!
I'M BODIE TROLL— FIERCEST MONSTER IN ALL THE VILLAGE OF HAGADORN!
I'M CHARLOTTE, AND I'M HAVIN' A TEA PARTY!
YOU WANT SOME TEA, MISTER BOOTY?
IT'S BODIE! AND YOU'LL NEVER GET ME T'DRINK THAT FANCY SLOP!!
IT'S JUST MOLDY LEAVES SOAKIN' IN HOT WATER!
ACTUALLY, THAT DON'T SOUND HALF BAD...

IT'S NOT REALLY TEA, MISTER BOOTY...

IT'S BEER!

LITTLE KIDS SHOULDN'T DRINK BEER!

IT TURNS 'EM INTO GROWN UPS, AND THERE'S NOTHIN' WORSE THAN THAT!

MY DADDY BREWED IT FROM ROOTS...

HE SAID EVEN LITTLE KIDS CAN DRINK IT!

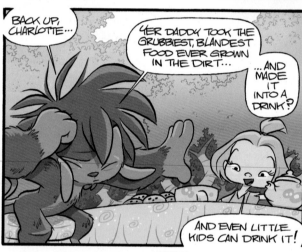

BACK UP, CHARLOTTE...

YER DADDY TOOK THE GRUBBIEST, BLANDEST FOOD EVER GROWN IN THE DIRT...

...AND MADE IT INTO A DRINK?

AND EVEN LITTLE KIDS CAN DRINK IT!

I NEED YOU T'FOCUS, CHARLOTTE! THE CRUDDIEST, BUTT-UGLIEST VEGETATION IN THE WHOLE KINGDOM, NOT TO MENTION THIS TROLL'S ALL-TIME FAVORITE SNACK, IS NOW A BEER? A ROOT BEER?!

YESH. Y'WUN SHUM, MISHER BOOPY?

WEEELLLL...

ONE LITTLE SIP COULDN'T HURT...

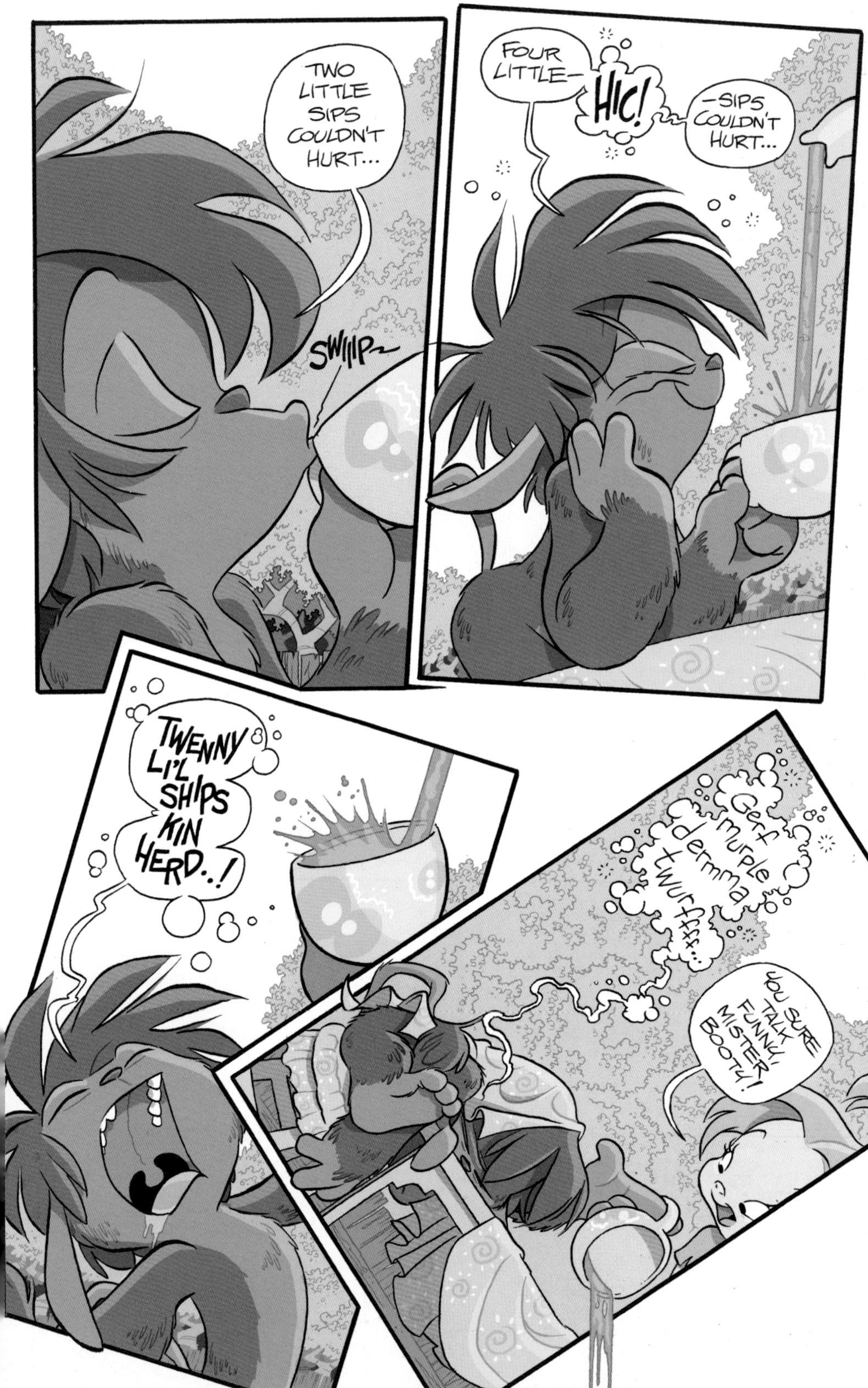
TWO LITTLE SIPS COULDN'T HURT...
SWIIIP
FOUR LITTLE—
HIC!
—SIPS COULDN'T HURT...
TWENNY LI'L SHIPS KIN HERD..!
Gerf murple dermma twurfff...
YOU SURE TALK FUNNY, MISTER BOOTY!

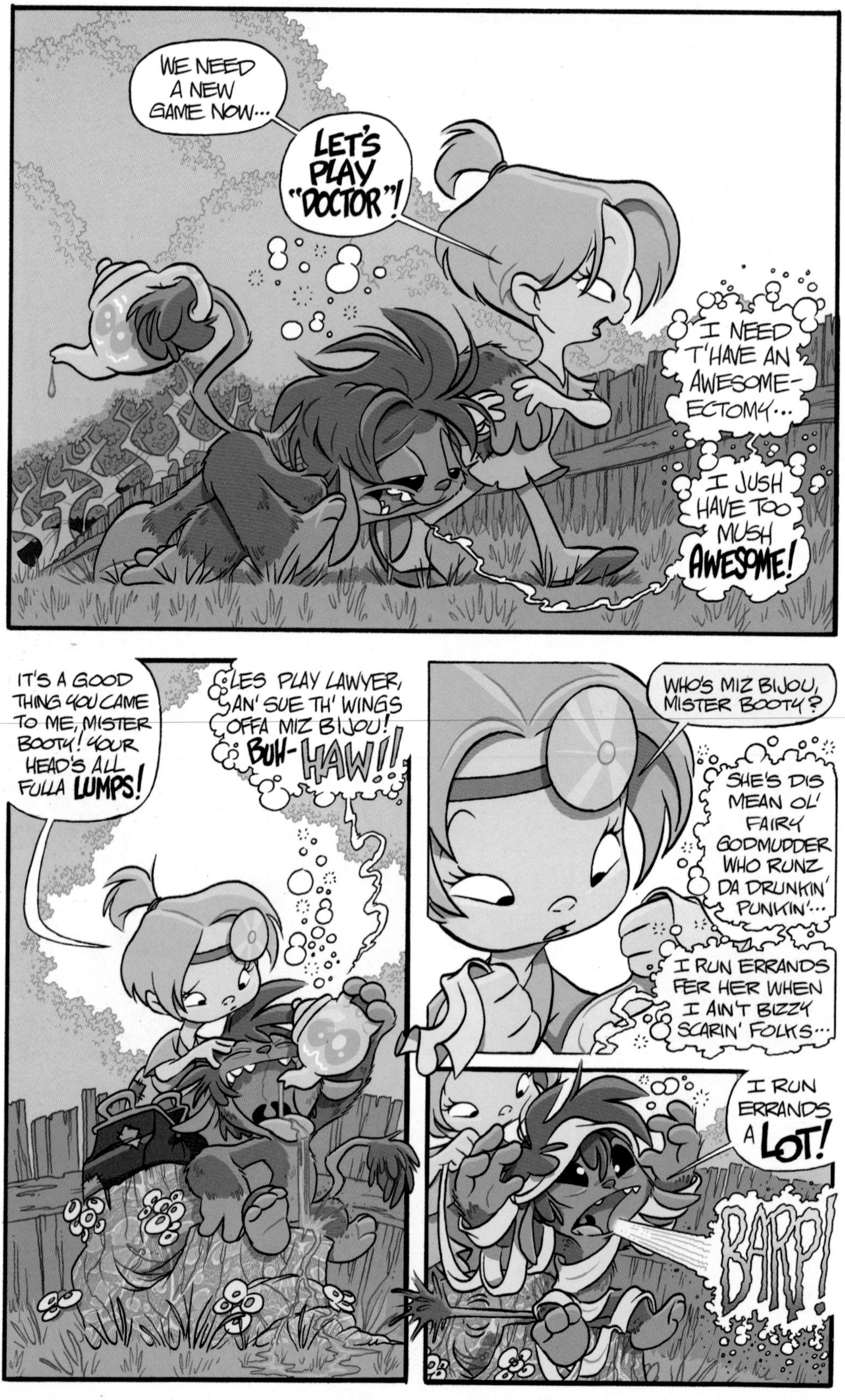

WE NEED A NEW GAME NOW...
LET'S PLAY "DOCTOR"!
I NEED T'HAVE AN AWESOME-ECTOMY...
I JUSH HAVE TOO MUSH AWESOME!
IT'S A GOOD THING YOU CAME TO ME, MISTER BOOTY! YOUR HEAD'S ALL FULLA LUMPS!
LES PLAY LAWYER, AN' SUE TH' WINGS OFFA MIZ BIJOU! BUH-HAW!!
WHO'S MIZ BIJOU, MISTER BOOTY?
SHE'S DIS MEAN OL' FAIRY GODMUDDER WHO RUNZ DA DRUNKIN' PUNKIN'...
I RUN ERRANDS FER HER WHEN I AIN'T BIZZY SCARIN' FOLKS...
I RUN ERRANDS A LOT!
BARP!

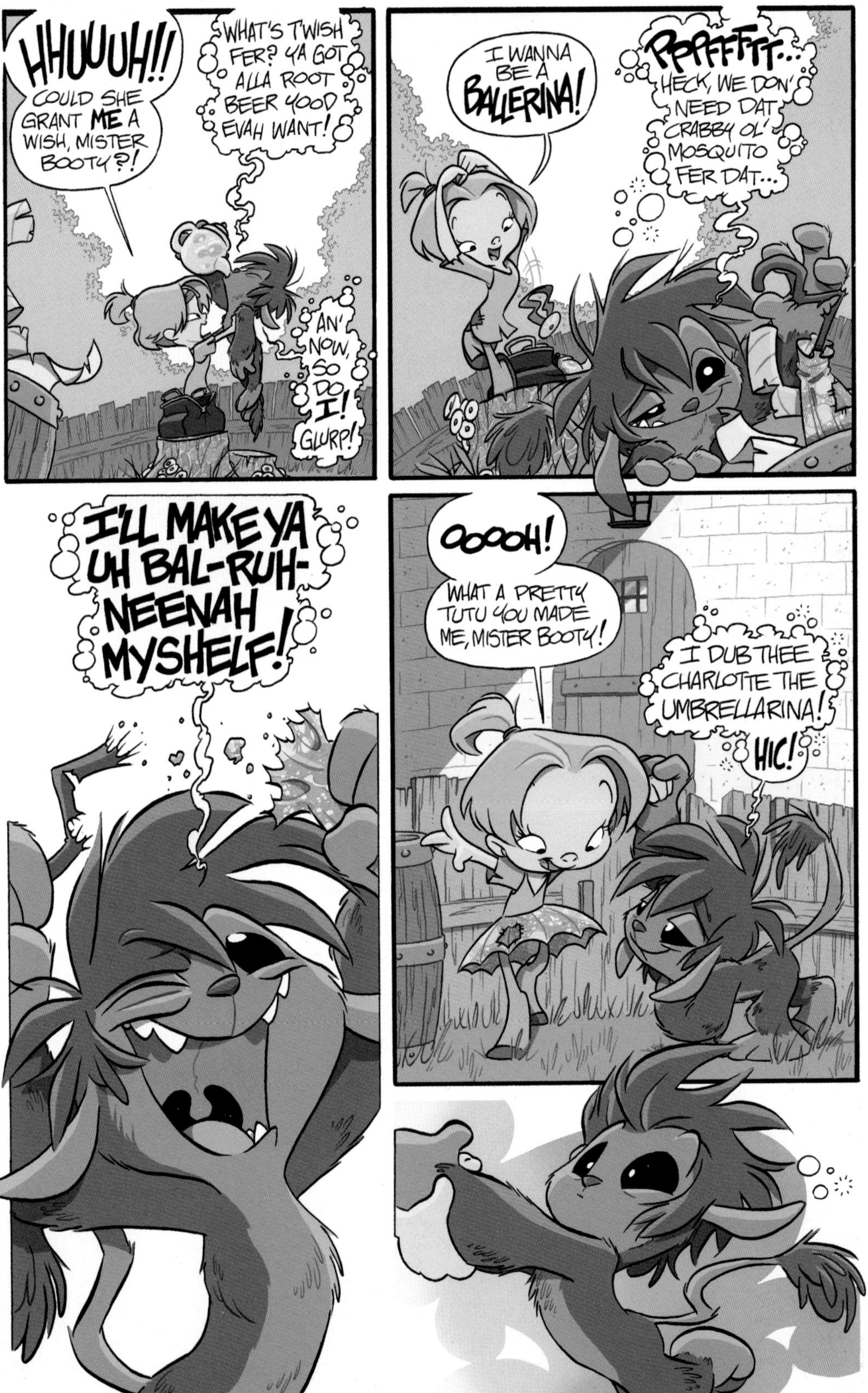
HHUUUH!! COULD SHE GRANT ME A WISH, MISTER BOOTY?!
WHAT'S T'WISH FER? YA GOT ALLA ROOT BEER YOOD EVAH WANT!
AN' NOW, SO DO I! GLURP!
I WANNA BE A BALLERINA!
PPPFFFTTT... HECK, WE DON' NEED DAT CRABBY OL' MOSQUITO FER DAT...
I'LL MAKE YA UH BAL-RUH-NEENAH MYSHELF!
OOOOH! WHAT A PRETTY TUTU YOU MADE ME, MISTER BOOTY!
I DUB THEE CHARLOTTE THE UMBRELLARINA!
HIC!

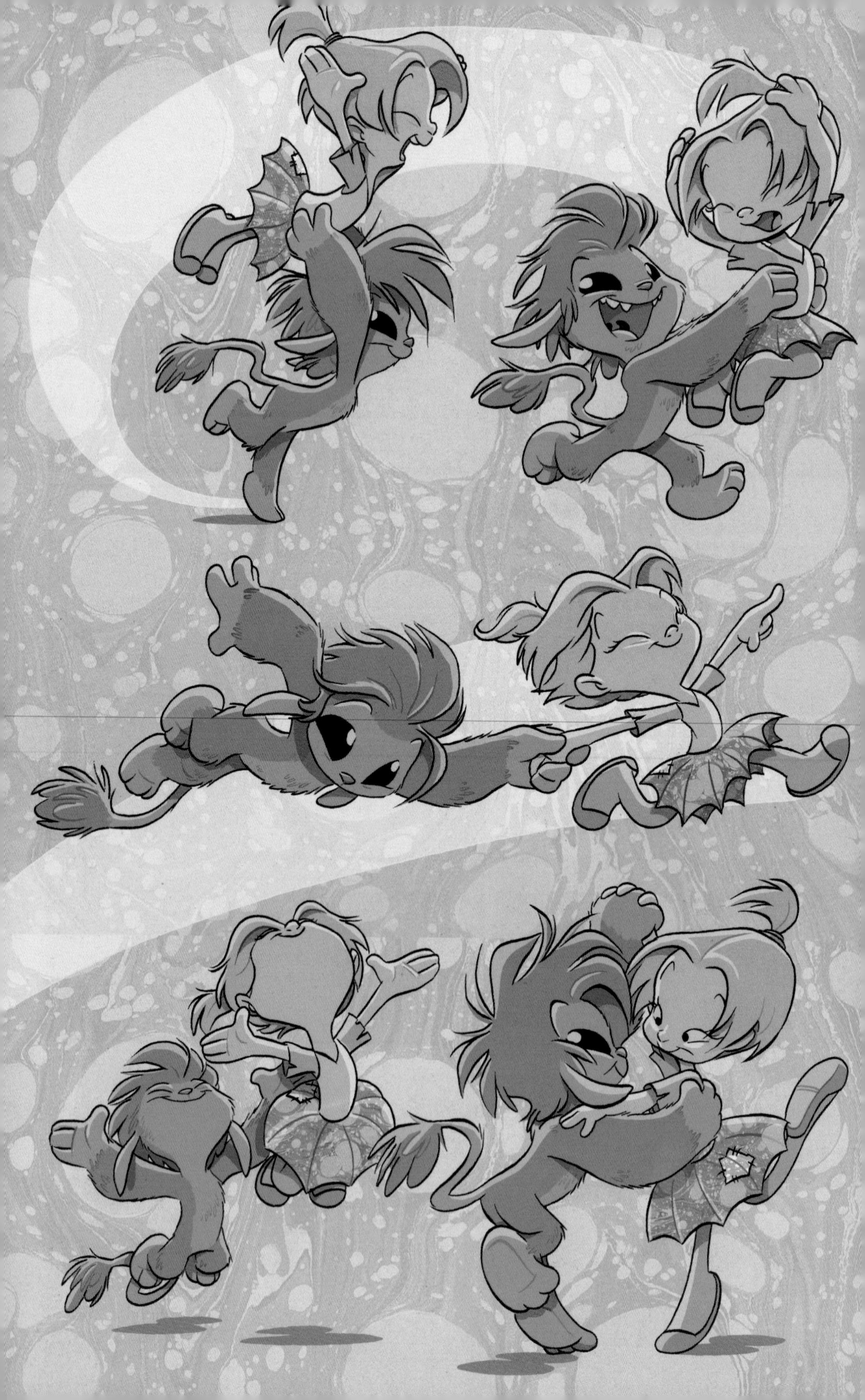

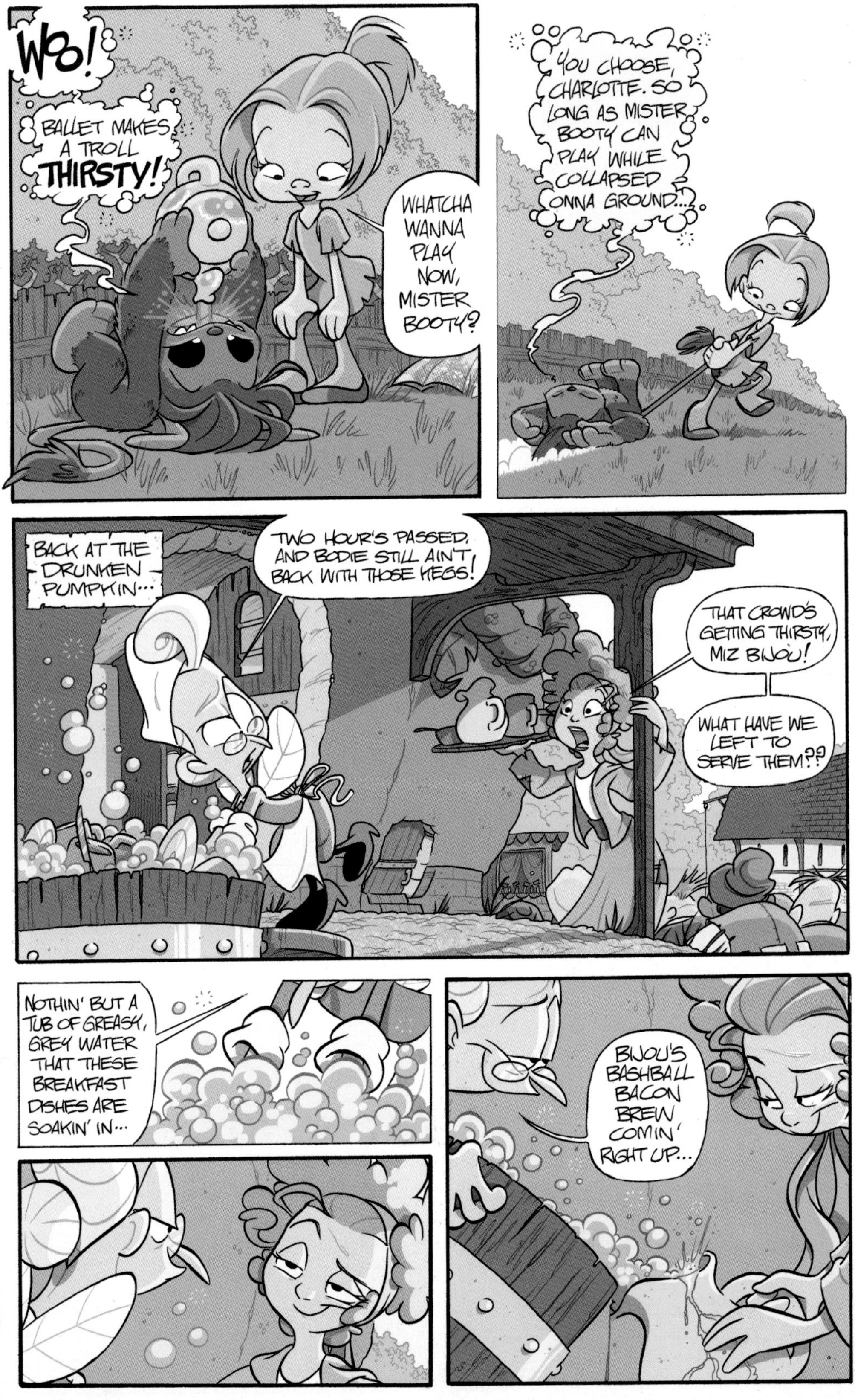
WOO!
BALLET MAKES A TROLL THIRSTY!
WHATCHA WANNA PLAY NOW, MISTER BOOTY?
YOU CHOOSE, CHARLOTTE. SO LONG AS MISTER BOOTY CAN PLAY WHILE COLLAPSED ONNA GROUND...
BACK AT THE DRUNKEN PUMPKIN...
TWO HOUR'S PASSED, AND BODIE STILL AIN'T BACK WITH THOSE KEGS!
THAT CROWD'S GETTING THIRSTY, MIZ BIJOU!
WHAT HAVE WE LEFT TO SERVE THEM??
NOTHIN' BUT A TUB OF GREASY, GREY WATER THAT THESE BREAKFAST DISHES ARE SOAKIN' IN...
BIJOU'S BASHBALL BACON BREW COMIN' RIGHT UP...

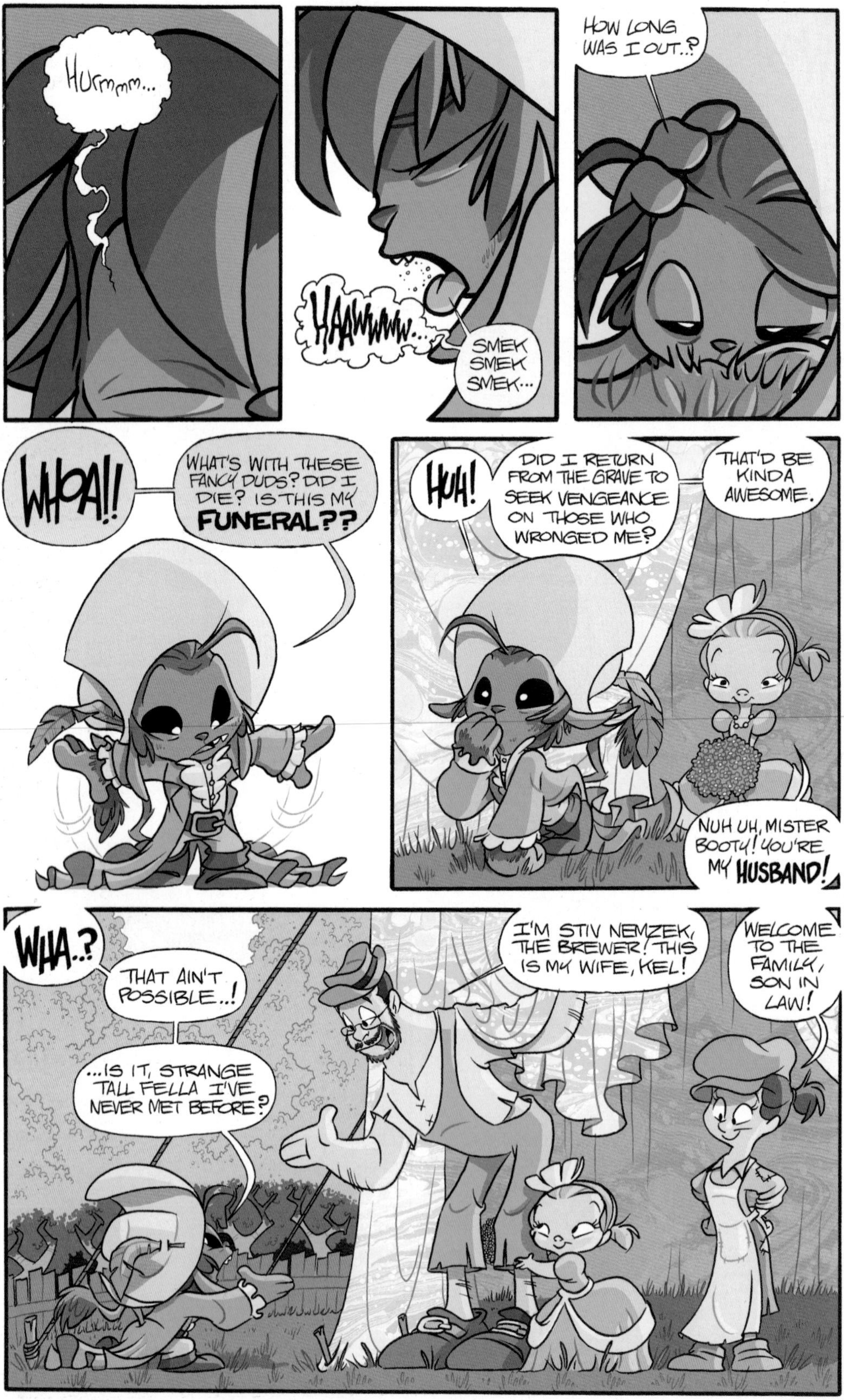

Hurmmm...
HAAWWWW...
SMEK SMEK SMEK...
HOW LONG WAS I OUT..?
WHOA!!
WHAT'S WITH THESE FANCY DUDS? DID I DIE? IS THIS MY FUNERAL??
HUH!
DID I RETURN FROM THE GRAVE TO SEEK VENGEANCE ON THOSE WHO WRONGED ME?
THAT'D BE KINDA AWESOME.
NUH UH, MISTER BOOTY! YOU'RE MY HUSBAND!
WHA..?
THAT AIN'T POSSIBLE..!
...IS IT, STRANGE TALL FELLA I'VE NEVER MET BEFORE?
I'M STIV NEMZEK, THE BREWER! THIS IS MY WIFE, KEL!
WELCOME TO THE FAMILY, SON IN LAW!

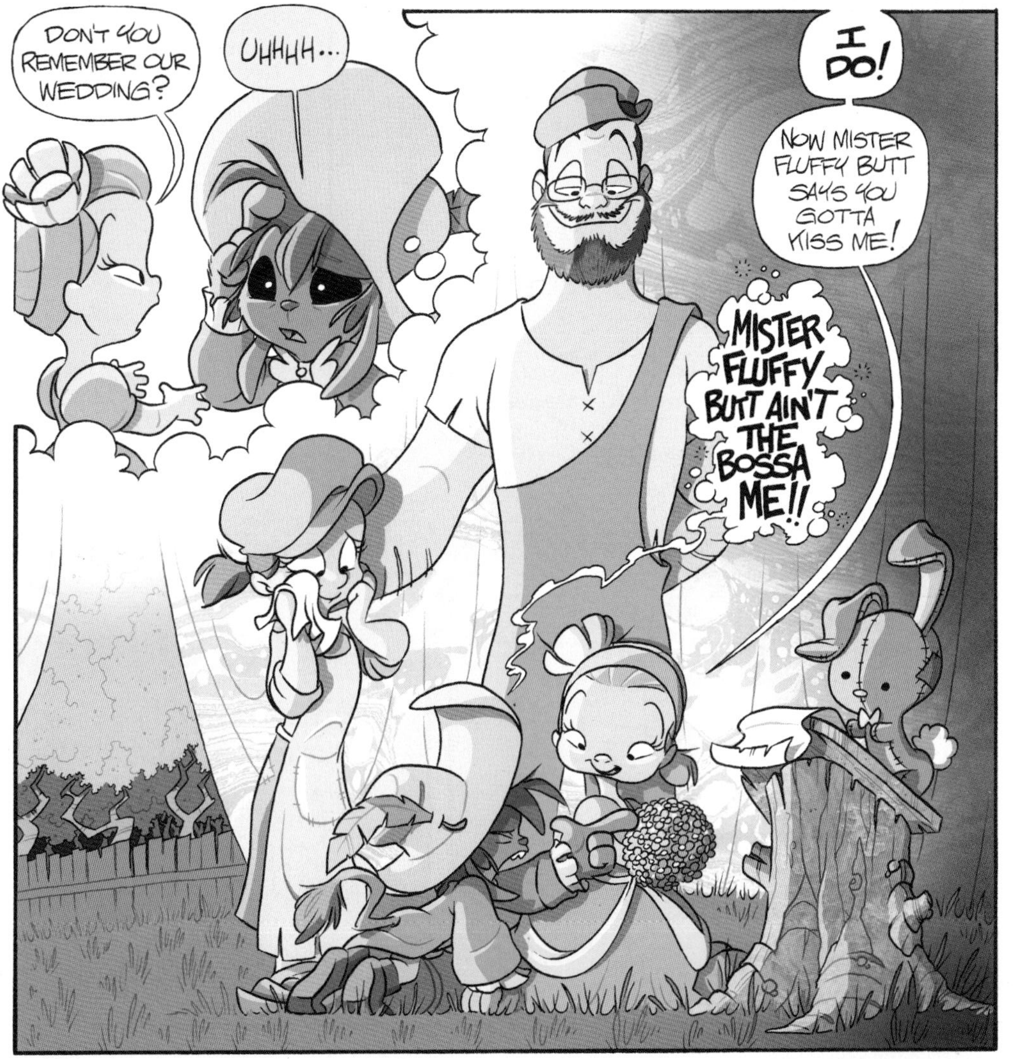
DON'T YOU REMEMBER OUR WEDDING?
UHHHH...
I DO!
NOW MISTER FLUFFY BUTT SAYS YOU GOTTA KISS ME!
MISTER FLUFFY BUTT AIN'T THE BOSSA ME!!

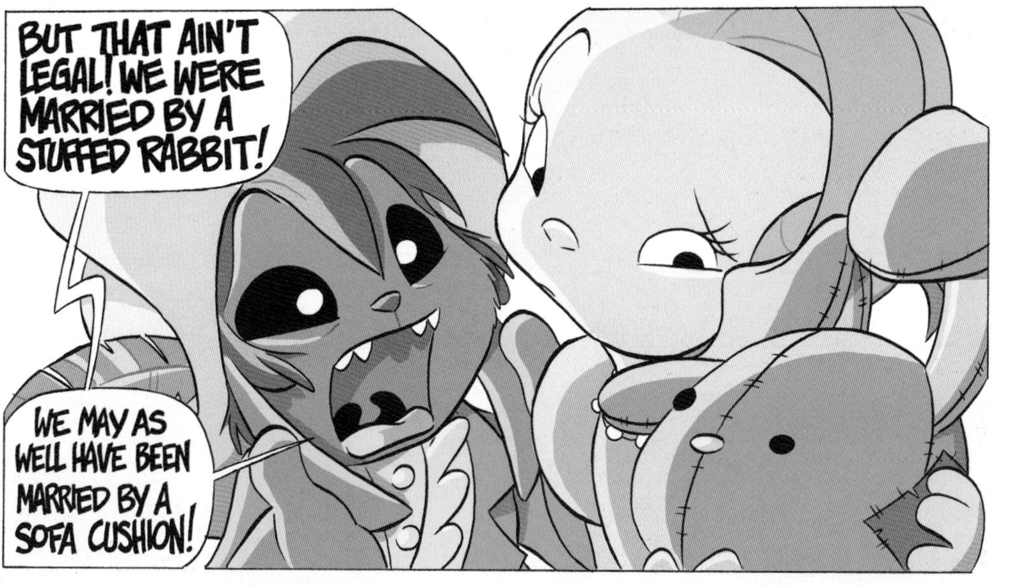
BUT THAT AIN'T LEGAL! WE WERE MARRIED BY A STUFFED RABBIT!
WE MAY AS WELL HAVE BEEN MARRIED BY A SOFA CUSHION!

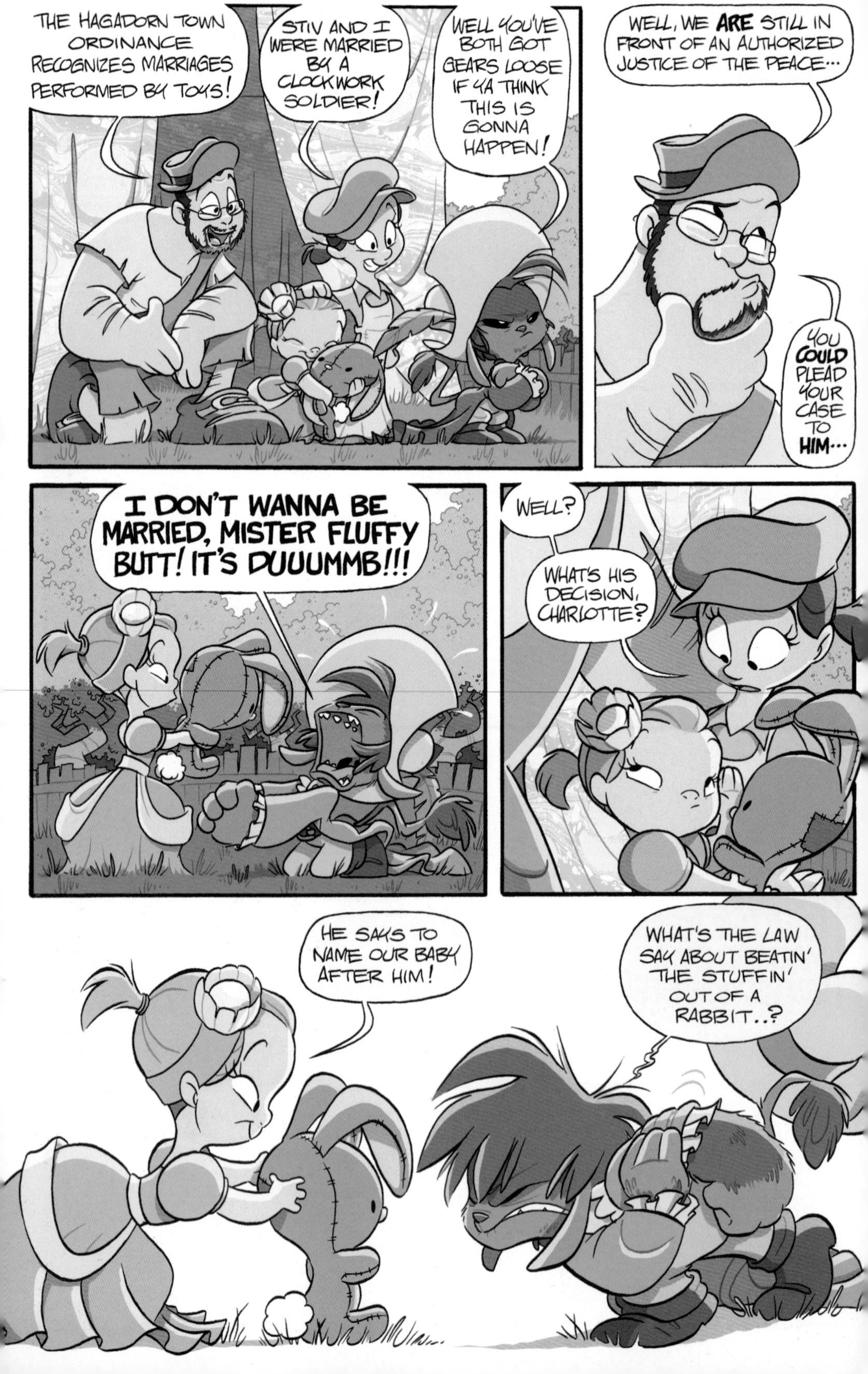
THE HAGADORN TOWN ORDINANCE RECOGNIZES MARRIAGES PERFORMED BY TOYS!
STIV AND I WERE MARRIED BY A CLOCKWORK SOLDIER!
WELL YOU'VE BOTH GOT GEARS LOOSE IF YA THINK THIS IS GONNA HAPPEN!
WELL, WE **ARE** STILL IN FRONT OF AN AUTHORIZED JUSTICE OF THE PEACE...
YOU **COULD** PLEAD YOUR CASE TO **HIM**...
I DON'T WANNA BE MARRIED, MISTER FLUFFY BUTT! IT'S DUUUMMB!!!
WELL?
WHAT'S HIS DECISION, CHARLOTTE?
HE SAYS TO NAME OUR BABY AFTER HIM!
WHAT'S THE LAW SAY ABOUT BEATIN' THE STUFFIN' OUT OF A RABBIT..?

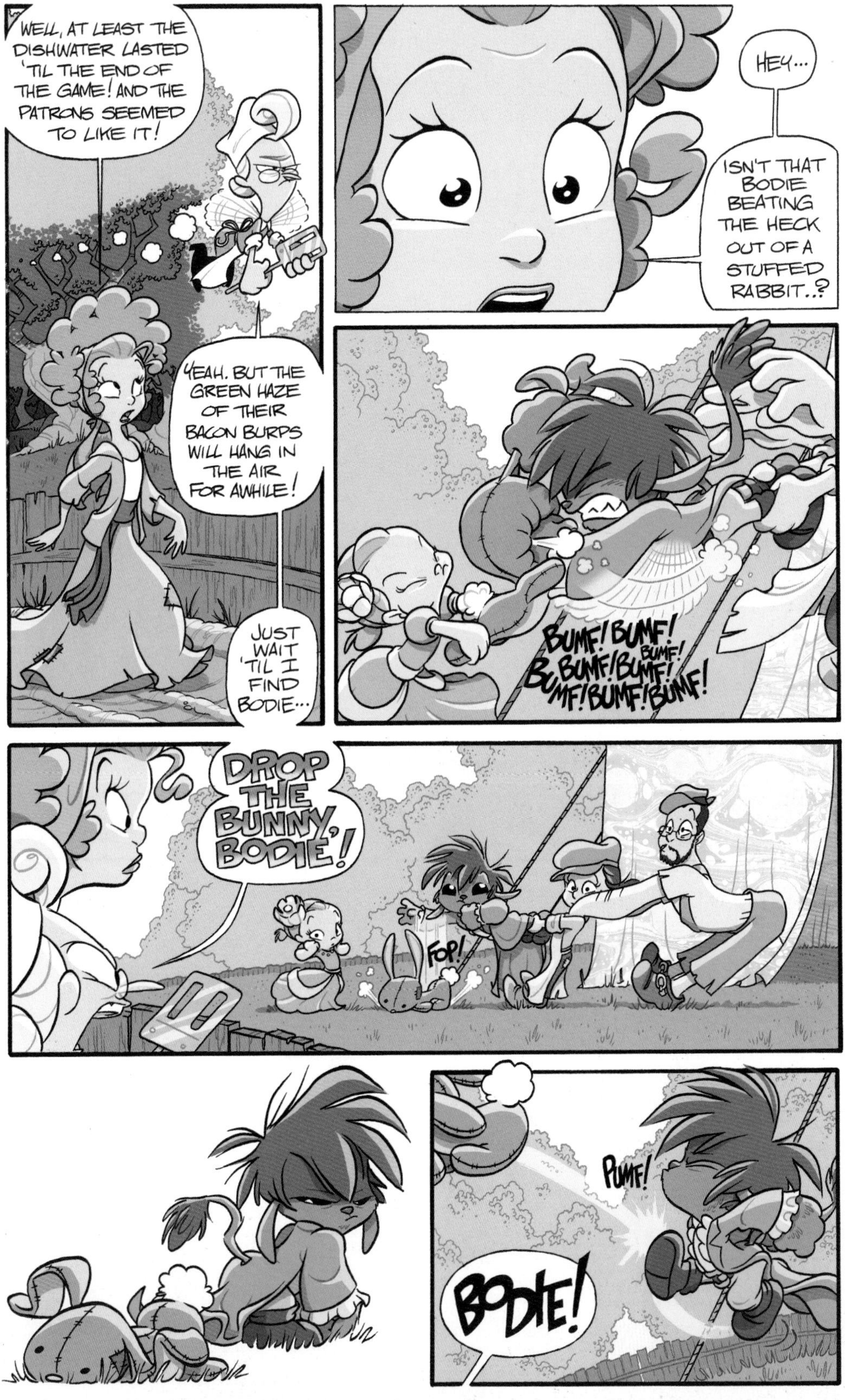
WELL, AT LEAST THE DISHWATER LASTED 'TIL THE END OF THE GAME! AND THE PATRONS SEEMED TO LIKE IT!
YEAH. BUT THE GREEN HAZE OF THEIR BACON BURPS WILL HANG IN THE AIR FOR AWHILE!
JUST WAIT 'TIL I FIND BODIE...
HEY...
ISN'T THAT BODIE BEATING THE HECK OUT OF A STUFFED RABBIT..?
BUMF! BUMF! BUMF! BUMF! BUMF! BUMF! BUMF! BUMF!
DROP THE BUNNY, BODIE!
FOP!
PUMF!
BODIE!

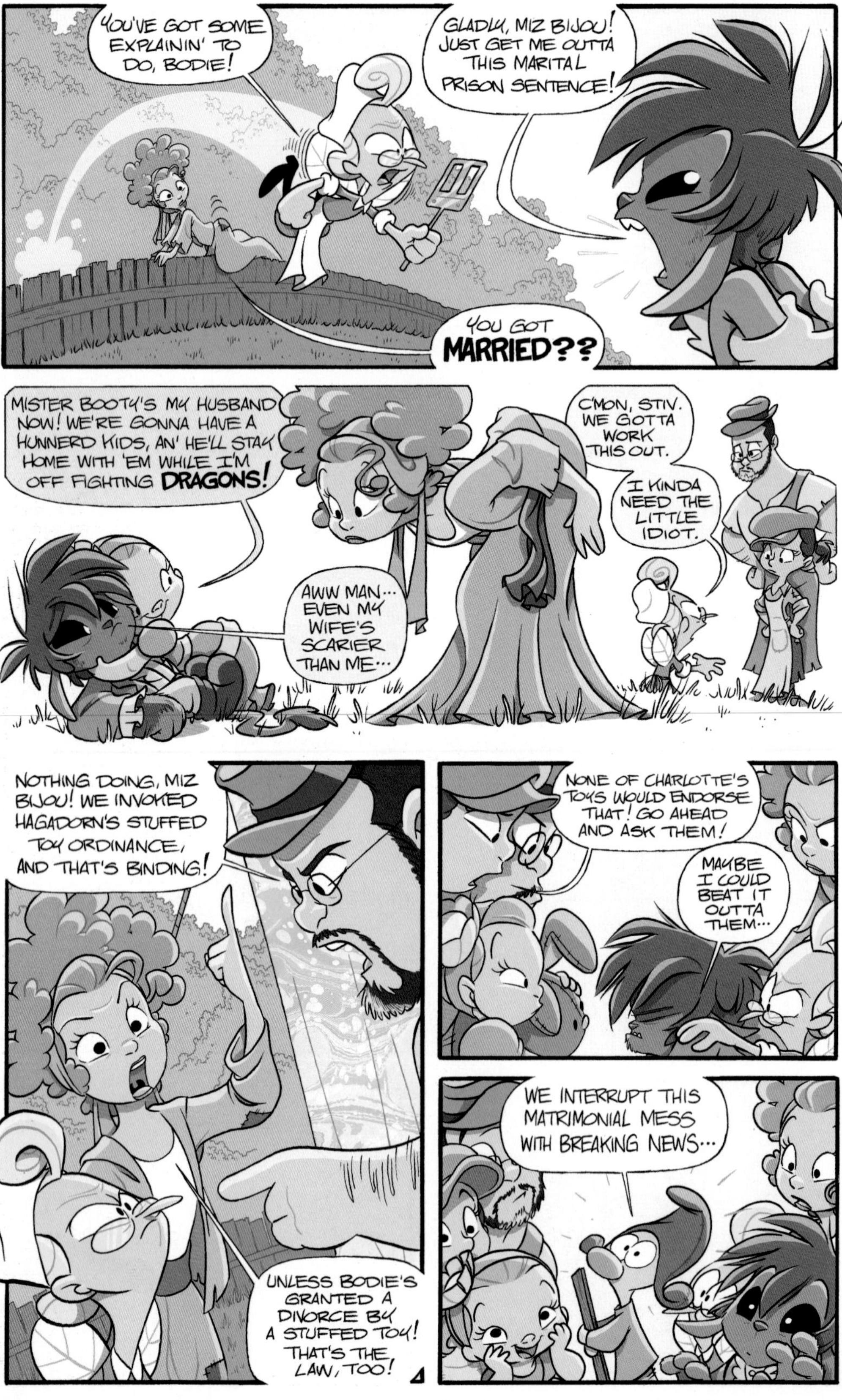
YOU'VE GOT SOME EXPLAININ' TO DO, BODIE!
GLADLY, MIZ BIJOU! JUST GET ME OUTTA THIS MARITAL PRISON SENTENCE!
YOU GOT MARRIED??
MISTER BOOTY'S MY HUSBAND NOW! WE'RE GONNA HAVE A HUNNERD KIDS, AN' HE'LL STAY HOME WITH 'EM WHILE I'M OFF FIGHTING DRAGONS!
AWW MAN... EVEN MY WIFE'S SCARIER THAN ME...
C'MON, STIV. WE GOTTA WORK THIS OUT.
I KINDA NEED THE LITTLE IDIOT.
NOTHING DOING, MIZ BIJOU! WE INVOKED HAGADORN'S STUFFED TOY ORDINANCE, AND THAT'S BINDING!
UNLESS BODIE'S GRANTED A DIVORCE BY A STUFFED TOY! THAT'S THE LAW, TOO!
NONE OF CHARLOTTE'S TOYS WOULD ENDORSE THAT! GO AHEAD AND ASK THEM!
MAYBE I COULD BEAT IT OUTTA THEM...
WE INTERRUPT THIS MATRIMONIAL MESS WITH BREAKING NEWS...

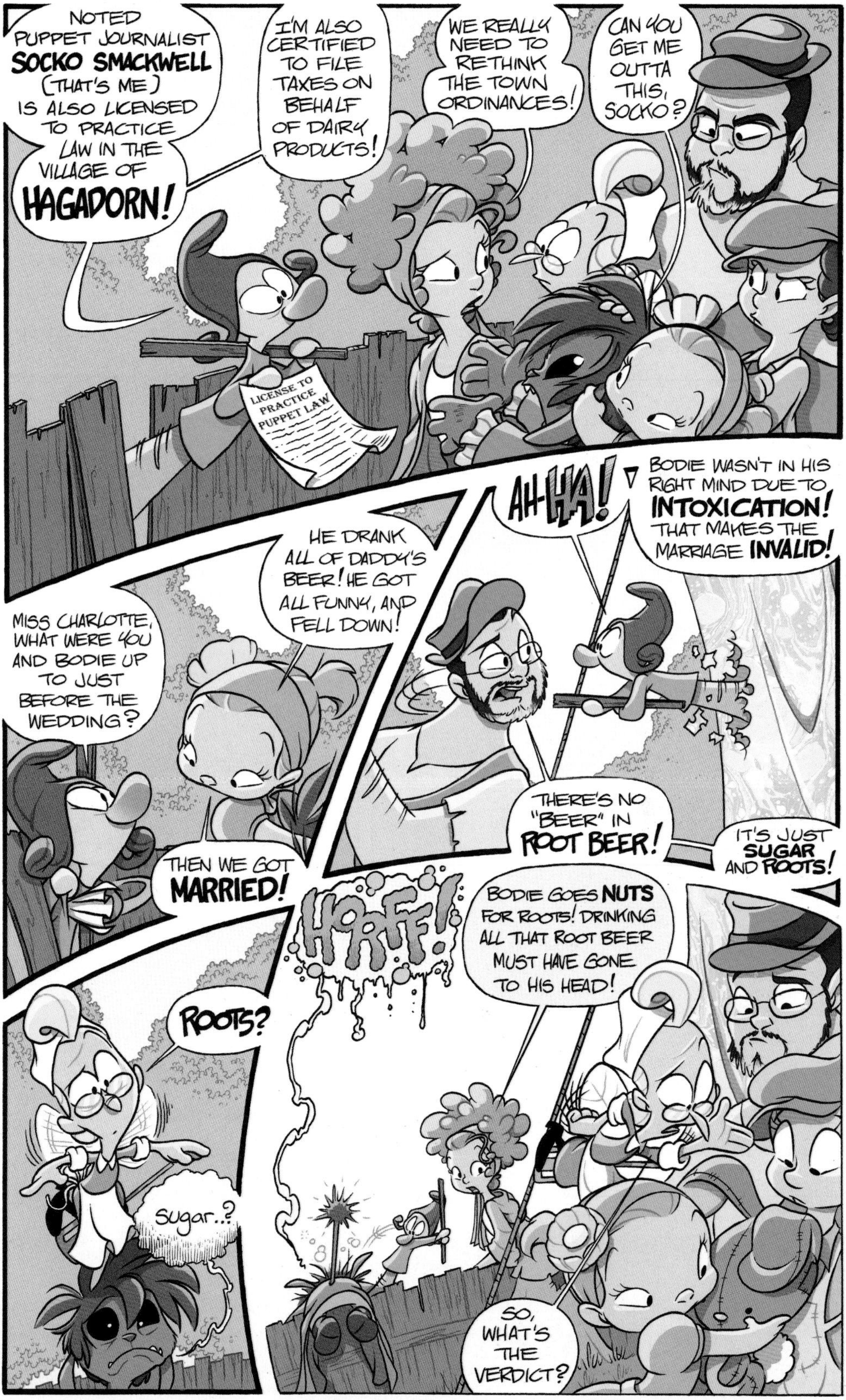
NOTED PUPPET JOURNALIST SOCKO SMACKWELL (THAT'S ME) IS ALSO LICENSED TO PRACTICE LAW IN THE VILLAGE OF HAGADORN!
I'M ALSO CERTIFIED TO FILE TAXES ON BEHALF OF DAIRY PRODUCTS!
WE REALLY NEED TO RETHINK THE TOWN ORDINANCES!
CAN YOU GET ME OUTTA THIS, SOCKO?
LICENSE TO PRACTICE PUPPET LAW
MISS CHARLOTTE, WHAT WERE YOU AND BODIE UP TO JUST BEFORE THE WEDDING?
HE DRANK ALL OF DADDY'S BEER! HE GOT ALL FUNNY, AND FELL DOWN!
THEN WE GOT MARRIED!
AH-HA!
BODIE WASN'T IN HIS RIGHT MIND DUE TO INTOXICATION! THAT MAKES THE MARRIAGE INVALID!
THERE'S NO "BEER" IN ROOT BEER!
IT'S JUST SUGAR AND ROOTS!
ROOTS?
sugar..?
HORFF!
BODIE GOES NUTS FOR ROOTS! DRINKING ALL THAT ROOT BEER MUST HAVE GONE TO HIS HEAD!
SO, WHAT'S THE VERDICT?

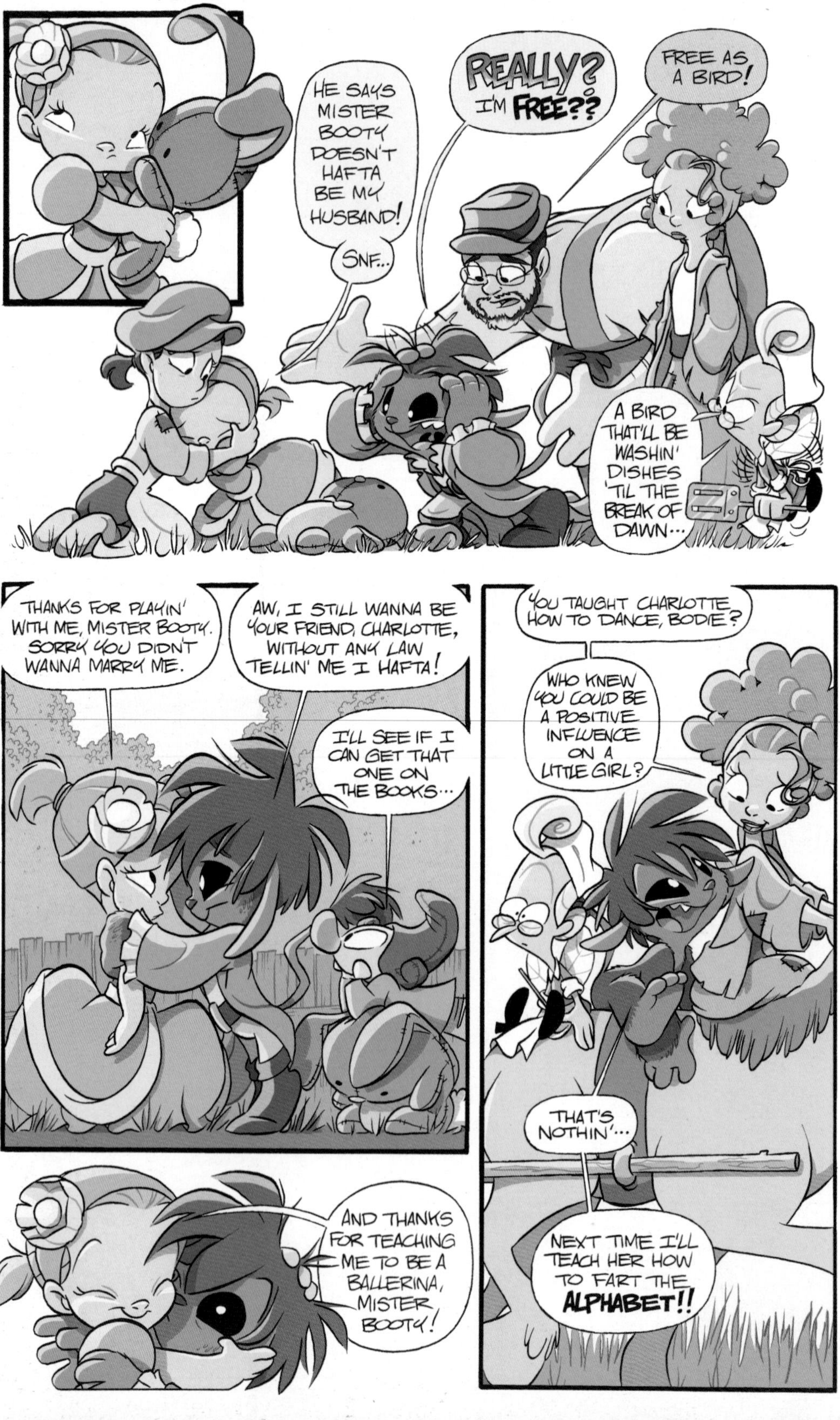

HE SAYS MISTER BOOTY DOESN'T HAFTA BE MY HUSBAND!
SNF...
REALLY? I'M FREE??
FREE AS A BIRD!
A BIRD THAT'LL BE WASHIN' DISHES 'TIL THE BREAK OF DAWN...
THANKS FOR PLAYIN' WITH ME, MISTER BOOTY. SORRY YOU DIDN'T WANNA MARRY ME.
AW, I STILL WANNA BE YOUR FRIEND, CHARLOTTE, WITHOUT ANY LAW TELLIN' ME I HAFTA!
I'LL SEE IF I CAN GET THAT ONE ON THE BOOKS...
AND THANKS FOR TEACHING ME TO BE A BALLERINA, MISTER BOOTY!
YOU TAUGHT CHARLOTTE HOW TO DANCE, BODIE?
WHO KNEW YOU COULD BE A POSITIVE INFLUENCE ON A LITTLE GIRL?
THAT'S NOTHIN'...
NEXT TIME I'LL TEACH HER HOW TO FART THE ALPHABET!!

CHAPTER 7
BAGGING A BODIE

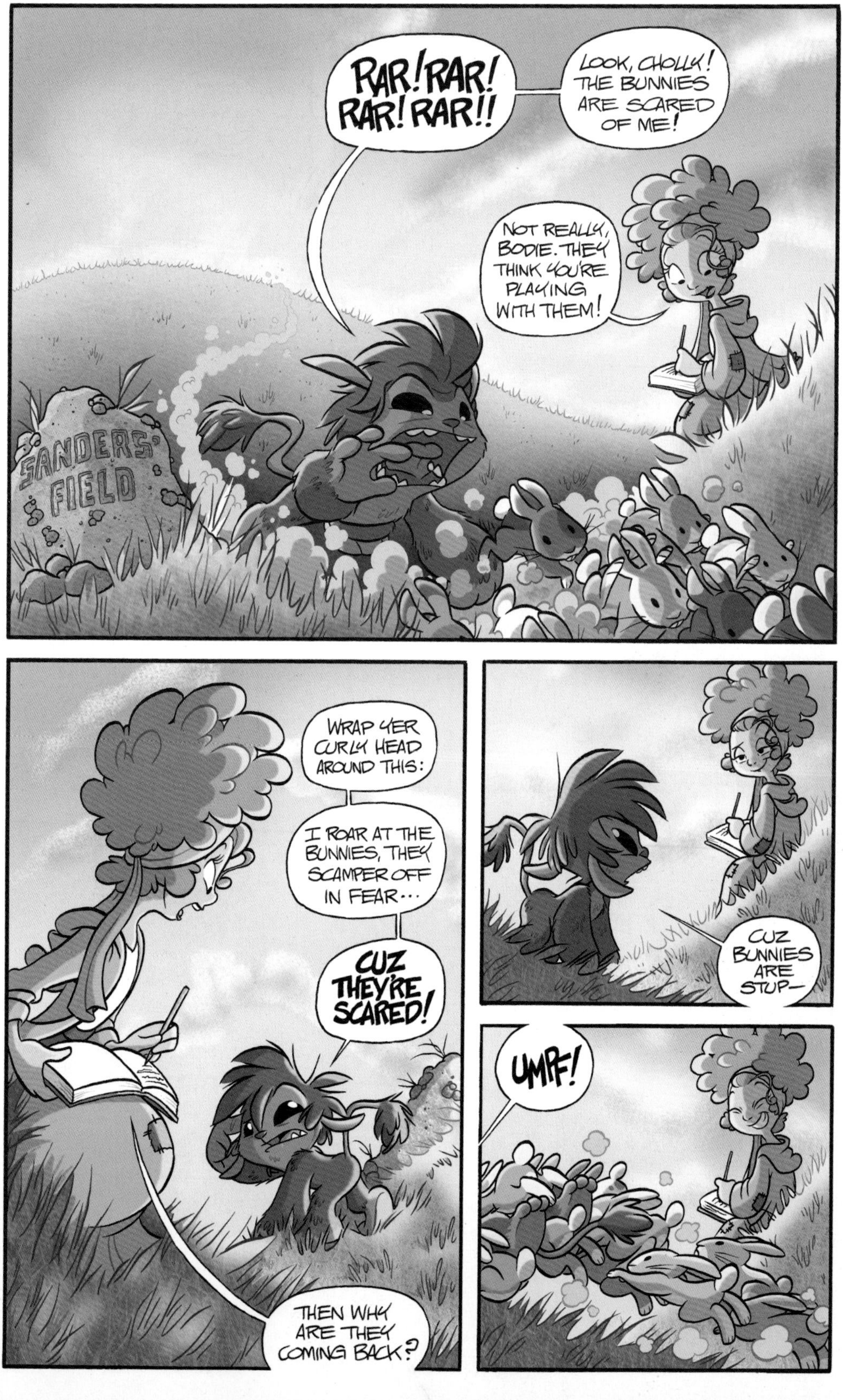
RAR! RAR! RAR! RAR!!
LOOK, CHOLLY! THE BUNNIES ARE SCARED OF ME!
NOT REALLY, BODIE. THEY THINK YOU'RE PLAYING WITH THEM!
SANDERS' FIELD
WRAP YER CURLY HEAD AROUND THIS:
I ROAR AT THE BUNNIES, THEY SCAMPER OFF IN FEAR...
CUZ THEY'RE SCARED!
THEN WHY ARE THEY COMING BACK?
CUZ BUNNIES ARE STUP—
UMPF!

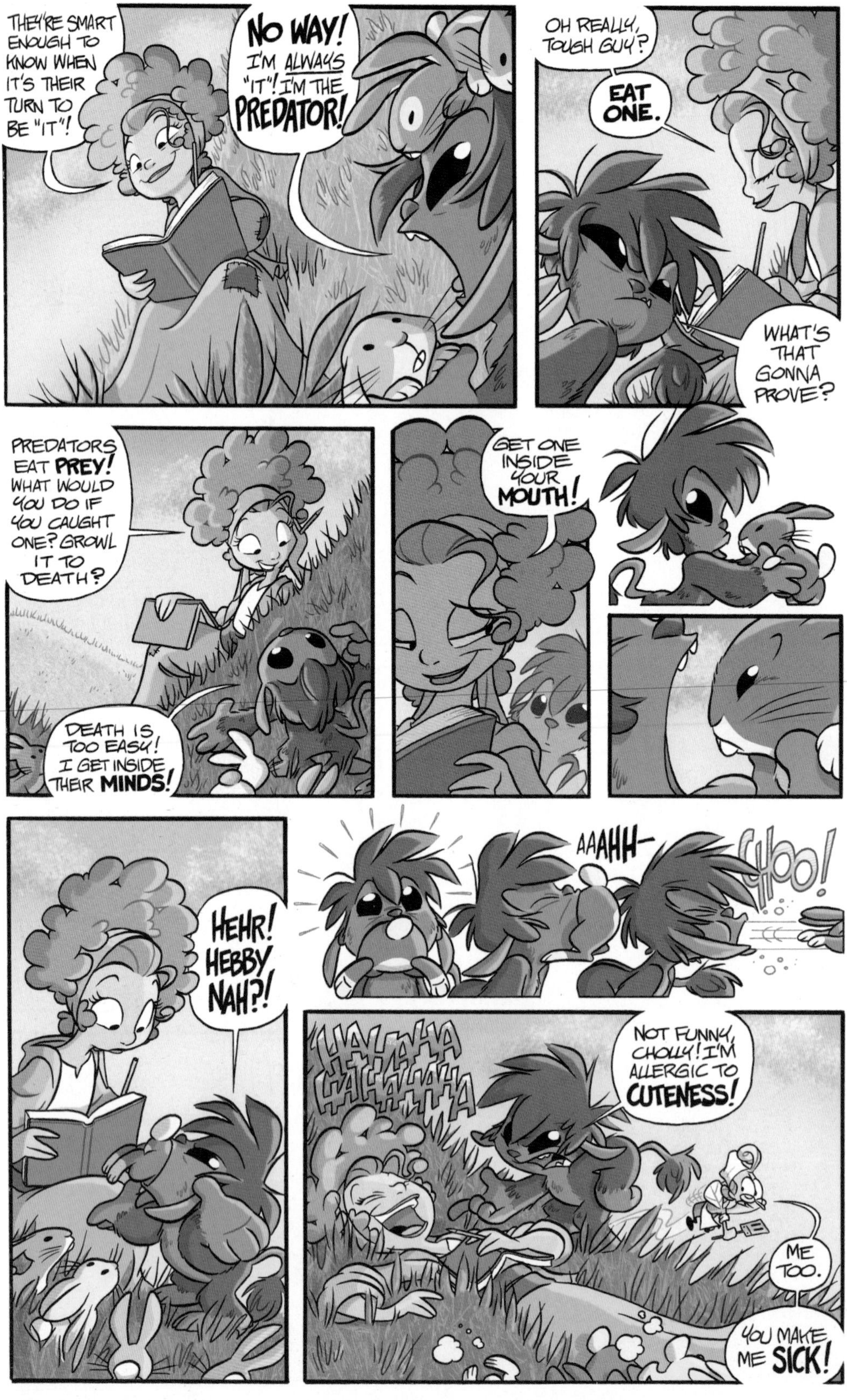

THEY'RE SMART ENOUGH TO KNOW WHEN IT'S THEIR TURN TO BE "IT"!
NO WAY! I'M ALWAYS "IT"! I'M THE PREDATOR!
OH REALLY, TOUGH GUY?
EAT ONE.
WHAT'S THAT GONNA PROVE?
PREDATORS EAT PREY! WHAT WOULD YOU DO IF YOU CAUGHT ONE? GROWL IT TO DEATH?
DEATH IS TOO EASY! I GET INSIDE THEIR MINDS!
GET ONE INSIDE YOUR MOUTH!
HEHR! HEBBY NAH?!
AAAHH-
CHOO!
HAHAHA HAHAHAHA
NOT FUNNY, CHOLLY! I'M ALLERGIC TO CUTENESS!
ME TOO.
YOU MAKE ME SICK!

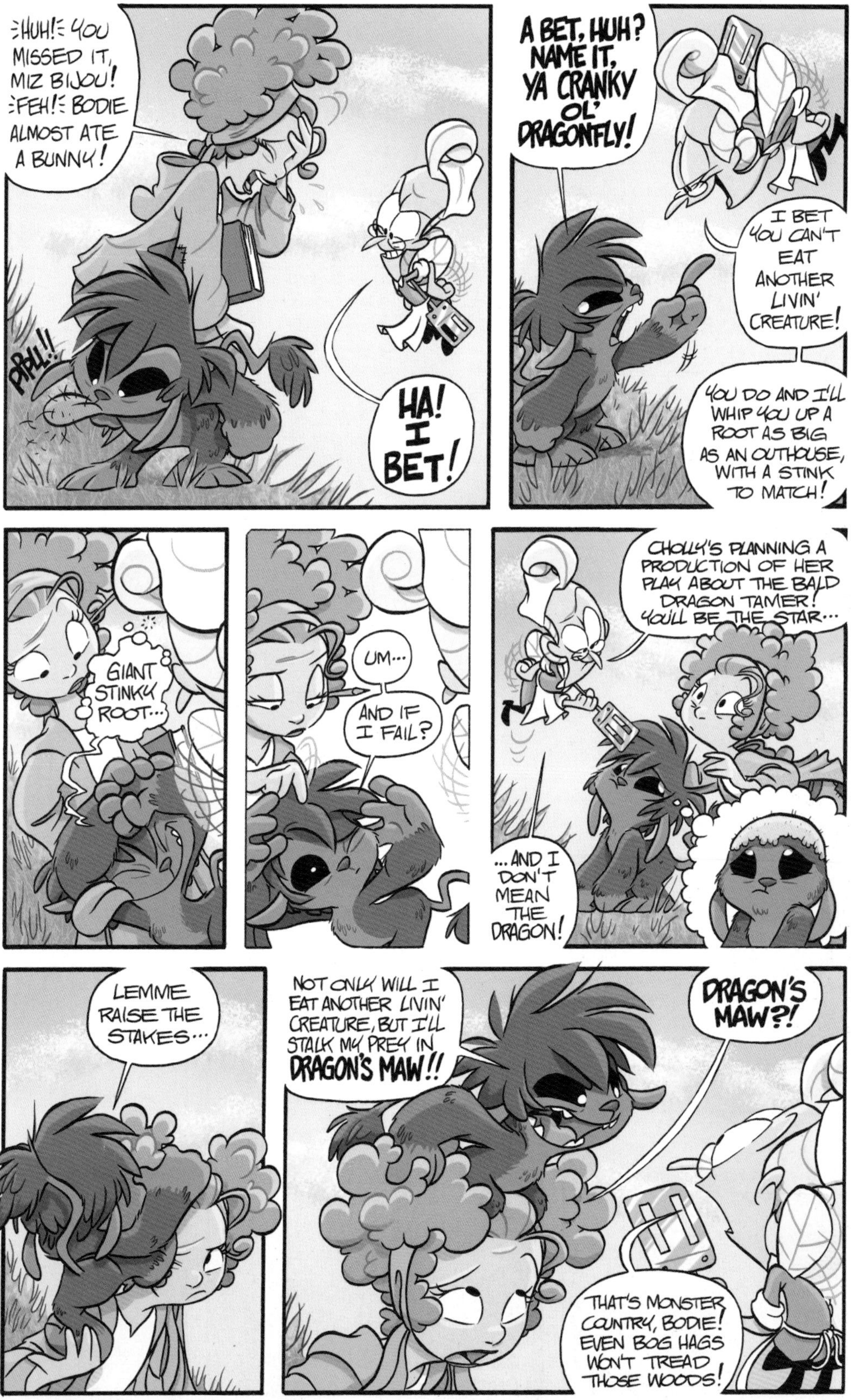

HUH! YOU MISSED IT, MIZ BIJOU! FEH! BODIE ALMOST ATE A BUNNY!
PPLL!!
HA! I BET!
A BET, HUH? NAME IT, YA CRANKY OL' DRAGONFLY!
I BET YOU CAN'T EAT ANOTHER LIVIN' CREATURE!
YOU DO AND I'LL WHIP YOU UP A ROOT AS BIG AS AN OUTHOUSE, WITH A STINK TO MATCH!
GIANT STINKY ROOT...
UM...
AND IF I FAIL?
CHOLLY'S PLANNING A PRODUCTION OF HER PLAY ABOUT THE BALD DRAGON TAMER! YOU'LL BE THE STAR...
...AND I DON'T MEAN THE DRAGON!
LEMME RAISE THE STAKES...
NOT ONLY WILL I EAT ANOTHER LIVIN' CREATURE, BUT I'LL STALK MY PREY IN DRAGON'S MAW!!
DRAGON'S MAW?!
THAT'S MONSTER COUNTRY, BODIE! EVEN BOG HAGS WON'T TREAD THOSE WOODS!

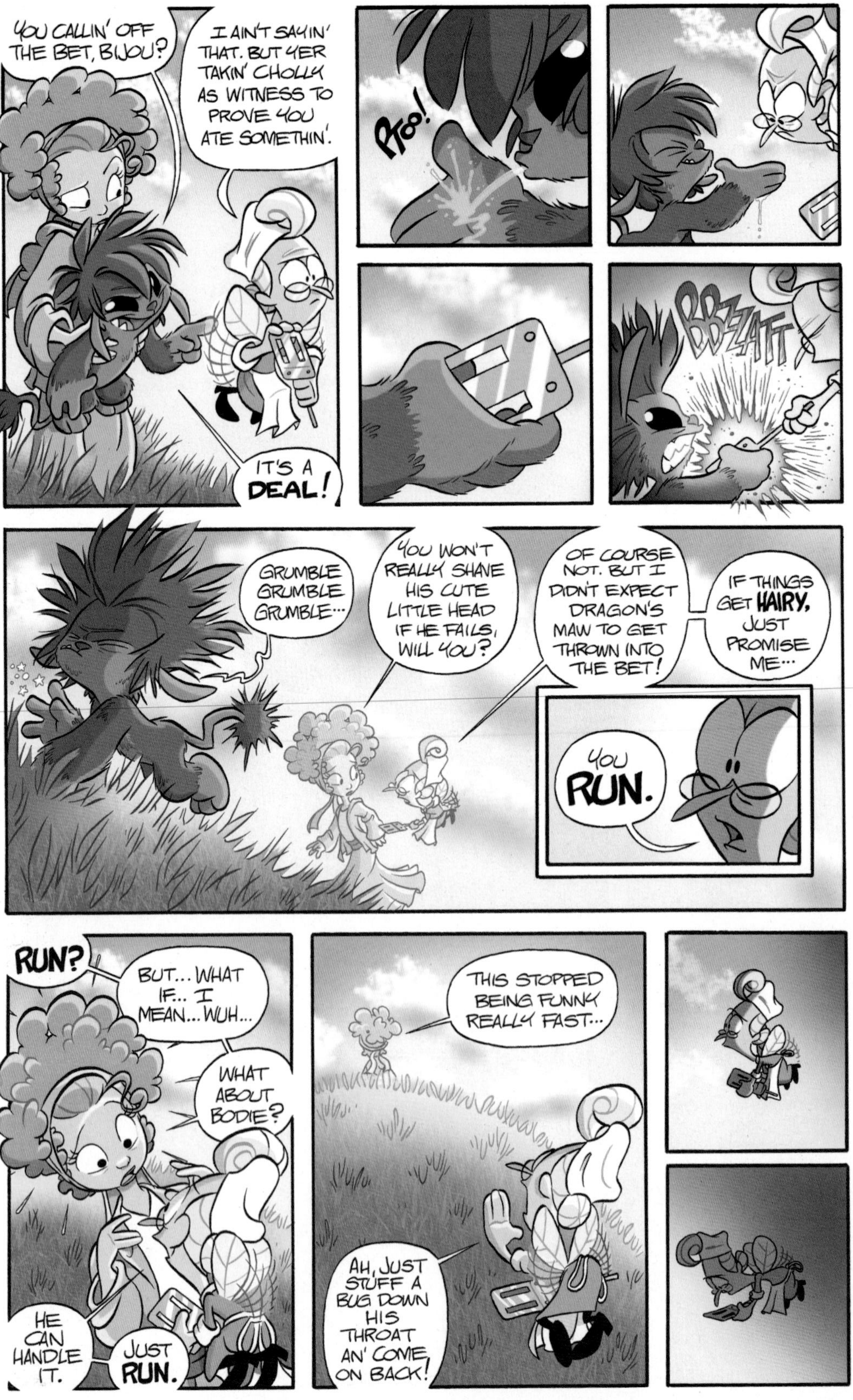
YOU CALLIN' OFF THE BET, BIJOU?
I AIN'T SAYIN' THAT. BUT YER TAKIN' CHOLLY AS WITNESS TO PROVE YOU ATE SOMETHIN'.
IT'S A DEAL!
PTOO!
BBZZAATT
GRUMBLE GRUMBLE GRUMBLE...
YOU WON'T REALLY SHAVE HIS CUTE LITTLE HEAD IF HE FAILS, WILL YOU?
OF COURSE NOT. BUT I DIDN'T EXPECT DRAGON'S MAW TO GET THROWN INTO THE BET!
IF THINGS GET HAIRY, JUST PROMISE ME...
YOU RUN.
RUN?
BUT... WHAT IF... I MEAN... WUH...
WHAT ABOUT BODIE?
HE CAN HANDLE IT.
JUST RUN.
THIS STOPPED BEING FUNNY REALLY FAST...
AH, JUST STUFF A BUG DOWN HIS THROAT AN' COME ON BACK!

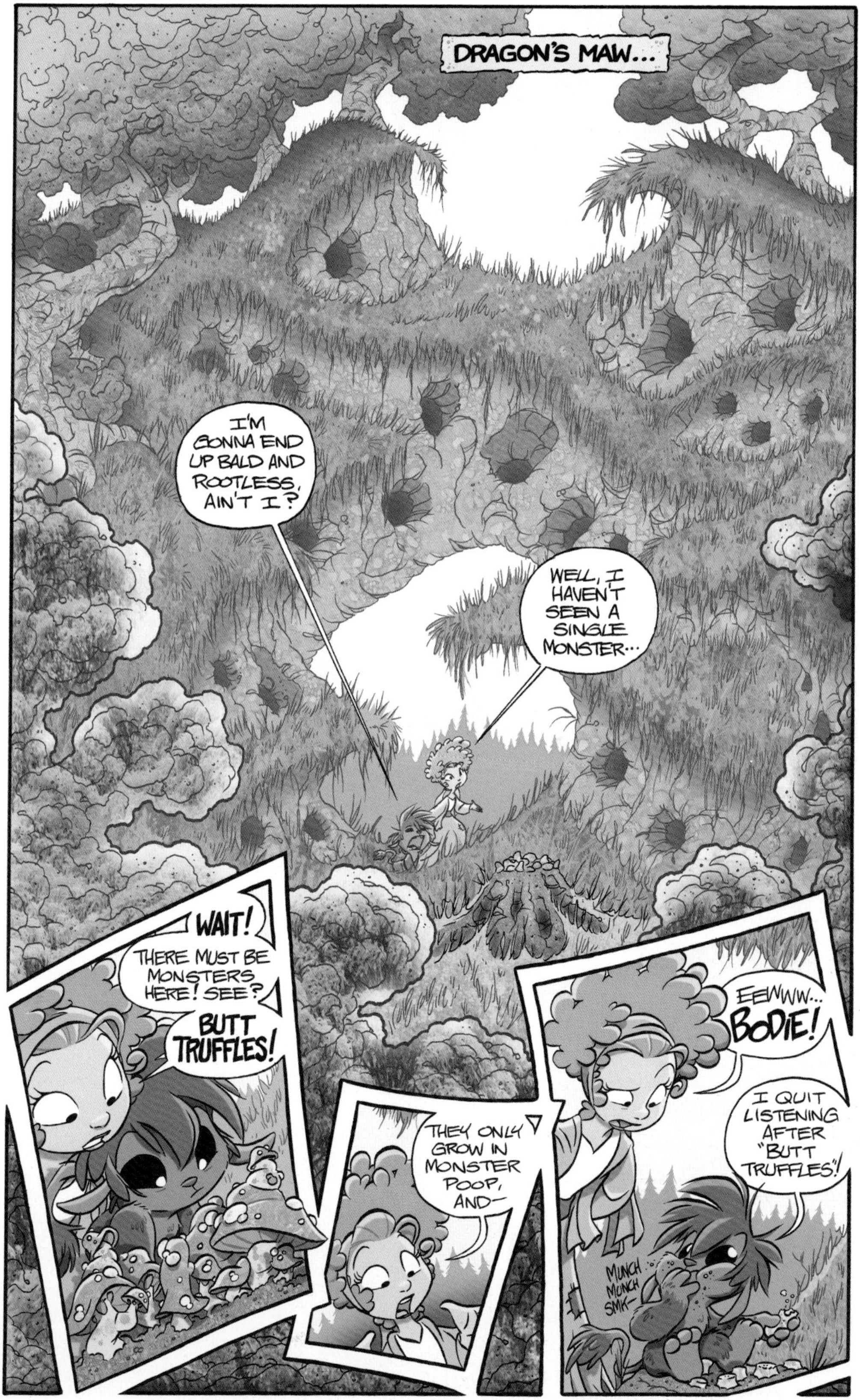
DRAGON'S MAW...
I'M GONNA END UP BALD AND ROOTLESS, AIN'T I?
WELL, I HAVEN'T SEEN A SINGLE MONSTER...
WAIT!
THERE MUST BE MONSTERS HERE! SEE?
BUTT TRUFFLES!
THEY ONLY GROW IN MONSTER POOP, AND—
EEWWW... BODIE!
I QUIT LISTENING AFTER "BUTT TRUFFLES"!
MUNCH MUNCH SMK—

KKRRAAK!

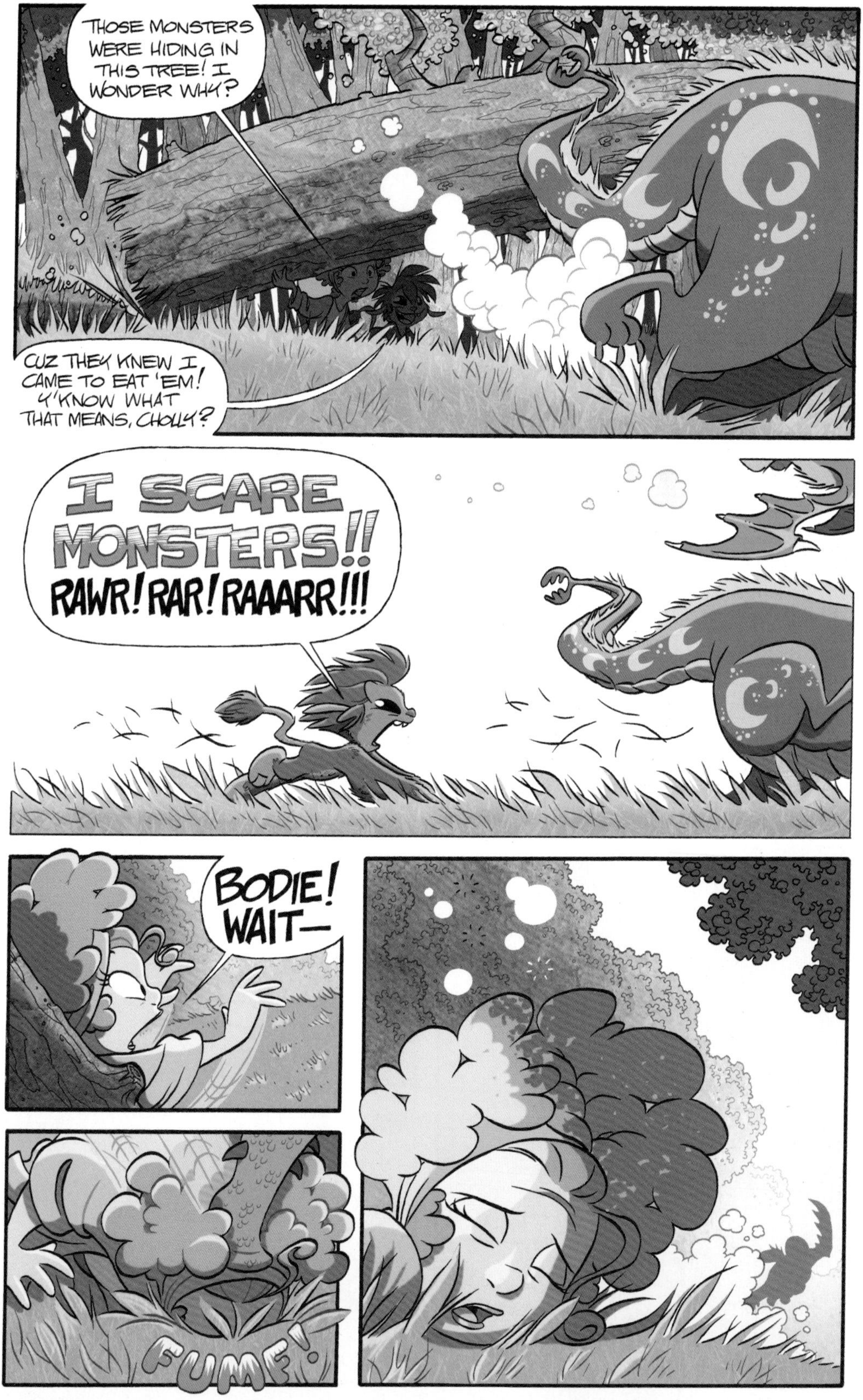
THOSE MONSTERS WERE HIDING IN THIS TREE! I WONDER WHY?
CUZ THEY KNEW I CAME TO EAT 'EM! Y'KNOW WHAT THAT MEANS, CHOLLY?
I SCARE MONSTERS!! RAWR! RAR! RAAARR!!!
BODIE! WAIT—
FUMF!

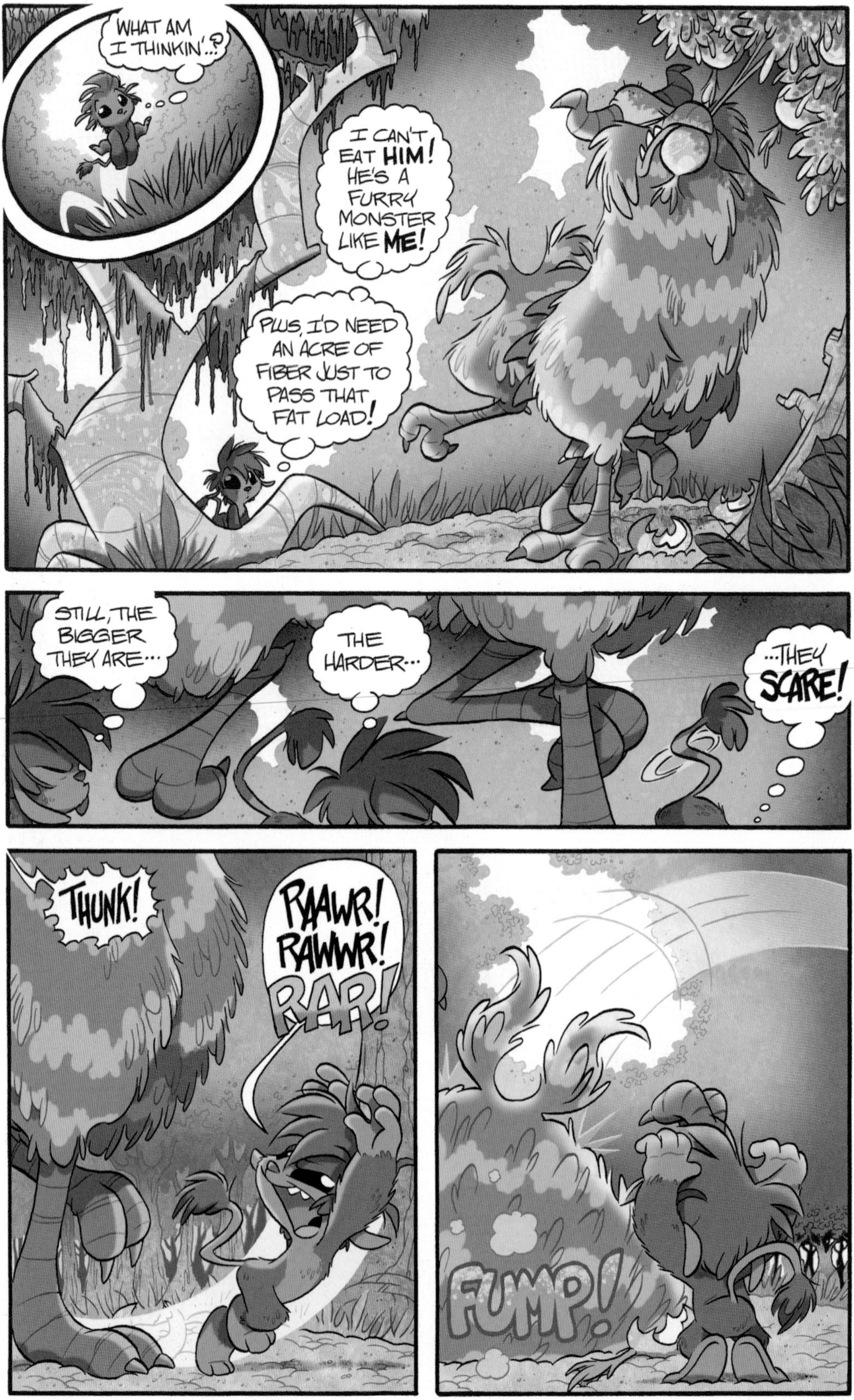
WHAT AM I THINKIN'...?
I CAN'T EAT HIM! HE'S A FURRY MONSTER LIKE ME!
PLUS, I'D NEED AN ACRE OF FIBER JUST TO PASS THAT FAT LOAD!
STILL, THE BIGGER THEY ARE...
THE HARDER...
...THEY SCARE!
THUNK!
RAAWR! RAWWR! RAR!
FUMP!

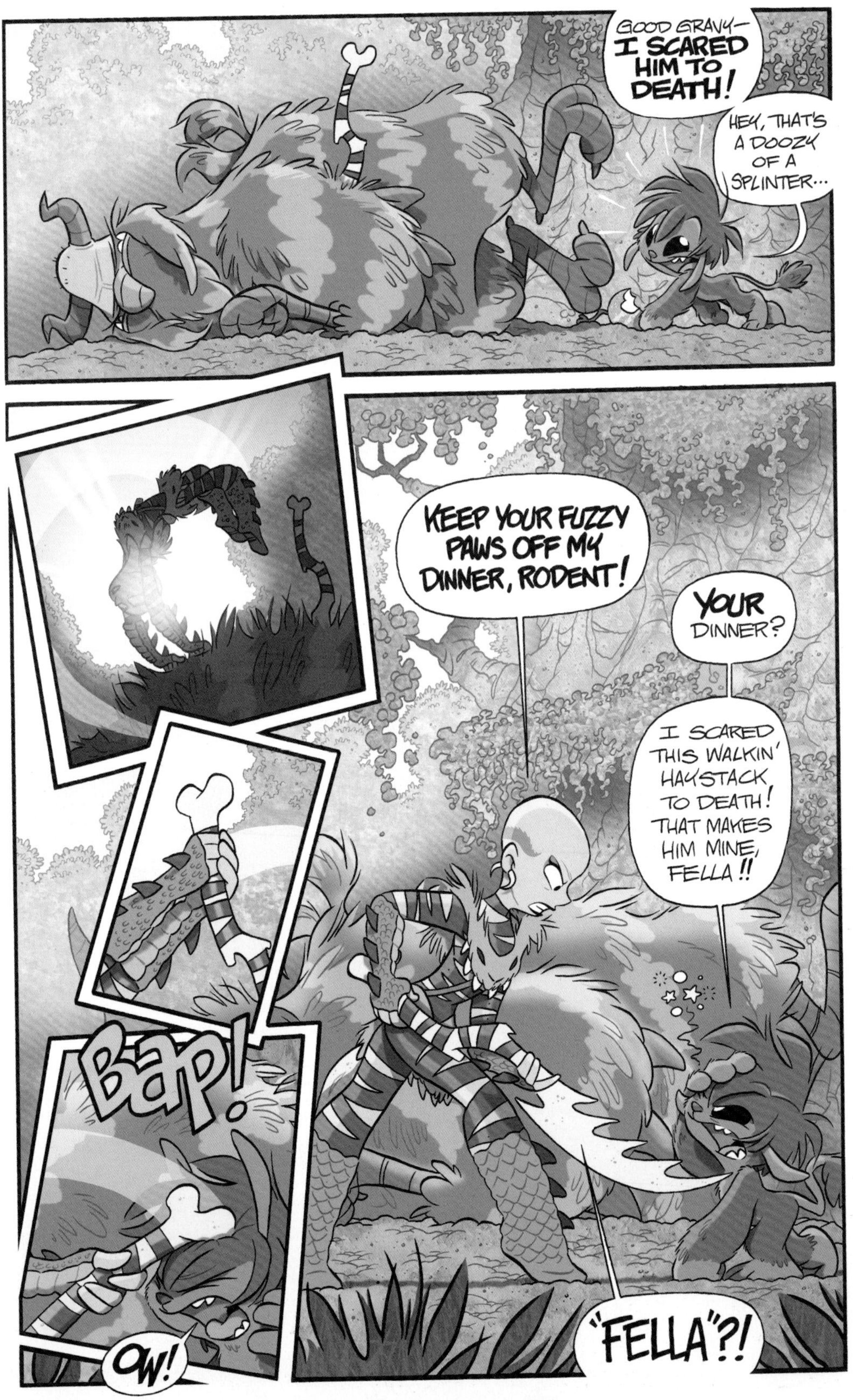
GOOD GRAVY— I SCARED HIM TO DEATH!
HEY, THAT'S A DOOZY OF A SPLINTER...
KEEP YOUR FUZZY PAWS OFF MY DINNER, RODENT!
YOUR DINNER?
I SCARED THIS WALKIN' HAYSTACK TO DEATH! THAT MAKES HIM MINE, FELLA!!
BLAP!
OW!
"FELLA"?!

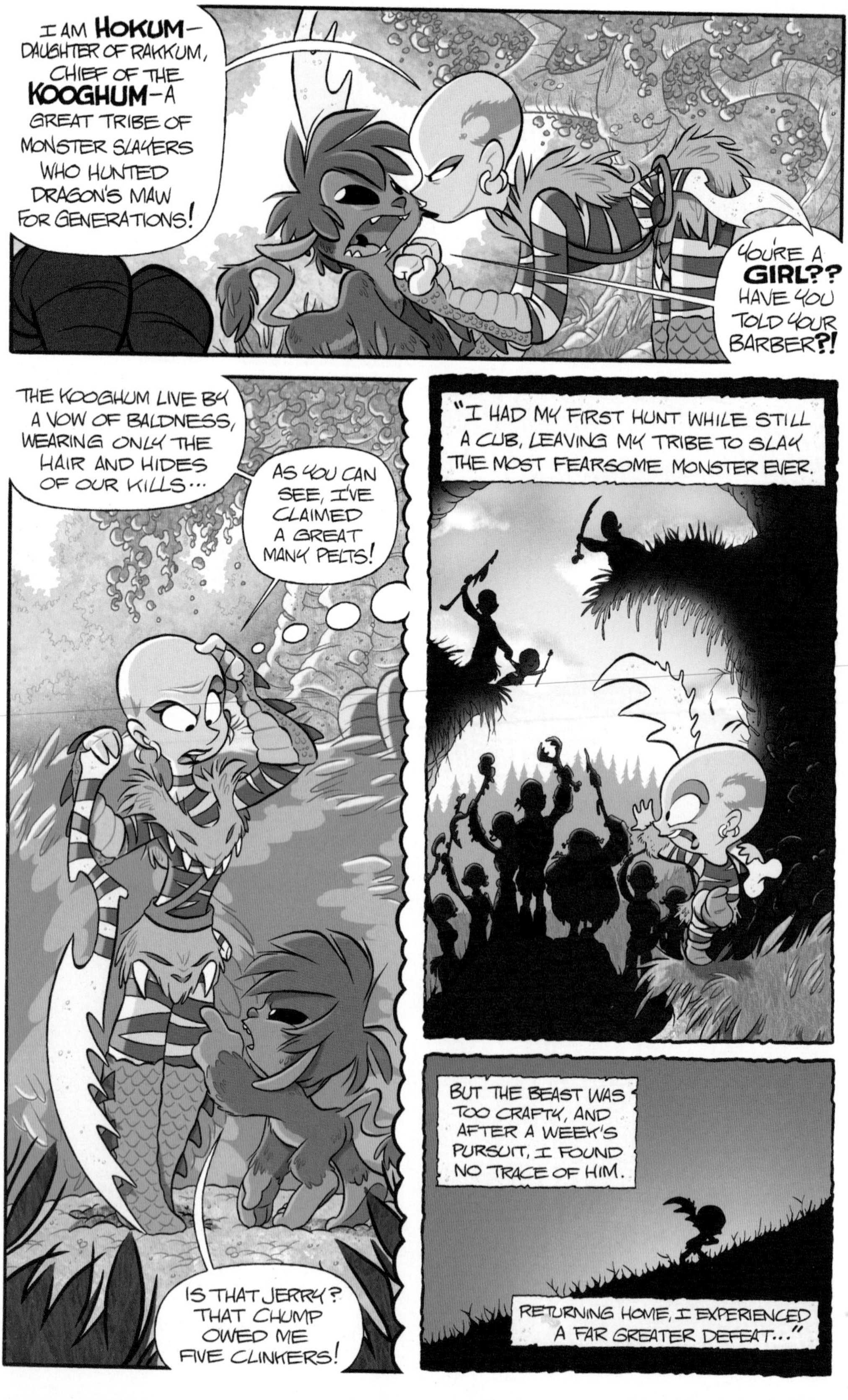
I AM HOKUM— DAUGHTER OF RAKKUM, CHIEF OF THE KOOGHUM—A GREAT TRIBE OF MONSTER SLAYERS WHO HUNTED DRAGON'S MAW FOR GENERATIONS!
YOU'RE A GIRL?? HAVE YOU TOLD YOUR BARBER?!
THE KOOGHUM LIVE BY A VOW OF BALDNESS, WEARING ONLY THE HAIR AND HIDES OF OUR KILLS...
AS YOU CAN SEE, I'VE CLAIMED A GREAT MANY PELTS!
IS THAT JERRY? THAT CHUMP OWED ME FIVE CLINKERS!
"I HAD MY FIRST HUNT WHILE STILL A CUB, LEAVING MY TRIBE TO SLAY THE MOST FEARSOME MONSTER EVER.
BUT THE BEAST WAS TOO CRAFTY, AND AFTER A WEEK'S PURSUIT, I FOUND NO TRACE OF HIM.
RETURNING HOME, I EXPERIENCED A FAR GREATER DEFEAT..."

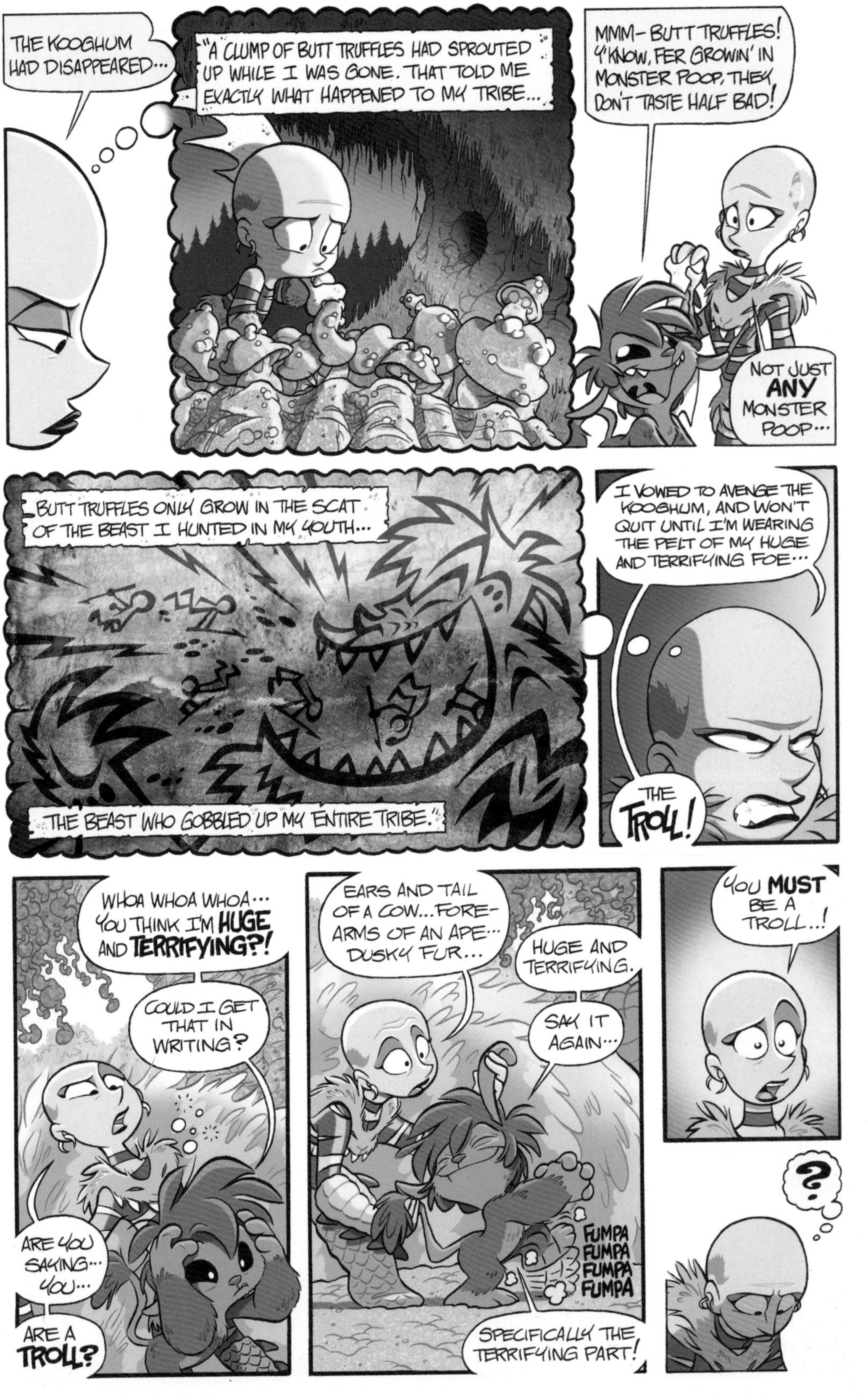
THE KOOGHUM HAD DISAPPEARED...
"A CLUMP OF BUTT TRUFFLES HAD SPROUTED UP WHILE I WAS GONE. THAT TOLD ME EXACTLY WHAT HAPPENED TO MY TRIBE...
MMM- BUTT TRUFFLES! Y'KNOW, FER GROWIN' IN MONSTER POOP, THEY DON'T TASTE HALF BAD!
NOT JUST ANY MONSTER POOP...
BUTT TRUFFLES ONLY GROW IN THE SCAT OF THE BEAST I HUNTED IN MY YOUTH...
...THE BEAST WHO GOBBLED UP MY ENTIRE TRIBE."
I VOWED TO AVENGE THE KOOGHUM, AND WON'T QUIT UNTIL I'M WEARING THE PELT OF MY HUGE AND TERRIFYING FOE...
THE TROLL!
WHOA WHOA WHOA... YOU THINK I'M HUGE AND TERRIFYING?!
COULD I GET THAT IN WRITING?
ARE YOU SAYING... YOU...
ARE A TROLL?
EARS AND TAIL OF A COW... FORE-ARMS OF AN APE... DUSKY FUR...
HUGE AND TERRIFYING.
SAY IT AGAIN...
FUMPA FUMPA FUMPA FUMPA
SPECIFICALLY THE TERRIFYING PART!
YOU MUST BE A TROLL...!
?

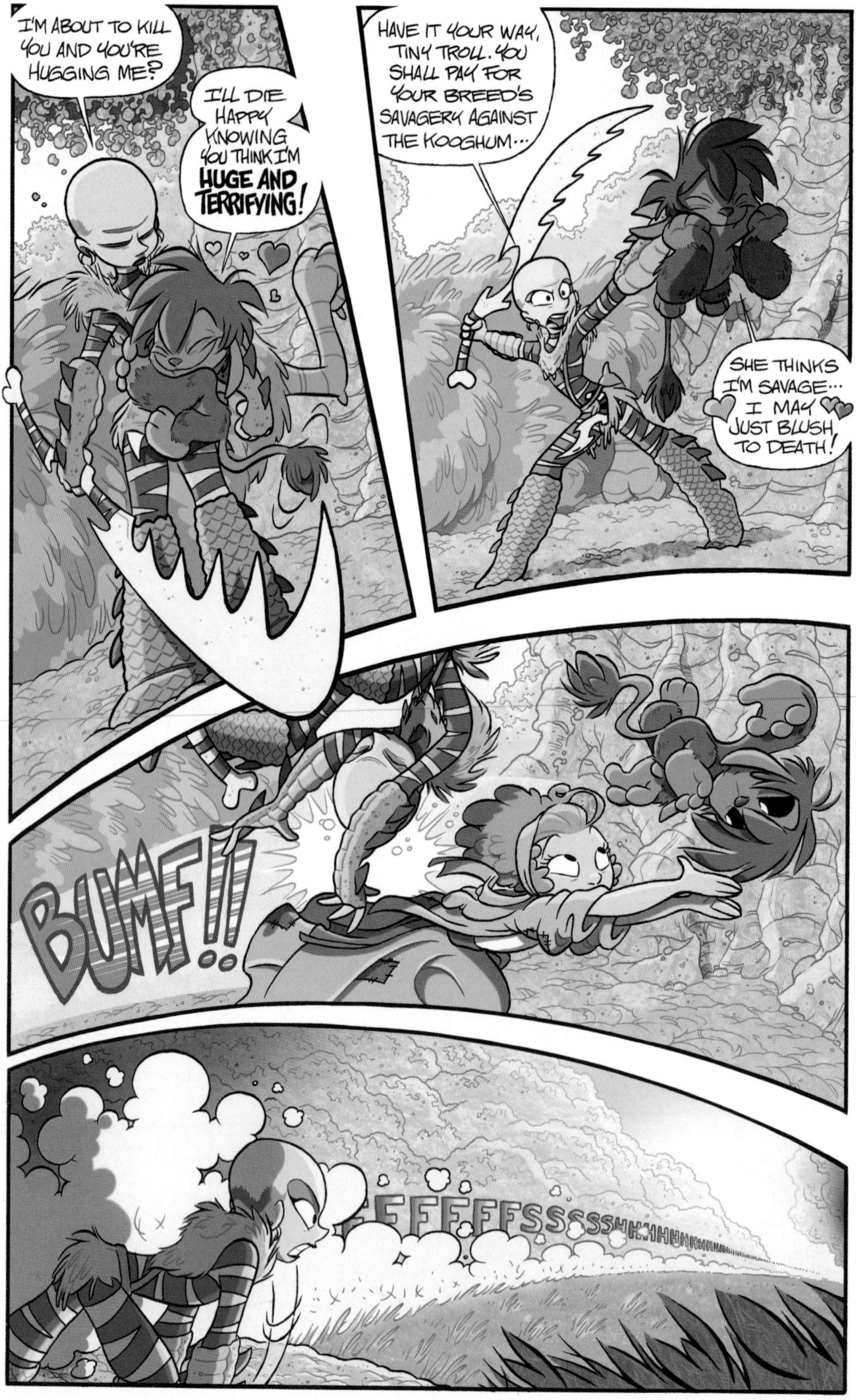
I'M ABOUT TO KILL YOU AND YOU'RE HUGGING ME?
I'LL DIE HAPPY KNOWING YOU THINK I'M HUGE AND TERRIFYING!
HAVE IT YOUR WAY, TINY TROLL. YOU SHALL PAY FOR YOUR BREED'S SAVAGERY AGAINST THE KOOGHUM...
SHE THINKS I'M SAVAGE... I MAY JUST BLUSH TO DEATH!
BUMF!!
FFFFFFFSSSSSSHHHHHHHHH

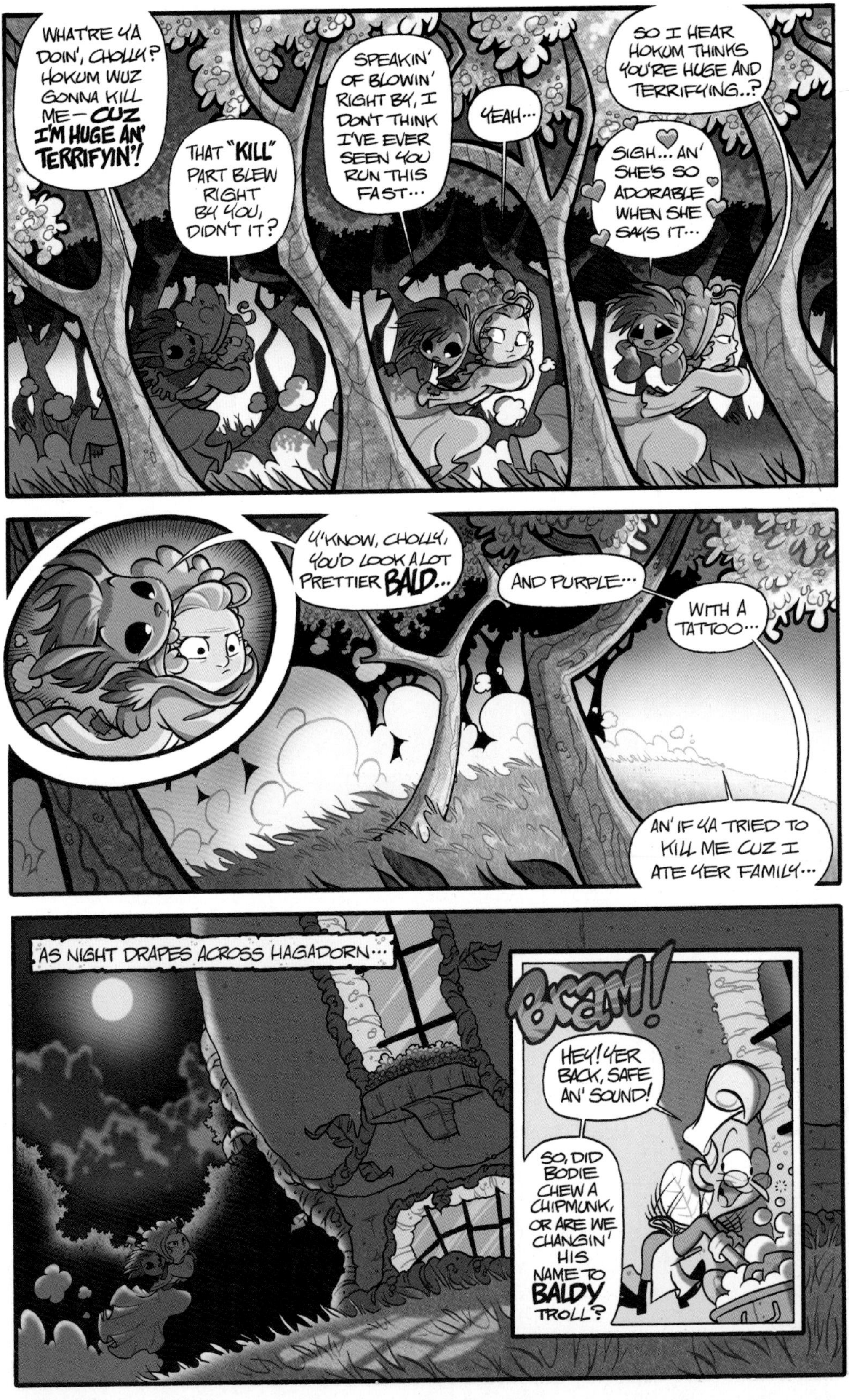
WHAT'RE YA DOIN', CHOLLY? HOKUM WUZ GONNA KILL ME— CUZ I'M HUGE AN' TERRIFYIN'!
THAT "KILL" PART BLEW RIGHT BY YOU, DIDN'T IT?
SPEAKIN' OF BLOWIN' RIGHT BY, I DON'T THINK I'VE EVER SEEN YOU RUN THIS FAST...
YEAH...
SO I HEAR HOKUM THINKS YOU'RE HUGE AND TERRIFYING...?
SIGH... AN' SHE'S SO ADORABLE WHEN SHE SAYS IT...
Y'KNOW, CHOLLY, YOU'D LOOK A LOT PRETTIER BALD...
AND PURPLE...
WITH A TATTOO...
AN' IF YA TRIED TO KILL ME CUZ I ATE YER FAMILY...
AS NIGHT DRAPES ACROSS HAGADORN...
BSCLAM!
HEY! YER BACK, SAFE AN' SOUND!
SO, DID BODIE CHEW A CHIPMUNK, OR ARE WE CHANGIN' HIS NAME TO BALDY TROLL?

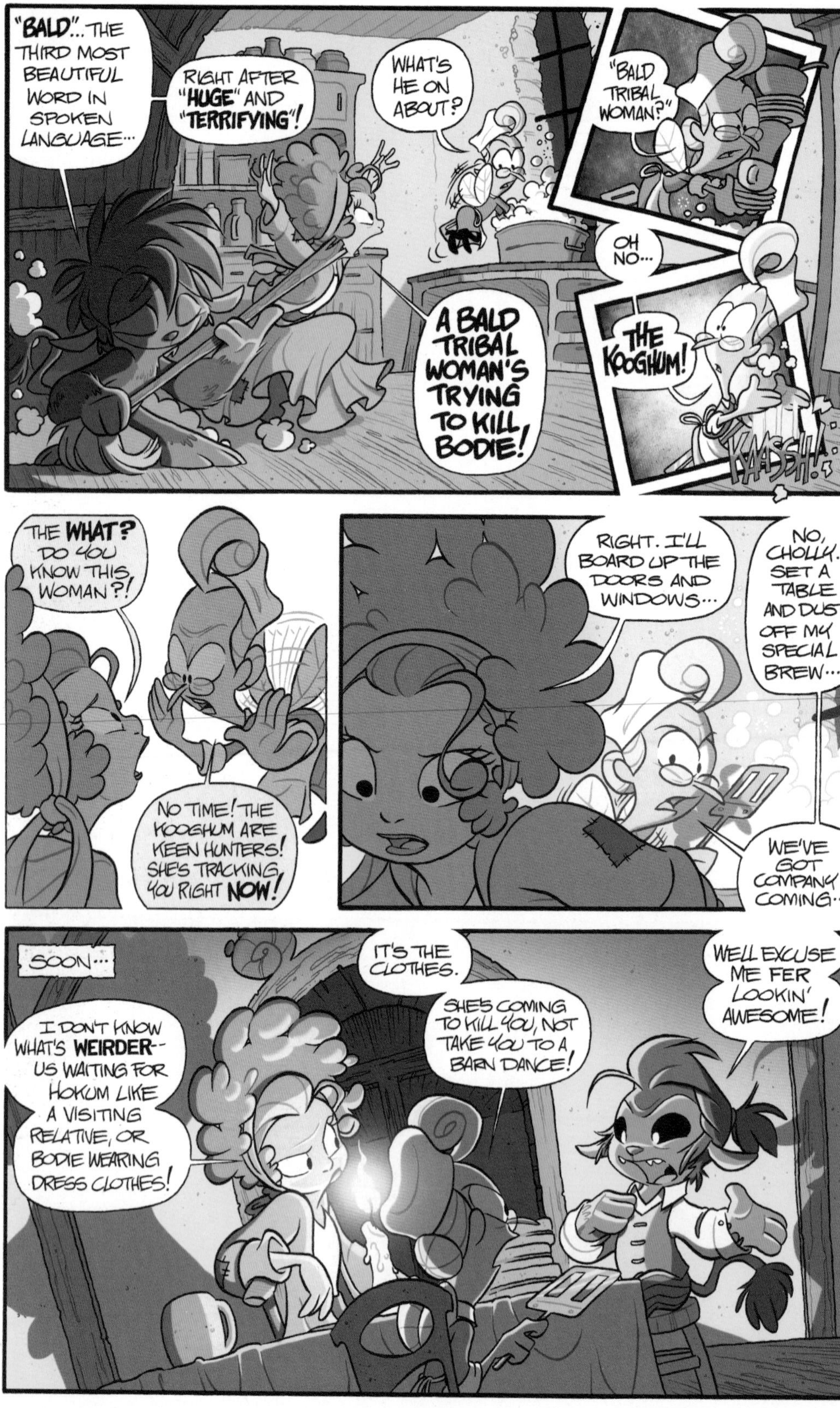
"BALD"... THE THIRD MOST BEAUTIFUL WORD IN SPOKEN LANGUAGE...
RIGHT AFTER "HUGE" AND "TERRIFYING"!
WHAT'S HE ON ABOUT?
A BALD TRIBAL WOMAN'S TRYING TO KILL BODIE!
"BALD TRIBAL WOMAN?"
OH NO...
THE KOOGHUM!
KAASSH!
THE WHAT? DO YOU KNOW THIS WOMAN?!
NO TIME! THE KOOGHUM ARE KEEN HUNTERS! SHE'S TRACKING YOU RIGHT NOW!
RIGHT. I'LL BOARD UP THE DOORS AND WINDOWS...
NO, CHOLLY. SET A TABLE AND DUST OFF MY SPECIAL BREW...
WE'VE GOT COMPANY COMING...
SOON...
I DON'T KNOW WHAT'S WEIRDER-- US WAITING FOR HOKUM LIKE A VISITING RELATIVE, OR BODIE WEARING DRESS CLOTHES!
IT'S THE CLOTHES.
SHE'S COMING TO KILL YOU, NOT TAKE YOU TO A BARN DANCE!
WELL EXCUSE ME FER LOOKIN' AWESOME!

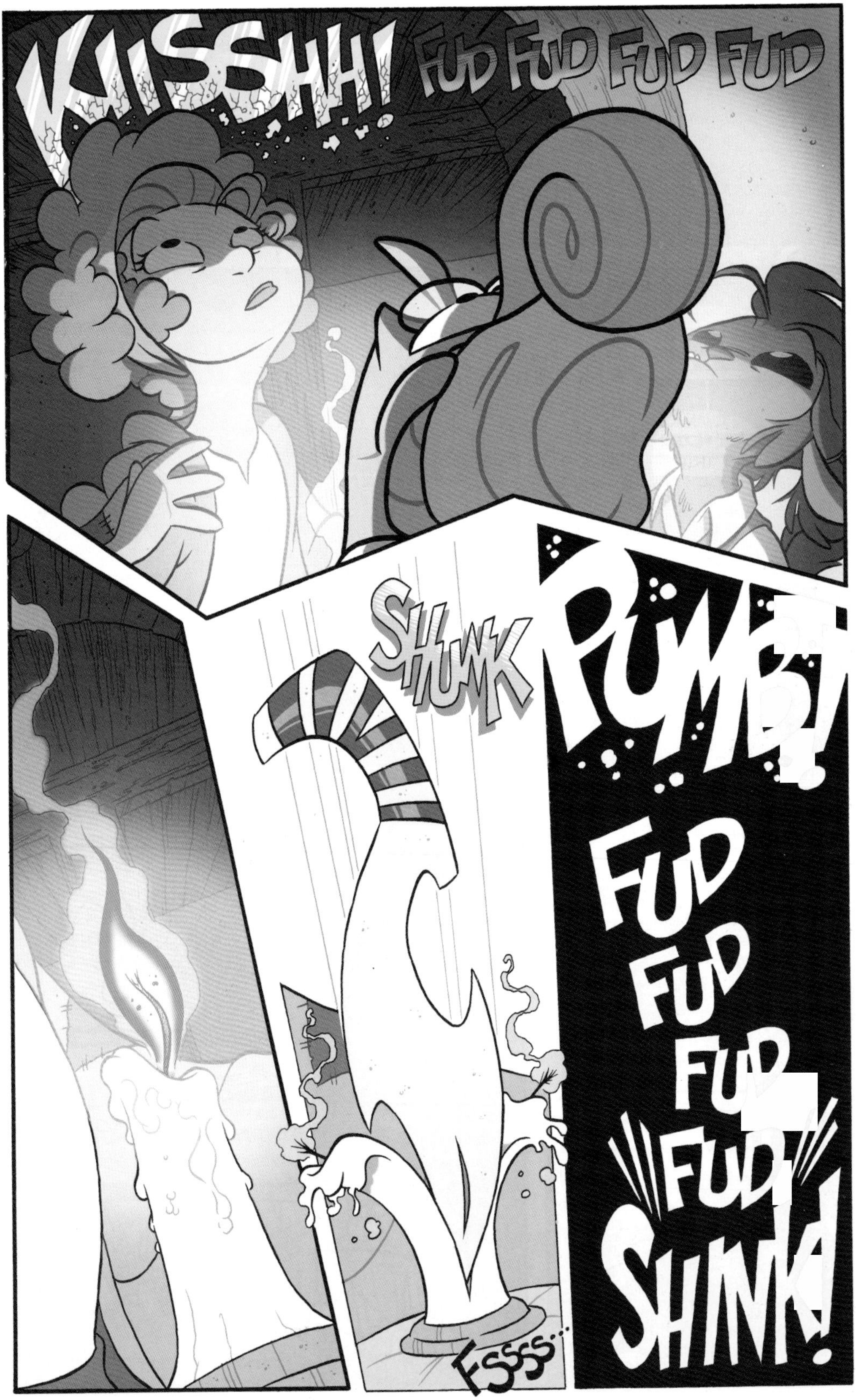
KKISSHH!
FUD FUD FUD FUD
SHUNK
PUM
FUD
FUD
FUD
FUD
SHINK!
FSSSS...

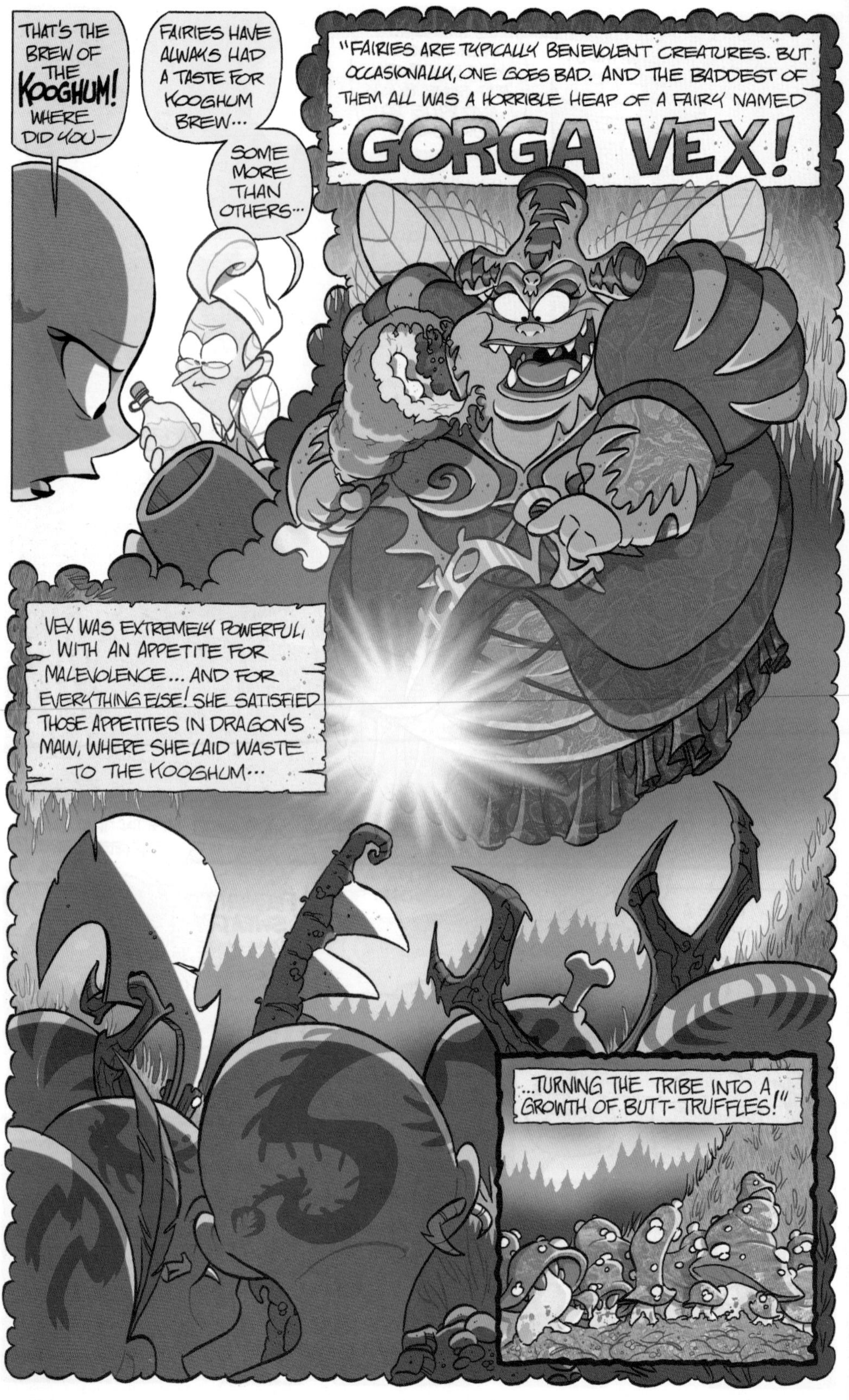
THAT'S THE BREW OF THE KOOGHUM! WHERE DID YOU—
FAIRIES HAVE ALWAYS HAD A TASTE FOR KOOGHUM BREW...
SOME MORE THAN OTHERS...
"FAIRIES ARE TYPICALLY BENEVOLENT CREATURES. BUT OCCASIONALLY, ONE GOES BAD. AND THE BADDEST OF THEM ALL WAS A HORRIBLE HEAP OF A FAIRY NAMED
GORGA VEX!
VEX WAS EXTREMELY POWERFUL, WITH AN APPETITE FOR MALEVOLENCE... AND FOR EVERYTHING ELSE! SHE SATISFIED THOSE APPETITES IN DRAGON'S MAW, WHERE SHE LAID WASTE TO THE KOOGHUM...
...TURNING THE TRIBE INTO A GROWTH OF BUTT-TRUFFLES!"

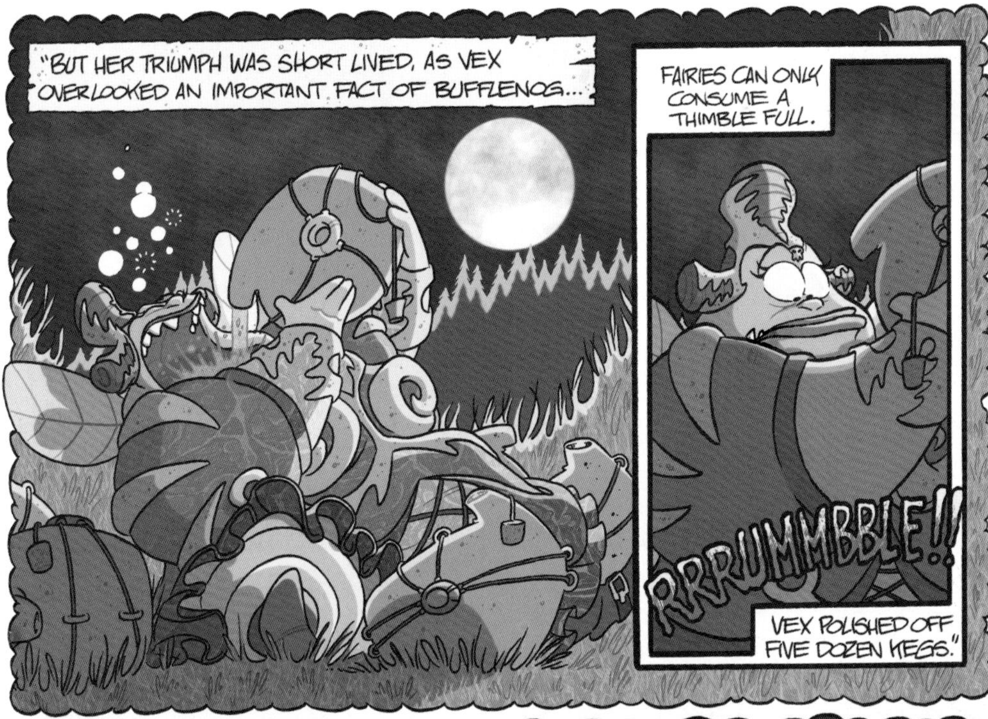
"BUT HER TRIUMPH WAS SHORT LIVED, AS VEX OVERLOOKED AN IMPORTANT FACT OF BUFFLENOG...
FAIRIES CAN ONLY CONSUME A THIMBLE FULL.
RRRUMMBBLE!!
VEX POLISHED OFF FIVE DOZEN KEGS."

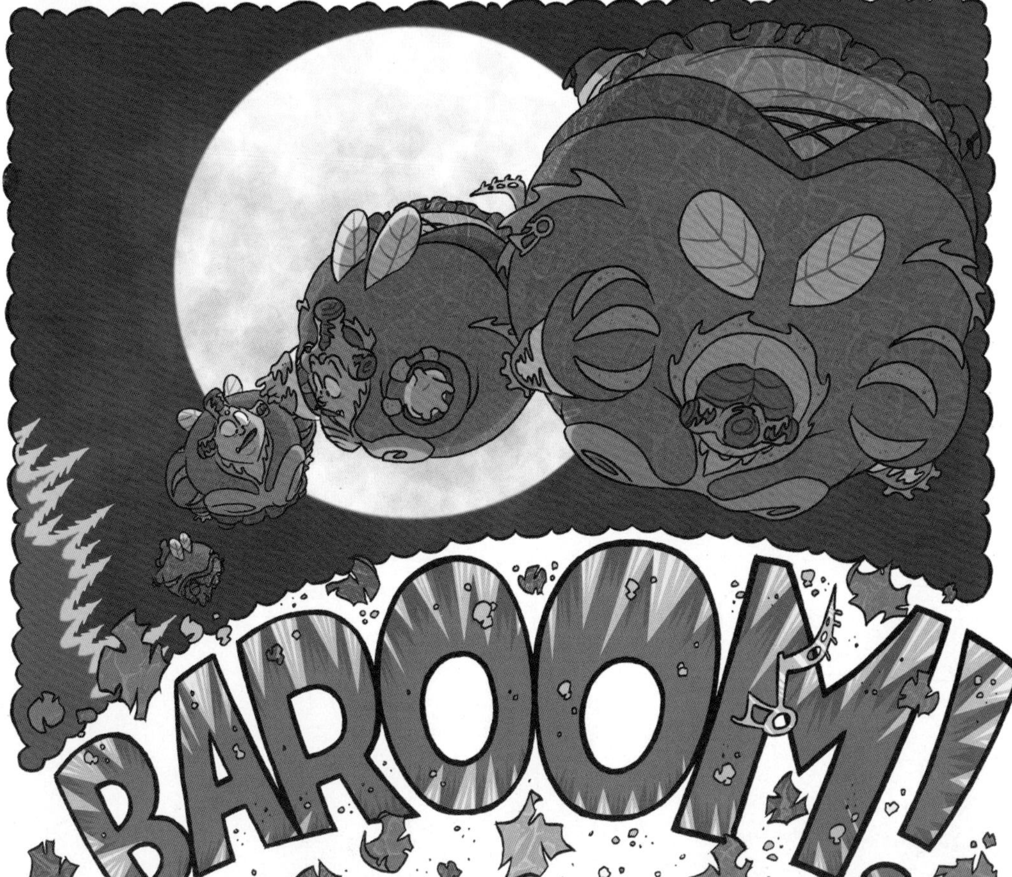
BAROOOM!

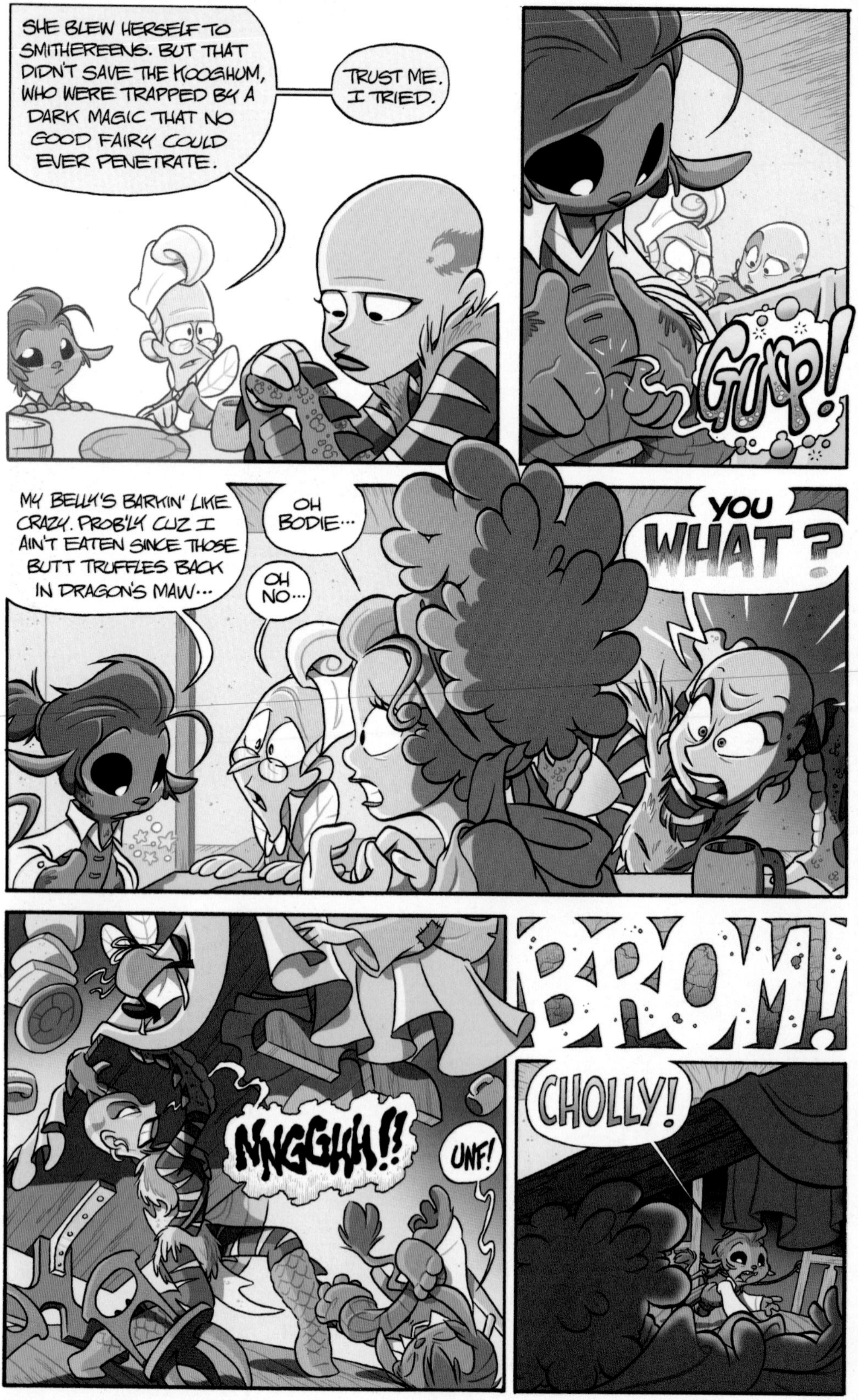

SHE BLEW HERSELF TO SMITHEREENS. BUT THAT DIDN'T SAVE THE KOOGHUM, WHO WERE TRAPPED BY A DARK MAGIC THAT NO GOOD FAIRY COULD EVER PENETRATE.
TRUST ME. I TRIED.
GUMP!
MY BELLY'S BARKIN' LIKE CRAZY. PROB'LY CUZ I AIN'T EATEN SINCE THOSE BUTT TRUFFLES BACK IN DRAGON'S MAW...
OH BODIE...
OH NO...
YOU WHAT?
BROM!
NNGGHH!!
UNF!
CHOLLY!

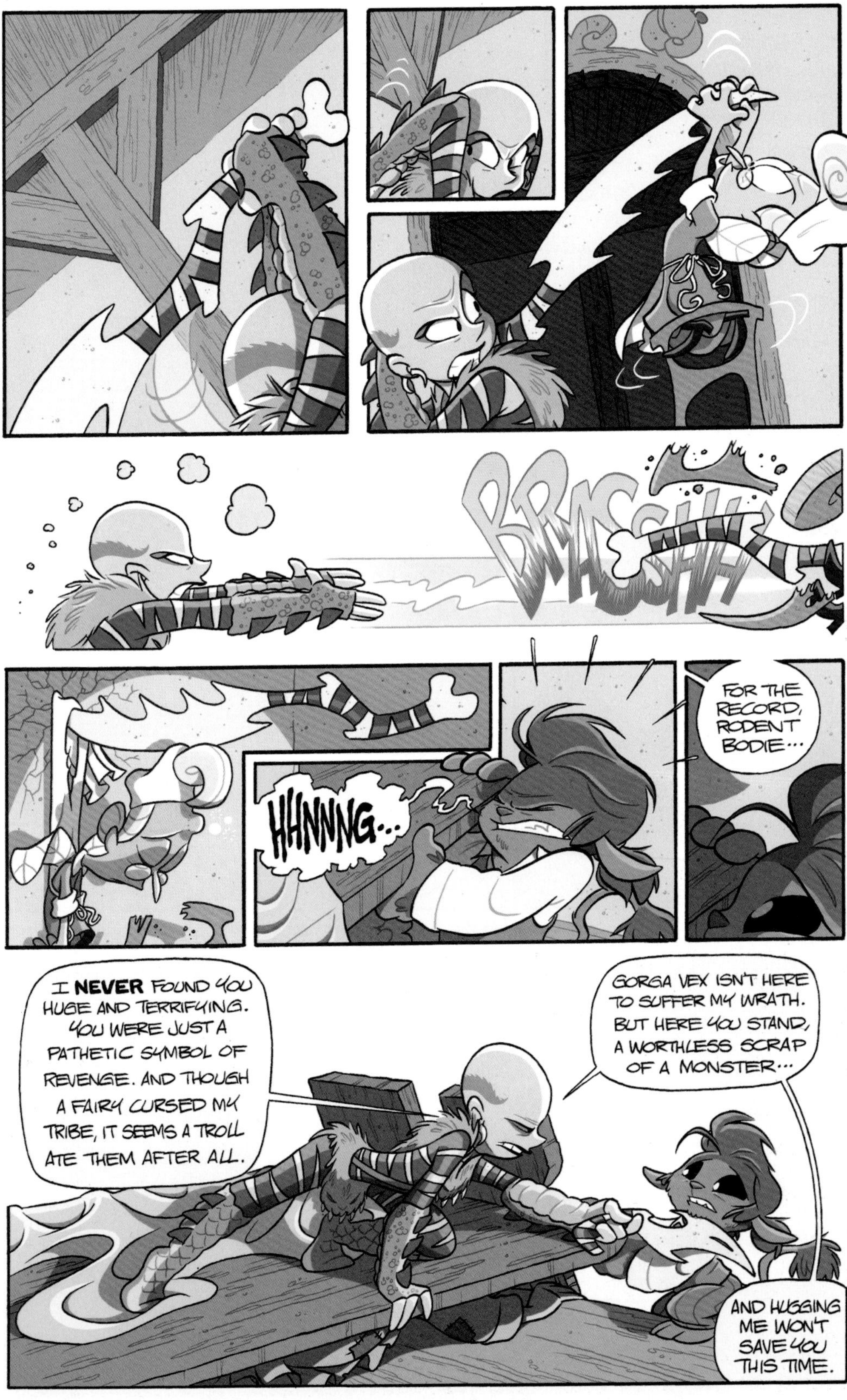
BRASSHH
HHNNNG...
FOR THE RECORD, RODENT BODIE...
I NEVER FOUND YOU HUGE AND TERRIFYING. YOU WERE JUST A PATHETIC SYMBOL OF REVENGE. AND THOUGH A FAIRY CURSED MY TRIBE, IT SEEMS A TROLL ATE THEM AFTER ALL.
GORGA VEX ISN'T HERE TO SUFFER MY WRATH. BUT HERE YOU STAND, A WORTHLESS SCRAP OF A MONSTER...
AND HUGGING ME WON'T SAVE YOU THIS TIME.

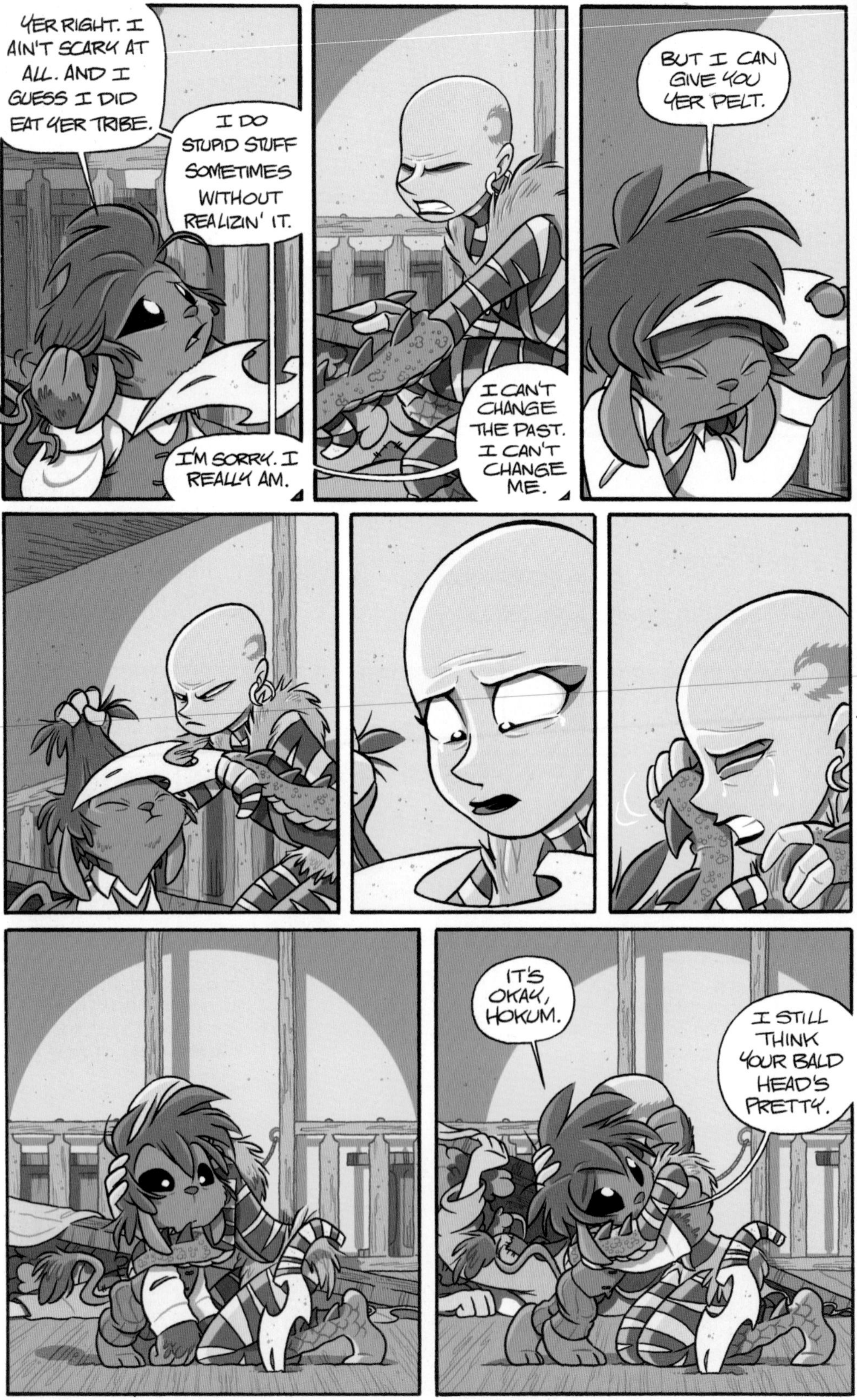
YER RIGHT. I AIN'T SCARY AT ALL. AND I GUESS I DID EAT YER TRIBE.
I DO STUPID STUFF SOMETIMES WITHOUT REALIZIN' IT.
I'M SORRY. I REALLY AM.
I CAN'T CHANGE THE PAST. I CAN'T CHANGE ME.
BUT I CAN GIVE YOU YER PELT.
IT'S OKAY, HOKUM.
I STILL THINK YOUR BALD HEAD'S PRETTY.

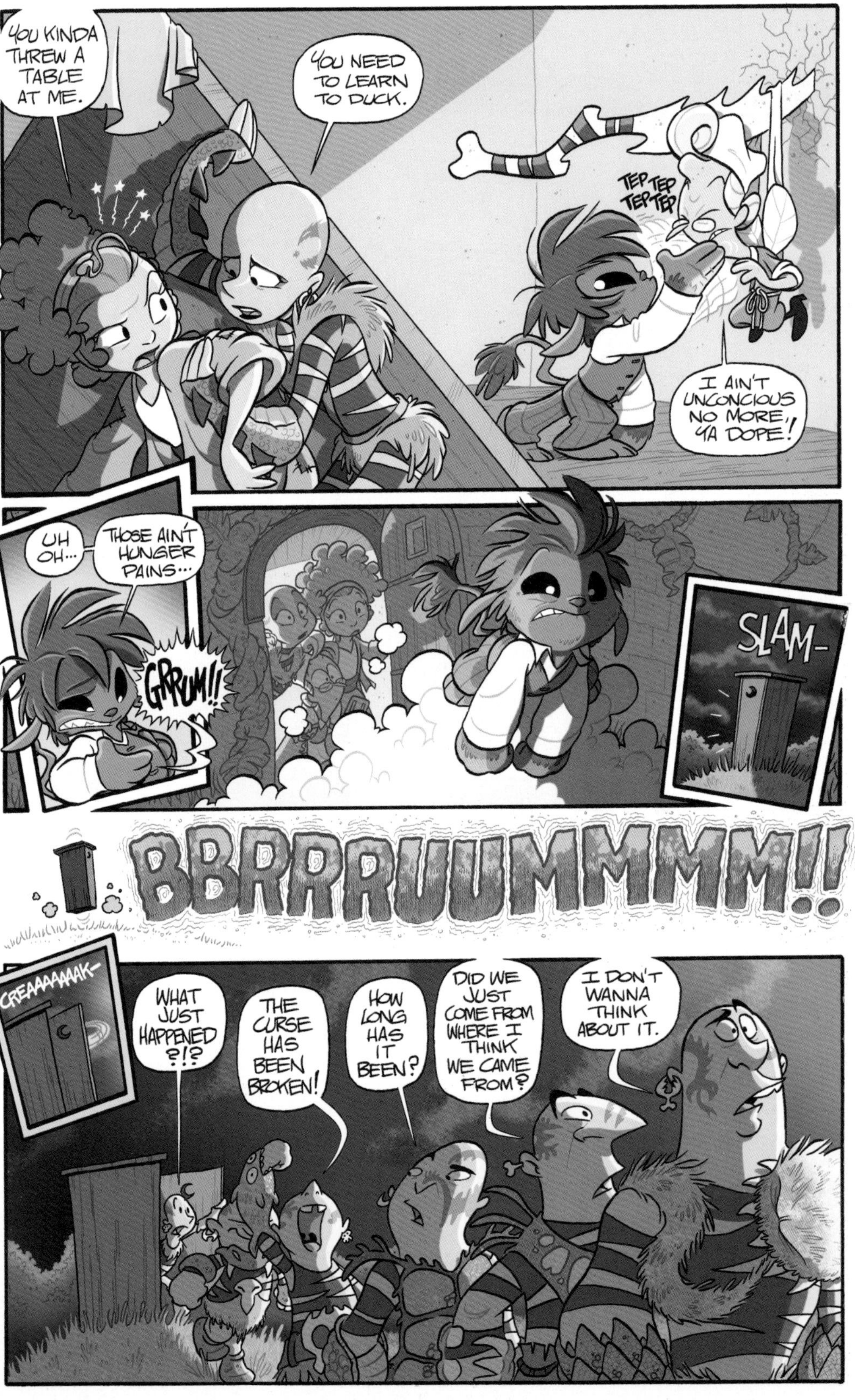

YOU KINDA THREW A TABLE AT ME.
YOU NEED TO LEARN TO DUCK.
TEP TEP TEP TEP
I AIN'T UNCONCIOUS NO MORE, YA DOPE!
UH OH...
THOSE AIN'T HUNGER PAINS...
GRRUM!!
SLAM-
BBRRRUUMMMMM!!
CREAAAAAAAK-
WHAT JUST HAPPENED ?!?
THE CURSE HAS BEEN BROKEN!
HOW LONG HAS IT BEEN?
DID WE JUST COME FROM WHERE I THINK WE CAME FROM?
I DON'T WANNA THINK ABOUT IT.

MUZZUM? KASSUM? HUNKUM? POZZUM?

RAKKUM...

FATHER!

I'M SO HAPPY, I COULD KILL SOMETHING!

THAT'S MY LITTLE GIRL!

BODIE! ARE YOU OKAY?

OH SURE.

JUST HATCHED A TRIBE OF NATIVES LIKE THEY WERE A DOZEN EGGS.

NOT HUMILIATIN' IN THE LEAST.

GET OVER HERE!

AW MAN, YER GONNA SHAVE MY HEAD CUZ I LOST THE BET!!

BODIE, YOU **WON!** YOU ATE A WHOLE TRIBE, AND YOU PUT RIGHT A TERRIBLE INJUSTICE!

THAT DESERVES SOMETHIN' **EXTRA!**

BBBBZZZZAAAPPP—B9MF!

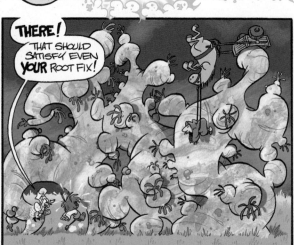

THERE!

THAT SHOULD SATISFY EVEN **YOUR** ROOT FIX!

MAN, IF YOU WUZ ALWAYS THIS NICE, I'D EAT PEOPLE MORE OFTEN!

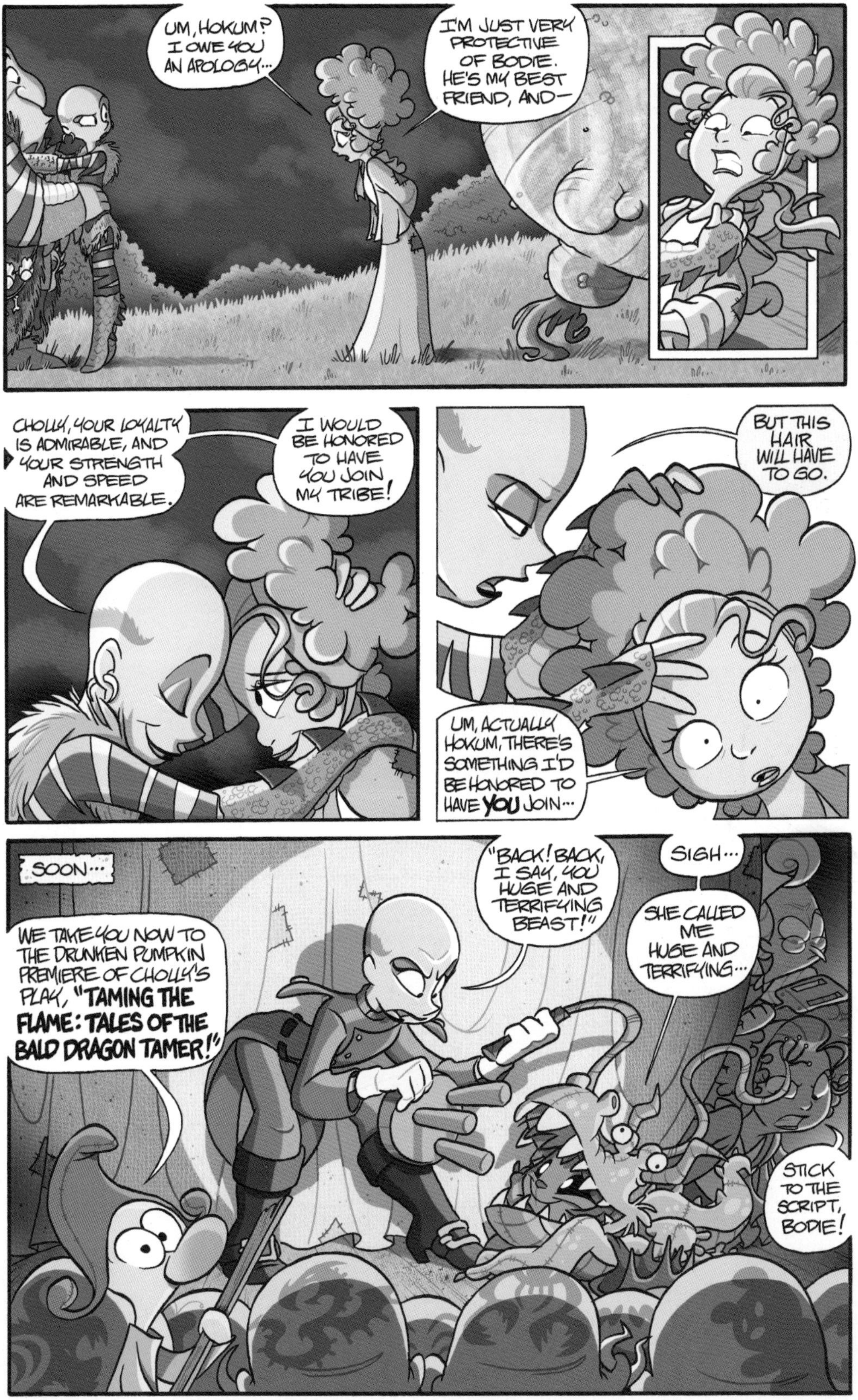
UM, HOKUM? I OWE YOU AN APOLOGY...
I'M JUST VERY PROTECTIVE OF BODIE. HE'S MY BEST FRIEND, AND—
CHOLLY, YOUR LOYALTY IS ADMIRABLE, AND YOUR STRENGTH AND SPEED ARE REMARKABLE.
I WOULD BE HONORED TO HAVE YOU JOIN MY TRIBE!
BUT THIS HAIR WILL HAVE TO GO.
UM, ACTUALLY HOKUM, THERE'S SOMETHING I'D BE HONORED TO HAVE **YOU** JOIN...
SOON...
WE TAKE YOU NOW TO THE DRUNKEN PUMPKIN PREMIERE OF CHOLLY'S PLAY, **"TAMING THE FLAME: TALES OF THE BALD DRAGON TAMER!"**
"BACK! BACK, I SAY, YOU HUGE AND TERRIFYING BEAST!"
SIGH...
SHE CALLED ME HUGE AND TERRIFYING...
STICK TO THE SCRIPT, BODIE!

CHAPTER 8
BITTERSWEET

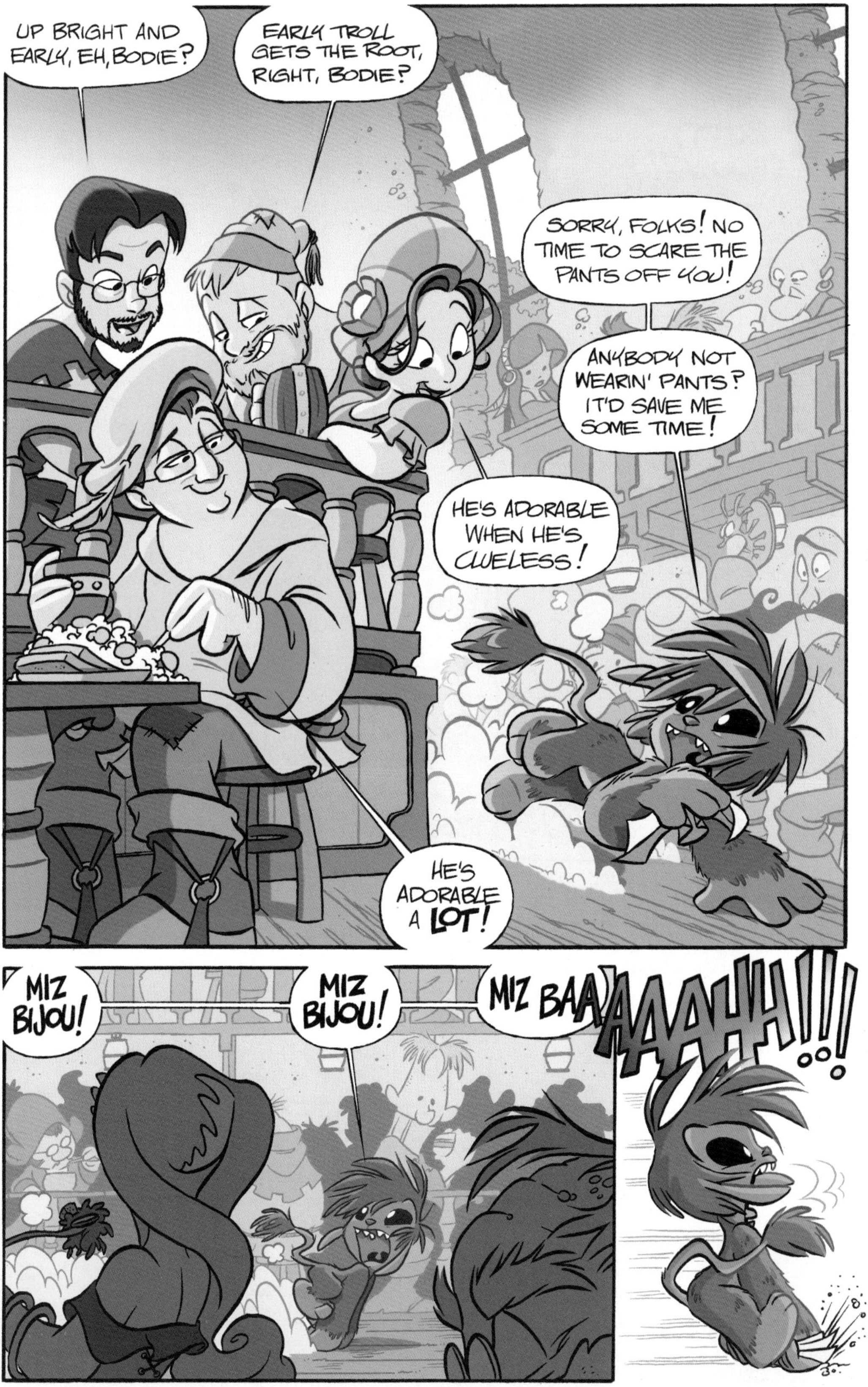
UP BRIGHT AND EARLY, EH, BODIE?
EARLY TROLL GETS THE ROOT, RIGHT, BODIE?
SORRY, FOLKS! NO TIME TO SCARE THE PANTS OFF YOU!
ANYBODY NOT WEARIN' PANTS? IT'D SAVE ME SOME TIME!
HE'S ADORABLE WHEN HE'S CLUELESS!
HE'S ADORABLE A LOT!
MIZ BIJOU!
MIZ BIJOU!
MIZ BAAAAAAHH!!!!

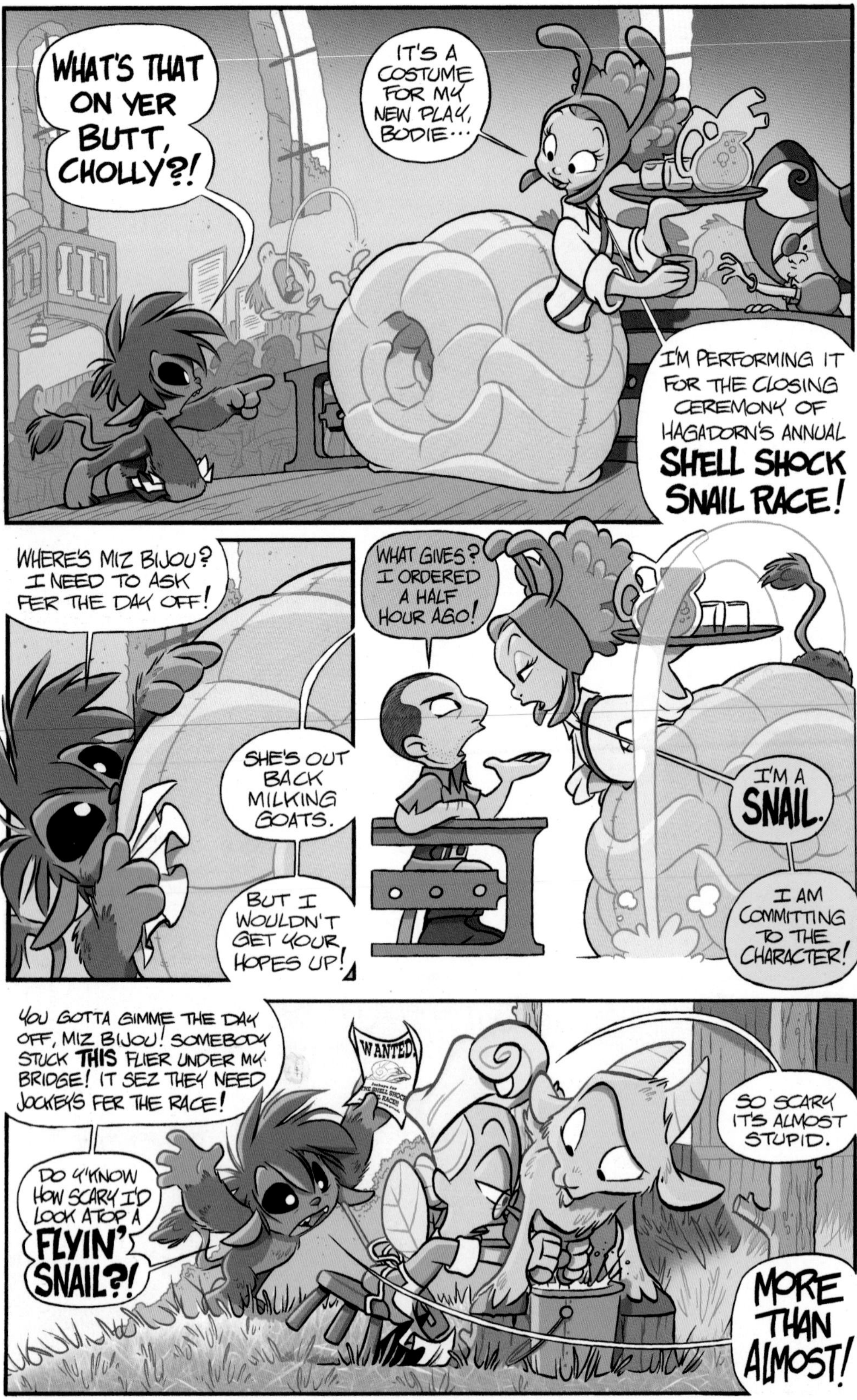
WHAT'S THAT ON YER BUTT, CHOLLY?!
IT'S A COSTUME FOR MY NEW PLAY, BODIE...
I'M PERFORMING IT FOR THE CLOSING CEREMONY OF HAGADORN'S ANNUAL SHELL SHOCK SNAIL RACE!
WHERE'S MIZ BIJOU? I NEED TO ASK FER THE DAY OFF!
SHE'S OUT BACK MILKING GOATS.
BUT I WOULDN'T GET YOUR HOPES UP!
WHAT GIVES? I ORDERED A HALF HOUR AGO!
I'M A SNAIL.
I AM COMMITTING TO THE CHARACTER!
YOU GOTTA GIMME THE DAY OFF, MIZ BIJOU! SOMEBODY STUCK THIS FLIER UNDER MY BRIDGE! IT SEZ THEY NEED JOCKEYS FER THE RACE!
WANTED
DO Y'KNOW HOW SCARY I'D LOOK ATOP A FLYIN' SNAIL?!
SO SCARY IT'S ALMOST STUPID.
MORE THAN ALMOST!

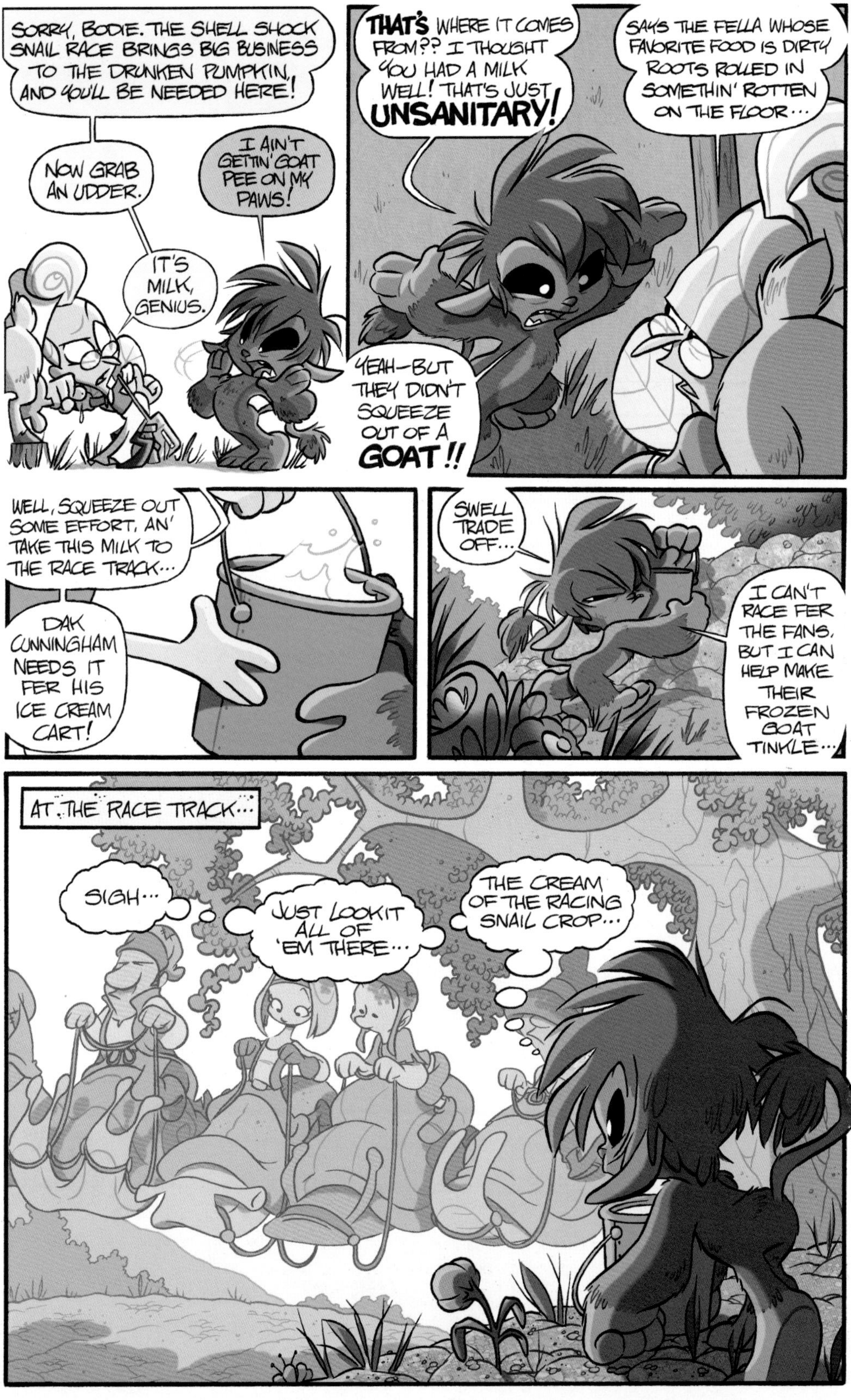
SORRY, BODIE. THE SHELL SHOCK SNAIL RACE BRINGS BIG BUSINESS TO THE DRUNKEN PUMPKIN, AND YOU'LL BE NEEDED HERE!
NOW GRAB AN UDDER.
I AIN'T GETTIN' GOAT PEE ON MY PAWS!
IT'S MILK, GENIUS.
THAT'S WHERE IT COMES FROM?? I THOUGHT YOU HAD A MILK WELL! THAT'S JUST UNSANITARY!
SAYS THE FELLA WHOSE FAVORITE FOOD IS DIRTY ROOTS ROLLED IN SOMETHIN' ROTTEN ON THE FLOOR...
YEAH—BUT THEY DIDN'T SQUEEZE OUT OF A GOAT!!
WELL, SQUEEZE OUT SOME EFFORT, AN' TAKE THIS MILK TO THE RACE TRACK...
DAK CUNNINGHAM NEEDS IT FER HIS ICE CREAM CART!
SWELL TRADE OFF...
I CAN'T RACE FER THE FANS, BUT I CAN HELP MAKE THEIR FROZEN GOAT TINKLE...
AT THE RACE TRACK...
SIGH...
JUST LOOKIT ALL OF 'EM THERE...
THE CREAM OF THE RACING SNAIL CROP...

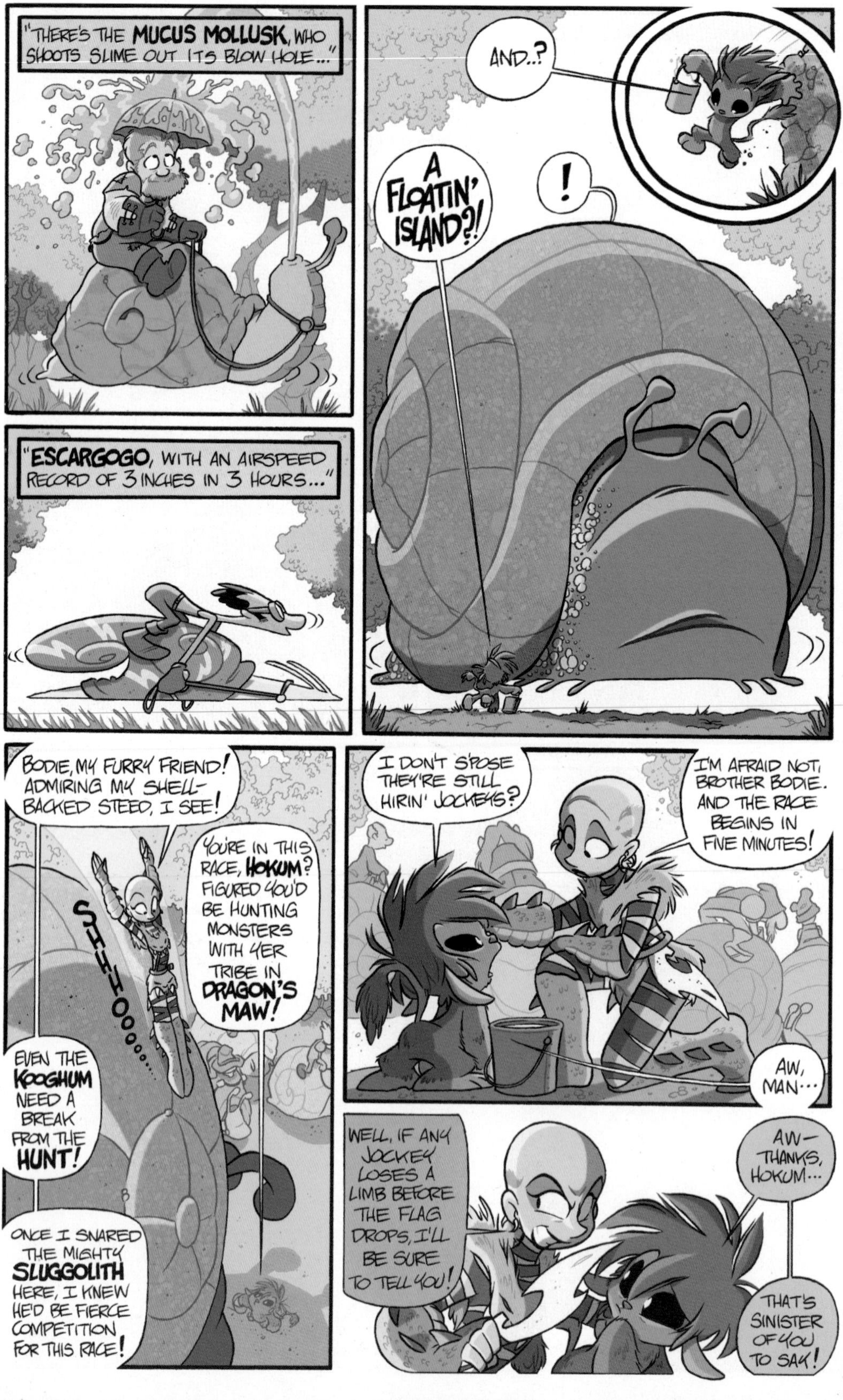
"THERE'S THE MUCUS MOLLUSK, WHO SHOOTS SLIME OUT ITS BLOW HOLE..."
AND..?
A FLOATIN' ISLAND?!
!
"ESCARGOGO, WITH AN AIRSPEED RECORD OF 3 INCHES IN 3 HOURS..."
BODIE, MY FURRY FRIEND! ADMIRING MY SHELL-BACKED STEED, I SEE!
SHHHOooo...
YOU'RE IN THIS RACE, HOKUM? FIGURED YOU'D BE HUNTING MONSTERS WITH YER TRIBE IN DRAGON'S MAW!
EVEN THE KOOGHUM NEED A BREAK FROM THE HUNT!
ONCE I SNARED THE MIGHTY SLUGGOLITH HERE, I KNEW HE'D BE FIERCE COMPETITION FOR THIS RACE!
I DON'T S'POSE THEY'RE STILL HIRIN' JOCKEYS?
I'M AFRAID NOT, BROTHER BODIE. AND THE RACE BEGINS IN FIVE MINUTES!
AW, MAN...
WELL, IF ANY JOCKEY LOSES A LIMB BEFORE THE FLAG DROPS, I'LL BE SURE TO TELL YOU!
AW— THANKS, HOKUM...
THAT'S SINISTER OF YOU TO SAY!

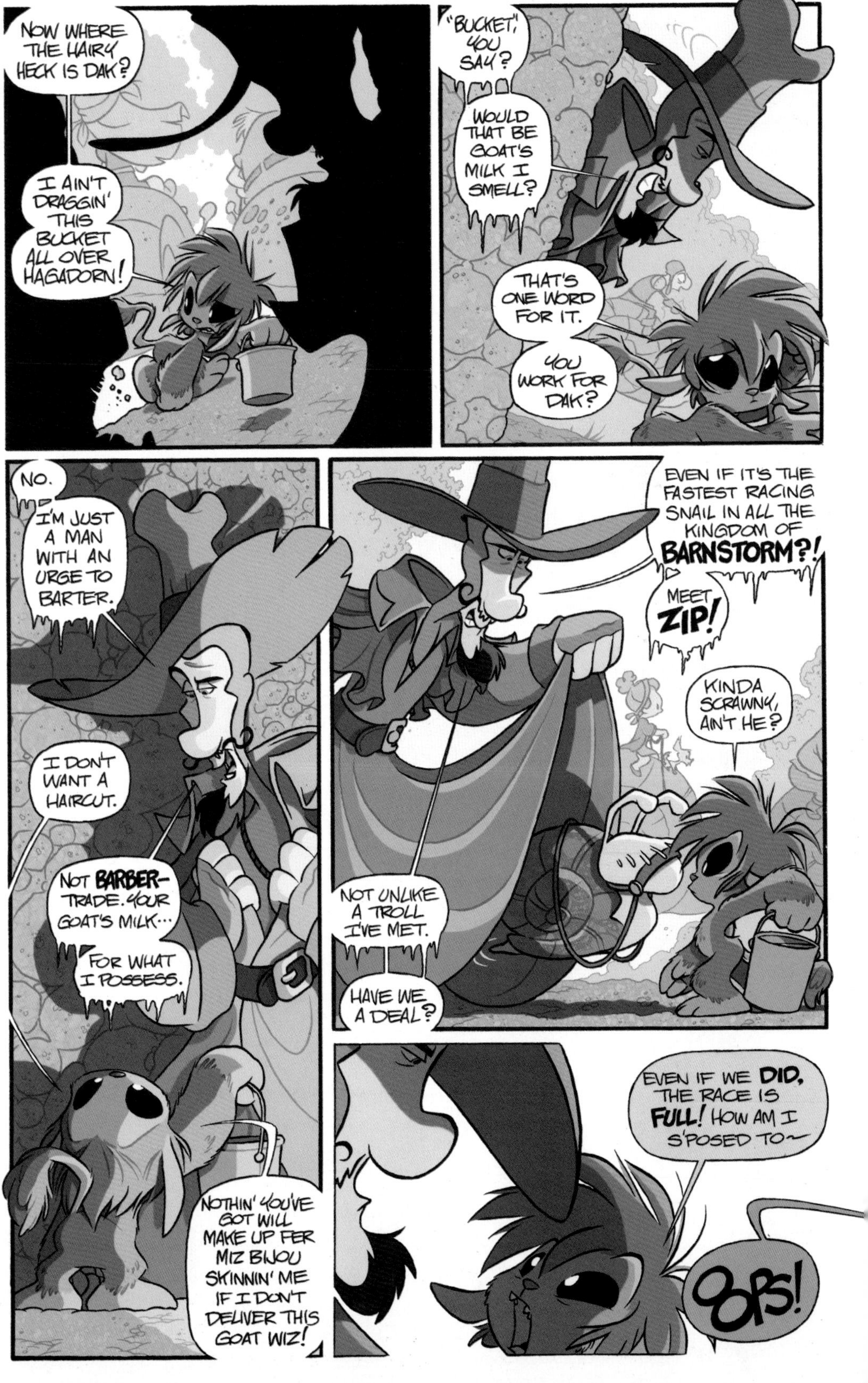
NOW WHERE THE HAIRY HECK IS DAK?
I AIN'T DRAGGIN' THIS BUCKET ALL OVER HAGADORN!
"BUCKET," YOU SAY?
WOULD THAT BE GOAT'S MILK I SMELL?
THAT'S ONE WORD FOR IT.
YOU WORK FOR DAK?
NO.
I'M JUST A MAN WITH AN URGE TO BARTER.
I DON'T WANT A HAIRCUT.
NOT BARBER-TRADE. YOUR GOAT'S MILK...
FOR WHAT I POSSESS.
NOTHIN' YOU'VE GOT WILL MAKE UP FER MIZ BIJOU SKINNIN' ME IF I DON'T DELIVER THIS GOAT WIZ!
EVEN IF IT'S THE FASTEST RACING SNAIL IN ALL THE KINGDOM OF BARNSTORM?!
MEET ZIP!
KINDA SCRAWNY, AIN'T HE?
NOT UNLIKE A TROLL I'VE MET.
HAVE WE A DEAL?
EVEN IF WE DID, THE RACE IS FULL! HOW AM I S'POSED TO~
OOPS!

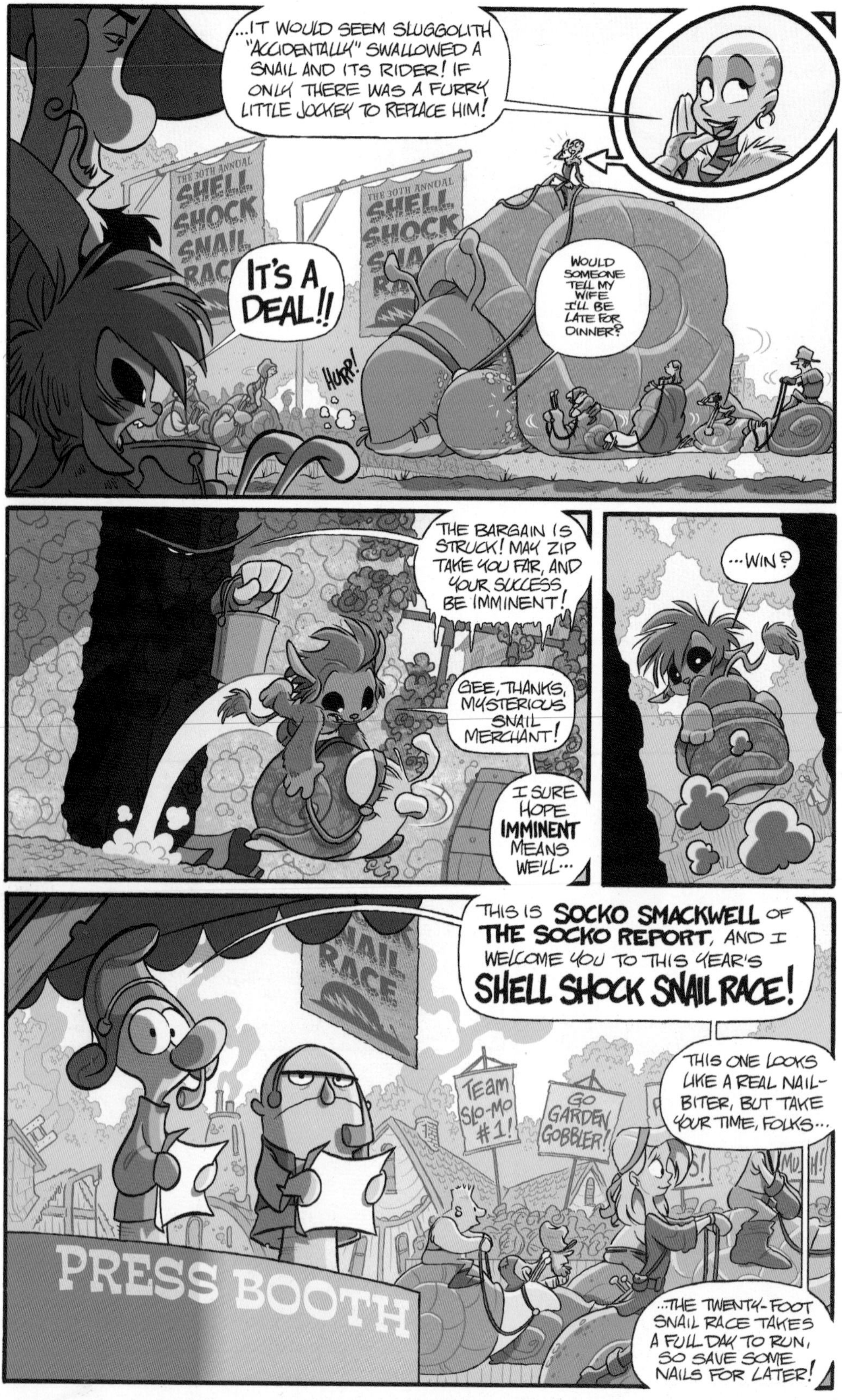
...IT WOULD SEEM SLUGGOLITH "ACCIDENTALLY" SWALLOWED A SNAIL AND ITS RIDER! IF ONLY THERE WAS A FURRY LITTLE JOCKEY TO REPLACE HIM!
THE 30TH ANNUAL SHELL SHOCK SNAIL RACE
IT'S A DEAL!!
WOULD SOMEONE TELL MY WIFE I'LL BE LATE FOR DINNER?
HURR!
THE BARGAIN IS STRUCK! MAY ZIP TAKE YOU FAR, AND YOUR SUCCESS BE IMMINENT!
GEE, THANKS, MYSTERIOUS SNAIL MERCHANT!
I SURE HOPE IMMINENT MEANS WE'LL...
...WIN?
THIS IS SOCKO SMACKWELL OF THE SOCKO REPORT, AND I WELCOME YOU TO THIS YEAR'S SHELL SHOCK SNAIL RACE!
THIS ONE LOOKS LIKE A REAL NAIL-BITER, BUT TAKE YOUR TIME, FOLKS...
...THE TWENTY-FOOT SNAIL RACE TAKES A FULL DAY TO RUN, SO SAVE SOME NAILS FOR LATER!
TEAM SLO-MO #1!
GO GARDEN GOBBLER!
PRESS BOOTH

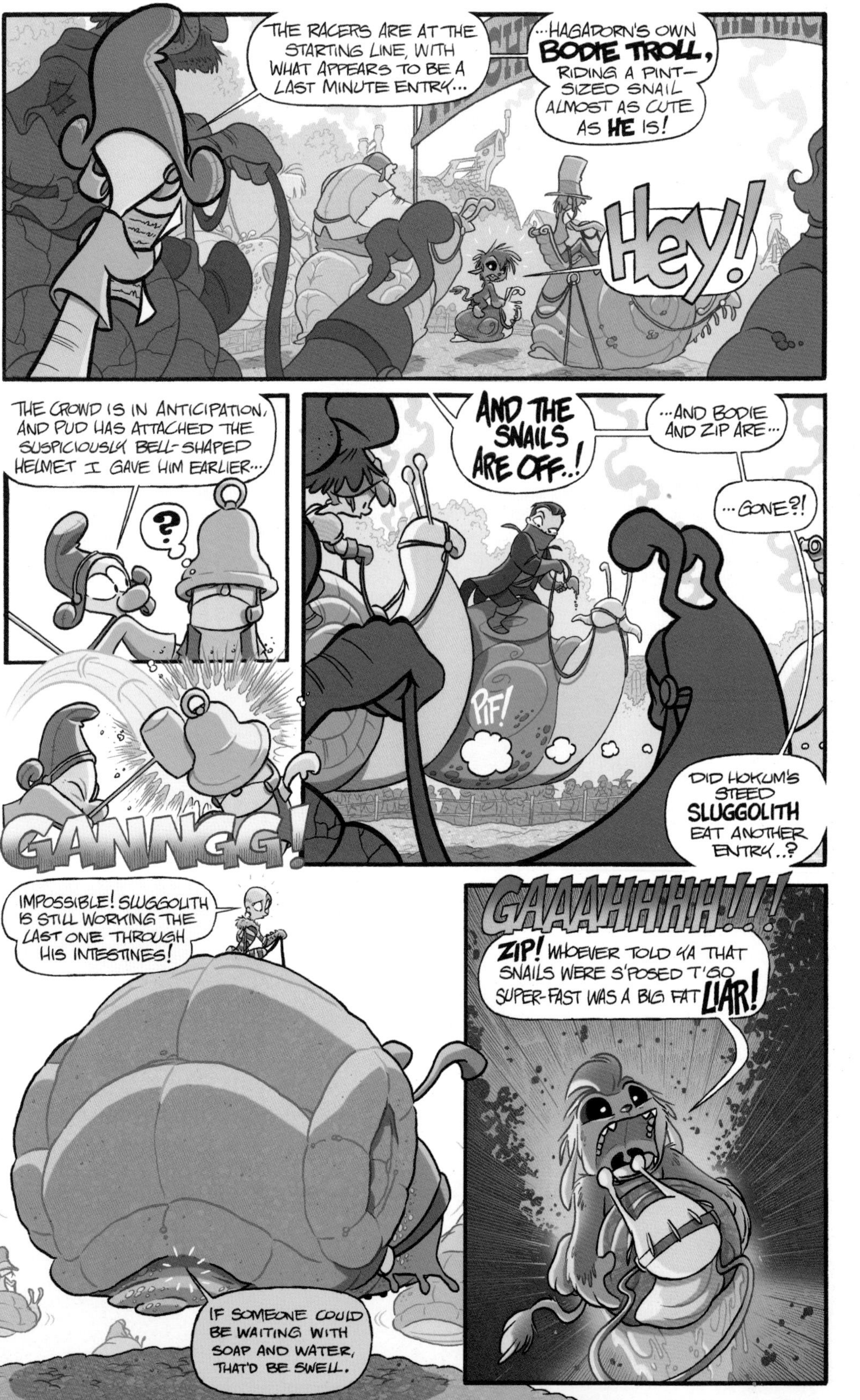

THE RACERS ARE AT THE STARTING LINE, WITH WHAT APPEARS TO BE A LAST MINUTE ENTRY...
...HAGADORN'S OWN BODIE TROLL, RIDING A PINT-SIZED SNAIL ALMOST AS CUTE AS HE IS!
HEY!
THE CROWD IS IN ANTICIPATION, AND PUD HAS ATTACHED THE SUSPICIOUSLY BELL-SHAPED HELMET I GAVE HIM EARLIER...
?
GANNGG!
AND THE SNAILS ARE OFF..!
...AND BODIE AND ZIP ARE...
...GONE?!
PIF!
DID HOKUM'S STEED SLUGGOLITH EAT ANOTHER ENTRY..?
IMPOSSIBLE! SLUGGOLITH IS STILL WORKING THE LAST ONE THROUGH HIS INTESTINES!
IF SOMEONE COULD BE WAITING WITH SOAP AND WATER, THAT'D BE SWELL.
GAAAHHHH!!!
ZIP! WHOEVER TOLD YA THAT SNAILS WERE S'POSED T'GO SUPER-FAST WAS A BIG FAT LIAR!

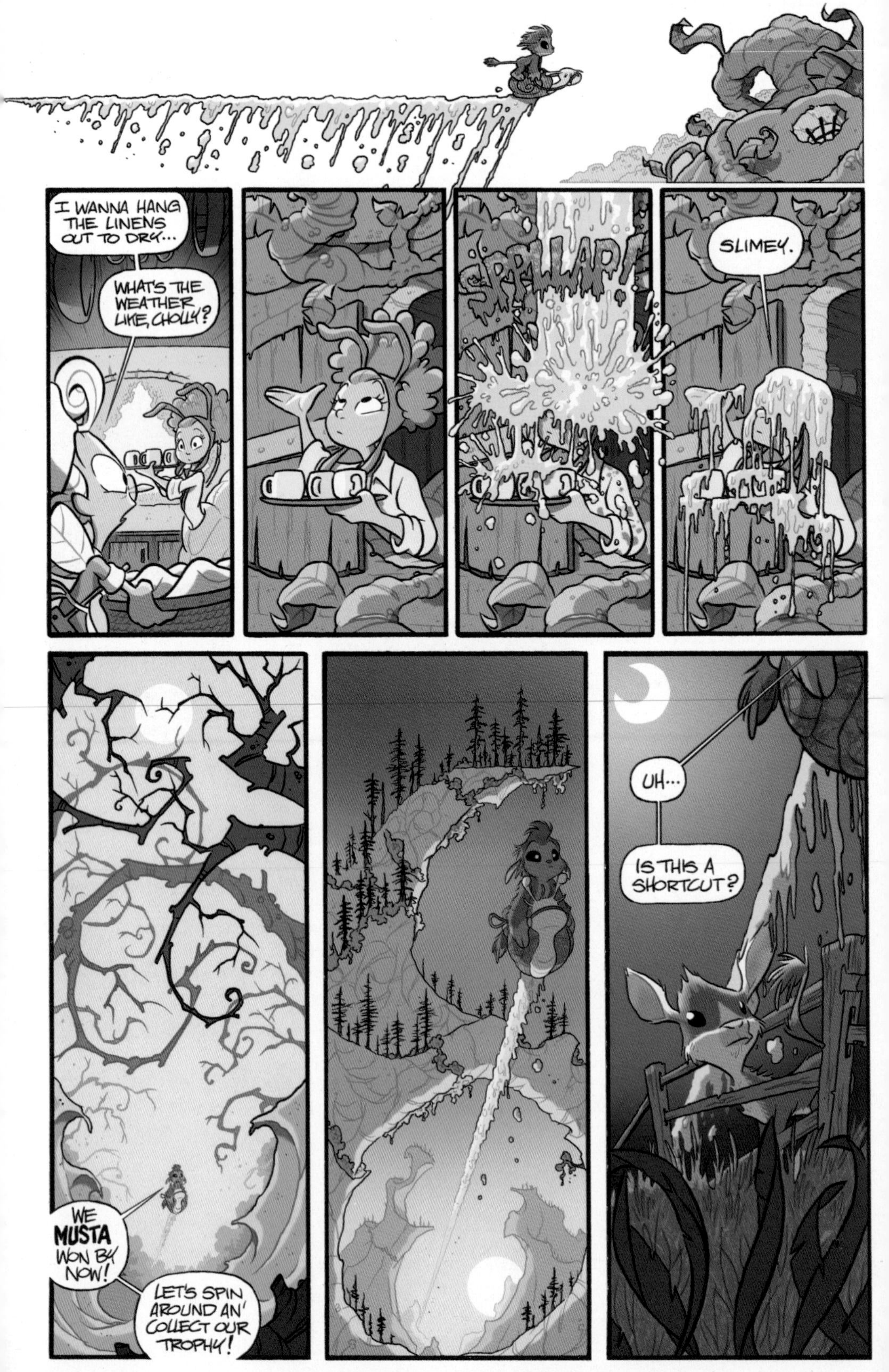
I WANNA HANG THE LINENS OUT TO DRY...
WHAT'S THE WEATHER LIKE, CHOLLY?
SPLLAP!
SLIMEY.
WE MUSTA WON BY NOW!
LET'S SPIN AROUND AN' COLLECT OUR TROPHY!
UH...
IS THIS A SHORTCUT?

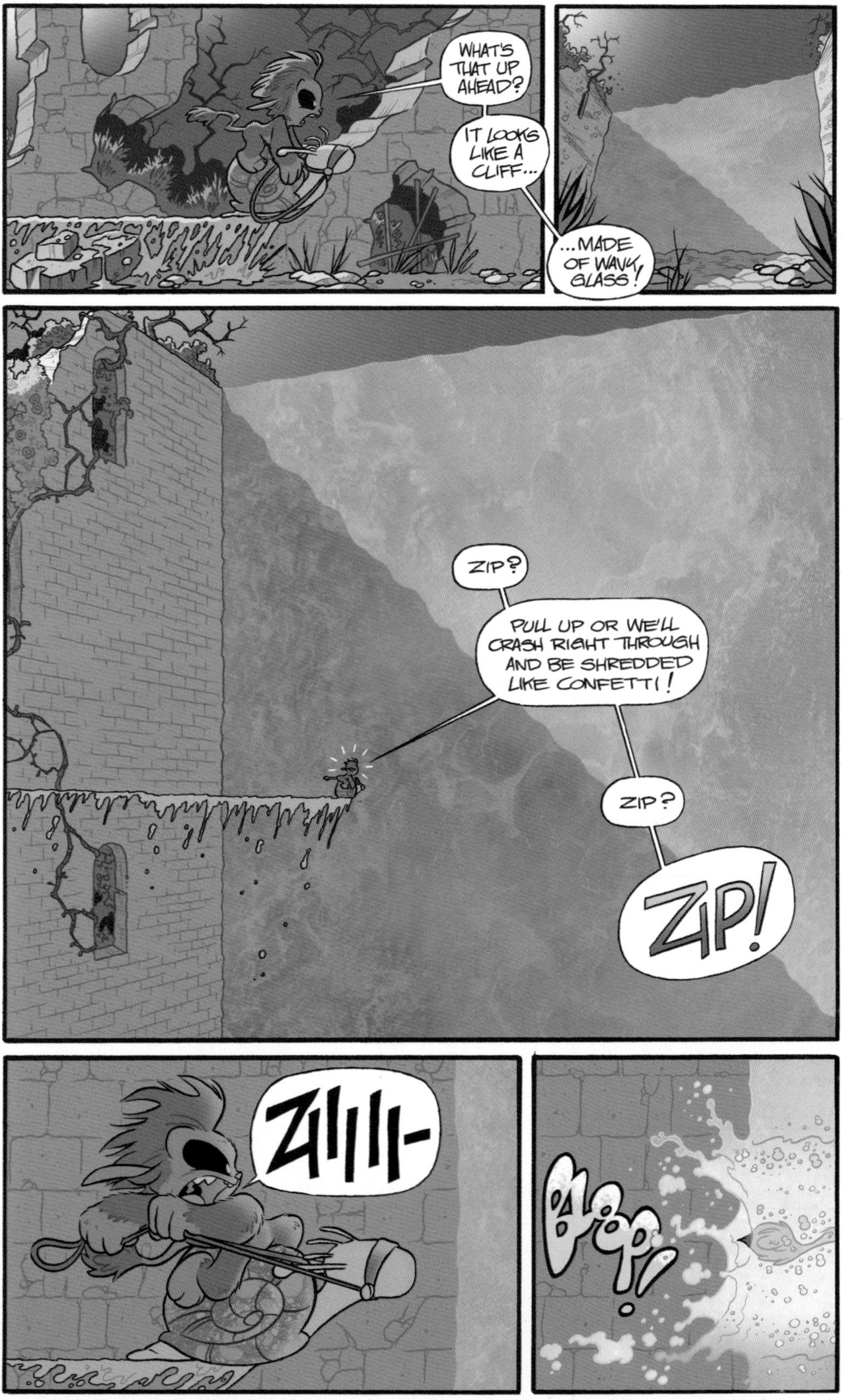
WHAT'S THAT UP AHEAD?
IT LOOKS LIKE A CLIFF...
...MADE OF WAVY GLASS!
ZIP?
PULL UP OR WE'LL CRASH RIGHT THROUGH AND BE SHREDDED LIKE CONFETTI!
ZIP?
ZIP!
ZIIII-
BLOOP!

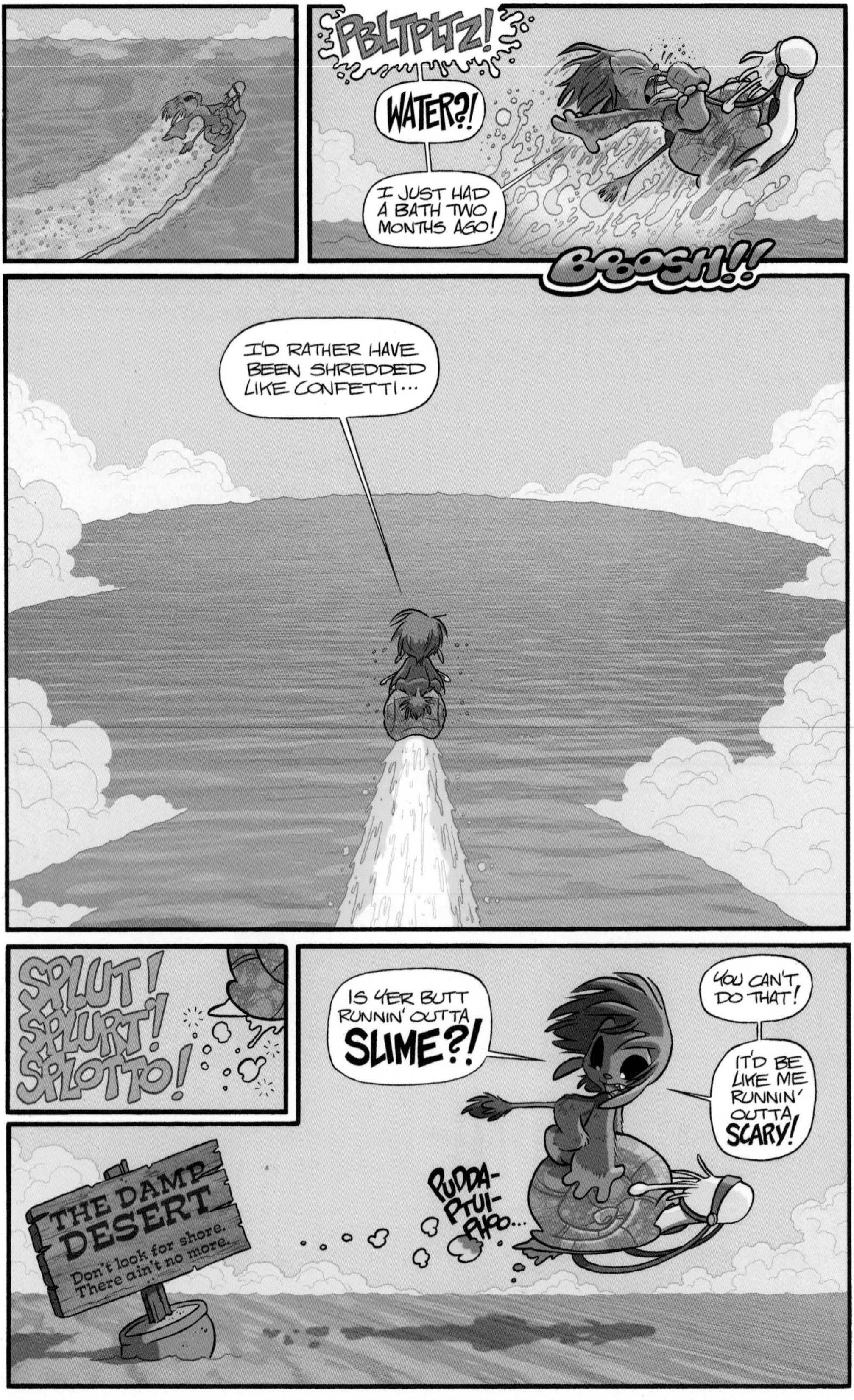
PBLTPLTZ!
WATER?!
I JUST HAD A BATH TWO MONTHS AGO!
BOOSH!!
I'D RATHER HAVE BEEN SHREDDED LIKE CONFETTI...
SPLUT! SPLURT! SPLOTTO!
IS YER BUTT RUNNIN' OUTTA SLIME?!
YOU CAN'T DO THAT!
IT'D BE LIKE ME RUNNIN' OUTTA SCARY!
PUDDA-PTUI-PHOO...
THE DAMP DESERT
Don't look for shore. There ain't no more.

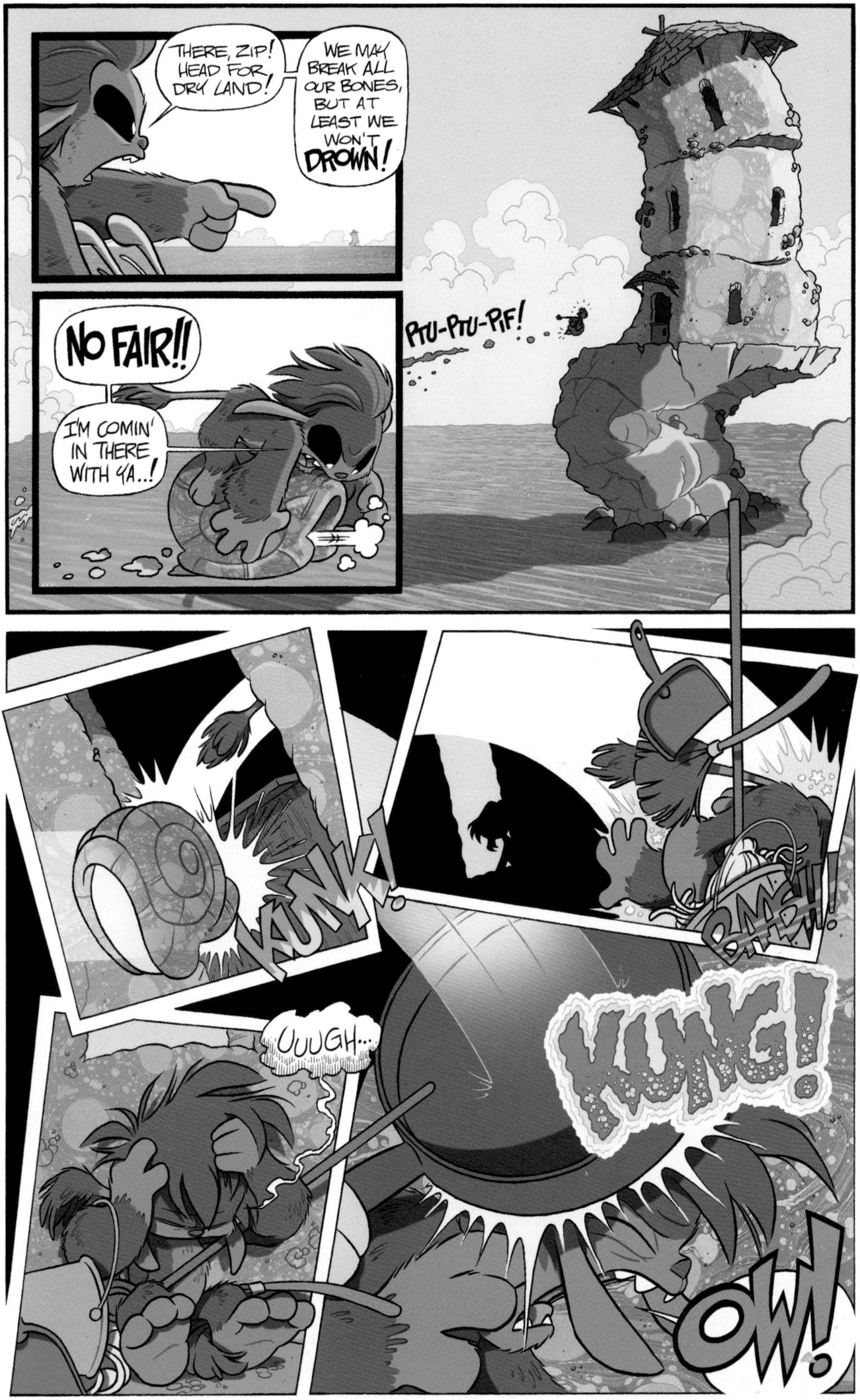
THERE, ZIP! HEAD FOR DRY LAND!
WE MAY BREAK ALL OUR BONES, BUT AT LEAST WE WON'T DROWN!
NO FAIR!!
I'M COMIN' IN THERE WITH YA...!
PTU-PTU-PIF!
KUNK!
BANG!!
KLUNG!
UUUGH...
OW!

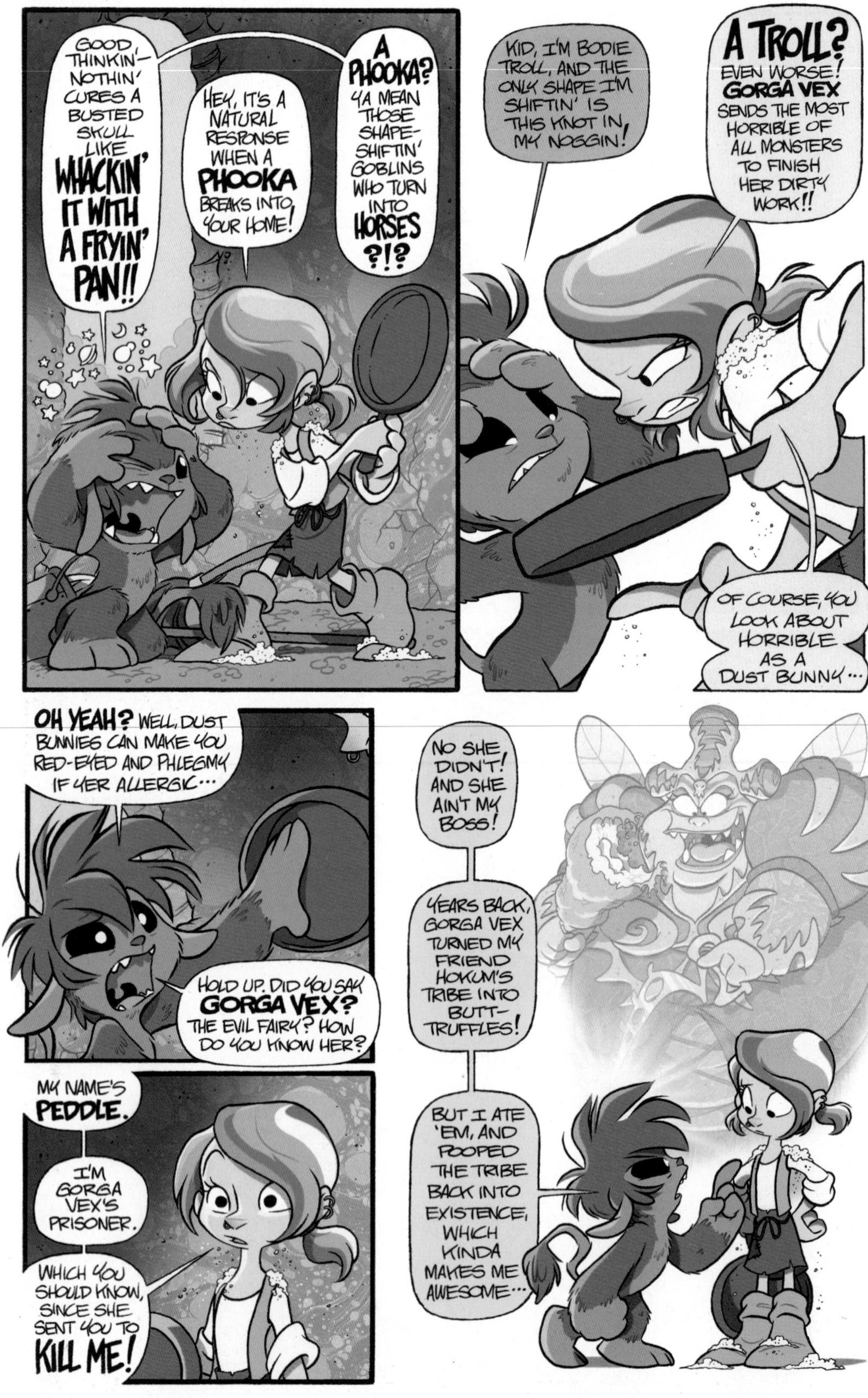
GOOD THINKIN'— NOTHIN' CURES A BUSTED SKULL LIKE WHACKIN' IT WITH A FRYIN' PAN!!
HEY, IT'S A NATURAL RESPONSE WHEN A PHOOKA BREAKS INTO YOUR HOME!
A PHOOKA?
YA MEAN THOSE SHAPE-SHIFTIN' GOBLINS WHO TURN INTO HORSES ?!?
KID, I'M BODIE TROLL, AND THE ONLY SHAPE I'M SHIFTIN' IS THIS KNOT IN MY NOGGIN!
A TROLL?
EVEN WORSE! GORGA VEX SENDS THE MOST HORRIBLE OF ALL MONSTERS TO FINISH HER DIRTY WORK!!
OF COURSE, YOU LOOK ABOUT HORRIBLE AS A DUST BUNNY...
OH YEAH? WELL, DUST BUNNIES CAN MAKE YOU RED-EYED AND PHLEGMY IF YER ALLERGIC...
HOLD UP. DID YOU SAY GORGA VEX? THE EVIL FAIRY? HOW DO YOU KNOW HER?
MY NAME'S PEDDLE.
I'M GORGA VEX'S PRISONER.
WHICH YOU SHOULD KNOW, SINCE SHE SENT YOU TO KILL ME!
NO SHE DIDN'T! AND SHE AIN'T MY BOSS!
YEARS BACK, GORGA VEX TURNED MY FRIEND HOKUM'S TRIBE INTO BUTT-TRUFFLES!
BUT I ATE 'EM, AND POOPED THE TRIBE BACK INTO EXISTENCE, WHICH KINDA MAKES ME AWESOME...

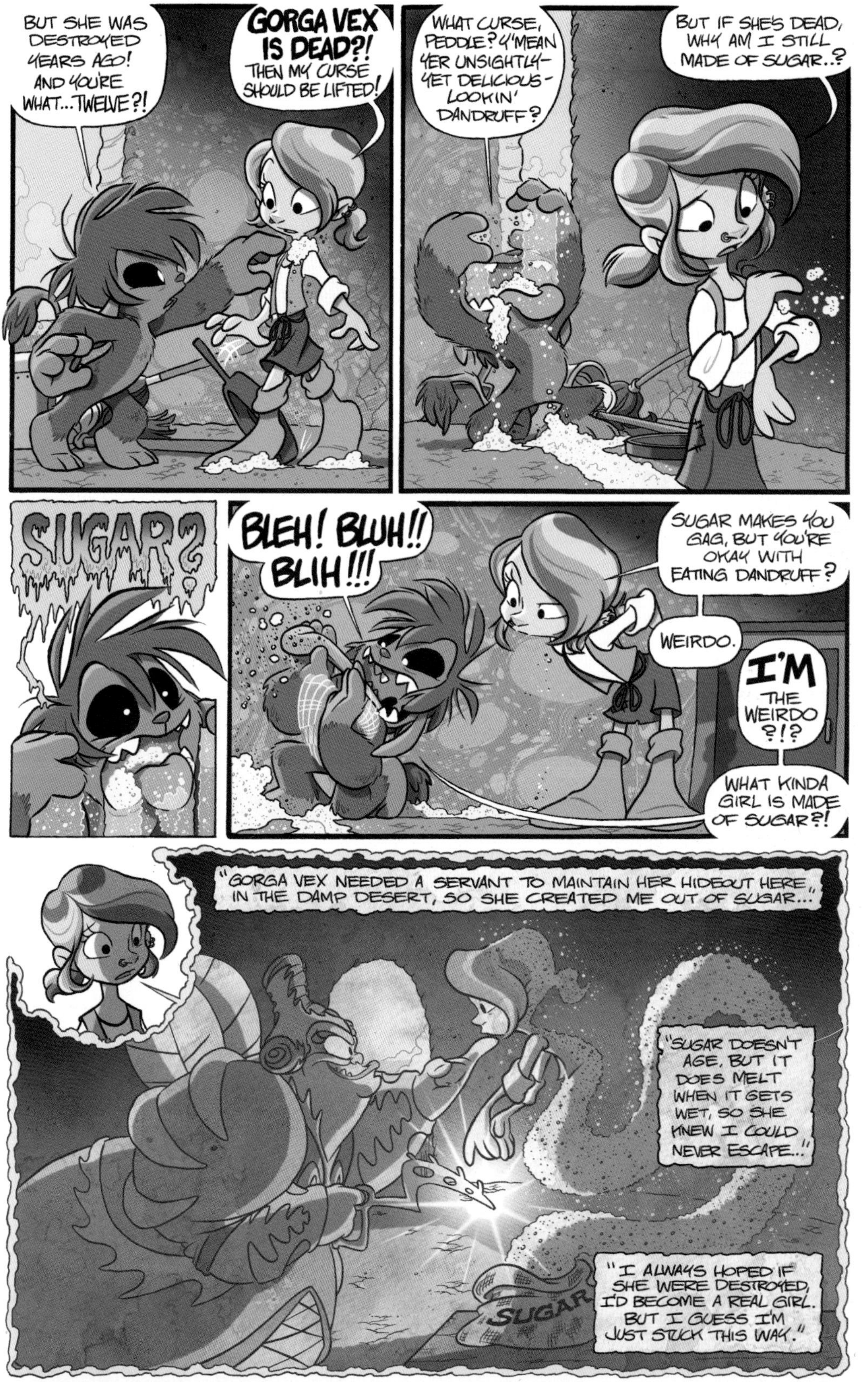
BUT SHE WAS DESTROYED YEARS AGO! AND YOU'RE WHAT... TWELVE?!
GORGA VEX IS DEAD?! THEN MY CURSE SHOULD BE LIFTED!
WHAT CURSE, PEDDLE? Y'MEAN YER UNSIGHTLY-YET DELICIOUS-LOOKIN' DANDRUFF?
BUT IF SHE'S DEAD, WHY AM I STILL MADE OF SUGAR..?
SUGAR?
BLEH! BLUH!! BLIH!!!
SUGAR MAKES YOU GAG, BUT YOU'RE OKAY WITH EATING DANDRUFF?
WEIRDO.
I'M THE WEIRDO?!?
WHAT KINDA GIRL IS MADE OF SUGAR?!
"GORGA VEX NEEDED A SERVANT TO MAINTAIN HER HIDEOUT HERE IN THE DAMP DESERT, SO SHE CREATED ME OUT OF SUGAR..."
"SUGAR DOESN'T AGE, BUT IT DOES MELT WHEN IT GETS WET, SO SHE KNEW I COULD NEVER ESCAPE..."
SUGAR
"I ALWAYS HOPED IF SHE WERE DESTROYED, I'D BECOME A REAL GIRL. BUT I GUESS I'M JUST STUCK THIS WAY."

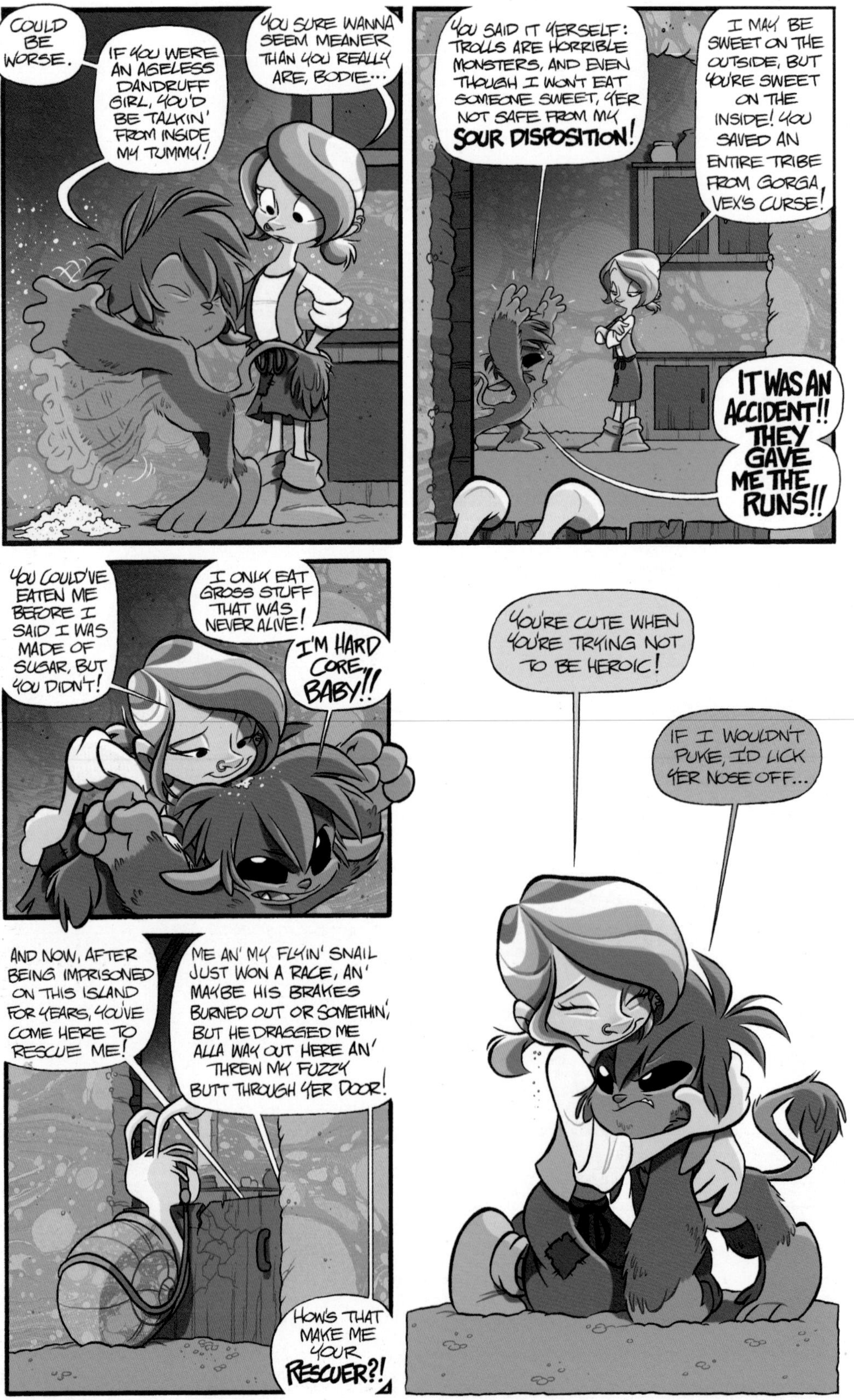

COULD BE WORSE.
IF YOU WERE AN AGELESS DANDRUFF GIRL, YOU'D BE TALKIN' FROM INSIDE MY TUMMY!
YOU SURE WANNA SEEM MEANER THAN YOU REALLY ARE, BODIE...
YOU SAID IT YERSELF: TROLLS ARE HORRIBLE MONSTERS, AND EVEN THOUGH I WON'T EAT SOMEONE SWEET, YER NOT SAFE FROM MY SOUR DISPOSITION!
I MAY BE SWEET ON THE OUTSIDE, BUT YOU'RE SWEET ON THE INSIDE! YOU SAVED AN ENTIRE TRIBE FROM GORGA VEX'S CURSE!
IT WAS AN ACCIDENT!! THEY GAVE ME THE RUNS!!
YOU COULD'VE EATEN ME BEFORE I SAID I WAS MADE OF SUGAR, BUT YOU DIDN'T!
I ONLY EAT GROSS STUFF THAT WAS NEVER ALIVE!
I'M HARD CORE, BABY!!
AND NOW, AFTER BEING IMPRISONED ON THIS ISLAND FOR YEARS, YOU'VE COME HERE TO RESCUE ME!
ME AN' MY FLYIN' SNAIL JUST WON A RACE, AN' MAYBE HIS BRAKES BURNED OUT OR SOMETHIN', BUT HE DRAGGED ME ALLA WAY OUT HERE AN' THREW MY FUZZY BUTT THROUGH YER DOOR!
HOW'S THAT MAKE ME YOUR RESCUER?!
YOU'RE CUTE WHEN YOU'RE TRYING NOT TO BE HEROIC!
IF I WOULDN'T PUKE, I'D LICK YER NOSE OFF...

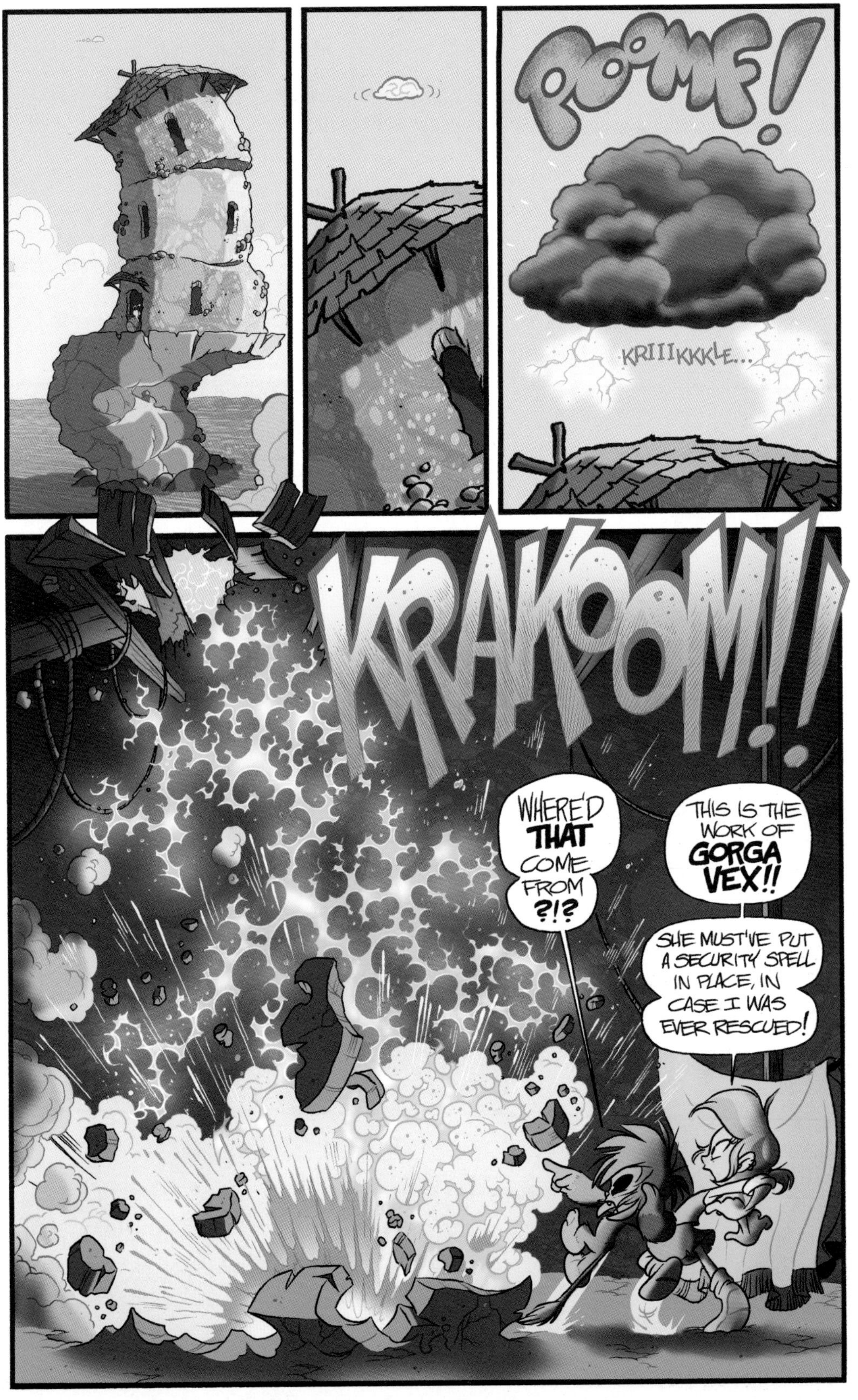
POOMF!
KRIIIKKKLE...
KRAKOOM!!!
WHERE'D THAT COME FROM ?!?
THIS IS THE WORK OF GORGA VEX!!
SHE MUST'VE PUT A SECURITY SPELL IN PLACE, IN CASE I WAS EVER RESCUED!

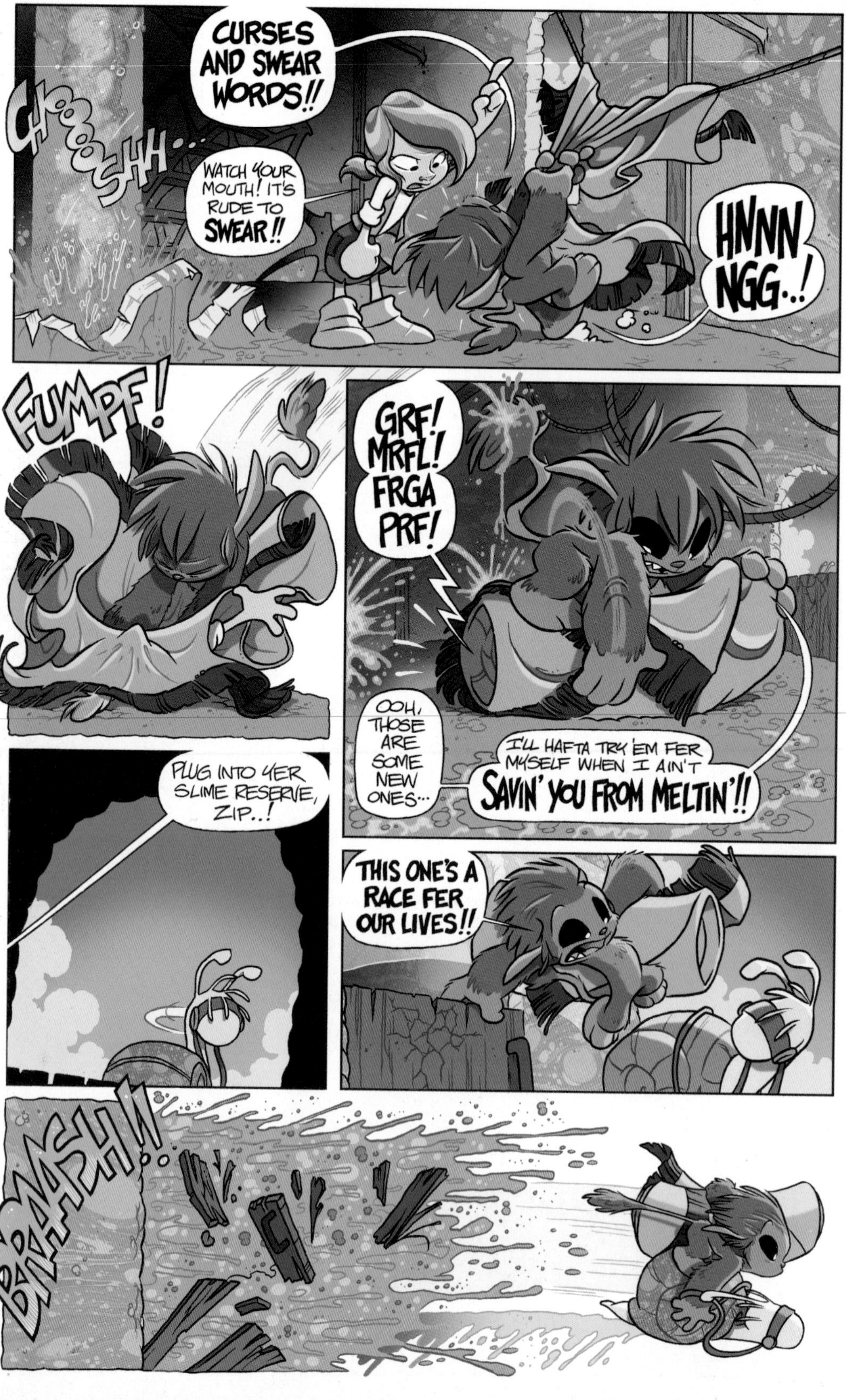
CURSES AND SWEAR WORDS!!
CHOOOSHH...
WATCH YOUR MOUTH! IT'S RUDE TO SWEAR!!
HNNN NGG..!
FUMPF!
GRF! MRFL! FRGA PRF!
OOH, THOSE ARE SOME NEW ONES...
I'LL HAFTA TRY 'EM FER MYSELF WHEN I AIN'T SAVIN' YOU FROM MELTIN'!!
PLUG INTO YER SLIME RESERVE, ZIP..!
THIS ONE'S A RACE FER OUR LIVES!!
BRAASH!!..

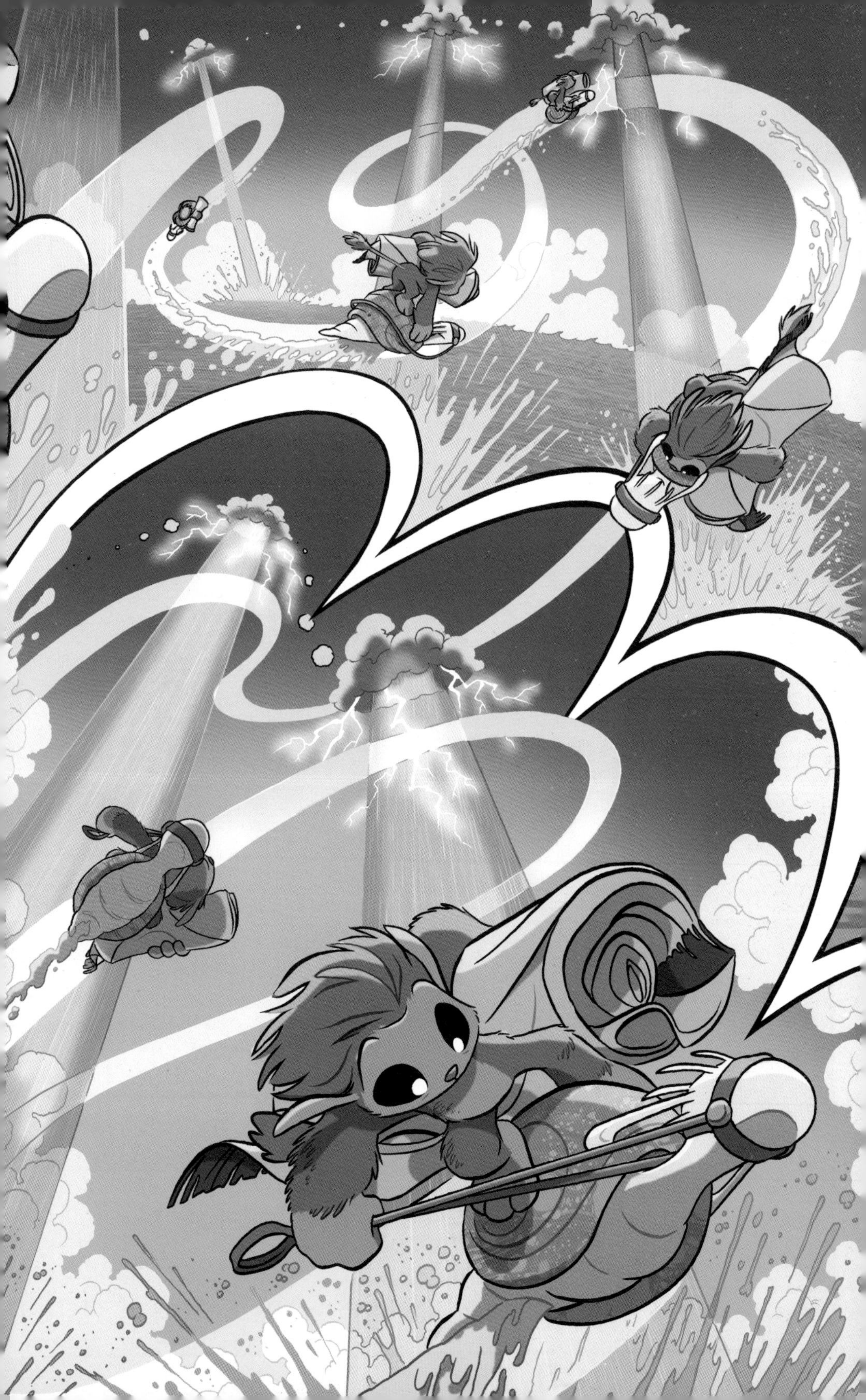

THERE'S THE EDGE!

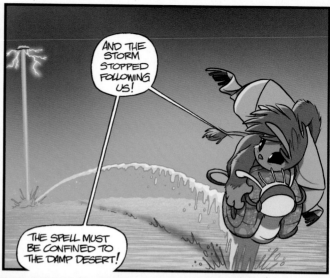

AND THE STORM STOPPED FOLLOWING US!

THE SPELL MUST BE CONFINED TO THE DAMP DESERT!

BZZZAAATT!

GRSSHH!

PWAK!

ZIP!

PUNK!

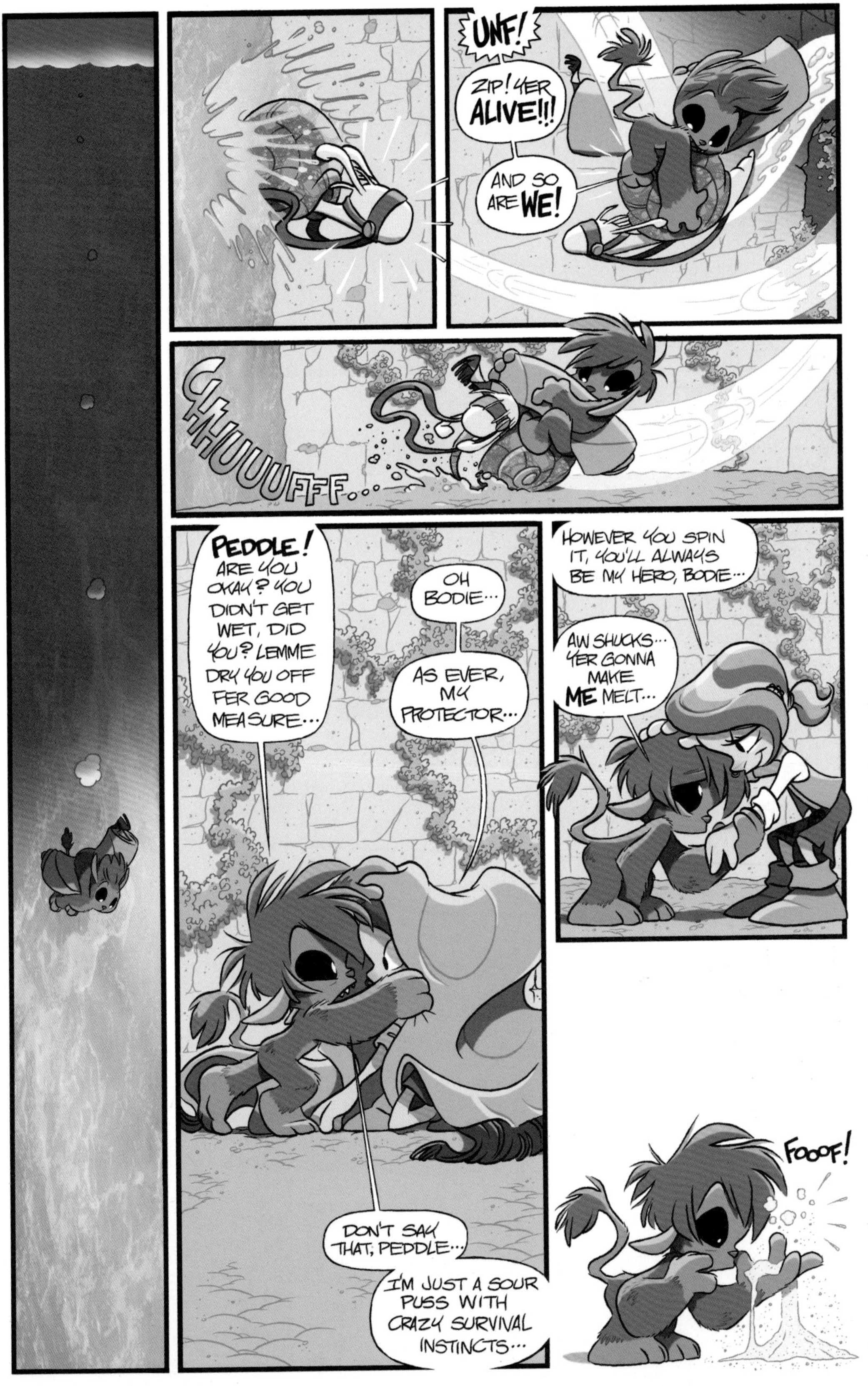
UNF!
ZIP! YER ALIVE!!!
AND SO ARE WE!
CHHUUUUFFFF...
PEDDLE! ARE YOU OKAY? YOU DIDN'T GET WET, DID YOU? LEMME DRY YOU OFF FER GOOD MEASURE...
OH BODIE...
AS EVER, MY PROTECTOR...
DON'T SAY THAT, PEDDLE...
I'M JUST A SOUR PUSS WITH CRAZY SURVIVAL INSTINCTS...
HOWEVER YOU SPIN IT, YOU'LL ALWAYS BE MY HERO, BODIE...
AW SHUCKS... YER GONNA MAKE ME MELT...
FOOOF!

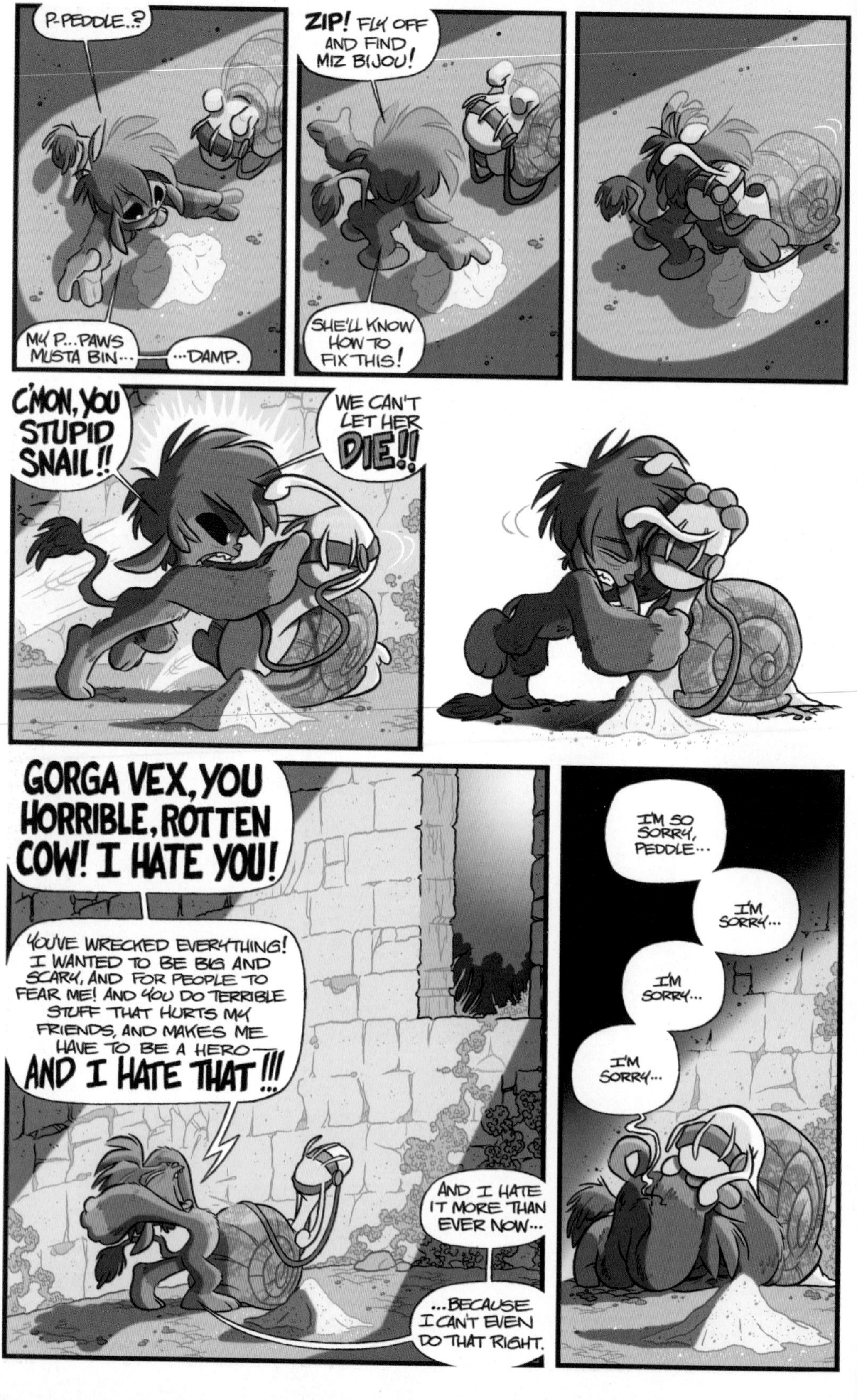

P-PEDDLE..?
MY P...PAWS MUSTA BIN...
...DAMP.
ZIP! FLY OFF AND FIND MIZ BIJOU!
SHE'LL KNOW HOW TO FIX THIS!
C'MON, YOU STUPID SNAIL!!
WE CAN'T LET HER DIE!!
GORGA VEX, YOU HORRIBLE, ROTTEN COW! I HATE YOU!
YOU'VE WRECKED EVERYTHING! I WANTED TO BE BIG AND SCARY, AND FOR PEOPLE TO FEAR ME! AND YOU DO TERRIBLE STUFF THAT HURTS MY FRIENDS, AND MAKES ME HAVE TO BE A HERO—
AND I HATE THAT!!!
AND I HATE IT MORE THAN EVER NOW...
...BECAUSE I CAN'T EVEN DO THAT RIGHT.
I'M SO SORRY, PEDDLE...
I'M SORRY...
I'M SORRY...
I'M SORRY...

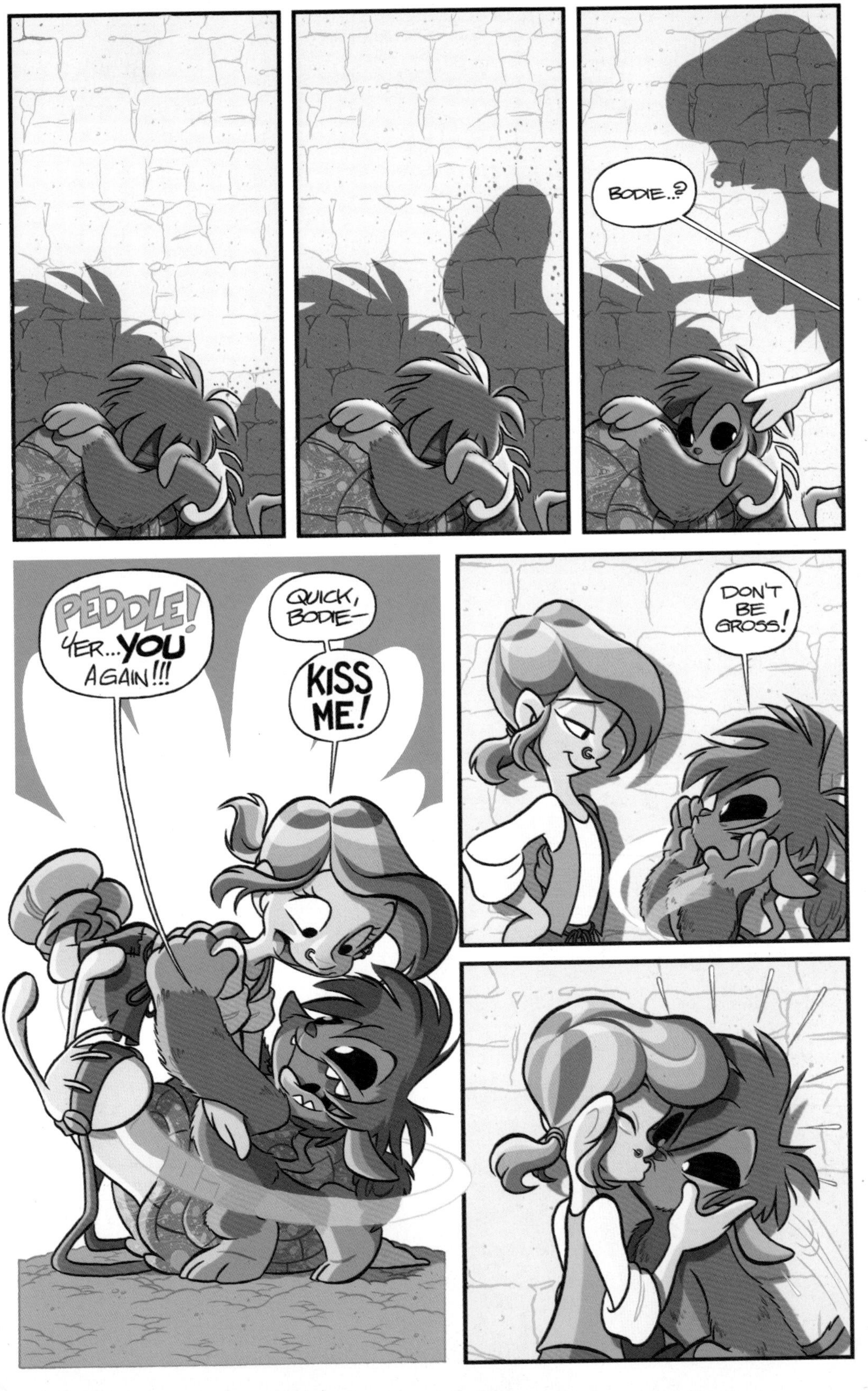
BODIE...?
PEDDLE! YER...YOU AGAIN!!!
QUICK, BODIE—
KISS ME!
DON'T BE GROSS!

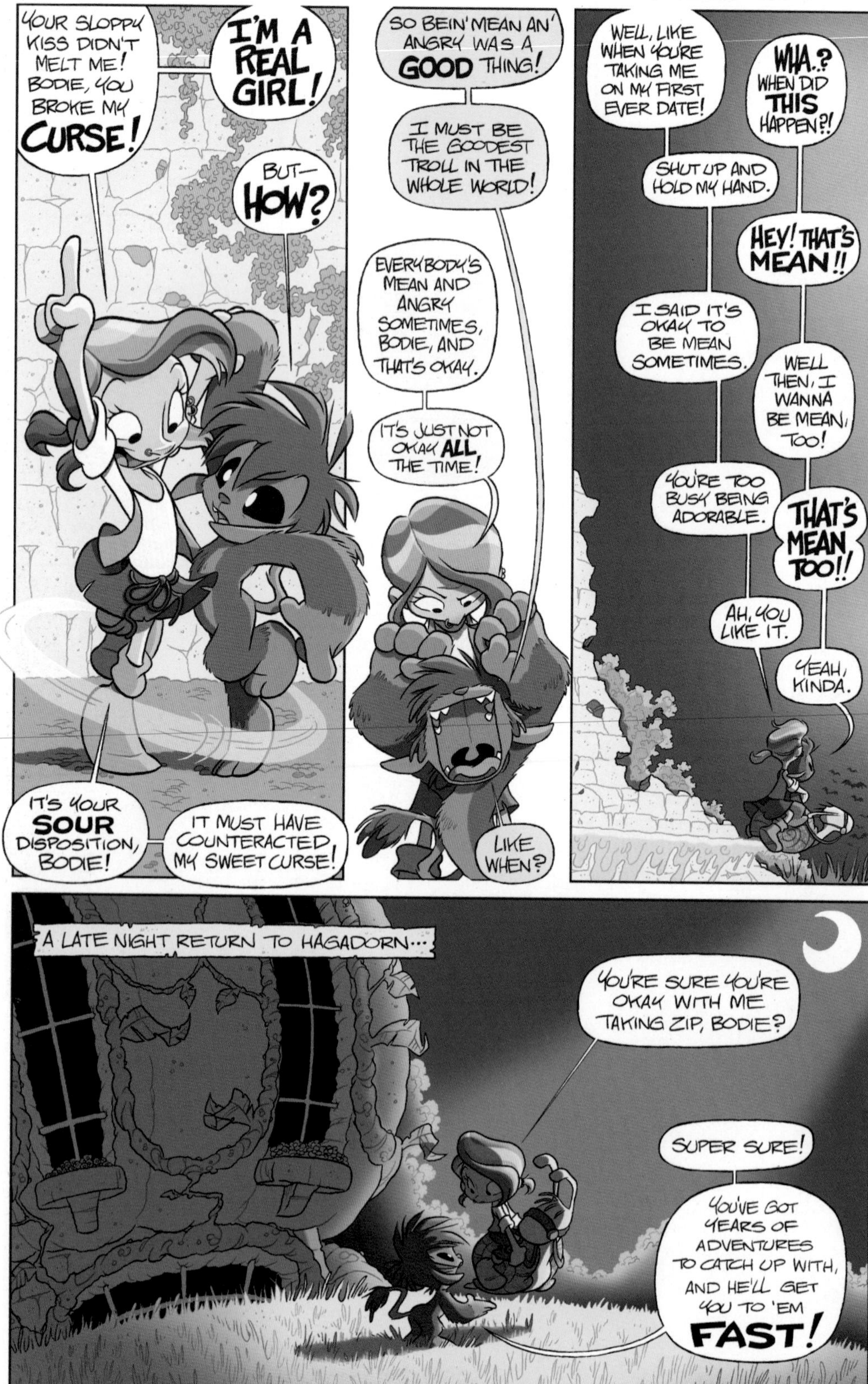

YOUR SLOPPY KISS DIDN'T MELT ME! BODIE, YOU BROKE MY CURSE!
I'M A REAL GIRL!
BUT— HOW?
IT'S YOUR SOUR DISPOSITION, BODIE!
IT MUST HAVE COUNTERACTED MY SWEET CURSE!
SO BEIN' MEAN AN' ANGRY WAS A GOOD THING!
I MUST BE THE GOODEST TROLL IN THE WHOLE WORLD!
EVERYBODY'S MEAN AND ANGRY SOMETIMES, BODIE, AND THAT'S OKAY.
IT'S JUST NOT OKAY ALL THE TIME!
LIKE WHEN?
WELL, LIKE WHEN YOU'RE TAKING ME ON MY FIRST EVER DATE!
WHA..? WHEN DID THIS HAPPEN?!
SHUT UP AND HOLD MY HAND.
HEY! THAT'S MEAN!!
I SAID IT'S OKAY TO BE MEAN SOMETIMES.
WELL THEN, I WANNA BE MEAN, TOO!
YOU'RE TOO BUSY BEING ADORABLE.
THAT'S MEAN, TOO!!
AH, YOU LIKE IT.
YEAH, KINDA.
A LATE NIGHT RETURN TO HAGADORN...
YOU'RE SURE YOU'RE OKAY WITH ME TAKING ZIP, BODIE?
SUPER SURE!
YOU'VE GOT YEARS OF ADVENTURES TO CATCH UP WITH, AND HE'LL GET YOU TO 'EM FAST!

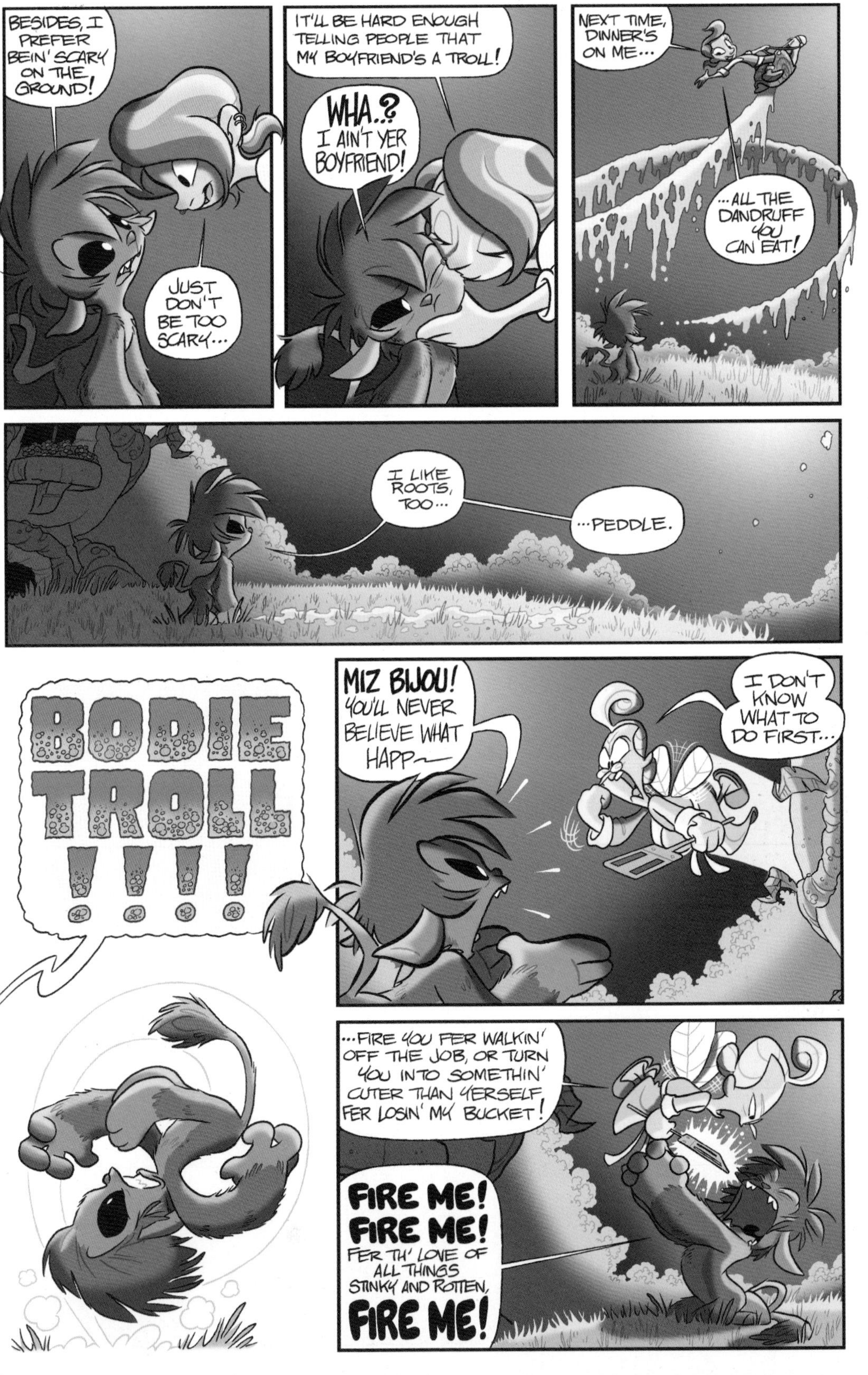
BESIDES, I PREFER BEIN' SCARY ON THE GROUND!
JUST DON'T BE TOO SCARY...
IT'LL BE HARD ENOUGH TELLING PEOPLE THAT MY BOYFRIEND'S A TROLL!
WHA..? I AIN'T YER BOYFRIEND!
NEXT TIME, DINNER'S ON ME...
...ALL THE DANDRUFF YOU CAN EAT!
I LIKE ROOTS, TOO...
...PEDDLE.
BODIE TROLL!!!!
MIZ BIJOU! YOU'LL NEVER BELIEVE WHAT HAPP—
I DON'T KNOW WHAT TO DO FIRST...
...FIRE YOU FER WALKIN' OFF THE JOB, OR TURN YOU INTO SOMETHIN' CUTER THAN YERSELF FER LOSIN' MY BUCKET!
FIRE ME! FIRE ME! FER TH' LOVE OF ALL THINGS STINKY AND ROTTEN, FIRE ME!

YOU'LL NOT GET OFF SO EASY.

I FOUND THE BUCKET IN THE VILLAGE SQUARE...

NOW GO CLEAN IT OUT...

WITH YOUR TONGUE.

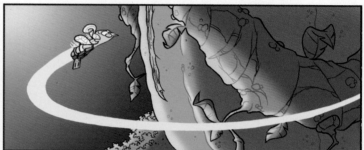

FIRST SUGAR, THEN GIRL KISSES, THEN GOAT PEE...

SOME REWARD FER BEIN' A HERO...

CHAPTER 9
PROSE AND CONS

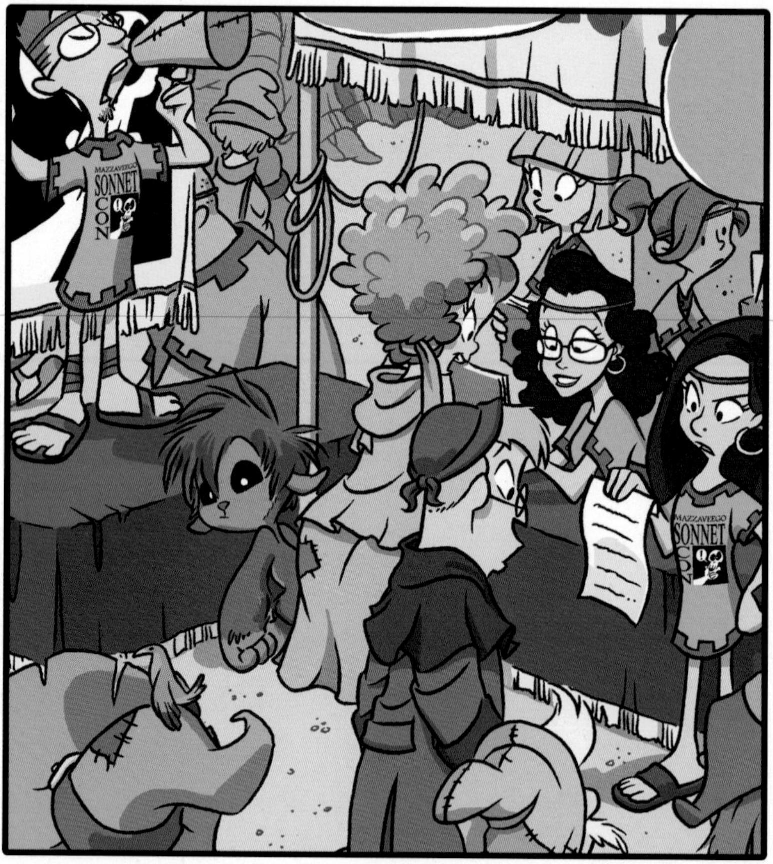
MAZZAVEEGO SONNET CON
MAZZAVEEGO SONNET CON

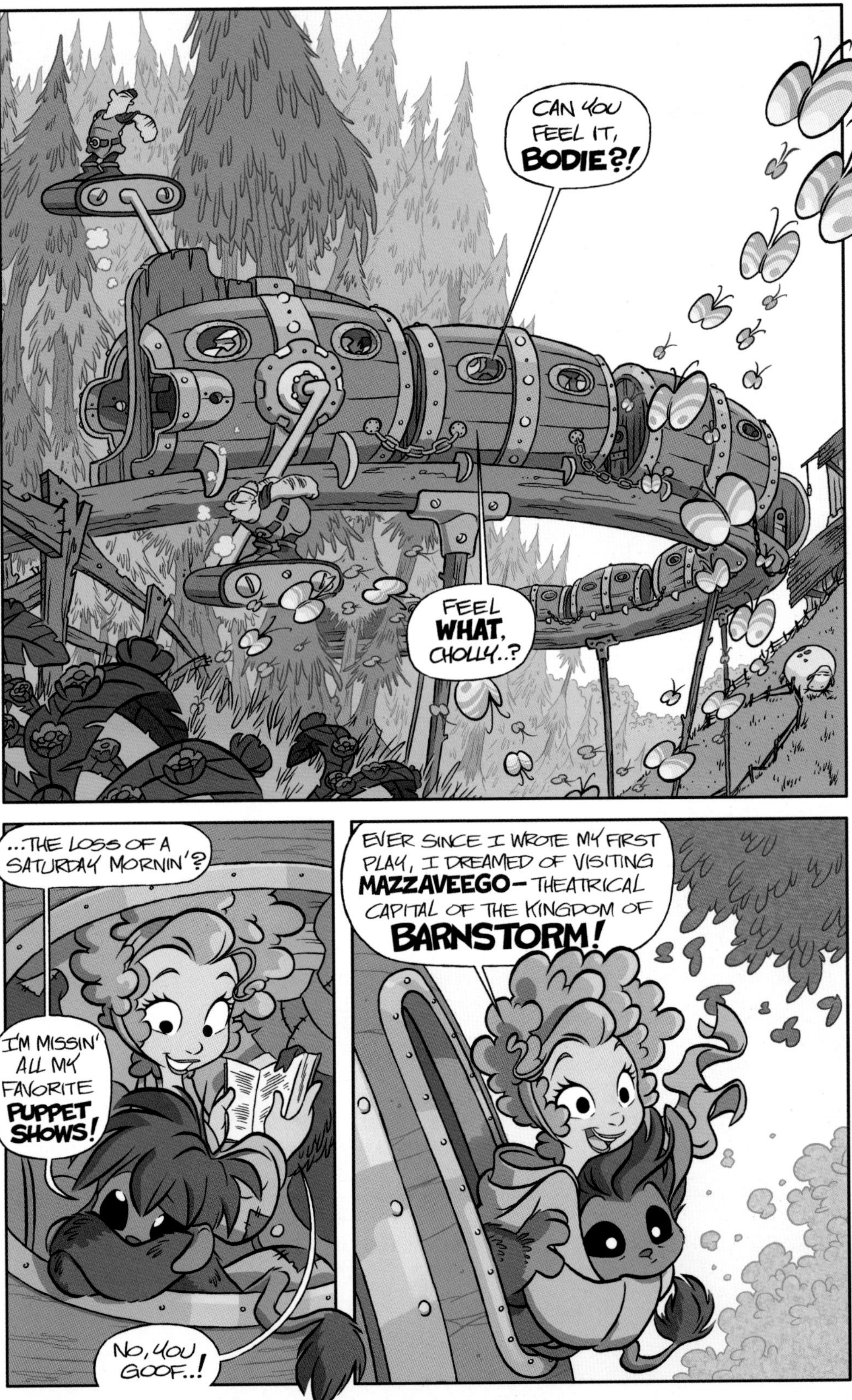
CAN YOU FEEL IT, BODIE?!
FEEL WHAT, CHOLLY..?
...THE LOSS OF A SATURDAY MORNIN'?
I'M MISSIN' ALL MY FAVORITE PUPPET SHOWS!
NO, YOU GOOF..!
EVER SINCE I WROTE MY FIRST PLAY, I DREAMED OF VISITING MAZZAVEEGO— THEATRICAL CAPITAL OF THE KINGDOM OF BARNSTORM!

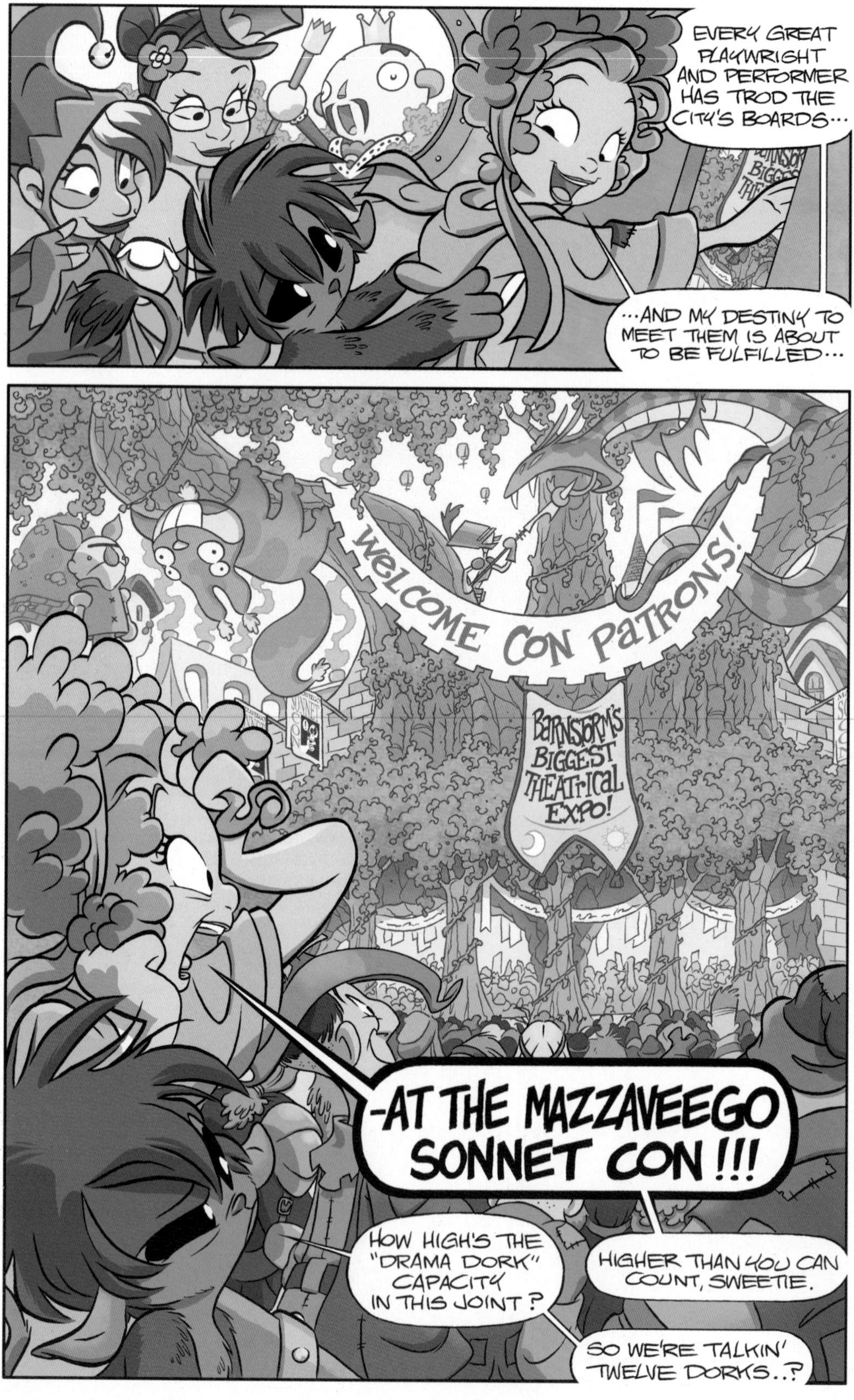
EVERY GREAT PLAYWRIGHT AND PERFORMER HAS TROD THE CITY'S BOARDS...
...AND MY DESTINY TO MEET THEM IS ABOUT TO BE FULFILLED...
WELCOME CON PATRONS!
BARNSTORM'S BIGGEST THEATRICAL EXPO!
-AT THE MAZZAVEEGO SONNET CON!!!
HOW HIGH'S THE "DRAMA DORK" CAPACITY IN THIS JOINT?
HIGHER THAN YOU CAN COUNT, SWEETIE.
SO WE'RE TALKIN' TWELVE DORKS..?

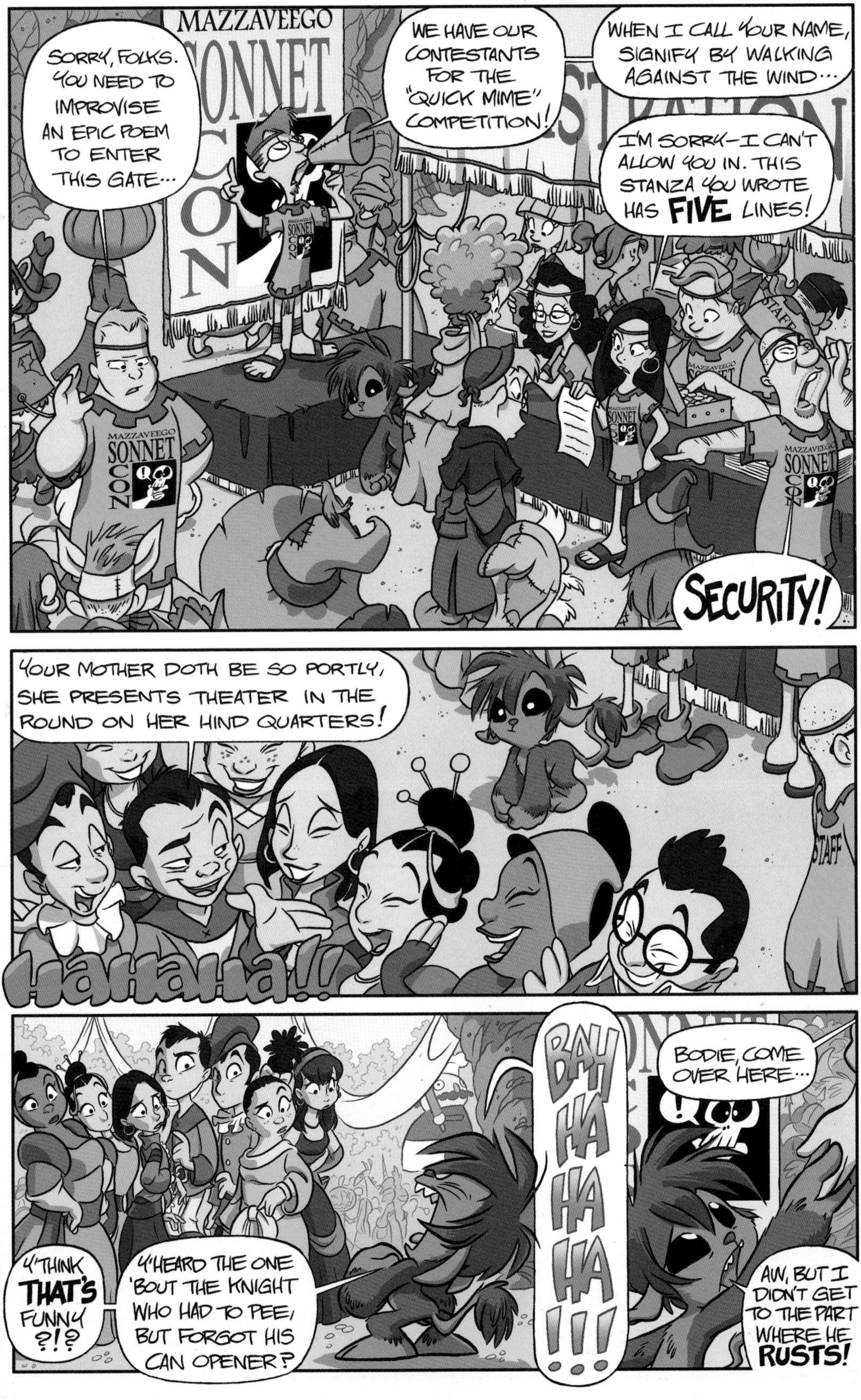
MAZZAVEEGO SONNET CON
SORRY, FOLKS. YOU NEED TO IMPROVISE AN EPIC POEM TO ENTER THIS GATE...
WE HAVE OUR CONTESTANTS FOR THE "QUICK MIME" COMPETITION!
WHEN I CALL YOUR NAME, SIGNIFY BY WALKING AGAINST THE WIND...
I'M SORRY—I CAN'T ALLOW YOU IN. THIS STANZA YOU WROTE HAS FIVE LINES!
SECURITY!
YOUR MOTHER DOTH BE SO PORTLY, SHE PRESENTS THEATER IN THE ROUND ON HER HIND QUARTERS!
HAHAHA!!!
Y'THINK THAT'S FUNNY ?!?
Y'HEARD THE ONE 'BOUT THE KNIGHT WHO HAD TO PEE, BUT FORGOT HIS CAN OPENER?
BAH HA HA HA HA!!!
BODIE, COME OVER HERE...
AW, BUT I DIDN'T GET TO THE PART WHERE HE RUSTS!

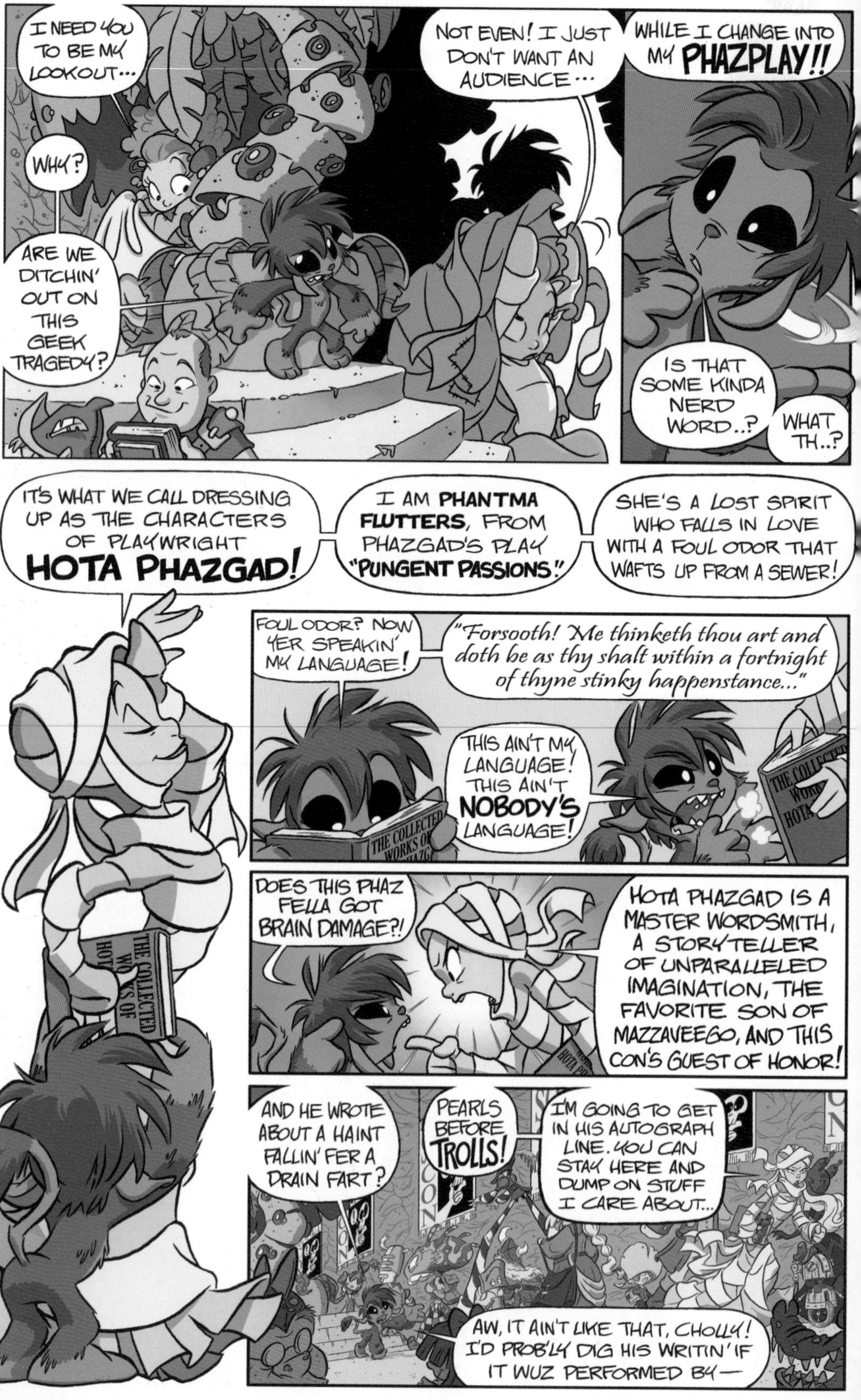
I NEED YOU TO BE MY LOOKOUT...
WHY?
ARE WE DITCHIN' OUT ON THIS GEEK TRAGEDY?
NOT EVEN! I JUST DON'T WANT AN AUDIENCE...
WHILE I CHANGE INTO MY PHAZPLAY!!
IS THAT SOME KINDA NERD WORD..?
WHAT TH..?
IT'S WHAT WE CALL DRESSING UP AS THE CHARACTERS OF PLAYWRIGHT HOTA PHAZGAD!
I AM PHANTMA FLUTTERS, FROM PHAZGAD'S PLAY "PUNGENT PASSIONS."
SHE'S A LOST SPIRIT WHO FALLS IN LOVE WITH A FOUL ODOR THAT WAFTS UP FROM A SEWER!
FOUL ODOR? NOW YER SPEAKIN' MY LANGUAGE!
"Forsooth! Me thinketh thou art and doth be as thy shalt within a fortnight of thyne stinky happenstance..."
THIS AIN'T MY LANGUAGE! THIS AIN'T NOBODY'S LANGUAGE!
THE COLLECTED WORKS OF
DOES THIS PHAZ FELLA GOT BRAIN DAMAGE?!
HOTA PHAZGAD IS A MASTER WORDSMITH, A STORYTELLER OF UNPARALLELED IMAGINATION, THE FAVORITE SON OF MAZZAVEEGO, AND THIS CON'S GUEST OF HONOR!
AND HE WROTE ABOUT A HAINT FALLIN' FER A DRAIN FART?
PEARLS BEFORE TROLLS!
I'M GOING TO GET IN HIS AUTOGRAPH LINE. YOU CAN STAY HERE AND DUMP ON STUFF I CARE ABOUT...
AW, IT AIN'T LIKE THAT, CHOLLY! I'D PROB'LY DIG HIS WRITIN' IF IT WUZ PERFORMED BY—

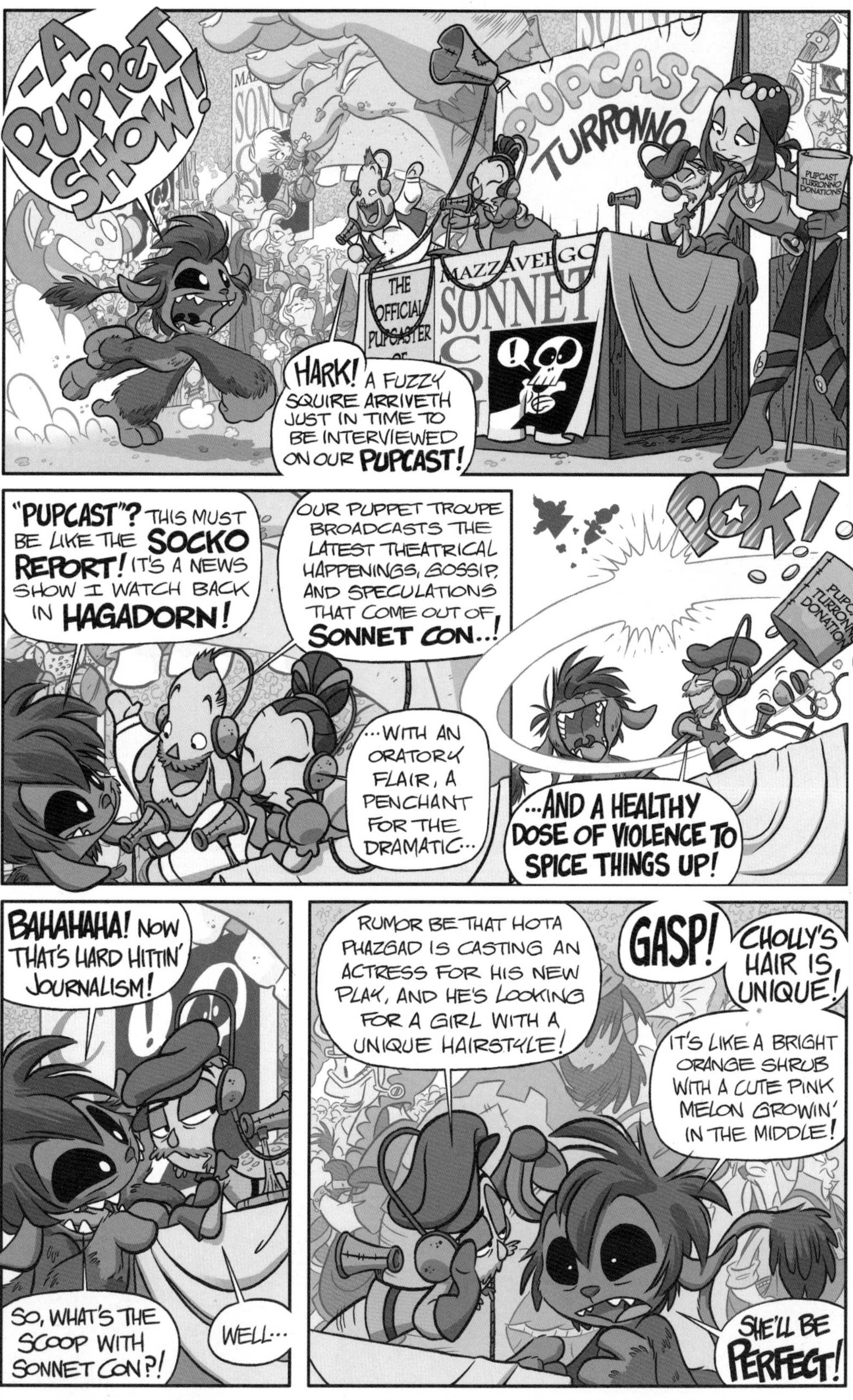

-A PUPPET SHOW!
PUPCAST
TURRONNO
MAZZAVERGO SONNET
THE OFFICIAL PUPCASTER
PUPCAST TURRONNO DONATIONS
HARK! A FUZZY SQUIRE ARRIVETH JUST IN TIME TO BE INTERVIEWED ON OUR PUPCAST!
"PUPCAST"? THIS MUST BE LIKE THE SOCKO REPORT! IT'S A NEWS SHOW I WATCH BACK IN HAGADORN!
OUR PUPPET TROUPE BROADCASTS THE LATEST THEATRICAL HAPPENINGS, GOSSIP, AND SPECULATIONS THAT COME OUT OF SONNET CON...!
...WITH AN ORATORY FLAIR, A PENCHANT FOR THE DRAMATIC...
POK!
PUPCAST TURRONNO DONATIONS
...AND A HEALTHY DOSE OF VIOLENCE TO SPICE THINGS UP!
BAHAHAHA! NOW THAT'S HARD HITTIN' JOURNALISM!
SO, WHAT'S THE SCOOP WITH SONNET CON?!
WELL...
RUMOR BE THAT HOTA PHAZGAD IS CASTING AN ACTRESS FOR HIS NEW PLAY, AND HE'S LOOKING FOR A GIRL WITH A UNIQUE HAIRSTYLE!
GASP!
CHOLLY'S HAIR IS UNIQUE!
IT'S LIKE A BRIGHT ORANGE SHRUB WITH A CUTE PINK MELON GROWIN' IN THE MIDDLE!
SHE'LL BE PERFECT!

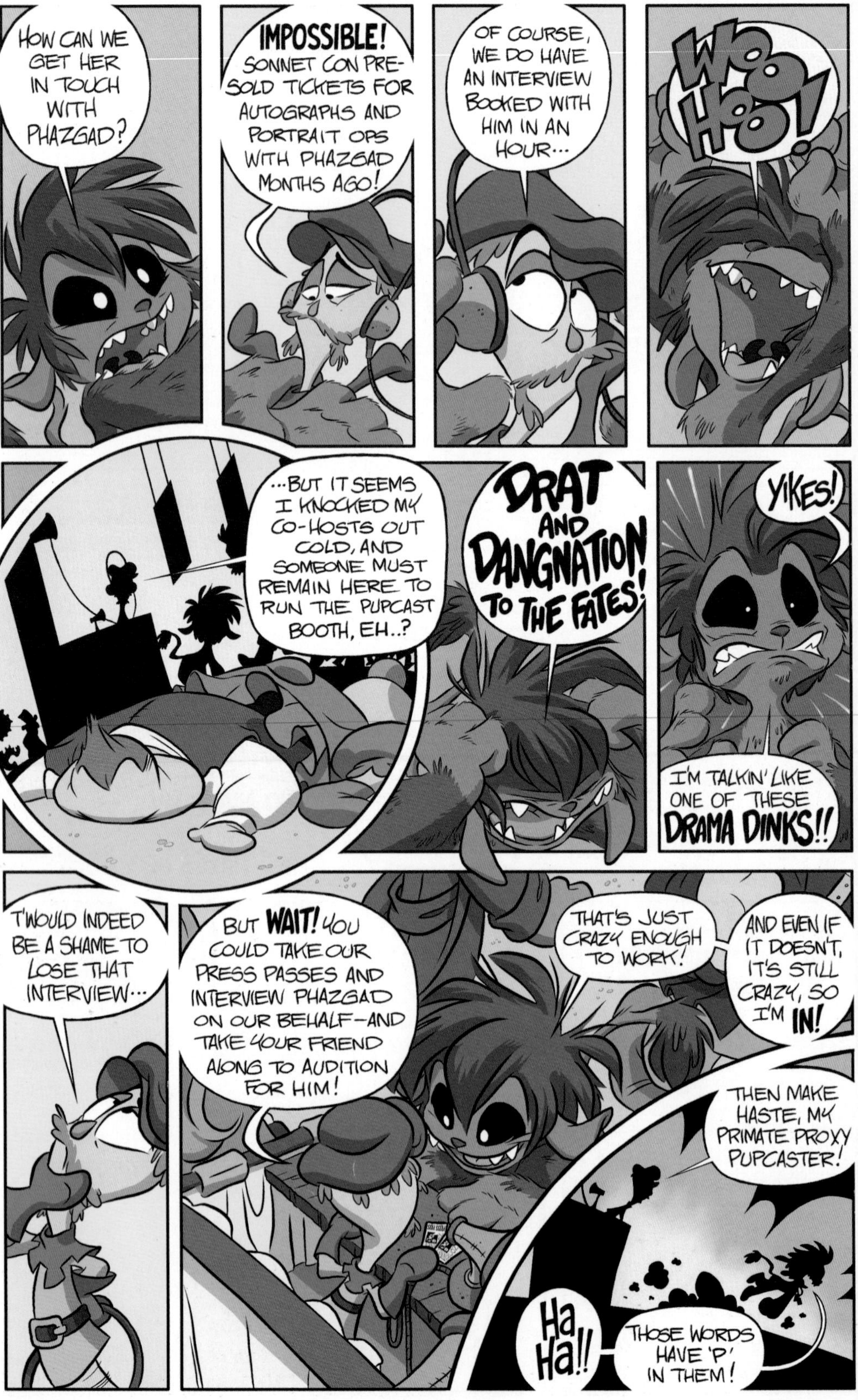
HOW CAN WE GET HER IN TOUCH WITH PHAZGAD?
IMPOSSIBLE! SONNET CON PRE-SOLD TICKETS FOR AUTOGRAPHS AND PORTRAIT OPS WITH PHAZGAD MONTHS AGO!
OF COURSE, WE DO HAVE AN INTERVIEW BOOKED WITH HIM IN AN HOUR...
WOO HOO!
...BUT IT SEEMS I KNOCKED MY CO-HOSTS OUT COLD, AND SOMEONE MUST REMAIN HERE TO RUN THE PUPCAST BOOTH, EH..?
DRAT AND DANGNATION TO THE FATES!
YIKES!
I'M TALKIN' LIKE ONE OF THESE DRAMA DINKS!!
T'WOULD INDEED BE A SHAME TO LOSE THAT INTERVIEW...
BUT WAIT! YOU COULD TAKE OUR PRESS PASSES AND INTERVIEW PHAZGAD ON OUR BEHALF—AND TAKE YOUR FRIEND ALONG TO AUDITION FOR HIM!
THAT'S JUST CRAZY ENOUGH TO WORK!
AND EVEN IF IT DOESN'T, IT'S STILL CRAZY, SO I'M IN!
THEN MAKE HASTE, MY PRIMATE PROXY PUPCASTER!
HA HA!!
THOSE WORDS HAVE 'P' IN THEM!

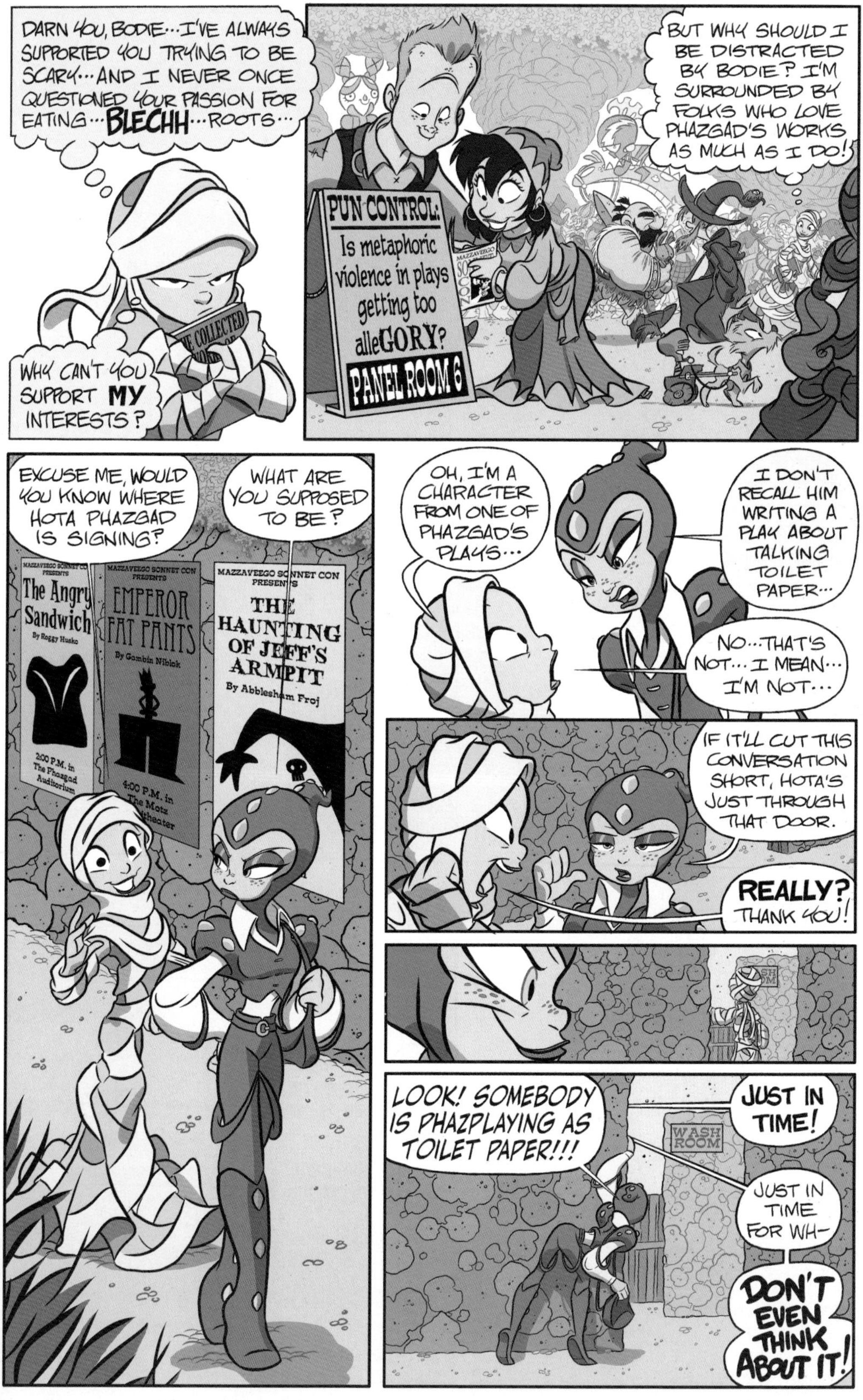
DARN YOU, BODIE... I'VE ALWAYS SUPPORTED YOU TRYING TO BE SCARY... AND I NEVER ONCE QUESTIONED YOUR PASSION FOR EATING... BLECHH... ROOTS...
WHY CAN'T YOU SUPPORT MY INTERESTS?
BUT WHY SHOULD I BE DISTRACTED BY BODIE? I'M SURROUNDED BY FOLKS WHO LOVE PHAZGAD'S WORKS AS MUCH AS I DO!
PUN CONTROL: Is metaphoric violence in plays getting too alleGORY? PANEL ROOM 6
EXCUSE ME, WOULD YOU KNOW WHERE HOTA PHAZGAD IS SIGNING?
WHAT ARE YOU SUPPOSED TO BE?
MAZZAVEEGO SONNET CON PRESENTS The Angry Sandwich By Roggy Husko 2:00 P.M. in The Phazgad Auditorium
MAZZAVEEGO SONNET CON PRESENTS EMPEROR FAT PANTS By Gambin Niblok 4:00 P.M. in The Mots
MAZZAVEEGO SONNET CON PRESENTS THE HAUNTING OF JEFF'S ARMPIT By Abblesham Froj
OH, I'M A CHARACTER FROM ONE OF PHAZGAD'S PLAYS...
I DON'T RECALL HIM WRITING A PLAY ABOUT TALKING TOILET PAPER...
NO... THAT'S NOT... I MEAN... I'M NOT...
IF IT'LL CUT THIS CONVERSATION SHORT, HOTA'S JUST THROUGH THAT DOOR.
REALLY? THANK YOU!
LOOK! SOMEBODY IS PHAZPLAYING AS TOILET PAPER!!!
WASH ROOM
JUST IN TIME!
JUST IN TIME FOR WH-
DON'T EVEN THINK ABOUT IT!

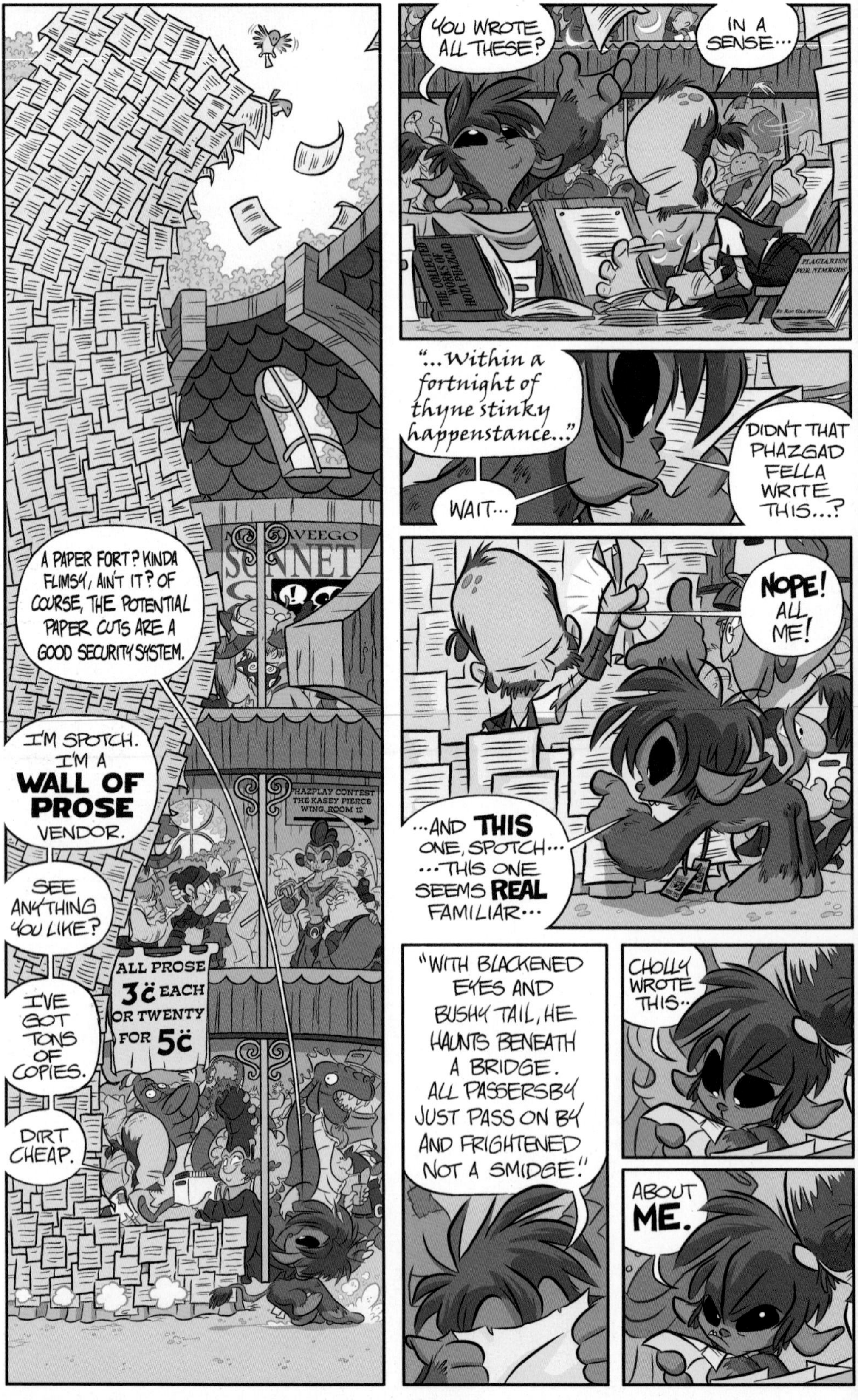
MASTAVEEGO SONNET
A PAPER FORT? KINDA FLIMSY, AIN'T IT? OF COURSE, THE POTENTIAL PAPER CUTS ARE A GOOD SECURITY SYSTEM.
I'M SPOTCH. I'M A WALL OF PROSE VENDOR.
SEE ANYTHING YOU LIKE?
I'VE GOT TONS OF COPIES.
DIRT CHEAP.
HAZPLAY CONTEST THE KASEY PIERCE WING, ROOM 12
ALL PROSE 3¢ EACH OR TWENTY FOR 5¢
YOU WROTE ALL THESE?
IN A SENSE...
THE COLLECTED WORKS OF HOJA PHAZGAD
PLAGIARISM FOR NIMRODS
"...Within a fortnight of thyne stinky happenstance..."
WAIT...
DIDN'T THAT PHAZGAD FELLA WRITE THIS...?
NOPE! ALL ME!
...AND THIS ONE, SPOTCH... ...THIS ONE SEEMS REAL FAMILIAR...
"WITH BLACKENED EYES AND BUSHY TAIL, HE HAUNTS BENEATH A BRIDGE. ALL PASSERSBY JUST PASS ON BY AND FRIGHTENED NOT A SMIDGE."
CHOLLY WROTE THIS...
ABOUT ME.

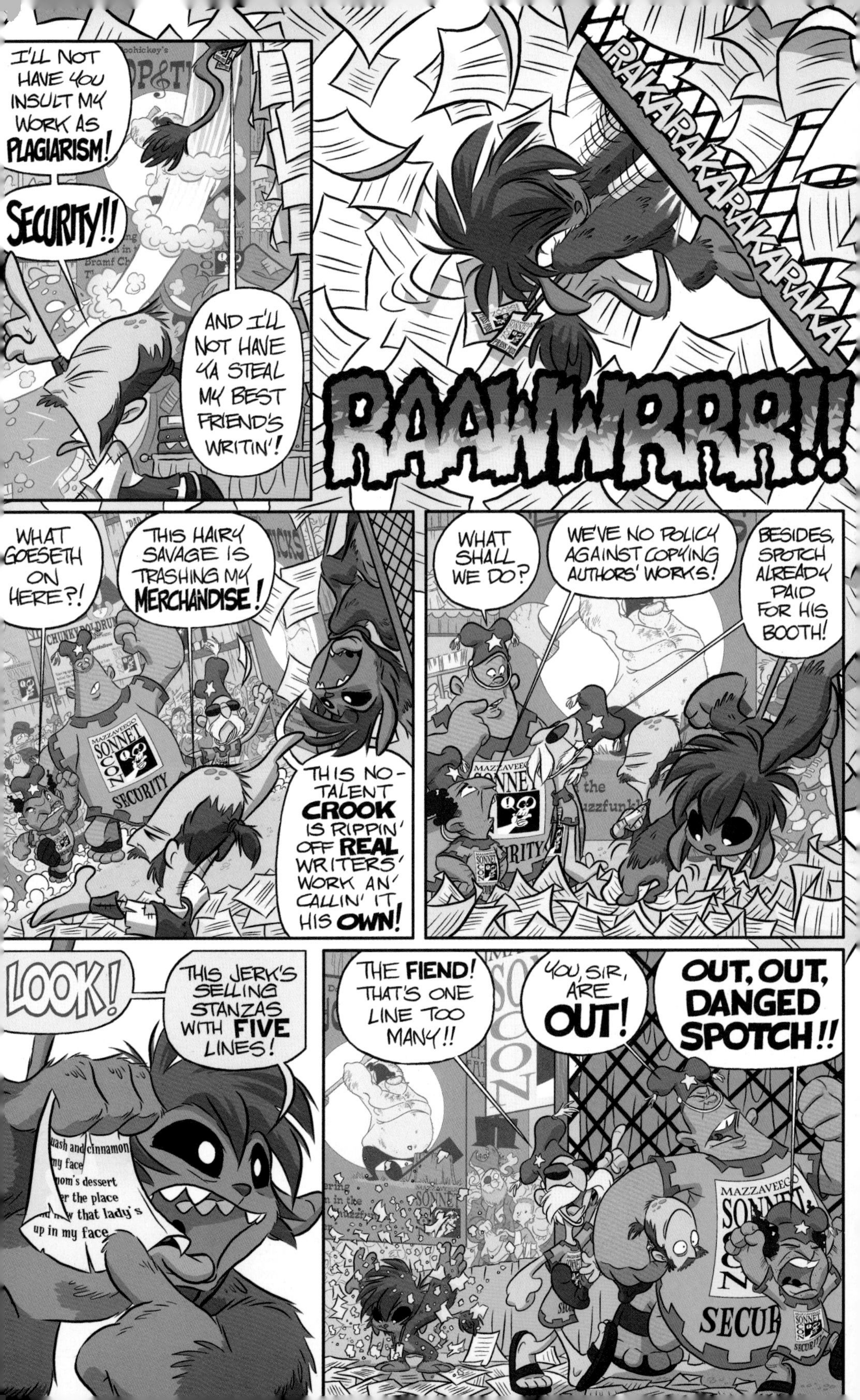
I'LL NOT HAVE YOU INSULT MY WORK AS PLAGIARISM!
SECURITY!!
AND I'LL NOT HAVE YA STEAL MY BEST FRIEND'S WRITIN'!
RAKARAKARAKARAKARAKA
RAAWRRR!!
WHAT GOESETH ON HERE?!
THIS HAIRY SAVAGE IS TRASHING MY MERCHANDISE!
THIS NO-TALENT CROOK IS RIPPIN' OFF REAL WRITERS' WORK AN' CALLIN' IT HIS OWN!
WHAT SHALL WE DO?
WE'VE NO POLICY AGAINST COPYING AUTHORS' WORKS!
BESIDES, SPOTCH ALREADY PAID FOR HIS BOOTH!
LOOK!
THIS JERK'S SELLING STANZAS WITH FIVE LINES!
THE FIEND! THAT'S ONE LINE TOO MANY!!
YOU, SIR, ARE OUT!
OUT, OUT, DANGED SPOTCH!!

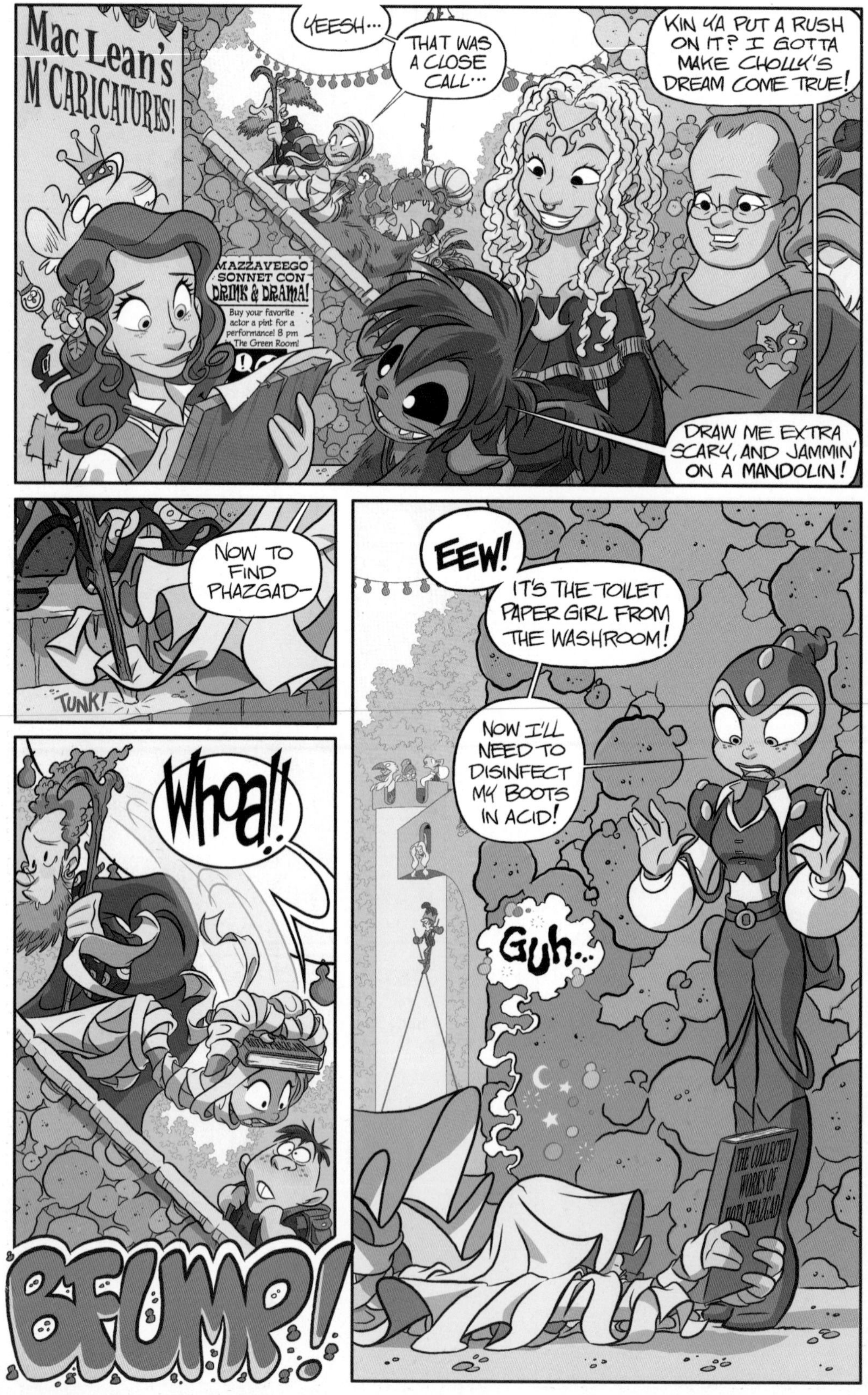
Mac Lean's M'CARICATURES!
YEESH...
THAT WAS A CLOSE CALL...
KIN YA PUT A RUSH ON IT? I GOTTA MAKE CHOLLY'S DREAM COME TRUE!
MAZZAVEEGO SONNET CON
DRINK & DRAMA!
Buy your favorite actor a pint for a performance! 8 pm
The Green Room!
DRAW ME EXTRA SCARY, AND JAMMIN' ON A MANDOLIN!
NOW TO FIND PHAZGAD-
TUNK!
Whoa!!
BFUMP!
EEW!
IT'S THE TOILET PAPER GIRL FROM THE WASHROOM!
NOW I'LL NEED TO DISINFECT MY BOOTS IN ACID!
Guh...
THE COLLECTED WORKS OF HOTA PHAZGAD

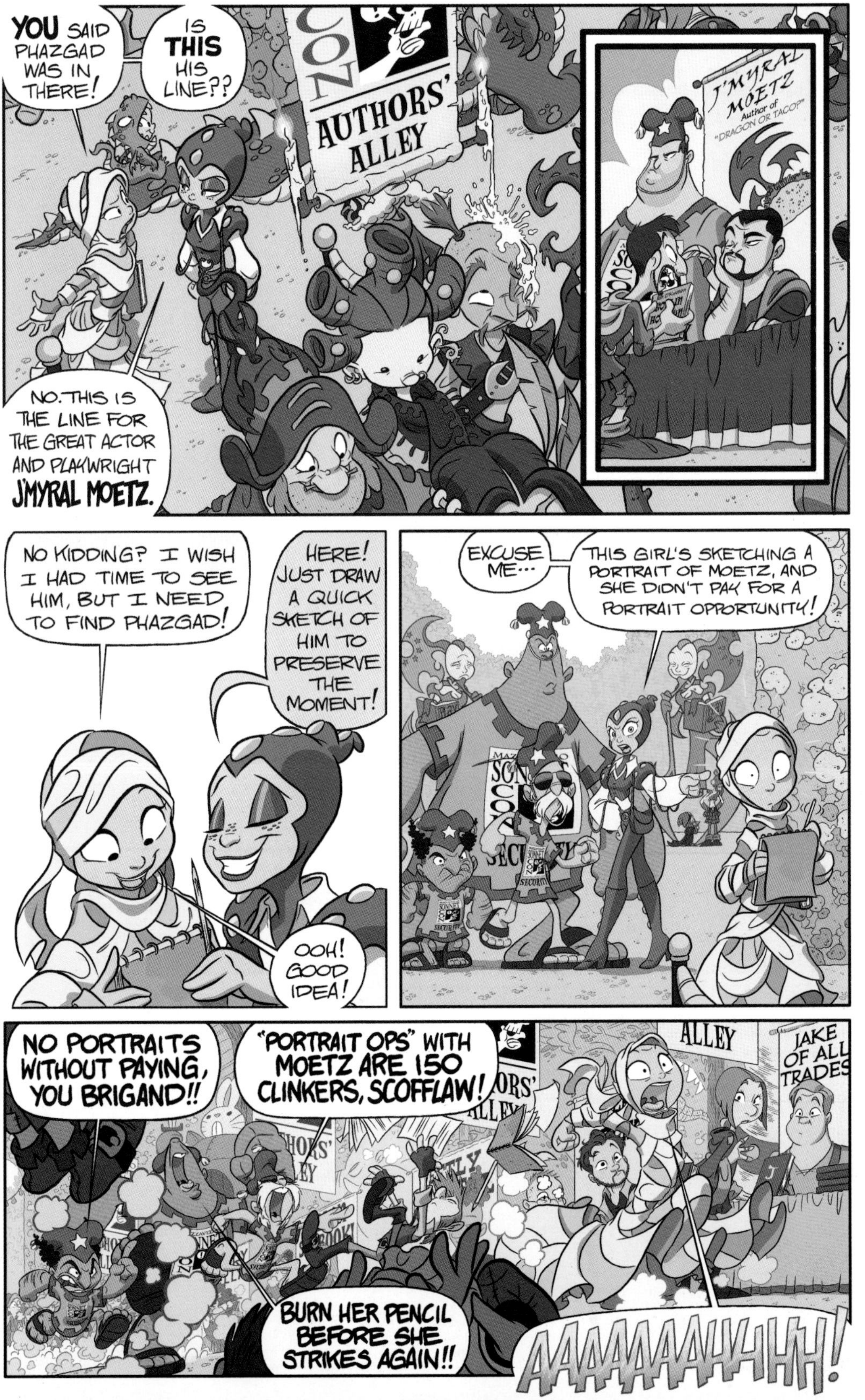
YOU SAID PHAZGAD WAS IN THERE!
IS THIS HIS LINE??
CON
AUTHORS' ALLEY
J'MYRAL MOETZ Author of "DRAGON OR TACO?"
NO. THIS IS THE LINE FOR THE GREAT ACTOR AND PLAYWRIGHT J'MYRAL MOETZ.
NO KIDDING? I WISH I HAD TIME TO SEE HIM, BUT I NEED TO FIND PHAZGAD!
HERE! JUST DRAW A QUICK SKETCH OF HIM TO PRESERVE THE MOMENT!
OOH! GOOD IDEA!
EXCUSE ME...
THIS GIRL'S SKETCHING A PORTRAIT OF MOETZ, AND SHE DIDN'T PAY FOR A PORTRAIT OPPORTUNITY!
SECURITY
NO PORTRAITS WITHOUT PAYING, YOU BRIGAND!!
"PORTRAIT OPS" WITH MOETZ ARE 150 CLINKERS, SCOFFLAW!
ALLEY
JAKE OF ALL TRADES
BURN HER PENCIL BEFORE SHE STRIKES AGAIN!!
AAAAAAAHHHH!

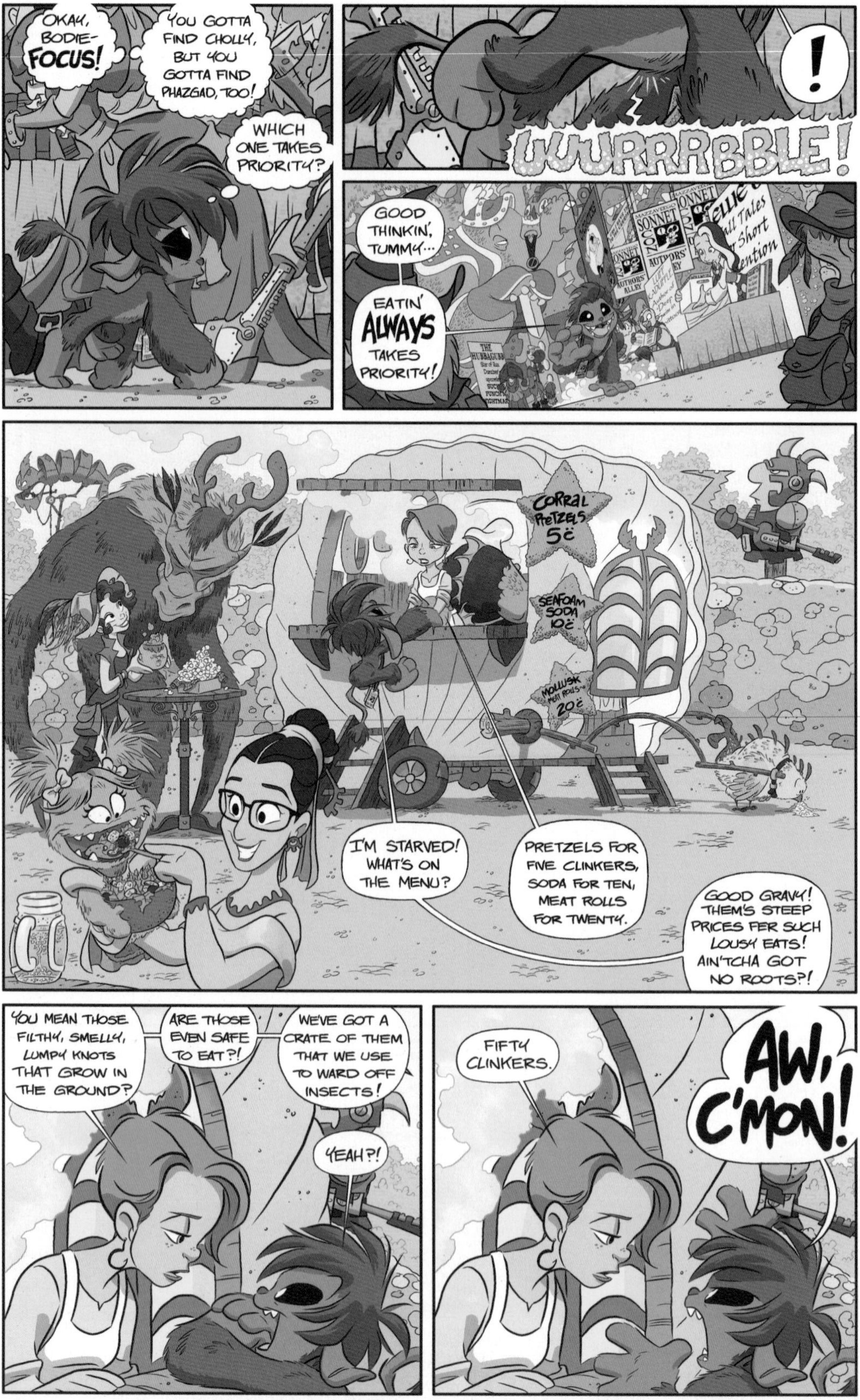
OKAY, BODIE- FOCUS!
YOU GOTTA FIND CHOLLY, BUT YOU GOTTA FIND PHAZGAD, TOO!
WHICH ONE TAKES PRIORITY?
!
UUURRRBBLE!
GOOD THINKIN', TUMMY...
EATIN' ALWAYS TAKES PRIORITY!
CORRAL PRETZELS 5¢
SEAFOAM SODA 10¢
I'M STARVED! WHAT'S ON THE MENU?
PRETZELS FOR FIVE CLINKERS, SODA FOR TEN, MEAT ROLLS FOR TWENTY.
GOOD GRAVY! THEM'S STEEP PRICES FER SUCH LOUSY EATS! AIN'TCHA GOT NO ROOTS?!
YOU MEAN THOSE FILTHY, SMELLY, LUMPY KNOTS THAT GROW IN THE GROUND?
ARE THOSE EVEN SAFE TO EAT?!
WE'VE GOT A CRATE OF THEM THAT WE USE TO WARD OFF INSECTS!
YEAH?!
FIFTY CLINKERS.
AW, C'MON!

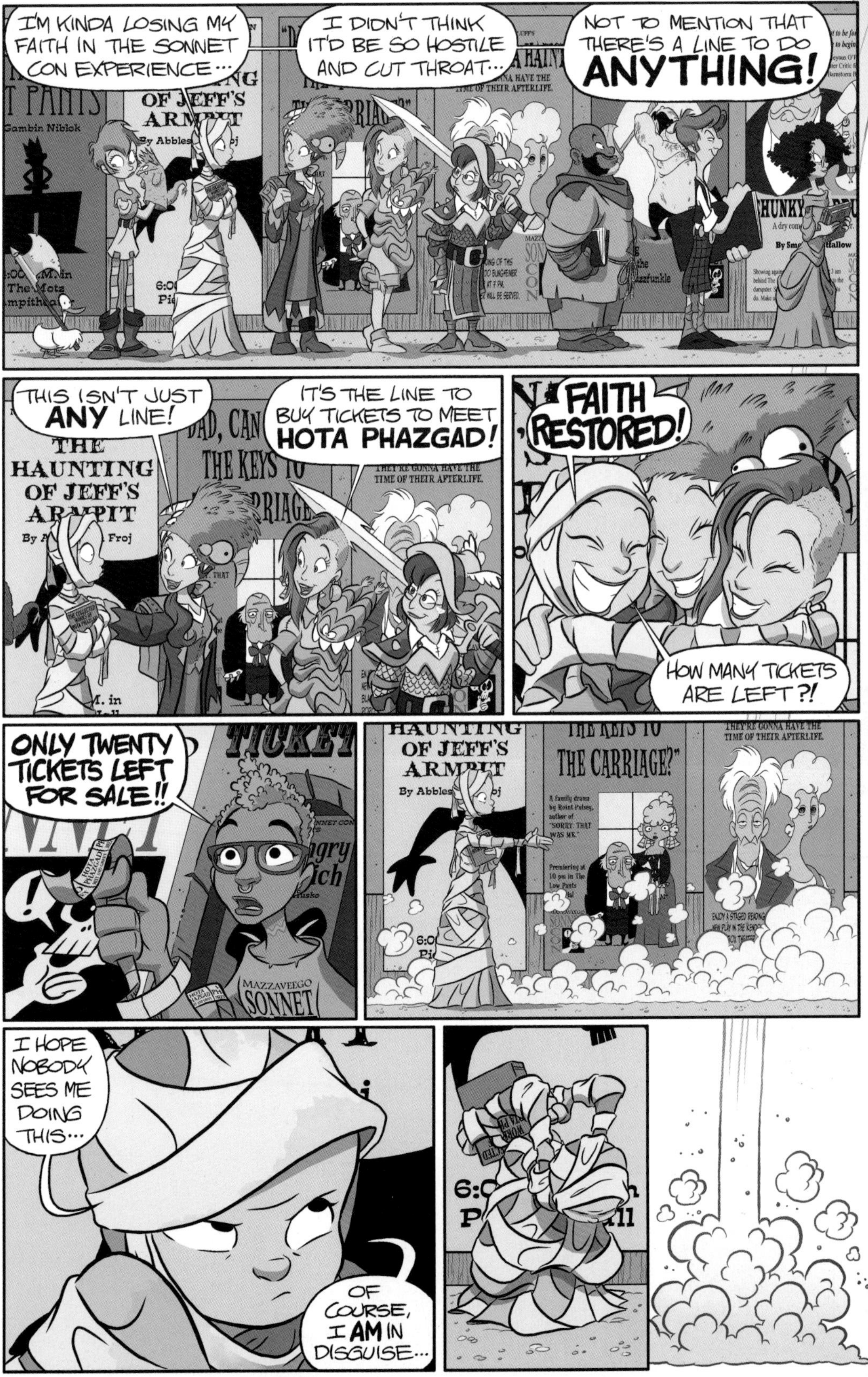
I'M KINDA LOSING MY FAITH IN THE SONNET CON EXPERIENCE...
I DIDN'T THINK IT'D BE SO HOSTILE AND CUT THROAT...
NOT TO MENTION THAT THERE'S A LINE TO DO ANYTHING!
THIS ISN'T JUST ANY LINE!
IT'S THE LINE TO BUY TICKETS TO MEET HOTA PHAZGAD!
FAITH RESTORED!
HOW MANY TICKETS ARE LEFT?!
ONLY TWENTY TICKETS LEFT FOR SALE!!
I HOPE NOBODY SEES ME DOING THIS...
OF COURSE, I AM IN DISGUISE...

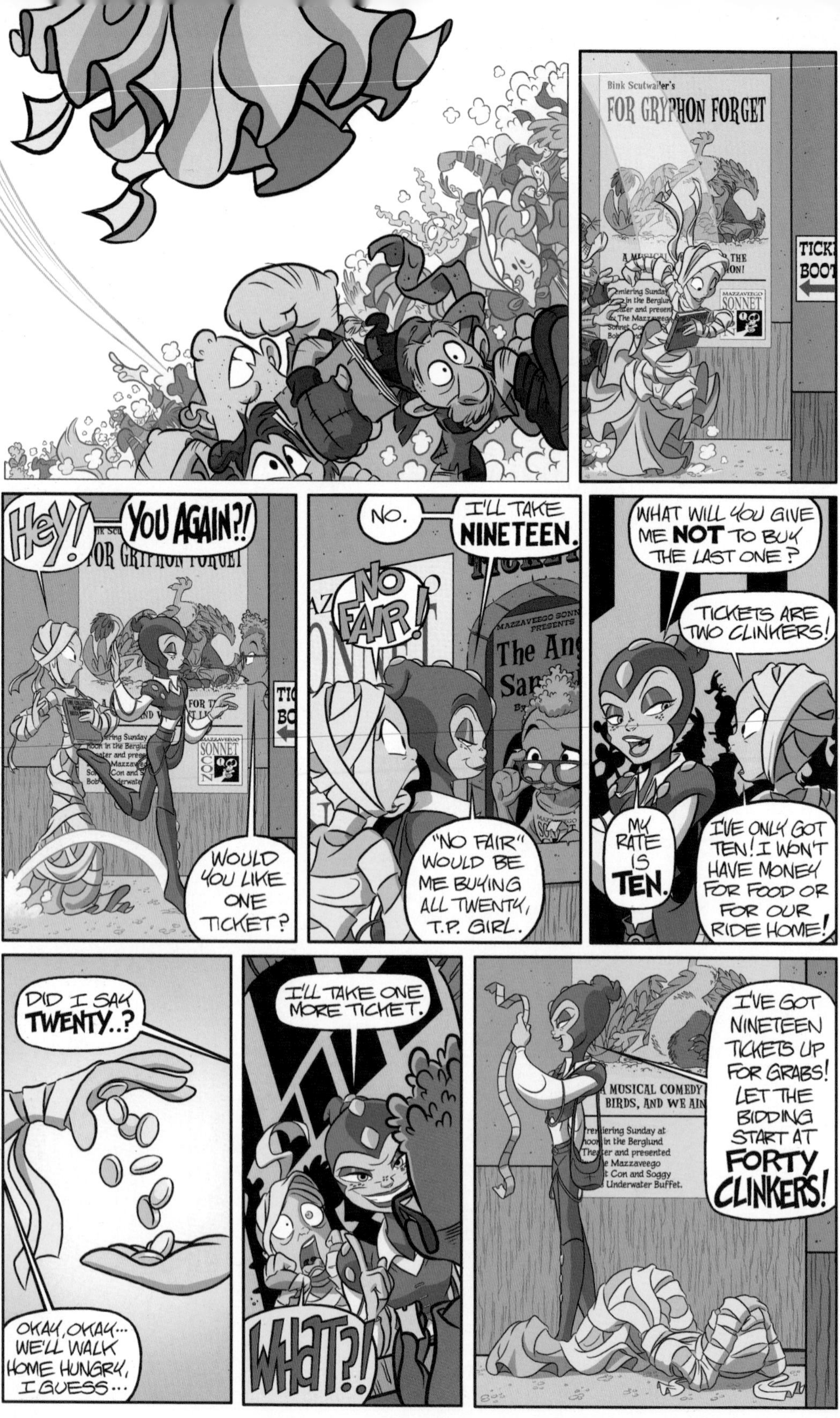

Bink Scutwaller's
FOR GRYPHON FORGET
MAZZAVEEGO SONNET
HEY!
YOU AGAIN?!
WOULD YOU LIKE ONE TICKET?
NO.
I'LL TAKE NINETEEN.
NO FAIR!
"NO FAIR" WOULD BE ME BUYING ALL TWENTY, T.P. GIRL.
WHAT WILL YOU GIVE ME NOT TO BUY THE LAST ONE?
TICKETS ARE TWO CLINKERS!
MY RATE IS TEN.
I'VE ONLY GOT TEN! I WON'T HAVE MONEY FOR FOOD OR FOR OUR RIDE HOME!
DID I SAY TWENTY..?
OKAY, OKAY... WE'LL WALK HOME HUNGRY, I GUESS...
I'LL TAKE ONE MORE TICKET.
WHAT?!
I'VE GOT NINETEEN TICKETS UP FOR GRABS! LET THE BIDDING START AT FORTY CLINKERS!

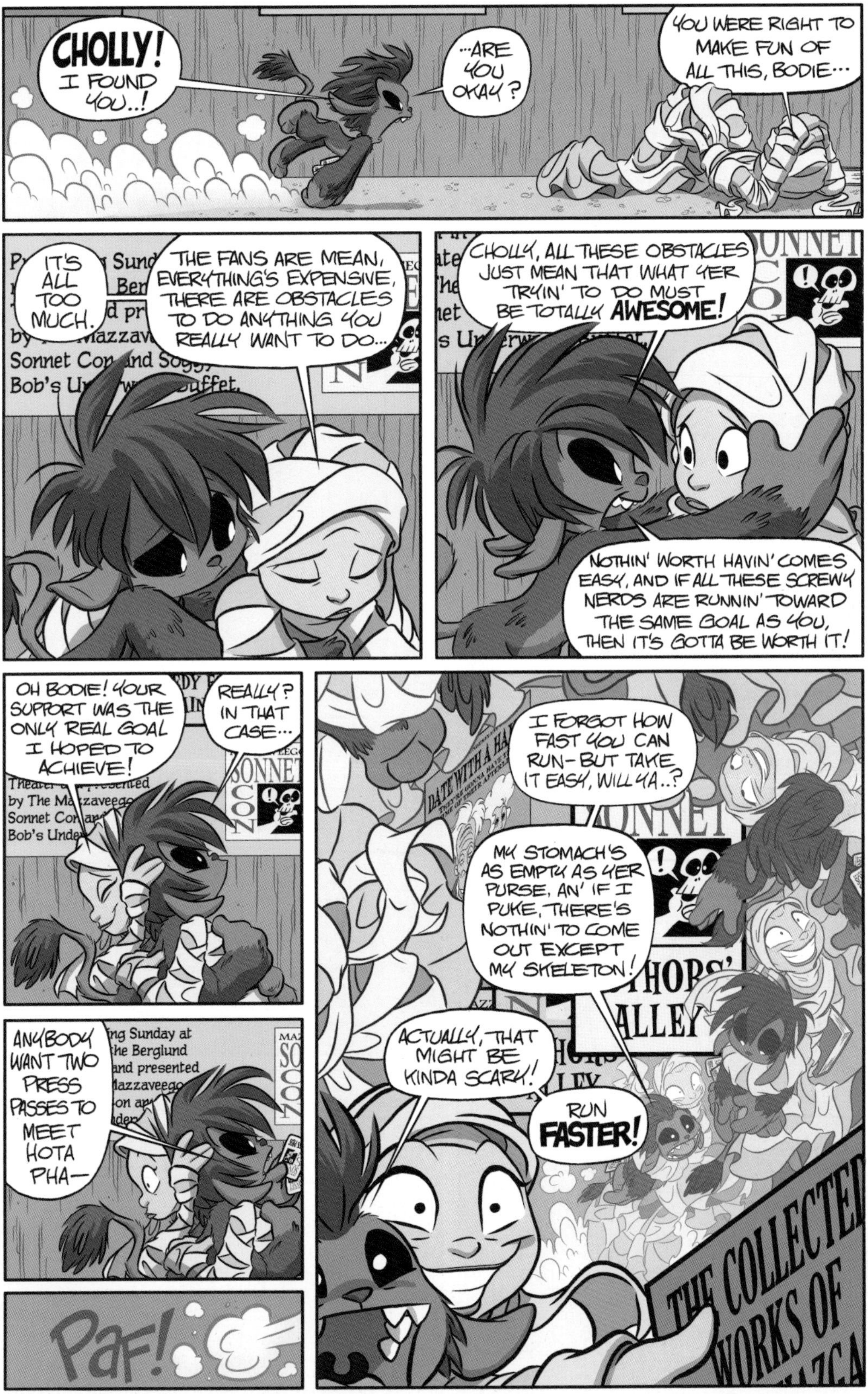
CHOLLY! I FOUND YOU..!
...ARE YOU OKAY?
YOU WERE RIGHT TO MAKE FUN OF ALL THIS, BODIE...
IT'S ALL TOO MUCH.
THE FANS ARE MEAN, EVERYTHING'S EXPENSIVE, THERE ARE OBSTACLES TO DO ANYTHING YOU REALLY WANT TO DO...
CHOLLY, ALL THESE OBSTACLES JUST MEAN THAT WHAT YER TRYIN' TO DO MUST BE TOTALLY AWESOME!
NOTHIN' WORTH HAVIN' COMES EASY, AND IF ALL THESE SCREWY NERDS ARE RUNNIN' TOWARD THE SAME GOAL AS YOU, THEN IT'S GOTTA BE WORTH IT!
OH BODIE! YOUR SUPPORT WAS THE ONLY REAL GOAL I HOPED TO ACHIEVE!
REALLY? IN THAT CASE...
ANYBODY WANT TWO PRESS PASSES TO MEET HOTA PHA—
PAF!
I FORGOT HOW FAST YOU CAN RUN– BUT TAKE IT EASY, WILL YA..?
MY STOMACH'S AS EMPTY AS YER PURSE, AN' IF I PUKE, THERE'S NOTHIN' TO COME OUT EXCEPT MY SKELETON!
ACTUALLY, THAT MIGHT BE KINDA SCARY!
RUN FASTER!
THE COLLECTED WORKS OF

Line starts here for HOTA PHAZGAD

CHHHHUUUFFFFFFF...

I'M SORRY, FOLKS. HOTA HAS RECEIVED HIS FINAL TICKET HOLDER FOR TODAY...

BUT WE'RE WITH THE PUPCAST! I'M SUPPOSED TO INTERVIEW HIM!

AND CHOLLY'S GONNA AUDITION FER HIM!

I AM?!

HOTA HAD AN ENGAGEMENT POP UP THAT HE MUST LEAVE FOR, RIGHT AFTER HE MEETS WITH...

...THIS YOUNG WOMAN.

I SOOOOO SHOULD HAVE SEEN THIS COMING...

T.P. GIRL! HOW PERFECT!

YOU CAN DRY YOUR EYES ON YOURSELF AS I AUDITION FOR YOUR HERO!

AND WHO MIGHT YOU BE, MISS?

GOSSAMER, GOOD SIR! I AM AN ACTRESS!

THE COLLECTED WORKS OF HOTA PHAZGAD

I'VE ONLY PERFORMED ONCE, BUT I ASSURE YOU, MY FATHER SAYS I WAS BRILLIANT!

WELL, YOU CAN CERTAINLY ACT CONFIDENT.

BUT I'M LOOKING FOR AN ACTRESS WITH THAT SPECIAL—

THE COLLECTED WORKS OF HOTA PHAZGAD

HAIRSTYLE?! SO I'VE HEARD!

LOOK NO FURTHER PHAZGAD..!

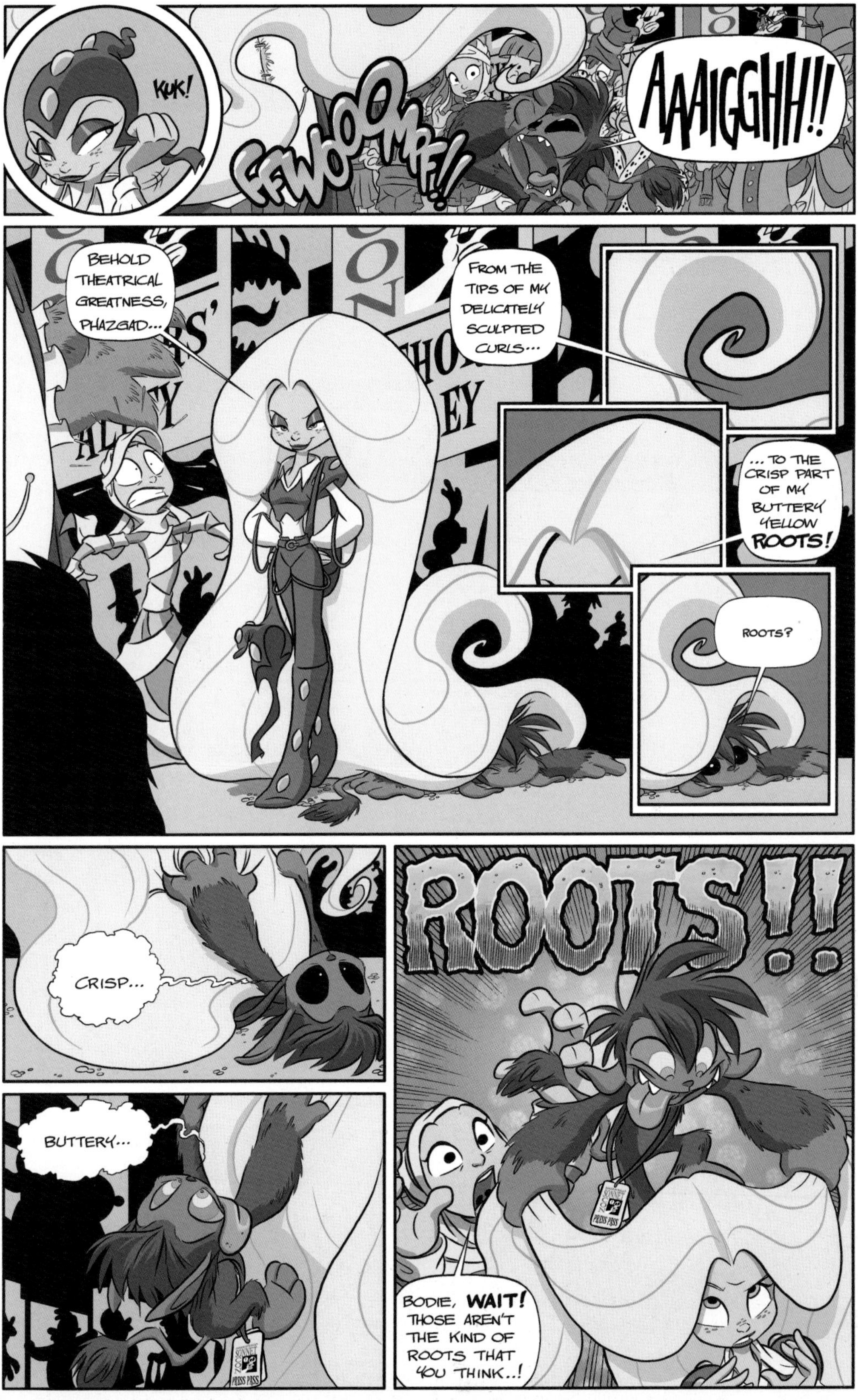
KUK!
FFWOOOMPF!!
AAAIGGHH!!
BEHOLD THEATRICAL GREATNESS, PHAZGAD...
FROM THE TIPS OF MY DELICATELY SCULPTED CURLS...
...TO THE CRISP PART OF MY BUTTERY YELLOW ROOTS!
ROOTS?
CRISP...
BUTTERY...
ROOTS!!
BODIE, WAIT! THOSE AREN'T THE KIND OF ROOTS THAT YOU THINK..!

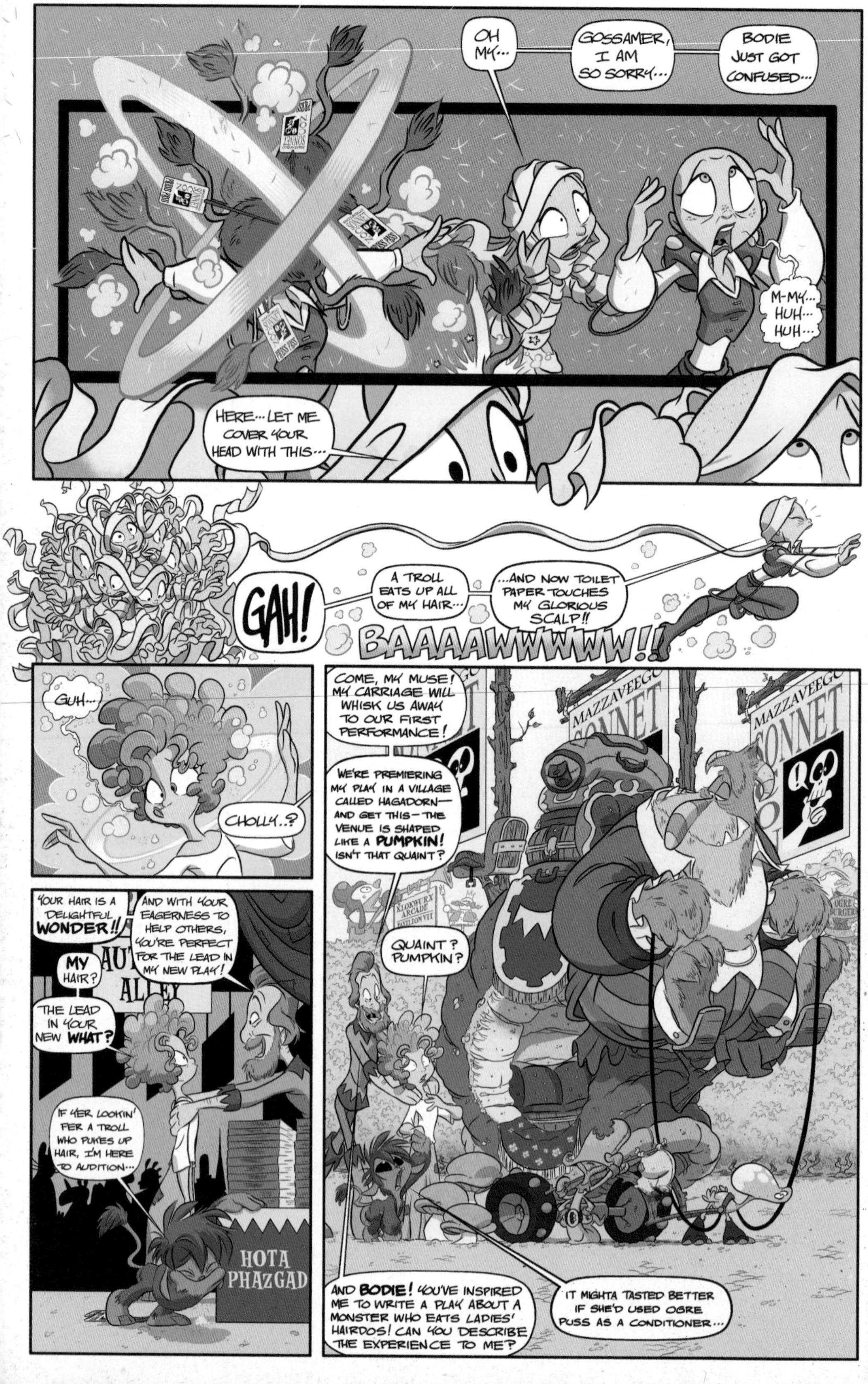

OH MY...
GOSSAMER, I AM SO SORRY...
BODIE JUST GOT CONFUSED...
M-MY... HUH... HUH...
HERE... LET ME COVER YOUR HEAD WITH THIS...
GAH!
A TROLL EATS UP ALL OF MY HAIR...
...AND NOW TOILET PAPER TOUCHES MY GLORIOUS SCALP!!
BAAAAWWWWW!!
GUH...
CHOLLY..?
COME, MY MUSE! MY CARRIAGE WILL WHISK US AWAY TO OUR FIRST PERFORMANCE!
WE'RE PREMIERING MY PLAY IN A VILLAGE CALLED HAGADORN— AND GET THIS— THE VENUE IS SHAPED LIKE A PUMPKIN! ISN'T THAT QUAINT?
QUAINT? PUMPKIN?
YOUR HAIR IS A DELIGHTFUL WONDER!!
AND WITH YOUR EAGERNESS TO HELP OTHERS, YOU'RE PERFECT FOR THE LEAD IN MY NEW PLAY!
MY HAIR?
THE LEAD IN YOUR NEW WHAT?
IF YER LOOKIN' FER A TROLL WHO PUKES UP HAIR, I'M HERE TO AUDITION...
HOTA PHAZGAD
MAZZAVEEGO SONNET
KLOKWURX ARCADE PAVILION VII
OGRE BURGERS
AND BODIE! YOU'VE INSPIRED ME TO WRITE A PLAY ABOUT A MONSTER WHO EATS LADIES' HAIRDOS! CAN YOU DESCRIBE THE EXPERIENCE TO ME?
IT MIGHTA TASTED BETTER IF SHE'D USED OGRE PUSS AS A CONDITIONER...

CHAPTER 10
BODIE GROWS TWO FEET

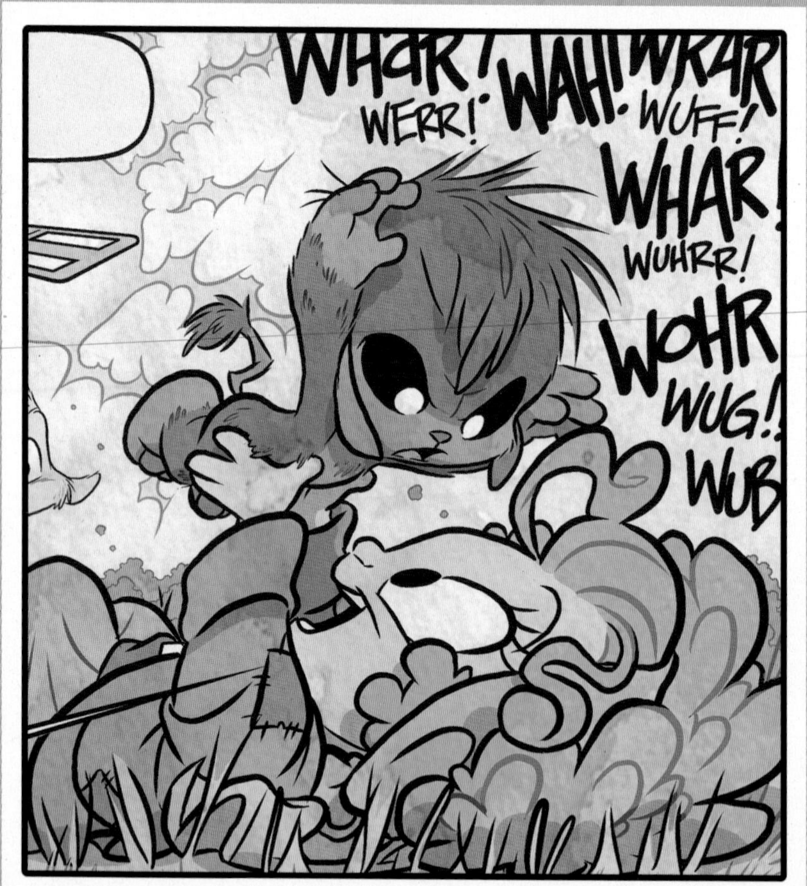
WHAR!
WERR!
WAH!
WRAR
WUFF!
WHAR!
WUHRR!
WOHR
WUG!
WUB

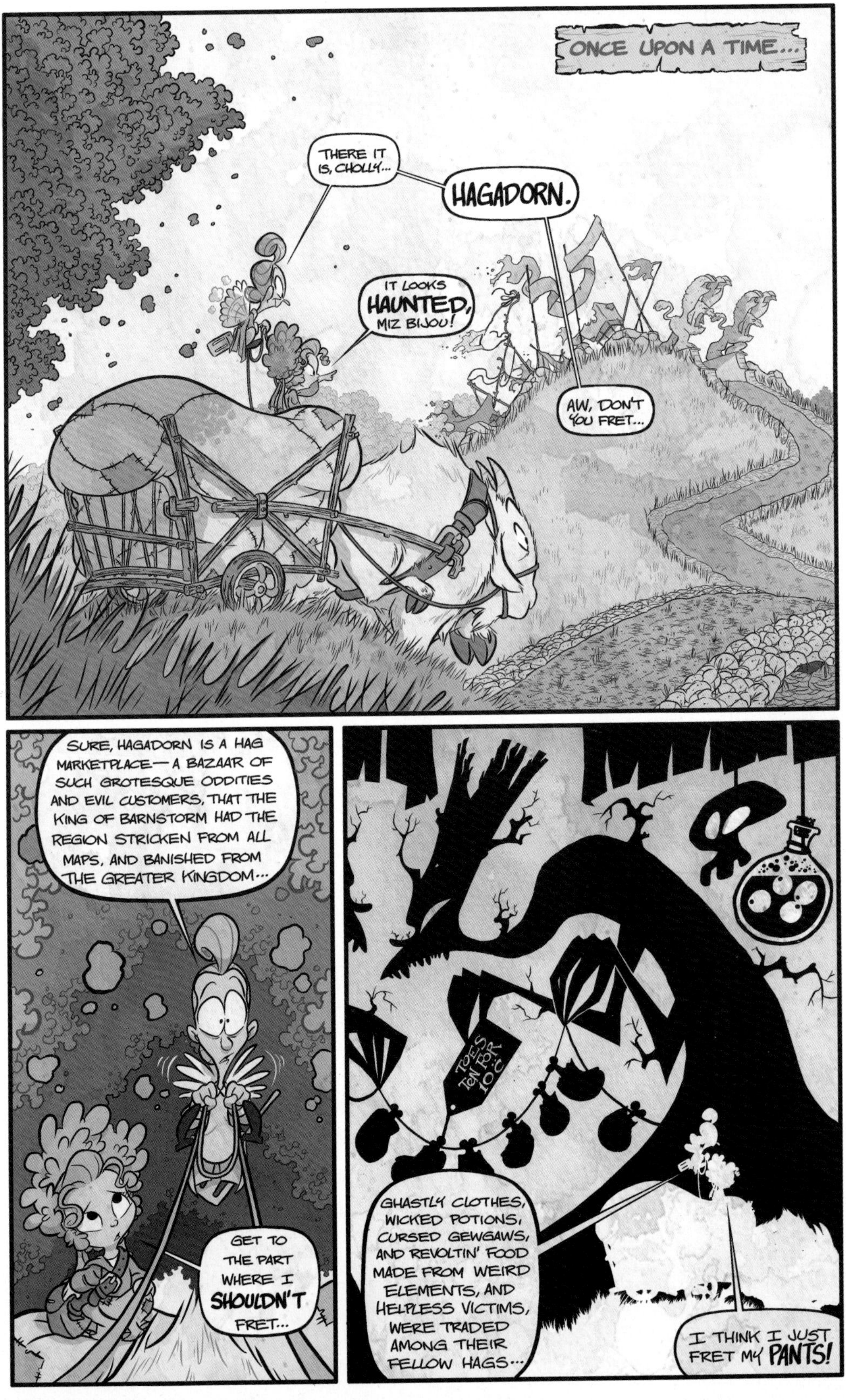
ONCE UPON A TIME...
THERE IT IS, CHOLLY...
HAGADORN.
IT LOOKS HAUNTED, MIZ BIJOU!
AW, DON'T YOU FRET...
SURE, HAGADORN IS A HAG MARKETPLACE— A BAZAAR OF SUCH GROTESQUE ODDITIES AND EVIL CUSTOMERS, THAT THE KING OF BARNSTORM HAD THE REGION STRICKEN FROM ALL MAPS, AND BANISHED FROM THE GREATER KINGDOM...
GET TO THE PART WHERE I SHOULDN'T FRET...
TOES TEN FOR 10¢
GHASTLY CLOTHES, WICKED POTIONS, CURSED GEWGAWS, AND REVOLTIN' FOOD MADE FROM WEIRD ELEMENTS, AND HELPLESS VICTIMS, WERE TRADED AMONG THEIR FELLOW HAGS...
I THINK I JUST FRET MY PANTS!

...BUT MY OLD FRIEND, **BAJ SANDERS**, HAS BEEN GRAZIN' HIS SHEEP OUT HERE FER THE PAST SEASON. HE SAYS THE HAGS ABANDONED HAGADORN, THOUGH HE DON'T KNOW WHY. SO IT OUGHTA MAKE A NICE PLACE FER US TO START OVER...

...UNNOTICED.

BESIDES, I'VE GOT A **MAGIC SPATULA** FER PROTECTION, DON'T I?

THE SAME MAGIC SPATULA THAT MISFIRED AND TURNED THE CANDY CLIFFS INTO PINK LEMONADE?

ELABORATIN' A LITTLE, AIN'T YA?

I GAVE ONE NAMELESS ROCK FACE AN ACCIDENTAL NOSE JOB...

WELL, IT SOUNDS COOLER THE WAY I'M WRITING IT IN MY STORY...

HAVE IT YER WAY, CHOLLY. JUST BE SURE TO WRITE ME AS A FOXY BABE...

THAT'S ODD.

I DON'T SEE SANDERS OR HIS SHEEP!

"FOXY... BABE..."

MAYBE HE TOOK 'EM TO MARKET IN HINKYDOO HAMLET...

WELL, SINCE THERE'S NO ONE TO SEE YA, WHY DON'T YA CUT LOOSE THOSE CRAZY LEGS OF YER'S AND TEAR UP **SANDER'S FIELD?**

ARE YOU SURE, MIZ BIJOU?

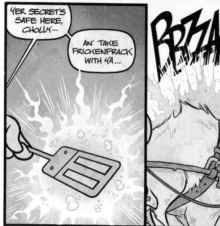

YER SECRET'S SAFE HERE, CHOLLY...

AN' TAKE FRICKENFRACK WITH YA...

BRZZAAP!!

THEY'RE PROB'LY DUE FER A TINKLE!

C'MON, FRICK! C'MON, FRACK!

I'LL RACE YA!

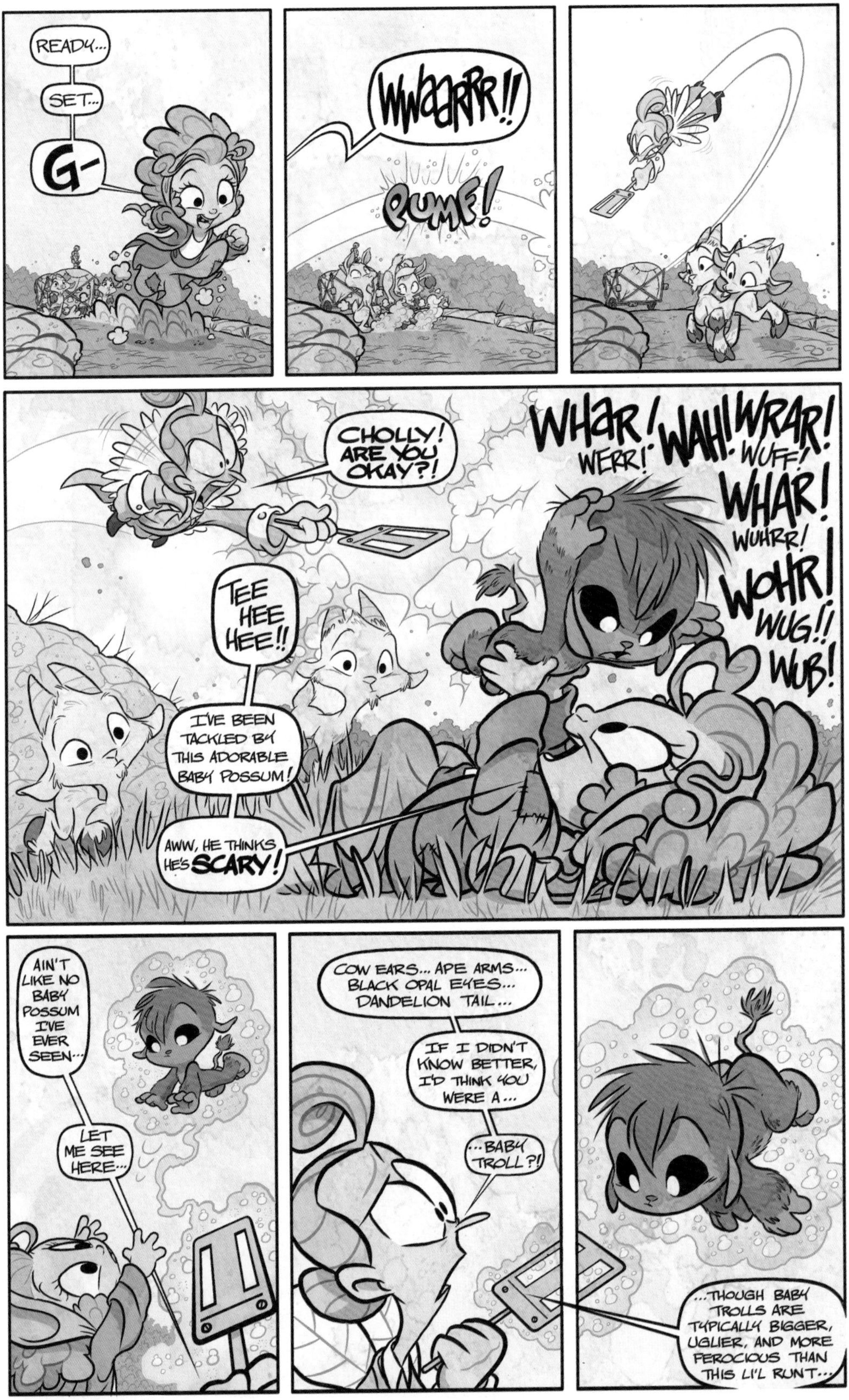
READY...
SET...
G-
WWAARRR!!
PUMF!
CHOLLY! ARE YOU OKAY?!
WHAR! WERR! WAH! WRAR! WUFF! WHAR! WUHRR! WOHR! WUG!! WUB!
TEE HEE HEE!!
I'VE BEEN TACKLED BY THIS ADORABLE BABY POSSUM!
AWW, HE THINKS HE'S SCARY!
AIN'T LIKE NO BABY POSSUM I'VE EVER SEEN...
LET ME SEE HERE...
COW EARS... APE ARMS... BLACK OPAL EYES... DANDELION TAIL...
IF I DIDN'T KNOW BETTER, I'D THINK YOU WERE A...
...BABY TROLL?!
...THOUGH BABY TROLLS ARE TYPICALLY BIGGER, UGLIER, AND MORE FEROCIOUS THAN THIS LI'L RUNT...

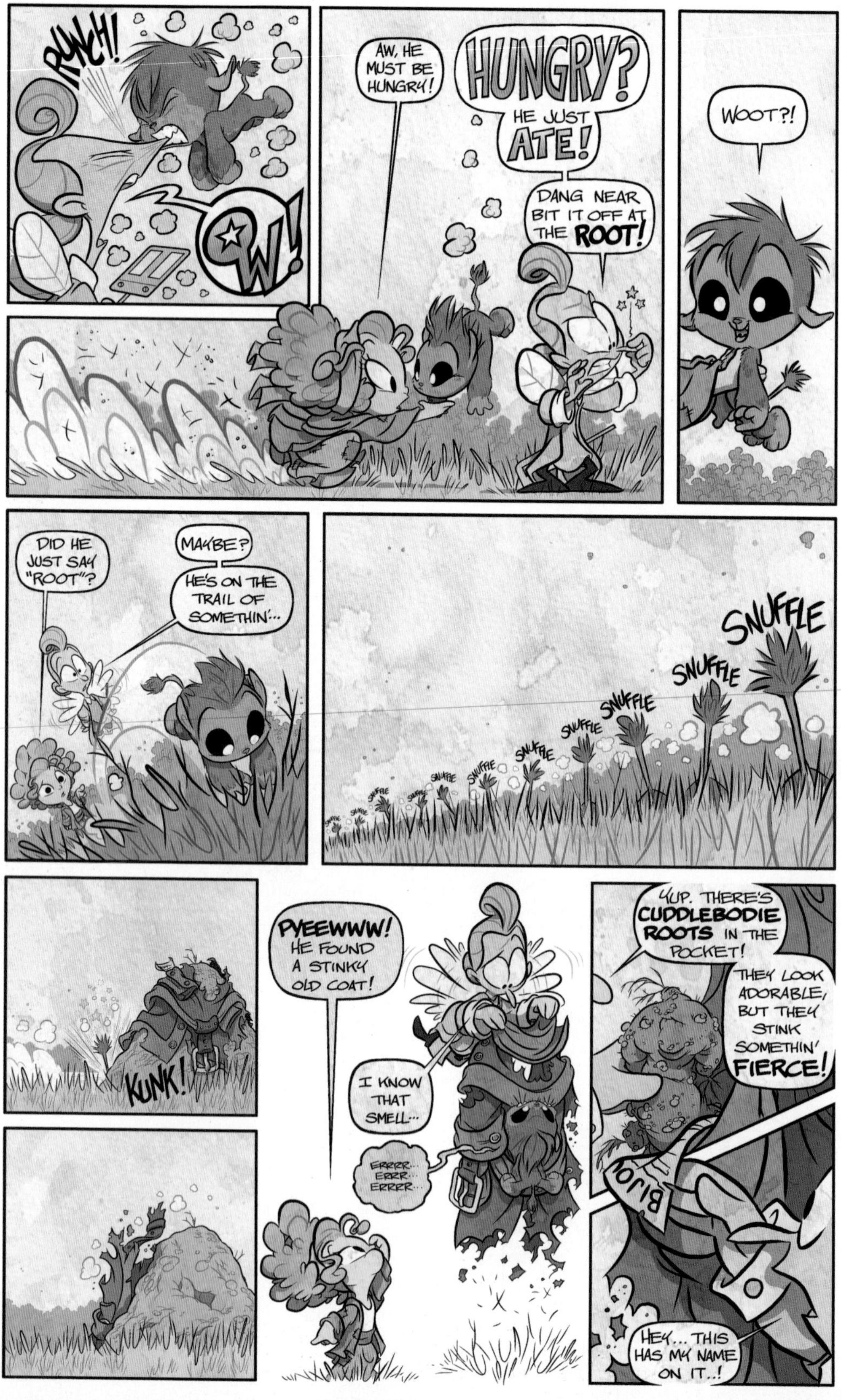

RUNCH!
OW!
AW, HE MUST BE HUNGRY!
HUNGRY? HE JUST ATE!
DANG NEAR BIT IT OFF AT THE ROOT!
WOOT?!
DID HE JUST SAY "ROOT"?
MAYBE?
HE'S ON THE TRAIL OF SOMETHIN'...
SNUFFLE
SNUFFLE
SNUFFLE
SNUFFLE
SNUFFLE
SNUFFLE
SNUFFLE
KUNK!
PYEEWWW! HE FOUND A STINKY OLD COAT!
I KNOW THAT SMELL...
ERRRR... ERRR... ERRRR...
YUP. THERE'S CUDDLEBODIE ROOTS IN THE POCKET!
THEY LOOK ADORABLE, BUT THEY STINK SOMETHIN' FIERCE!
BIJOU
HEY... THIS HAS MY NAME ON IT..!

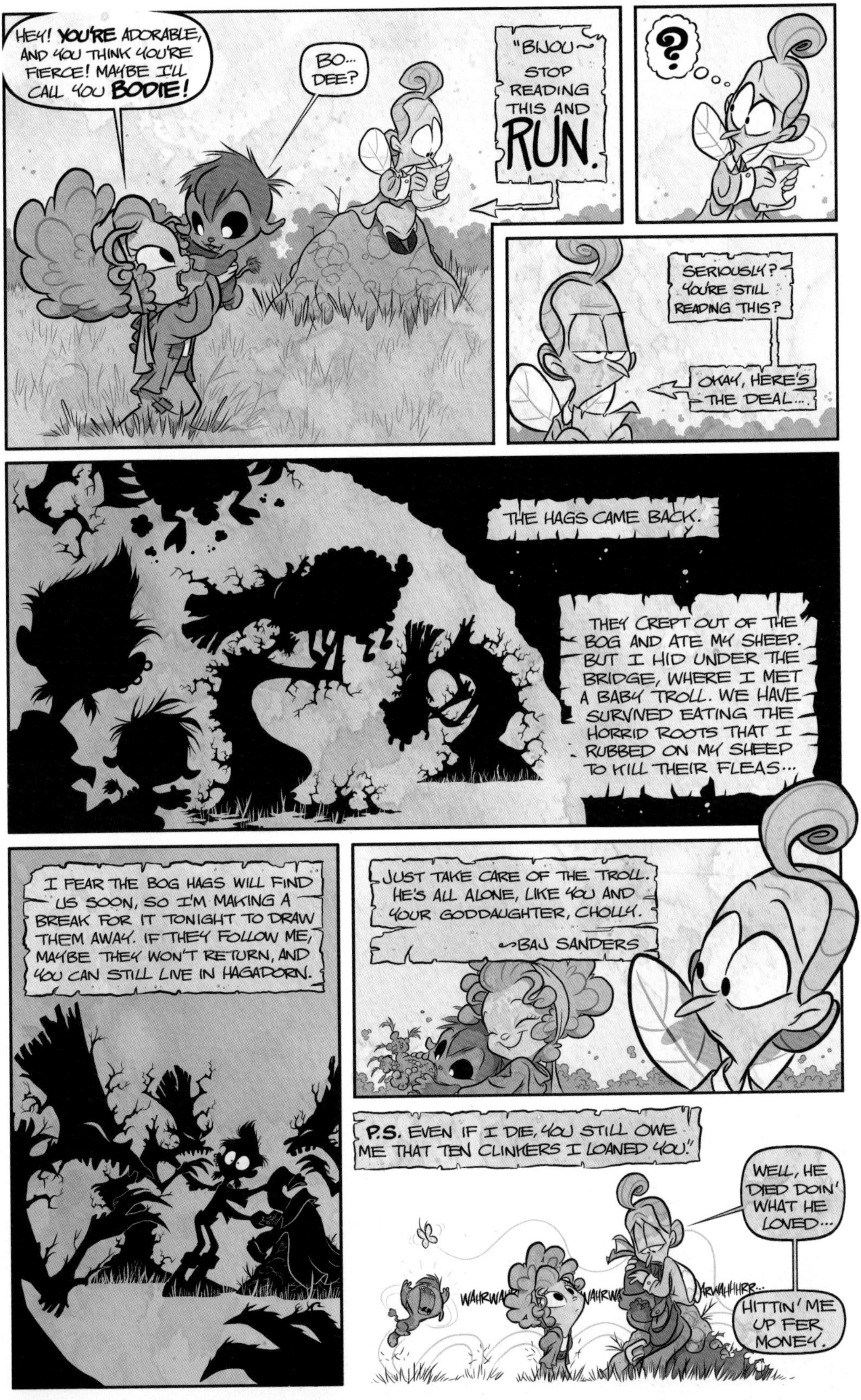
HEY! YOU'RE ADORABLE, AND YOU THINK YOU'RE FIERCE! MAYBE I'LL CALL YOU BODIE!
BO... DEE?
"BIJOU~ STOP READING THIS AND RUN.
?
SERIOUSLY? YOU'RE STILL READING THIS?
OKAY, HERE'S THE DEAL...
THE HAGS CAME BACK.
THEY CREPT OUT OF THE BOG AND ATE MY SHEEP. BUT I HID UNDER THE BRIDGE, WHERE I MET A BABY TROLL. WE HAVE SURVIVED EATING THE HORRID ROOTS THAT I RUBBED ON MY SHEEP TO KILL THEIR FLEAS...
I FEAR THE BOG HAGS WILL FIND US SOON, SO I'M MAKING A BREAK FOR IT TONIGHT TO DRAW THEM AWAY. IF THEY FOLLOW ME, MAYBE THEY WON'T RETURN, AND YOU CAN STILL LIVE IN HAGADORN.
JUST TAKE CARE OF THE TROLL. HE'S ALL ALONE, LIKE YOU AND YOUR GODDAUGHTER, CHOLLY.
~BAJ SANDERS
P.S. EVEN IF I DIE, YOU STILL OWE ME THAT TEN CLINKERS I LOANED YOU."
WELL, HE DIED DOIN' WHAT HE LOVED...
HITTIN' ME UP FER MONEY.
WAHRWA
WAHRWA
WAHHHHRR...

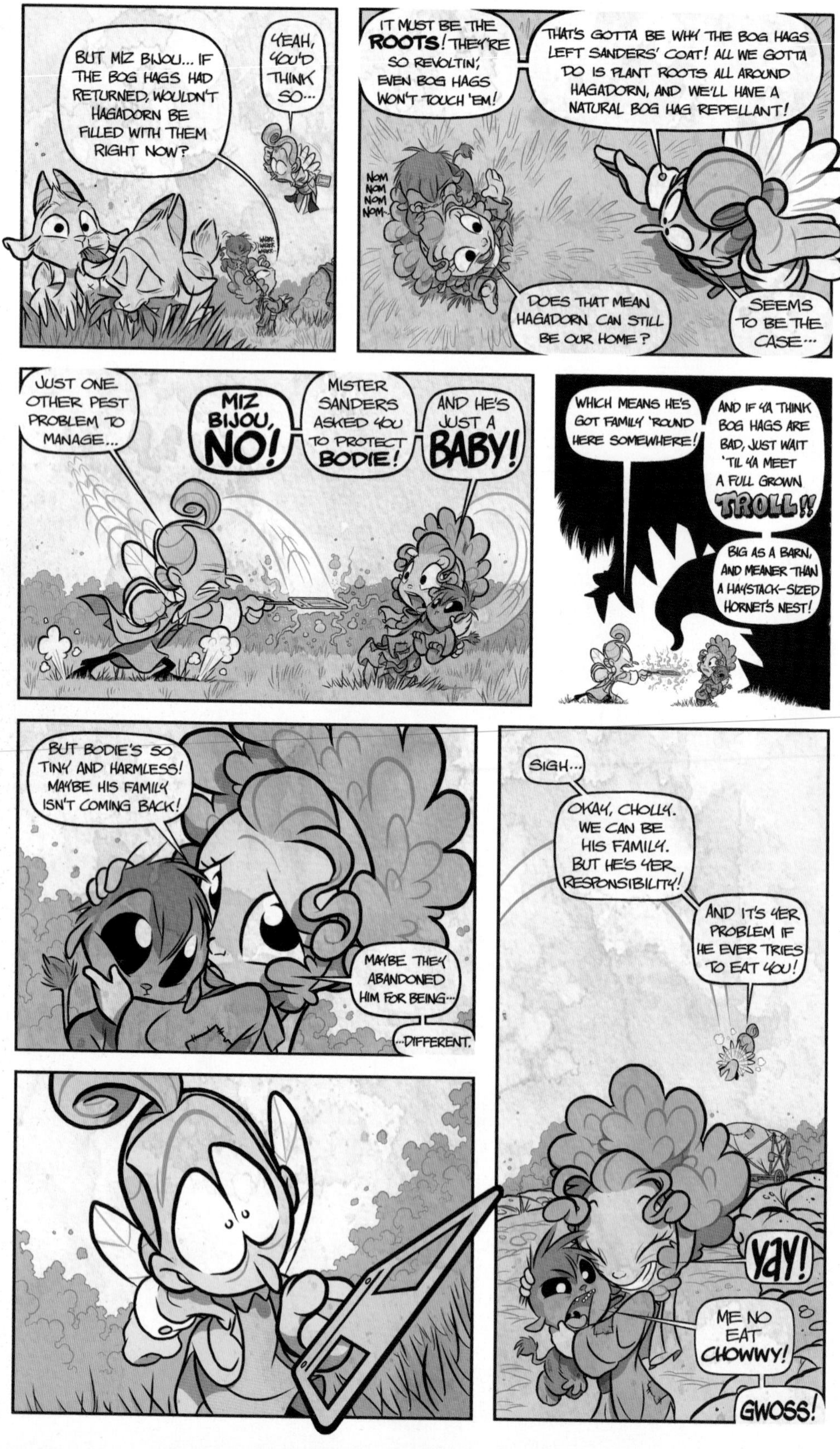
BUT MIZ BIJOU... IF THE BOG HAGS HAD RETURNED, WOULDN'T HAGADORN BE FILLED WITH THEM RIGHT NOW?
YEAH, YOU'D THINK SO...
IT MUST BE THE ROOTS! THEY'RE SO REVOLTIN', EVEN BOG HAGS WON'T TOUCH 'EM!
THAT'S GOTTA BE WHY THE BOG HAGS LEFT SANDERS' COAT! ALL WE GOTTA DO IS PLANT ROOTS ALL AROUND HAGADORN, AND WE'LL HAVE A NATURAL BOG HAG REPELLANT!
NOM NOM NOM NOM...
DOES THAT MEAN HAGADORN CAN STILL BE OUR HOME?
SEEMS TO BE THE CASE...
JUST ONE OTHER PEST PROBLEM TO MANAGE...
MIZ BIJOU, NO!
MISTER SANDERS ASKED YOU TO PROTECT BODIE!
AND HE'S JUST A BABY!
WHICH MEANS HE'S GOT FAMILY 'ROUND HERE SOMEWHERE!
AND IF YA THINK BOG HAGS ARE BAD, JUST WAIT 'TIL YA MEET A FULL GROWN TROLL!!
BIG AS A BARN, AND MEANER THAN A HAYSTACK-SIZED HORNET'S NEST!
BUT BODIE'S SO TINY AND HARMLESS! MAYBE HIS FAMILY ISN'T COMING BACK!
MAYBE THEY ABANDONED HIM FOR BEING...
...DIFFERENT.
SIGH...
OKAY, CHOLLY. WE CAN BE HIS FAMILY. BUT HE'S YER RESPONSIBILITY!
AND IT'S YER PROBLEM IF HE EVER TRIES TO EAT YOU!
YAY!
ME NO EAT CHOWWY!
GWOSS!

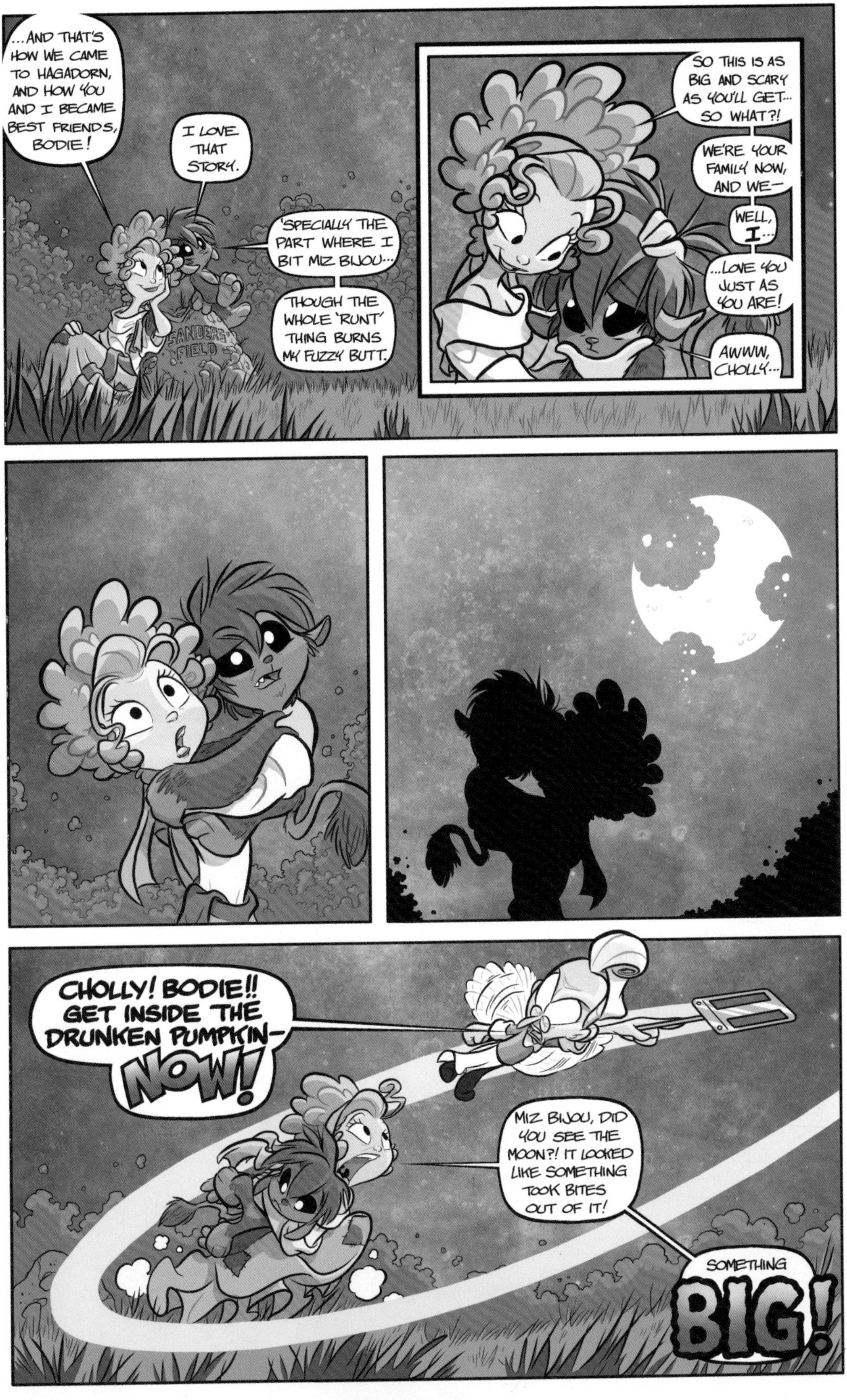
...AND THAT'S HOW WE CAME TO HAGADORN, AND HOW YOU AND I BECAME BEST FRIENDS, BODIE!
I LOVE THAT STORY.
'SPECIALLY THE PART WHERE I BIT MIZ BIJOU...
THOUGH THE WHOLE 'RUNT' THING BURNS MY FUZZY BUTT.
SANDERS' FIELD
SO THIS IS AS BIG AND SCARY AS YOU'LL GET... SO WHAT?!
WE'RE YOUR FAMILY NOW, AND WE—
WELL, I...
...LOVE YOU JUST AS YOU ARE!
AWWW, CHOLLY...
CHOLLY! BODIE!! GET INSIDE THE DRUNKEN PUMPKIN— NOW!
MIZ BIJOU, DID YOU SEE THE MOON?! IT LOOKED LIKE SOMETHING TOOK BITES OUT OF IT!
SOMETHING BIG!

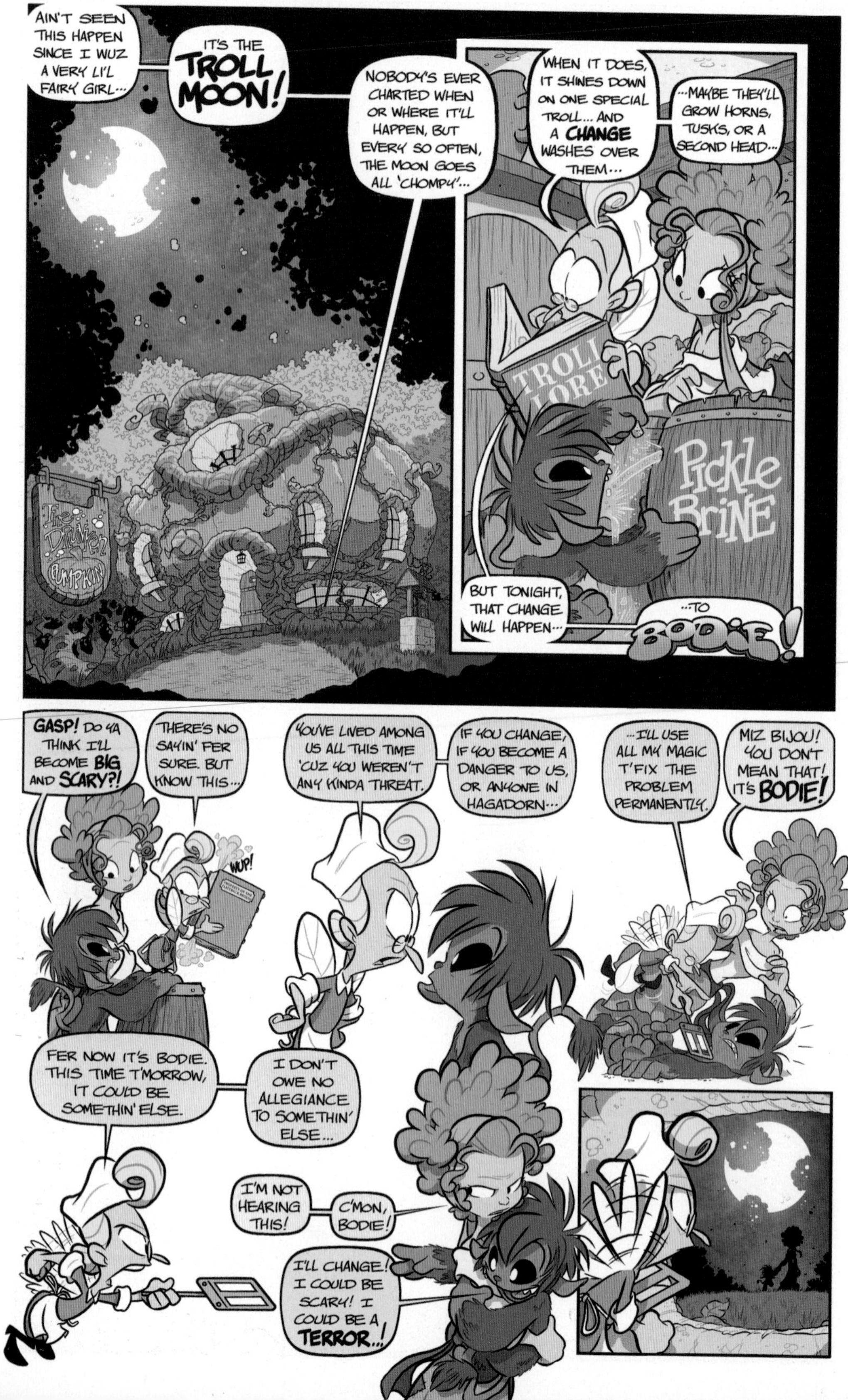
AIN'T SEEN THIS HAPPEN SINCE I WUZ A VERY LI'L FAIRY GIRL...
IT'S THE TROLL MOON!
The Drunken Pumpkin
NOBODY'S EVER CHARTED WHEN OR WHERE IT'LL HAPPEN, BUT EVERY SO OFTEN, THE MOON GOES ALL 'CHOMPY'...
WHEN IT DOES, IT SHINES DOWN ON ONE SPECIAL TROLL... AND A CHANGE WASHES OVER THEM...
...MAYBE THEY'LL GROW HORNS, TUSKS, OR A SECOND HEAD...
TROLL LORE
Pickle Brine
BUT TONIGHT, THAT CHANGE WILL HAPPEN...
...TO BODIE!
GASP! DO YA THINK I'LL BECOME BIG AND SCARY?!
THERE'S NO SAYIN' FER SURE. BUT KNOW THIS...
WUP!
YOU'VE LIVED AMONG US ALL THIS TIME 'CUZ YOU WEREN'T ANY KINDA THREAT.
IF YOU CHANGE, IF YOU BECOME A DANGER TO US, OR ANYONE IN HAGADORN...
...I'LL USE ALL MY MAGIC T'FIX THE PROBLEM PERMANENTLY.
MIZ BIJOU! YOU DON'T MEAN THAT! IT'S BODIE!
FER NOW IT'S BODIE. THIS TIME T'MORROW, IT COULD BE SOMETHIN' ELSE.
I DON'T OWE NO ALLEGIANCE TO SOMETHIN' ELSE...
I'M NOT HEARING THIS!
C'MON, BODIE!
I'LL CHANGE! I COULD BE SCARY! I COULD BE A TERROR..!

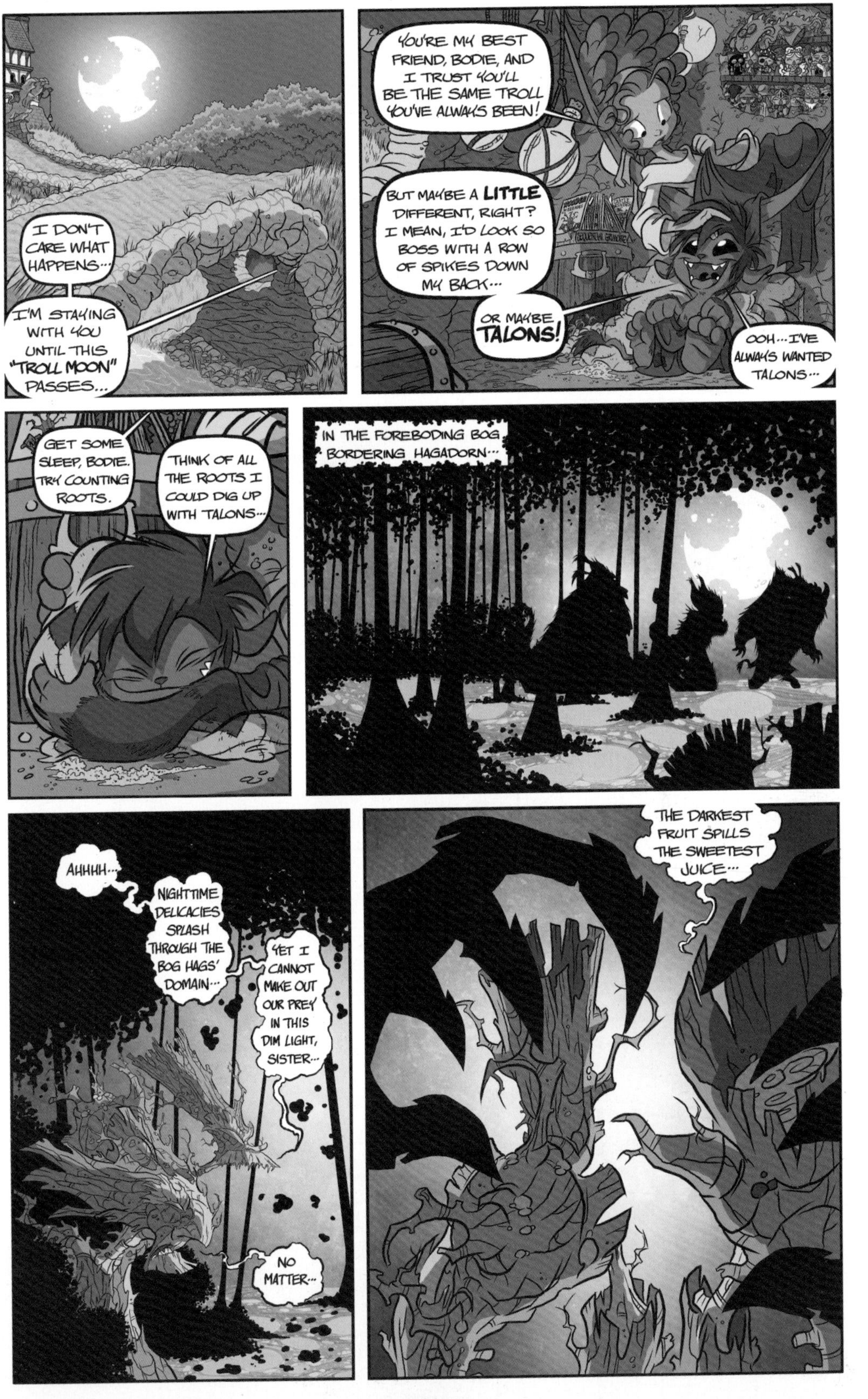
I DON'T CARE WHAT HAPPENS...
I'M STAYING WITH YOU UNTIL THIS "TROLL MOON" PASSES...
YOU'RE MY BEST FRIEND, BODIE, AND I TRUST YOU'LL BE THE SAME TROLL YOU'VE ALWAYS BEEN!
BUT MAYBE A LITTLE DIFFERENT, RIGHT? I MEAN, I'D LOOK SO BOSS WITH A ROW OF SPIKES DOWN MY BACK...
OR MAYBE TALONS!
OOH... I'VE ALWAYS WANTED TALONS...
GET SOME SLEEP, BODIE. TRY COUNTING ROOTS.
THINK OF ALL THE ROOTS I COULD DIG UP WITH TALONS...
IN THE FOREBODING BOG BORDERING HAGADORN...
AHHHH...
NIGHTTIME DELICACIES SPLASH THROUGH THE BOG HAGS' DOMAIN...
YET I CANNOT MAKE OUT OUR PREY IN THIS DIM LIGHT, SISTER...
NO MATTER...
THE DARKEST FRUIT SPILLS THE SWEETEST JUICE...

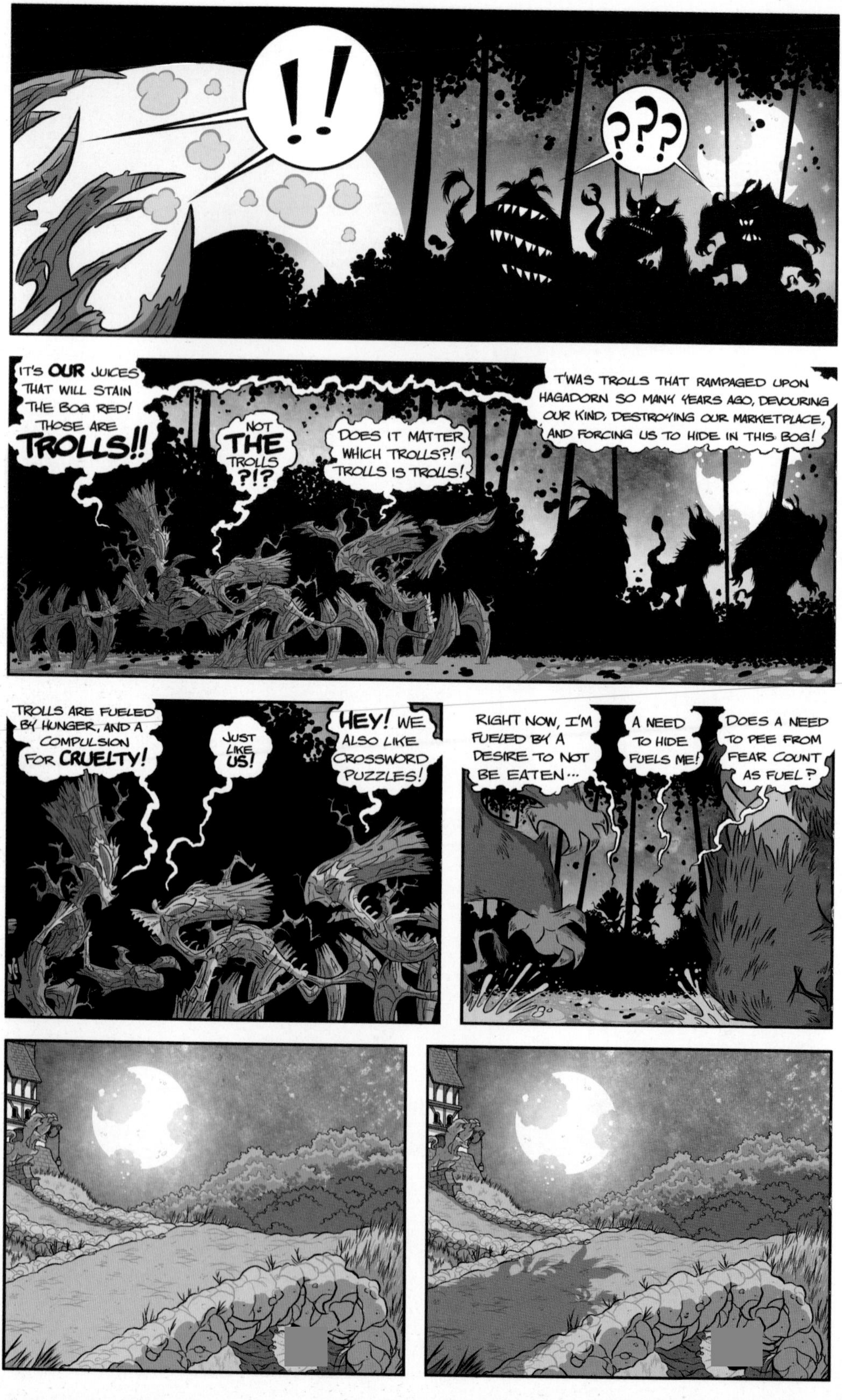
!!
???
IT'S OUR JUICES THAT WILL STAIN THE BOG RED! THOSE ARE TROLLS!!
NOT THE TROLLS ?!?
DOES IT MATTER WHICH TROLLS?! TROLLS IS TROLLS!
T'WAS TROLLS THAT RAMPAGED UPON HAGADORN SO MANY YEARS AGO, DEVOURING OUR KIND, DESTROYING OUR MARKETPLACE, AND FORCING US TO HIDE IN THIS BOG!
TROLLS ARE FUELED BY HUNGER, AND A COMPULSION FOR CRUELTY!
JUST LIKE US!
HEY! WE ALSO LIKE CROSSWORD PUZZLES!
RIGHT NOW, I'M FUELED BY A DESIRE TO NOT BE EATEN...
A NEED TO HIDE FUELS ME!
DOES A NEED TO PEE FROM FEAR COUNT AS FUEL?

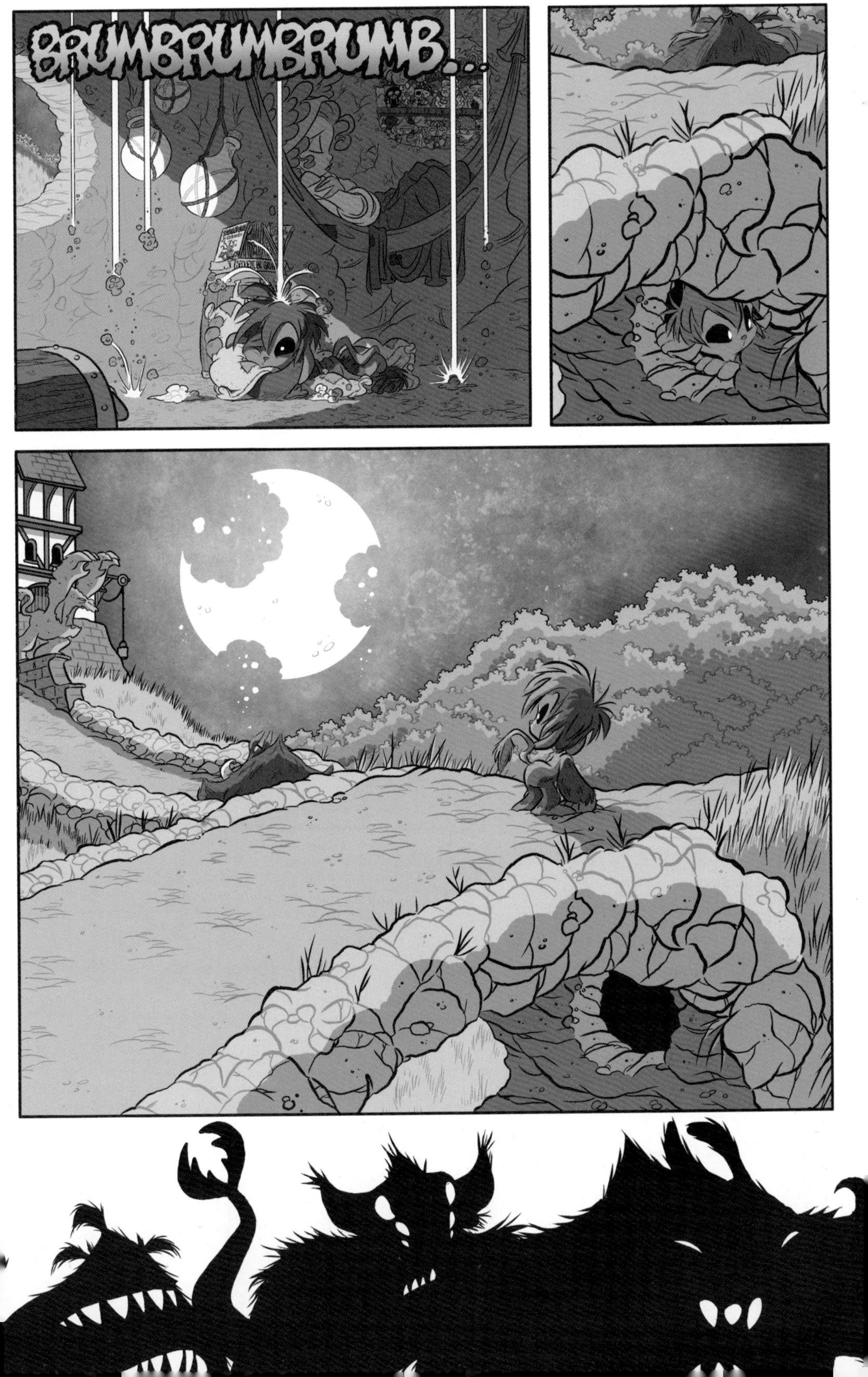
BRUMBRUMBRUMB...

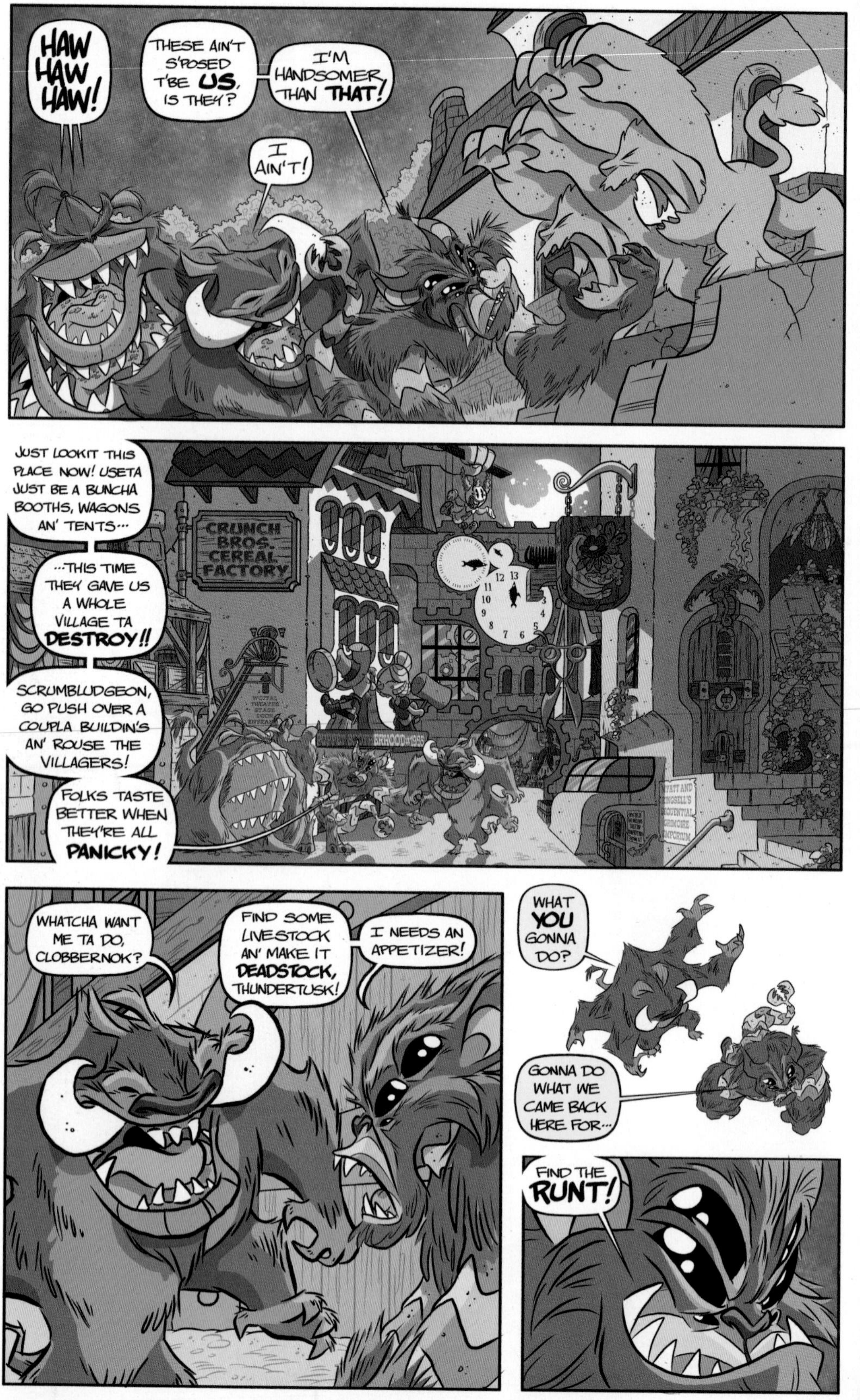
HAW HAW HAW!
THESE AIN'T S'POSED T'BE US, IS THEY?
I'M HANDSOMER THAN THAT!
I AIN'T!
JUST LOOKIT THIS PLACE NOW! USETA JUST BE A BUNCHA BOOTHS, WAGONS AN' TENTS...
...THIS TIME THEY GAVE US A WHOLE VILLAGE TA DESTROY!!
SCRUMBLUDGEON, GO PUSH OVER A COUPLA BUILDIN'S AN' ROUSE THE VILLAGERS!
FOLKS TASTE BETTER WHEN THEY'RE ALL PANICKY!
CRUNCH BROS. CEREAL FACTORY
WHATCHA WANT ME TA DO, CLOBBERNOK?
FIND SOME LIVESTOCK AN' MAKE IT DEADSTOCK, THUNDERTUSK!
I NEEDS AN APPETIZER!
WHAT YOU GONNA DO?
GONNA DO WHAT WE CAME BACK HERE FOR...
FIND THE RUNT!

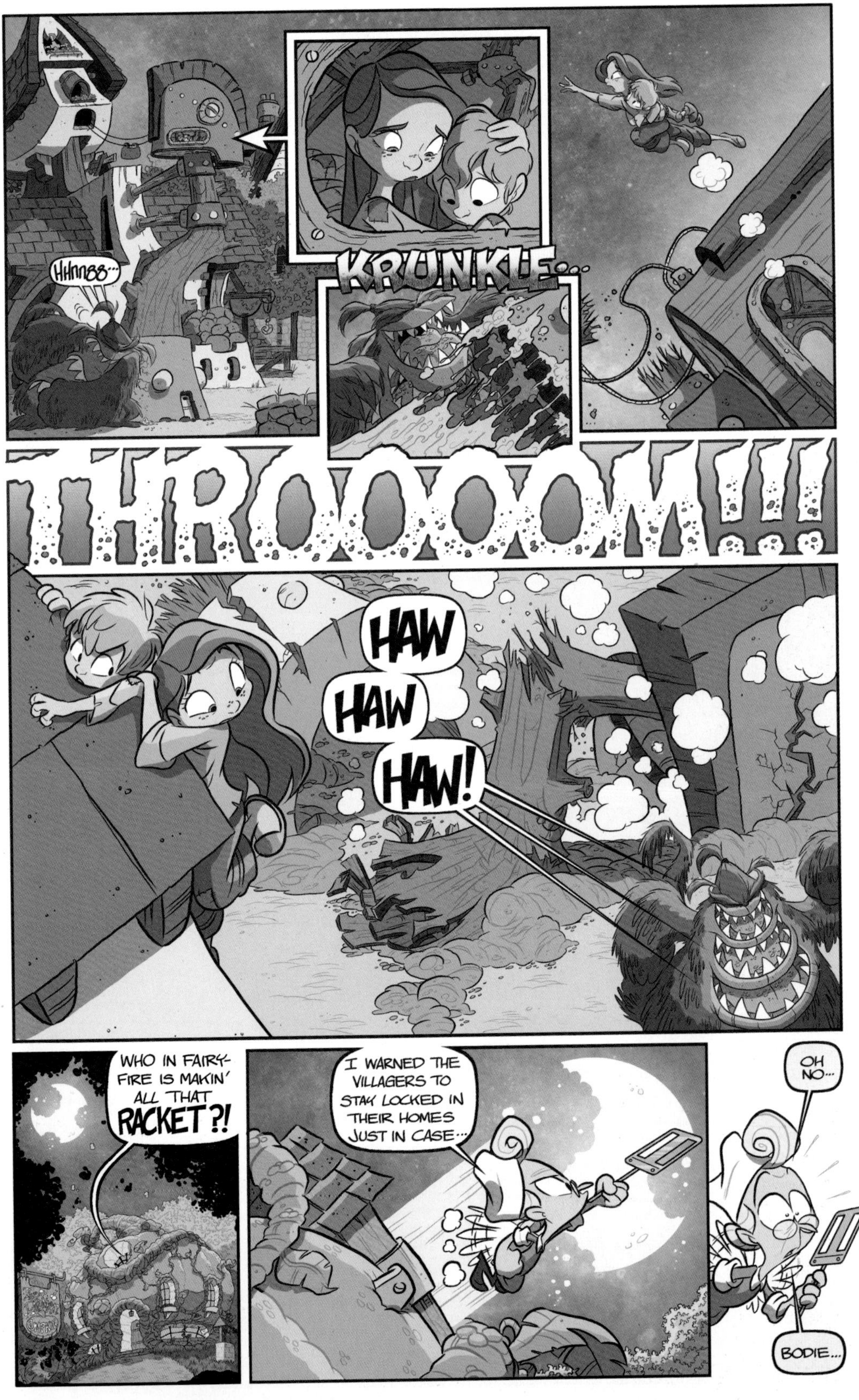
HHnngg...
KRUNKLE...
THROOOOM!!!
HAW
HAW
HAW!
WHO IN FAIRY-FIRE IS MAKIN' ALL THAT RACKET?!
I WARNED THE VILLAGERS TO STAY LOCKED IN THEIR HOMES JUST IN CASE...
OH NO...
BODIE...

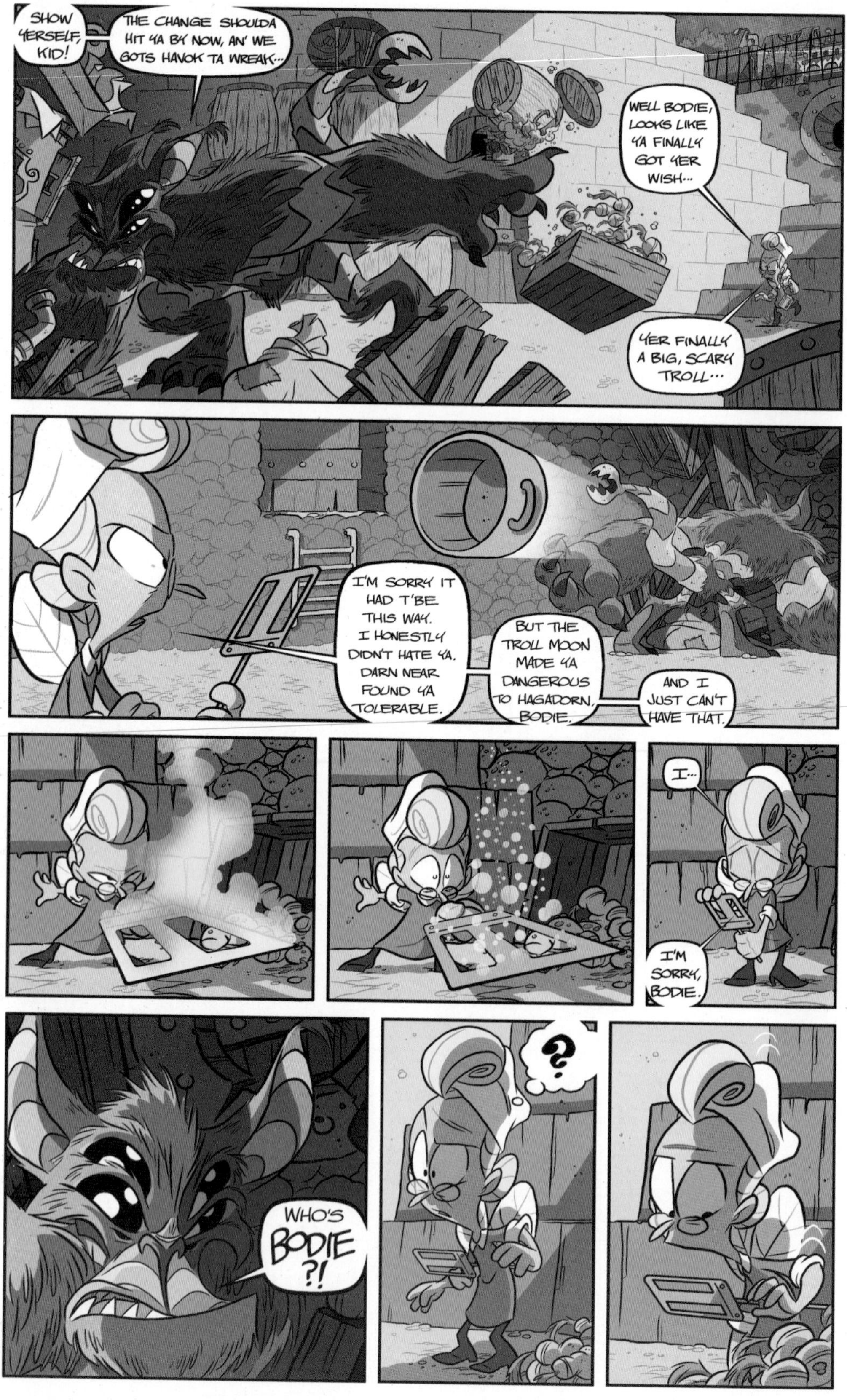
SHOW YERSELF, KID!
THE CHANGE SHOULDA HIT YA BY NOW, AN' WE GOTS HAVOK TA WREAK...
WELL BODIE, LOOKS LIKE YA FINALLY GOT YER WISH...
YER FINALLY A BIG, SCARY TROLL...
I'M SORRY IT HAD T'BE THIS WAY. I HONESTLY DIDN'T HATE YA. DARN NEAR FOUND YA TOLERABLE.
BUT THE TROLL MOON MADE YA DANGEROUS TO HAGADORN, BODIE.
AND I JUST CAN'T HAVE THAT.
I...
I'M SORRY, BODIE.
WHO'S BODIE ?!
?

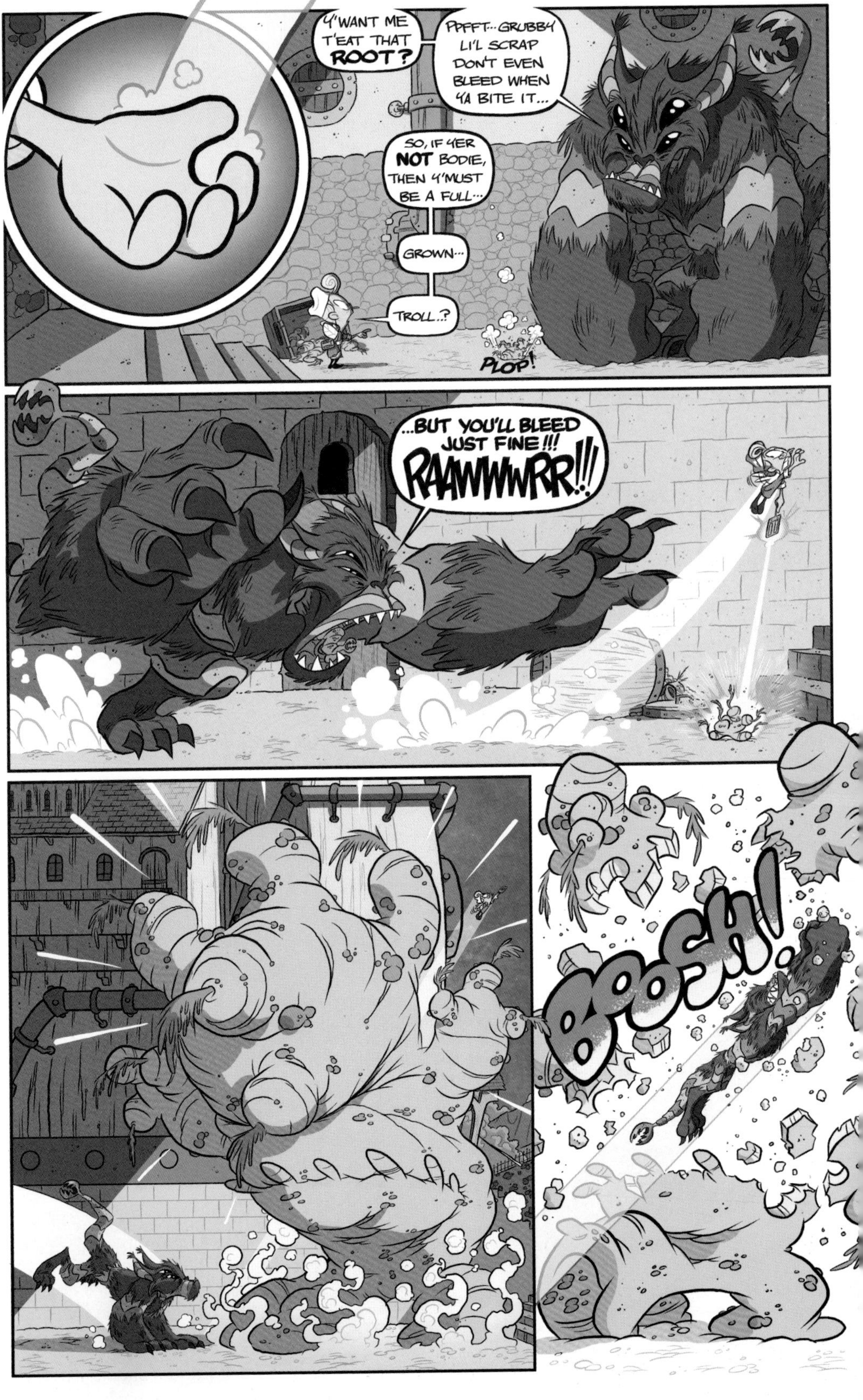
Y'WANT ME T'EAT THAT ROOT?
PPFFT... GRUBBY LI'L SCRAP DON'T EVEN BLEED WHEN Y'A BITE IT...
SO, IF YER NOT BODIE, THEN Y'MUST BE A FULL...
GROWN...
TROLL..?
PLOP!
...BUT YOU'LL BLEED JUST FINE!!!
RAAWWWRR!!!
BOOSH!!

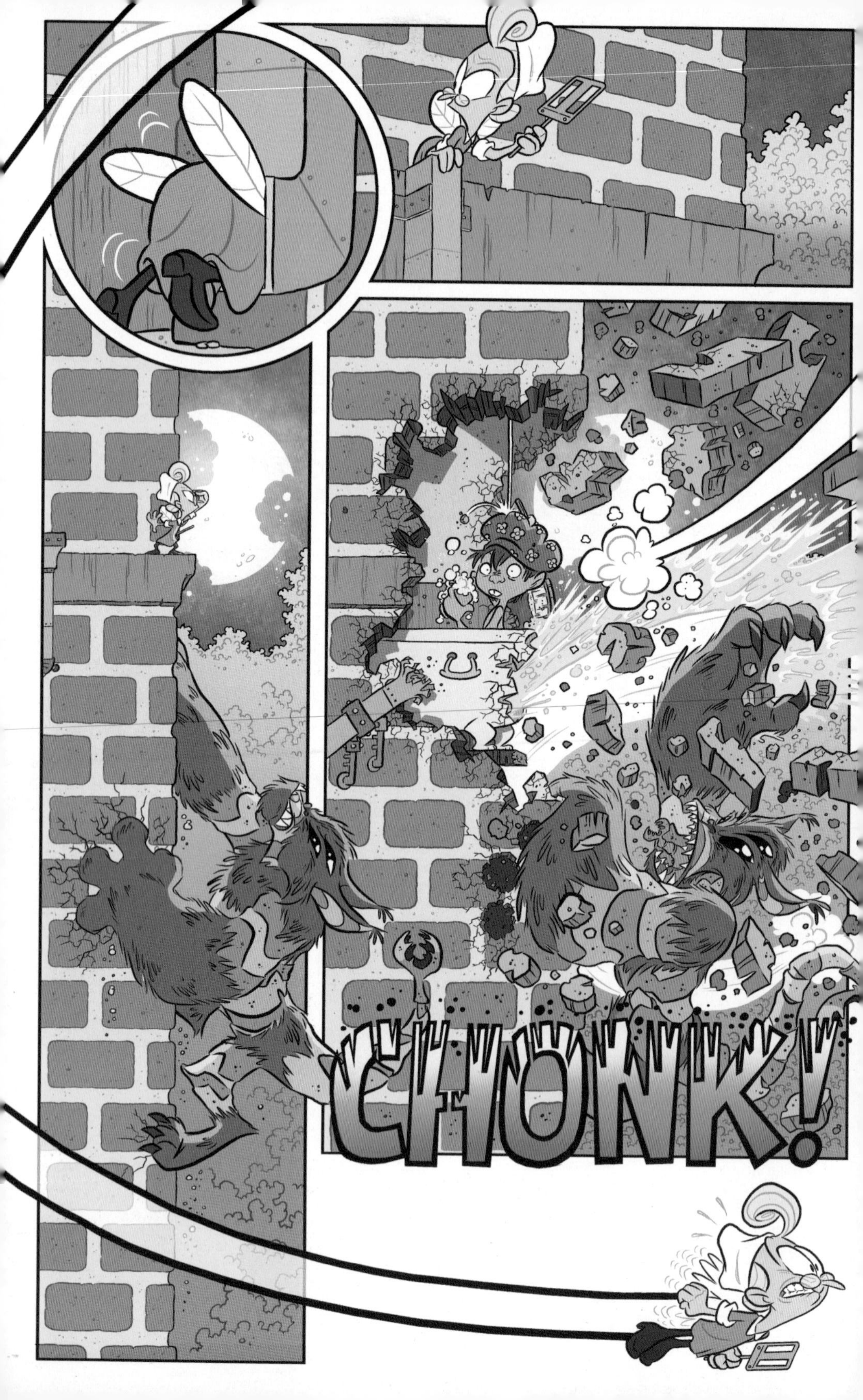
CHONK!

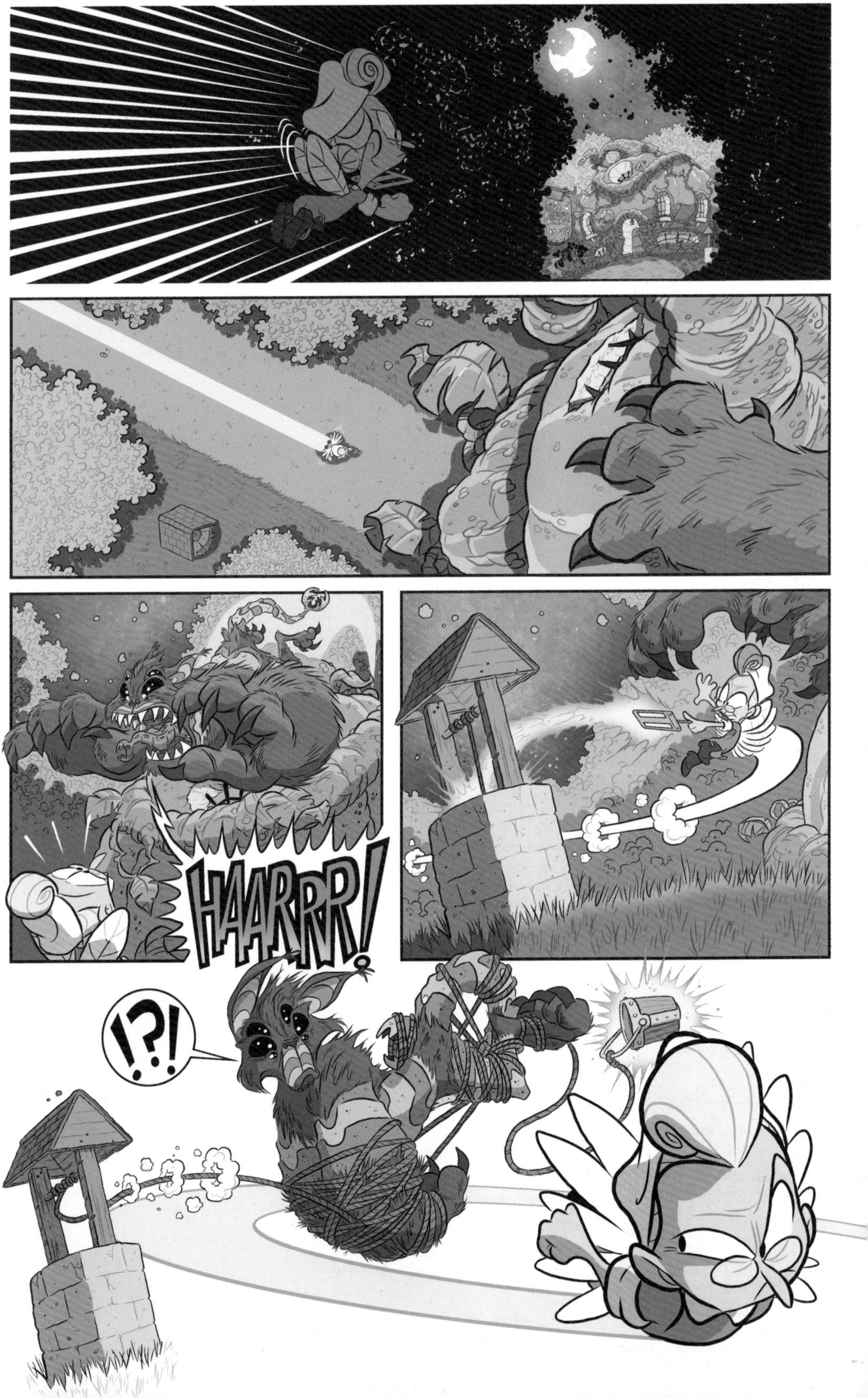
HAARRR!
!?!

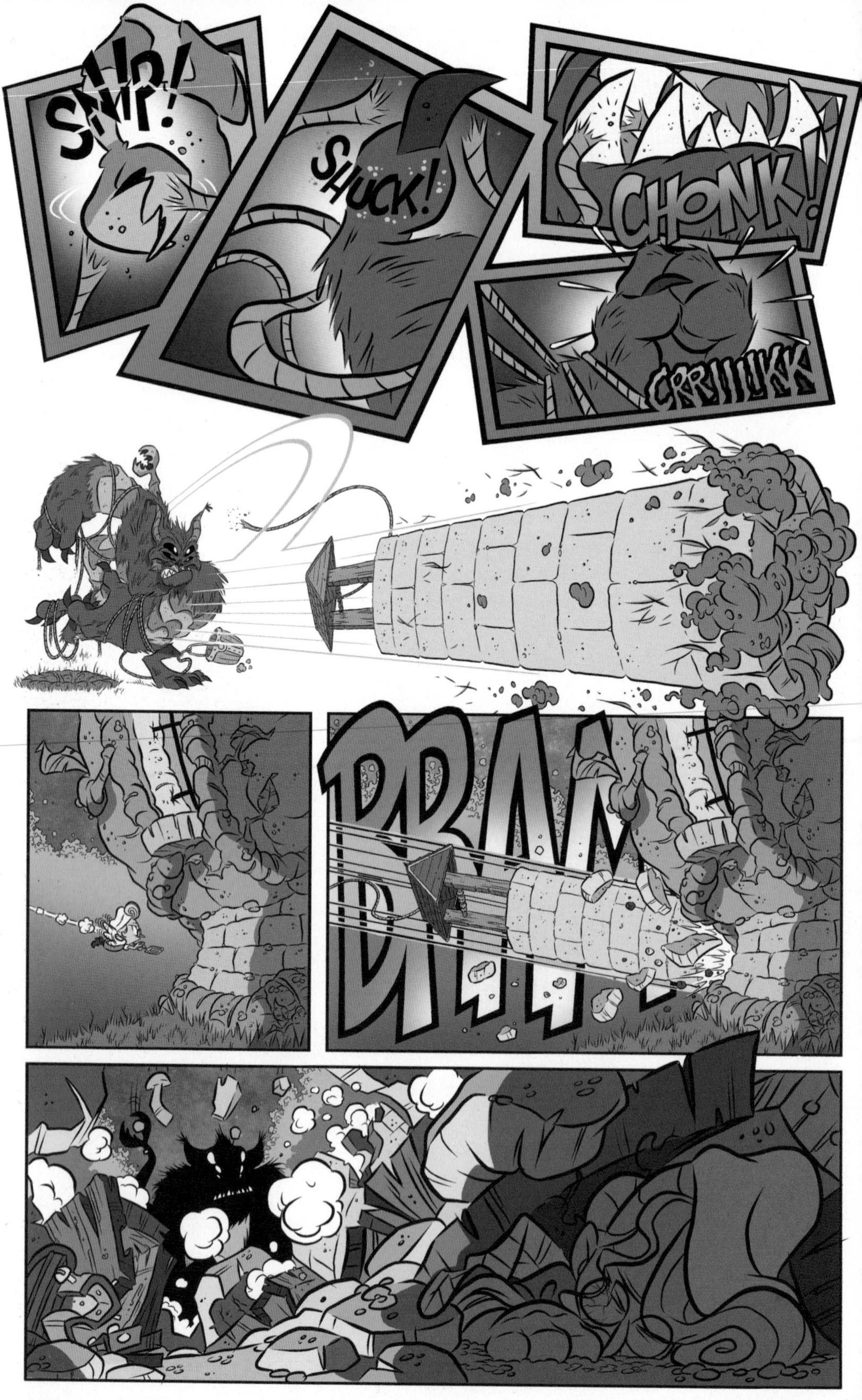
SNIP!
SHUCK!
CHONK!
CRRUUUNK
BRAM

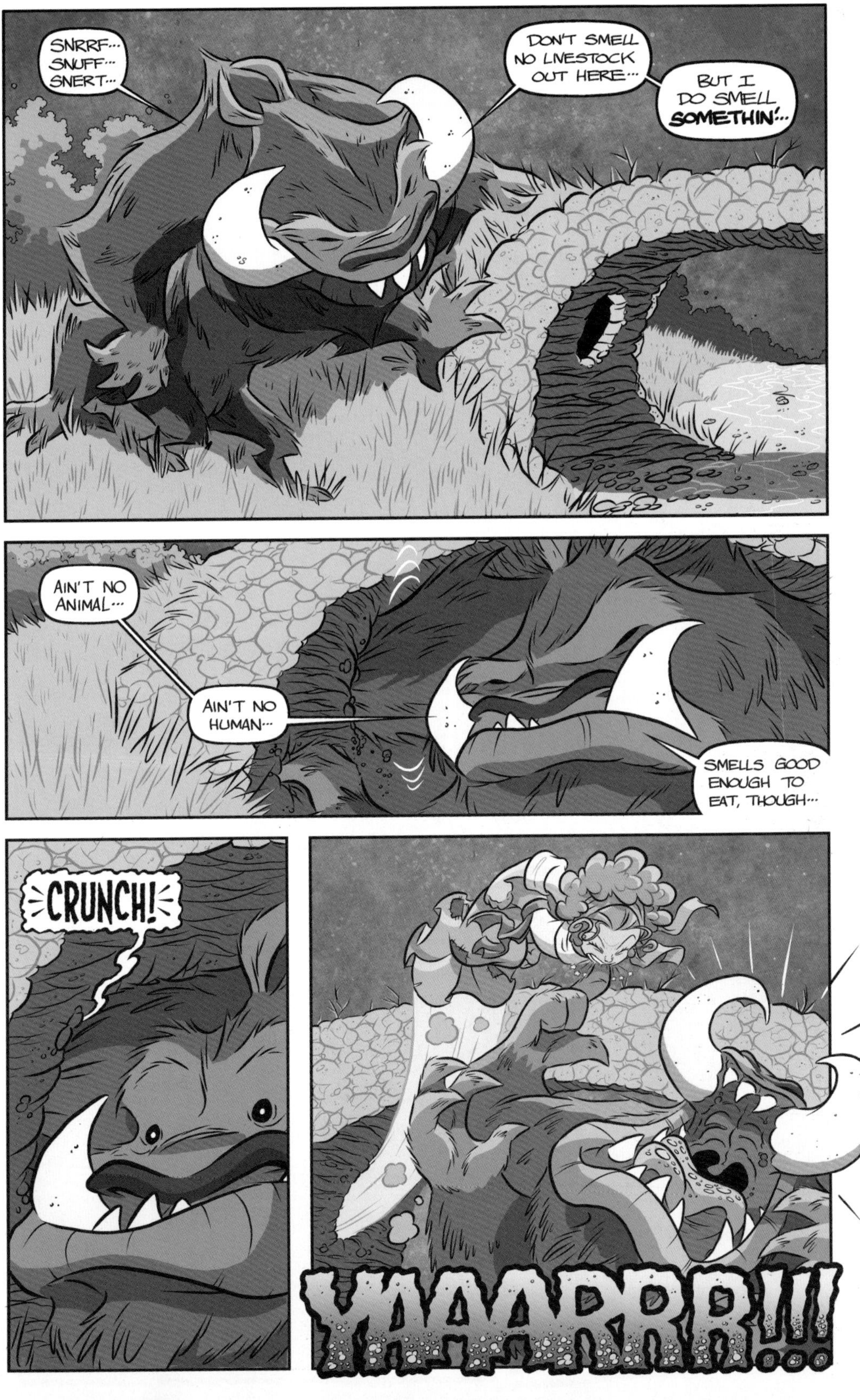
SNRRF... SNUFF... SNERT...
DON'T SMELL NO LIVESTOCK OUT HERE...
BUT I DO SMELL **SOMETHIN'**...
AIN'T NO ANIMAL...
AIN'T NO HUMAN...
SMELLS GOOD ENOUGH TO EAT, THOUGH...
CRUNCH!
YAAARRR!!!

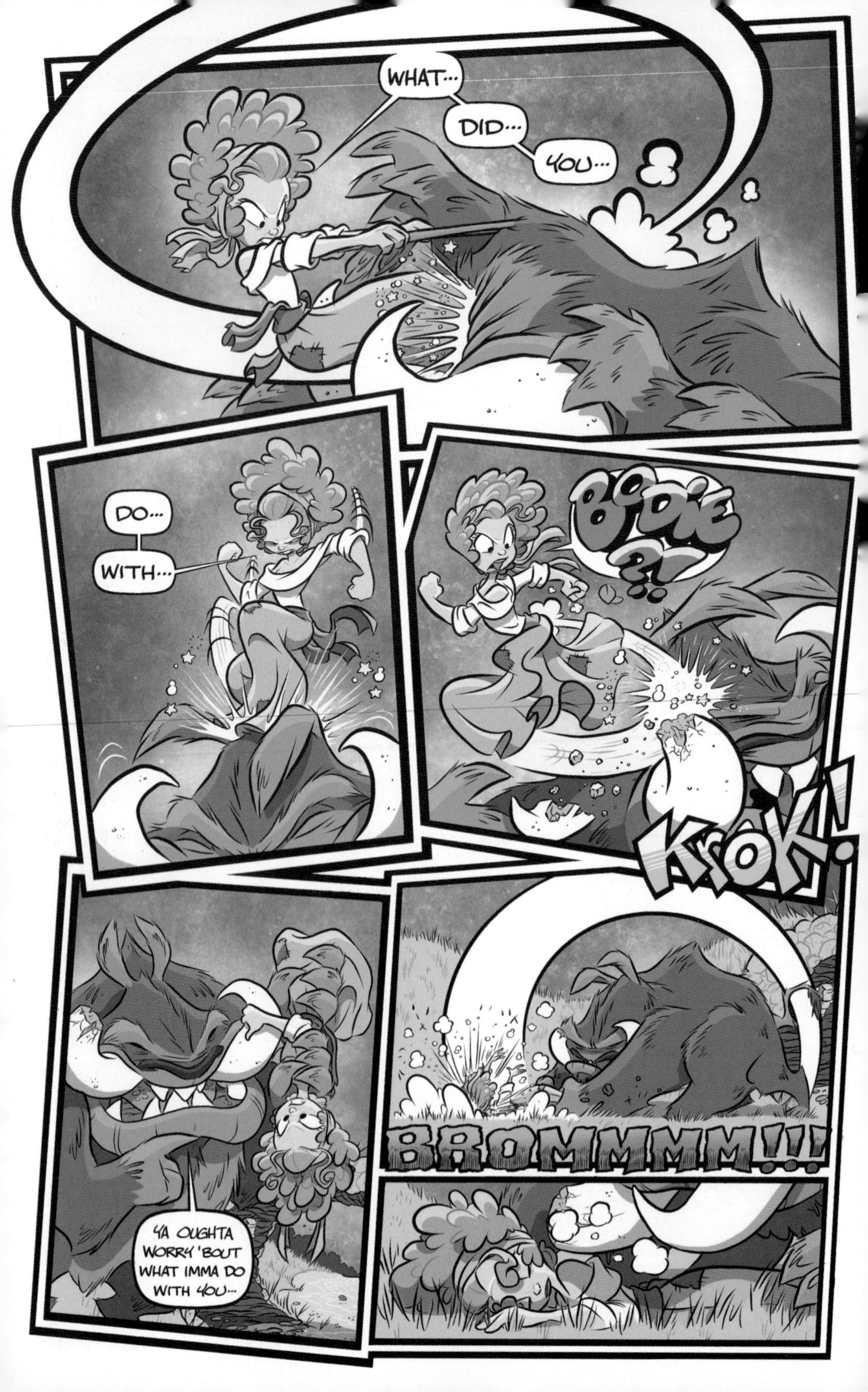
WHAT...
DID...
YOU...
DO...
WITH...
BODIE?!
KROK!
YA OUGHTA WORRY 'BOUT WHAT IMMA DO WITH YOU...
BROMMMM!!!

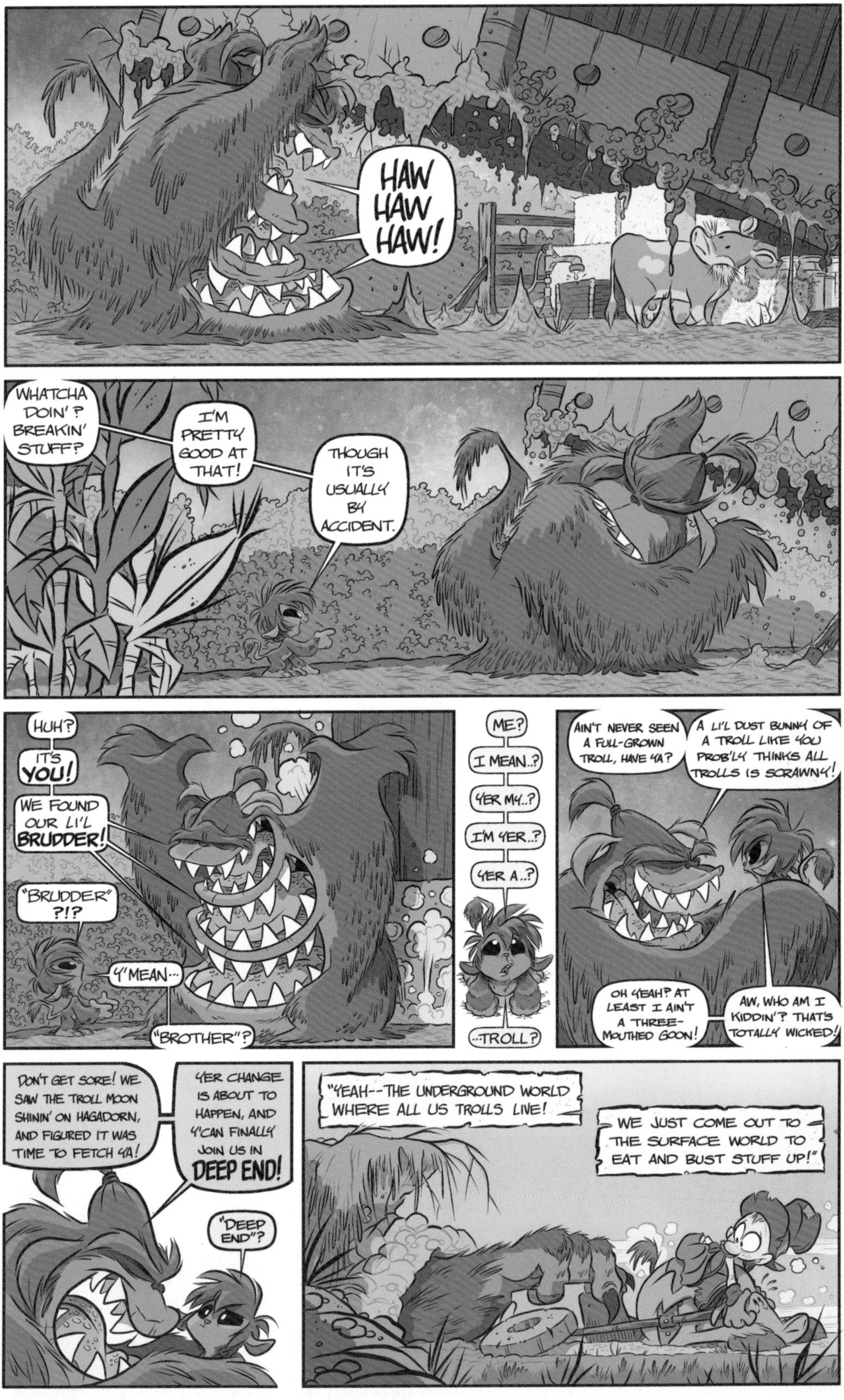
HAW HAW HAW!
WHATCHA DOIN'? BREAKIN' STUFF?
I'M PRETTY GOOD AT THAT!
THOUGH IT'S USUALLY BY ACCIDENT.
HUH?
IT'S YOU!
WE FOUND OUR LI'L BRUDDER!
"BRUDDER"?!?
Y'MEAN...
"BROTHER"?
ME?
I MEAN..?
YER MY..?
I'M YER..?
YER A..?
...TROLL?
AIN'T NEVER SEEN A FULL-GROWN TROLL, HAVE YA?
A LI'L DUST BUNNY OF A TROLL LIKE YOU PROB'LY THINKS ALL TROLLS IS SCRAWNY!
OH YEAH? AT LEAST I AIN'T A THREE-MOUTHED GOON!
AW, WHO AM I KIDDIN'? THAT'S TOTALLY WICKED!
DON'T GET SORE! WE SAW THE TROLL MOON SHININ' ON HAGADORN, AND FIGURED IT WAS TIME TO FETCH YA!
YER CHANGE IS ABOUT TO HAPPEN, AND Y'CAN FINALLY JOIN US IN DEEP END!
"DEEP END"?
"YEAH--THE UNDERGROUND WORLD WHERE ALL US TROLLS LIVE!
WE JUST COME OUT TO THE SURFACE WORLD TO EAT AND BUST STUFF UP!"

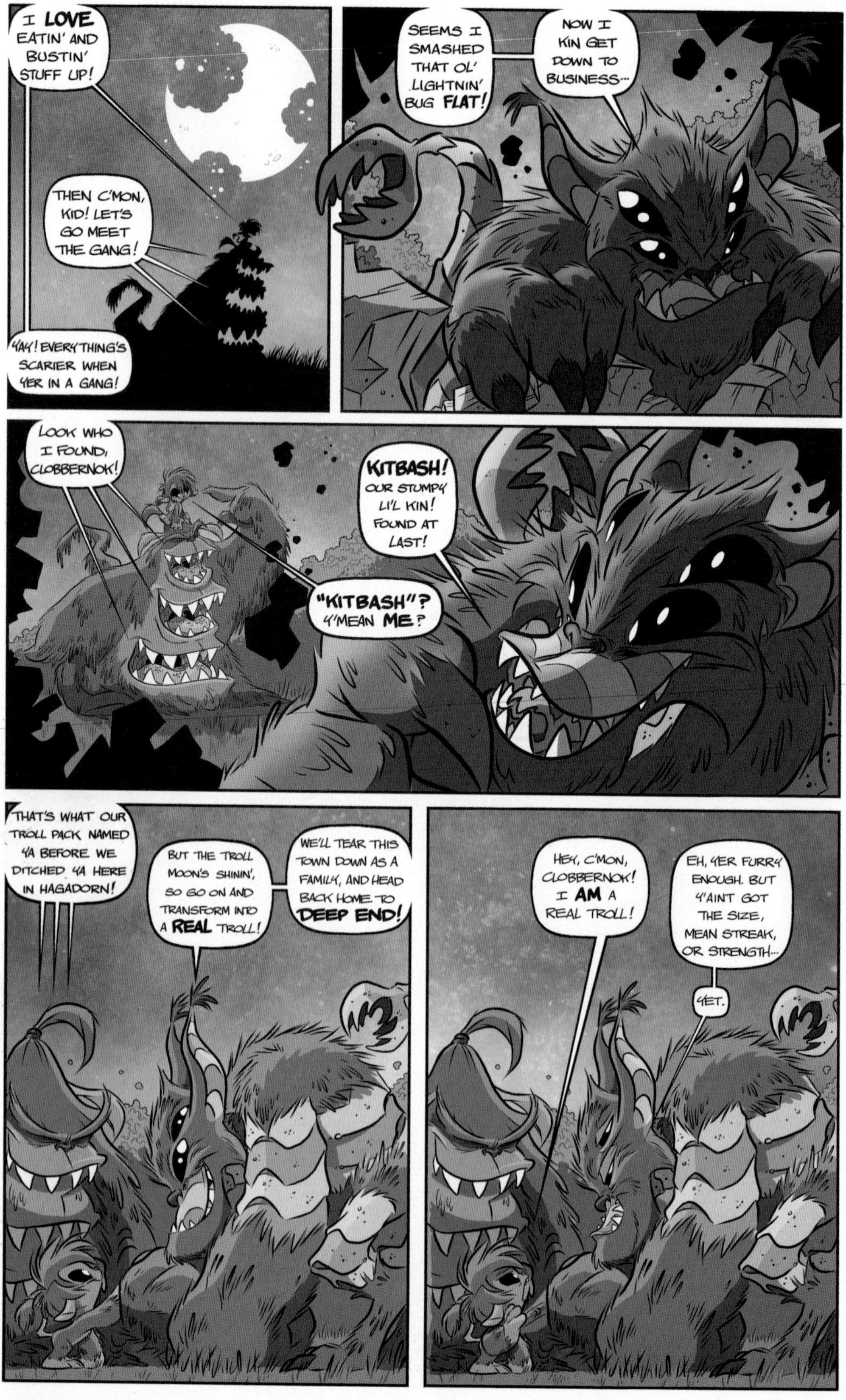
I **LOVE** EATIN' AND BUSTIN' STUFF UP!
THEN C'MON, KID! LET'S GO MEET THE GANG!
YAY! EVERYTHING'S SCARIER WHEN YER IN A GANG!
SEEMS I SMASHED THAT OL' LIGHTNIN' BUG **FLAT**!
NOW I KIN GET DOWN TO BUSINESS...
LOOK WHO I FOUND, CLOBBERNOK!
KITBASH! OUR STUMPY LI'L KIN! FOUND AT LAST!
"**KITBASH**"? Y'MEAN **ME**?
THAT'S WHAT OUR TROLL PACK NAMED YA BEFORE WE DITCHED YA HERE IN HAGADORN!
BUT THE TROLL MOON'S SHININ', SO GO ON AND TRANSFORM INTO A **REAL** TROLL!
WE'LL TEAR THIS TOWN DOWN AS A FAMILY, AND HEAD BACK HOME TO **DEEP END**!
HEY, C'MON, CLOBBERNOK! I **AM** A REAL TROLL!
EH, YER FURRY ENOUGH. BUT Y'AINT GOT THE SIZE, MEAN STREAK, OR STRENGTH...
YET.

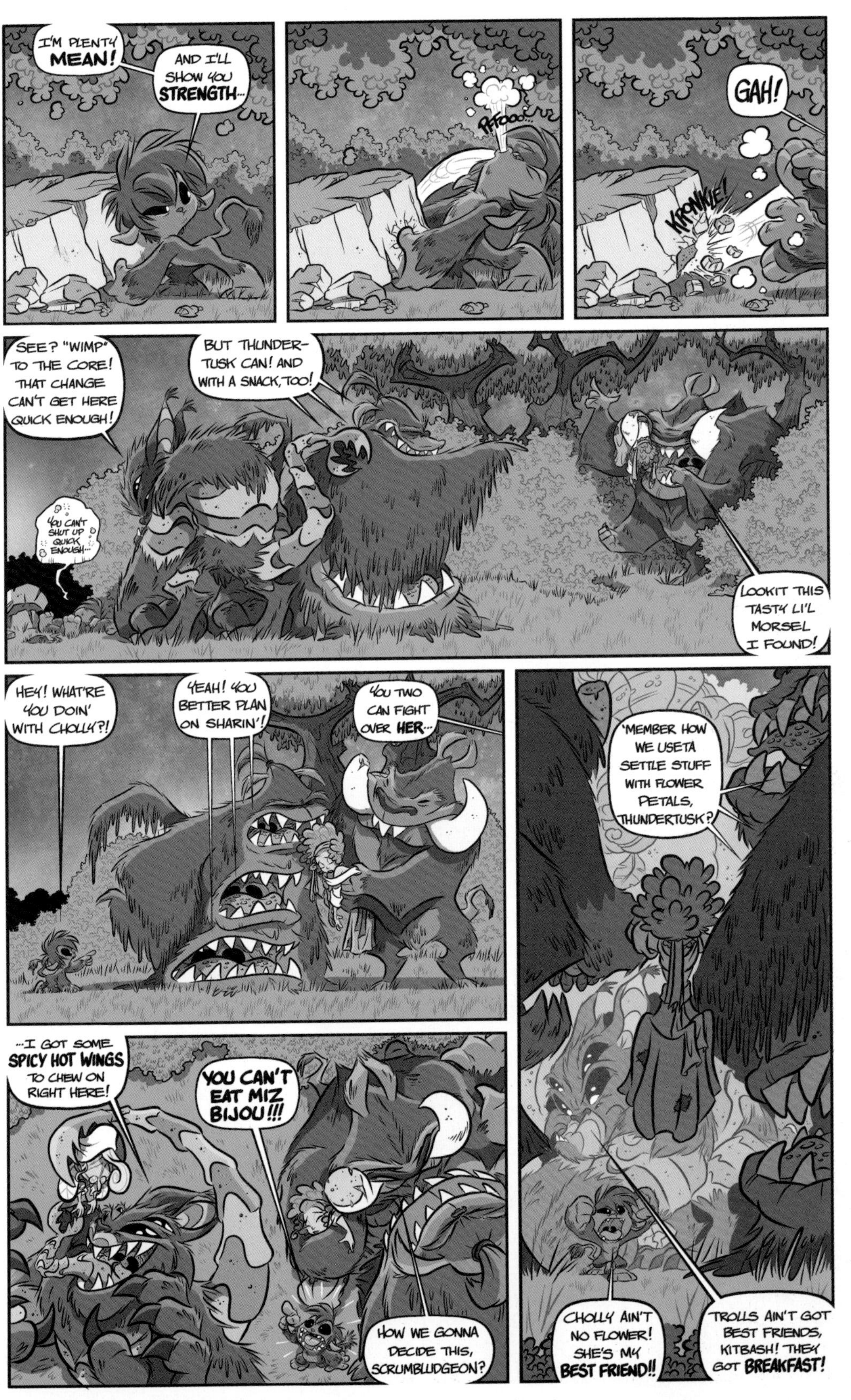
I'M PLENTY MEAN!
AND I'LL SHOW YOU STRENGTH...
PFFOOO...
GAH!
KRONKLE!
SEE? "WIMP" TO THE CORE! THAT CHANGE CAN'T GET HERE QUICK ENOUGH!
YOU CAN'T SHUT UP QUICK ENOUGH...
BUT THUNDER-TUSK CAN! AND WITH A SNACK, TOO!
LOOKIT THIS TASTY LI'L MORSEL I FOUND!
HEY! WHAT'RE YOU DOIN' WITH CHOLLY?!
YEAH! YOU BETTER PLAN ON SHARIN'!
YOU TWO CAN FIGHT OVER HER...
...I GOT SOME SPICY HOT WINGS TO CHEW ON RIGHT HERE!
YOU CAN'T EAT MIZ BIJOU!!!
HOW WE GONNA DECIDE THIS, SCRUMBLUDGEON?
'MEMBER HOW WE USETA SETTLE STUFF WITH FLOWER PETALS, THUNDERTUSK?
CHOLLY AIN'T NO FLOWER! SHE'S MY BEST FRIEND!!
TROLLS AIN'T GOT BEST FRIENDS, KITBASH! THEY GOT BREAKFAST!

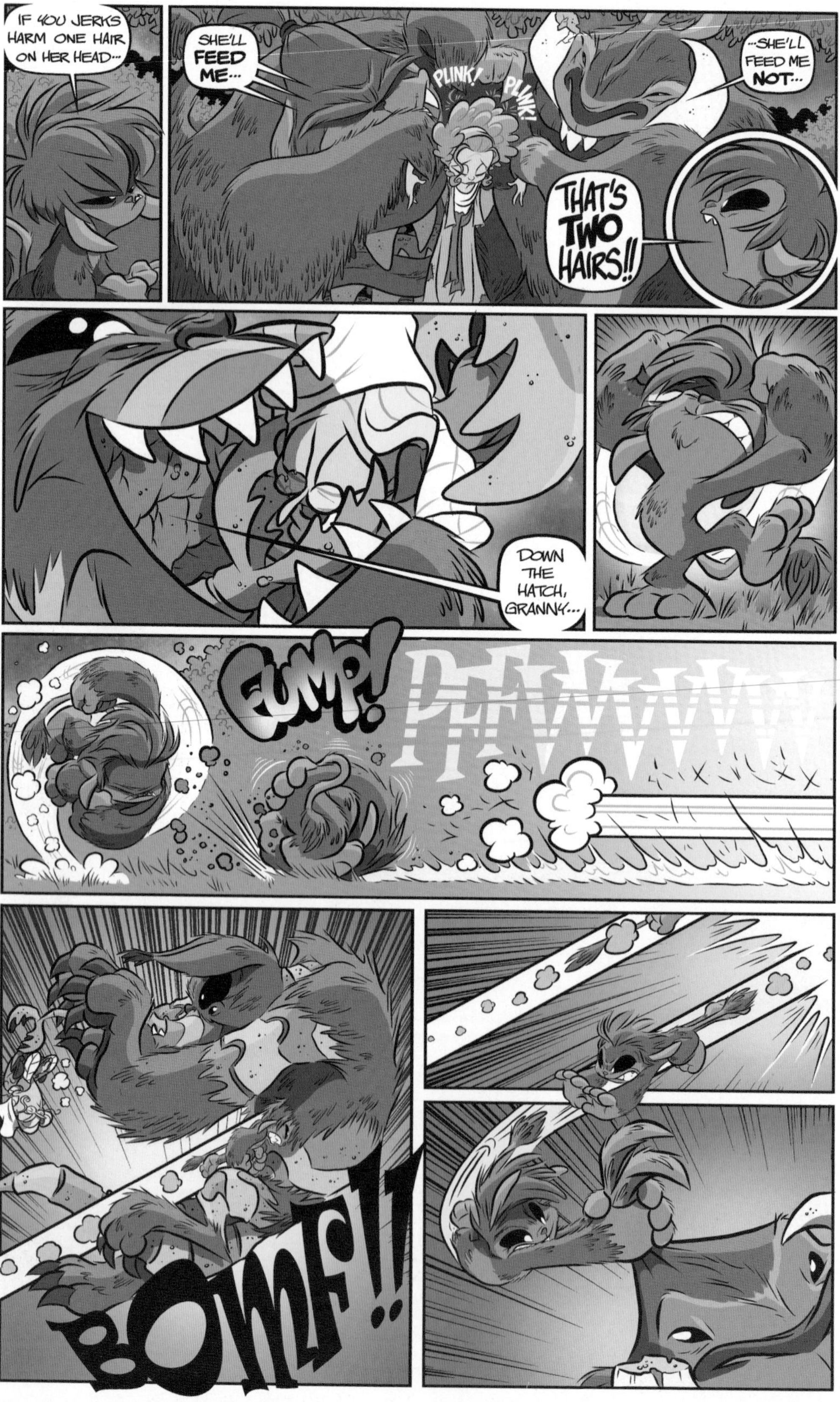
IF YOU JERKS HARM ONE HAIR ON HER HEAD...
SHE'LL FEED ME...
PLINK!
PLINK!
...SHE'LL FEED ME NOT...
THAT'S TWO HAIRS!!
DOWN THE HATCH, GRANNY...
FUMP!
BOMF!!

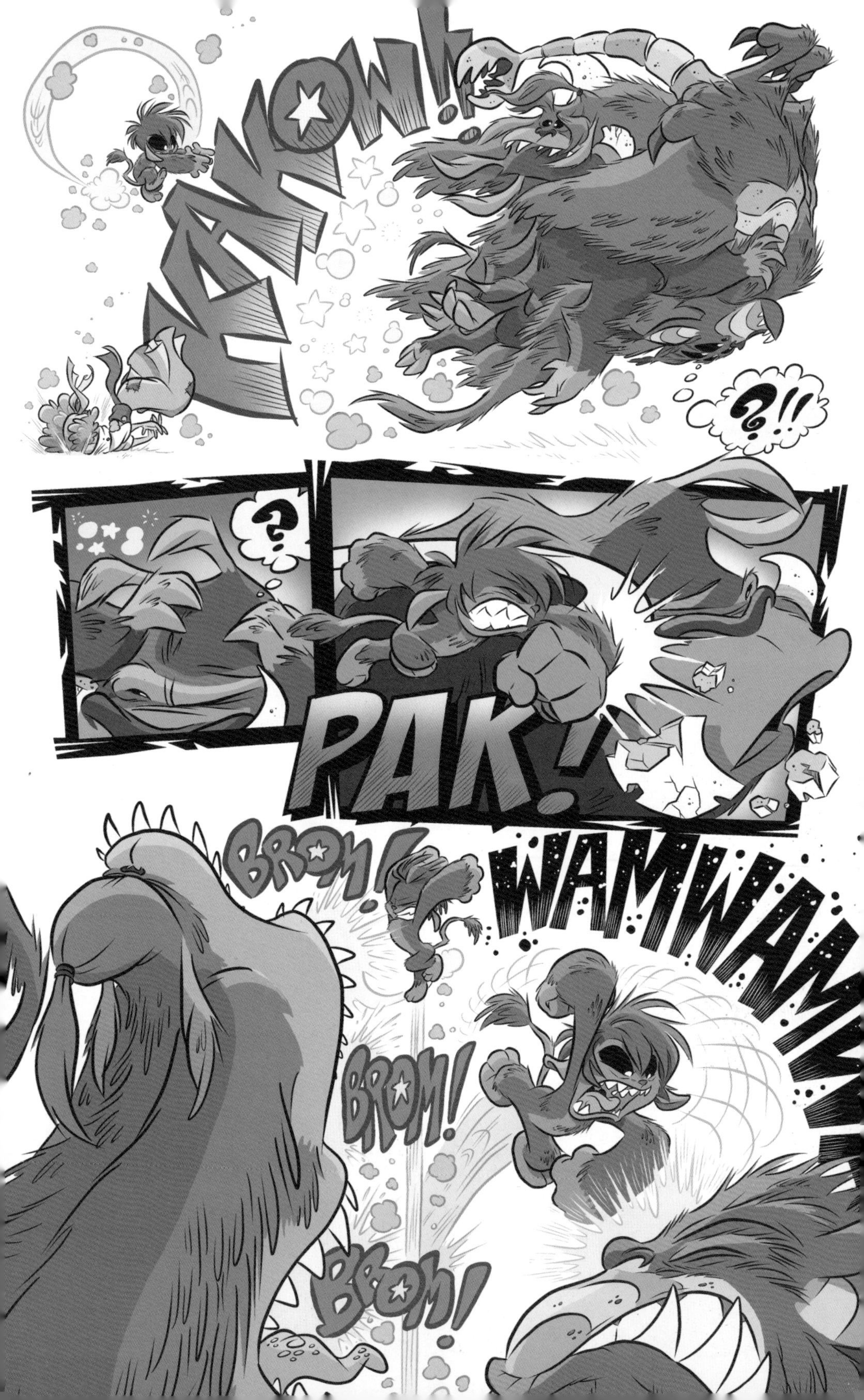
KAKOW!!
?!!
?
PAK!
BROM!
WAMWAMW
BROM!
BROM!

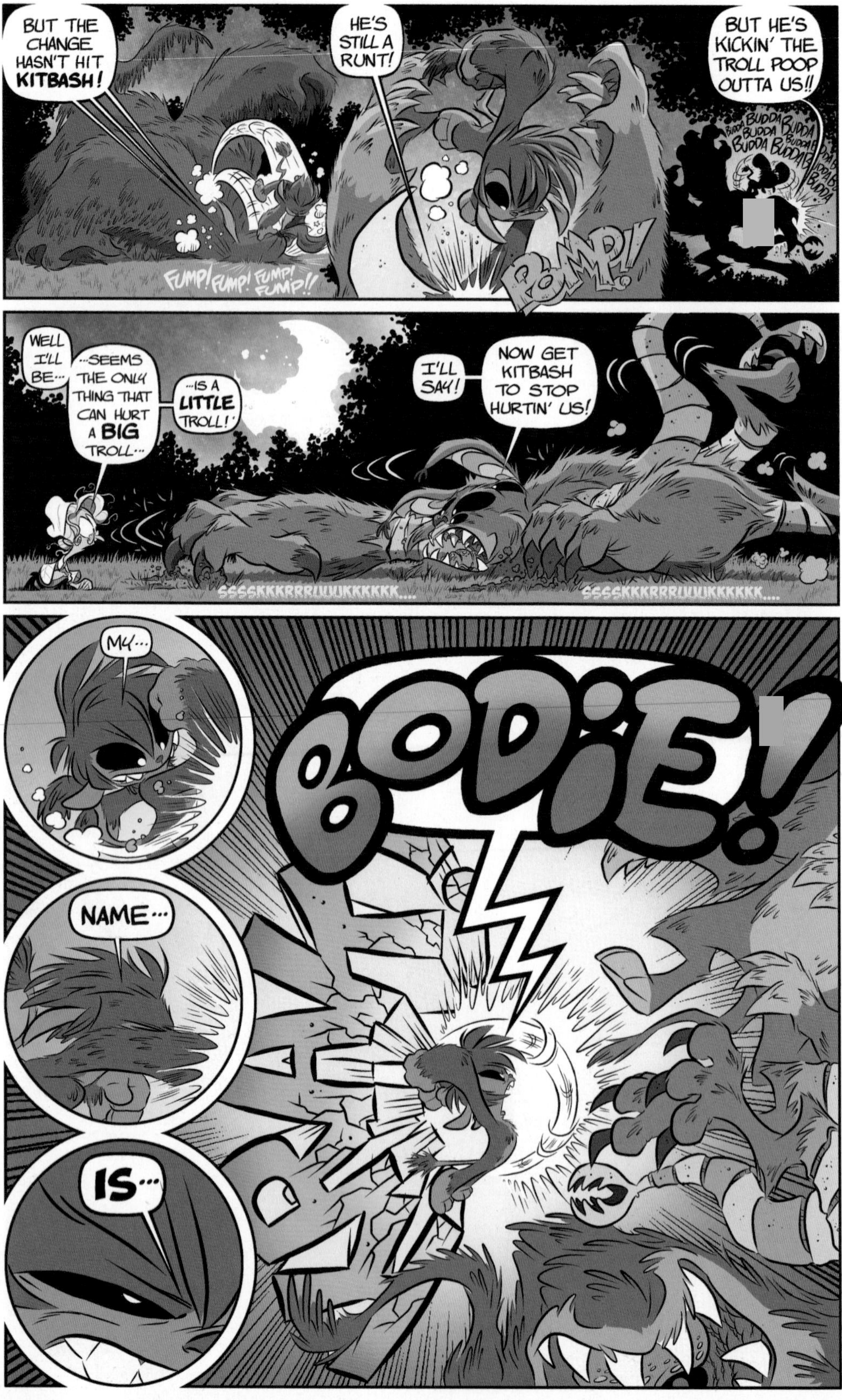

BUT THE CHANGE HASN'T HIT KITBASH!
FUMP! FUMP! FUMP! FUMP!!
HE'S STILL A RUNT!
POMP!!
BUT HE'S KICKIN' THE TROLL POOP OUTTA US!!
BUDDA BUDDA BUDDA BUDDA BUDDA BUDDA BUDDA BUDDA BUDDA BUDDA
WELL I'LL BE...
...SEEMS THE ONLY THING THAT CAN HURT A BIG TROLL...
...IS A LITTLE TROLL!
I'LL SAY!
NOW GET KITBASH TO STOP HURTIN' US!
SSSSKKKRRRUUUKKKKKK...
SSSSKKKRRRUUUKKKKKK...
MY...
NAME...
IS...
BODIE!

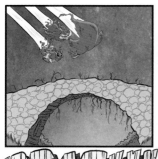

BRASH!
CRUNKLE...

HEAD FER DEEP END, AND DON'T LOOK BACK!

HAGADORN IS OFFICIALLY OFF LIMITS!

BUT KITBASH-- I MEAN "BODIE"-- IS FIERCE ENOUGH TO REJOIN OUR PACK!

WE GOTTA CONVINCE 'EM!

I'M FER CONVINCIN' MY'SELF TO AVOID HIM LIKE A SALAD AND A BATH! HE'S TOO FIERCE EVEN FER US!

HE MAY BE THE FIERCEST TROLL WHO EVER LIVED!

TOLD YOU.

SHUT UP.

GRRR...

BODIE, HONEY... IT'S OKAY... THEY'RE GONE. THEY WON'T RETURN, THANKS TO YOU.

BUT CHOLLY... SHE'S HURT REAL BAD. WE GOTTA TEND TO HER.

CHOLLY..? I...

I... I CAN'T... SHE'S TOO HEAVY... BUT I CAN'T LEAVE HER ON THE GROUND...

YER CRAZY STRENGTH MUST ONLY WORK AGAINST OTHER TROLLS. BUT DON'T WORRY...

I'VE GOT HER...

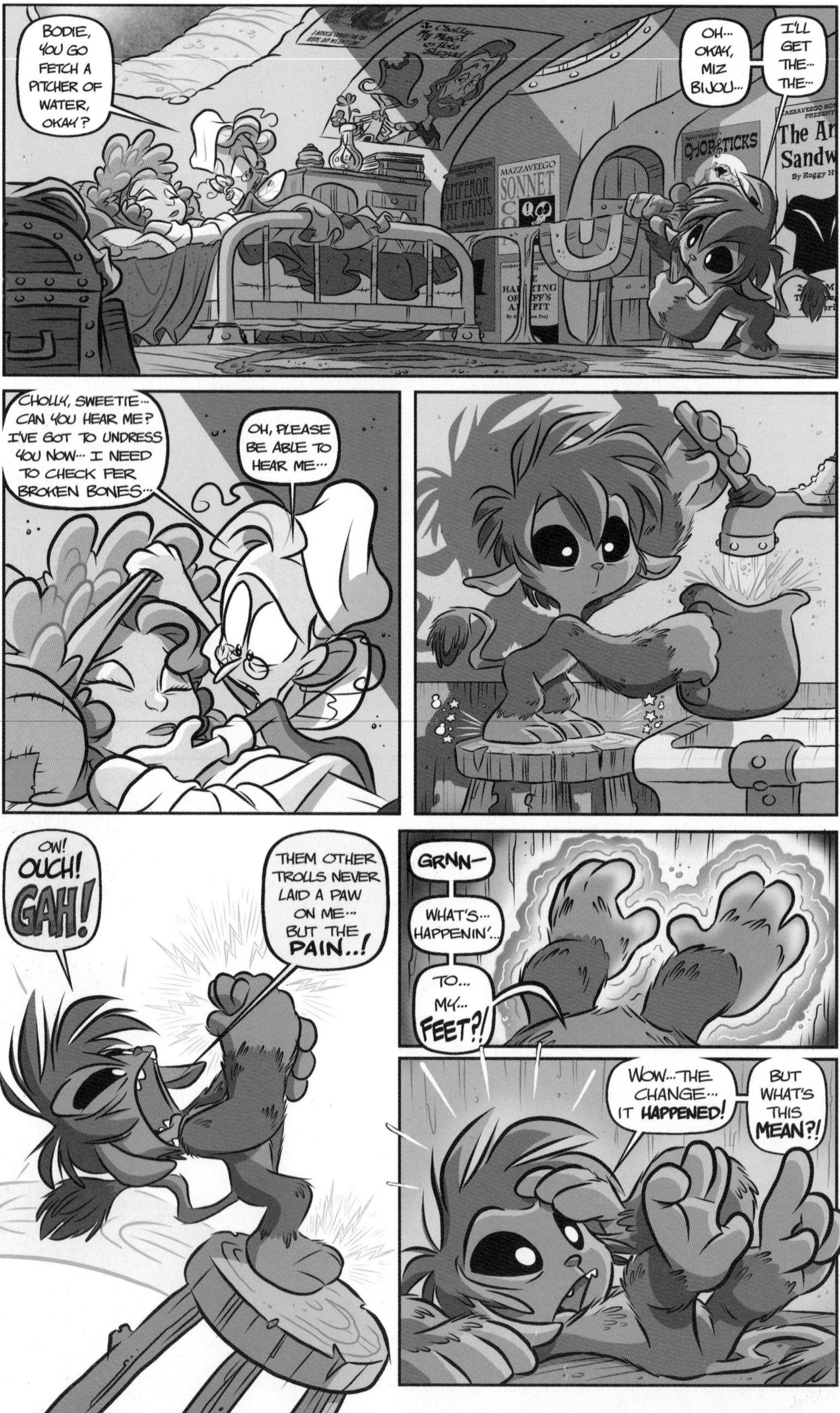
BODIE, YOU GO FETCH A PITCHER OF WATER, OKAY?
OH... OKAY, MIZ BIJOU...
I'LL GET THE... THE...
EMPEROR FAT PANTS
MAZZAVEEGO SONNET
CHOPSTICKS
CHOLLY, SWEETIE... CAN YOU HEAR ME? I'VE GOT TO UNDRESS YOU NOW... I NEED TO CHECK FER BROKEN BONES...
OH, PLEASE BE ABLE TO HEAR ME...
OW! OUCH! GAH!
THEM OTHER TROLLS NEVER LAID A PAW ON ME... BUT THE PAIN..!
GRNN—
WHAT'S... HAPPENIN'...
TO... MY... FEET?!
WOW... THE CHANGE... IT HAPPENED!
BUT WHAT'S THIS MEAN?!

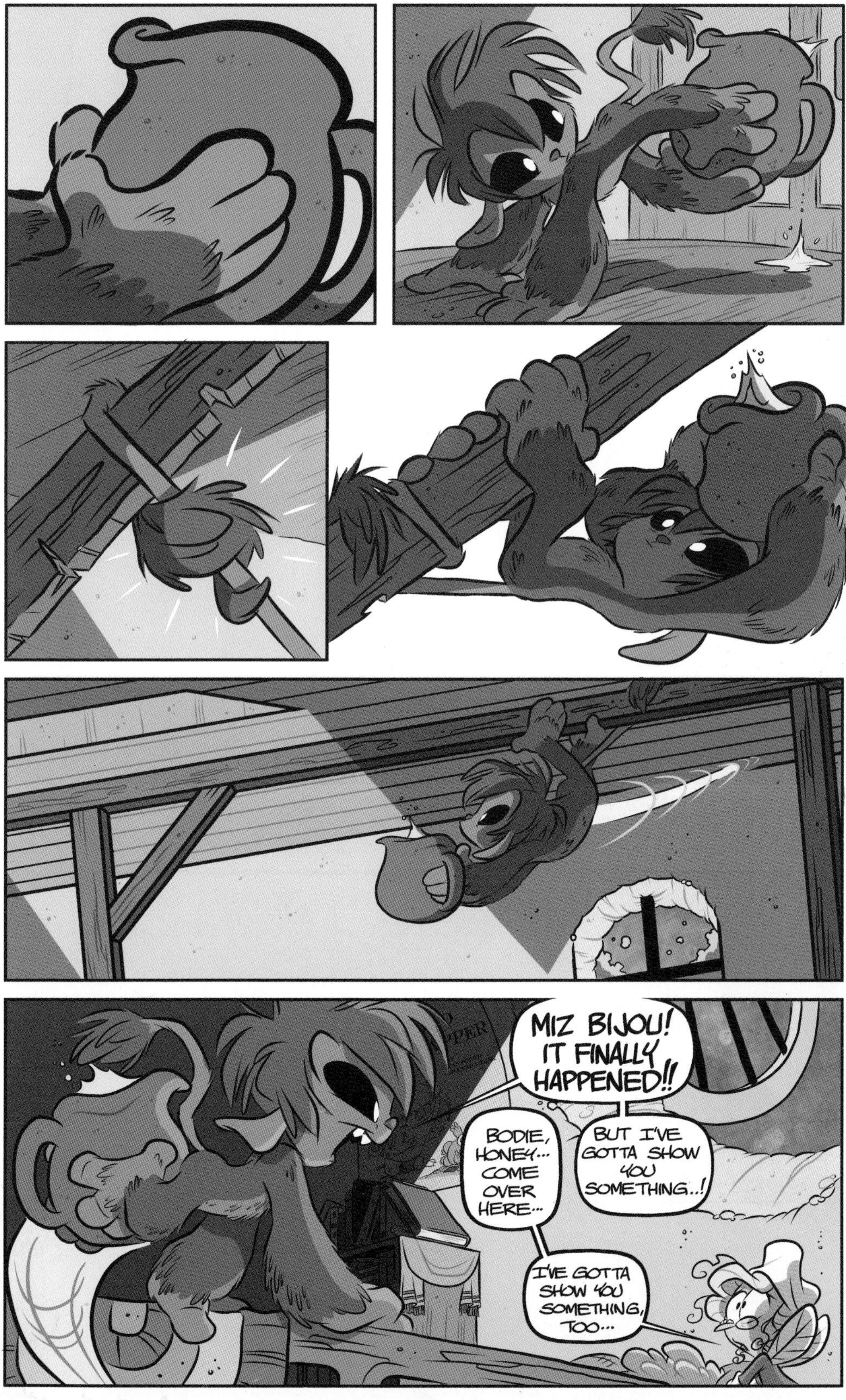
MIZ BIJOU! IT FINALLY HAPPENED!!
BUT I'VE GOTTA SHOW YOU SOMETHING..!
BODIE, HONEY... COME OVER HERE...
I'VE GOTTA SHOW YOU SOMETHING, TOO...

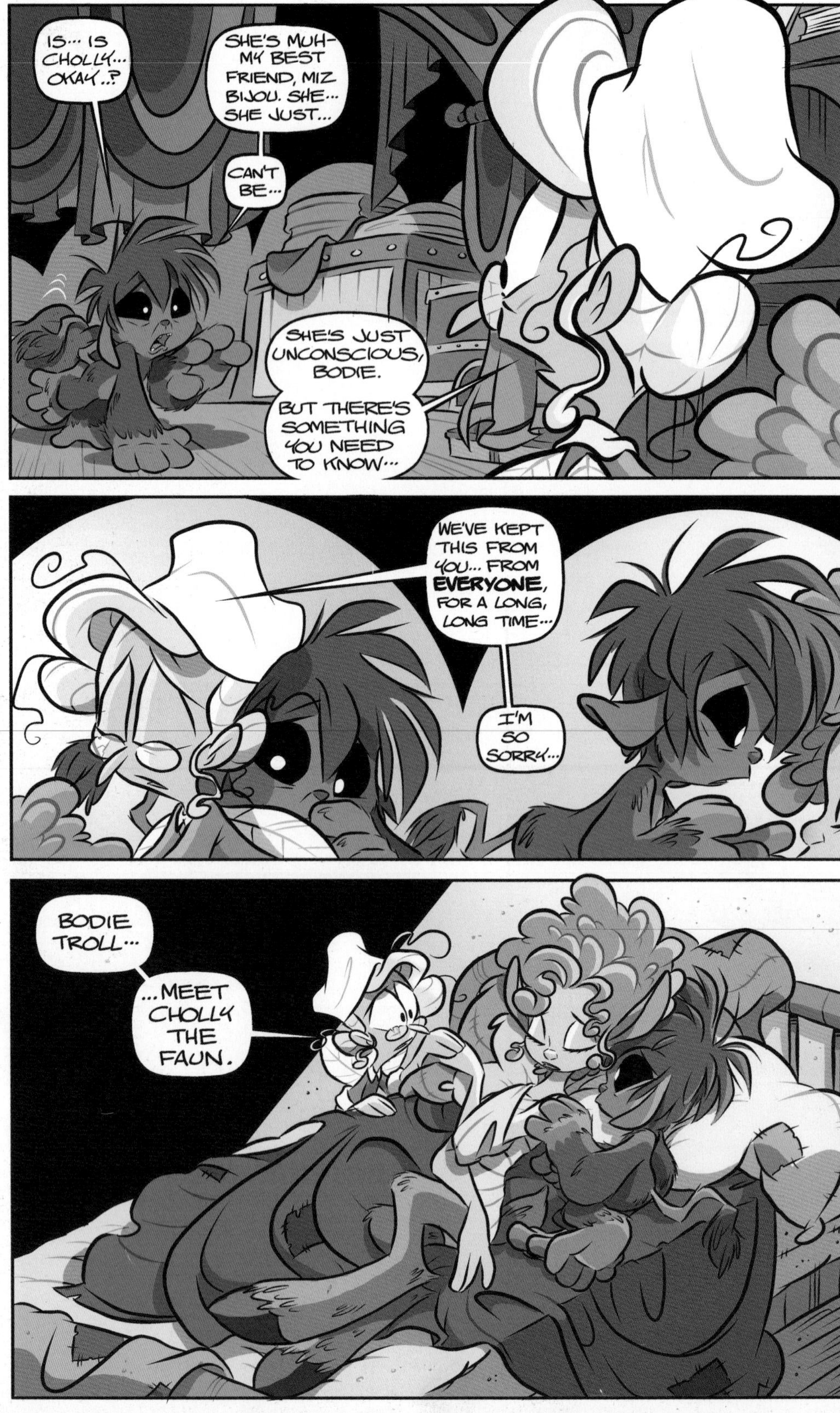
IS... IS CHOLLY... OKAY...?
SHE'S MUH-MY BEST FRIEND, MIZ BIJOU. SHE... SHE JUST...
CAN'T BE...
SHE'S JUST UNCONSCIOUS, BODIE.
BUT THERE'S SOMETHING YOU NEED TO KNOW...
WE'VE KEPT THIS FROM YOU... FROM **EVERYONE**, FOR A LONG, LONG TIME...
I'M SO SORRY...
BODIE TROLL...
...MEET CHOLLY THE FAUN.

THANK YOU!

I grew up loving folk and fairy tales, from the classical texts, to the Disney versions, to satirical takes seen in Jay Ward's *Fractured Fairy Tales* and through *Jim Henson's Muppets*. I even experienced them through the oral tradition, as my grandmother would tell me folk tales that fit the classic mold, but were her own homespun creations. In keeping with the fairy tale theme, you could almost say is was prophesied that I'd create my own fairy tale. Least wise, the odds were pretty darn good.

But nothing written in the stars or foreseen in a crystal ball would have been enough to make my fantasy a reality. I've had so many wonderful people who helped me along the path to publishing *Bodie Troll*. To those people: thank you all for clapping your hands and saying you believed in me.

To my family, for your love and unwavering support of my talent and dreams. A special mention to my late Grandpa Bill--without your unique childhood nickname for me, Cholly would never have come to be.

To my friends, for your encouragement, inspiration, advice, and for allowing yourself to be characters within Bodie's world.

To all the artists who contributed pin-ups to this first *Bodie Troll* mini-series. Thank you for your talents, and for giving me such impressive artistic heights to aspire towards.

To Jay Jacot, for being a rapid-fire color flatter, an amazing support system for all things Bodie and beyond, and for being an incredible friend.

To Evan Shaner for being Bodie's first colorist and helping me discover the palette of his world. And to Nathan Pride for his own amazing color skills when I needed his help at the end.

To Mike Mignola, for allowing me to run my Kid Hellboy pitch in this collection. You've helped me show my readers where Bodie began.

Lastly, to my lifelong hero, Jim Henson. Thank you for being a continual source of hope and inspiration, and for showing me at a young age that monsters could be funny and loveable. And to Karen Falk, a dear friend who reunited me with Jim when I needed him the most.

And thank you, my readers, for being such a great audience for my fairy tale. I look forward to continuing Bodie's adventures for years to come, and having you with me at every step of the journey!

—Jay

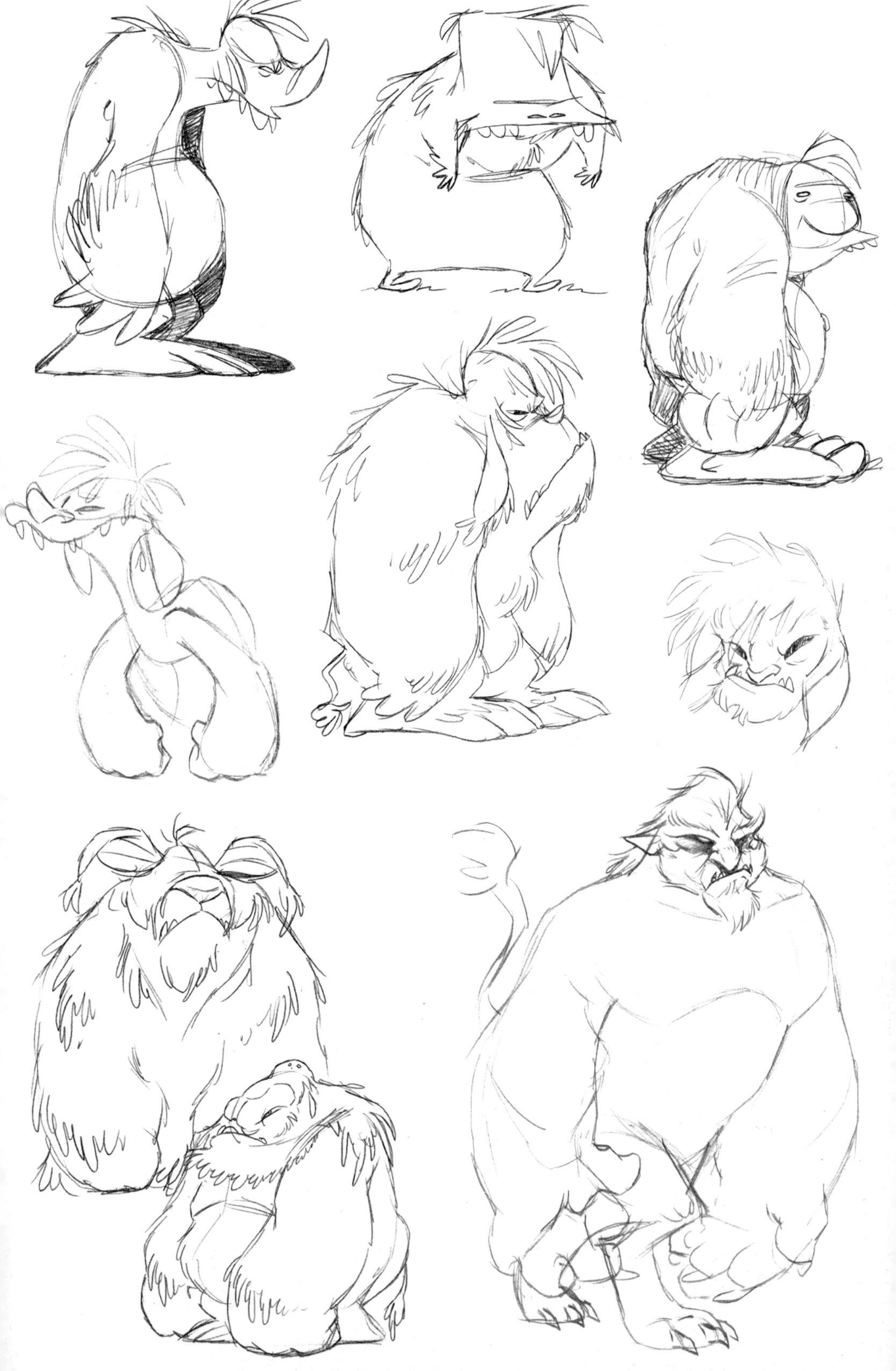

Origin of Bodie

Bodie began life in a supporting role, and as a girlfriend to a demon, no less.

in 2010, I pitched a "Kid Hellboy" story to creator Mike Mignola. In it, I showed Kid Hellboy visiting Norway, where he has his first crush--a girl troll who smacks him with a rock. Mike enjoyed the story, but had no place for it within Hellboy's current publication schedule. Any disappointment was quickly quashed by my surprising interest in this troll character I'd created.

As I began developing the troll, it took on more of my personality, resulting in she becoming a he. A rapid-fire naming session resulted in "Bodie" winning out, just beating out "Henny", a play off of my hero, Jim Henson. Once in an interview, I

was asked if I got "Bodie" from "Bodhi", the Buddhist word for enlightenment. I admitted that "Bodie" had just sounded fun when I came up with it, but suggested they print the Buddhist story to make me sound more interesting.

There were only a few remaining cosmetic decisions made in Bodie's development. A last minute choice to switch from blue to brown as his color scheme was my attempt to avoid comparison to other cuddly pop culture icons. Bodie had nostrils in his first story, but lost them for a more streamlined snout from the second story onward. And by the end of his fourth story, the shines of Bodie's eyes would serve as pupils to give the typically scatter-brained little runt better focus.

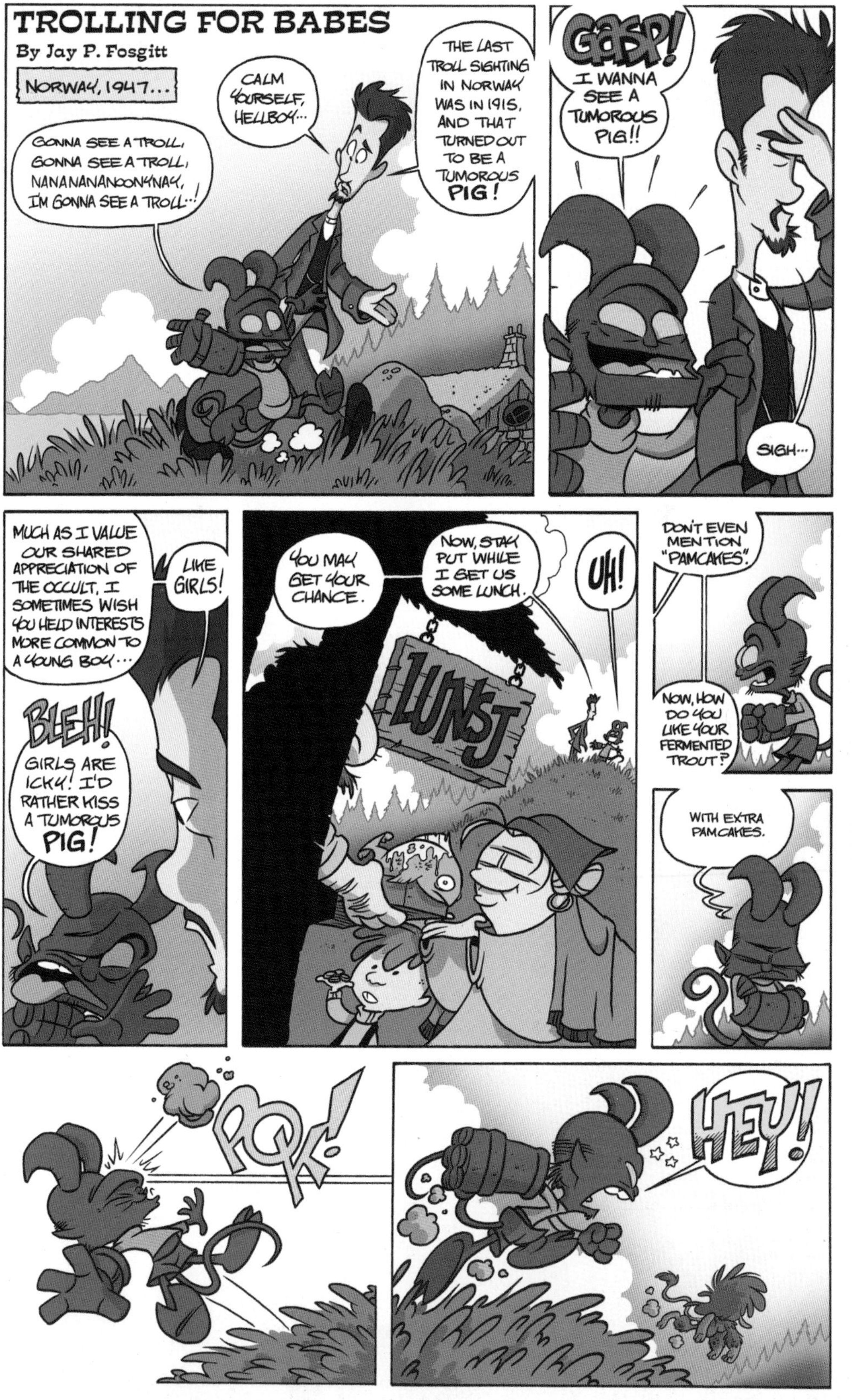
TROLLING FOR BABES
By Jay P. Fosgitt
NORWAY, 1947...
GONNA SEE A TROLL, GONNA SEE A TROLL, NANANANANOONYNAY, I'M GONNA SEE A TROLL--!
CALM YOURSELF, HELLBOY...
THE LAST TROLL SIGHTING IN NORWAY WAS IN 1915, AND THAT TURNED OUT TO BE A TUMOROUS PIG!
GASP!
I WANNA SEE A TUMOROUS PIG!!
SIGH...
MUCH AS I VALUE OUR SHARED APPRECIATION OF THE OCCULT, I SOMETIMES WISH YOU HELD INTERESTS MORE COMMON TO A YOUNG BOY...
LIKE GIRLS!
BLEH!
GIRLS ARE ICKY! I'D RATHER KISS A TUMOROUS PIG!
YOU MAY GET YOUR CHANCE.
NOW, STAY PUT WHILE I GET US SOME LUNCH.
UH!
LUNSJ
DON'T EVEN MENTION "PAMCAKES".
NOW, HOW DO YOU LIKE YOUR FERMENTED TROUT?
WITH EXTRA PAMCAKES.
POK!
HEY!

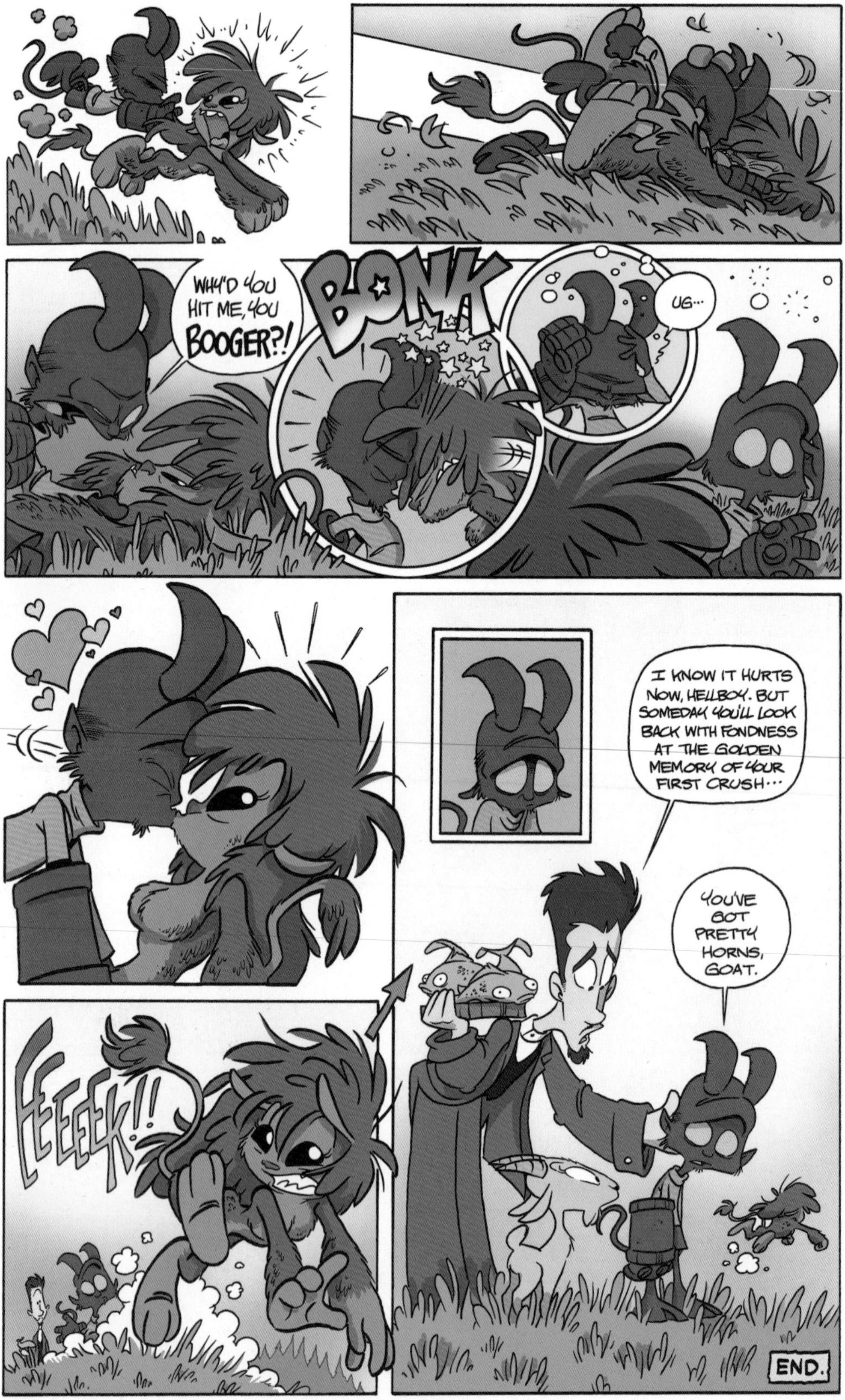
WHY'D YOU HIT ME, YOU BOOGER?!
BONK
UG...
I KNOW IT HURTS NOW, HELLBOY. BUT SOMEDAY YOU'LL LOOK BACK WITH FONDNESS AT THE GOLDEN MEMORY OF YOUR FIRST CRUSH...
YOU'VE GOT PRETTY HORNS, GOAT.
EEEEEK!!
END.

BODIE SKETCHES

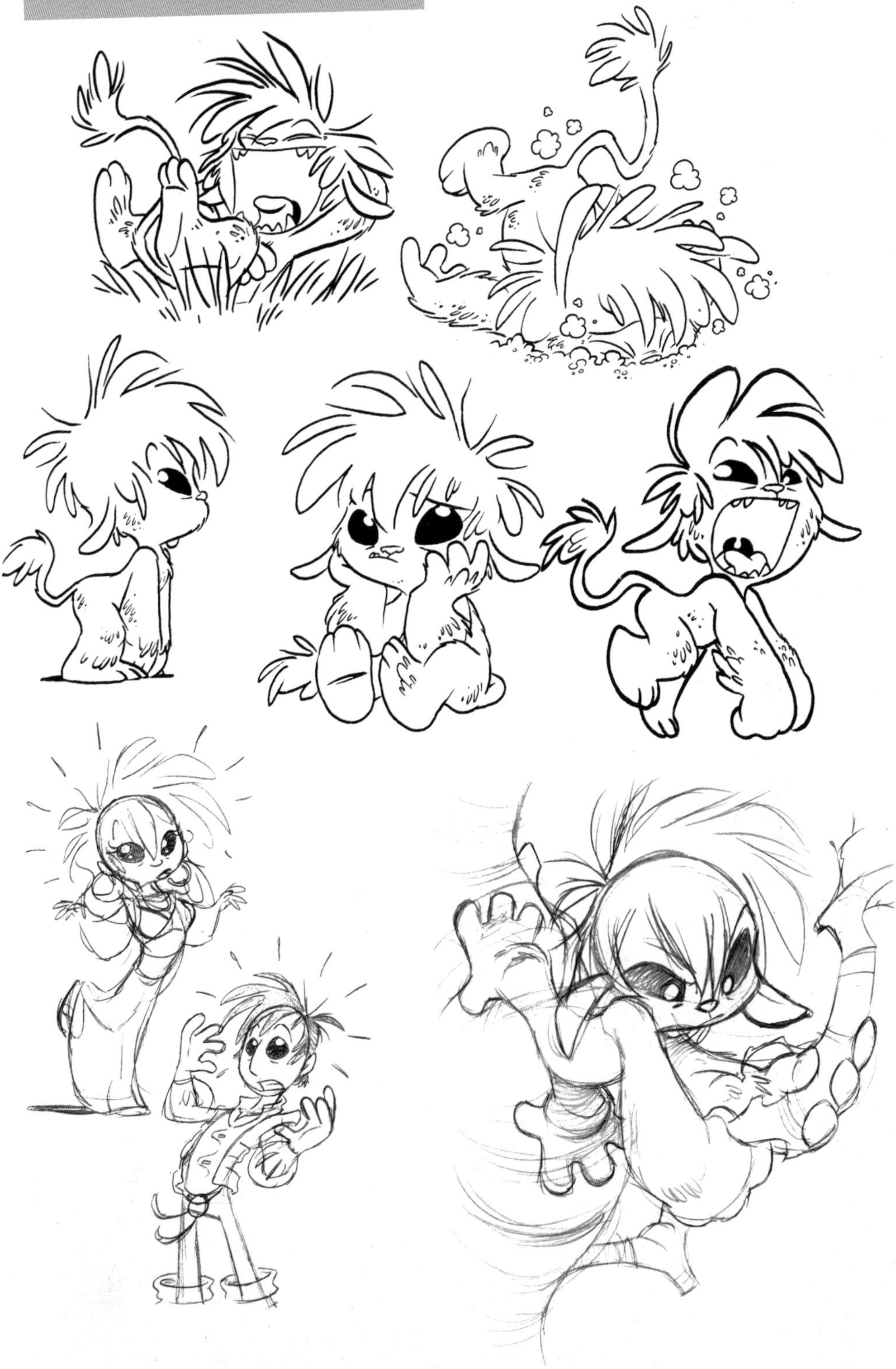

CHOLLY

I created Cholly in 1998 while I was working on my college newspaper as staff cartoonist. I was attempting to create a comic strip about a girl in college--a two-fold challenge, because I'd never written a female character at that time, and the college theme was imposed upon me by my editor. I'd have preferred to do a fantasy strip. But I managed to slip fantasy elements into the comic by giving Cholly an imaginary friend named Gunk--a more abrasive template for the relationship Cholly would one day have with Bodie. Even the strip's title, *The Epic of Cholly*, suggested grander adventures than running late for class or late night study sessions.

Cholly's personality was inspired by a girl I'd had a crush on in college, who happened to be an aspiring writer. Cholly's name was my childhood nickname, given to me by my grandfather. I never knew where he got it, though he did enjoy the "funny papers" and could have been riffing on Charlie Brown.

In 2000, I attempted an actual fantasy strip, also called *The Epic of Cholly*. It never saw publication, but it became the genesis for *Bodie Troll*.

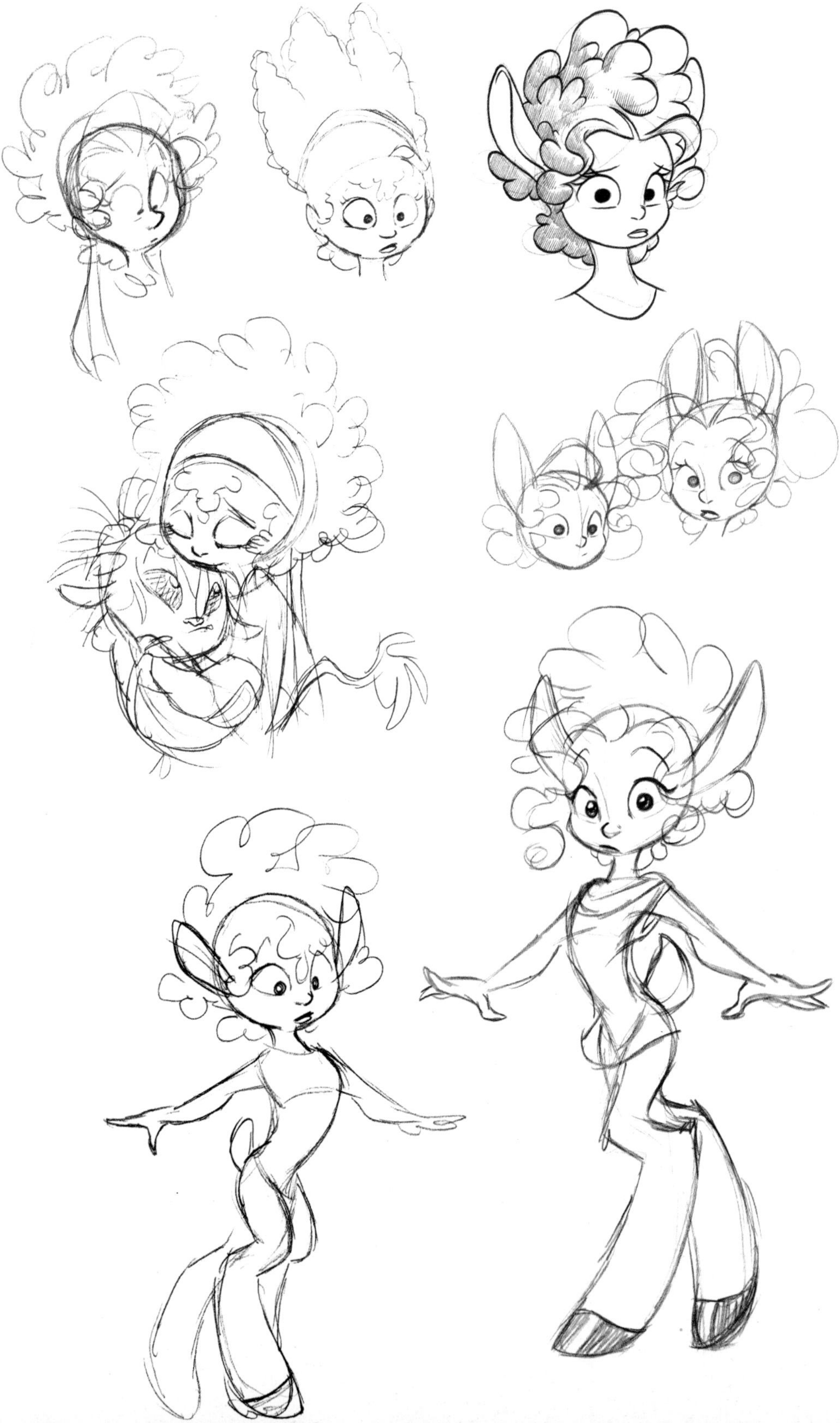

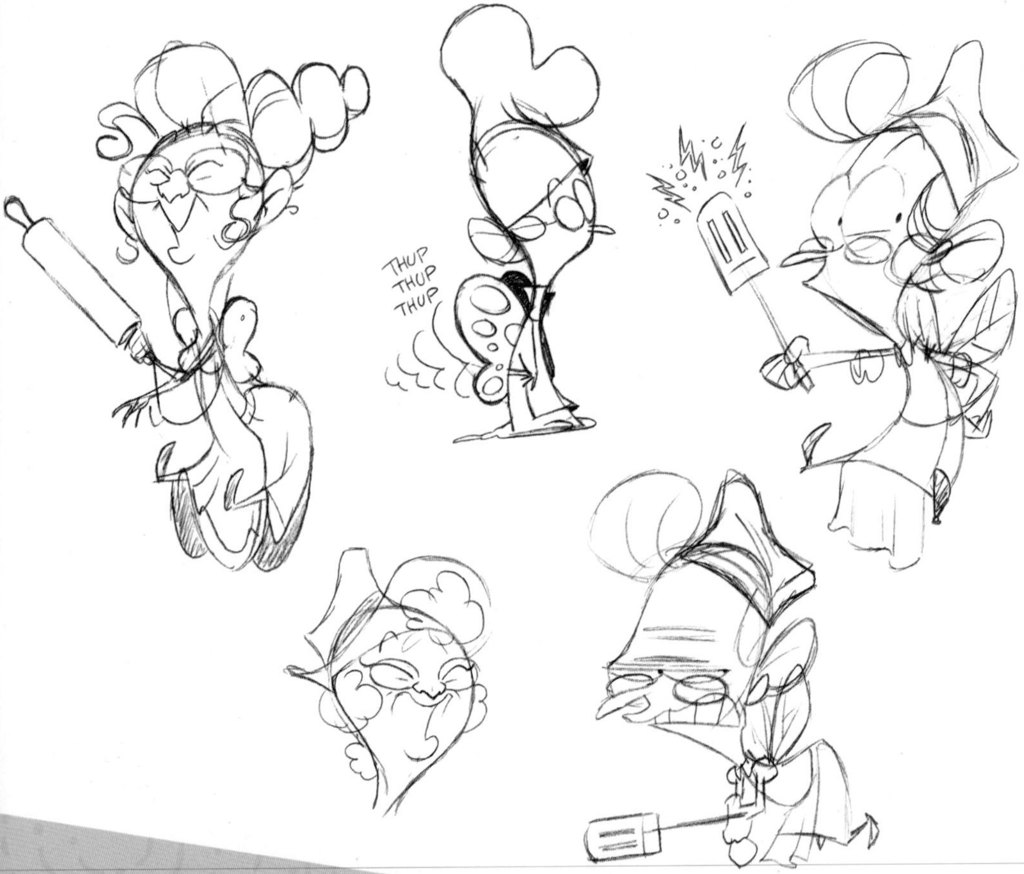
THUP
THUP
THUP

MIZ BIJOU

Miz Bijou began as Auntie Bijou in the original " The Epic of Cholly" comic strip in 1998. She was a far more kindly parental figure than the hair-trigger spatula-slinger she'd become in *Bodie Troll*, and was loosely based on my grandmother.

When I switched gears to developing "The Epic of Cholly" as a fantasy strip in 2000, Auntie Bijou became Miz Bijou, a retired fairy godmother and proprietor of The Drunken Pumpkin. She was also the guardian of Cholly, her god daughter and barmaid, who aspired to be a playwright. This concept only saw one completed strip drawn from it, along with piles of fairytale archetype sketches that would eventually become incidental, and not so incidental, characters in *Bodie Troll* ten years later.

Because "Bijou" is an antiquated term for a movie theater, which doesn't figure into a technology-free fairy tale world, I worried about using the name in *Bodie Troll*, and came close to changing her name to Granny Bastian, after my friend and *Cursed Pirate Girl* creator Jeremy Bastian. But then I looked up the definition of bijou: "Something small, delicate, and exquisitely wrought." That was a perfect description of a fairy, so the name stayed.

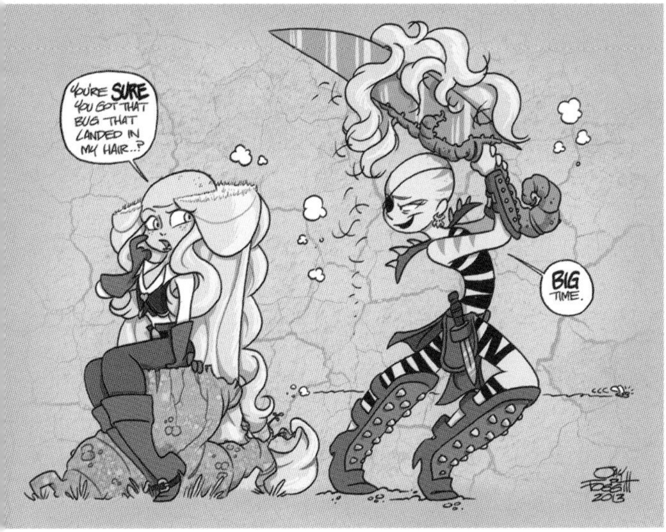
YOU'RE SURE YOU GOT THAT BUG THAT LANDED IN MY HAIR...?
BIG TIME.

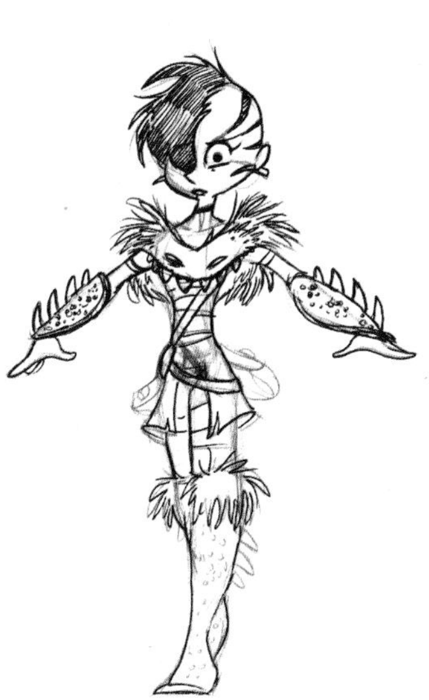

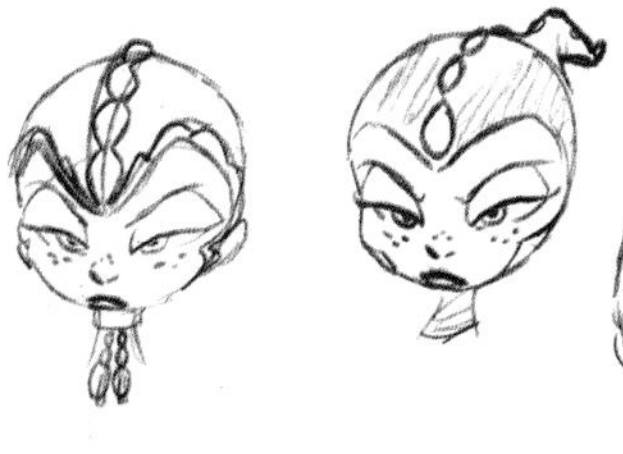

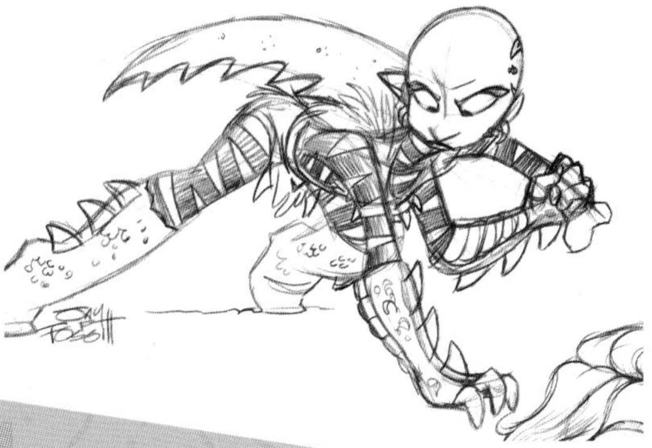

HOKUM & GOSSAMER

Hokum began as Cholly's weird goth college roommate in "The Epic of Cholly". She originally wore all black, had pale white skin, and had a boyfriend named Pud who spoke in gibberish.

When "The Epic of Cholly" was being retrofitted as a fantasy strip, Hokum was being considered for a role as either an apprentice witch or a warrior woman, though she never got past the design stages.

When *Bodie Troll* was in early development, Hokum came close to being a malevolent spirit in a magic mirror before I settled on the previously considered warrior identity.

Gossamer was originally Cholly's editor and adversary on their college newspaper. Her obsession with her hair was her hook from the start.

Gossamer nearly starred in the second "Epic of Cholly" strip. But I decided she made a better troublemaker that the cheery protagonist Cholly would be.

Gossmer's hair is the whole reason Bodie is obsessed with roots. I needed a weird thing for Bodie to obsess over. I had a gag in mind where he ate Gossmer's hair. Then I thought of hair roots, and suddenly this idea of Bodie eating all kinds of roots became as natural as Popeye eating spinach.

PIN UP GALLERY

DAVID PETERSEN

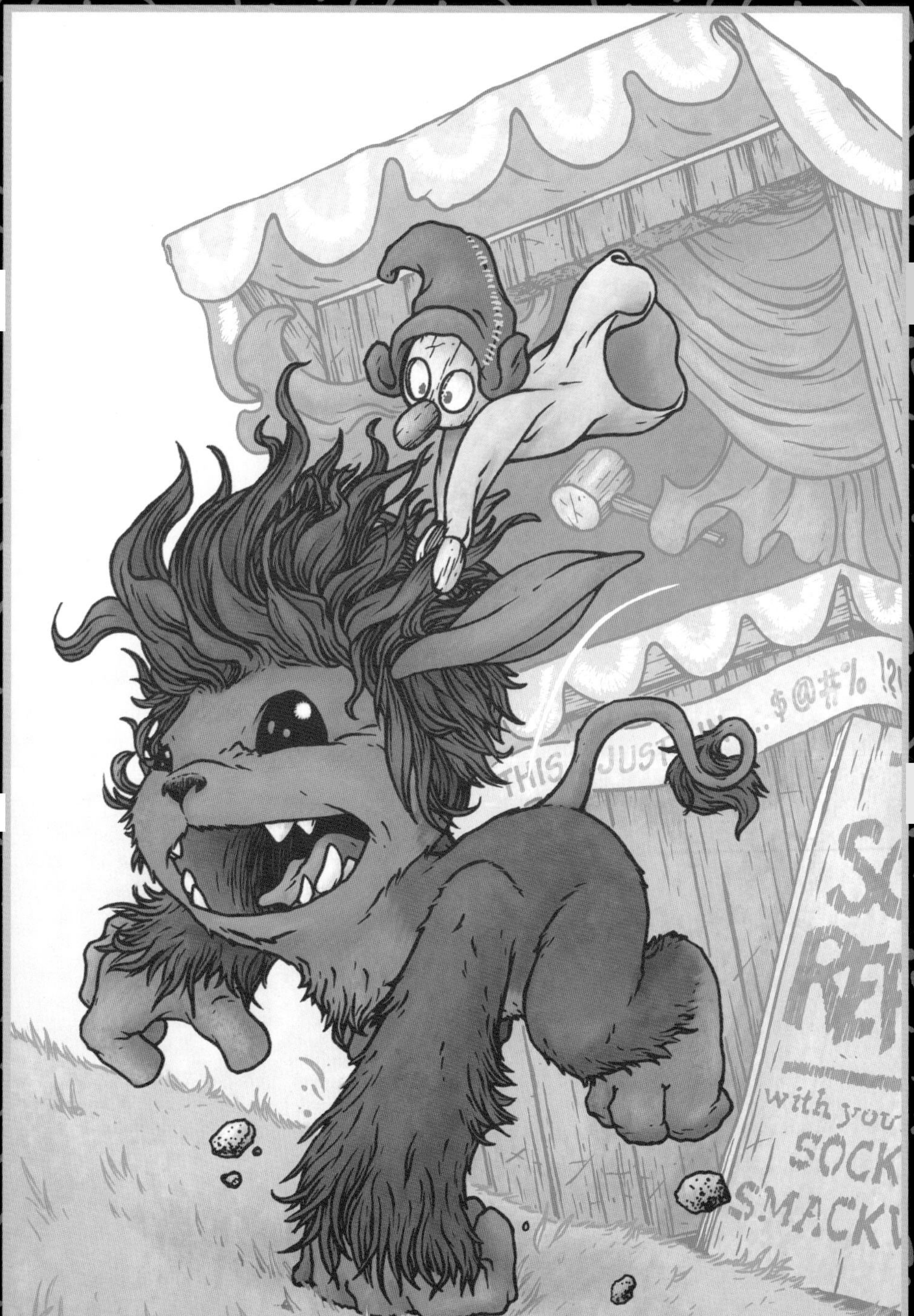
THIS JUST
$@#%

Snack Time!

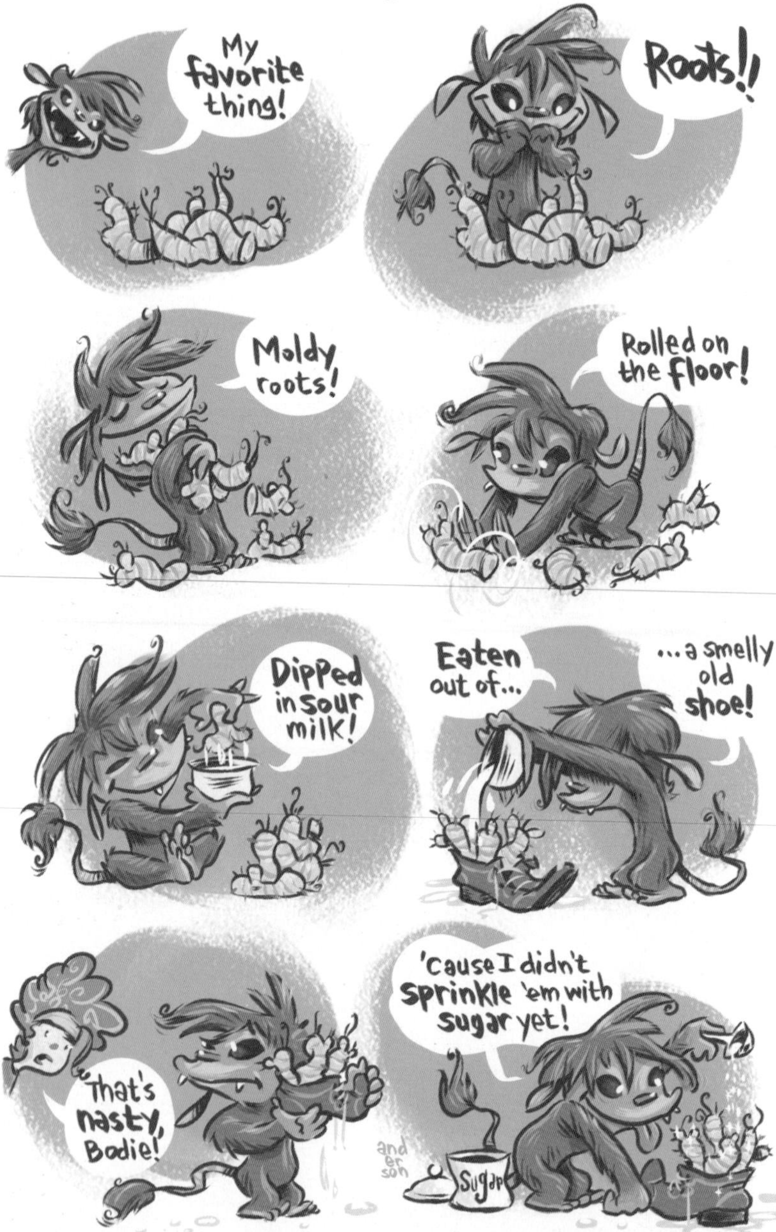
My favorite thing!
Roots!!
Moldy roots!
Rolled on the floor!
Dipped in sour milk!
Eaten out of...
...a smelly old shoe!
That's nasty, Bodie!
'Cause I didn't sprinkle 'em with sugar yet!
Sugar
anderson

JEREMY BASTIAN

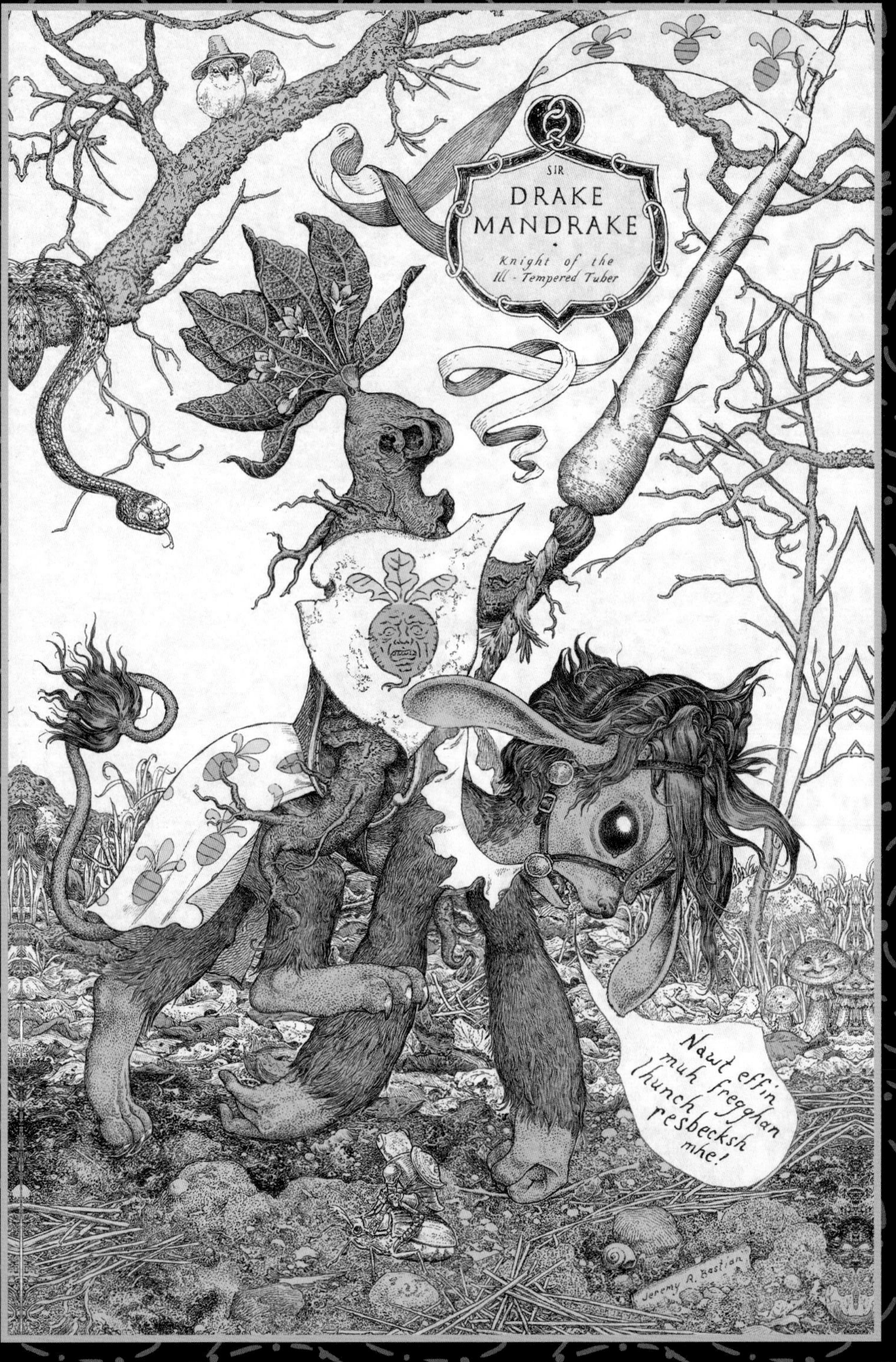
SIR
DRAKE
MANDRAKE
Knight of the
Ill - Tempered Tuber
Nawt effin
muh fregghan
lhunch
resbecksh
mhe!
Jeremy A. Bastian

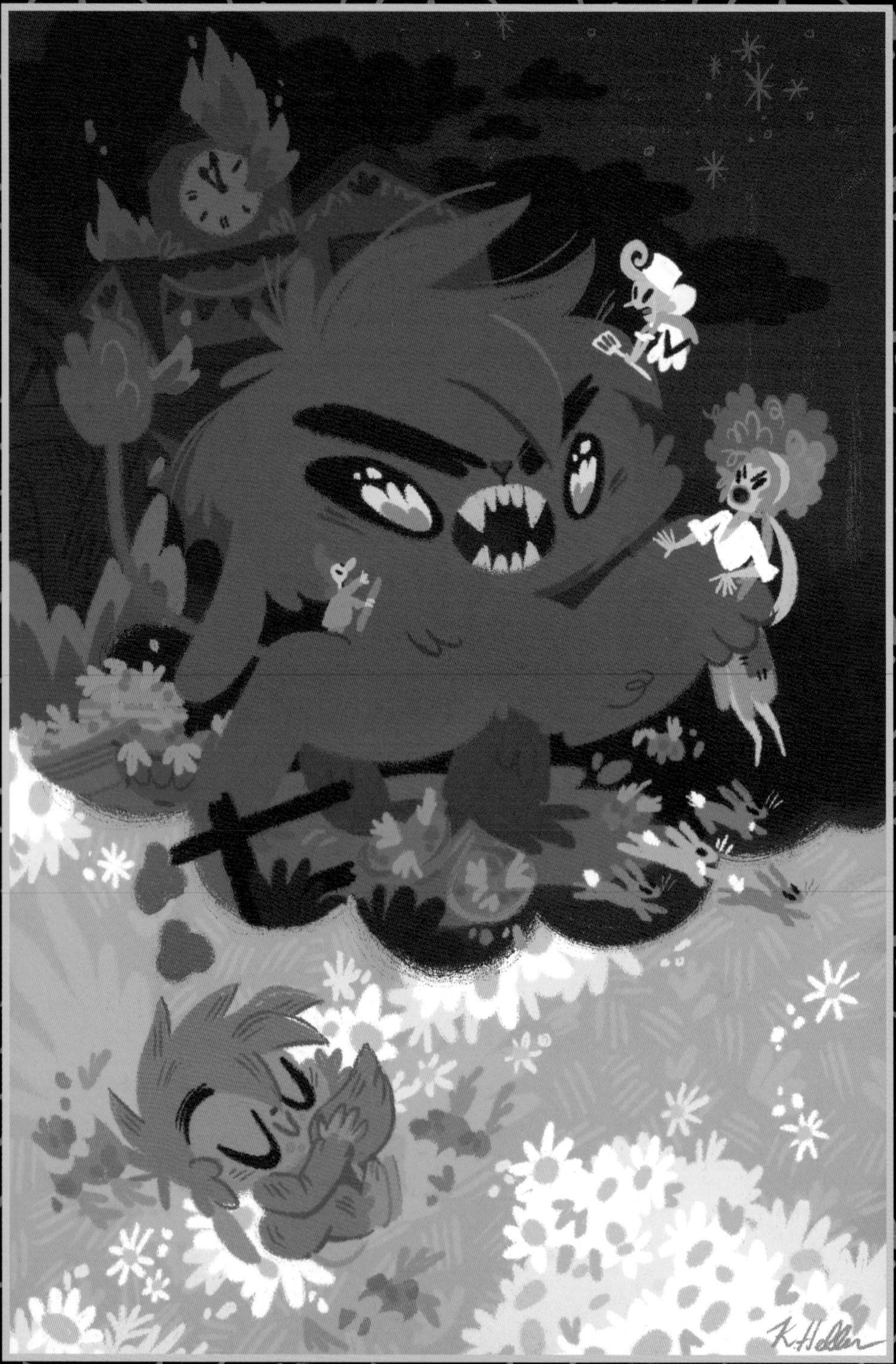
K.Heller

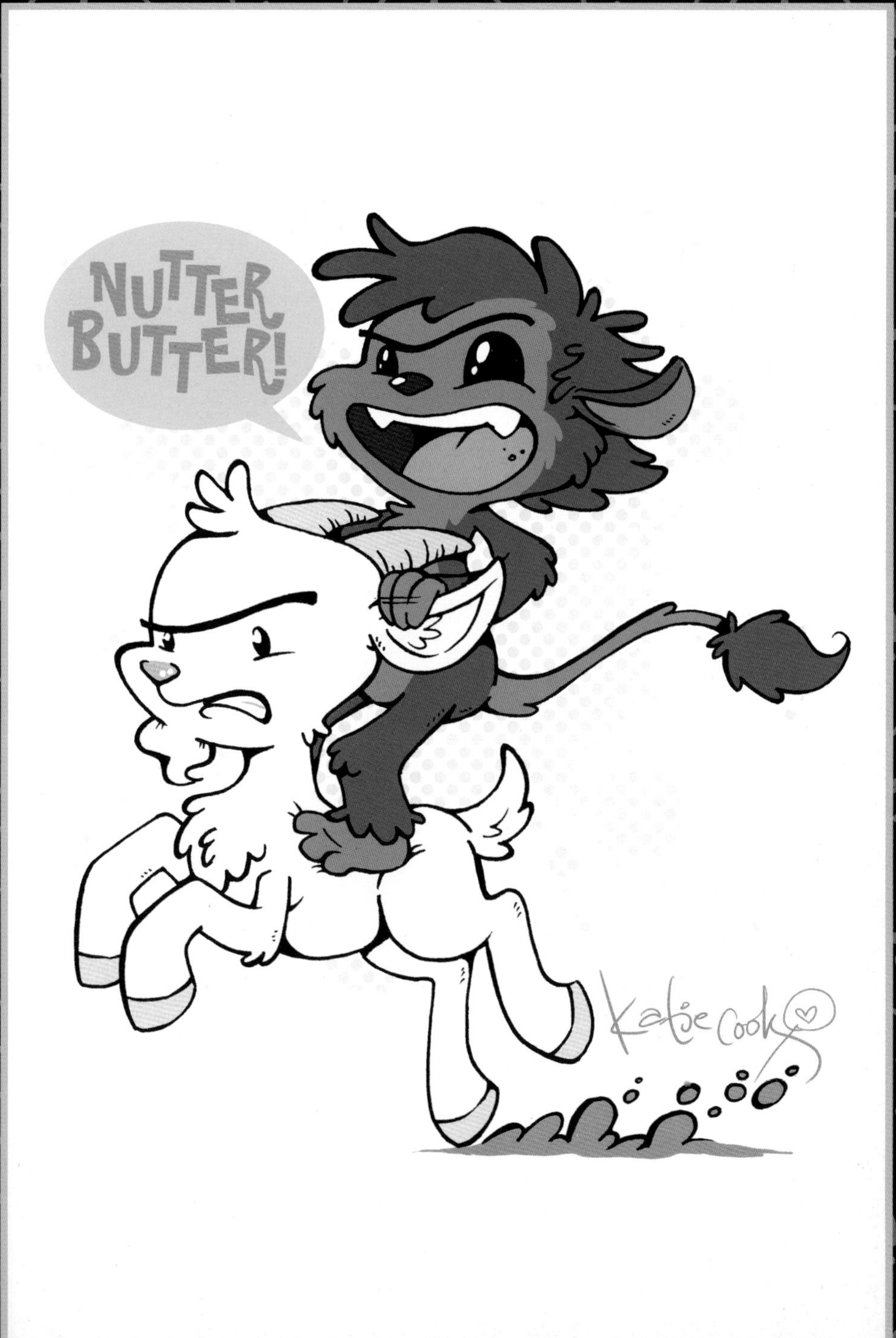
NUTTER BUTTER!
Katie Cook

ROBB MOMMAERTS

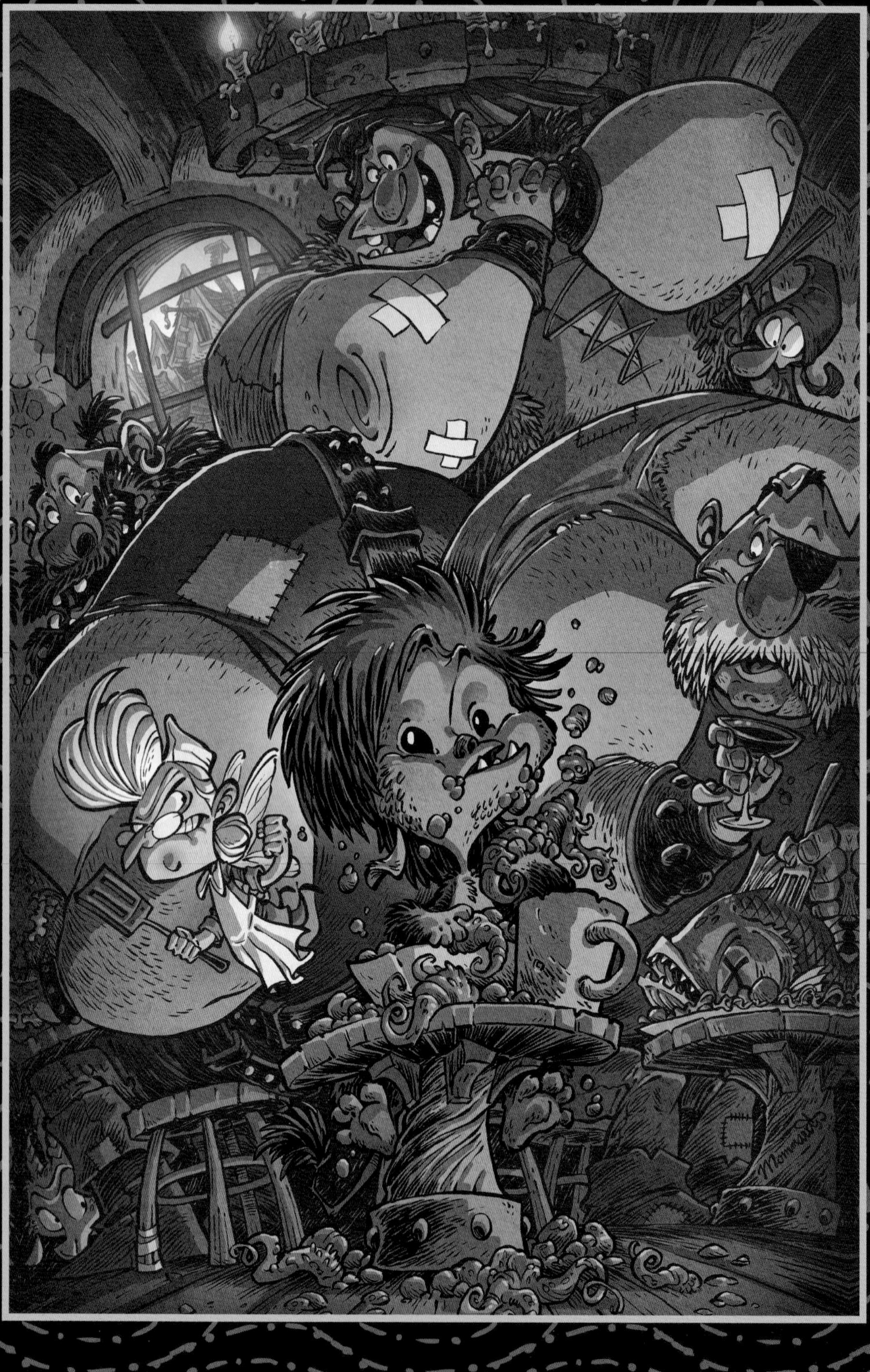

GUY DAVIS

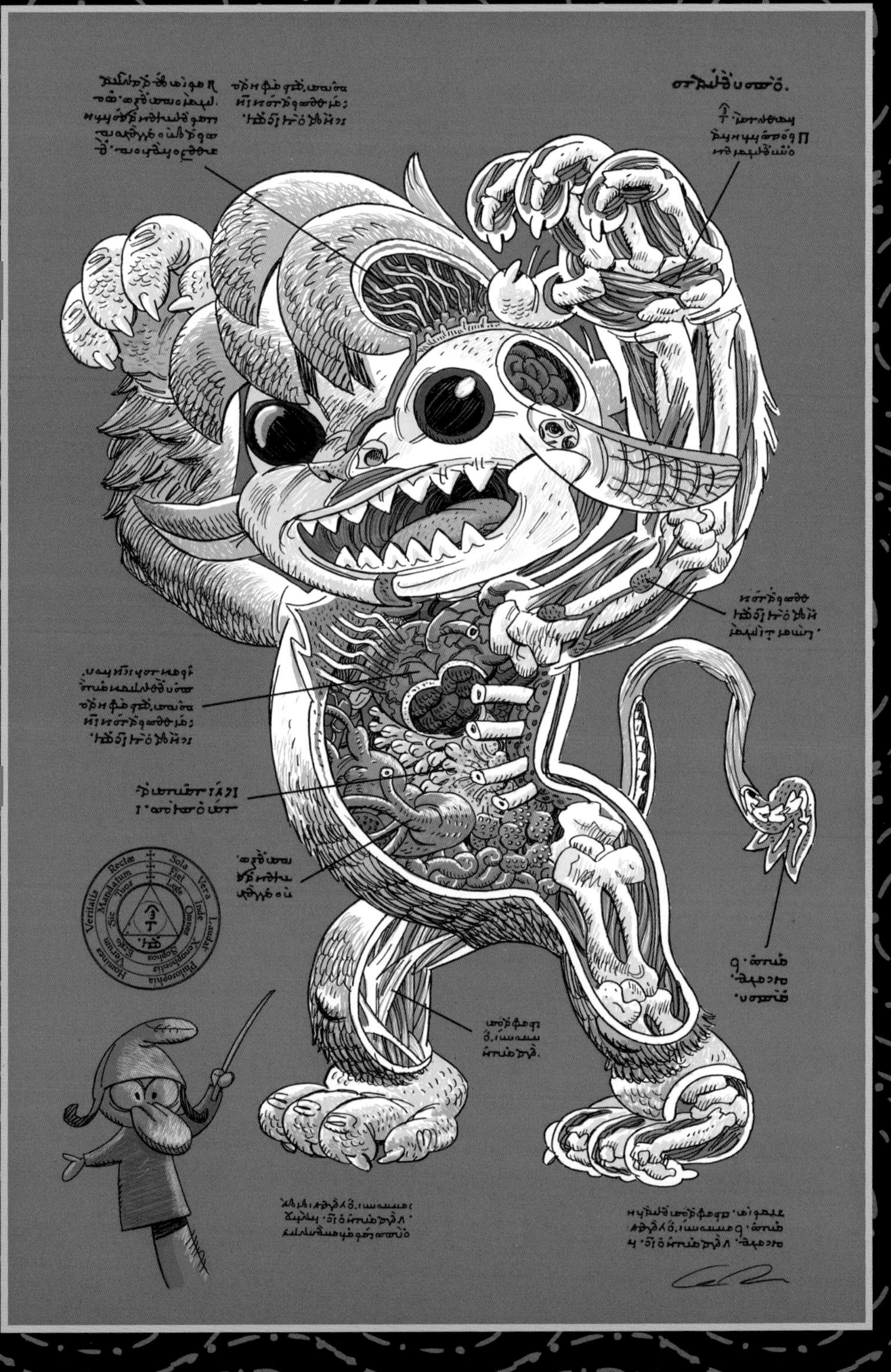

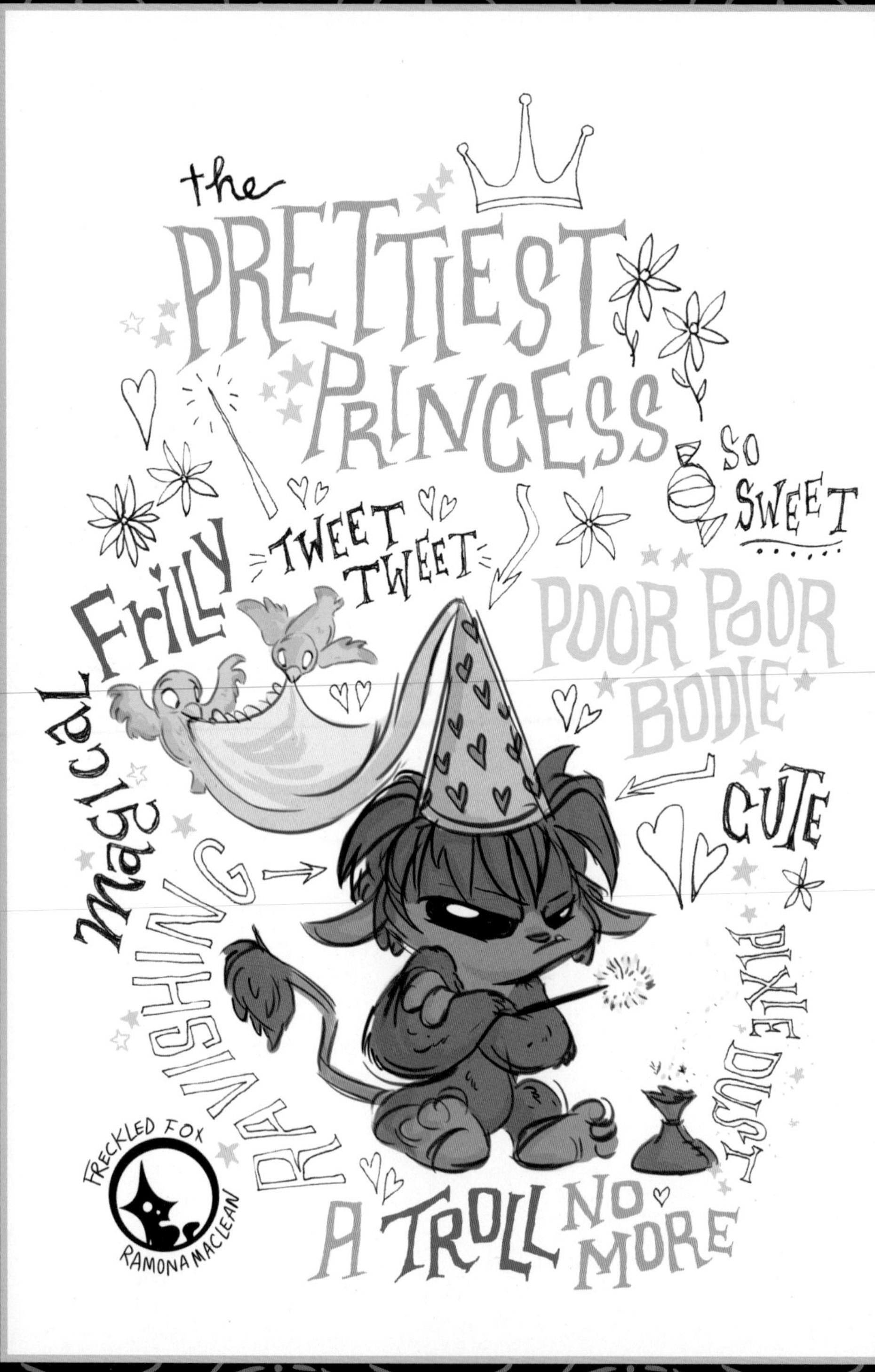
the PRETTIEST PRINCESS
SO SWEET
FRILLY
TWEET TWEET
POOR POOR BODIE
MAGICAL
CUTE
RAVISHING
PIXIE DUST
A TROLL NO MORE
FRECKLED FOX
RAMONA MACLEAN

KYLE LATINO

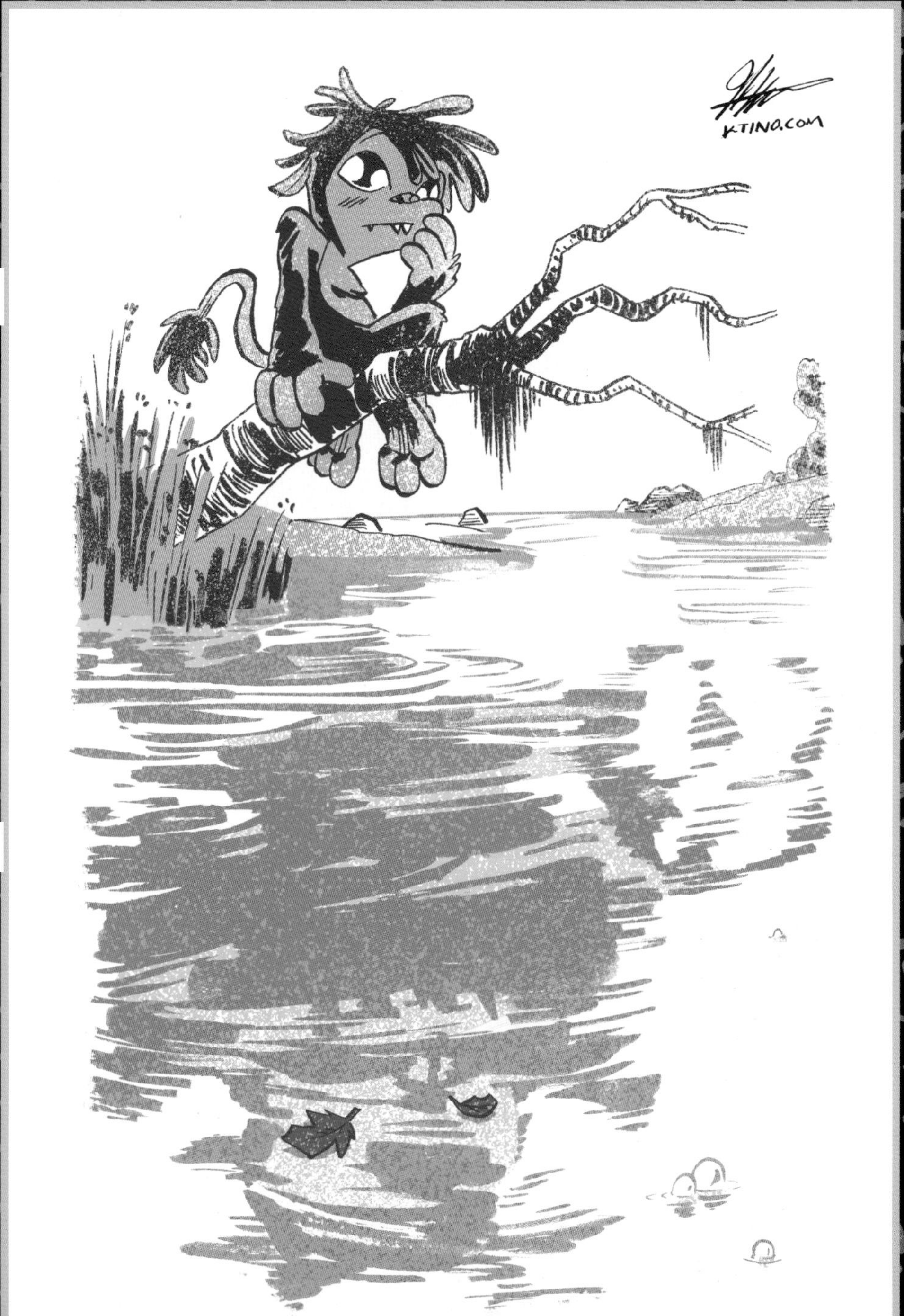
KTINO.COM

CRAIG ROUSSEAU

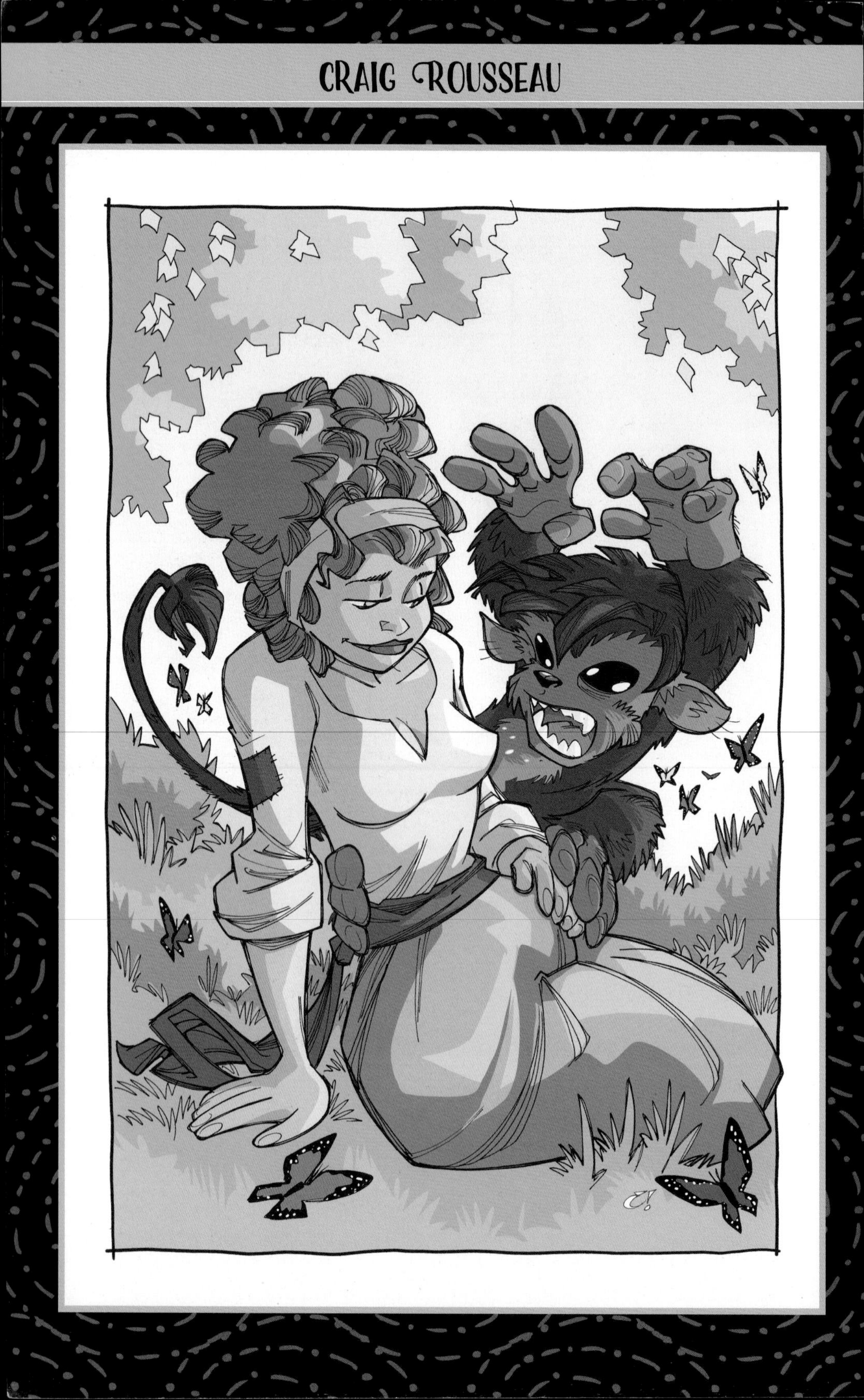

BEN CALDWELL

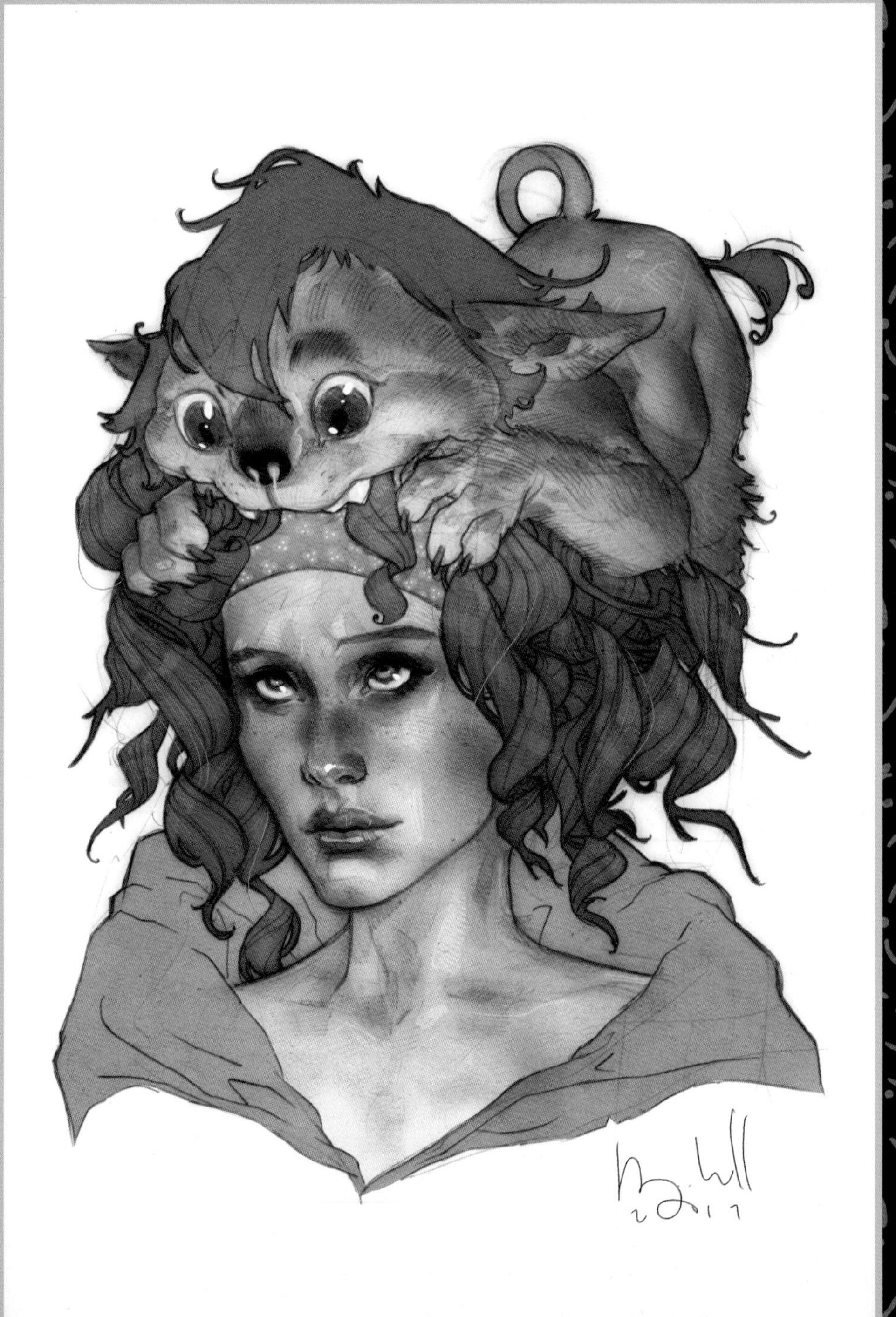

COVER GALLERY

CHAPTER ONE

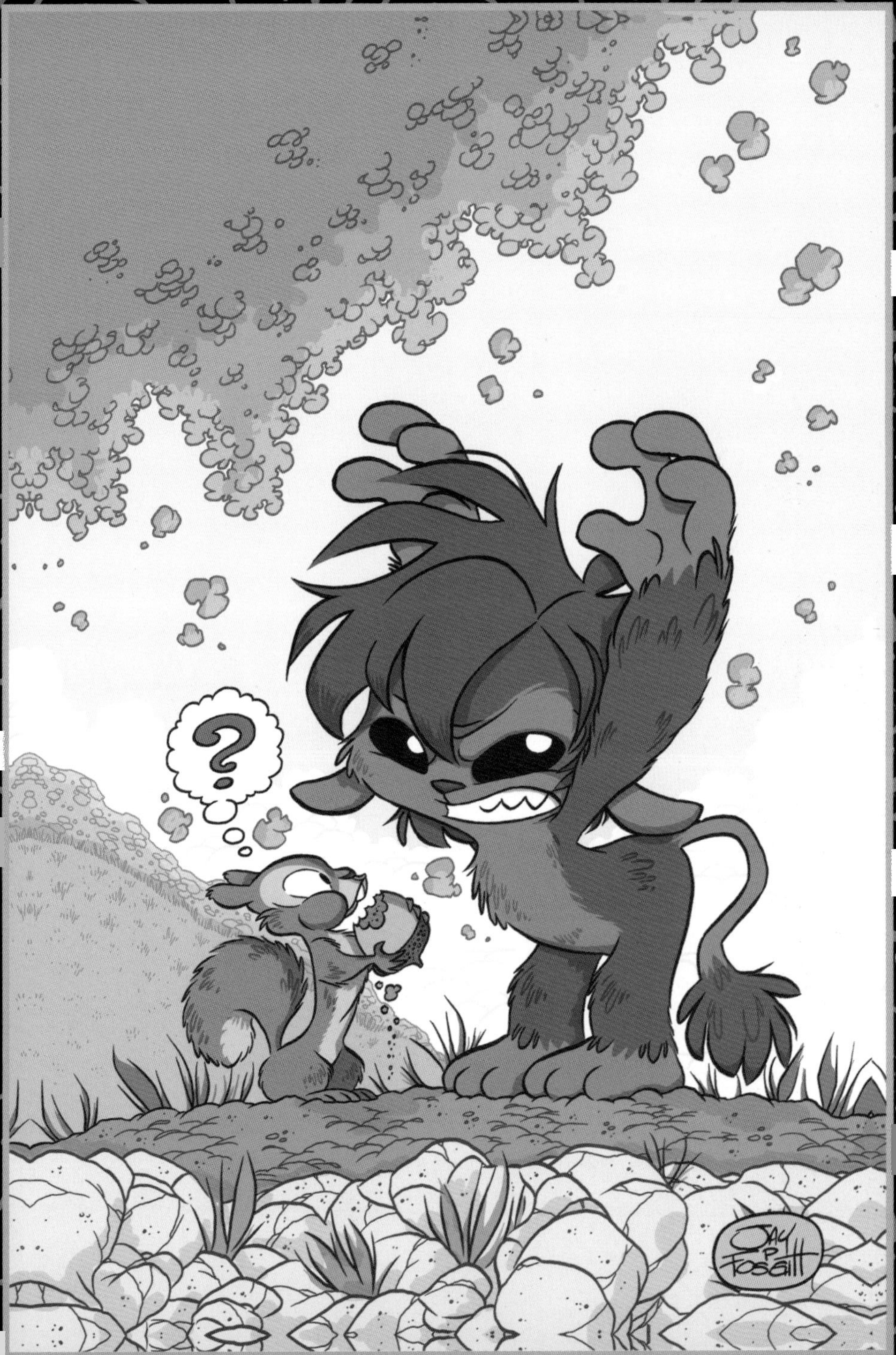
?
JAY P FOSGITT

CHAPTER TWO

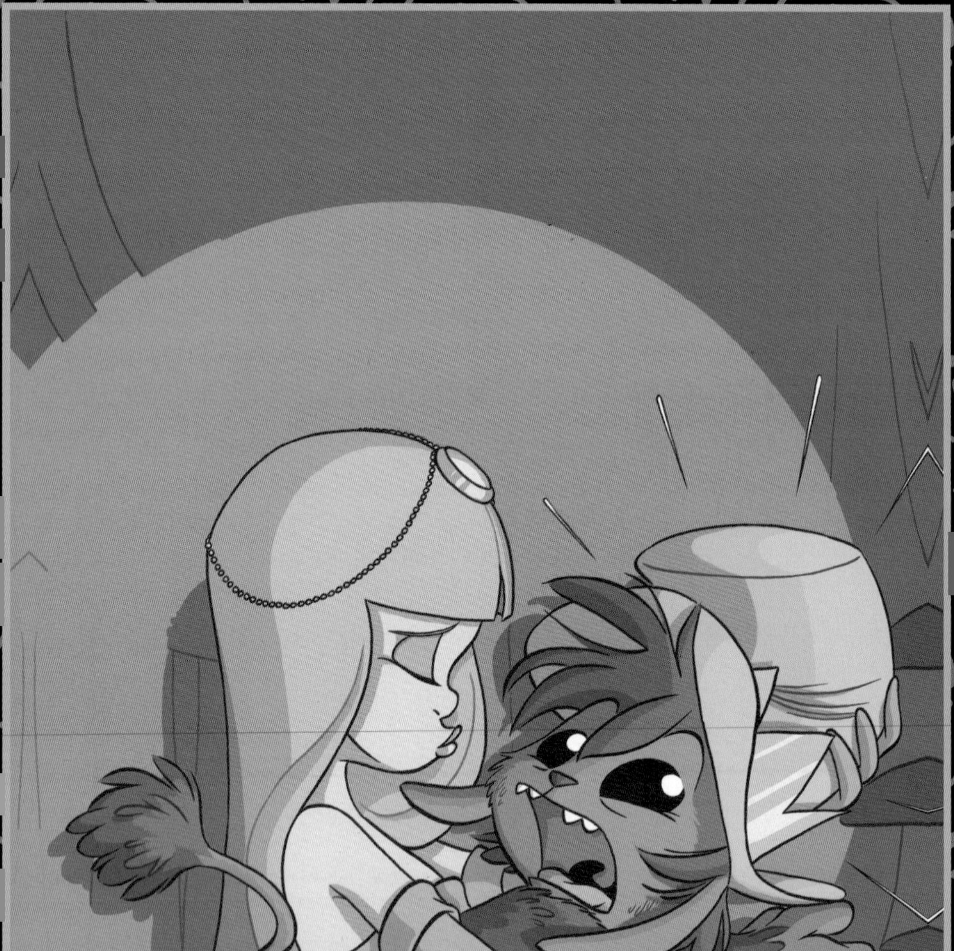

CHAPTER THREE

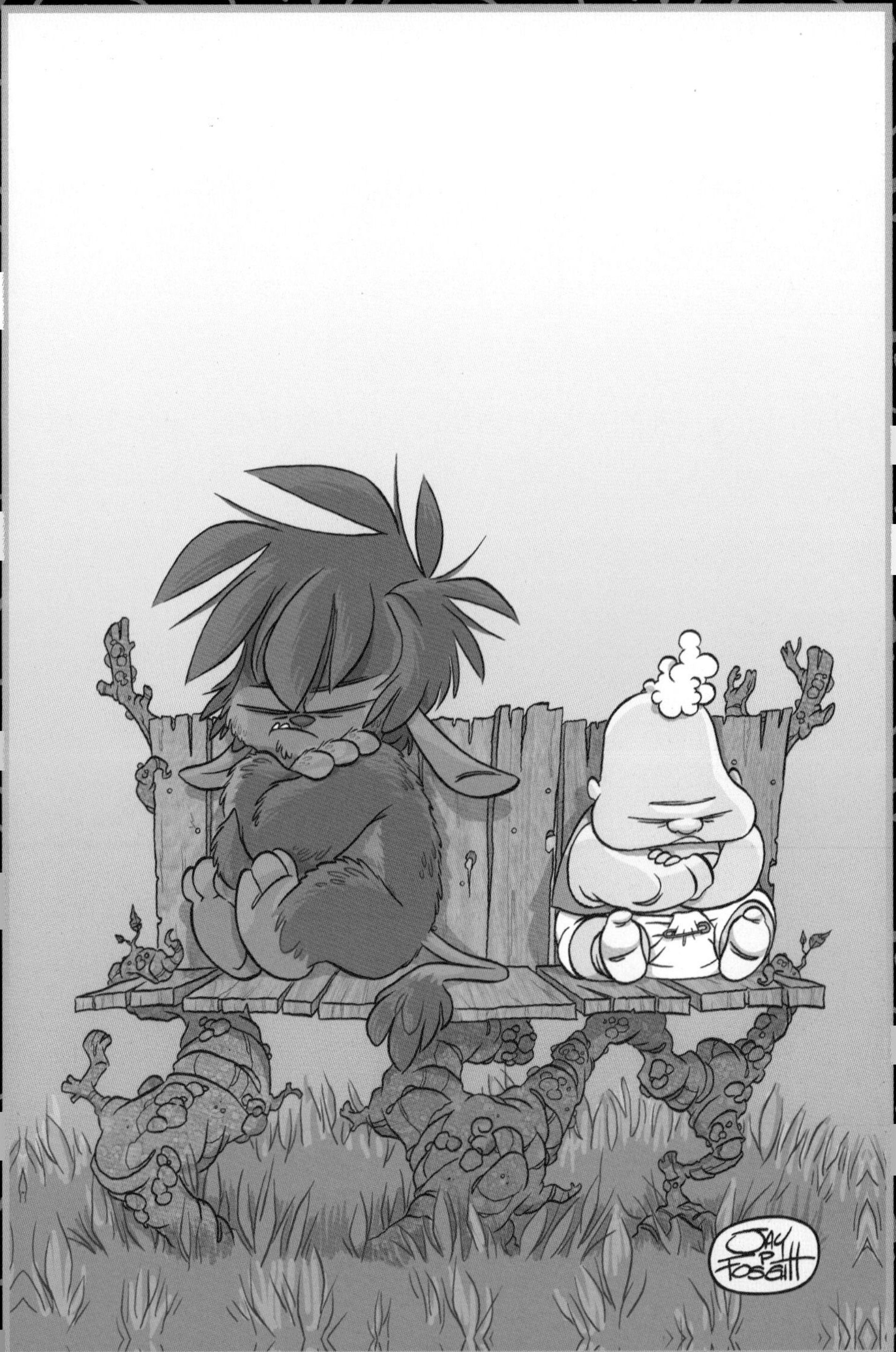
JAY P FOSGITT

CHAPTER FOUR

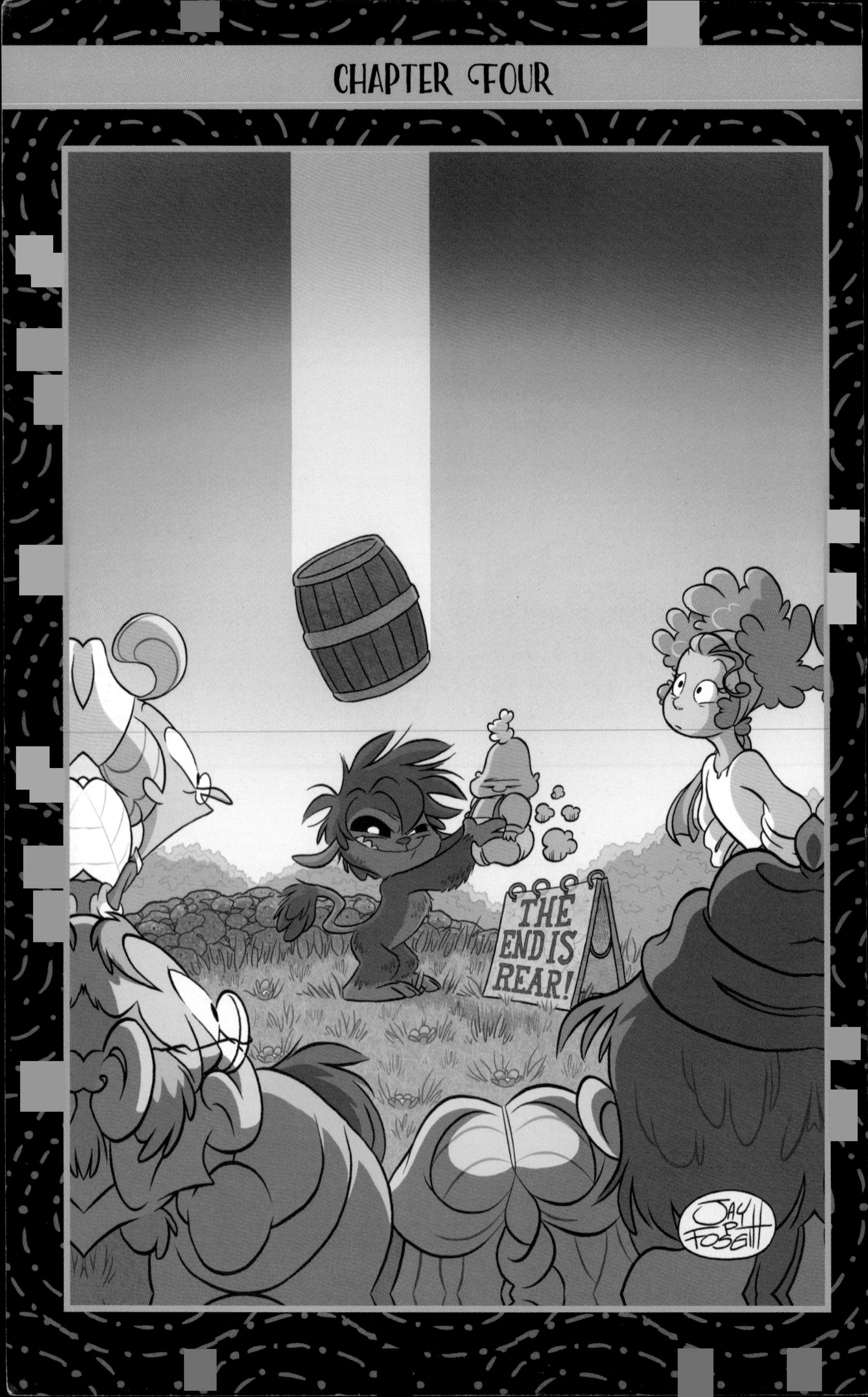
THE
END IS
REAR!
JAY P FOSGITT

CHAPTER FIVE

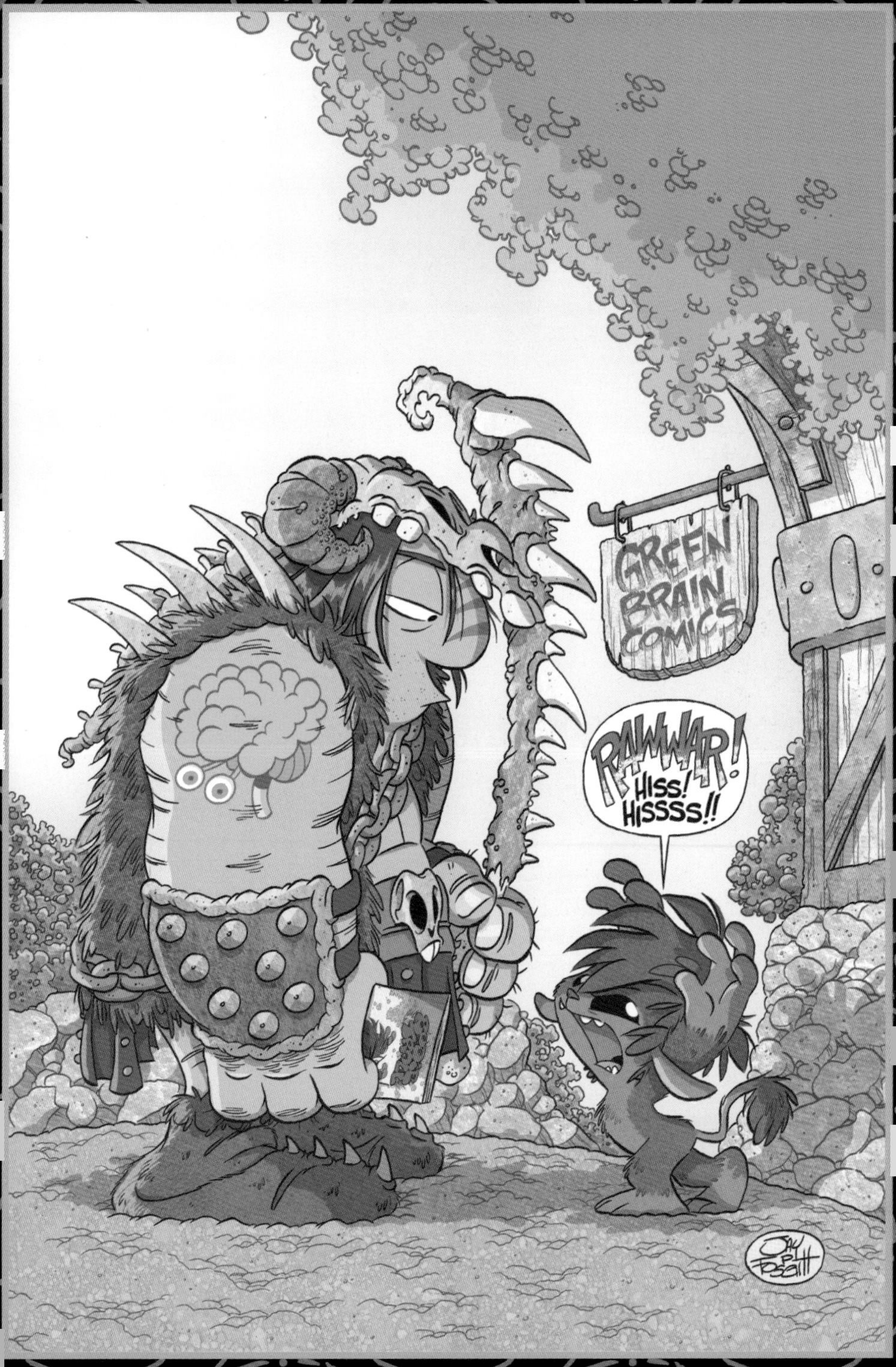
GREEN BRAIN COMICS
RAWWAR! HISS! HISSSS!!

CHAPTER SIX

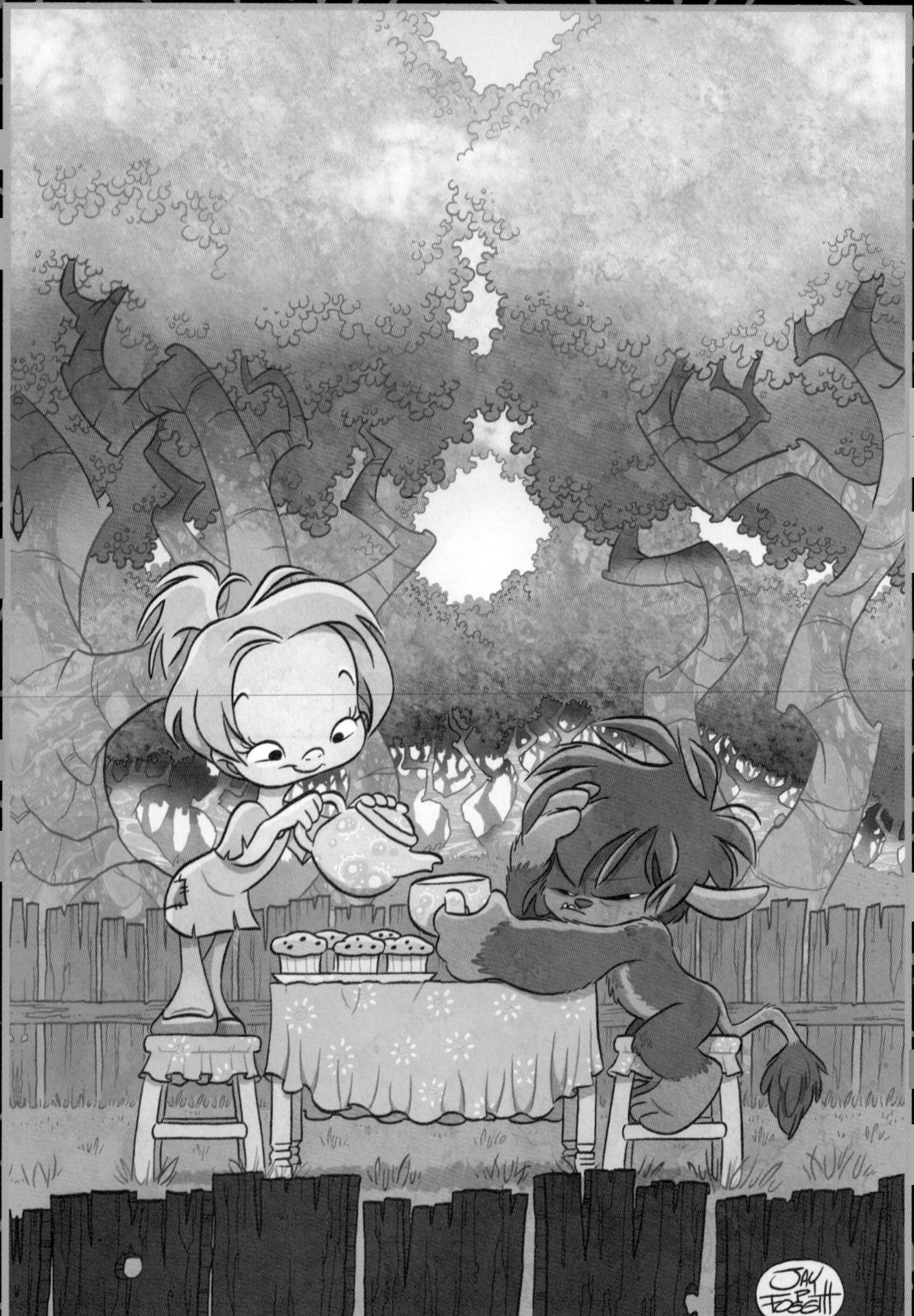

CHAPTER SEVEN

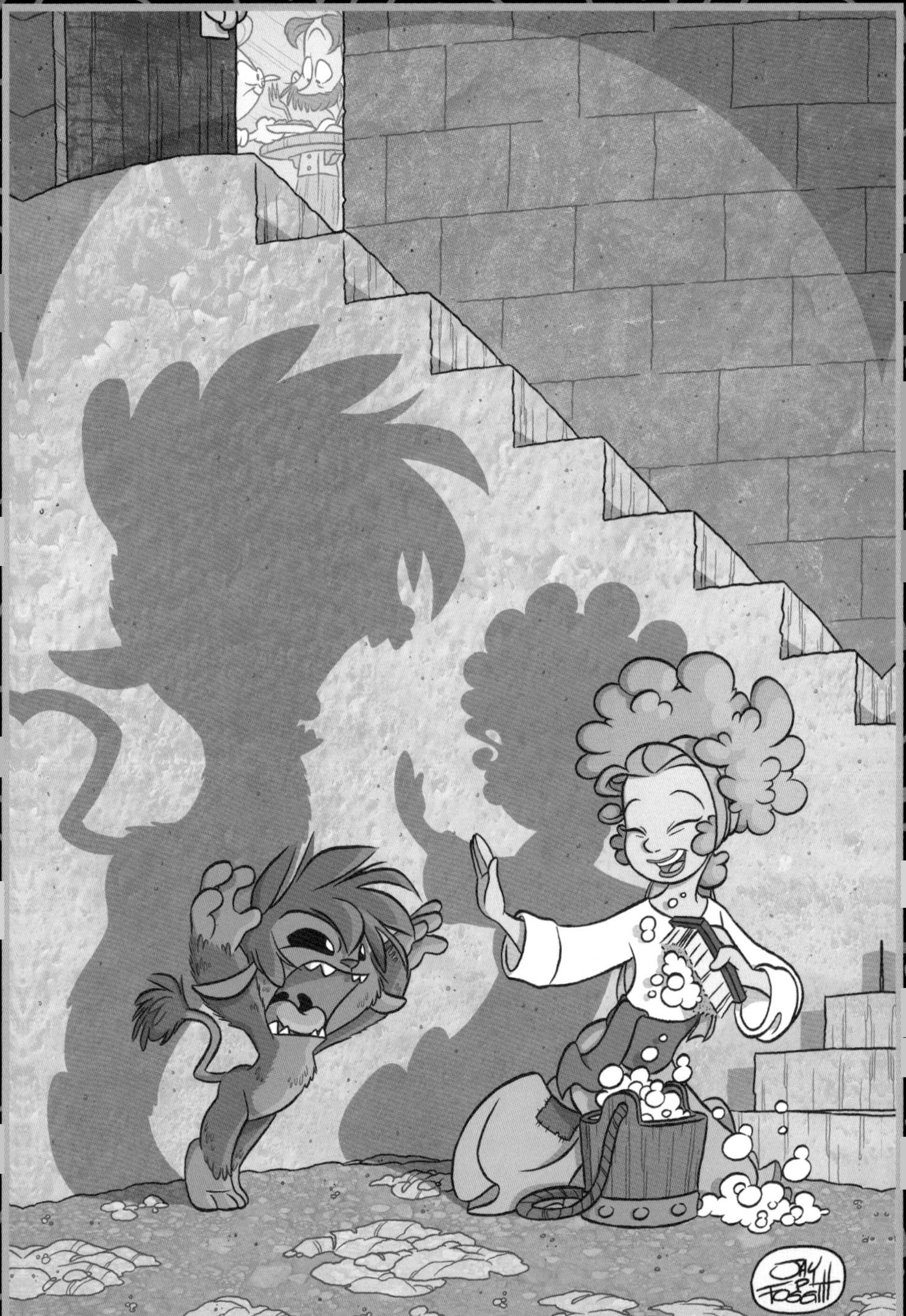

CHAPTER EIGHT

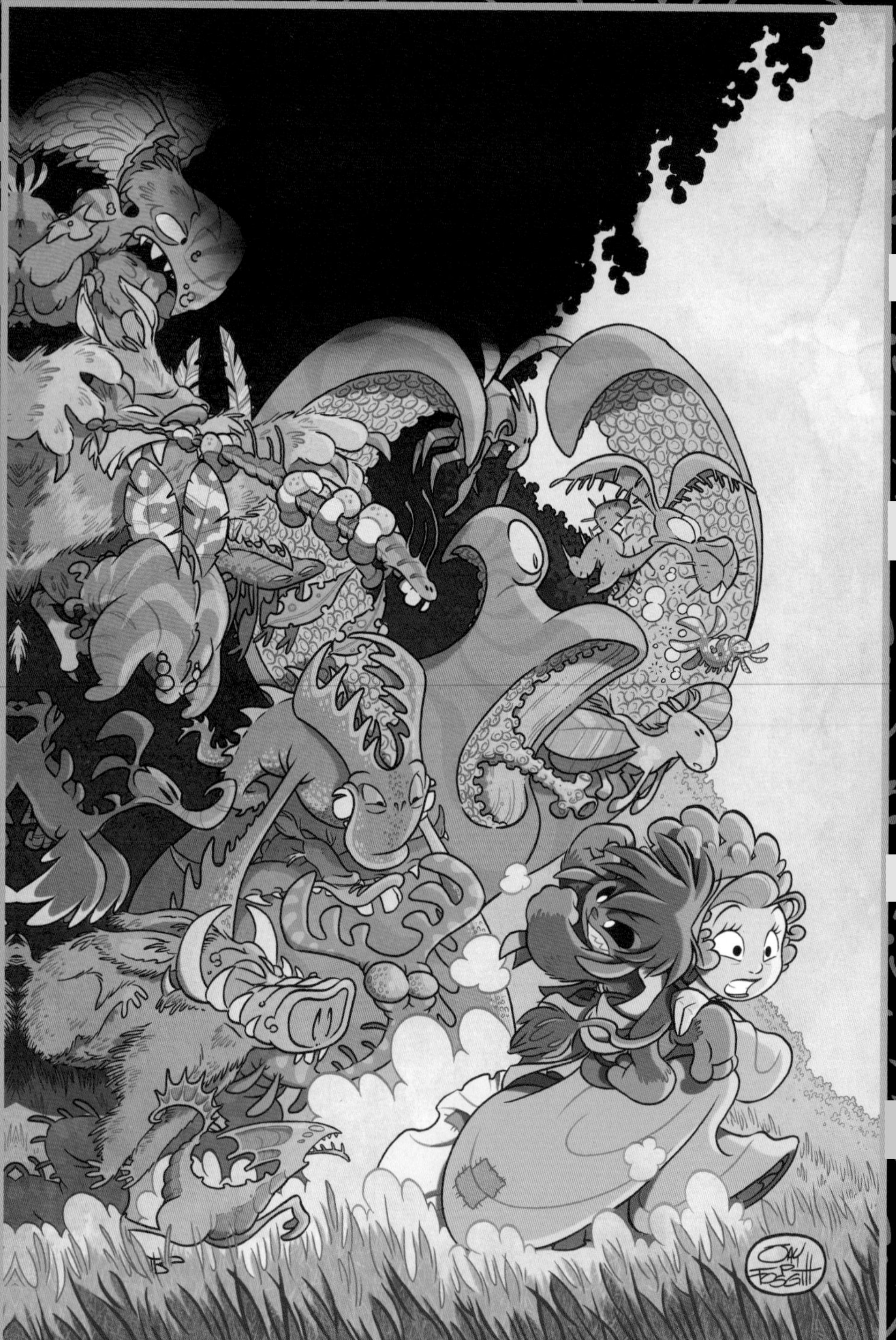

CHAPTER NINE

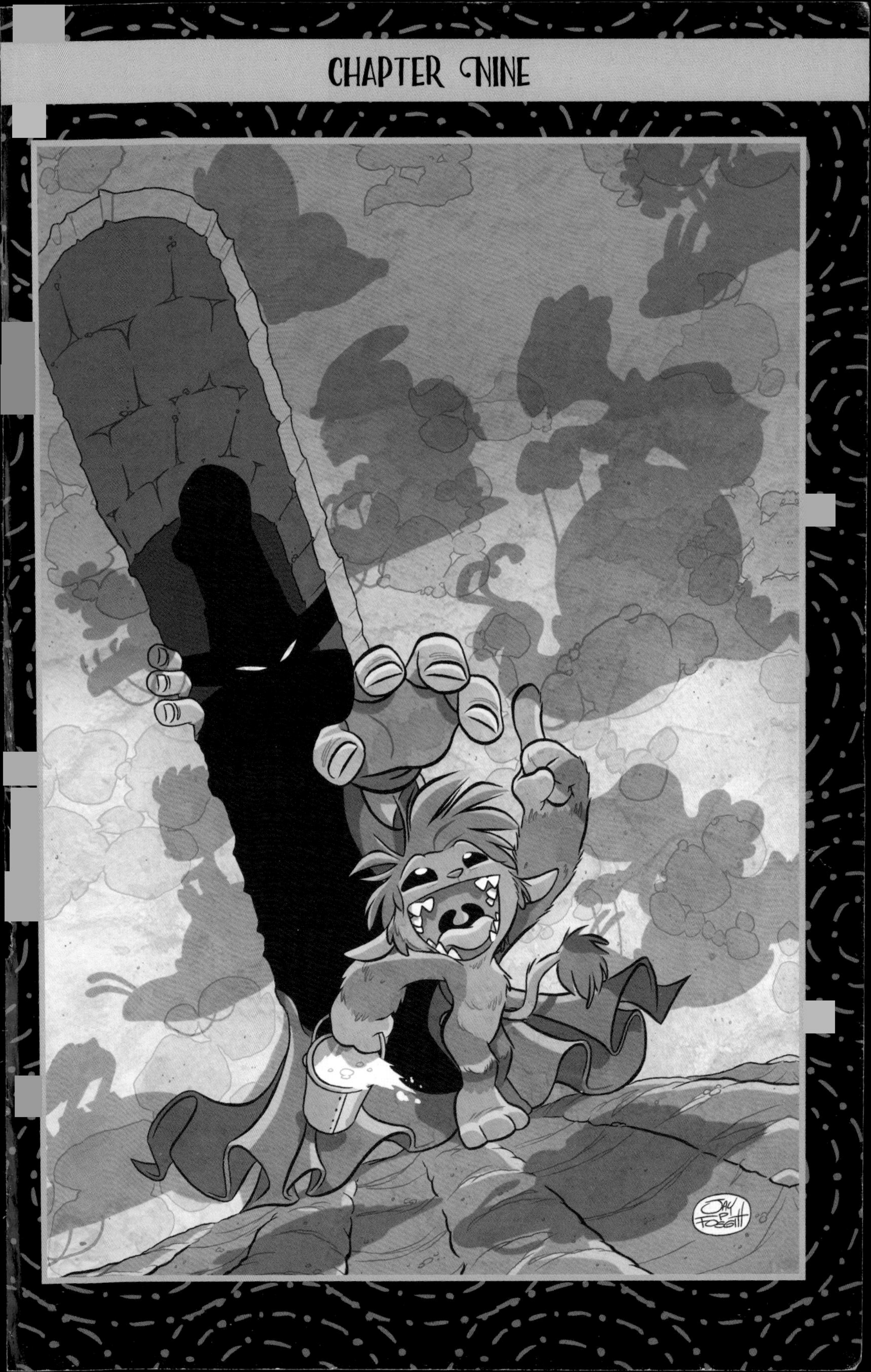

DISCOVER
EXPLOSIVE NEW WORLDS

ADVENTURE TIME

sam sykes · selina espiritu · sarah stern
BRAVE CHEF BRIANNA

KELLY THOMPSON BRIANNE DROUHARD M. VICTORIA ROBADO
MEGA PRINCESS

THE NOT-SO SECRET SOCIETY
DALEY · CRAFTS · CLARK · BRUNI

OVER THE GARDEN WALL

STEVEN UNIVERSE
VOLUME ONE

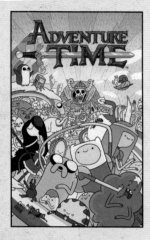

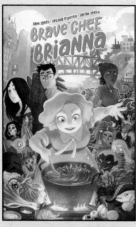

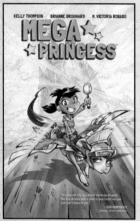

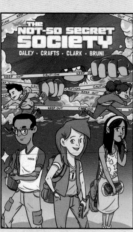

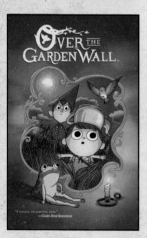

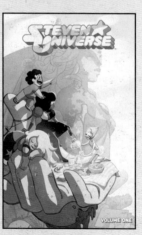

Adventure Time
Pendleton Ward and Others
Volume 1
ISBN: 978-1-60886-280-1 | $14.99 US
Volume 2
ISBN: 978-1-60886-323-5 | $14.99 US
Adventure Time: Islands
ISBN: 978-1-60886-972-5 | $9.99 US

The Amazing World of Gumball
Ben Bocquelet and Others
Volume 1
ISBN: 978-1-60886-488-1 | $14.99 US
Volume 2
ISBN: 978-1-60886-793-6 | $14.99 US

Brave Chef Brianna
Sam Sykes, Selina Espiritu
ISBN: 978-1-68415-050-2 | $14.99 US

Mega Princess
Kelly Thompson, Brianne Drouhard
ISBN: 978-1-68415-007-6 | $14.99 US

The Not-So Secret Society
Matthew Daley, Arlene Daley, Wook Jin Clark
ISBN: 978-1-60886-997-8 | $9.99 US

Over the Garden Wall
Patrick McHale, Jim Campbell and Others
Volume 1
ISBN: 978-1-60886-940-4 | $14.99 US
Volume 2
ISBN: 978-1-68415-006-9 | $14.99 US

Steven Universe
Rebecca Sugar and Others
Volume 1
ISBN: 978-1-60886-706-6 | $14.99 US
Volume 2
ISBN: 978-1-60886-796-7 | $14.99 US

Steven Universe & The Crystal Gems
ISBN: 978-1-60886-921-3 | $14.99 US

Steven Universe: Too Cool for School
ISBN: 978-1-60886-771-4 | $14.99 US

kaboom!™

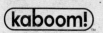

AVAILABLE AT YOUR LOCAL COMICS SHOP AND BOOKSTORE
To find a comics shop in your area, call 1-888-266-4226
WWW.**BOOM-STUDIOS**.COM